COLD TEA ON
A HOT DAY

AT THE CORNER
of LOVE AND
HEARTACHE

COLD TEA ON
A HOT DAY

AT THE CORNER
of LOVE AND
HEARTACHE

Curtiss Ann Matlock

MIRA

ISBN: 0-7394-2693-1
COLD TEA ON A HOT DAY Copyright © 2001 by Curtiss Ann Matlock
AT THE CORNER OF LOVE AND HEARTACHE Copyright © 2002 by Curtiss Ann
Matlock

Printed in the USA

COLD TEA ON
A HOT DAY

One

In the hazy glow of first morning light, a gleaming red Mercedes, a Roadster with its top up, sat on the side of the blacktopped county road. The engine idled gently, and headlights shone on the patchy grass and weeds.

The driver was slumped in the seat, comfortably, as if taking a nap. He was dead.

A dog lay with his head upon the man's thigh. He had lain there for some time, out of loyal respect to a friend.

In a nearby tree, a meadowlark gave out a shrill morning call.

The dog, perking his ears, sat up and then went over to poke his wet nose out the window, fully open because the man had been driving along in the cool spring night with the passenger window down so that the dog could enjoy putting his face in the wind.

Fairly certain the man would no longer notice being abandoned, the dog hopped through the window with graceful ease and landed on the dewy wet grass.

After a moment of the sniffing the damp, pungent air, the dog trotted off in the easterly direction that the car had been heading. It was pleasant in the cool first light. A little way along he came to a fresh armadillo run over in the road. He sniffed it, but he was yet far above the depths of eating roadkill. An owl perched on a fence post was kind enough to tell the dog that a town, where likely he could find breakfast, was just over the hill.

Sure enough, when he topped the hill, a town lay before him. The dog sat and looked at it. The morning sun was just beginning to peek over the horizon and cast its pink glow upon this world of humans. Where families of buffalo once wallowed and great herds of cattle once crossed on their way to the rowdy markets in Kansas, there now existed a place springing out of the prairie with tree-lined streets and brick buildings and clapboard houses.

The dog had come to the town in the same manner that he went everywhere and to each of his humans, following the direction led by his heart. The day he had come to the large concrete parking lot and to the man with the glasses, he had known that was the place for him and the human for his dog's loyal work of companionship.

Now, looking down on the town, he knew this was a new place for him and a new human awaited his ministrations.

The dog started down the hill, taking in the lay of the land and ready for any opportunity that presented itself.

The garbage trucks were starting on their first runs, and early risers all over began tuning kitchen radios to the morning weather report and going out on front porches to hang up flags in support of the campaign to keep Valentine's distinction as the Flag Town of America.

Fayrene Gardner, who had come into the Main Street Café a half an hour early because she had been unable to sleep due to the excitement of expecting a visit from her first ex-husband, came out the café door and set the United States flag in its holder.

A few yards down the sidewalk, at the doors of *The Valentine Voice,* Charlotte Nation was doing likewise. Charlotte, who was a little dismayed to see Fayrene had beat her to it, thought it important for the *Voice* to get their flag out first, as they were a leader in the community.

Setting the pole in the slot with some haste, she hurried back inside to get a cup of coffee for Leo, Sr. before he got off on his deliveries. Since their circulation manager quit three weeks earlier, Leo had been handling the job. Charlotte was thrilled, as now Leo was there early each morning, like herself. He got all the other deliverers off, and then was the last to leave on a route of his own.

"Thanks, Charlotte," Leo said, taking the cup she handed him and sipping. "Well, I gotta get goin' now."

"Yes . . . you do." She followed him to the doorway and stood there as he slipped into the delivery van and drove off down the alley, watching with the eyes of a woman in love with a man she could never have.

Up on Church Street, Winston Valentine was glad to be able to manage the job of getting out the front door of his house with the aid of a cane, while carrying two folded flags under his arm. One of his lady boarders, a piece of toast jammed in her mouth, came after him.

He told her with poorly tempered impatience, "I'm all right, Mildred . . . you cain't help me and eat toast at the same time!"

She had already dropped jelly on her ample bosom; Winston didn't want her to get jelly all over his flags. He felt guilty for having the thought that she could in that minute drop dead and he would gladly step over her. He was relieved when she got more concerned about her toast and jelly than about helping him.

He got himself down the front steps and over to the flag pole in the front yard, where he raised the Confederate flag, followed by the Stars and Bars. He could still raise his flags, and once more all by himself, thank God, and he wasn't yet pissing in his pants, so the day looked good.

Across the street, his neighbor Everett Northrupt, younger by better than ten years, was raising his flags, too, only the Stars and Bars of the U.S. of A. was on top and a lot bigger. Everett was from up North.

Both men stood at attention as music, a mingling of "Dixie" and "The Star Spangled Banner," blared out from speakers from each man's home. Winston, not wanting Everett to have anything on him, stood as straight as he could and saluted the flags and the day.

Then, as most days, he saw Parker Lindsey jogging down the street. Parker, a single fellow who no doubt had plenty of pent-up energy, would jog from his veterinary clinic at the edge of town, cut through the school yard and behind houses along a path that came out east of the Blaine's house, then go down Church Street to Porter and make several jogs to get to the highway and back east to his own place. It was a distance of five miles. Winston played a game of judging the younger man's state of sexual energy by how hard he was running when he went past.

"G'mornin', Doc," Winston called to him, remembering what it was like to be a virile man in his prime. He admired Parker Lindsey, who was going at a pretty good clip this morning.

" 'Mornin'." Puffing, Parker raised a hand in a wave and kept on going.

From the opposite direction came Leo, Jr., pedaling past with his teenage legs on his Mountain Flier. " 'lo, Mr. Winston!" he said and sent a rolled newspaper flying into the yard and landing two feet away.

"Bingo!" Winston called back with a wave.

He bent carefully to get the paper, considering it exercise. When he came up, he saw a woman in bright pink on a purple bicycle pumping along toward town. It was his niece, Leanne, who sometimes jogged and sometimes rode a bicycle. A professional barrel racer, Leanne worked to keep her legs strong.

" 'lo, Uncle Winston!"

Winston waved back, while averting his gaze from the sight of her. Leanne wore the skimpy attire so popular with women these days, and being her uncle, Winston did not consider it polite to stare. Leanne was a fine specimen of a woman. It was a little too bad she liked to display that around a lot. Winston felt women today had forgotten mystique. He liked to watch women on exercise shows on television, though.

Walking stiffly, but grateful to be walking, he went around the side of the house, where he clipped blossoms from his dead wife's rosebushes. *I'm keepin' on, Coweta.* He would miss his wife until his dying day.

Further up Church Street, Vella Blaine, wearing a lilac flowered apron and a big straw hat over her greying hair, was out in her backyard, snipping fresh blooms from her own rosebushes. She held each to her nose to inhale the delicious, soothing scent. Her very favorite were the yellow Graham-Thomas blossoms. She was so proud of her roses this spring.

Hearing a car, she looked up to see her husband behind the wheel of his big black 80s Lincoln as it chugged away, carrying him onward to his twelve-hour day at his drugstore.

Perry had not bothered to tell her goodbye. Again.

Gripping the stems of the cut roses so tightly that the thorns pricked her hands, Vella walked purposefully up the back steps and went inside to prepare a fresh pot of coffee for herself and Winston, who had, with the arrival of balmy spring, begun once more to join her for an early-morning chat. She got out the blue pottery mug Winston seemed to favor. In the mirror hung on the inside of the cabinet door, she paused to put on lipstick.

Down on Porter Street, the sun had risen high enough to shine its first golden rays on the roof of a small house dating from the forties that Realtors called a bungalow. In bed in the back bedroom, Marilee James, who was definitely not a morning person, was awakened by her eight-year-old son.

"Maa-ma . . ."

Marilee managed to crack an eyelid.

"Maa-ma . . ." He peered into her face, his blue eyes large behind his thick glasses.

Marilee tried to focus enough to see the clock. Willie Lee simply had no sense of time at all. He woke up when he woke, and slept when he slept, never minding the rest of the world . . . or his mother, who had not had a decent night's sleep since Miss Porter had suddenly and fantastically thrown the newspaper management into her hands and run off with a husband.

Was that red numeral a five or a six? She was going to have to get a bigger clock. The thought caused her to close her eyes.

"Ma-ma, can I have a dog?" Willie Lee spoke in a whisper and slowly, carefully pronouncing each word, as was his habit.

"Not right this minute," Marilee managed to get out with as hoarse a voice as she used to have when she smoked a pack and a half a day of Virginia Slims.

She gathered courage and stretched herself toward the clock. The red numerals came in more clearly. It was 6:10. Giving a groan, she rolled over and thought that she could not get up. That was all there was to it. She *would not* get up.

"I want this dog in this pic-ture." Willie Lee shoved a book in her face.

Marilee, who could not respond in any way, shape or form, stared with fuzzy vision at a picture of a spotted dog in one of her son's picture books.

Willie Lee, not at all bothered by not being answered, sat back on folded legs and said, "I will ask God for this dog."

Marilee's sleepy gaze came to rest upon her son, upon his head bent once more to study the picture book. His short white-blond hair stood on end in all directions, as was usual.

Her Willie Lee, who had put up a mighty struggle to enter the world and ended up with brain damage that cast doubt still upon his future ability to lead anything resembling a normal life without someone to watch over him.

Her heart seemed to swell and her heartbeats to grow louder . . . *thump . . . thump . . . thump . . .* echoing in her ears, broken only by the clink of dishes from the kitchen, where Corrine was no doubt readying the table for breakfast, as she had each morning since coming to stay with them.

With the aroma of coffee floating in to reach her, Marilee pictured the slight figure of her young niece at the counter. Likely she had to pull a chair over and stand on it in order to fill the coffeemaker.

Two of them, two little souls, depending upon only her, Marilee, a mere woman alone.

The idea so frightened her that in an instant she had flung back the covers and gotten to her feet, moving in the manner of generations of women before her who had struggled with the overwhelming urge to run screaming out of the house to throw themselves in front of the early-morning garbage truck. The saving answer to that urge was to propel herself headlong into the day of taking care of those who needed her.

"Let's get you dressed, buster," she said to her son, scooping him up, causing him to giggle.

"Time to get go-ing," he said, mimicking her usual refrain.

"Yes . . . time to get going."

When focusing on the needs of those around her, she did not have to face the needs clamoring inside herself.

"Here they are," Corrine said and brought Marilee the car keys she had been searching for, as the child did each morning at seven-thirty—or any other time, really.

"Thank you, hon . . . now, let's get goin'. . . ."

The children trooped before her out the front door, and they all piled into the Jeep Cherokee for the five-minute drive to school, where Marilee let them out on the wide sidewalk in front of the long, low brick building.

The two, taller and very thin Corrine and shorter, slight Willie Lee, did not run off with the other screaming and laughing children but stood there side by side, forlornly watching her drive away.

Marilee, who caught sight of them in the rearview mirror, felt like a traitor abandoning her delicate charges.

Pressing firmly on the accelerator, she focused on the road and reminded herself that she was a working mother, just like a million other working mothers, trying to keep a roof over all their heads, and that her children needed to learn to deal with real life.

As she whipped the Cherokee into its accustomed place in the narrow lot behind the brick building that housed *The Valentine Voice,* she realized that she had been doing the same thing for most of seven years. *Where did the years go? When had twenty-one turned into forty?*

It was Miss Porter running off into a new life who had caused this unrest, Marilee thought with annoyance, hiking her heavy leather tote up on her shoulder. The next instant, having the disconcerting impression that she was beginning to resemble Miss Porter, she dropped the bag to her hand.

"My computer is down," Tammy Crawford said immediately when Marilee came down the large aisle of the main room.

"Call the repairman." Marilee threw her bag on her already full desk and picked up the day's edition of the *Voice.* She had not had time to read it at home. She had not had time for weeks.

"Mrs. Oklahoma is going to visit the high school this mornin'," Reggie said. "Principal forgot to call us . . . I'm goin' right over there."

" 'kay." Marilee didn't think everyone really needed to report to her.

Charlotte strode forward with a handful of notes. "Here's the first morning complaints of late papers ... and Roger, that new guy they've hired up at the printer, wants you to call him ... and here's a note from the mayor for tomorrow's 'About Town' column. City hall has lost those flags they thought they had left."

Marilee took the notes and sank into her chair.

June, who was now working on their ad layouts since their top ad layout person had quit last week, came over and said, "I can't read this note Jewel put on this ad. Do you think that is supposed to be a two or a five?"

"Call the Ford dealer and ask. I don't think they would appreciate us guessing."

"Okay. I can do that." June generally needed to convince herself of action.

Marilee, giving a large sigh, fell into her chair and flopped open the paper to see how it had come out, and if she would need to be making any retractions and groveling apologies. She thought she was learning to grovel quite well.

"Another day in paradise," she said to no one in particular.

The Valentine Voice
About Town

by Marilee James

For the one or two people in town who have not heard by now, Ms. Muriel Porter, former publisher of *The Valentine Voice,* and Mr. Dwight Abercrombie, who met last year on a Carribean cruise, were married yesterday afternoon in a small ceremony at St. Luke's Episcopal Church. Immediately afterward the two left on a world tour they estimate will take them upward of eighteen months. Following their world tour, the couple plan to settle in either Daytona Beach or possibly Majorca, Spain. Ms. Porter-Abercrombie wanted everyone to know she will always remain a Valentinian, however far she may roam.

"Valentine will always be my home," Ms. Porter stated. "My ties there are as necessary to my life as cold tea on a hot day."

The new publisher and editor in chief of *The Valentine Voice,* Tate Holloway, will be arriving this weekend to officially take over the paper. Mr. Holloway is Ms. Porter-Abercrombie's cousin and a veteran newspaper journalist with thirty years experience on a number of the nation's leading newspapers.

An open house will be held in honor of Mr. Holloway on

Monday at the *Voice* offices. Cake and coffee will be served courtesy of Sweetie Cakes of Main Street. Come by and welcome Mr. Holloway, or address to him your complaints.

Until Monday, I will continue as managing editor. All news stories should be reported to me, and you can call me at my home number, 555-4743, afternoons and until 8:00 p.m. Please save all complaints for Mr. Holloway on Monday.

Other important bits of note:

The first meeting of the Valentine Rose Club will be held tonight, 7:00 p.m., at the Methodist Church Fellowship Hall. Vella Blaine will head the meeting and wants it stressed that all denominations are welcome and there will be no passing of a collection plate.

Jaydee Mayhall has formally declared his candidacy for city council. Thus far he is the first candidate to declare intentions of running for the seat being vacated by long-time member Wesley Fitzwater, who says he is tired of the thankless job. Mayhall invites anyone who would like to talk to him about the town's needs to stop by to visit with him at his office on Main Street.

Mayor Upchurch has ten Valentine town flags left at city hall, for anyone who wants to fly one outside their home or shop. The flags are free; the only requirement is a proper pole high enough that the flag does not brush the ground.

Two

Looking in the Wrong Direction

"**H**ow long has he been missing?" Principal Blankenship demanded of the teacher standing before her.

"Since lunch recess," Imogene Reeves answered, wringing her hands. "I don't care if he is retarded and looks like an angel. He knows how to slip away. He is not just wanderin' off."

The principal winced at the word *retarded* spoken out loud. There were so many unacceptable words and phrases these days that she couldn't keep up, but she was fairly certain the term *retarded* fell in the unacceptable category. She checked her watch and saw it was going on one o'clock.

She headed at a good clip out of her office, asking as she went, "Has anyone spoken to Mr. Starr . . . checked the storerooms?"

It could very well be a repeat of that first time, she thought, calming herself. It had been Mr. Starr, the custodian, who had found Willie Lee the first time. That time the boy had been all along playing with a mouse in the janitor's storeroom. This had been upsetting—a little fright that the mouse might bite and the boy get an infection—but it was better than the second time, when the boy had gotten off the school grounds and all the way down to the veterinarian's place a half-mile away. That time Principal Blankenship had been forced to call the boy's mother, because the veterinarian was a *friend* of the boy's mother.

Oh, she did not want to have to tell the mother again. Marilee James wrote for the newspaper. This would get everywhere.

Imagining what her father, a principal before her, would have said, would have *yelled,* Principal Blankenship just about wet her pants.

The storeroom had been searched and the custodian Mr. Starr consulted; involved with changing out hot water heaters, he had not seen Willie Lee since the beginning of the school day. The closets were searched, and the storerooms a second time, and the boys' bathrooms.

At last the principal resorted to telephoning down to the veterinarian's office.

"I haven't seen Willie Lee," the young receptionist at the veterinarian's told her. "And Doc Lindsey has been out inoculatin' cattle since before noon."

The principal, with a sinking feeling, went along the corridors of her small school, peeking into each classroom, searching faces, hoping, praying with hands clasping and unclasping, for Willie Lee to appear.

In her heart she knew that Willie Lee had escaped the school grounds a second time, but she did not want to think of such a failure on the part of one of her teachers. Or herself. And truly, she didn't want anything to happen to the child.

She did wish he could go to another school.

At last, with pointy shoulders slumping, she broke down and spoke over the school intercom: "Attention, teachers and students. Anyone who has seen Willie Lee James since lunch recess, please come to the office."

In Ms. Norwood's fourth-grade class, Corrine Pendley heard the announcement of her cousin's name. Face jerking upward, she stared at the speaker above the classroom door. Then she saw all eyes turn to her.

Her face burned. Bending her head over her notebook, she focused her eyes on the lined paper in front of her and concentrated on being invisible.

The teacher had called her name several times before Corrine was jolted into hearing by Christy Grace poking her in the back with a pencil. "She's callin' you."

Corrine looked up at the teacher, who asked if Corrine had seen Willie Lee. Corrine said, "No, ma'am." She wondered at the question. Maybe the teacher thought she was a little deaf. Or else she thought Corrine would lie.

Why didn't everybody mind their own business and quit looking at her?

Bending her head over her math problems, she made the numbers carefully, trying to concentrate on them, but thinking about her cousin. Willie Lee was only eight, and little for his age.

He was slow, but this did not mean he didn't know about some things. *One thing he seemed to know was how to get away when he wanted to.* Corrine wished she had gone with him.

Her anxiety increased. She felt responsible. She should have been looking out for him. She was older, and he didn't have any brothers or sisters, just like she didn't.

All manner of dark fantasies paraded through her mind. She hoped he didn't get run over. Or fall in a muddy creek and drown. Or get picked up by a stranger.

Her pencil point broke, startling her.

Carefully, she laid the pencil down, got up and walked as quietly as possible, so as not to become too visible, to the teacher's desk to ask in a hurried whisper to go to the rest room.

In the tiled room that smelled strongly of bleach, she used the toilet and then she washed her hands. She kept thinking about the front doors. When she came out of the rest room, she turned left instead of right and walked down the hall and right out the double doors. She did this without thinking at all, just following an urge inside.

All the way down the front walk, she felt certain a yell was going to hit her in the back. But it didn't. Then she was running free, running from school and then running from herself, scared to death to have done something that was very wrong and would make everyone mad at her.

She would have to find Willie Lee, she thought. If she found him, no one would be mad at her. The sun felt warm on her head and the breeze cool to her face.

At that very instant, when finding her cousin and being a hero seemed totally possible, she looked down the street and saw her Aunt Marilee's brilliant white Jeep Cherokee coming.

The Jeep's chrome shone so brightly, Corrine had to squint. Still, she saw Aunt Marilee behind the wheel. Corrine stopped in her tracks, and her life seemed to drain right out her toes.

Likely she was going to get it now. And she deserved it. She never could seem to do things right.

The vehicle pulled up beside her, and the tinted window slid down. Aunt Marilee said, "Where are you goin'?"

Corrine, who could not read her aunt's even tone or blank expression, said slowly, "They announced 'bout Willie Lee being missin'. I was goin' to find him."

Her aunt said, "Well, that makes two of us. Get in. I have to go see the principal first."

Corrine opened the door and slipped into the seat in a manner as if to disappear. Carefully, she closed the door beside her. In the short drive to the school parking lot, she tried to read her aunt's attitude but could not. She had never seen her aunt look like this. She thought desperately of what her aunt might be thinking, in order to be ready for what to say or do.

But all Aunt Marilee said to her when they got to the school was, "Come on back in with me. You'll need to get your stuff from class."

Aunt Marilee went to Corrine's class with her and told Ms. Norwood that she was taking Corrine home early. Corrine, who was used to moving from an entire apartment in just a few minutes and therefore was not in the habit of accumulating needless trifles, stuffed all her books and notebooks from her desk into her backpack in scarcely a minute. As she lugged it to the classroom door, she could feel everyone looking at her, but it didn't matter. She was leaving, at least for today.

The heels of Aunt Marilee's Western boots echoed sharply on the corridor floor all the way back to the principal's office, where Aunt Marilee said to her, "Sit right here. I don't want to lose you, too."

Without a word, Corrine sat. Aunt Marilee disappeared into the principal's office.

The secretary, who had bleached blond hair teased up to amazing heights, looked at her. Corrine looked around the room and swung her feet that only brushed the floor.

Aunt Marilee had not fully closed the door, but even if she had, the voices would probably have been heard. Aunt Marilee had the furious tone she used when she and Corrine's mother got into their fights. Corrine imagined her aunt was standing how she did when she meant business: feet slightly apart and eyes like laser rays.

Aunt Marilee wanted to know how people supposedly educated in child development could not manage to keep track of one little boy who was diagnosed as learning disabled and not able to think above five years old. The principal answered that the school was not a prison and did not have guards.

"We are trying to mainstream Willie Lee to the best of our ability," the principal said. "We do not lose normal children, who are taught to participate."

Corrine held her breath, afraid that her Aunt Marilee was going to reveal finding Corrine halfway down the block. And maybe, since she had gotten away—since she had even *attempted* to leave—maybe she was not quite normal.

"We are doing the best we can with your children, Mrs. James," the principal said in a low tone.

Corrine saw the big-haired secretary's eyes cut to her, as if thinking, You're one of those troublemakers. Corrine swung her feet and looked at the wall, feeling the empty hole in her chest grow until it seemed to swallow her.

"Arguing will not find Willie Lee. I apologize. Now, tell me when and where my son was last seen." Aunt Marilee's voice, sounding so very calm and firm, enabled Corrine to draw a breath.

"I'll tell you," Aunt Marilee said when they got back in the Cherokee, Aunt Marilee slamming the door so hard the entire vehicle rattled. "Willie Lee knew exactly what he was doin'. I don't care how dumb people think he is."

"He is only dumb in some things," Corrine said.

Aunt Marilee didn't seem to hear her. She started off fast, gazing hard out the window. "Oh, Willie Lee," she said under her breath, and for an instant Corrine thought her aunt might cry. This was very unnerving to Corrine, who instantly turned her eyes out the window, looking hard, thinking that she just had to find Willie Lee. She had to make everything all right again for her aunt.

They drove slowly down to the veterinary clinic, looking into yards as they went. They went into the veterinarian's office, where two people waited with their dogs, a yippy little terrier and a trembling Labrador.

The girl behind the counter told them that Doc Lindsey had been out most of the day, was at that moment tending a sick horse at some ranch but was expected back any moment.

Dr. Lindsey was Aunt Marilee's boyfriend. Parker Lindsey, which Corrine thought was a lovely name. He was so handsome, too. Clean and neat, and he smiled at her and Willie Lee. He smiled at just about everyone, and had very white, even teeth. Sometimes, although she never would have told anyone on this earth, Corrine imagined having a boyfriend just like Parker Lindsey.

Aunt Marilee did not want to take the office girl's word that Willie Lee wasn't there. Corrine, who never took anyone's word for anything, was glad to accompany her aunt and search along the outside dog runs and look into the cattle chutes and pens. Corrine even called Willie Lee's name softly. He might come to her first, she thought, because Aunt Marilee was getting pretty mad now.

They got back inside the Cherokee and drove around a couple of streets surrounding the school. Aunt Marilee said that they should be able to spot Willie Lee's blond hair, because it shone in the sun. They stopped and asked a couple of people they saw in yards if they had seen Willie Lee. At one falling-down house, a man sat in his undershirt on the front step, drinking a beer. Aunt Marilee got right out of the car and went up to ask him about Willie Lee, but Corrine stayed rooted in the seat, watching sharply. She made it a point not to talk to men with beers in their hands.

Then Aunt Marilee headed in the direction of home, saying out loud, "Maybe he's on his way home."

Corrine, who was beginning to get really scared for her cousin and for her aunt and for her whole life, scooted up until she was sitting on the edge of the seat, looking as hard as she was able.

It was a long walk to home, but only about a five-minute drive. Maybe Willie Lee knew the way, and he wouldn't have to cross the highway or anything. Still, no telling where he might go, and again all sorts of fearful images began to race across her mind, such as cars running over her cousin's little body, and snakes slithering out to bite him, or maybe a black widow spider like in the movies, or maybe a bad man would get him, or a bunch of big, mean boys.

At one point she said, "Willie Lee doesn't like school. Some of the kids tease him and call him dumb and stupid, and it's hard for him to sit still all day." She didn't want her aunt to make Willie Lee go back to school.

Aunt Marilee said, "I know."

"I don't like school, either," Corrine said, quietly, in the manner a child uses when she has to speak her feelings but does so in a way and time that she believes the adult might not hear. Then her throat got all thick, and she hated herself for being so stupid as to risk making Aunt Marilee mad. She would die if Aunt Marilee got mad at her.

Aunt Marilee, her gaze focused out the windshield, said, "We'll talk about it later." And a moment later, she whispered, "God, help us find Willie Lee."

They searched the streets on the way home, following the route Aunt Marilee took when driving them to and from school. Again Aunt Marilee questioned several people who were outside.

A man who was roofing a house said, "Yeah, Marilee, I saw him over there on the corner. I'm sorry, I didn't recognize him as your boy. And I didn't see what direction he went."

At least when the man had seen him, Willie Lee hadn't been dead yet, Corrine thought.

Aunt Marilee drove the rest of the way home, where she went immediately to the backyard and checked to see if Willie Lee might be there with his rabbits or up in his tree fort. Corrine climbed the ladder to look in the fort, even though no one answered when they called. "He's not here," she called back to her aunt.

Aunt Marilee went to the front yard and hollered, "Willie Lee! Willie Lee!"

There was no answer.

Aunt Marilee unlocked the front door and went inside and straight to the answering machine on her desk in the corner of the living room. There were no messages. Aunt Marilee immediately picked up the telephone and called the school, asking if Willie Lee had been found there. He had not. Next Aunt Marilee telephoned the sheriff's office to ask for help.

Afterward, she snapped the receiver back on the hook and looked at Corrine. "He's all right. God watches over all of us, and most especially little ones like Willie Lee."

Corrine, who had reason to doubt God watched over her, thought her Aunt Marilee was speaking to calm herself. She felt guilty for the thought.

"Well, we've done all we can," Aunt Marilee said, rising straight up. "We'll wait here and let God handle it."

Aunt Marilee let God handle it for about the length of time it took to make a pot of tea and fix a cup with lots of sugar for Corrine, and search for a pack of cigarettes, which she didn't find, and then she went to telephoning people.

From the chair at the table, where she could look clear through the house to the front and watch her aunt hold the phone to her ear while pacing in long strides that pushed out her brown skirt, Corrine felt helpless and desperate.

Three

Tate Holloway drove into Valentine from the east along small, bumpy roads because he had taken a wrong turn and gotten lost. He never had been very good at directions. A couple of his city desk editors used to say they hated to send him out to an emergency, because he might miss it by ending up in a different state.

He slowed his yellow BMW convertible when he came into the edge of town. He passed the feed and grain with its tall elevator, and the car wash, and the IGA grocery. Anticipation tightened in his chest. Right there on the IGA was a sign that proclaimed it the Hometown Grocery Store.

This was going to be his own hometown.

Driving on, he entered the Main Street area and spied *The Valentine Voice* building. He allowed it only a glance and drove slowly, taking in everything on the left side of the street, turned around at the far edge of town and took in everything on the opposite side of the street.

He had seen the town as a child of nine, and surprisingly, it looked almost as he remembered. There were the cars parked head-in on the wide street. There was the bank, modernized nicely with new windows and a thorough sandblasting job. There was the theater—it had become something called The Little Opry. There was the florist . . . and the drugstore, with the air conditioner that dripped. The air conditioner was still there, although he could not tell if it dripped, as it was too cool in April to need it. He imagined it still dripped, though.

There were various flags flying outside the storefronts: the U.S. flags, the state flag of Oklahoma, what appeared to be the Valentine City flag, and a couple of Confederate flags, which surprised him a bit and reminded him that people in the west tended to be truly individualistic. There was a flag with flowers on it at the florist, and at least one person was a Texan, because there was a Texas flag flying proudly.

Tate thought the flags gave a friendly touch. He noted the benches placed at intervals. One thing the town needed, he thought, was trees.

He liked a town with trees along the sidewalks to give shade when a person walked along.

Back once again to *The Valentine Voice* building, he turned and parked the BMW head-in to the curb. Slowly he removed his sunglasses and sat there looking at the building for some minutes. It sat like a grand cornerstone of the town, two-story red brick, with grey stone-cased windows and The Valentine Voice etched in a granite slab beside the double doors.

Emotion rose in his chest. Tears even burned in his eyes.

There it was—his *own* newspaper.

It was the dream of many a big-city news desk editor to become publisher of his own paper, and Tate had held this dream a long time. A place where he could express his own ideas, unencumbered by the hesitancies and prejudices of others less inclined to personal responsibility and more concerned with being politically correct and watching the bottom line dollar. Newspaper publishing as it once was, with editors who spoke their fire and light, drank whiskey from pint bottles in their desk drawers and smoked big stogies, with no thought of the fate of their jobs or pensions, only the single-minded intent to speak the truth.

The good parts of the old days were what Tate intended to resurrect. Here, in this small place in the world, he would pursue his mission to speak his mind and spread courage, and to enjoy on occasion the damn straight wildness for the sake of being wild.

Yes, sir, by golly, he was on his way.

Tate alighted from the BMW, slammed the door and took the sidewalk in one long stride. A bell tinkled above as he opened the heavy glass front door and strode through, removing his hat and taking in the interior with one eager glance: brick wall down the left side, desks, high ceiling with lights and fans suspended. Old, dim, deteriorating . . . but promising. A city room, by golly.

"Can I help you?"

It was a woman at the front reception desk, bathed in the daylight from the wide windows. A no-nonsense sort of woman, with deep-brown hair in a Buster Brown cut and steady black eyes behind dark-rimmed glasses. Cheyenne, he thought.

"Hello, there. I'm Tate Holloway." He sent her his most charming grin.

"You're not."

That response set him back.

"Why, yes, ma'am, I believe I am." He chuckled and tapped his hat against his thigh.

She was standing now. She had unfolded from her chair, and Tate, who was five foot eleven, saw with a bit of surprise that he was eye to eye with her.

"You aren't supposed to be here until Saturday."

"Well, that's true." He tugged at his ear. He had expected to be *welcomed*. He had expected there to be people here, too, and the big room was empty.

"But here I am." He stuck out his hand. "And who might you be, ma'am?" he drawled in an intimate manner. It had been said that Tate Holloway could charm the spots off a bobcat.

This long, tall woman was made of stern stuff. She looked at his hand for a full three heartbeats before offering her own, which was thin but sturdy. "Charlotte Nation."

"Well, now . . . nice to meet you, Miss Charlotte."

She blinked. "Yes . . . a pleasure to meet you, Mr. Holloway." She wet her lips. "I'm sorry I didn't say that right away. It's just that Marilee said you weren't coming until Saturday." There again was the note of accusation in her voice. "We aren't prepared. We are . . ." She looked around behind her at the room and seemed to search for words. "Well, everyone is busy working for the paper, just not here."

"I'm glad to see that," Tate said. "I didn't expect a welcoming committee."

A spark of suspicion about that statement shone in her eyes, before she blinked and said, "I'm assuming you know that Chet Harmon, Harlan Buckles and Jewel Luttrell have all quit in the last month. June Redman has taken on the layout, and she's out gettin' her mammogram this afternoon. She used to just work part-time, anyway. Imperia is out on some sales calls. Leo and Reggie and Tammy are on stories, and Marilee's had to go find her little boy." She paused, then added, "Zona's here, of course."

"Marilee James? Her little boy is missing?" He recalled the woman's voice on the phone, deep and soft, like warm butter. He had been anticipating seeing her and felt a bit of disappointment that she wasn't here. Actually, saying that he didn't want a welcoming committee was a fib, as this woman recognized. Tate had anticipated being greatly welcomed . . . at least, he had expected to be received with some enthusiasm.

The woman nodded. "Willie Lee. He's wandered off from school again. He's eight years old but learning disabled."

"I see."

"He is sweet as the day is long, but he tends to drift away. And he is not afraid of anybody in this world. That's the worry . . . so many strangers come down here these days from the city."

He felt vaguely guilty, since he had just driven in from a city. "Well, I'll just have a look around."

The woman blinked, as if surprised.

Just then a door from an office down on the left opened. A person— a small woman—appeared, saw Tate, and stepped back and shut the door. It happened so quickly that the only impression Tate had was of a small, grey-haired mouse of a woman. The office had window glass, but dark shades were drawn.

Tate looked at the brown-haired woman, who said, "That is Zona Porter—no relation—our comptroller."

Tate waited several seconds to hear more, to possibly be introduced to this woman, but just then the phone on the desk rang, and the brown-haired woman immediately snatched it up.

"*Valentine Voice,* Charlotte speaking." She gripped the telephone receiver. After several seconds, she told whoever was on the other end, "I'll have Marilee call you back about that. She's had to go out after Willie Lee. He's wandered off from school again." Her eyes lit on Tate. "Oh, wait! Mr. Holloway, the new publisher, is here. You can talk to him. Hold on a minute while I switch you over to another line . . . yes, he's the new owner, Ms. Porter's cousin. . . . I know it isn't Saturday, he came early. Now I'm switching."

She said to Tate, "It's the mayor. They've landed the detention center after all, and he wants to give you the story."

He stood there staring at her, and she stared back. Then a ringing sounded from a room behind Ms. Nation.

"Go on and get it in Ms. Porter's office," the woman ordered, shooing him with her hand. "I have to keep this phone clear in case anyone calls about Willie Lee."

Tate turned and strode down the wide reception area to the opened doorway, the office he remembered as his uncle's. Two long strides and he reached the enormous old walnut desk. Almost in a single motion, he tossed aside his hat and answered the phone, at the same time pulling a pad and pen from the breast pocket of his brown denim sport coat.

His journalist's instincts had kicked in. He was a newspaper owner, by golly.

The mayor, a meek but earnest man with extremely thin fingers and hair, drove Tate out to see the site for the new detention center that would employ a hundred people right off the bat.

There was a lot of controversy over the center, the mayor admitted. He stuttered over the word *controversy*. Tate listened to the man's explanations and read a bit between the diplomatic lines. Many people didn't want what they thought of as a prison in their midst.

The mayor drove him all around, giving him a guided tour of the town and surrounding area. He took him into the Main Street Café and introduced him around, and then over to Blaine's Drugstore and introduced him to Mr. Blaine, the only person in the store at the time and who seemed reticent to break away from his television. His only comment on the detention center was, "They'll need a pharmacy, those boys."

After that Tate walked with the mayor, who shyly requested being called Walter, up and down both sides of the street, the mayor introducing him to various shop owners, who all said more or less, "Hey, Walter," and slapped the mayor's back fondly and got a warm back-slapping in return. The mayor was generally beloved, Tate saw.

When he finally begged off from a supper invitation by the mayor and returned to the newspaper offices, Miss Charlotte was on her feet. "I'm glad you are back. It's after five o'clock, and time for me to go home. Leo took the disks for the mornin' edition up to the printer. We didn't think we could wait for you," she added in the faintly critical tone Tate was beginning to recognize. "Harlan used to handle it. Since he quit, we're all just sort of filling in for the time being." There was an air of expectancy in that comment, too.

"That's just fine. I didn't realize it was after five. I'm sorry to hold you up."

"I waited because I wasn't sure you had keys. I didn't want to lock you out." She pulled a purse as big as a suitcase from beneath the desk.

Tate felt a little embarrassed to tell her that he didn't have any keys. She strode out from behind her desk, and he stepped out of her way, having a sense she might walk right over him. She continued on into his cousin's—*his*—office, reached into the middle drawer of the desk and pulled out keys that she handed over to him.

She was through the front door when he thought to ask, "Did they find Marilee James's little boy?"

She looked over her shoulder at him. "No. I'm going over to her house now and take some fried chicken."

The door closed behind her, and Tate watched through the big plate glass window as she walked away down the sidewalk and turned the corner. Miss Charlotte wore an amazingly short skirt and high heels for a prim-and-proper woman. And she didn't walk; she marched.

* * *

He went out to the BMW that he'd left right there with the top down, his computer in full sight. He had figured a person could do that in Valentine.

Making a number of trips, he carted the computer, monitor and then a few boxes into his new office. After he'd set the things down, he stood smoothing the back of his hair. That he ought to be doing something to help in the search for little Willie Lee James tugged at him. He felt helpless on that score. There didn't seem anything he, not knowing either the child or the town, could do.

He left the boxes in a stack and started to connect up his computer, but then decided he was too impatient to see his new home. He wanted to get a look around while the light was still good. He locked the front doors and was one step away when he stopped, remembering the small grey woman he had earlier seen appear. Was she still in there?

He didn't think she could be, since Miss Charlotte hadn't said anything about her. Still, the thought caused him to go back inside to check.

On the door glass of the office was printed: Zona Porter, No Relation, Comptroller. He did not hear sound from beyond the walls. He knocked. No answer. Very carefully he turned the knob and stuck his head in the door. The office, very small and neat, even stark, was empty.

Well, good. He felt better to have made certain.

Back at the front door again, he locked the door of *his* newspaper, wondering if one even needed to bother in such a town. Whistling, he strode to his BMW, where he jumped over the door and slid down into the seat. He backed the BMW out of its place and had to drive the length of town and turn around and come back to the intersection of Main and Church Streets. His cousin Muriel's house, which he had bought sight unseen since he was nine years old, was on the second block up Church Street, on the corner. He heard Muriel's clipped tone of voice giving him the directions.

The town was pretty as a church calendar picture in the late-afternoon sunlight that shone golden on the buildings and flags, houses and big trees. Forsythia blooms had mostly died away, but purple wisteria and white bridal wreath were in full bloom.

It struck him how he knew the names of the bushes. He had learned a few things from his ex-wife, he supposed. He experienced a sharp but brief stab of regret for what he had let pass him by. He had not cared about houses and yards during his married years; he had not valued building a home and a family.

Then he immediately remembered all that he had experienced in place of domesticity, and he figured his life and times had been correct for him. In fact, that was what Lucille had told him: "You need to be a newspaperman, Tate, not a married man."

Funny, he hadn't thought of Lucille in a long time. Her image was fuzzy, and her voice came only in a faint whisper from deep in memory. She had been a rare woman, but neither of them had fit together in a marriage. Set free, she had blossomed as a psychologist, mother, political activist.

To everything there is a season, a time for every purpose under heaven, he thought as his gaze lit on the big Porter house that came into view—the *Holloway* house, he mentally corrected.

He thought of his season now, as he pulled the BMW to a stop in the driveway just outside the portico. His season had come to put down roots. He had reached that point, by golly, finally, at the age of fifty-one. It was a fact, he thought, that might daunt a lesser man.

His strides were long and swift. He took the wide front steps two at a time and unlocked a door that needed refinishing. It creaked loudly when opened.

He stepped inside, into a wide hallway. There was a pleasant scent of old wood. He walked through the musty rooms, the oak flooring creaking often beneath his steps as he gave everything a cursory, almost absent look, noting the amazing fact that Muriel had pretty much left everything just as it was.

When Muriel had decided to leave, she had definitely decided to *leave.*

He poked his head out the back door, the screen door that definitely needed replacing, then walked more slowly around the kitchen that had not been painted in twenty years. His cousin had not been a domestic type, any more than he had been. On into the dining room, where he unlocked the French doors and stepped out on the wraparound porch. By golly, he *liked* the porch! He was going to sit out here on hot afternoons and smoke his cigars and drink iced tea thick as syrup with sugar.

Just then his gaze fell on the wicker settee, where he saw a little boy asleep.

A little boy, a dog, and a big orange cat who regarded Tate with definite annoyance.

Four

Vast Stretches of the Heart

When Parker's blue pickup truck, with the white-and-gold Lindsey Veterinary Clinic emblem on the side, came pulling up in her driveway, Marilee went running out to meet him. There was in the back of her mind the idea that he would be bringing Willie Lee.

She saw immediately that he had not.

"I heard about Willie Lee. Is he home yet?" Parker strode around the front of his truck toward her.

"No . . . all this time, Parker . . ." Her arms pried themselves from her sides, and she reached for him.

He took her against him and held her tight. Then, as he walked her back into the house, with his arm around her shoulders, Marilee told him of her conversation with the principal, of having searched the neighborhoods, of calling Sheriff Oakes, and of the helplessness of just having to wait. She did not mention the fear that was rising to choke her throat, that maybe this time Willie Lee was truly gone, a fear that had haunted her since the night she had delivered him early, blue and choking for breath.

"He is just out diggin' in a ditch for crawdads or explorin' ant trails or something that boys do," Parker said with perfect reasonableness.

Recriminations for having felt the burden of being a mother echoed in her brain, bringing shame and self-loathing.

"He'll turn up, Marilee. It'll be okay," Parker whispered in her ear as he again drew her close.

What was great about Parker was his solidity in any crisis. Probably it had something to do with being a veterinarian, facing life and death on a regular basis. He was not daunted by a crisis, but was, in fact, better in a crisis than at normal times. He could offer himself in a crisis, whereas during normal everyday times, he withheld himself and kept his affability around him like a shield.

"Did you bring any cigarettes?" she asked.

"No. Why would I have cigarettes?" He looked startled.

"Parker, don't you keep any, just in case?"

"I quit three years ago, and so did you, remember?" he said with a righteousness that Marilee thought uncalled for in the situation.

Annoyed, she almost asked him to go get her a pack, but then the phone rang.

Phone calls had been coming in from people as they heard about Willie Lee. Each time Marilee would jump to answer, hoping it was the sheriff calling to say Willie Lee was found. After three more such calls, she waved at Parker to answer.

Then Charlotte Nation drove up in her little red Grand Am. Marilee, sitting at the window, watched Charlotte unfold her long legs out of the car and come swiftly up the walk, her arms loaded with brown bags. Charlotte had brought containers of fried chicken and potato salad from the Quick Shop that had put in a delicatessen.

Marilee looked at the food and felt sick; it was like funeral food.

Charlotte reported that June had managed to correct both the Ford and IGA ads in time for Leo's delivery of the disks to the printer for tomorrow's edition. And that their new publisher, Tate Holloway, had arrived before schedule.

"He did?" Vaguely, Marilee tried to be concerned about this.

"Don't worry about him," Charlotte said, giving a dismissive wave. "He took it upon himself to come early, so he had to take what he got. And when Willie Lee comes home, you are going to be worn out, so sleep in tomorrow morning and just come on down when you get ready."

When Willie Lee comes home . . .

As Charlotte's Grand Am pulled away from the curb, Marilee, who felt the need to keep vigil out the front window, was dismayed to see her mother's Cadillac pull in. The car bore a front license plate that said CCoopers, which was advertising of a sort for the discount appliance store owned by her mother's second husband—Carl Cooper— one of those stores that plastered the television with cluttered and tasteless ads. What this did for Marilee's mother, however, was give her the fame she craved.

Watching her mother, a small woman with Lady Clairol blond hair who walked in short, quick strides, Marilee had the thought to run and hide, but like one inextricably caught, she kept sitting there.

Her mother had come to talk about Marilee helping her get new tires for her Cadillac, because her husband could not be counted on to do this to her satisfaction.

"Carl won't take the time," she said, having launched immediately into her request. "He insists on just goin' down to the discount tire warehouse and getting the cheapest ones slapped on there . . . and he doesn't pay attention if they balance them or not."

Marilee jumped in to say, "Mother, I can't talk to you about this now. Willie Lee is missing."

Upon being told of her grandson's disappearance, her mother became very agitated. Her entire countenance became one of doom, so much so that to look at her made Marilee have trouble breathing.

Her mother then launched in with comments of a dire sort. "Anything could happen to him out there, all these perverts in the world." And, "The boy is too friendly, doesn't know a stranger. I hope he didn't get in a car with somebody." Then, "You never should have sent the boy to school anyway. He isn't capable of regular school," and, in a whisper that really wasn't one and that Parker heard very well, "You should marry Parker, and then you could stay home with the boy."

Invariably her mother called Willie Lee the boy.

"He has a name, mother. It is *Willie Lee*."

"Well, I know that," her mother said, looking confused and hurt and more fearful than ever. Marilee felt like a toad but did not apologize.

Parker, who could stand no conflict, said, "Norma, would you like more coffee?"

Marilee turned and went and shut herself in the bathroom, where she stared at her reflection in the medicine cabinet mirror for a long minute, asking all sorts of unintelligible questions of herself and God.

Finally, her spinning brain settling somewhat, she opened the medicine cabinet and began a thorough search. Surely she had some pills left in here from the time when Stuart had walked out on her. Surely she did. Oh, Lordy, she felt like she was coming apart.

A knock sounded at the door. Marilee, wondering if word had come of her son, whipped the door open to see standing there her tall and sturdy Aunt Vella.

"Hello, sugar. I'm sorry, I'm not Willie Lee." Her eyes, all sympathetic, went beyond Marilee to the sink strewn with the stuff out of the medicine cabinet. "What are you doing?"

"Looking for any of my old pills. I don't have any, though. I threw them all out."

"Well, yes, you did. I was here that day. Now, I've brought you what you need—a big chocolate shake."

"Chocolate?"

"Yes, sugar . . . it's in the kitchen."

"Bless you." Marilee threw herself on her aunt, who hugged her tight and then kept an arm around her all the way to the kitchen, where her mother saw and frowned. There had always been animosity between Marilee's petite mother and her statuesque Aunt Vella, who was her father's sister.

Marilee disengaged herself from her aunt and sat down, taking up the large paper cup and spooning the thick shake into her mouth. Her Aunt Vella and Uncle Perry owned Blaine's Drugstore and Soda Fountain, and Aunt Vella knew exactly how Marilee liked her chocolate shakes, with an extra squirt of chocolate syrup.

Then Marilee saw that Corrine had her own shake, too. Corrine's black eyes met Marilee's for an instant, in which Marilee summoned forth an encouraging smile from the place mothers always keep them. She had forgotten about her niece and wanted to make up for it. The child had enough of being forgotten in her life.

Corrine quickly looked away, though, as if needing to protect herself.

"Well, I have to go," Marilee's mother said. "I have to get Carl's supper."

"That's okay . . . there's nothing you can do here." God forbid Carl's supper be interrupted. Marilee breathed deeply.

"You call me as soon as you have news . . . and I can come back down." She was edging toward the door, and turned and told Parker, "Good seeing you, Parker—you call me if Marilee needs me."

Parker nodded politely, wisely not committing himself.

"Vella, it was good seein' you."

"Norma . . ."

Different as night and day, the two women managed to tolerate each other.

For a second Marilee's mother hovered uncertainly, and then she patted Marilee's arm and stroked Corrine's dark hair away from her forehead, saying, "Honey, can't you clip your hair out of your eyes?"

Marilee saw Corrine quietly keep sipping her milk shake, while beneath the table her legs swung about ninety miles an hour.

"Well, I'll get with you this weekend about the tires," Marilee's mother said before leaving.

Marilee played the straw around in her milk shake and suffered guilt at the thought of telling her mother to cram the tires up her ass.

Vella, feeling the need to be polite and thoroughly cover the annoyance she always felt in the other woman's presence, hopped to her feet and escorted her ex-sister-in-law to the front door. And needing to make certain the woman did indeed get out the door. It was, Vella thought as she saw her ex-sister-in-law get into her car, a great failing on her part that, after all these years and the death of her brother, Norma Cooper should still have the power to irritate the fire out of her.

When she returned to the kitchen, Parker was massaging Marilee's shoulders and joking with Corrine, producing a rare smile from the child. Although she had always found Parker Lindsey vaguely wanting, Vella thoroughly admired the way he could lighten a moment when he put his mind to it.

Marilee said to her, "Don't you have the Rose Club meeting tonight?"

"Yes. And I'm going. There's plenty of time. Perry can get supper over at the café, and I can go straight to the meeting from here." Perry always took himself off to the café, if he came home and she wasn't there and no supper was on the table. Then he would come home, turn on the television and fall asleep in his La-Z-Boy.

She went to the counter to unpack a grocery sack from the IGA, where she had bought chocolate cookies and bananas. In her estimation a person could live on bananas for a meal and cookies for desert. She noted then on the counter a big bucket of fried chicken and a container of potato salad. With a small slice of alarm over possible food poisoning, she put the potato salad in the refrigerator.

The phone rang, and all of them jumped. Parker was the first to reach the receiver hanging on the wall. "James house," he answered in an uncharacteristically clipped tone.

They all stared at him, not a breath being breathed. He said, "Hmmm . . . okay," and hung up then said, "That was Neville. He said they haven't found Willie Lee, but they have talked to five people who saw him this afternoon. He was definitely heading this way home."

Marilee wished she had talked to the sheriff herself. Hearing his voice would have been something. Then she imagined the sheriff telling her that they were searching all the drainage culverts.

"Where *is* he?"

They all stared helplessly at her. She swung around and pushed out the back screen door and down the steps to the yard, hardly realizing what she was doing.

Please, Lord, bring my baby home. I will do anything. Please, Lord . . . just please. How will I bear it if you take him from me? If anything happens to him . . .

Thankfully, those in the kitchen knew her well enough to let her go alone. She went to the foot of the tree that housed the little fort Marilee and Willie Lee had built together and looked upward. She did not cry. She never cried in a crisis. As she saw it, crying had never changed anything, and if she cried, then all would be lost.

She went to the rabbit cages and realized it was way past time the two rabbits inside were fed their evening meal. She got their food from the garage and filled their dishes, changing their water, too. She thought how Willie Lee loved animals. He seemed more comfortable with them than with people.

As she stood gazing at the rabbits, a squeal sounded . . . the familiar squeal of the gate in the back fence.

She whirled around to see a man coming through the gate. A tall man . . . Charlotte had said Tate Holloway . . .

Then she saw, standing beside the man, her much smaller son.

"This boy says he lives here," the man said.

"Oh, my . . . *Willie Lee!*"

It was not until that instant of seeing the small boy's figure and then her eyes falling on his upturned face that she realized she had truly begun to believe she would never see Willie Lee alive again, and that what she had been wrestling with all these hours was the inner imagining of his limp little body being pulled from some muddy ditch.

But here he was, his blond hair standing on end and his blue eyes peering out from his thick glasses, regarding her calmly.

"Hey, Ma-ma."

She had scooped him against her. He pushed away and put a hand on her cheek, looking deep into her eyes.

"Why are you cry-ing, Ma-ma?"

"Because I missed you . . ." She was crying so hard that she could hardly speak. "I didn't know where you were, and I've been so scared, because you were lost."

She hugged him close again.

"I was not lost," he said, again pushing away to look at her with his dear blue eyes blinking behind his glasses. "I was com-ing home."

"Oh, honey . . ." She caressed his dear, unruly hair, so glad for the feel of it. "It is a long way from school. You shouldn't come home all by yourself."

"I was not all by my-self. I had Mun-ro with me."

For an instant of confusion, Marilee thought he meant the man, but then he was reaching to bring forward a dog. A shaggy, spotted small type of shepherd.

"Mun-ro," Willie Lee introduced happily.

The man was Tate Holloway, which was a little surprising, but not so much, because Marilee had recognized his deep Southern drawl. He explained that he had been looking around his cousin's house and had discovered Willie Lee sleeping on the wicker settee on the porch, with the dog and a big orange cat that had, as Mr. Holloway put it, "skeddaddled faster than a hog skatin' on ice."

Tate Holloway's voice was as it had been when Marilee had spoken to him on the phone, all deep and smoky, and he drew his words out like he purely enjoyed each one on his tongue.

"Bub-ba," Willie Lee said, turning concerned eyes up to her. "I was going to feed Bub-ba, but his food is all gone, and he ran away from us."

Understanding dawned as to what had brought Willie Lee home by way of the back gate. "We've been going through the gate each night to feed Bubba on the back step," Marilee explained. "Bubba is—or was—Ms. Porter's cat. We've been feeding him until you came. She said you got the cat with the house."

Willie Lee said, "Bub-ba needs food."

"We'll let Mr. Holloway take Bubba some of this chicken," Marilee told him.

They all sat around the big oak table in Marilee's kitchen, eating the meal friends had brought earlier. It was very much like a party. Marilee kept Willie Lee sitting on her lap, where she could repeatedly touch him. On one side, within touching distance whether she wished it or not, sat Corrine, who seemed to grin an awfully lot for her, and on the other side, with his arm often on the back of Marilee's chair, sat Parker. Aunt Vella hovered, a good hostess attending everyone. Marilee soaked up this time of contentment, of safety after threat.

"I was going to call you," Tate Holloway said, having gone over the story a second time and embellishing with how *Miss* Charlotte had taken him to task for coming before his scheduled Saturday arrival and how surprised he had been to see a boy on his settee.

"I had your telephone number, but Willie Lee here—" he winked and pointed at Willie Lee with a chicken leg "—said he would show me the way over. I sure wondered where he was goin' when he led me into those cedar trees, but by golly, there was the gate right in the midst of those ramblin' roses, just like he said."

Marilee, putting warm chicken meat in her mouth with her fingers, watched the man and her son grin at each other. Tate Holloway had a charming grin.

"I knew the way. I was not lost," Willie Lee said. Then he looked at Marilee, squinting with one eye behind his thick glasses. "Well, oncet I was lost, but Mun-ro led me home."

Taking a roll from his and Marilee's plate, he slipped from her lap and went to feed it to the dog lying on the spiral rug in front of the sink, as was the right of a dog who had protected her son.

Marilee, approving of how gently the dog ate from her son's hand, felt a sinking feeling. "Honey, Munro may belong to someone. He has a collar."

Willie Lee said, "No . . . he was look-ing for me, to come live here. I told God I want-ed him. Re-member?"

Marilee glanced at Parker.

"I don't think I've seen that dog before," Parker said. "But not everybody 'round here brings me their pets. Most, but not everyone. And he doesn't have any tags . . . may not have had a rabies shot," he added as caution.

Everyone looked at the dog, who blinked his kind eyes.

Tate Holloway said, "You just can't separate a boy and a dog, oncet they've chosen each other," and winked at Willie Lee. "Plain secret of life is a good dog."

Now Marilee knew where Willie Lee had picked up saying "oncet."

"How come you to name him Munro, Willie Lee?" Aunt Vella asked.

"That is his name."

At this good sense, all of them chuckled, except Corrine, who had begun to help Aunt Vella clear the table and who informed them, "It says Munro on his collar."

When they all looked at her, she added, "It's printed in white. M-U-N-R-O."

Parker took a look, pulling the collar out of the dog's hair. "Yep. Munro." He petted the dog.

"Who told you his name?" Marilee asked.

"Mun-ro told me," Willie Lee said practically, stroking the dog.

"Did he tell you if he has had his shots?" Parker wanted to know, giving Marilee a wink.

Willie Lee looked at the dog and then said, "He does not want shots."

They all chuckled. Marilee looked closer at the dog, who smiled happily back at her. She had to admit the name fit him perfectly.

The sheriff and friends and neighbors and Marilee's mother had been alerted that the crisis was over, and Willie Lee had been returned home safe and sound. Vella, who had made a majority of the telephone calls, left to go to her Rose Club organizational meeting. Now that all was safe and sound, she was in a hurry, backing her Crown Victoria with racing speed.

Tate Holloway decided he would walk home on the sidewalk. "Think I'll see a bit more of the neighborhood," he said.

Parker went with Marilee to see their new neighbor out the front door. It occurred to Marilee that in all the years she had worked for Ms. Porter and lived just beyond the rose-lined fence from the big Porter home, the woman had never even once visited her home. Here, in the first hours of his arrival, Tate Holloway had not only visited, he had returned her beloved son and eaten a celebration meal with them.

Streetlights were on now, sending their silvery glow up and down the street and casting shadows into yards.

"Thank you for the delightful meal," Tate Holloway said, stopping at the foot of the steps and turning to look upward at Marilee and Parker on the edge of the porch. "And for this fine fare for Bubba," he added, lifting the plastic bag containing the leftover chicken pieces.

Marilee said, "Thank *you*, Mr. Holloway, for returning Willie Lee."

Tate Holloway grinned. "Well, now, I think it would be more accurate to say that Willie Lee led me over here."

He gazed at her with that grin.

"And I'd prefer it, Miss Marilee, if you would call me Tate," he said in his deep, slow East Texas drawl.

His eyes that seemed to twinkle, even at this distance, rested on her. There was a contagious inner delight in Tate Holloway.

"All right. Tate. I'm glad to meet you."

"I'm glad to know you, Marilee James, and your family. I won't be a stranger . . . you can count on that."

Marilee gazed down at the tall man who grinned up at her, until Parker slipped his arm around her and said, "We are sure grateful for you bringing Willie Lee home, Tate."

Tate's eyes shifted to Parker. "Ah . . . yes, well, sir . . . I'm just glad things turned out so fine. Good night." With another glance at Marilee and a wave of the little bag of chicken, he was off down the walkway.

Marilee's eyes followed, seeing that his fine, white-blond hair caught the light and shone like sun-warmed silk, and that his shoulders were strong, his torso lean, and his strides long, in the way of a man who is all muscle and purpose.

Then Parker was turning her from the sight. They walked back into the house with his arm around her shoulders. Just inside the closed door, in the dimness, he drew her to him and kissed her.

"Your Willie Lee came home safe and sound, just like I said," he reminded her.

"Thank you for being here, Parker." She was very grateful.

He pulled her against him and kissed her neck. She felt him wanting a lot more, but she could not give any thought to it right now. She was too busy clutching to her what she had feared she had lost. There was no energy left at this moment to consider her relationship with Parker.

She tucked Corrine and Willie Lee into bed.

"Honey, we will have to run an announcement in the paper about finding Munro," she told Willie Lee, taking off his glasses and setting them on the night table.

"He is my dog now." He put his hand on the dog, who lay beside him.

"He has a collar with his name on it. That means someone bought it for him. Someone who cares for him. What if you had lost him? Wouldn't you want whoever found him to do their best to get him back to you?"

Willie Lee frowned, and his lower lip quivered. "Mun-ro found me. I did not find-ed him."

"We will run an ad in the paper for two weeks. That is the right thing to do, the most we can do."

Willie Lee turned on his side and clutched the dog to him.

Marilee kissed him and considered not running the ad. Maybe just the Sunday paper.

She kissed Corrine and turned out the light, then went to the kitchen to prepare the coffeemaker for the morning. She thought it a wise course to tone down the strength of the brew that Corrine made. Maybe lessening her caffeine intake would help her nerves, which seemed so on edge these days.

At the moment of stretching her hand to the light switch, her eye came to rest on Willie Lee's picture book lying on the edge of the table. The book he'd had that morning, when he had been trying to show her the picture of the dog.

She took it up and thumbed through the pages, until she came to the one with the dog picture that jumped right out at her.

She scanned the print below, which was a description of the dog. An Australian Shepherd, it said, bred for herding sheep. The dog in the picture had his tail bobbed. Marilee had seen similar dogs in the rural areas.

Taking the book, she went to the open door of the children's room, where the dog lay on the rug beside Willie Lee's bed. The dog opened his eyes and looked at her. His tail thumped.

In the dim light cast from the bathroom, Marilee consulted the book, then looked again at the dog.

She would check again in the clear light of day, she thought. So many wild things could occur to a person in the night and be cleared up in the light of day.

When the morning came, Marilee found that Munro did look remarkably like the dog in the picture book, although, he *was* darker.

Her eyes followed the dog and her son walking through the kitchen. No matter the dog's appearance, she thought, her son had asked for a dog and been given one. She wondered what she would ask for . . . and wished she could believe it would be given.

Five

The Beauty of the World

It was bare first light of his first full day in his new town when Tate, dressed in brand-new, grey sweatpants, brand-new, bright-white T-shirt with the words *Just Do It* emblazoned on the front, and brand-new top-of-the-line jogging shoes, came out on his very own front porch.

Tate had jogged intermittently off and on for years, and had profited from it, too, but now he wanted to really make it routine. He was in the prime of his life and wanted to honor that by making the most of himself physically and mentally. That was the spirit!

Stretching his arms wide, he sucked in a deep breath. Ahh! The brisk morning, quite different from the heavily humid air of Houston.

He jogged down the steps and out to the sidewalk of the quiet street. As he turned along Porter Street, in the direction of Marilee James's house, the yellow cat, Bubba, streaked out from beneath a lilac bush and joined him, bouncing along behind Tate, looking like an orange basketball with a tail.

Tate wanted to see Marilee's house clearly in the light of day. He wondered if she was an early riser.

He had a sudden fantasy of her being on the porch and seeing him, jogging along manfully, her waving and him waving back. He smiled at his fanciful notion, although he did experience a little bit of disappointment when his gaze found her front porch, white gingerbread trim, and empty.

Not only was all quiet at the James house, but along most of the street. At the house on the corner, a young man wearing a UPS uniform was chinning himself with bulging arms on a beam across the middle of his porch ceiling. He dropped to his feet, headed for his car at the curb, casting Tate a wave as he came. Friendly fellow! Tate waved back.

Turning up First Street, heading for the commerce area of Main, Tate slowed. He had begun to breathe quite hard. He sure didn't want to have a heart attack on his first day in town. He glanced back and saw that Bubba had deserted him.

Tate continued on, a sort of jog, meeting two ladies who were race walking, pumping arms, talking at the same rate they were walking. They exchanged swift hellos with Tate.

On Main Street, a woman was unlocking the door of her shop— Sweetie Cakes Bakery painted across the window. She nodded and slipped in the door. Further down the street, he looked across at *The Valentine Voice* building. By golly, it was his!

He was walking now.

Just then Charlotte came through the front doors of the *Voice,* surprising him somewhat, and put up the flag, setting it quickly and returning inside before Tate got close enough to holler a good morning

He was perhaps breathing a little too hard to offer a hearty good morning.

For the past two weeks his attention and time had been taken up with his move to Valentine; that he had not been routinely jogging was telling on him now.

At the corner of the police station, from where he thought he smelled coffee brewing, he turned up Church Street, heading for home. The golden rays of the sun now streaked the horizon.

Funny how he had not realized that the street went up a hill.

Ah, there was another jogger coming toward him. Tate felt the need to push himself into a jog. Didn't want to be out jogging and not doing it.

A minute later he was sure glad he was jogging, because the young man coming toward him turned out to be not quite so young, and to be Parker Lindsey. By golly, he looked all youthful male in a sleeveless shirt and jogging shorts that showed tanned hard thighs.

The two approached the intersection.

"Good mornin'." Tate raised his voice and refused to sound breathless.

" 'Mornin'," Lindsey returned, cruising along at a good clip. He even wore a sweatband around his forehead, like a marathon runner.

Tate put some strength into his jog. He might have a few years on Lindsey, and a lot of grey in his hair, but where there was snow on the mountaintop, there was a fire in the furnace. He thought of the old saw as he continued on across the intersection toward his driveway, intent on at least jogging around to the back of the house, out of view.

Just then he saw, coming along down the hill, a shapely blond young woman in a skimpy exercise outfit, jogging and smiling at him. He might have stopped to talk to her, but the young woman's attention was captured by Tate's older neighbor on the opposite corner, who came from her house in walking shorts and shoes, waving and calling the blond woman by name.

The town was a haven for health enthusiasts!

He continued up his driveway, which had much more of an incline than he had before noted, and around to the back steps, where Bubba now lay, sunning himself. The cat gave Tate a yawn.

"I feed you . . . no comments."

Tate dragged himself in the door and sank down upon the floor, going totally prostrate on the cool linoleum.

Marilee sat holding her coffee cup in both hands and thinking that she should have made it stronger. She had gotten used to Corrine's brew and seemed not to be able to function well on a weaker variety.

Across from her, Corrine, looking for all the world like she was about to be shot, played with her food. Willie Lee, who ate slowly, asked if Munro could go to school with him.

"He will be lone-ly with-out me," he said.

Marilee, watching Corrine play the fork over her egg, thought, there are only three weeks left to the school year.

"I think we can have the ending of our school year today," she said, suddenly getting up and taking her plate to the sink. "You two do not need to go back this year."

She looked over her shoulder to see their reactions.

Willie Lee's eyebrows went up. "I do not have to go to schoo-ol to-day?"

"No, not today, and no more until fall. We'll see about it then."

Corrine was looking at Marilee with a mixture of high hope and sharp distrust on her delicate features.

"I'll call Principal Blankenship and see what we can do about you finishing your work at home," Marilee told her.

The relief that swept the girl's face struck Marilee so hard that she had to turn away and hide her own expression in her coffee cup. She thought of her sister, Anita. Corrine's mother. She had the urge to toss the coffee cup right through the window.

Then Willie Lee was at her side and tapping her thigh. "Mun-ro needs breakfast."

Looking into his sweet face, Marilee smiled. "He does, doesn't he."

"I can give him my egg," Corrine said.

"Please, make him toast, too, Ma-ma."

"Yes, darlin' . . . I'll make toast for Munro." She looked at the dog, now eating the egg very gently from Corrine's plate.

* * *

Marilee's reasoning mind told her to force the children to go to school and face what they would have to face sooner or later, a regimen and self-control, and those few cruel and mean and inept people one will come across on many an occasion. Life was a tough row of responsibility to hoe, and the sooner the children, even Willie Lee, learned this, the better.

She all but took out a gun and shot her reasoning mind. It wisely shut up.

Thinking of both the principal and her new boss, who she would now ask to let her work at home, she got herself dressed nicely in a slim knit skirt and top in soft blue, accented with a genuine silver concho belt from her more prosperous days of no children and a husband who earned quite good money as a world-renowned photojournalist. She managed to talk herself into doing a thorough makeup job and brushed her hair until it shone.

Then she sat at her cherry-wood desk to telephone Principal Blankenship and secure from the woman the promise that Corrine would be kept with her grade. The principal was surprisingly agreeable, even eager, at the idea of releasing the child, whom she all but labeled troubled straight out.

"Corrine has perfect straight A's," the principal said. "Her grades are not a question. She is a very bright girl. That is not at all her problem in class. I'm sure we can accommodate you in order to help Corrine have the rest she needs." Then she tacked on, "Ah . . . I have the name of a child therapist you might want to consider."

For Willie Lee, the principal promised to consult his teacher about work that might possibly help him. Marilee, who had from her teenage years been unable to shake her faith in her own mental capacity, told the principal not to bother Mrs. Reeves. "I'm going to pick out a curriculum for Willie Lee."

The principal definitely disapproved of this action, labeling it risky, but stopped short of pressing, no doubt fearful Marilee would change her mind and bring the children back to school.

Marilee thanked Principal Blankenship for all her help and hung up, sitting there for some minutes, her hand on the telephone, gazing at nothing, until she realized she was gazing at a pattern on the Tibetan rug that fronted the couch. She remembered, then, buying it in Calcutta, on one of hers and Stuart's trips. Her gaze moved about the room, noting a painting on the wall that had been purchased in New Orleans, and a pottery vase picked up in the Smoky Mountains.

Her eyes moved to the small picture of her ex-husband that she kept, still, on her desk.

Stuart James grinned at her from the photo. She picked it up, remembering how handsome she had found him the first time she had laid eyes on him, remembering how wonderful he had made her feel when he touched her body. Stuart was a man who greatly enjoyed making love.

Into these deep thoughts came the sound of childish voices. She blinked and got up, following the sound to the back door.

Willie Lee and Corrine, with the dog between them, sat on the back stairs in the dappled morning sunlight that shone through the trees. They did not hear her footsteps, and she was able to watch them for some minutes through the screen door.

Corrine was talking to the dog, right along with Willie Lee. And she was actually smiling.

"Ma-ma . . . Mun-ro needs to come, too." He spoke as if scolding her for not remembering the dog.

Marilee looked at her son and then the dog. "Okay, Munro . . . get in."

As she backed the Jeep Cherokee from the drive, she gave thanks for the all-purpose vehicle. She supposed she might as well accept that the dog was destined to go everywhere with them. He could, in Valentine, America.

A new vehicle, a yellow convertible BMW, was parked in the block of spaces behind *The Valentine Voice* building. The top was down, and with a raised eyebrow, Marilee peered into the vehicle, noting the soft leather seats. Obviously, coming from Houston, Tate Holloway was unaware of how serious dust could be in this part of the country.

The two-story brick building that housed the newspaper had changed only marginally since it was first built in 1920. The back area of the first floor, which had once housed the printing press, had been converted into a garage and loading area. Printing was now done by a contract printer who did a number of small-town newspapers; *The Valentine Voice* was one of the last small-town dailies in the nation.

The front half of the first floor was pretty much as it had been built. The original bathroom had been enlarged and a small kitchen sink area added. Several offices had been made by adding glass partitions, one of which had dark-green shades all around and a door with a dark-green shade. The name on the glass of the door read: Zona Porter, No Relation, Comptroller. Everyone respected that Zona preferred privacy. One could go in and speak to Zona in the office, but Zona rarely came out. Had a bathroom been installed off her office, Zona would not have come out at all. She had her own refrigerator, coffeemaker, cups, glasses, tissues. She did not care to touch things after other people.

E. G. Porter's original office remained at the right, with tall windows that looked out onto the corner of Main and Church Streets.

Entering through the rear door, Marilee felt a little like she was leading a parade, with the children and the dog Munro trailing behind her.

Leo Pahdocony, Sr., a handsome dark-haired Choctaw Indian who wore turquoise bolas, shiny snakeskin boots and sharply creased Wranglers, was pecking away at the keyboard of his computer and talking on the telephone at the same time, with the receiver tucked in his neck. He gave her a wave and a palm-up to Willie Lee.

His wife, Reggie, a petite redhead who handled news in the schools, churches and most of the photography, popped out of her swivel chair and came to greet them with delight. Reggie, who had for the past five years been trying to conceive another child, extended her arms to capture the children in a big hug. Corrine managed to sidestep her way to Marilee's chair and sat herself firmly, but Willie Lee, always loveable, let Reggie lift him up and kiss him.

"You gave us a scare, young man, running off," Charlotte told him, coming forward with messages for Marilee.

Willie Lee said, "I did not run off. I was com-ing home."

"Uh-huh. Good thinking." Charlotte turned her eyes on Marilee. "Tammy phoned. She's got a horrible toothache."

Marilee saw that Charlotte was thinking the same thing she was: that Tammy had a job interview elsewhere. Without Miss Porter's money pouring in, no one expected the newspaper to continue much longer than a year, if that.

A pounding sounded from the office of the publisher. Marilee looked at the closed door and noticed that Muriel Porter's name plaque was gone, leaving a dark rectangle on the oak.

Pounding again.

"He's hangin' pictures," said Imperia Brown, smacking her phone receiver into the cradle. "It's drivin' me crazy. I'm outta here." She grabbed up her purse and headed for the front door.

Charlotte strode over to the large, gilded frame of the newspaper's founder's portrait now propped on the floor against the copy machine, and said to Marilee, "He took down Mr. E. G. first thing." Charlotte definitely disapproved.

"Might be one of us next," Reggie said.

Marilee and Charlotte cast each other curious glances, and Reggie said she wondered if Ms. Porter might not be feeling her skin crawling at the removal of her daddy from the wall.

"I've been halfway waitin' for the wall to cave in, E.G. having his say from the grave," she said.

"The walls are apparently holding," Charlotte said, "and he's hanging them with all sorts of pictures. He has one of him with President Nixon. I don't know why he'd want to advertise it," she added.

"He has one of him with Reba," Reggie put in with some excitement. "He did a feature piece on her for *Parade Magazine.*"

Reggie had every one of Reba McEntire's albums. She suddenly grabbed up a pen to hold in front of her mouth like a microphone and began singing one of Reba's songs. This was something she often did, pretending either to be a singer or a television commentator. Reggie was every bit pretty enough to be either; however, she could take clowning and showing off to the point of annoyance, as far as Marilee was concerned. Right then was one of those points, and Marilee felt her temper grow short as Reggie kept jutting her face in front of Marilee's and singing about poor old Fancy.

"Reggie, would you keep an eye on Corrine and Willie Lee for me?" she said, thus diverting the woman to more quiet childishness, while Marilee went to their publisher's solid oak door and knocked.

The sound of hammering drowned out her knock, and she had to try again, and when still no answer came, she poked her head in the door. "Mr. Holloway?" She was unable to address him as Tate, being at the office.

He turned from where he was hanging a picture. "Marilee! Come in . . . come in. Just the person I've been waitin' for. You can come over here and help me get this picture in the right place."

It was a picture of him with Billy Graham, black-and-white, as all the photographs appeared to be. He placed it against the wall and waited for her instructions, which she gave in the form of, "Higher . . . a little to the left . . . a little lower. Right there."

Having, apparently, a high opinion of her ability to place a picture, he marked the spot and went to hammering in a nail.

In a flowing glance, Marilee, wondering how an accomplished journalist of Tate Holloway's wide experience would manage in tiny Valentine, took in the room. The sedate, even antiquated office that had belonged to Ms. Porter was gone. Or perhaps a more accurate description was that it was being *moved out,* as pictures and books and boxes full of articles, a number of them antiques, were in a cluster by the door. Next to that, in a large heap, lay the heavy evergreen drapes, which had been ripped from the long windows, leaving only the wooden blinds through which bright light shone on the varied electronic additions: a small television, a radio scanner, a top speed computer and printer, a laptop computer, and one apparatus that Marilee, definitely behind the electronic times, could not identify.

The major change, however, was to the big walnut desk, which had been moved from where it had sat for eons in front of the windows, facing the wall with E. G. Porter's portrait. Marilee had always had the impression that Ms. Porter would sit at the desk and look at her father on the wall and worship him. Or maybe throw mental darts at him.

Now the desk sat in front of that wall, looking away from it, and behind, where E.G.'s august portrait had hung, was an enormous black-and-white photograph of Marilyn Monroe in the famous shot with her dress blowing up.

After eyeing that for a startled moment, Marilee's gaze moved on to the clusters of photographs already hung—the ones of Tate Holloway with Reba and President Nixon, and ones of him receiving awards, and with soldiers, and a curious one of a boy plowing with a mule. She stepped closer for a better look at that one. Next to the faded snapshot of the boy and the mule was one of a lovely blond woman in the front yard of an old house, her arms around two boys.

"That's my mother," Tate told her, coming up behind her. "With me and my brother, Hollis. I'm the older, skinnier one."

"And that's you, plowing with a mule?"

"Yep. Farmin' in East Texas in the fifties. My mother took that picture. Mama liked to take pictures."

He had come to stand very close behind her. Close enough for his breath to tickle her hair.

"This is Mama in front of the house me and Hollis bought her." His arm brushed her shoulder as he pointed at another photograph. "And this is how my daddy wound up."

He tapped a photograph of a mangled black car stuck to the front end of a Santa Fe Railroad engine.

"I like to see where I've come from and how far I've journeyed and remind myself where I don't want to go," he said with practicality. Then, the next second, "You smell awfully good, Miss Marilee."

That comment jerked her mind away from the horror of the mangled car. She turned, and her shoulder bumped his chest, because he didn't move but stood there gazing at her with a light in his clear, twinkling blue eyes that just about took every faithful breath out of her lungs.

His gaze flickered downward, and hers followed to stop and linger on his lips.

The next instant she stepped quickly away from him and said as casually as possible, "And just what does that picture mean in your journey?" She gestured at the photograph of Marilyn Monroe.

"Well—" he sauntered to the desk and laid down the hammer "—I like the touch Marilyn gives the place."

"What touch are you going for, exactly?"

"Oh . . . I think a photograph like that sets people off balance, for one thing." He folded his arms, and his strong shoulders stretched his shirt. "And it is lively. I might come in here feelin' a little too serious about myself and things in general, and I'll look up there at that beautiful woman—" he looked up at the picture and grinned "—with a laugh like that and those legs goin' to heaven, and it makes me remember the true secret of life." He gave a little wink.

Marilee took that in and took hold of the solid walnut back of the visitor chair, feeling the need to have the chair between herself and Tate Holloway.

She looked at him, and he looked at her in the manner of a man who was intent on having what he wanted. It was both flattering and unsettling.

Breaking the gaze, she said, "I need to discuss my job here."

His eyebrows went up, "Well, you go ahead, Miss Marilee . . . as long as you aren't about to tell me you're gonna quit."

Marilee reacted to this with a mixture of gratification and annoyance. There was something very commanding in the way he spoke, as if he would not *allow* her to quit.

"Do you want a raise?" he asked before she could speak. "I can spare twenty more a week—okay . . . I'll go to thirty."

"I don't want a raise . . . but I'll take it."

"I won't force it on you, if you don't want it."

"I want it. I only meant that a raise wasn't what I was going to discuss, but now that you've offered, I will take it."

"Well, since it isn't a question of a raise, there's no sense in talkin' about it."

"But we *are* talking about it now, and I'll take it. My workload has greatly increased since Harlan and Jewel left."

"Okay, twenty dollars a week it is."

"You said thirty."

He cocked his head to the side and regarded her. "What was it you wanted to discuss about your job, Miss Marilee?"

Keeping her hands pressed to the chair back, she told him of her decision to remove her children from the final weeks of school and therefore her need to work from home. That she had been so bold as to take the raise before explaining this, and the glint in his eye that showed admiration, gave her courage.

She explained that until this year, when she had enrolled Willie Lee in school, her arrangement with Ms. Porter allowed her to often work from home, and she had managed very well.

"I have made arrangements with a high school girl to help me in the summer," she told him, "but until school ends, I will only have her occasionally in the evening hours."

"Well now, I don't see any problem at all with you workin' from home," said her new boss and publisher. "I already have laptop computers coming for everyone, and we'll be installing a networking system so that any of us can work from anywhere in town, or in the nation, if need be."

Marilee thought that *The Valentine Voice* was suddenly on a rocket, being blasted into the twenty-first century.

Moving purposefully, her boss went to stand behind his desk, placed his hands on it and leaned forward. "I want you to keep this to yourself for a few days. I'll tell everyone shortly, but for now, I'm just telling you." He paused. "We're going to have to cut the paper to a twice weekly."

She took that in.

He said, "I don't imagine that comes as any shock to you."

"No . . . it doesn't." It saddened her, but it was no surprise. Everyone knew that Ms. Porter had been subsidizing the paper for years, and Marilee, having taken over for Ms. Porter, had consulted a number of times with Zona and knew the great extent to which that subsidizing had run.

Tate Holloway eyed her with purpose so strong that he leaned even farther forward. "It is my intention to get this paper to be payin' for itself. I'm out to build somthin' here, Miss Marilee. And I'm going to need your help to do it."

"I'll do what I can."

"I'm countin' on that, Miss Marilee. . . . I sure am."

Gazing into his twinkling baby-blue eyes, Marilee kept tight hold on the chair back, as if holding to an anchor in the face of a rising, rolling sea.

Six

Maybe She's Human

Marilee came out of Tate Holloway's office and closed the door firmly, then held on to the doorknob for some seconds. Behind her, through the door, the low tones of music began—Charlie Rich singing from Tate Holloway's stereo.

Pushing away from the door, Marilee wrestled with high annoyance at her new boss. Tate Holloway was way too full of himself.

The next instant Reggie was sticking a pen in front of her face, saying, "Tell us the news, Ms. James. Are we all goin' to be swept out to make way for new employees to go with the new publisher?"

This had been a major worry of Reggie and Leo's, both being employed at the same place. Mainly it appeared to be a great worry of Reggie's, since Leo wasn't given to worrying over steady employment. Before coming to work at *The Valentine Voice,* he had held various positions in automobile sales, insurance, cattle brokering, photography, trucking and a half-dozen others, several for no more than a week or two before either quitting or being fired. While Reggie defended her husband as trying to find himself and being a victim of too much feminine attention, it had been fact that he had not been able to keep a job of any secure endurance, until he had landed the one of sports reporter at the *Voice.* He proved excellent at it, and the one time he had shown any inclination to quit, Reggie had come in behind him and finagled a job of her own, thereby being on the scene to make certain he kept his position.

A part of Marilee's brain tried to be sensitive to all of this, but seeing everyone's eyes, even Willie Lee's and Corrine's, turned in her direction made her very irritated.

"Don't put that thing in my face, Reggie. I need both my eyes." She pushed Reggie's hand aside and strode to her desk and began shuffling through files to take home.

"Okay. So are you pissed off because you do not want to tell us that we are all about to be fired?"

The breathlessness of the question struck Marilee, and she looked up to see Reggie's thoroughly uneasy eyes. The precariousness of all their positions came fullblown into her mind, and she felt sorry for her short temper.

"Of course we aren't all going to be fired. Who would he get to replace us? The paper can barely pay for itself now." Just a mild fib. "He can't afford to be hauling in a whole new crew of Pulitzer prize winners to Valentine. Right now he's dependent on us. We are all he's got."

She felt as if she were withholding from her friends, being unable to tell the entire truth about the change from a daily to twice weekly. Darn him for confiding in her.

Turning from this dilemma, and from Reggie's searching eyes, she said, "He said it will be fine for me to work at home," and went on to briefly explain about Willie Lee and Corrine not going back to school. "I want to be home with them, like I used to be with Willie Lee, and this will work fine, because Mr. Holloway is getting us all laptop computers and a networking system."

"Wow," Reggie said. "Guess there's more money than we thought." She jumped from Marilee's desk and went over to hug Leo, who said quite practically, "Doesn't mean money. Just good credit."

"I finally got my machine working how I like it," Charlotte said, frowning. She had gotten so furious with the technician who had first set up her computer that she had refused to allow him to touch it again, read the manual front to back and now knew enough to maintain her machine herself.

Marilee, who was gazing at her typed up notice for Lost and Found, crumpled up the paper and tossed it into the trash. The dog was Willie Lee's now, she figured, and she was going to let it be.

"Let's go get some ice cream," she said to the children. "You, too, Munro," she added, when Willie Lee opened his mouth to remind her.

With Willie Lee holding one hand and Corrine the other, and Munro running along beside them, Marilee headed directly to where she went whenever she felt her spirits in disarray—to her aunt and uncle's drugstore.

Blaine's Drugstore and Soda Fountain had been in business for over seventy years, in the same spot on Main Street. There was a rumor that the outlaws Bonnie and Clyde had once gotten lemonade and bandages from the distant relative of Perry Blaine who had opened the store in 1920. Perry had taken over from his father in '57, when he had come home from Korea. Things had been booming in Valentine in the fifties, with oil pumping all around, and farming and cattle going okay. That same year Perry had installed the sign with the neon outline that still hung between the windows of the second story.

Ever since the fateful summer of '96, when it had been featured in both the lifestyle pages of the Lawton paper and then on an Oklahoma City television travel program, Blaine's Drugstore had received visitors from all over the southern part of the state. People, enough to keep them open on Friday and Saturday evenings in the summertime, came to order Coca-Colas and milk shakes and sundaes in the thick vintage glassware. Some of the glasses were truly antiques, and to keep the visitors coming, once a year Vella drove down to Dallas to a restaurant supply to purchase new to match. She would covertly bring the boxes into the storeroom and place them behind the big boxes of napkins and foam to-go containers.

When taken to task by her daughter Belinda for perpetrating a hoax, Vella said with practicality, "People like thinkin' the glasses are old, and they would rather not be apprized of the truth. Besides, they *will* be antiques in another fifty years—and I sure pay enough for them to be looked at."

As Marilee and the children entered the store, the bell above the door chimed out. Immediately Marilee was engulfed by the dearly familiar scents of old wood, simmering barbecue and faint antiseptic of the store that had not changed since she was a nine-year-old child and so often came running down the hill to escape the sight of her father sitting in his cracked vinyl recliner, beer in hand and glassy eyes staring at the flickering television, and her mother in the kitchen gone so far away into country songs on the radio that she would not speak.

"We have come for ice cream," Willie Lee said as he went directly to his Great-Aunt Vella, who was sitting at the rear table, with glasses on the tip of her nose so she could more easily read the IGA ads in the newspaper spread wide before her.

"You've come to the right place then, mister," said Winston Valentine, who was sitting across from their aunt and who nudged an empty sundae dish that sat in front of him. Being yet spring and midmorning, the place was empty except for these two.

"Hel-lo, Mis-ter Wins-ton," Willie Lee said.

"Hello, Mister Willie Lee."

Willie Lee extended his hand, as Winston had taught him, and Winston shook the small offered hand with great respect.

Marilee saw that Winston's big, gnarled hand, when it released Willie Lee's, shook slightly. The blue veins showed clearly when he used that same hand to push his tall frame up from the table.

"If you ladies and gentleman will excuse me," he said, polite as always, "I have to walk on home and make sure Mildred has not drowned Ruthanne in her bath this mornin'. The nurse has the day off." He checked his watch. "They ought to be done by now."

Mildred Covington and Ruthanne Bell, two elderly ladies, shared Winston Valentine's home. Since Winston's stroke the year before, a home health nurse came in to check on all three of them three times a week. Aunt Vella had once told Marilee that on the days the nurse did not come, Winston, after making certain the women had breakfast, tried to leave home at midmorning, so as to not be present when the women were getting bathed and dressed; Mildred seemed to have a penchant for running around naked in front of him whenever she had the chance.

"Winston's really aging now," Marilee said, watching the old man lean heavily on his cane as he went out the door. He was eighty-eight this year, and only since his stroke had he slowed any.

"There's more life in him than many a man I know," Vella said, and in a snapping manner that startled Marilee a little. It only then occurred to her that her Aunt Vella was not getting any younger, either; no doubt it was distressing to her aunt to see a dear friend declining and heading for the border.

Marilee found the fact depressing, as well. She felt as if her life were going down a hole, and she could not seem to find the stopper.

"Now, what's this about my darlin's wantin' ice cream?" Aunt Vella asked.

"We want sun-daes," Willie Lee told her and scampered over to haul himself up on a stool at the counter.

"We'll have three chocolate sundaes, please," Marilee said, slipping onto a stool.

She set herself to getting into a better mood. Children learned by example and picked up on things easily. She did not need to add to any of their numerous wounds by being in a poor mood.

"Me and Mun-ro want va-nil-la," Willie Lee said. "Cor-rine says dogs should not ev-er have choc-o-late."

Marilee only then remembered the dog and looked down to see him already curled beneath Willie Lee's feet, as if knowing that he would need to be quiet and unseen to remain.

Aunt Vella took a cursory look around the end of the counter, then said, "We surely can't leave Munro out."

"No, we can-not," Willie Lee said.

"Is your choice chocolate, too?" Aunt Vella asked Corrine.

Corrine frowned in contemplation.

"I'll give you another minute." Aunt Vella went about lining up four dishes and making the sundaes— cherry for Corrine, it turned out. While doing this, she threw conversation over her shoulder, telling about the Rose Club meeting held the previous evening—"We had ten people!"—and how they had already voted as a first project to plant roses around the Welcome to Valentine signs at each end of town.

"Winston and I are goin' up to Lawton tomorrow to buy bushes," Vella reported, feeling increasing excitement with the telling.

She had been very pleased with the respectable turnout of people for the first Rose Club meeting, and felt a glow that her idea of a rose club had proven out. Especially after Perry had rather pooh-poohed the idea as frivolous. She almost had not pursued the idea, after his attitude, but it had turned out that a number of people, such as their mayor's wife, Kaye Upchurch, had liked the idea immensely. While Kaye Upchurch could be on the frivolous side, she was truly knowledgeable about what was good for the town. Her enthusiasm for the Rose Club's place in the community was heartening.

Vella was also becoming more and more excited about going up to Lawton with Winston. She had never been anywhere with Winston, outside of her own backyard or here at the store.

"We'd like to get the bushes in the ground soon. It's already so late to be planting," she added, bringing her thoughts back to the moment. "We could very well get a repeat of last summer and all that heat. Winston thought we could install some sort of watering system by the welcome signs," she said, focusing on a plan. "If the city doesn't want to pay for it, Winston said he would."

In Vella's opinion, Winston was a little free with his money, and this was both quite amazing and refreshing. Her husband Perry pinched a penny until it gave up the ghost. Vella thought she needed to take lessons from Winston in being more free and easy. She did not want to spend her remaining years being as controlled as she had spent her entire life to this point.

Marilee, only halfway listening to her aunt's conversation, other than to observe that the Rose Club seemed to make her aunt very happy, watched the loose skin at the back of her aunt's arm wiggle, while her biceps worked sturdy and strong. Marilee had lately been trying to exercise the backs of her own arms, which were the first thing to go on a woman; she was amazed that her aunt was so strong, though, despite the sagging back of her arm.

Then Marilee found herself looking over the counter, at the age-spotted long mirror, the shelf of neatly lined and glimmering tulip glasses, the modern licenses in dingy frames, and the yellowing menu with the Dr Pepper sign at the top. The drone of Uncle Perry's television reached her from the back room of the pharmacy, where her uncle would be sitting in his overstuffed brown chair.

Aunt Vella brought a dish of ice cream around the end of the counter and set it down for Munro. "I didn't think he needed whipped cream or a cherry," she said, then stood there, watching the dog, as they all were.

"I sure hope this doesn't give him a headache," Vella said, as the dog began to lick the cold sweet ice cream with some eagerness.

"He likes it," Willie Lee pronounced quite happily.

"Hmmm . . ."

Aunt Vella went back to put the finishing touches on the people's sundaes; they definitely got whipped cream and a cherry. She then set the children's sundaes on the granite counter, with a "There you go, sugars," pronouncing the word as *shu*-gahs in a way that caused a particularly strong pull on Marilee's heart.

As her aunt scooted a sundae across toward her, Marilee looked at it and suddenly realized she was sitting on the last stool at the far end of the counter, right where she had always sat as a child when she came running into the drugstore, dragging Anita by the hand. Aunt Vella would lean over the counter, dab at Anita's tears and ask, "What can I get for my two *shu*-gah girls today?"

Marilee would be choking back tears but would manage to get out quite calmly that she and Anita would like chocolate milk shakes, please. Her Uncle Perry always called Marilee a little lady because she never yelled or screamed or cried. There were so many times when she wished she *could* yell and scream and cry.

Now, as then, she took up the long-handled spoon and smoothed the chocolate syrup around on the vanilla ice cream. She liked to let the ice cream get a little soft and then mix it with the chocolate syrup. She would have to admit to being addicted to chocolate, but after having taken tranquilizers for too long after her heartbreak with Stuart, she thought chocolate a fairly harmless aid to getting along in turbulent times. Chocolate tasted good and felt good going down, and it did not make her brain so fuzzy as to spin out of the world.

As she spooned the chocolate and vanilla ice cream onto her tongue, she looked across and caught hers and Corrine's reflections in the wide old mirror. Corrine's dark eyes, for a moment, met hers in the mirror, before looking down at her sundae. Marilee watched Corrine's reflection, the bend of the dark head, the way she tilted it slightly, looking for all the world like her mother at that age.

Marilee's gaze returned to her own reflection. It struck her quite hard that here she was staring at middle-age and still employing the same coping skills she had employed as a ten-year-old girl.

"You've been workin' way too hard," Aunt Vella said. "You just need a little boost. You should take a potent mixture of B's for three months, and it wouldn't hurt for you to start taking calcium . . . you need to start thinkin' about keepin' your bones. Every woman's bones start to fade after thirty-five."

Marilee had followed Vella over to the pharmacy shelves, where her aunt perused the bottles of vitamins and herbs, while the children occupied themselves twirling on the stools at the counter. Actually, it was Corrine being twirled by Willie Lee. She held on to the stool with her thin little hands, while Willie Lee got a kick out of spinning her around. Corrine was always so patient with Willie Lee. She displayed strong mothering instincts with him, and very often she did things for him that he was capable of doing for himself. Willie Lee allowed this, in the pleasing way he always went along with people.

"You worry about them too much. They'll be fine. They have God, just like you do. He cares for you. Trust Him."

At her aunt's statement, Marilee looked over to see that the older woman had noticed her wandering attention.

"Then who looks after the children who are abused and forgotten all over the place?" Marilee asked, more sharply than she had meant to.

"I don't know," her aunt answered in the same fashion. "I'm not smart enough to know that. I only know what I know, that there is a God who cares for us, and that worrying never solved a thing. Change what you can, accept what you can't, and leave off worrying. It just wears you out."

Marilee sighed, her mind skittering away from a discussion she didn't wish to get into.

"I couldn't stand it anymore," she said. "I took them out of school for the rest of this year. Corrine looks like she's going to face the firing squad each day she goes to school, and Willie Lee just keeps runnin' away. Maybe I'm not even addressing the true problem. . . . I know I'm not . . . but it just seemed the one thing I could do."

"Good. You changed something. And there aren't enough days of school left to worry about it, anyway." Vella was peering at the labels on the vitamin bottles through her reading glasses at the end of her nose. "Do you have the kids on vitamins?"

"Dailies."

"Not enough."

Marilee watched her aunt set about deciding which vitamins would be sufficient for the children. She felt an anger well up inside.

"Can vitamins fix a brain damaged by birthing?" she asked. "Or a heart broken by an irresponsible mother who prefers to drink rather than take care of her daughter?"

Vella's dark eyes came up sharply. "No one prefers to drink. Anita is sick, Marilee, just like your daddy was."

Marilee could not address this. She felt guilty for feeling so angry at her sister. Even as she thought about being angry, the anger began to ebb and slip into sadness and guilt, which she hated worse. The guilt threatened to consume her. She kept thinking there ought to be something she could do to help her sister, but everything she had tried had failed. She could not look at it anymore.

"Mrs. Blankenship thinks Corrine needs a therapist," she said, the words falling out almost before she realized.

"Half of America needs a therapist," Aunt Vella said, "but where do you find a sane one?"

Marilee had to chuckle at this, said so seriously. She gazed at Corrine, who was now twirling Willie Lee on the stool. "I think a therapist is worth trying, but I just don't know how I can afford it."

"Children have an amazing ability to survive. Don't discount it."

"That's another question," Marilee said, her gaze coming back to her aunt. "What's goin' to happen if Corrine gets really sick? How will I pay the doctor bills? My doctor charges sixty dollars a visit." The limit of those could plainly be seen. "She isn't my daughter, so I can't put her on my insurance."

"Oh, my heavens, don't go makin' up worries that likely won't happen."

Marilee looked at her aunt.

Her aunt looked back and said, "We'll help you, Marilee. You know that."

"I know it, but how far can we all go? You know perfectly well a catastrophe could bankrupt us all without insurance."

Aunt Vella said very quietly, "Have you thought about adoption?"

"I've thought about it." Marilee felt guilty for admitting what seemed a very bad thought. "But I don't think Anita would willingly go along with it. I could press it. I could take her to court and prove she isn't able to care for Corrine, but what would that do to her?"

"You can't take on Anita's burdens for her, Marilee. She has to own up to being responsible for her own actions. If she's going to be a drunken sot, she'll have to take the consequences. You don't help her by letting her off. Maybe if you pressed, Anita would have more reason to try to get herself straight."

Marilee clamped her mouth shut. Discussing this was making her too depressed. She did not have faith in Anita, certainly. And now she was having doubts about having faith in herself. She was sinking into a full decline when the bell above the front door rang out.

It was Fayrene Gardner entering the store. She came swiftly toward the pharmacy counter and presented Aunt Vella, who stepped forward, with a prescription. Fayrene, sniffing loudly, was clearly distraught.

"We'll get this straight away," Aunt Vella said and immediately stepped through to the back room, calling, "Perry . . . we need this filled. Perry!"

Fayrene noticed Marilee, who just then found she was staring, feeling connected by her own distress.

"Are you all right, Fayrene?" Marilee asked, feeling the need to say something, and hoping Fayrene wasn't about to confess to having fallen victim to some horrible disease.

"Men," Fayrene said vehemently. "I wish they'd all drop dead."

Marilee wasn't certain what to say to that, and became more uncertain when Fayrene's face crumpled and she went to crying into a tissue. Feeling comfort was required, and needing to give it, Marilee reached out a hand to possibly take hold of the woman and provide what assistance she could.

But Fayrene pulled herself up tight and called, "Vella, I'll be back to get it after lunch," then pivoted and strode out of the store, again holding a tissue over her mouth to block a sob.

"Well, mercy," Aunt Vella said.

"I don't think I have ever seen Fayrene in such a state," Marilee said.

"I haven't, either."

"What was the prescription? Is she really sick?"

Vella stepped back to the pharmacy area, then returned and said, "Tranquillizer. A good one," she added with approval.

Marilee felt quite fortunate in that instant. Or perhaps it was more accurate that she no longer felt quite so alone, after having witnessed another person in despair. It reminded her that life was difficult, and this was a plain fact that, once recognized, made living if not smooth, at least not quite so shockingly distressing. It pointed up that people did continue to live on, no matter how often the will to live seemed to be challenged.

And at least she herself was within the control of chocolate. Her eye fell to a Hershey bar in front of the prescription counter, and she quickly grabbed it and threw it in with the vitamins Aunt Vella was now sacking.

"I might need that tonight," she said. She thought maybe she ought to take a chocolate bar over to Fayrene.

When they came out of the drugstore, Corrine went skipping over in the direction of the florist next door. In fact, to Marilee's eye, it seemed Corrine was drawn to the tubs of colorful spring flowers on display outside as if by a cord. But when just a foot away, the girl suddenly stopped and turned back to Marilee, in the manner of correcting a wrong action.

Marilee, who had herself entertained a first thought that flowers were an unnecessary extravagance, said with purpose, "Would you like some flowers? I think I would."

As she spoke, she walked to the tubs of mixed bouquets that a few weeks ago Fred Grace, Jr. had begun setting out in front of his florist shop.

"If it works for Wally-world, it's sound," Fred told everyone, referring to the big Wal-Mart chain of stores. Within a week he gleefully reported that impulse buying had doubled.

"Which ones do you like?" Marilee asked the children.

Corrine, not quite meeting Marilee's gaze, shrugged her small shoulders. Her eyes slid again to the flowers.

"I *need* some daisies," Marilee said, reaching for a bouquet. "Absolutely need them."

One thing she intended to teach Corrine was a hard-learned lesson she herself had experienced, and that was that beauty was a necessary part of life. She felt society in general had forgotten this, and that fact might just be a major cause of wars. Often, against every cell in her body that told her to be frugal, she would buy flowers or a pretty picture, because she felt her very life might depend on it.

"You can both choose a bouquet for yourselves," she told the children as she examined the bouquet she had chosen, peering at little purple things that looked suspiciously like weeds.

Willie Lee wanted Marilee to pick him up so he could see better, which she did, and he gleefully pulled a bouquet of red carnations from one of the tubs.

"Cor-rine, you like yel-low," he said.

Corrine chose very slowly and reverently a bouquet of yellow daisies and white carnations.

"Oh, those are lovely, Corrine."

"Mun-ro needs flow-ers, too."

"He can enjoy ours," Marilee told her son.

Her son sighed heavily and bent to let the dog sniff his flowers.

Pulling a twenty-dollar bill out of her purse, she had Corrine help her figure out the total cost of the three bouquets, which Corrine did with amazing speed. Then Marilee handed the bill to Corrine and told her to go inside and pay Mr. Grace.

Corrine hesitated, and Marilee wondered if she had asked too much of the painfully shy girl, but Willie Lee spoke up and said, "Mun-ro says he will go with you, Cor-rine," and indeed, the dog stood ready at the girl's side.

Corrine turned, and Marilee watched her niece's oh, so slight figure disappear into the store. She felt like hurrying after her, to be there beside her, guarding for any type of hurt that might come her way.

Then, peering through the window while trying not to appear to be peering, Marilee saw Corrine walk up to the cash register and hand up the money to Fred Grace. Munro stood right at Corrine's leg, his head next to her knee, looking upward, too. Fred handed down Corrine's change, and then out Corrine and Munro came, a smile playing at the girl's lips.

"Thank you, Aunt Marilee," she said softly, depositing the change in Marilee's hand.

"Thank you, Corrine. And Munro." She and Corrine grinned at each other.

The three of them, accompanied by the dog, started down the sidewalk. Marilee, seized by a warm happiness, felt certain they were all walking straighter and marveled at the power of a handful of colorful flowers. The few people they passed along the way smiled, and one man tipped his ballcap.

The colorful flowers gave way to a spontaneous idea.

"Let's grow our own." Marilee looked at the children. "Let's have a garden."

Willie Lee gave back an enthused, "Yes," and Corrine raised an eyebrow, as if wondering if it could be done.

At the temporary plastic greenhouse set up at MacCoy's Feed and Grain, they ran everywhere at once, picking out flats of pansies and the biggest marigolds in the world. Corrine liked the blue cornflowers. Then the tomato plants looked so perky, and the idea of sweet home-grown tomatoes seemed so inviting, that Marilee got a half dozen of them.

The revolving stand of crisp and colorful seed packets caught

Willie Lee's attention. When Marilee went to pull him away, she selected several packets.

Into the back of the Cherokee went containers of perky little plants, seed packets, bags of fertilizer, a new shovel for Marilee, and two small-size shovels for the children, all paid for with the ease of a card. Felt like she wasn't even spending money.

They sped home, where the first business was to get their cut flowers into vases of water. Marilee, determined to make everything a learning opportunity, showed the children how to cut the stems slanted to soak up the water and taught them as much as she knew about how flowers took water up their stems.

Afterward they trooped out to the backyard and hauled out shovels and their tender plants and seed packets. Watching Willie Lee attack the ground the best he could with his small shovel, Marilee found her hopes resurface for being able to teach her son simple skills that would enable him to function on a more or less adequate scale with everyday living in the world. Perhaps he would not ever be able to read or to count sufficiently, but learning to plant and grow and cut, and to clean up after himself, would see him a long way when his mother was no longer available to care for him.

Seven

"What's for supper?" Parker asked after giving Marilee a kiss on the cheek.

"I have no idea."

Sprawled on the couch, having been gazing blankly at the television news, she felt incapable of any endeavor involving getting up and moving around.

"We dug a garden today. Shovels, half the backyard." At least it had seemed like half.

"Why didn't you go rent a tiller?" He shifted her legs over and sat beside her.

"I didn't plan to make it fifteen by fifteen. I just wanted a small garden for the children to grow some flowers, but then I saw the tomato plants, and they came in a container of six, and then Willie Lee saw the cantaloupe seed packets and wanted to grow those—they always put seeds in packets with beautiful pictures of perfect fruit, without all the hard work and bugs. I was just as bad as Willie Lee—I got carried away and bought zucchini seeds because of the picture, and I didn't remember the awful bugs until I was on the way home. Anyway, I figured before planting the seeds, we needed to get the ground turned and let it sit there for the grass to die.

"I don't know. It just seemed to . . . mushroom," she ended lamely.

She really was unclear as to how she and two children had gotten into digging up a good portion of the backyard. Thinking of it now, she was amazed at the accomplishment, and as Parker began massaging her legs, she told him all about the activity with the children, painting word pictures of their funny antics for him. She had enjoyed digging in the dirt, had gone at it with a vengeance, for which she was now paying.

"Why weren't the children in school?" Parker asked, having now worked himself upward to leaning over and nuzzling her neck.

Marilee, vaguely aware of his scent and the warm, moist touch of his lips on her neck, realized she had not told him of her decision to remove the children from school.

"I took them out of school for the remainder of the school year," she said, now experiencing a rising certainty for the decision.

Parker quit nuzzling her neck and sat up. "You took them out of school?"

"Yes, there are less than three weeks left of the school year anyway." Seeing the disapproval bloom on his face, her certainty faltered. She realized two things at once: she had counted on his approval, and she had not been paying sufficient attention to his manly attentions moments earlier. No man was ever happy to have his advances ignored.

She felt at fault and annoyed at the same time. She was tired and not in the mood to deal with his male needs, nevertheless, this seemed a poor attitude on her part, so she sat up and tried to work up the stamina required of her.

"I believe that more than anything they can learn in the few remaining weeks of school, the children need to be secure and reassured," she said. "They need to be home for a while."

"What about your job?"

She saw he was determined to focus on obstacles, instead of swinging immediately into support.

She went on to explain her reasoning for her actions, which had begun to sound truly logical and reasonable when she had told it all to Aunt Vella, yet, in the light of Parker's expression now, Marilee had to work hard to keep on track.

"Tate doesn't have a problem with me working at home. He's giving us all laptop computers. Hooking them up on a network. I had already planned to try to work half days at home during the summer, anyway."

She thought that despite whatever Parker might be thinking behind his frown, her enthusiasm to proceed with what she saw as a viable healing endeavor for her children remained intact. She became more annoyed at Parker for not immediately grasping this concept.

"I know there is a curriculum available," she said, continuing to explain her plans for educating the children, "and I've heard of some support groups that I want to investigate. I'm going to draw up something for them to study every day. Especially Corrine. She is really smart, and one of her problems at school may have been boredom. Would you discuss ideas with me over supper? I want to start putting a plan in place for the summer."

If she could get Parker involved, he would come around. And, while she considered herself fully intelligent, she thought Parker better at critical, organized thinking. He could be, if he would apply himself, a great deal of help.

Parker, however, gave a remote shrug that Marilee did not find at all an acceptable reaction. She told herself not to be surprised. Parker could get into a very remote mood, as could every man of her experience.

But here she was more or less inviting him into her life, and he was not responding with any small bit of gusto. She supposed she wanted too much from him, and she felt at fault but couldn't figure out why, other than that her plans had brought on his disapproval. She felt herself getting all jangled inside, and angry because of it.

When the telephone rang, she grabbed it, as if grabbing some remedy for the conflicting moment. Unfortunately, she heard her mother on the other end of the line.

"Marilee? Marilee, this is your mother." Her mother had the habit of saying her name twice.

"Yes, Mom."

Her mother wanted Marilee to take her car for new tires tomorrow.

As Marilee listened to this, Parker stepped close and whispered, "Ask her to take the kids for the evening."

Marilee, amazed that he would suggest such a thing, scowled at him. "I can't do it tomorrow, Mom. I can on Saturday."

Why couldn't she take it tomorrow, her mother wanted to know.

"Ask her . . ." He encircled her from behind and whispered in her ear about how they could drop the kids off at her mother's house.

She wiggled away from him and tried to think of how to put her mother and the tires off until Saturday without getting into a long explanation of having taken the children out of school. She finally got the arrangements straight, promising to go up to Lawton on Saturday morning for tire shopping.

"I have to go fix supper now, Mom. I'll see you Saturday." She hung up with a hard click and looked at Parker, who had turned from her and was stroking the back of his head.

"You know I do not leave the children with my mother. She does not want the care of them. She won't half watch them, and I am not going to leave them up there at her house, with her husband drinking every night." She wondered what in the world had gotten into him to suggest such a thing.

"Marilee, I want us to go out to dinner. The kids will be okay at your Mom's for a couple of hours. So what if Carl gets drunk? He doesn't bother the kids."

She gazed at him for several seconds, knowing he could not understand that taking them to her mother's was the same as setting them adrift for a few hours on a vast, turbulent ocean. The thought of it scared the daylights out of her.

"Corrine has had enough of that," she said flatly.

She averted her gaze, biting back all manner of words she was certain she would regret. She could not sort out what she truly felt. Likely she was overreacting, as was her habit. She just had to get some sort of control of herself.

"How 'bout gettin' a baby-sitter for the kids, then?" Parker asked.

"I am too tired to shower and dress, much less call to get a baby-sitter on last-minute notice," she said, unwilling to move in body or mind. "Besides, I have my pieces for Sunday's issue to write tonight." She would have to be writing more at nights now, and she thought him shortsighted not to get this point.

"But I can make hamburgers," she offered, swept with the urge to make up for her stubbornness, "and you can sit at the table and talk to me while I cook."

This would mean energy spent on cooking, which she should save for her writing job. How much easier if he would have been just as pleased with a can of soup thrown on the stove.

But hamburgers were Parker's very favorite food, as long as there were buns to go with them—Parker would not eat a hamburger on plain bread. Marilee was fairly certain she had buns in the freezer, and she wanted him to talk with her about the children. She wanted him to understand. She wanted him to share.

He did not fall into the plan with enthusiasm, but he did fall in and follow her into the kitchen, where he went straight to the refrigerator and pulled himself out a canned cold drink, while she peered out the back door to check on the children, who were playing in the dirt at the corner of their newly turned garden. At least Willie Lee was digging in the dirt for some reason, with Munro lying in it and watching. Corrine was sitting nearby in a yard chair; Corrine was a neat person who seemed to avoid dirt.

Seeing the children thus apparently contentedly occupied, and finding hamburger buns in the freezer, Marilee's spirits revived somewhat, and she had hope that she could set everything right with Parker by serving up both a good meal and the correct, upbeat attitude.

She set about winning him over as she went about preparing supper. She told him of her plans for the summer with the children. She hoped to better prepare them for school in the fall, and to enable herself to take a more forward part of their education, even when they went back to school. She felt she had been expecting too much from the school, a place made for the masses, to deal with the special particulars of her children's needs. It was her responsibility as a parent to see to those particular needs.

Parker, who had settled himself at the table with his cold drink, waiting for his supper to be served, replied to her remarks with "Hmms" and "Yes, I guess you can do that," all basically cautionary in nature, and all much less than satisfying.

Finally Marilee said, "Parker, I really would appreciate some support here."

To which he replied with raised eyebrows, "I'm listening."

"But you do not seem to be putting forth helpful ideas," Marilee said. "I do want your ideas, Parker."

"I don't think you want my ideas. You already have your mind set."

She gazed at him, telling herself not to overreact. One thing that she felt always got her into a lot of trouble was her habit of getting so emotional. Both Stuart and Parker had often accused her of this, and she determined at that minute not to give Parker ammunition.

"One thing you need to think about," Parker said, "is what Anita might think of you takin' her daughter out of school."

"Anita wasn't seeing that Corrine got to school half the time," Marilee answered, stung to the core. "And I don't see that she is here, making any of the decisions."

"Anita is still her mother. You're makin' all these plans for a child that isn't yours. You're gettin' way too involved, Marilee. You are referring to Corrine as your child. What if Anita shows up tonight at the door and wants to take her daughter with her? What are you goin' to do then?"

"I don't know," Marilee said. "I'm just tryin' to deal with 'right now' the best I can. I won't worry about 'then' until it happens."

Now that he had brought the concern to the front of her mind, she experienced fear of exactly that happening. This made her angrier at him for making her more fearful.

"And I don't know what you expect me to do. Should I just drop Corrine? Not look after her to the best of my ability? Well, who *is* goin' to do it, then?"

Clamping her mouth shut, she turned to the stove to remove the hamburgers from the hot pan before they burned. She herself was burning pretty good and didn't want to say something she would regret.

Parker didn't say anything more about it, and Marilee found this good thinking on his part.

The atmosphere at the supper table proved strained, despite all Marilee's good intentions for happiness. She and Parker were patently polite to each other in front of the children. Corrine's dark eyes moved from Marilee to Parker in a furtive fashion, and seeing this, Marilee brought up the subject of their gardening and the fun they had enjoyed. She managed to get Corrine to smile.

It had been a good idea, Marilee realized. The children had rosy faces. They had been outside, where they needed to be in the spring, and she had the sudden inspiration that tomorrow she would keep them outside most of the day. There were a lot of things she could teach them outside. So many things that must be experienced and could not be found in books. Being stuck at desks in school had no doubt been a major problem for them. They were souls who at this time needed to be out in the sun. And she could give them that.

The thought so pleased her that in a flush of warmth for everyone, she looked at Parker and smiled. He saw and smiled in return.

Marilee and Parker were alone in the lamplight in the living room. After supper Willie Lee had, with the innocence of an untroubled mind, simply lain down on the kitchen rug beside Munro, closed his eyes and gone instantly to sleep. Marilee had put him to bed in his underwear and simply wiped his hands with a damp rag; he had not awakened. Corrine was in the bath.

Parker wanted to make out.

"Corrine will be coming out of the bathroom any minute," Marilee said, pushing away from him after a particularly stimulating kiss that in truth she was reluctant to end. But the idea that Corrine might see them in a sexual encounter, even one with all their clothes on, was unnerving.

"We'll hear the door," Parker said, trying to pull her back against him. He had a very insistent manner this evening that aroused in Marilee both desire and irritation.

"Parker . . . I am not going to make love with you on this couch."

"Don't tell me you don't want it," he said in a sultry tone, moving his hand to her breasts.

She did not like his crude phrase, a dislike made even more annoying because, unfortunately, she wanted it very badly and even responded to his touch.

"Parker . . . I have the children to consider. Corrine could come in here at any moment."

His pushing the matter made her resolve return, and she was able to extricate herself from his embrace.

Parker gave a sigh of clear irritation. He had been sighing a lot that evening.

"What are you tryin' to show Corrine?" Parker wanted to know. "Don't you think you should be more honest? We are goin' together, Marilee. Most adults goin' together do have a sexual relationship. Corrine should be aware of this."

"She is eleven years old and aware of the facts of life, and I have little doubt that she's seen way more than she needs to see. Heaven only knows what she has seen with Anita." In Marilee's view, her sister changed men about like she changed underpants.

"She doesn't need to deal with any further information about sex right now," Marilee said. "And I'm not ready to deal with it with them." This was closer to the truth than was comfortable.

Deep inside Marilee, where even she could not clearly see, was a child who longed still for the loving, nurturing mother she had not experienced. Could she have articulated her vision of a mother, she would have ended up describing Snow White. A way to get this fantasy mother was to *be* such a mother to these children given into her care, and that left little room for any type of sexuality.

"How long do you expect me to go on like this, Marilee?"

Marilee gazed at him. "I have never believed that a man and a woman could not control themselves until both of them were emotionally ready to handle the complications of sex."

"It isn't only that. When was the last time we had time for just us— you and me?"

Marilee could not answer him. She averted her gaze.

"Marilee, I want some time with you. Is that some sort of crime? I like the kids fine, but there is a time and place for grown-ups . . . that's us. You and me."

"I have the children. That isn't going to change." She thought Parker tended to remain on the childish side, too.

He sighed again, with clear irritation. "If you would marry me, we wouldn't have so many complications. We could sleep together, and you wouldn't be havin' to work at night but could be spendin' that time with me, and you could be free to do whatever it is you want to with the kids during the day."

A number of things went through her mind, the last being how he said *do whatever it is you want with the kids,* as if her daily endeavors in raising children were flights of fancy.

"Are you serious about marriage, Parker?"

Parker, never one for any confrontational question, regarded her carefully before saying, "I guess I'm the one who has brought it up, more than once."

That did not quite seem an answer to her.

"Yes, you are," she said. "And I suppose I've thought you were speaking in the passion of the moment. And marriage isn't like that. Passion fades, Parker, but everything else remains . . . the dirty laundry, the headaches and backaches, and the children."

She paused, giving him time to say something to that. He did not.

"I'm a woman with a handicapped son who will always need my greatest attention and a niece who will always have a part of my life. Marrying me means that suddenly you will have a wife and two children."

He nodded slowly. "I guess my life has included that for the past two years now, and I'm still here."

He guessed a lot.

"Yes, but there is a world of difference when you cannot simply walk out that door."

He blinked at that.

The rest of her doubts got all blocked up inside of her. She would have preferred some response on his part to her last statement, but he remained silent and did not jump in there with passionate proclamations of readiness right that minute to take on her and her children. This did not surprise Marilee. And she could give him credit for using his head and not thinking with his needs.

Consistently using one's head could be the secret of life, she thought, remembering Tate Holloway's use of the phrase.

Corrine, dressed in her yellow pajamas and having carefully combed her wet hair, went to tell her Aunt Marilee that she was ready for bed. She went quietly and with some hesitancy, a little fearful of being an interruption to her aunt and Parker.

She paused in the opening from the hallway. Her aunt and Parker were at the door, kissing. She ducked behind the wall and then peered out, watching until Parker left. Then she stepped back into the bathroom, shut the door silently and counted to ten, then stepped out again.

"I'm ready for bed, Aunt Marilee."

Her aunt was now standing at her desk, looking over some papers. Her head came up, and she smiled at Corrine. Corrine felt glad she had not let Aunt Marilee know she had seen her and Parker. Her aunt might have been mad at her. Aunt Marilee didn't get mad as fast as her mother did, but still, Corrine figured it best not to take chances. She liked when her aunt smiled at her, and the way her aunt always came with her after her bath, to pull back the sheets on the narrow bed and then tuck them around Corrine.

They would have to whisper, because of Willie Lee already being asleep. Although her aunt said, "I don't know why we bother to whisper—a two-ton cannon goin' off under his bed won't wake him." And then Aunt Marilee would chuckle. Aunt Marilee was beautiful when she smiled or laughed.

Smiling now, her aunt said, "I sure had a good time planting today. Did you?"

Corrine nodded. She had enjoyed herself, but even if she had not, she would have nodded, because she knew instinctively she was supposed to have had a good time.

Aunt Marilee leaned down and said softly, "Bless and keep Corrine, Lord. Thank you." Then she kissed Corrine on the forehead, adjusted covers that didn't need adjusting, turned out the light and left.

Corrine lay awake for a long time, as she normally did. She generally had a hard time sleeping, and she figured something was wrong with her, since other people, like Willie Lee, just went to sleep, while she could not. Sometimes her legs ached, and they did tonight. Sometimes her feet cramped up painfully, and if she could not get this to stop, she would have to get up and put on a shoe, to keep her foot from balling in a cramp.

Tonight, however, it was only her legs, and only a little bit, so she just lay there and watched the moonlight come and make patterns in the room. She thought about when they had bought tomato plants and chosen seeds. It had been late for the plants, so the man at the store had said, but Aunt Marilee said she didn't see why that should stop them. Corrine had liked picking the plants and seeds more than turning the dirt in the garden. Dirt was dirty. But she did like the smell of the dirt.

She guessed she liked the whole thing of making the garden, but she didn't want to like it too much. The things she liked too much were frequently taken away. She usually tried to pretend to the world—and whatever governed Bad Luck—that she did not like anything very much, because that way the Bad Luck wouldn't know she did like it and then take it from her.

Thinking all of this, she was awake when the telephone rang. Likely it would have awakened her anyway, because Corrine slept lightly and awakened with the smallest sound. She knew immediately that it was her mother. She couldn't have said how she knew this, only that she knew it positively. Maybe because a phone call in the night meant trouble, and trouble meant her mother, and indeed, she heard her aunt Marilee say, "Hello, Anita."

Corrine's heart leaped, and she almost jumped out of bed to run to the phone. Her mother had remembered her! But then she registered the tone of her aunt's voice, which was sharp.

"It is nearly eleven o'clock, Anita." Then her aunt's voice dropped, and there were footsteps—her aunt going away into the kitchen.

Heart pounding, Corrine slipped out of bed and crept to the edge of the living room entry. She could see into the kitchen, only she couldn't see Aunt Marilee. She could hear, though, listening really hard.

"Anita . . . no. I'm not goin' to do that."

Corrine saw her aunt come into view. Her aunt was talking while she strode around the kitchen.

"I know you haven't spoken to her in two weeks, but that's your own doin'. It is eleven o'clock, and I'm not going in there and waking her up for her to talk to her drunk mother."

At *drunk mother,* Corrine put her head down. She could hardly breathe.

"Okay, you aren't drunk, but I can tell you have been drinkin'." Aunt Marilee spoke in a hushed, angry voice. "I'm not trying to keep you from Corrine . . . I'm just tellin' you that I am not going to go wake her up. Why don't you call back in the morning?"

Corrine's heart pounded. "Around ten o'clock would be a good time." Aunt Marilee walked out of view over toward the sink. "Call collect . . . it's okay, Anita . . . you're my sister."

Aunt Marilee's voice fell, and Corrine could only hear the tone, which was sad. Then her aunt came back into view at the table, where she laid down the phone. Her head came around, and she stared into the hallway. Corrine drew back into the deep shadow and bumped into something that almost made her scream. She clamped her hand over her own mouth and saw that she had bumped into Munro. He licked her face. She pressed against the wall, not daring to move for fear Aunt Marilee would see her there and guess she had been spying. The memory of what had happened once when her mother had caught her spying came full into her mind, and her stomach turned. Corrine thought for a horrible minute that she was going to throw up.

After several long moments of holding her breath, Corrine dared to peek out. There was Aunt Marilee in the kitchen, having sat at the table, with her head in her hands. Her body was shaking.

Aunt Marilee was crying.

Corrine scampered back to bed so fast she forgot about trying to be quiet. She pulled the covers up tight. Tears were coming out of her eyes now, and her chest felt like it would burst, but she did not want to make a lot of noise and have Aunt Marilee come see. Then Munro was there, licking her face. She put her arms around him, buried her face in his hair and wished she could disappear. She wished she had never been born. Everyone would be a lot better off if she had never been born. She had heard her mother say that once to Aunt Marilee.

The Valentine Voice
About Town

by Marilee James

The new publisher and editor in chief of *The Valentine Voice*, Tate Holloway, has arrived. Don't forget the open house to be held on Monday, here at the *Voice* offices. Cake and coffee will be served courtesy of Sweetie Cakes of Main Street. Everyone is invited to come by and welcome Mr. Holloway.

Other important bits of note:

Ms. Porter-Abercrombie, who as of this writing is somewhere in Tangiers, has sent in her first travel report, an overview of the Miami airport. Look for it in the travel section of Sunday's edition. Anyone who plans to pass through the Miami airport will find Ms. Porter's report invaluable.

The upcoming race for the city council post being vacated by longtime member Wesley Fitzwater heats up with G. Juice Tinsley throwing his hat into the ring. Mr. Tinsley, owner of the IGA, says that his platform rests on being for everything that Jaydee Mayhall, his opponent, is against.

Motorists and pedestrians, beware of a sinkhole on First Street, near the Methodist parsonage. Pastor Stanley Smith discovered it when the front right tire on his car, parked in front of his house, sank up to the hub. It had to be towed out of the hole. The City Works Department has put out a caution sign until they can get this hole repaired.

The mayor retracts his offer of city flags. There are none left.

Eight

Bright New Day

Tate walked the length of Main Street so that he was able to jog at a fresh pace homeward on Church, where he expected to and did meet Parker Lindsey just as the sun popped up.

"Mornin'," Lindsey said, coming to a stop.

"Good mornin'," Tate replied, a little surprised at Lindsey stopping.

"So, how's it goin', Editor?" Lindsey began a series of leg-stretching exercises.

Editor. Tate liked that, although he was a little annoyed at the way Lindsey said it.

"Goin' mighty fine," Tate said. He decided he could do stretching exercises, too. As he bent, he saw Bubba sitting like a fat Budda in his yard, watching with squinting eyes.

"I imagine you come into town to take advantage of the paved streets for jogging," Tate said. He knew the veterinarian's house and clinic were on the outskirts of town.

"Yep," Lindsey answered. "I jog in. Five miles a day."

Sounded like bragging.

"I guess I like reading better," Tate said. "Expands the mind."

"And the gut," Lindsey returned.

Oh, boy. He had stepped in there with that one, trying to be too smart.

When Winston came into his kitchen through the back door, bringing the day's supply of rose blossoms, both Mildred and Ruthanne were sitting at the kitchen table. That both women were rising early these days was a high annoyance. They were cutting into his solitude time.

"I can't find a one of those cheese-and-crackers samples we got up at the Wal-Mart the other day." Mildred was emptying the contents of her large purse on the table.

"I think you ate them all on the way home." Winston filled a jelly glass with water for the rose blossoms.

"Oh, really? That nice man gave me extra ones. . . . I was just sure I saved one or two." She was now raking out her purse and covering the table with everything imaginable: comb, hair spray, mayonnaise packets, sugar packets, tea bags, loose change, little box of Sugar Smacks cereal. "Oh, here's one!" She held it up with triumph.

Winston, who decided there was no room on the little table for the flowers, noticed that Ruthanne had not said a word, not even hello. Her eyes were closed.

He looked closer, seeing that she had her normal angelic countenance.

"She's asleep," Mildred said in a loud whisper.

"Oh."

Yes, she appeared to be breathing. He was relieved. It was something; she was sitting right there in the chair, only slumped a little bit. She was falling into an instant sleep more often these days, and he doubted that could be a good sign. He experienced increasing discouragement at the inevitable fact that Ruthanne, whose mind had never been fully with them, was now slipping away in body also.

As everyone did sooner or later, he thought with a large sigh.

He put a hand on Ruthanne's shoulder and called her name.

Ruthanne's eyes came slowly open. "Good morning, Winston. Is it time for me to get up now?"

"You're up, Ruthanne."

"Oh, how nice." One thing about Ruthanne, she was easily happy.

"Winston, let's have fried potatoes for breakfast." Mildred dug a cracker into the plastic square of cheese as she spoke.

"I was visitin' with my Mama," Ruthanne said and smiled at Winston.

"Fried potatoes with those Vidalia onions Charlene brought over," Mildred said, her mouth full of cracker.

"You're havin' cheese and crackers," Winston pointed out. "I'm goin' on down to Vella's for coffee."

"Oh, this is just a snack." She pointed at the cheese with a cracker. "A real breakfast would be so nice . . . and you know Marie won't make us fried potatoes," she added, her bottom lip quivering.

Marie was their day help, who came at noon to make one hot meal a day and to pick up for an hour. Marie was dedicated to nutrition, and anything fried was off-limits.

"I'm goin' on down to Vella's for coffee."

By durn, he had to get out of there. He felt a little guilty, thinking of the possibility that Ruthanne could die while he was gone, but he guessed it would happen when it happened. And mostly he wanted to live until he died, and not be smothered by Mildred Covington's love of food.

"Winston, you are mean not to make fried potatoes."

"I'll make 'em for you tonight." He was getting out the door.

"What you are makin' right now is a spectacle of yourself with that Vella Blaine," Mildred threw at him.

"I'm just goin' for coffee." He had stopped in the doorway, surprised at the accusation.

"Uh-huh."

"I'm eighty-eight years old, for Pete's sake."

Mildred started crying, but he knew if he stopped to comfort her, he would not get away. "Have toast and jelly, and I'll make fried potatoes tonight," he told her as he went down the steps.

He started across the yard, which was a little soft, so that his cane tip sank in. He knew he was hurrying away to a woman, but it was not what anyone could understand. It had to do with a longing for his wife, and for life as he once knew it, and the desire to get away from where he found himself, old and declining.

There was no running away from old age, he thought angrily. But he guessed he had better do whatever he could to enjoy the current moment, because he could wake up dead tomorrow.

The phone rang while Corrine was rinsing their breakfast plates. Willie Lee was coloring at the table, and said, "Get it, Cor-rine."

Corrine turned off the water and grabbed a towel as she ran to get the telephone.

"Hello," she said hesitantly.

"Corrine? Oh, Corrine, honey, this is Mama."

"Hello, Mama." Her heart beat very fast. Her mother had called her! And she sounded fine!

"I know it's early. Have y'all been up long . . . is Marilee up?"

"Aunt Marilee is in the shower," she said slowly, cautiously judging what to tell her mother, who easily could get angry at her aunt. "We've had breakfast," she added quickly, wanting her mother to know that they had not been lazing in bed.

"Well, that's good. I was afraid I might wake you up, but I needed to call while I'm on break. I got a job, honey—I'm workin' at the Tarrant County Court House."

"That's good." Corrine wished she could think of more to say.

"Yes, it is. It's a real good job. I'm a secretary, and I dress up every day."

"That's neat," Corrine said, pleased to have thought of the word.

There was a bit of silence, and then her mother said, "Well, honey . . . how are you doin' up there?"

"Okay."

Another pause and what sounded like her mother puffing on a cigarette. "I talked to your Aunt Marilee last night. She said she's taken you out of school."

"Yes." She answered cautiously, then thought to add quickly, "I'm still doin' my school work, though. I'll pass."

"Your Aunt Marilee is teachin' you, huh?"

"Yes."

"Well, she's good at that, I imagine." It was a question.

Corrine had a panic about which way to go with this. Finally she said, "Yes."

"Don't you miss goin' to school with the other kids? You can go back to school, if you want. I'll tell Marilee to take you back."

"I don't want to go back."

"Well, okay. I just wanted you to know I'd get you back in, if you wanted to go."

"I don't."

"All right. There's only a few weeks left of school anyway, and it won't be long until I can get you back down here with me. I'm makin' good money, and I have health benefits and everything. I'm savin' to get us a nice place, with your own room. Won't you like that?"

"Yes, Mama."

"Oh, honey, I sure miss you."

"I miss you, too, Mama."

"You do?"

"Yes."

"Well, it won't be too long now, and I'll be straight again and can come get you."

"Okay."

Aunt Marilee came in just then, and Corrine said, "Here's Aunt Marilee. You want to talk to her?"

"Yes, just real quick. Here's a kiss from Mama." A smooching sound came over the line.

"Here's one back," Corrine said quickly and did a faint smooching sound that made her feel silly, then handed the phone to her aunt.

Having no inclination to hear any of her aunt's end of the conversation, she went hurriedly to the back door and out into the sparkling sunshine flitting through the trees. She was quickly followed by Munro and then Willie Lee.

Willie Lee said the strangest thing. "Cor-rine, Munro says you need a hug." And then he threw his arms around her middle.

Corrine about jumped out of her skin. "Stop that, Willie Lee." She pushed him away. "Come on, let's go up in your tree house."

She jumped up and took hold of the steps and then the branches, enjoying the feeling of strength in her body. She could climb trees. Someday she would be able to do everything and wouldn't need anybody to take care of her.

The Valentine Voice

Sunday, April 30

Today's Highlights:
—The *Voice* goes to twice weekly. Beginning May 7, *The Valentine Voice* will be published on Sunday mornings and Wednesday evenings. Story page 1.
—Controversial detention center becomes major campaign issue in city council seat race. Story page 1.
—Death proves of natural causes, but identity of man found dead in his car on the outskirts of town turns to mystery. Story page 2.
—Rose Club to plant bushes to beautify town. Open invitation to join the fun. Story page 3.
—Sinkhole on First Street grows. Warning sign falls in. Story page 4.

Nine

Come Sunday Morning

Spring had sprung and summer was taking over. Lilacs were gone, so were most of the irises, and Doris Northrupt's newly potted dahlias were poking out of the soil.

Young Leo Pahdocony, who was working to save money for the university next year, was mowing lawns in his spare time. He was getting so much business that his father was urging him to start a lawn maintenance business instead of going away to school. Leo, Sr., said he could handle the business end; Reggie was determined her son was going to get an education and her husband not handle anything.

Charlotte Nation was putting flea repellant on her terrier, and Parker Lindsey was working his butt off giving animal vaccines, so that come Sunday he turned off his alarm and slept in.

Winston went out later on Sunday morning to put up the flag. There wasn't anyone out early anyway on a Sunday, so he and Everett Northrupt had an agreement to do their respective flag raising one hour later.

This Sunday Winston worked up a damp sweat doing his patriotic duty. Northrupt yelled over after they had finished the ceremony, "Hot!"

"Yep," Winston returned, thinking, What did the man expect at this time of year? Northrupt was originally from up in one of those Northern states, like Indiana or somewheres.

Going around to the back door of his house, he checked the thermometer fastened there on the corner. The dawning sun rays had not yet hit it, and the needle pointed to seventy degrees. That did not look good. He didn't think he would wear a sport coat to church. He couldn't stand heat in his old age, and besides, he didn't need to impress anyone.

"The fella at the national weather channel says just a bit dry, is all," Perry Blaine reported to his wife Vella from where he sat in his easy chair, catching the early-morning television report. All week long,

Perry got up at the same time, 5:00 a.m., but on Sundays he remained at home until the drugstore opened at noon, to serve the church crowd soft drinks and ice-cream sundaes. Perry did not ever work the soda fountain—they hired two high school kids for Sundays—but he opened the pharmacy, since the store was open anyway. Most of the time he could sit back there and nap and watch John Wayne movies. People didn't like to get sick on Sundays; it cut into their weekend time. He did a heck of a business on Mondays, though.

If they had another hot summer, that meant they would make another killing with ice cream, he reminded Vella, who was pulling on her floral smock and straw hat.

At least this year they were having sizeable amounts of rain, and that meant war with leaf molds on the roses. Vella didn't make a breakfast on Sunday, but threw some jellied toast at Perry and went out to spray her bushes in an attempt to stave off powdery mildew and black spot.

Her roses were starting off better this year than last, she thought, clipping several long stems of fragrant Chrysler Imperial blossoms and carrying them inside to put in a vase for the preacher at that morning's services. She intended to get to church early. She always intended this, and seldom made it. Perry said she'd been born late and kept it up.

Sunday morning was the only morning Marilee got up early and with some anticipation. A long time ago, during one of her trips with Stuart, she had met an old black man sitting on the front porch of one of the tiny grocery stores that in those days inhabited dozens of small towns of Tennessee. He had offered her a cold drink and some wisdom. She had at the time been very annoyed with Stuart for going off on a story and leaving her flat at this grocery store; knowing Stuart as she did by then, she had been concerned with finding a ride back to their hotel. The old man had observed this.

"Me," he said, "I allow all week for worryin', but not on Sunday. Worryin' is a lot of work, and man is supposed to rest on Sunday so he'll be able to go fresh in the new week. Anything comes up on Sa'dy night, I just put it aside 'til Monday, when I'll be refreshed from a day of rest. Anger . . . frettin' . . . stewin' . . . it all waits. And sometimes, while it waits, it just seems to disappear."

When Stuart had decided he needed to be free, and she was going crazy with the idea of being alone and raising a handicapped son, she had remembered this bit of advice. Since then, Sunday was her No-Worry Day. Sunday morning she would make herself a cup of coffee thick with sugar and real cream—the only day she allowed herself cream, because she wasn't worrying about fat and cholesterol—and would go out on the front porch and sit in the swing. Even in winter, unless the weather was too inclement, she followed this routine, wearing heavy wool and wrapped up in a blanket, the warm coffee mug in her hands.

This was her time to simply be. A time to let go of striving and struggling to be something and think what needed to be thought. A time to listen to the stillness of the world, and to her own heart, and to the possible whisper of the Lord inside. A time to savor peace from the normal turmoil of her emotions.

Sometimes she would nod off, as she did this morning, until Leo, Jr. passing and the newspaper landing smack-dab on her porch woke her. She caught a glimpse of Leo, Jr. peddling on, then, right behind him, came a jogger.

It was Tate Holloway. She recognized him with a jolt of surprise. And here she was in her bathrobe.

He waved, and she waved back.

Okay. She snapped open the newspaper. As she was reading, her neighbor across the street came out in his pajamas to retrieve his newspaper, and on the corner, Buddy, the young man who worked for UPS, pulled his Mustang to the curb, in from an all-nighter, which was the liberty of the young and single. Apparently his mother didn't quite see it this way. She met him at the door, and her angry voice, if not the words, echoed down to Marilee.

When she went inside, she was curious at the quiet—no television cartoons. She heard hushed voices and splashing water in the bathroom. Corrine and Willie Lee were hanging over the side of the tub, bathing Munro.

"Mun-ro has to go to church with us," Willie Lee said.

Corrine became very still and did not look up.

"I suppose he should come," Marilee said, wondering at her sanity.

She and the children, and Munro, who smelled like a wet dog, had a leisurely breakfast, after which the humans dressed, and Marilee spritzed Munro with perfume. After a ten-minute wait on Parker—he sometimes joined them for church—she and the children and the dog walked down the block to First Street, then turned south for two blocks to the Methodist Church, where they viewed the sinkhole in front of the parsonage. The Sunday school classes had let out, and the pastor was giving a tour of the sinkhole, now about the size of a family dinner table. A big yellow caution sign sat inside it, just barely visible at the top. The City Works had now strung yellow tape around the hole.

Inside the sanctuary, Marilee directed the children into the rear row, moving from their customary second-row seats, in order to have Munro lie at Willie Lee's feet. The few people who noticed the dog only smiled. Munro was smart enough to keep a low profile.

Their change in seating, however, proved quite flustering to Aunt Vella, who invariably came after the first hymn had begun. This morning she came racing in to take advantage of everyone standing and singing, blew past Marilee and the children on up to set a bud vase with a red rose on the corner of the pulpit, and then returned to the second row, where she stopped, perplexed at finding Imogene Reeves and her husband and grandchildren taking up the pew.

"They're back there, Vella." Norm Stidham leaned over from the opposite side.

"What?"

Iris MacCoy raised her voice over the singing. "In the back, honey . . . Marilee and the kids are in the back."

"Oh . . . my . . ."

"They have a dog," Minnie Oakes said.

Marilee was in the aisle, motioning her aunt, who put a hand to her pillbox hat and hurried back to join them. She lifted an eyebrow on sighting Munro, and then went right into the middle verse of "In the Garden."

The light came through the golden glass windows and shone warmly on the walls and the congregation. On Marilee's left side, Aunt Vella, smelling of Avon powder, sang out the old hymn with feeling. On her right, Willie Lee repeated, "Dew on the ro-ses . . ." and Corrine held her hymnal open on the back of the pew in front of them; her mouth moved but made no perceptible sound. Munro lay with his eyes closed, either in misery or prayer.

Oh, Lord.

She was surrounded by blessings. In that moment, for a slice of time, it was as good as it gets.

"Is the paper really goin' to twice a week, Marilee?" It seemed as if the facts of the newspaper article could not be taken seriously. People had to hear it confirmed from her lips.

"Durn shame."

"I knew Ms. Porter leavin' was goin' to be the death of the paper."

"Well, I'm paid up. What will happen to my money? Can I get a refund?"

Marilee repeated, almost word for word, because she had written the article, what it said in that morning's newspaper, that the change would save the paper and enable it to continue operation, that the editions would in time grow in size, and that accounts would be adjusted.

By the time she left church she found her No-Worry Day seriously invaded. On the way past the sinkhole she made Willie Lee and Corrine hold her hand, having a vague apprehension that the hole would reach over and grab her children.

On Monday morning Tate drew on new jogging shorts and a muscle shirt and checked himself out in the mirror. His legs were white. He could stand it, though, but he could not go that muscle shirt, no-sir.

Changing into a T-shirt, he thought maybe he would buy one of those sleeveless T-shirts. He could go to that, he decided, and was annoyed that he had not bought one at the sport shop. He was further annoyed that he was feeling the childish need to compete with Lindsey.

Ah, well, if he were perfect, he wouldn't have any need to be on earth.

The phone rang as he went out the door. He left it and jogged down Porter, with Bubba bouncing along behind him like a meandering basketball. Passing the James house, he looked at it with his usual fantasy and was startled to see a figure on the front step. A little dark-haired figure in yellow pajamas.

He waved, and Corrine gave a hesitant wave in return, then hopped up and skedaddled in the front door.

At the corner the young UPS man chinned himself three times on the porch beam, hopped down and, with biceps bulging, came to his car parked at the curb. "My mother sure is irritated at you for cuttin' the paper to two days," he said.

"I'm sorry." He might have wished for better first words between them.

He continued on, turning toward Main Street. Bubba dropped out of sight, as had become his habit. As if the cat was hesitant to be seen in public with him, Tate thought.

He came abreast of the walking-talking ladies. Their morning nod to him seemed decidedly cool.

The bakery lady's car was out front, but the door to the shop was closed, and all quiet there. All quiet on the entire street. Halfway along he had to drop to a walk. The calf of his right leg twinged, and he shook it out.

Turning east at the police station, with the aroma of coffee that stirred his taste buds, he saw Lindsey in the distance, coming down the hill right on time.

Okay. Get moving.

Pushing himself into an energetic pace, he met Lindsey at the intersection. Thankfully Lindsey came to a stop, so Tate could, too. His chest was burning.

"Mornin', Editor," Lindsey said, stretching his legs. "Hell of a change in the paper."

"Everythin' changes," Tate said, stretching his legs and trying not to pant.

Just then, here came the young blond woman, this time on a bicycle, wearing bright-blue short-shorts and a yellow halter top, showing lots of smooth, tanned skin. She slowed a fraction. "Hello, y'all," she said and cruised on past between Tate and Lindsey as they both offered hellos.

Tate's head turning as if on a swivel, he followed her with his eyes, seeing her lovely rounded rump undulate as she pumped the bicycle, heading east on Porter. Nothing wrong with appreciation, Lord. He was not lusting. He doubted he could keep up with such a woman.

Then he saw Lindsey had been watching, too.

Tate said, "If you hurry, maybe you can catch her, you bein' in such good shape and all."

Lindsey grinned a slow grin. "Why, I got a girl, Editor."

Tate thought a half a minute and said, "I don't think you have much more than I do . . . we're both out here joggin' our brains out."

Lindsey kept his mouth shut and headed off at a rate designed to show Tate what he did not have.

Tate pushed himself to semijog up his drive and around the back of his house, where he didn't bother to go inside but collapsed on the step. Bubba came and sat down to stare at him.

"Remember, I feed you," Tate told the cat.

Behind him, through the screen door, came the ringing of the telephone.

Another complaint about the changes in the paper, he surmised, remaining right where he was.

He met Marilee at the intersection of their respective streets. Seeing her face behind the Cherokee windshield, he tooted his horn and waved out the window, going so far as to holler, "Where are you goin' so early?" It was just eight-thirty.

Corrine's small head poked out the passenger window of the Cherokee. "To get doughnuts for the paper." The girl's voice came thinly across the distance.

Tate pulled his BMW through the intersection and up alongside

Marilee. Her window and the rear passenger window, where Willie Lee poked his head out, came down at the same time.

"Hi, Mis-ter Tate."

"Hello, Willie Lee . . . hello, Munro," he added to the dog, who brought its head alongside the boy's.

Then he shifted his gaze to Marilee. Big dark glasses hid her eyes.

She said, "We're goin' to get doughnuts to take down to the paper."

"I thought we were going to have some cakes delivered." He tried to see through the dark lenses. It was disconcerting to be talking to emotionless dark glasses.

"Too early. Bonita isn't deliverin' the cakes until around ten, and the office is already filling up with people . . . who all pretty much want to smack you for darin' to change an institution of the town."

"I know." How well he knew. "Phone's been ringin' since yesterday. I got a call this mornin' before I even got my shower." Annoyance crawled over him, and he focused it on Marilee's sunglasses. He considered reaching out and yanking them right off her face so he could look her in the eye.

"Charlotte called to ask me to bring my tea maker," she said, "and to go get another three dozen doughnuts. She brought in a dozen herself, and they're gone."

"I'd best scoot down there, then, and give her a hand with crowd control." He could not believe the uproar over the tiny newspaper.

"Yes, you had better."

"Get me some jelly doughnuts," he thought to sling out the window as Marilee drove on.

He put his vehicle in gear and headed down the street, thinking that he should have anticipated a strong objection to changing the paper from a daily. Such outcry should be a cause for celebration on his part; it showed a lot more people than he had imagined read it.

He suspected, though, that the outcry had less to do with the number of people who read the paper and more with the simple fact that human beings did not take readily to change, even to change that meant improvement.

He shook hands and offered a friendly welcome and an attentive ear, which he had long ago learned was the best way to deal with complaints. Most people were content, once they had been heard out. There was not much more he needed to offer than a true listening ear.

The place had cleared out, and Tate had made it to his office, when a short but ramrod-straight grey-haired man in a dark cardigan, plaid shirt and creased khakis appeared at his door.

"Charlotte isn't out here," the man said to Tate. "No one is out here."

"Well, now, I'm sorry. Charlotte was just here." Tate came to the door and looked out at the empty room where only minutes before at least three women had been working at their desks.

"I guess everyone has stepped out. Can I help you?"

"Hmmm . . . Everett Northrupt," the man said, sticking out his hand.

"Nice to meet you, sir. I'm Tate Holloway."

"I figured." The man's eyes narrowed. "I want to know how you will handle my account. I'm paid up for a year of dailies. I expected to receive them. I have received them for eight years, since I moved down here. Always paid on time. I tip the boy ten dollars, twice a year, Easter and Christmas."

"I'm sure the young man appreciates that, sir. And we appreciate you as a customer. Don't you worry about your account. It will be adjusted. You won't lose any money."

"I paid for a daily. I expect a daily." The man stared intently at Tate.

"Well, sir . . . we can give you a refund." Tate pulled at his ear.

"I don't want my money back. I want my daily paper. I paid for a daily, and I expect a daily."

Tate saw Charlotte out of the corner of his eye, coming out of the rest room. She looked his way, but he did not think he should wave her down for help.

"Sir—" he felt compelled to sir the man "—as I explained in my editorial, I am sorry for the disappointing change, but it is my hope that by going to a twice weekly, we can save this important institution and turn it into even a grander paper than it has been for many years."

The man's mouth got tighter. "So then you'll go bankrupt, and I'll lose my payment anyway."

The man had a definite negative outlook.

Tate took hold of the man's elbow. "Would you like a cup of coffee, Mr. . . ." He was embarrassed to have forgotten the man's name.

"Northrupt. I've had my coffee this mornin'."

"Well, sir, I find I'm in need of several cups this mornin'." He decided it was time to get Charlotte's help, no matter how blatant the request appeared. But she was busy at her computer. It was nearly impossible to get Charlotte's attention once she determined to focus on the computer screen.

Thank heaven, there was Marilee! She came through the door with the children, each carrying a white doughnut box and going over to the long, white-linen-draped table.

"Well now, here's doughnuts," Tate said. He hauled Northrupt along by the elbow. "Just look at this spread . . . fresh doughnuts . . . fresh coffee. Thank you, Miss Marilee."

Marilee, opening the boxes of doughnuts, said to him, "I have to go back to the Jeep for the tea maker and distilled water."

Tate was left there with his irritated customer, staring at Marilee and Corrine's backs disappear out the door.

"Hel-lo, Mis-ter North-rub."

It was Willie Lee, with Munro beside him, standing there looking up and holding out his hand for a shake.

Mr. Northrupt shook the boy's hand. "Hello, Willie Lee."

Willie Lee gave his hand to Tate for a shake, too.

Then Northrupt looked expectantly at Tate.

"How about a doughnut, Mr. Northrupt? Let's see, there's glazed, chocolate covered, cinnamon . . . and jelly. Jelly doughnuts are a secret to life, you know."

"I want a jell-y dough-nut," Willie Lee said.

"You betcha', son. Here you go." Tate handed a doughnut to the boy. "What kind would you like, Mr. Northrupt?"

"I have diabetes," Mr. Northrupt said.

"I'm sorry to hear that. You look fit, though, sir." He had a sudden disturbing vision of a newspaper headline that read: Editor Kills Man With Doughnut.

He filled a foam cup with steaming coffee and held it toward the older gentleman.

Mr. Northrupt looked at the cup. "I said I've had my coffee. And I don't drink from a foam cup, anyway. Tastes bitter."

Tate withdrew the cup, brought it to his lips and sipped. He didn't like foam cups, either.

"I don't see how goin' to a twice weekly paper delivered at fifty cents each can make you more money than a daily at forty cents each," Mr. Northrupt said.

"Cut down on outlay. Paper costs dearly these days. Over all, we'll cut down on paper costs, printing costs and delivery costs."

The man's frown deepened.

"I believe it will be a better paper. We'll have a lot more in each issue. We'll be adding two pages to start, another two in two more months, as well as special inserts from time to time."

"You're set to do this thing, then."

"Yes, sir, I am. It's gotta be done." He looked down to see Willie Lee standing there, jelly on his face, and his eyes behind his thick glasses intently looking up at them. The dog sat at his feet, doing the same thing.

Just then Marilee came in bearing the tea maker and a sack, and Corrine came right behind her, lugging two gallons of distilled water. Tate jumped to take the heavy gallon containers from the small girl.

"You have met the *Voice*'s senior editor, haven't you, Mr. Northrupt?" Suddenly he realized the need to give her the title. Her eyes came quickly to his. "This is Marilee James."

"Everett and I have known each other for quite a while. Hello, Everett. How is Doris doin'? I heard she took first prize for her water-color at the Spring Fair."

"Yep, she did." Northrupt turned to the table and took up two napkins. "I think I'll just wrap up a couple of these cinnamon rolls and take them with me."

"What about your diabetes?" Tate said, a little alarmed.

"I'm takin' these to Doris. I need to get some of my money back." He left with a napkin-wrapped cinnamon roll bulging in each pocket of his cardigan sweater.

For a few minutes—dare he hope for the rest of the day?—the visitors had stopped. Feeling frazzled, Tate got his ceramic cup, now appearing very dear to him, and poured himself a cup of coffee from the pot that sat on the cloth-covered table.

Marilee, who was adding fresh doughnuts to the plates, said, "I'll take twenty dollars more a month as senior editor."

"That is what the thirty was for. I just forgot to mention it."

"If I had known, though, I would have asked for fifty."

"When the paper makes money."

"Good enough. I'll remind you."

"Would you mind stayin' a while? I think we really need a hostess for this open house."

Charlotte didn't appear inclined to leave her desk, and if she did, Tate thought she seemed more intimidating than welcoming. He realized he felt a little desperate, and this made him feel silly, yet he still cast Marilee a hope-filled look.

"You're the boss," Marilee told him in that smooth, snappy way she had of speaking.

Her eyes looked very blue. He could never tell for certain when she was joking. He liked this about her— admired it, a trait he admired in himself.

"I doubt that very much where you're concerned, Miss Marilee," he drawled, relieved and happily taking up a jelly doughnut.

"I think I'll do a lot better to ask you, rather than to tell you," he added, and bit into the doughnut, raspberry, his favorite.

Her gaze was on him. He smiled, keeping his full mouth closed, savoring the jelly on his tongue and the sight of her blue eyes. Enjoying the electricity between them.

By golly, he wanted powerfully to kiss her. This struck him so hard that for an instant he forgot to chew his doughnut and almost choked on it.

Then she had lowered her eyes and was saying cooly, "I'll stay until noon. Then I'll need to get the children home for lunch, and Willie Lee generally takes a nap."

Tate, inhaling a deep breath and allowing his gaze to drift downward over her body, her back now turned to him, thought, Marilee James is one heck of an attractive woman.

He had experience attending parties to welcome some pretty prominent dignitaries, however, he had always been in the capacity of observer. He knew how to blend in and watch others pay welcome and receive welcome, pay homage and receive homage. He had never been the one stuck out there in the thick of it.

He smiled until his smile felt pasted on, and shook hands until he thought his arm might be permanently stuck into position. Every third minute he was blinded by flashes from Reggie's camera.

"Let's get one of you and the mayor shaking hands," she said, going so far as to physically position Tate and Mayor Upchurch in front of the big spray of flowers sent over by Fred Grace. "Free advertising for town merchants never hurt anything."

"Wait! I want in the picture," said Kaye Upchurch, the mayor's wife, who bustled herself over, slipped her arm through Tate's and smiled at the camera.

Reggie snapped the picture, then told them to hold it. "I always take two shots, just to make sure."

Reggie took two shots of Tate with Sheriff Oakes and Jaydee Mayhall, who was a prominent—not to mention the only—local attorney, and then two of him with Adam and Iris MacCoy, who owned the feed-and-grain store and were building a senior living community, and two of him with Winston Valentine, who presented him with a key to the Senior Citizens' Center.

"Let's get a shot of the publisher and his staff," Reggie commanded, assembling everyone who had returned to the offices—except Zona, of course, who might or might not have been holed up in her office behind the pulled shades.

"Marilee, you get there in front of Mr. Tate—" Reggie sighted through her camera "—Imperia, you get on his left, and, Tammy, you right here. June, get there beside Marilee, and, Charlotte, you stand behind his right shoulder, you're so tall . . . get in close. And, Leo, get closer in with Charlotte.

Tate caught a sweet citrus scent from Marilee's hair. He put his hand on her waist and felt her jump. A flash went off. Marilee moved away, but then Reggie made them all get back together for another shot, after which she enlisted Bonita Embree of Sweetie Cakes Bakery to take a shot with Reggie squeezing in.

"Nobody move! Take another one, Bonita, just to make sure."

Tate paused to look at the room for a minute. In his mind's eye, he constructed how he wished the room to take shape. He would hire a new layout manager and assistant as soon as he could find them, and two more staff writers. Two more desks along there, updated, pleasant partitions, maybe of blue . . . modern, while leaving the antique brick walls. They had to have new lighting, but he didn't intend to install a lowered ceiling, no, sir.

He was sinking all he had in the world into this place.

He turned out the lights and went out the front door to the curb, where he had begun parking his BMW in an effort to avoid what dust he could. He jumped over the door and into the seat, in the manner he liked to do to keep himself fit, or to display his fitness to himself and anyone else who might notice, and simply for the fun of it.

Backing out, he headed down the street drenched with early-evening sunlight. It rained a lot more down in Houston than here, and he was enjoying the dryness. He enjoyed seeing the play of golden setting sunlight on the buildings and trees as he drove the few blocks to his house.

When he saw the Victorian house, he reminded himself that it was his new home.

He pulled beneath the portico, got out and slammed the door, went easily up the stairs and in through the side door that wasn't locked. He didn't see a reason to lock the house. Most everything he owned was still in taped boxes that had been delivered on Saturday, which would make robbery pretty easy, he thought, glancing into the rooms at the stacked boxes. Although he figured that people exiting his house with boxes would likely be noticed and questioned in Valentine, America, where his neighbor across the street was often sitting on her porch and watching everything like a hawk.

Even when he had lived in the big city, though, Tate never had been much for locking anything. Lucille used to say he didn't lock doors because he had nothing worth stealing, not outside himself nor in.

Funny how he thought of Lucille these days. As if he was seeing a review of his life in order to see clearly the mistakes, so as not to make them again in the future.

The silence of the house engulfed him, and he had the dreary thought that he had not successfully built up riches of the spiritual sort, either. He had for too many years kept people at a distance, kept himself running after a journalism career so hard that he did not have time or energy to face the nagging bite of emptiness in his soul.

It was only when he had been brought to an abrupt halt, when he was face-to-face with the emptiness that was on the brink of swallowing him, that he had attempted to change his life. Sometimes, like right then, he wearied of the attempt.

Living life took a great deal of fortitude.

He thought of all this as he opened the refrigerator—a five-foot, curved-top vintage fifties Kelvinator that revealed his cousin's total lack of concern with either the house or modernization. Or perhaps it stood as a testament to solid craftsmanship from another era. Tate found himself reluctant to part with it.

He wished for a good glass of sweet iced tea, but having none made, he took the easier route of pulling a small bottle of Coke from the wire shelf, then slammed the door. He popped the cap from the bottle, shook five cat treats from the container on the counter, and walked out the back door, where Bubba had already learned to wait for him each evening.

"You're a pretty smart boy," he said to the cat, as the animal sat up to receive each treat. "You take the good things of life immediately."

Immediately after the final treat, Bubba gave him a satisfied look and then turned and ambled away.

"Got what you wanted, and now you're off," Tate said to the cat's retreating behind. "I feel used."

Straightening, he drank deeply from the cold bottle.

The big, blooming lilac bush buzzed with bees. He was going to have to get a mower for the lawn. He had never owned a power mower. He had never owned a lawn. He'd *had* a lawn once, with Lucille, but he didn't think it could be called owning one. He had paid a lawn maintenance crew to handle it for the five months or so they had lived in the house.

Just then he heard childish voices, laughter and a dog's bark. A woman's voice cut in. Marilee's voice, from her yard just beyond the cedar trees.

His spirit perked up, and he started toward the sound, drawn along as surely as if by a cord. Through the break in the trees and to the gate in the fence covered with rambling rose vines, letting himself through the gate even before being invited by Marilee, who stood in front of a smoking grill, while Willie Lee and Corrine raced around with Munro in the shadowy yard.

"Well, you already have your drink," Marilee said to him, her eyes on the bottle in his hand. "Would you like to join us for hot dogs?" Her eyes came to his, and her smile was warm.

"Yes, ma'am, that sounds right fine," he replied.

He allowed himself the enjoyment of studying her womanly beauty, even when she looked away. Tate had always considered it one of his finest traits that he could appreciate the delicacies of a woman.

"My mama always said there was nothin' like these little Co-Cola's," Tate explained. "The Coke in them tastes better than in the bigger bottles. Lots better than in plastic."

They were sitting on the back concrete steps, eating their hot dogs and beans off plates in their laps. Marilee had said she once possessed a picnic table and benches, but that during a power outage in a bad winter storm, she had burned them and had never replaced them.

Tate was in the midst of explaining how his mother used to take him and his brother down to the corner grocery every afternoon to get a cold drink out of the cooler of ice. "We didn't even have 'lectric in those little country stores when I was a kid," he explained to the children he doubted could imagine not having electricity.

"Is it dif-fer-ent?" Willie Lee asked, breaking into Tate's tale.

"What different?" Tate asked. "Not havin' electricity?"

"What is in the bot-tle?" Willie Lee was looking at the now empty bottle in Tate's hand.

Marilee said, "It's all the same Coke, Willie Lee. Just some people think the little bottles taste different."

"They do taste different," Tate stated.

"Matter of opinion," Marilee returned.

Tate took exception to an opinion he found poor, and into this Corrine inserted with a hesitant voice, "The little bottles are glass. The bigger bottles are plastic."

Tate and Marilee regarded her, and then Tate said, "We should do a taste test." He grabbed the idea with enthusiasm. "We'll gather the different bottles of Coke and taste each one to see if there is a difference. It will be a great experiment. You can give the children points for a science project," he added to Marilee, thrilled with himself for thinking of a way to contribute to the children's education, and thrilled even still further at the bright smile that came across Marilee's face.

"I think that's a super idea," she said.

"Well, by golly, then . . . come on and finish up those dogs, kids, so we can get to it."

Ten minutes later, he was a little surprised when Marilee threw him the keys to her Cherokee and told him, "It's your idea, so you go buy the Cokes. I'll stay here and get the kitchen cleaned up."

"Okay. You kids want to go with me?"

"Yes," Willie Lee said immediately.

Tate saw Corrine looking uncertainly at Marilee, and noticed that Marilee hesitated.

"Yes, you guys can go," Marilee said.

"Mun-ro, too." Willie Lee put in.

"You bet, Munro, too," Tate said, pleased that Corrine was joining them as they went out the door.

It had been many years since he had been alone with children. He had on a number of occasions, years ago, enjoyed his brother's three children, but they were long grown. This experience with Willie Lee and Corrine somehow struck him as quite special. He realized he felt pretty important and grand, helping to improve children's spirits with an openness about life.

He supposed he was getting a little carried away about a short trip to the IGA, but nevertheless, there was something about being a man of his ripe age with children that enabled him to jump back into his own childhood. He supposed he'd had to grow up enough to be childish again.

He took an index card from his pocket and jotted a note on it. Then he noticed Corrine looking at him curiously.

"Just jotting down a thought I don't want to lose," he told her. "That's what newspapermen do." He thought maybe she should know that trait; it might prove helpful to her in the future, should she get interested in a newspaperman.

At the checkout counter, Tate told the young clerk, who looked quizzically at the array of Coca-Cola in the different-size bottles, and some in cans, too, "We are conducting an experiment. I have with me budding scientists—" he put a hand on each of the children's shoulder "—who might in another twenty years possibly develop soft drinks that can feed the world."

"Yeah, whatever," said the clerk, who was young enough to know everything.

Eager to get back to Marilee and share the fun of the experiment with her, Tate zoomed along the streets at a good clip. His mind was zooming on ahead, too, in the manner of a man who is powerfully attracted to a woman. That he had not been so strongly attracted to a woman in years came to him. Maybe it was simply the new changes in his life, he thought. Maybe the attraction would pass.

Still, Marilee James excited him, by golly. Each time he came into her presence, he felt like a man in a manner he had somehow forgotten along the way. His mind took off with a strong fantasy of drawing her to him, slowly and seductively . . . hoping he hadn't forgotten how to do that. He imagined kissing her.

It was at this part in the fantasy that he was brought to an abrupt halt, in both mind and vehicle, by the sight of Parker Lindsey's truck sitting in Marilee's driveway.

"Parker's here," Corrine said, as Tate pulled the Cherokee to the front curb. Her delight was apparent, and irritating.

"Yes, he is," Tate said, carefully, mindful that Corrine's young eyes had turned on him with some curiosity.

"Hello, Parker. Good to see you." Tate put the sacks of Coca-Cola on the table and held out his hand for a shake.

"Hello, Tate."

The man's grasp was very firm. Parker Lindsey was an inch taller than Tate and a good ten years younger, maybe, but Tate judged himself to be on the high end of any comparison with the man. He let Lindsey see this in his eyes.

"Marilee says you all are about to run an experiment," Lindsey said.

"Guess we're intent on havin' fun, too."

Tate lined the can and various bottles of Coke on the counter. Marilee brought glasses for each of them, and they began to taste.

"Better rinse with water between each taste," Lindsey advised.

Tate had been going to say that.

The one opinion everyone shared was that the cola in bottles, either the plastic or the small glass, tasted different from the canned cola. Everyone but Willie Lee, whose concentration went to the bubbles in each glass he was handed. He liked how the bubbles tickled his nose when he stuck his nose in the glass. At one point he inhaled too many bubbles and choked, causing Marilee to retire from the testing to keep an eye on him, as he wanted to continue experiencing the bubbles tickling his nose.

"Yep," Tate said. "These smaller bottles of Coke taste a whole lot better."

"I like the canned," Parker said. "And I really doubt you could tell the difference in Coke out of the small bottle or the big one, if you weren't lookin' at it."

"Try me. I won't look."

Tate, aware of being on the childish side but unable to stop himself, handed Lindsey his empty glass, picked up his water glass and swished water in his mouth, then turned his back.

Corrine was looking up at him, a curious expression on her small, heart-shaped face, and he winked at her. "You keep track of what bottle, missy, so there aren't any mistakes." Then he smiled at Marilee, who raised an eyebrow.

Lindsey handed him a glass with a couple of swallows of cola. Corrine watched him as he drank from it.

"Small bottle." Tate handed his glass back to Lindsey.

"Lucky guess. Three tries."

There was the sound of liquid splashed in a glass.

Lindsey gave Tate the glass again. Tate tasted, then tasted again. "One liter."

"Okay."

Lindsey disappeared with the glass behind Tate's back. Tate took a quick swish of water, and repositioned himself for the final taste.

Lindsey handed him the glass with several swallows of brown liquid. Tate drank deeply, swished the cola around his tongue. Lindsey and Corrine gazed at him. Marilee, holding a droopy-eyed Willie Lee, suppressed a grin.

"Small bottle," Tate said.

"You're a good guesser, I give up," Parker said.

Marilee chuckled aloud, which was Tate's reward.

Tate looked at black-and-white photographs of the prairie on the living room wall, while Lindsey, on the sofa like he was used to being there, flipped channels on the television. They were alone. Willie Lee was put to bed, and Marilee was helping Corrine in her bath.

"Why don't you go on home?" Lindsey said suddenly.

Tate looked around. "Why don't you?"

"I belong here."

"Do you?"

Lindsey gazed at him. "Marilee and I are engaged."

"Oh? I hadn't heard that."

He let himself survey Lindsey, and saw the man gearing up to say something more, but just then Marilee and Corrine appeared out of the hallway. "Corrine's ready to say good-night."

"Well, good night, missy. I sure enjoyed our taste testin'." He always fell into a deep Southern drawl with young ladies.

"Good night, Corrine." Lindsey did not have much of an accent.

"Good night," Corrine responded in a faint, shy voice.

Marilee disappeared with Corrine, and reappeared a few minutes later. She looked uncertain, and Tate figured he would do best to take the initiative of making things easier on her. People always greatly appreciated the person who made things easier.

"I'd best be goin'," he said. "Thanks a lot for the dinner and the company. Good seein' you again, Parker."

At the door, he looked long into the deep pools of Marilee's blue eyes and wondered if he dared kiss her.

"Thank you for an evenin's hospitality. I enjoyed it mightily, Miss Marilee."

"I did, too."

"Good night." He leaned over and kissed her cheek.

She became very still. "Good night, Tate."

He turned and walked away. When he reached the sidewalk, he briefly looked back. Marilee was standing there, gazing after him. He waved, and she waved. As he continued on walking beneath the streetlights, he mulled things over and decided Marilee was not thoroughly engaged as yet. And what he needed to do was give her a proper kiss. A kiss would reveal the possibilities between them.

The Valentine Voice

View from the Editor's Desk
by Tate Holloway

I would like to start this new era of *The Valentine Voice* off with a public thank you to all the people who have made me welcome and voiced support for the newspaper. An anonymous gifter left a basket of homemade jams and fruit on my front porch. Thank you. It was all *Delicious*. I wouldn't mind if you left another.

In speaking with people these weeks since my arrival in this beautiful town, I've been asking questions and compiling a number of concerns from the citizenry. I thought I would share the main ones with you here.

Mr. Winston Valentine says, "I think the town needs more public benches. We have a few on Main Street, but we older people don't live on Main Street. We need benches on the streets where we live and walk."

It was reported that Lucy Kaye Sikes felt faint during a recent walk and had to sit to rest on the curb of East Porter Street, and would still be there if Winston had not come along to help her to her feet.

Miss Julia Jenkins-Tinsley, our postmistress, says, "I would appreciate people paying attention when the wind is up and close the post office door behind them. It gets caught in the wind every couple of months, and that thingamajig that's supposed to close the door gets ripped right off. If people would read the sign I put up, it wouldn't keep happening."

Mr. Jaydee Mayhall, who is a candidate for city council, says, "I don't like a prison in our midst, and if I had been on the council when the matter came up, we would not be having to deal with it now. Vote for me."

Mr. Juice Tinsley, who is also a candidate for the city council, had this to say in response to Mr. Mayhall, "For one thing, it is a detention center, not a prison, and it will bring jobs and more people spending money in this town. I'm all for it, and I intend to support it, if elected or not."

My own suggestion to the city council is for planting trees along the sidewalks of Main Street. I'm heading up a petition for signatures of citizens who would like to see these trees, and I'll be taking the petition to next month's meeting of the council.

Please come by the *Voice* offices and sign the Tree Petition, or simply come by to visit and give us your views on what improvements you would like to see in your town, or what it is you like about your town. We want to be your voice in the community. The coffee is always hot and the door always open.

Charlotte, given the dubious honor of editing her boss's work, did not approve of the editorial. She thought it way too familiar in tone, and that he was opening them up for all sorts of kooks and weirdos and just plain time wasters. She thought the paper should set a more formal standard of leadership and not *mingle*. Ms. Porter, who everyone knew was a kind and compassionate soul, nevertheless had known the wisdom of retaining her place as a leader, not a mingler.

Charlotte brought this argument up to her boss and suggested he might want to rework his editorial, especially the last paragraph.

But Tate Holloway was a man set on his own way. "Keep an open mind, Charlotte, or you get old. Change can be good."

"You could put down a time we are open for visitors," she suggested, motioning with her pencil. "Maybe Wednesdays, after noon." That was going to be their least busy time from now on.

"People won't remember that." He gazed at her and then said, "How 'bout you just check my spellin' and punctuation and let it go?"

"You were the one who gave it to me to edit," she pointed out, tapping her pencil on the paper. "You have spell-checker on your machine."

"Yes, but it makes mistakes. Won't catch *there* and *their,* you know, and I interchange those a lot."

"Do you want *delicious* capitalized?"

"No . . . that was a mistake. Glad you caught that."

"There isn't such a word as *gifter,*" she pointed out.

"Well, hmmm . . ." He knotted his eyebrows and rubbed his cheek. "I guess we should change that. Put *citizen* in place of *gifter.* I don't like it, but we have an educational standard to uphold."

She was glad he had some standard, even if she found it lacking.

"If you decide to reconsider about inviting all and sundry to come in here, I will be able to change it until 10:00 a.m. tomorrow." She placed the editorial in the layout, with a reminder to check before sending it to the printer.

Ten

Life's Unexpected Moments

Munro lay on the rug in front of the kitchen sink. His children sat at the table, doing something that caused them to speak in low voices and every once in a while laugh.

His lady came in to speak to the children. Munro liked her voice, most especially when it held a smile. Lying there, his eyes contentedly closed, he listened to his humans; that was how he thought of them, as *his* humans.

"I made a gir-affe, like in my bo-ok," Munro's boy said.

"Well, it sure is. Good job, honey. Did Corrine help you?" It was his lady's voice; it made Munro's tail twitch happily.

"No." This was Munro's girl, her voice soft, slow and true, like a sun-warmed creek in summer. "All I told him was to use the yellow clay, that giraffes are yellow with brown spots. He made it all by himself, though."

"He did?"

"Yes, I did."

"Well, my goodness . . . this is really something. . . ."

Quite suddenly, Munro's ear detected another sound, and his head came up. Someone was at the front door. *Someone was opening the front door.* Instinct had him up and at the kitchen door, peering around the jamb and through the house. The person entering the front door was a stranger.

Munro went in a silent, streaking motion toward the door.

"Marilee . . . Marilee!" The stranger's eyes fell on him and went wide. "Yeeaaw!" A bulging brown bag came flying at Munro, and the woman's scream ripped the air.

Munro ducked the bag, at the same time seeing the contents— which were nothing but cloth—spill out across the floor.

"Mother? What is the problem?" It was his lady, her footsteps clicking, her voice now filled with alarm.

Munro, peeking out from around the big chair, watched and listened to the two humans, trying to judge if he might need to defend his charges or hide himself.

"That dog just about attacked me." The stranger pointed at Munro and her voice was sharp enough to cause him to wince.

"Munro?"

His lady's voice held a question. He looked upward to see eyes searching him. Then she smiled in a way that made him feel he'd done a good thing after all, even if he had not been going to attack this silly woman. He had been ready for attack, though, and he knew he had done right with that.

"Well, I guess he didn't realize . . . since you let yourself in. He doesn't know you, Mother. It's okay, Munro. She can come in." His lady patted his head, causing his heart to swell up in the right place.

Although still a little embarrassed, and quite annoyed with this stranger, Munro returned confidently to his rug in the kitchen.

"You should watch that dog," the woman with the sharp voice said. "He slips around, and he could have a vicious streak. You don't know. . . ."

She went on in that sharp voice, and Munro thought maybe she would profit by his giving her a bite on the ankle.

Corrine went into Aunt Marilee's room to try on the clothes her grandmother had brought her: two dresses and a skirt and blouse. They all came from the secondhand thrift store, and so did the red plastic car Willie Lee played with in their room. The car looked brand-new. The clothes did, too. But they weren't.

Wearing the first dress, Corrine looked at herself in the mirror. She wondered if the dress was supposed to look like this on her. She wanted to tear it off and stomp on it. But doing that would make everyone mad at her.

Slowly she opened the door and went out to display herself to her aunt and grandmother. She was in sock feet, and they did not hear her.

Her grandmother was saying, "She's dating a lawyer from the district attorney's office. He's taken her out three times in a week."

Aunt Marilee said something in a low voice.

"Well, Anita says he is quite a big-wig . . . and he drives a Jaguar."

Corrine, not wanting to hear another word about her mother having a boyfriend, entered the room.

"Well, now . . ." Her grandmother's head came around. "That looks really pretty. It's a little big, but she'll grow into it."

Corrine jerked her eyes over to Aunt Marilee to judge what was the truth, seeing immediately that the dress was not right.

"Mom, she isn't goin' to grow into that until next year."

"Well, then it'll last her. Turn around, honey, let's get a good look."

Corrine did as she was told. Her eyes coming around again to her Aunt Marilee, she had the urge to run and throw herself into her aunt's arms.

"It's not that big. Children grow."

Corrine headed back to Aunt Marilee's room. Just inside the door, she stopped, hearing her grandmother and Aunt Marilee.

"Mom, why can't you buy her something new? Something that fits now?"

"You have to buy big for children. I always did for you girls. You and Anita grew so fast at that age, I couldn't keep clothes on your back. It's no sense buying new, when she'll be right out of it before you know it."

Corrine pushed the door closed and went to the bed, ripped off the dress and took up the second one. It was green and looked like a melon.

Then she plopped on the bed and brought her legs up and clutched them, wishing to make herself very small. She wished she could just disappear and not be any more trouble to anyone.

Marilee walked her mother to her car in the driveway.

"I don't think Corrine liked the dresses." Her mother was hurt.

"She thanked you for them, Mom." This was the best Marilee could think to say.

"She should wear dresses more. Anita hasn't taught her, and now you have to teach her, Marilee. You need to teach her to wear dresses and fix her hair, to be ladylike. Pretty is as pretty does. If you let her keep on wearing jeans and overalls—" her voice dropped "—she'll turn out strange."

"Oh, she will not, Mom. She's only eleven, for heavensake. What do you want—her to paint her fingernails and start dyin' her hair?"

Her mother said with a knowing air, "Eleven is a lot older these days than what it used to be when you were a child."

Marilee wanted to say that eleven had been quite old enough when she had been there, but she stopped all the resentful thoughts that tried to crowd into her mind.

"There is plenty of time for Corrine to grow up," she said. "She needs to just be a child and not think anything about growing up."

"Life doesn't allow us much *not* thinking about tomorrow," her mother said primly. "And that is what Anita is doing. She's looking down the road for some security, and it is a fact of life that she will be more secure with a husband who has a successful career than she will be alone, trying to make it on a secretary's salary. You need to think about that with Parker. Don't throw away what Parker could give you, Marilee. There's nothing wrong with finding a man with a future."

Marilee took a breath. "How are the tires doin'?"

"Oh . . . they're fine, I guess. Carl thought they were too expensive. I was afraid of that when you picked these." She looked at the front tire and frowned.

Marilee looked at the tire and held her lips together.

"Well, I guess I'd better go." Her mother cast her that rather help-less expression, as if knowing things were not right between them but not having a clue as to what to do about it. Marilee felt the same.

Marilee hugged her mother. At least she could do that. "Goodbye, Mom. Drive careful."

She stood politely in the drive, thinking she was glad to give her mother a daughter who watched and waved as her mother drove away in the gleaming Cadillac with the brand-new, too expensive tires.

Willie Lee and Corrine were both in their bedroom. Marilee went on to her own room and saw the clothes Corrine had left neatly spread upon the bed. Corrine was the neatest eleven-year-old Marilee had ever seen.

She held up one of the dresses, and then the other, and then the skirt and blouse, looking them over, shaking her head at both the colors and the large size. Painful memories of her childhood flitted across her mind. For a long time Marilee had believed that all children stuffed newspaper in the toes of their shoes to keep them from flopping off at the heel. There had been that black coat that she had hemmed two full turns; she had thought that made it the correct size, but then someone had pointed out how it hung off her shoulders. One day she had glanced at her image in the girl's bathroom mirror at school and seen a child's face in an old-lady's coat. She had been seventeen when she finally realized that she was not likely to wear a large in anything, because she wasn't going to grow much further.

Hearing a sound, she turned and saw Corrine in the doorway.

"Do you really like any of these?" Marilee gestured to the clothes.

"They're okay." Corrine's expression, as usual, was carefully guarded.

"You don't have to like them. You did the polite thing by thanking your grandmother, but you don't have to wear any of these."

Marilee tried to read her niece but couldn't. She wanted very much to shake the child and say, "Speak up. Tell me what you want."

Corrine gave a small shrug.

"Well, they're too big for you right now. We'll store them in my closet for a while." She reached into her closet for hangers, and her eyes fell on a bit of fur peeking out at the end of the closet rod. Beginning to chuckle, she wrestled the piece from the press of clothing and held it out for Corrine to view.

Corrine's eyes went wide.

"This was a present from your grandmother."

Marilee held the pink robe with the fake fur collar up in front of her and then sashayed a two step. "Can't you just see me wearing this when I take out the garbage?"

She was rewarded by Corrine's grin.

"Your grandmother tries to please. It's just that her ideas don't quite match ours. But still, it is the thought that counts. This is the only way she knows to show her love."

Her niece's heart-shaped face relaxed with understanding, and she nodded.

Marilee put the robe and Corrine's dresses in the back of the closet.

"You know, all of us really do need some summer clothes. Let's go shoppin' tomorrow." Now, there was an outstanding idea!

"Okay," Corrine said, and there seemed to be a glimmer of eagerness in her face.

Anita telephoned late that afternoon. She spoke for five minutes to Corrine and then wanted to speak to Marilee.

"I'm in a hurry," her sister said, sounding somewhat breathless. "I got a date, and he's pickin' me up in half an hour. He's an attorney."

"Mom told me this afternoon. She brought Corrine some clothes."

"Oh, Lordy, are they like what she used to buy us?"

"Pretty much." Marilee felt a warm connection to her sister flow over her. "Corrine does need some new clothes. She's grown quite a bit. I'm going to take her shopping tomorrow." Marilee thought how much fun it would be if her sister could join them in shopping.

"Okay. I'll send you some money from my next check."

The fantasy of them shopping together disintegrated. "When are you comin' up to visit?" she asked.

"I don't know. I can't get any time off, with just startin' and all."

"There are weekends."

"I'm tryin' to save money, Marilee. It takes money to get a nice place and everything. And I really don't think my car will make it up there and back."

"Corrine needs to see her mother, Anita." Marilee was aggravated at herself; she sounded as harping as her own mother.

"Look, things are really goin' good for me right now. I got this new job, and I've met Louis, and he's so great. I'm gettin' myself together, and who knows—maybe soon I'll have a new daddy for Corrine. I'd just love to do that for her. Oh . . . Louis is here. I gotta run. Kiss my baby for me."

"Anita! She likes the cards you send. Don't stop." Marilee wasn't quite certain why she felt the need to say that. She was feeling a strange panic, as if she needed to reach through the phone and grab hold of her sister to keep her with them and safe.

"Great, I won't . . . bye now." Then she was gone and the line went dead.

Marilee hung up and stood there for a long minute trying to believe that her sister would actually send money, and experiencing the strong urge to run down there and get Anita.

She always felt the need to save Anita, only she was not exactly sure what from.

As she checked the cabinets and tried to drum up interest in making supper, wondering if Parker might find Chef Boyardee canned spaghetti acceptable, it came to her that it had been almost two weeks since she had promised Parker to consider marrying him.

Receiving this thought with some alarm, she checked the Stidham Texaco calendar hanging on the kitchen wall beside the telephone and saw that this was exactly the case.

Guilt assailed her. She had not given the question much thought at all. It was not that she did not care, but so many other things seemed to have taken precedence since then. Researching and developing lesson plans for teaching the children, planning their days to include stimulating activities, adjusting to new conditions at the paper and new working arrangements—all of that left little time to consider meals, much less marriage.

And Parker had been very busy these last weeks, too, as he always was with each springtime. She had seen him only on brief occasions, and a number of days they had only spoken on the telephone. In fact, Parker had not made one tiny mention of the marriage proposal in these weeks.

While she remained uncertain about marrying Parker, Marilee did know that she did not want to lose him altogether. She and Parker had enjoyed a good friendship; they knew each other quite well in ways that some people could only imagine.

Certainly Parker deserved much more than the neglectful attention she had given him of late. And now that her guilt was working on her, she began to berate herself for foolish behavior in throwing away something dear and precious that she had with Parker.

She reached for the telephone and dialed his number at the veterinary clinic. Parker himself answered.

"Would you like to come to supper this evening?" she asked straight away, thinking maybe she should have identified herself. It was possible he had forgotten her voice during these days of little communication.

"Ah . . . yeah, that'd be great." He seemed surprised but eager as he explained he had surgery on a dog to complete before he could get away.

"That will be fine," she said, pleased to accommodate him. "We will have lasagna."

She hung up and threw herself into motion.

Eleven

It was growing dark when Marilee spread the cream-colored linen cloth over the small table in the dining area. She set two tapered candles in crystal candlesticks in the middle of the table, then stood back to observe the look, wondering if she was getting carried away.

She was not trying to get Parker all worked up. It was just that she felt she owed him something for her recent neglect of him, for disappointing him in the sexual department, and for his patience in waiting for her to make up her mind about his marriage proposal. He deserved repayment for putting up with her indecisiveness.

She had, since phoning him about supper, been trying to decide about marriage. The question had lodged like a splinter in her brain, and she had not been successful in working it to one side or the other. She simply could not bring either a yes or a no to the forefront. What she hoped to accomplish tonight was to be able to work herself more in the direction of yes, and to keep Parker over on that side, too.

She was gathering silver and the good china plates when there came a rap at the back door. Tate smiled at her through the glass. She was not all that surprised. Had she been thinking of it, and not so much about her dilemma, she would have expected him; he had been dropping by for brief visits every few days since moving into the big house beyond her fence.

"Hello," he said when she opened the door.

"Hello."

She stepped back, letting him enter, glad to see the appreciation in his eyes as he looked at her, glad to know that she could get a man's blood up.

Then all this gladness produced a great anxiety. She was, of course, dressed for Parker, so she did not need to be so glad to see Tate. Of course it was simply a normal thing, pleasure at a man's appreciation. But she had everything planned out here. She didn't need Tate Holloway interrupting.

"Wow, it smells good in here," Tate said.

"Lasagna." Then she hurriedly added, "I'm having Parker for supper."

Tate's eyebrows went up. "You are? Does that mean you cooked him . . . or you're havin' him . . . here, I mean?"

"Parker is coming to supper," she stated, ignoring his innuendo and heading into the dining room with the plates and silverware.

Tate, of course, came right on her heels. Setting the two places and folding the linen napkins, she refused to look at him. It paid to be cautious around Tate Holloway, who was such an unpredictable man. He seemed to awaken tendencies that she did not need to have. She hoped he left quickly. She had already experienced the awkwardness of trying to deal with the two men together. They had been a handful together the previous week, during the Coke taste-testing episode.

"Well, looks like a romantic dinner for two," Tate said.

"Yes." She felt his intense gaze and didn't want to meet it. Best not to encourage him.

He followed her back into the kitchen.

She told him that she was sorry she didn't have time to visit with him, but Parker would be arriving any minute.

He pulled out a chair and sat down anyway. "I wanted to let you know that a new notebook computer will be delivered tomorrow . . . probably in the afternoon. A technician will bring it and make certain it is all set to work on the network. I should be able to get a firm time tomorrow morning, and I'll call you."

"Okay. Oh . . . I'd planned to do some shopping. I'll do it in the morning and try to be home by one." She got the lasagna out of the oven.

"I'll make sure the tech works around that schedule." He leaned forward and sniffed the air with appreciation. "Woo-ee, that smells delicious."

She set the casserole on a trivet and admired it.

"The kids aren't goin' to get any of that?" he asked.

"They ate earlier. They're in bed."

"Too bad." He was eyeing the dish. "I just had a ham sandwich a couple of hours ago. No cheese, either." He looked at her.

She jerked her gaze away and popped the foil-wrapped Italian bread into the oven, then wiped her hands on a towel. "Is that all you needed—to tell me about the computer?"

His eyebrows went up. "Yes, I suppose so."

To her relief, he rose and started for the door. Then, his hand on the doorknob, he stopped. "You know, Lindsey isn't the man for you."

It took her a few seconds to process this startling comment.

"He isn't?"

"No, not at all. A woman like you needs a more mature type."

What could she say to this outrageous statement? And what did he mean *"a woman like you?"*

"My first husband was older by fifteen years."

"I said mature type, not necessarily getting on in years."

"I suppose you have come to know me, and Parker, enough in two short weeks to form this opinion?"

"I've been a journalist for a long time. It's a job that teaches you about people. Parker Lindsey isn't up to you."

Up to her? It made her sound like she was a trial.

She gazed at him, with his arm propped on the doorjamb and his body draped there like so much sovereign male.

"Well, thank you for your opinion. You'll understand if I feel I have to make my own decision." He had managed to draw her along where she did not want to be.

"Oh, yes, I suppose you do. Everyone has to find things out for themselves."

"Yes, and now you can leave." Her strong urge to have him out propelled her into incivility. She quite suddenly could not face him and Parker together, and went so far as to step forward, motioning with her hands, as if to sweep him out.

A foot from him, she found herself eye to eye with him.

She gazed at him, and he gazed at her.

She thought for an instant he was going to kiss her, to reach out and take her to him with his strong arm on which blond hairs shone and kiss the fire out of her. She turned her head, in the manner of veering away, knowing she could not, under any circumstances, let him kiss her.

"I have a dinner guest due to arrive any moment." She adjusted the apron around her waist.

He opened the back door and then stopped, saying, "Oh, could I borrow some tea? I meant to ask for that right off. I'd like to have some iced tea, but I don't want to have to go to the store."

She went directly to the cabinet, opened the door and reached in for the box of tea bags. He wanted to know if she had loose tea.

She threw the box of tea bags back on the shelf and strode to the freezer.

As she delved into the freezer for the box of tea, she heard Parker's soft call from the living room and his footsteps approaching.

"Well, good evenin', Lindsey," Tate said. He had planned this.

"Yeah . . . hi." Parker's eyes went from Marilee to Tate and back again.

"Tate was just borrowin' some tea. He's leaving."

"Yes, you two have a nice evenin'," Tate said, casting a wave before letting himself out the back door.

"Is that guy over here all the time now?" Parker frowned as he rolled his sleeves to wash his hands.

"He has only been over here a couple of times." She got the bread out of the oven.

What in the world had he meant, *"a woman like you?"*

"What is this?" Parker asked, observing the formally set table with surprise and wonder that gave her great pleasure.

Marilee, who was lighting candles, blew out the match and smiled. "I thought we could have a quiet meal and relax. That's all, relax a bit, talk a bit. We need to talk. The children ate earlier. Willie Lee's already asleep. Corrine's reading, or she was. I'll check on her in a minute."

She went to the kitchen for the food, and Parker stepped quickly to help her.

"I'm starved," he said, eyeing the food with an enthusiasm that made her feel she had done a very good deed after all.

So, Tate Holloway . . . you and your opinion can go jump.

"Here," she said, handing him the bottle of wine. "Please pour our glasses, while I go check on the children."

She left him in the kitchen and went to peek in the children's bedroom, hoping to find both children asleep. They were. Willie Lee was out with his face buried in the pillow, as usual for him. Munro, who had taken to sleeping with Corrine in something of a sentry manner, opened his eyes but didn't move. Corrine had fallen asleep with the book on her chest. Marilee removed the book and turned out the lamp, and could not resist touching each child's head.

Returning, she paused in the hallway. She stood there, with her breath held and time stopped, looking across the living room at Parker sitting in the glow of the candlelight. The wine in their glasses sparkled.

Did she dare tell him she would marry him? It was time. She should not let him get away. She *did* care for him, and her heart swelled with feeling.

She stepped out, determined to follow where the night led.

"Kids asleep?" he asked, eating heartily from his salad.

"Yes. Corrine fell asleep reading. She's been such a light sleeper, but Munro seems to have helped that. She seems to be sleeping through the night since he started staying with her."

"Hmmm." He was eating quite hungrily, in the way that satisfies a woman.

Marilee passed the plate of Italian bread toward him. "Try the bread. I got it fresh at the bakery today."

He bit into a slice of the buttery bread and made an appreciative sound. "This is delicious, just delicious," he said, pointing to all the food with his fork.

"Thank you."

Serving herself, she looked at her plate and inhaled the rich aromas of butter and garlic. She looked across at Parker. She realized that she was attempting to feed Parker a full luscious meal in order to make up for denying him an intimate portion of herself. Apparently she was succeeding.

She took up her own fork and began to eat. It was delicious. She had outdone herself. She should have made two dishes of lasagna and frozen one.

Parker lifted his wineglass. "To the cook."

She lifted hers, clinked against his, and then drank deeply.

Attempting to start the conversation off with easy topics, Marilee asked Parker if he'd had any interesting cases lately. He replied that he hadn't had anything out of the ordinary, although he *had* had the tragic case of a mare dying in foal.

"Real nice barrel-racing mare," he said, and he paused in his eating, his shoulders slumping, and sat there with a dark stare at the table. Even knowing the facts of life, Parker always blamed himself a great deal when he lost an animal, and Marilee always felt helpless, because she could do nothing for him.

Trying to retrieve a positive focus, she asked about the mare's baby, and he said, brightening, that it was a healthy filly, that he had secured a wet mare for it from Ray Horn, and the mare had taken the filly immediately. "Ray didn't think the mare would take the baby, but I've done it before. Some mares do, some don't. This one did."

"Well, that's wonderful," Marilee said. "Who owns the baby?"

"Leanne Overton. She's Charlene's cousin. I guess she's livin' out there with Charlene and Mason for a while. Some trouble with an ex-husband, I gather."

Marilee tried to remember Leanne but could not.

Parker offered the information that she was quite a successful barrel racer and that she had three high-dollar horses, another one ready to foal any time.

"Do you suppose that the children and I might come along with you sometime and see a live birth?" Marilee asked, feeling enthused at the idea.

Parker said, "I guess so."

Marilee had the uncharitable thought that she could do with him giving up the word *guess*.

"Aren't they a little young for that sort of thing?" he asked.

Marilee, who found his hesitant tone annoying, pointed out Willie Lee's early acquaintance with his rabbits. "If children are acquainted with the facts of life in a natural way, they accept it as natural, as it should be. And Corrine is already so far advanced in biology. I've been looking at schoolbooks for her for next year. It is amazing what kids are taught these days."

"So you plan to have Corrine with you next year?" He frowned with disapproval.

"I don't know. . . . I guess I'm not planning anything." Oh, dear, now *she* was using the word. "But I *am* prepared."

She didn't like the feeling of needing to defend herself. Maybe it had something to do with "a woman like her." Tate's phrase repeatedly echoed in the back of her mind—and in his voice, too. She wished she could slap the image.

She drank the rest of her wine and then pointed out that she planned on next year in the same manner that most people planned on next year. "I hope to be alive, and thus far I am given to believe that Corrine will for some time need me to be looking after her."

Parker nodded, appearing to take that in. After a minute, he said, "How is Anita doing? Have you heard from her?"

"She's been sending Corrine cards, and she called twice this week." She felt pleased to give this report. "She has a job at the Tarrant County Courthouse. Secretary, to a judge, I think."

"Sounds encouraging. Benefits and everything?"

"She says so."

"This may be the time she gets her act together," Parker said.

Marilee tore a slice of bread. "Anita has been trying to get herself together for all of her life. Unfortunately, about the time she does, she gets herself hooked on something and comes unraveled again." Marilee was a little ashamed at this bit of sarcasm popping out.

Parker raised an eyebrow at her.

"Okay, Anita is trying and is doing very well," she said more properly. "But past history has me on the cautious side. I don't know if Corrine will still be here for school in the fall or will be able to return to Anita, but it seems prudent, given past experience, to make plans for her schooling and to remain available, just in case.

"The chances are high that I will have Corrine popping in and out of my life. I am, as I have said, a woman with two children. That is how it is, and I'm sorry if it displeases you."

Maybe her sharp attitude answered the question of what "a woman like her" was. *Contentious* came to mind.

"I didn't say it displeased me." He seemed awkward with the word. "I just don't want to see you get hurt, Marilee. Corrine is not your child, and you will have to give her back to Anita when Anita decides to take her. You don't want to look at this. You are gettin' way too involved with her. You are making a burden for yourself that you don't need to have."

"A burden? I don't consider my niece a burden."

"I didn't mean it like that. I meant that you are complicating your life in a way that you don't need to."

"And therefore I complicate your life."

"Well, yes, it does that. And you don't seem to care how it will affect me."

Marilee stared at him. The truth in his words stung, and she wanted to sting back.

"You are an adult, Parker. She is a child. Virtually a motherless child. You condemn me for what I give her? You feel neglected because of it?"

He got all red in the face.

They were now more or less in a good argument. Parker pointed out once again, in different words and with the aid of his fork, that she had no legal claim to Corrine, and that Anita could come and take her at any moment, and there was nothing Marilee could do about it.

"Forgive me if I don't care to see you hurt," he added.

Marilee pointed out that she knew this fact very well, and that Corrine was her niece and would always be her niece.

"I have to be there for her. There isn't anyone else."

It came to her that Parker was an only child of two rather cool and distant parents. His father had been dead some years, and his mother had remarried and moved to Colorado. It would be difficult for him to relate to feelings for one's sister's child.

"I know this is hard for you to understand, because you have no brother or sister, but Corrine is a blood relative, as close to me as my own child. I was there with Anita when she was born," she added, remembering it all for an instant—the excitement, the wonder, the bit of sadness that the child was not her own and that she had known even then, that Corrine was in for a rough road with Anita, and that she, Marilee, was hopeless to prevent so many painful problems.

She gazed at Parker with her heart full of emotion that spilled over to him.

He pretty well wiped this out, however, by saying, "The best thing you can do for Corrine is to help her with her own mother and quit buttin' in."

She was shocked by her urge to reach across and slap him.

She said evenly, "I am not *butting in.* It was Anita who asked me to come get Corrine, Parker."

Each recognizing how close they were coming to the line, they shut up. Marilee ate her lasagna, which was now sticking in her throat, and Parker mopped up the sauce on his plate.

They finished the meal in comparative silence broken only by occasional overly polite comments, in the manner of two people who are afraid one more cross word might be the last hot straw that ignites a flame to burn down the house.

Parker helped her to clear away the dishes; then he kissed her neck and cajoled her into kissing him, right there at the kitchen sink.

"I'm sorry we argued. I really am." He gave her his best little-boy grin.

"I am, too." Perhaps it had been more her fault than his.

She kissed him good and wondered what in the world was wrong with her. Pushing lingering resentment aside, she took his hand and led him to the couch, where they settled close together in the low light and talked softly of this and that, all innocuous subjects, while Parker kept getting more and more intimate with his hands, and Marilee kept getting more anxious.

She was annoyed with herself for not coming out and asking, *Do you still want to marry me? Let's get this stuff straight.* She was annoyed with him for not taking the initiative to speak up on the matter.

She could not say any of this. She certainly could not bring up the marriage question. Better to let him bring it up. It was a man thing.

When he did bring it up, she would say yes. That was it. She would say yes. She kissed him deeply with this thought.

And then Parker's mobile phone went off, his answering service relaying an emergency message.

"It's Leanne's mare," he told Marilee, as he clicked off from the service and began punching numbers on the little phone.

He spoke into it and said the name Charlene in a brief exchange, ending with, "I'll be right out. I'm leavin' from Marilee's."

He clicked off the phone and rose. "After what happened to the other mare, Leanne's real nervous over this one. I said I'd be right out."

"Charlene and Mason's?"

"Yeah. Mason's there . . . he's 'bout as good as needs be, too."

She hurried with him to the door and out onto the porch. He broke into a trot to his truck. She held on to the porch post and watched as if he were going off to war, sending prayers with him as he backed out and headed off down the road.

God, please don't let anything happen to this mare. It is so hard for him to have that happen.

She went back inside and softly closed the door, leaned against it and fought back sudden tears that somewhat baffled her.

She was struck with the knowledge that she could pray for the life of a mare, but she could not seem to pray about this situation with Parker.

Brushing her teeth, Marilee glanced into the mirror and stared at herself. She bent to rinse her mouth, and then she stared at her reflection again.

Up to a woman like you.

She was a woman who was quite contrary, she thought. Here she had a good man that she really cared for and she kept picking fights with him.

She was afraid of marriage.

This, of course, was only natural, given her experience with Stuart, and what she had seen with her own father and mother. Marriage was serious business, not to be entered into lightly, so she was showing good sense to be cautious.

It was more. *Some unnamed fear.*

It was fear of life passing by, and of making the wrong choices and being stuck with them.

With a hard tug on the belt of her robe, she pivoted and left the bathroom, stalking into the kitchen, where she made a cup of chamomile tea, sat at the table and sipped it, while alternately staring and looking away from her reflection in the night-black window.

She went to the back door and peered through the window, but all she could see was dark yard. Trees obscured Tate Holloway's house. She wondered about him.

She did not intend to worry about Tate Holloway. Lord knew she had enough to think about, without going *there*.

Seating herself again at the table, she sipped her tea while her gaze wandered in a slow circle from the redchecked tablecloth to her reflection in the window, to the telephone, then again to the tablecloth.

Finally she pushed herself from the table with a deliberate motion and dialed Parker's home number, halfway expecting the impersonal voice of his answering service.

She was startled to hear a "Hello" in an unfamiliar voice. A *woman's voice.*

"I'm calling Parker Lindsey."

"Oh, this is his phone. Marilee? This is Charlene. Parker left his phone here on the table."

"I'd dialed his home phone. I thought his service would answer, if he wasn't home." Marilee felt confused, but somewhat relieved to recognize Charlene MacCoy's voice. Charlene was a warm person, and her voice was warm, too.

"Well, I guess they've already switched over here. He's out in the barn with Leanne. Do you want me to go get him?"

"Oh, no, it's not important. How is the mare?"

"She's fine. She had the prettiest baby." Charlene's voice became excited. "Not a paint, like Leanne was expectin', but black, with a white star and white feet. A really nice filly. And there was no trouble at all. That mare just popped her out, when she got ready. Parker swore she was holding things up just because." Someone in the background said something, and Charlene said, "That was Mason, and he says that mare was waitin' for the full moon to get up." She laughed.

"Parker was in here havin' coffee just a few minutes ago, and then him and Leanne went back out there to watch the mare and the baby again. Do you want me to have him call you?"

"No . . . I imagine he'll be tired. I'll call him in the morning."

"Well, Mason's just goin' out there now. He'll tell him you called."

When Marilee hung up, she laid her forehead against the phone and gave thanks for the healthy filly.

And she wished she did not feel so dissatisfied. It made her feel selfish.

Lying in bed, with the moonlight filtering through the window and making patterns on her coverlet, she contemplated herself and her life. She had the strong urge to pick up the telephone and call Tate Holloway, and she wondered at herself.

She simply had too much of a fondness for telephone talk in the night.

Twelve

In Matters of the Heart

Tate jogged along in front of Marilee's house just as golden light shone into the elms that towered over the blue roof of the squatty white cottage.

With relief, he saw that her Cherokee sat alone in the driveway. No sign of Lindsey's truck.

He jogged on over to Main, where his burning lungs and rubbery legs forced him to walk for over half the block. He was getting better, though, because he recovered by the time he got to the police station. When he turned up Church and was past the police station and getting close to the intersection, he began to wonder what might have happened to Lindsey. There was no sign of the man.

What might have happened at the evening's previous candlelit supper? Was the man too worn-out to jog this morning? He did not like that particular train of thought.

He had dropped to something only resembling a jog and was approaching his driveway when a figure came pounding around the curve in the street half a block ahead, accompanied by a rider on a bicycle.

It was Lindsey jogging, and the blond-haired woman on the bicycle.

"Mornin'," Lindsey said, when he came near.

"Mornin'," Tate replied and gave a wave.

"Hi," the woman said.

"Hello."

Tate watched the two pass, Lindsey jogging and the woman on her bicycle beside him. *Together?*

Tate jogged up his driveway and around to the back door, up the steps and inside and all the way upstairs and into his bathroom for a shower.

He did not think he should jump to hopeful conclusions about the disintegration of the romance between Marilee and Lindsey. Sometimes things were not always what they seemed. A major rule for a journalist was to get the facts.

But he whistled as he showered. By golly, he was showing improvement in the jogging area. Don't count him over the hill yet.

"We'll see you tomorrow, Editor," called Sherry, the waitress who worked the late-afternoon shift at the Main Street Café.

The few other patrons added their friendly goodbyes.

"Later, buddy," from Juice Tinsley, and a wave from Norm Stidham, who had a mouth full of raisin pie.

"Don't forget to send Marilee to cover the Homemakers meeting on Thursday. We're showing the video Ms. Porter sent from Cairo," said Kaye Upchurch, who was sitting with her mother, Odessa Collier.

"Marilee'll be there."

"Good to have seen you, Tate." Odessa gave her sultry smile.

Odessa Collier had to be pushing seventy but was still hot enough to strip wallpaper, Tate would bet.

He winked at her.

Folding the newspaper beneath his arm, he stepped out into the brightness of a May afternoon.

Thank you, Lord, for this happy minute. He thought of it with the feeling of a man who had been in combat in the jungles of Viet Nam, not to mention all the painful stories he had covered in his life as a journalist. He knew how fleeting happiness was in life on earth.

On this wonderful afternoon he was living what he considered the epitome of his dream. He had formed the habit to head to the Main Street Café at midafternoon each day, where he would get a glass of iced tea and sometimes a slice of pecan pie, and enjoy an informal chat with anyone there. After about fifteen minutes he would head on over to Blaine's Drugstore, where he would get another glass of iced tea or maybe an ice-cream cone, and chat some more with Vella Blaine and whoever came in.

In this way, he got a pulse on the town. He discreetly jotted down the names of people he met, and at night he went over the names and recalled the faces in order to have them handy on his tongue for the next time he met them, or to mention in his editorials. In this fashion, he felt he was making a lot of people happy, and at the same time he built circulation, which was already up by nearly a hundred people. People liked to see their names in print, and he liked to place the names there. It was a happy merging of desires.

This afternoon, upon leaving the drugstore after an ice-cream cone and a chat with Miss Vella, Miss Dixie Love and Gerald Overton of the Citizens Bank, he felt somewhat victorious, as if he'd scaled a tall mountain. He supposed he had only arrived at the first plateau—he had simply gotten moved into town and made some necessary decisions and implemented the biggest one of those, which was keeping the paper going and changing it to a twice weekly. So far he was living his dream and keeping a number of people employed and able to feed their families. Well and good. He tried not to think about the enormous precipice before him in the form of a giant debt, and the somewhat daunting matter of how he would live out the rest of his life.

One day at a time, he reminded himself, as he hopped over the door of his convertible and directed his BMW around the block to drive by Marilee's house and saw only her Cherokee parked in the driveway. His curiosity over what had transpired with the candlelit supper was about to eat a hole in his brain.

Whipping his car on around the corner and into his driveway, he grabbed the bag of groceries out of the seat and went straight to the kitchen, where he made a pitcher of sweet iced tea. He picked up the pitcher and the new box of loose leaf tea he had bought to replace what he had borrowed. Then he stopped and tossed the box of tea back on the counter, before heading out the back door and across the yard to the gate in the fence.

It squealed as he opened it. Late-afternoon sunlight filtered through the trees down onto the garden patch. Tate looked at it and thought that Marilee needed a plow.

When he reached the back steps of the little bungalow, he glanced upward and saw Corrine gazing out the kitchen window at him. She disappeared, and a moment later the door swung open to him.

"Hello, Mr. Tate."

"Evenin', missy. How are you? Why, is that a new bow in your hair?"

"Yes," she replied with her normal solemness. "Aunt Marilee is in cursin' at the computer you had sent over today."

"Oh, she is?"

He grinned, coaxing a grin in return from the girl, whose eyes looked so much deeper than her years. He had already formed an idea of her situation, a formation based on his instincts about people and bits and pieces of knowledge discreetly picked up along the way about Marilee James, her sister and her family. He, having been a similar child, felt great empathy for this one.

"I brought some sweet tea. Let's see if we can sugarcoat the situation."

She said quite quickly and in a low voice, "Mr. Parker was here, but he doesn't know anything about computers, and she ran him off." She shook her head. "I hope you can help."

"Well, I imagine I can." So Lindsey had been there and had not been a help.

Corrine quietly assisted him in getting the glasses and ice cubes. Then she pushed a package of cookies at him. "I think you'd better add chocolate."

When Tate entered the living room, it was with a glass of iced tea in one hand and a chocolate cookie in the other.

Marilee looked up and saw him and glared. "I don't like this new computer."

He lifted the glass and cookie. "I come in peace, to return your tea . . . made." And then he determinedly grinned his very warmest grin.

"I had peace until I had to learn a new computer. My old one worked just fine."

"Well, now, you couldn't use the Internet with your old one. It is time to get on the information highway or get left behind."

"I might prefer being left behind."

Feeling a little desperate, he held out the glass and cookie, and she took them very slowly.

He watched her bite into the cookie and then look up at him, her eyes deep blue, and chocolate smearing her moist lips. An immediate full-blown fantasy filled his mind of kissing her until she moaned and writhed like a wild woman in his arms.

"You have a cookie crumb on your chin . . . let me just . . . there. Now, let's see how I can help you with this computer."

He pulled a chair over and sat on it backward, right next to her, continuing to look at her lips with anticipation. He knew quite suddenly that he was right where he wanted to be.

The sun was far to the west and the breeze dying down. In the process of deadheading her roses, Vella paused and ran a gardener's appreciative gaze over the spring greenery of her rosebushes and upward into the elm trees. "Thank you, God," she whispered, as she almost invariably did at such a sight.

Then she caught sight of Perry's big black car arriving. Anticipation and an ache slipped across her heart at the same moment.

She hurried up the steps and in the back door and straight to the oven, where she checked the meat loaf. It was good and dark, crusty as she liked it to be. She made a superb meat loaf; Winston always praised it all over when she brought it to the church fellowship supper.

"Got the Wednesday *afternoon* edition of the paper," Perry said as he came into the kitchen. He was a big chunk of a man and seemed to fill the kitchen. Just like every other day of the week, on his way to the sink, rolling up his sleeves, he turned on the little television.

Vella looked over her shoulder at the set that sat on the counter. She had a sudden and disturbing fantasy of herself with a shotgun, blasting out the screen.

"I made meat loaf," she said, showing it proudly as her husband sat at the table.

"Hmmm." He glanced at it, then looked at the newspaper. "That Juice Tinsley's goin' all out with advertisin' for the city council seat. Don't know why anyone in their right mind would want the job."

Vella focused on setting the food on the table. She liked the supper table to be colorful, like a bouquet of roses. There was the browned meat loaf with red tomato sauce on top, light-green-and-gold succotash, steamy ivory potatoes, golden butter and tan kissed rolls.

Perry, who had been using the remote control to flip channels on the television until he got to his favorite news program, said, "Looks like we're gonna get in another mess over there with them I-rackees." With one eye on the television, he served himself a slice of meat loaf.

Vella wondered, as she had for years now, how a man as educated as Perry—he had big university education from University of Oklahoma and the pharmacist degree, plus lots of courses every year to keep up-to-date—could have slipped back into such poor grammar.

She looked at her gleaming china plate and then at the array of food. She watched her husband fold open the newspaper and hold it with one hand, while eating with the other, and dividing his attention between the newspaper and the television.

"Perry, how is the meat loaf?" She still had not served herself.

"Hmmm . . . oh, pretty good," he said, his eyes on the newspaper.

"Perry." Vella, who had not yet served her plate, began unbuttoning the front buttons of her shirtwaist. Her heart began a rapid pumping. It was as if her hand was working all by itself.

Perry was now looking at the television. Vella noted the paleness of his complexion, the blue veins over his nose and at his neck. Yet he still had that little cowlick at the top of his head that she had loved from the very first.

"Perry." She now had the top of her shirtwaist fully unbuttoned.

"Huh?" He did not turn his head from the television.

"Perry!"

In an instant she had pushed to her feet so hard that the chair scooted back and bumped the counter. Then she yanked her shirtwaist wide open to reveal her voluptuous breasts, full and heavy in their support bra.

"Look at me!"

Perry was looking. He gazed straight at her breasts, with his mouth hanging open and his eyes wide as saucers so that she saw the blue irises, which she had not seen in years.

Vella felt triumphant. She had, at long last, succeeded in getting his attention. She felt, too, that she had gone completely mad, but she could not grab hold of caring.

"I'm alive, Perry! I'm alive and sittin' here with you every night!"

"Well, my god," he said.

"Is that all you have to say?"

He closed his mouth and swallowed.

Letting go of her dress, she swept an arm at the table, sending half the dishes and food crashing onto the floor. Her pendulous bosom heaved and swayed.

"I am sick to death of you actin' like I am dead. Like I don't exist, when day after day I work in your store, wash your clothes, cook your supper and clean your pee drips off the toilet. I am a flesh-and-blood woman who goes to bed with you night after night. I have worn perfume and new rayon gowns and put myself in front of you, and you don't even see." She had begun sobbing. "Look at me! I may be old, but I am not dead. *You* are not dead."

Just then some bit of reasoning sliced into her brain, and she saw herself mirrored in his shocked expression. Covering her face with her hands, she fled the kitchen.

Perry, stunned so exceedingly that he could for some seconds only manage to move his head and watch his wife running away, thought, She's gone crazy.

Then fear pierced his brain enough to propel him into action. He struggled to get out of his chair, but his brain was a little ahead of his body in coming awake, so he had a bit of a time getting going and ended up knocking his chair over.

"Vella?" he said hoarsely, and found the name was not familiar on his tongue.

He went upstairs to find her in their bedroom, grabbing clothes out of her dresser drawers and throwing them into two suitcases that lay wide-open on the bed—the suitcases she had bought when she made that trip to New Orleans to look at roses a couple of years ago and that he thought were way too high priced.

"I am leavin' you, Perry. I can't go on like this another minute."

Perry didn't know what to say. He tried to think of something, but nothing would come. He had a sense of being in the *Twilight Zone* television show.

She wouldn't leave. She was a sixty-four-year-old woman. Or maybe she was sixty-five, he wasn't certain.

The next minute she fastened the bulging suitcases, grabbed each handle with her blue-veined hands, dragged the cases off the bed and past him, and threw them down the stairs, denting and scratching the wall they'd paid big bucks to have painted six months ago, and the banister and the floor at the bottom. One by one she hauled the cases out of the house and threw them into her car and drove off into the hot ball of a western sun.

Perry blinked against the glare. The picture left in his mind was of her enormous breasts in white cotton swaying as she slipped behind the steering wheel.

When Vella flew past in her car and saw Winston in his yard taking in his flags, which he could finally do alone these days, she pressed the accelerator harder to keep from stopping and flinging herself into his arms.

It wasn't until she got to Main Street and passed the drugstore, where her daughter Belinda would be working the counter, that she realized she had no place to go. She could not go in and talk about this to Belinda, for heavensake. Belinda was no more a conversationalist than her father, except with Deputy Midgett, with whom she now lived in sin; thank God she had moved out at last, even if it was to the apartment over the drugstore.

There was Minnie Oakes, but generally Vella found Minnie's brain stuffed with straw. Minnie rarely had an original thought, and their friendship was one of sharing stain removal tips and ice-cream cones, not confidences.

Outside of Minnie, Vella could not name a close friend. At least, not a woman friend. There was Winston, but she could not go to him. She certainly didn't want to be included in his "old lady collection."

She drove on along the highway. Maybe she would just keep on driving clear to California and the ocean, take off all her clothes on the beach and walk right into the water naked.

That she was repeatedly coming back to sensuous thoughts became clear to her. She had been battling them for months, and yet they kept getting stronger and stronger.

Tears streamed down her face. *Oh, Lord, what has happened to me? What have I done?*

About five more miles and the cool air blowing on her breasts brought it to her attention that she needed to pull over and fasten up her blouse.

Tate Holloway *was* flirting with her.

Marilee could no longer dismiss the fact of his flirting, as she had tried to do ever since her very first meeting with the man. Trying, and mostly succeeding, to not let Tate's attention be unduly flattering, she nevertheless admitted to herself that she would have to be dead not to find it quite nice.

And she kept recalling how he had told her, in her own kitchen that Lindsey was not a man up to "a woman like her." She wanted very much to question him about that provocative statement, however, she did not think she would like his opinion. She told herself to focus on his instructions for the use of the new whiz-bang computer.

She knew instantly that she had a fine mind to be able to handle so many conflicting thoughts coming into it at one time, yet she did not overly congratulate herself on such a trait, because science had shown that the ability was present in all women. She thought maybe God had sensibly installed it into the female species as a strategy for survival in a man's world.

"Now, Miss Marilee . . . you don't have to hit that button. You can just tap this little mouse window you're usin' with your finger."

"Oh, that's right." She liked that.

"Are you havin' trouble seein'? Maybe the screen isn't bright enough. All you have to do is use this button. See?"

"Oh, that *is* better!"

"Who is that in the picture?"

"What? Oh, that's my ex-husband, Stuart." It was silly to feel uncomfortable about being asked about Stuart. She noticed that Tate had blue eyes, like Stuart.

"Devil-may-care fellow."

"Yes . . . he was, pretty much."

"He looks familiar to me." But his blue eyes were on Marilee's, as if he were trying to see into her mind.

She averted her eyes. "You might have seen his work, or even met him. He was quite a well-known photographer. Lots of his stuff in *National Geographic, Life,* a few in *Time.*" And *he* had been a flirt, too.

Tate frowned thoughtfully. "Maybe I have . . . but I think he more reminds me of Parker Lindsey."

Gazing at the screen, Marilee typed. The letters came out crazy.

"Your left hand needs to move over a key," Tate pointed out.

"This keyboard is awkward."

"You can plug in your big one. I've got the ergonomic ones on order."

"Oh."

"Want me to plug your big one in now?"

"Yes, that might be a good idea."

He did all he was supposed to, quite efficiently; he apparently knew electronic gadgets. She tried the bigger keyboard and found it worked well.

"Does this little thing do the same as a mouse?"

"Yep."

"It's annoying."

"Your choice."

When they finally closed the computer, Marilee was so relieved and delighted to be able to work it that she not only felt compelled to apologize for her sharp behavior but was actually able to do so.

"I'm sorry for being so snippy earlier," she said, almost choking on the words. She thought of how she had been sharp with Parker and knew that she would probably never master the art of apology.

"Ah, Miss Marilee, I don't think I'd give a penny for a woman without some spunk."

He was looking at her in that way of his, as if thoroughly pleased with every bit of her that he saw. A warm flush fell over her and gathered between her legs.

Averting her eyes, she rose and headed for the kitchen. Willie Lee and Munro had fallen asleep together on the couch, and Corrine was sitting in the big chair, reading an *American Girls* book. Marilee didn't think Corrine should see her in that moment. Corrine was too observant by far; she would understand immediately that Marilee felt an attraction for this man. Good Lord, Marilee didn't want anyone to see her being such a fool.

She poured two glasses of iced tea and turned, intent on taking his into the living room, but there he was draped in the doorway.

"Thank you for bringing the iced tea." She held out the glass, and he came over to take it from her.

Drinking deeply from her own, she thought the best course was to drink the tea quickly down and then tell him good-night. She would not ask him about his comment the previous evening. She was going to ignore it.

"You're welcome," he returned quite happily. "It is my way of returning what I borrowed."

"You borrowed an entire box."

"I know. I'll return it a little at a time, all made up."

Then, without benefit of invitation, just as he had done the previous evening, he pulled out a chair and sat himself at the table, saying, "The important thing to know about brewing good iced tea is to use distilled water. And tea bags are okay, but I prefer to use loose tea—black-and-orange pekoe—and pour the hot water over it. You can't go off and let the tea sit there longer than eight minutes, either, because then you get the tannic acid comin' out, and that makes the brew bitter. 'Course, tea made in the sun can sit longer."

"You are quite a connoisseur of cold tea," Marilee said, both impressed with a man who would take care with such a small thing and wondering how in the devil she would tell him goodbye now with him sitting himself down.

"Good cold tea on a hot day is the secret of life," he replied.

She gazed at him. "I think I've heard you pronounce about three different things as being *the* secret to life."

"Well, you know, Miss Marilee . . ."

Tate pulled on his ear and grinned that grin, charming enough to coax bees from their hive, ". . . I'm still searchin' for that one major secret to life."

Marilee wrapped an arm around her middle and held on to herself, quite possibly to keep from going straight to him, throwing herself on his lap and seeing what the kiss in his eyes would feel like on her lips.

The idea was preposterous. The idea of kissing him scared her pants off.

Thankfully, he quite suddenly quit flirting and led the way into discussing the needs down at the newspaper. He said he had that afternoon hired a new layout man, a young guy fresh from college with a graphic art degree. "With the salary I can pay, my choices of experienced people are limited," he said. "He'll be here the end of next month."

Marilee asked him forthrightly if he intended to let any of them go.

"No," he replied instantly. "I may need to switch people around to different jobs, but I'll find a place for everyone."

"You won't be able to switch Zona to another job," Marilee said and moved to sit opposite him at the table. She had to find a way to make certain Zona remained protected.

But Tate said in an understanding manner, "No, I won't be switchin' Zona," and gave a wry smile. "I've begun to wonder if she sleeps in that office. I don't ever see her come or go."

"She does not intend anyone—especially you—to see her. Give her time, though. She'll thaw a little when she gets to know you. It's just that she has a very hard time with change. And with men."

"What's wrong with her?" he asked bluntly.

"The gossip is her overbearing father. What is known, however, is that she suffered severe schizophrenia in her twenties. Treatment has helped her, allows her to operate outside a hospital, anyway. After her parents died, she was destitute. Then one day Ms. Porter brought her in and made her the bookkeeper. It turned out Zona is a genius with numbers, and somehow Ms. Porter had discovered this. I think Ms. Porter had been trying to help Zona all along."

"Muriel was always like that," he said with a thoughtful nod. "She doesn't look like an altruistic pudding heart, but she is."

Marilee watched his eyes drift down to the table and saw emotions flow across his face. She looked at the tender spot where his hair curled behind his ear. It was white hair there, mingling in with the sun streaked blond.

Then he was looking back at her, cocking his head. "How many know that Charlotte is in love with Leo?"

Marilee, quite struck by this further proof of his powers of observation, said, "Well, I know, and now you know. I'm not certain Leo knows. He is so used to women doing for him that Charlotte getting coffee for him each morning isn't going to mean much. And Charlotte may be denying it to herself. She's so hungry for a romantic relationship and scared to death of it at the same time."

"That's a common place to be," he said.

"Yes, it is."

She thought his eyes most remarkable, and then she realized he was gazing at her in that way that was sizing her up.

"I read your piece on the detention center," he said. "You did a very good job of keeping to the middle ground."

"I can take that as approval?" She decided to size him up in return.

"Oh, yes, ma'am . . . I think your ability to present a story without biasing it with your opinions is very good. I think, too, that when you decide to move people with a feature, like the piece I read in the files that you did about the retirement community the MacCoys are building, or the one you did about the young man getting crazed on drugs and threatening people with an unloaded gun, you're even better. You are good at putting your heart in your work. You should do more of it."

Marilee had not before heard much analytical praise for her writing; Ms. Porter had never been one for even the mildest praise of one of her writers. Either what you had written was adequate or it was not, that was all there was to it. Now Marilee wasn't certain how to respond. She felt decidedly uncomfortable.

Tate said, "I want you to do a feature on detention centers across the state, and how each community has been impacted. I want you to show the good and the bad. Then when you come to your own conclusion, you write a piece reflecting that."

"What if I don't come to a conclusion?" she asked right off.

"Then reflect that."

She nodded, thinking immediately of the children.

As if he heard her thoughts, he added, "It'll mean some traveling, but I believe you can take the children with you." He raised an eyebrow.

"Yes," she said slowly. "I can take them with me, or get someone to stay with them." Her interest was spiraling upward at a rapid rate, but caution sat on it. "I haven't ever done that sort of reporting. I wasn't trained as a journalist. I just answered the ad Ms. Porter put in the paper, and there wasn't anyone else who had the least writing ability, so I got the job. Everything I've written has been set right here in Valentine."

"I got all my journalism training on the job, too," he said. "I went to school to be a Baptist minister. While I was at it, I took a job as a sports reporter for the college paper, and, well, once I saw my name in print, I was hooked."

Marilee was busy looking him up and down. There he sat in cowboy boots, faded denims and a soft khaki shirt. She could not identify what type he looked like, but she did not think it was in any way a minister.

He must have picked up her thoughts, as he then said that had all been almost thirty years ago. "I was infinitely more suited to journalism," he said. "I tended to have a certain type of curiosity about people that was less suitable for a minister but quite well suited for a journalist. And at the time I enjoyed whiskey way too much to be a Baptist preacher." He grinned.

"I'm a farm boy from East Texas, who came up narrow and went wide. I was married one time and divorced some fifteen years ago because I wasn't a very good husband. I gave up drinkin' a long time ago, but I sure can get as high on reading history and sweet tea and good blues music."

He paused, and she was not at all certain what was going on, although she felt certain that something was going on.

"What about you, Miss Marilee?"

"Me?" She straightened her spine.

"What can you tell me about you?"

"I'm certain you know all there is to know about me." She fingered her glass and saw that it was empty . . . his was, too.

"I know you are a native of Valentine but have traveled some," he was saying. "That Vella and Perry Blaine are your aunt and uncle, and that you are divorced from that devil-may-care fellow in the picture, who I believe you said was fifteen years your senior."

My heaven, the man had a memory.

"You have one son, and now your niece, your sister's child. I know you enjoy motherhood. I've seen that myself in the way you extend yourself for those children. I know you write well, don't like computers, enjoy my sweet tea and are quite addicted to chocolate." He grinned at her. "I'd like to know more."

"Why?"

She remembered quite clearly what he had told her the evening before, and she saw in his eyes that he remembered, and knew she did, too.

He said, "Because we'll be working closely together, and I will most likely have to make decisions that involve you." He paused, then added, "And because, as I have already been trying to get across, I am attracted to you and would like to explore the possibilities between us."

Realizing she had let things go too far, she fixed him with the skeptical eye that she felt would let him know she wasn't in the market for such flirting. "There are no possibilities between us." She got to her feet.

He did not move. "Word on the street is divided about whether or not you are actually engaged to Parker Lindsey."

"Word on the street?"

"Rumor . . . and I've asked around. Are you and Lindsey engaged? Was that what that little candlelight supper was about last night?"

Marilee wasn't certain which way to go with this. "Nooo . . . but Parker and I . . . we have an understanding."

"Ahhh . . . an understanding. Is that like 'going together'?"

When he said it, it sounded childish. "Yes. We've been dating for a number of years, and we are considering being engaged."

"I see." He frowned. "And you still keep your ex-husband's picture on your desk."

Marilee felt the barb sting. "*If* it is any of your business—which it is not—I keep my ex-husband's picture there so Willie Lee can see a picture of his father."

She took their glasses to the sink, thinking that he would take the hint to leave.

But all he did was scoot his chair back and slouch down more comfortably. She looked over her shoulder. His gaze was on her, and he seemed to be doubling something inside himself that perhaps she had better prepare to rebuff.

Maybe she would ask him to explain his term: *a woman like her.*

At that rather intense moment, however, the doorbell rang, causing Marilee to jump and just about holler "Ohmygod," which was a word not far from her thoughts at that minute. Thank goodness she held herself in check enough to say politely, "Excuse me just a minute."

She hurried for the front door, a part of her not thinking so much of letting someone in as of letting herself out. In her mind, she was practically running down the street.

Corrine had already answered the door, with Munro right at her heels. Willie Lee remained on the couch, as normal for him, fast asleep.

The door swung wide to reveal the caller to be Aunt Vella. On sight of her aunt in quite a disheveled state, Marilee knew instantly that some disaster had occurred.

"I've left Perry," were Aunt Vella's first words.

It was a sight Marilee had never in her life seen, nor expected to see, her aunt crumbling before her eyes. She reached out and took hold of the older woman, who burst into sobs.

"I don't have anywhere to go!" Aunt Vella cried.

Marilee, struck to the core, said instantly, "Oh, yes you do, Aunt Vella. You have right here!"

Putting an arm around her aunt, she led her into the kitchen and sat her at the table, where Tate immediately poured her a glass of sweet iced tea. Aunt Vella took up the glass and knocked the tea back as if it were a shot of whiskey.

When Vella had not come home by the time the late-night news program finished, Perry called his daughter, Belinda, who had finally moved out on her own three months earlier. Likely, he thought, Vella had shown the first signs of going crazy on Belinda's thirty-first birthday, when she had packed all of their youngest daughter's things and told her to move out to the apartment over the drugstore.

"Let me speak to your mother," he said when his daughter's voice came on the line.

"What? Daddy?" Belinda had never had a phone call from her father.

Perry, gripping the receiver, listened to his daughter say that her mother was not there. She had not seen her mother. She wanted to know what had happened, and Perry told her that her mother had gone crazy and driven off.

Belinda, who had little capacity for alarm, said, "Well, if she shows up here, I'll let you know. Did you check out by her roses? Maybe she's out there on the bench."

Perry hung up and padded in his sock feet to peer out the back door window. Vella had planted solar lights in the ground at the edges of her rose garden. They had cost a mint.

He peered hard. The lights lit things up considerably. The bench was bare.

He went back and telephoned Belinda again and told her that her mother was not on the bench.

"Well, I imagine she'll turn up tomorrow mornin', Daddy," said Belinda, with obvious impatience at being again interrupted. "If she doesn't, I'll have Lyle put out an APB."

Belinda hung up and relayed the information about her mother and father to Lyle, who lay beside her in the bed. "They had a spat. Must have really been somethin' this time. Usually Mama just quits talkin' to him," she said, welcoming Lyle's hard body against hers, which was the one thing in life that she had found could sustain her interest for any length of time.

"Mama isn't gonna leave her roses. She'll be in the kitchen makin' breakfast in the mornin'." Then she focused her thoughts on what Lyle did for her.

Tate, his reading glasses on his nose, folded up the yellowed newspaper he was reading and threw it atop the others in a pile on the opposite side of the bed, old editions of *The Valentine Voice* from the archives on the second floor of the *Voice* building. At least the newspapers provided a weight, something in bed with him.

Experiencing a wave of loneliness, he thought of Marilee and imagined her in bed with him.

Immediately he swung his legs to the floor. He rubbed his eyes and checked the clock—1:33, and sleep still wouldn't come.

He got up and dressed in sweatpants and a shirt and running shoes and headed out for a jog. He figured Bubba would be asleep somewhere, but the cat streaked out from beneath the lilac bush and fell in behind him.

Once again, Tate headed along the street in front of Marilee James's house. He saw with some comfort that Marilee's Cherokee was alone in the driveway. He slowed, peering to see if there was a light in the rear bedroom. There was, a low glow. Either Marilee was awake or she slept with the lamp on.

Dragging himself from the sight, he continued on around to Main Street, where he was surprised to meet up with Winston Valentine walking, with his cane tapping, from the opposite direction.

"Winston?" he said involuntarily.

"Hello, Editor."

"Can't sleep, either?"

"Old people never sleep, son." Winston did not stop his slow strides.

Tate kept on going, too, turned at the police station and jogged along Church Street toward his own house. On the opposite side of the street another jogger, a woman whose silver-bright leotard glowed beneath the streetlight, gave proof to hidden lives going on throughout the night.

Marilee gave up trying to sleep. Reaching into her nightstand drawer, she pulled out half of a Hershey bar kept there for emergencies. Punching her pillows, she sat up against them, broke pieces of the Hershey bar and stuffed them into her mouth.

She knew exactly what was wrong with her. She wanted a man. *Yes, Lord, it was true.*

Lying there, listening to her Aunt Vella's snores reverberate from the other room where she slept in Willie Lee's bed, Marilee wished for a man to hold her and fill her with wild feelings that took her away from the loneliness that struck so deeply this night.

She admitted this to herself, hoping to get rid of the desire, trying to give it up to God, but she kept holding on to it, thinking maybe some miracle of a perfect life with a perfect man would appear before her. The lonely yearning tugged ever harder, giving her fantasies of both Parker and Tate, which was about as foolish as could be.

Taking the telephone on her lap, she called Parker. He answered in a sleepy voice.

"Parker, it's me, Marilee."

"Oh . . . what time is it?"

She told him it was almost two o'clock and that she couldn't sleep. "I need to talk to you for a while," she said, choking so badly on the words that her voice broke.

"What?"

"Could we just talk?" she whispered.

"Okay." His voice was way too sleepy to be satisfying.

"Parker? Parker are you awake?"

"Barely."

He explained that he had been busy that night with an epileptic dog and a horse cut by barbed wire.

Marilee listened, then told him about Aunt Vella, who lay in Willie Lee's bed, snoring louder by the minute. "They've been married forty-five years. I doubt either of them has had a full week apart in all that time."

"I imagine she'll go home tomorrow," Parker said.

Marilee, whose mind seemed to be jumping all over the place, wasn't thinking about Vella any longer. "Parker . . . would you come over?"

"Now?"

"Yes." She had gone out of her mind. "Come over and sit on the couch with me."

"Okay," Parker said with questionable enthusiasm, despite how he had been after her.

Marilee hung up and stared at the telephone. Good grief. How did she get herself into such nonsense? She slipped into her bathrobe and went to open the front door a crack, so that Parker wouldn't make any noise coming in.

Turning, her gaze fell on Willie Lee. She had forgotten about leaving him sleeping on the couch. She was truly losing her mind. With him here, that left her bed as the only empty place in the house. She imagined herself and Parker falling into her bed.

Propelled by a bit of panic, she hurriedly lifted Willie Lee and carried him into her bed. He never woke up for anything until he was ready, and likely that would probably be when Parker arrived.

On her way back to the living room, she saw Munro come out of the bedroom where he had been sleeping with Corrine. He gave her a curious look.

"Come lie with me," she told him, sitting on the couch and patting the space beside her.

After a few seconds of debate, he came and hopped up beside her, circled twice and lay against her. He felt nice, warm and comforting, and a peace began to steal over her. She thought that she should have thought of Munro before. Sleeping with a dog could have true advantages over a man; a dog wasn't going to make all those demands and then run off and leave you.

She fell asleep and didn't know until morning that Parker had never come. He telephoned while she was having coffee with Aunt Vella.

"Did you call me last night?" he asked.

"Yes," she said, paused and then added, "I was just wantin' to talk, but you were too tired."

"I sure was," he said. "You didn't ask me to come over there, did you?"

"No, you must have dreamed that."

The Valentine Voice

Sunday, May 14

Today's Highlights:

—Detention Center again at the center of conflict. One injury, one arrest as a result of an altercation at Thursday's city council meeting. Story on page 1.

—Identity confirmed of man found dead in his car. Local woman makes a positive identification. Story on page 3.

—Sinkhole repair falls short. City Works loses dirt down hole. Story page 3.

—Valentine High School seniors prepare for graduation. Largest graduating class in school history. Story page 6.

Thirteen

A Fine State of Confusion

She had made a poor decision in not arranging for a sitter for the children or leaving them with Aunt Vella when she went on a research trip to a juvenile detention center up near Oklahoma City. As a result, the three of them, plus Munro, had endured almost six hours of structure and confinement, and were now hot, tired and cranky.

With a pounding head, Marilee felt great relief to see the outskirts of Valentine up ahead. She also saw a bunch of vehicles parked off the road and a group of people clustered around the Welcome to Valentine sign.

"There is Aunt Vel-la." Willie Lee, disobeying the rule by being out of his seat belt, was on his toes and peering over the front seat.

"It's the Rose Club," Corrine put in.

Marilee, slowing down, saw Reggie taking pictures. And there was Tammy with her notebook, talking with Winston for the article in the paper.

She pulled off the road, and she and the children, and Munro, who'd had to wait in the car at the detention center, tumbled out of the Cherokee with great relief to move after the long drive. Munro was apparently doubly glad; he went directly to hike his leg on a tree.

"Hello, Mis-ter Win-ston," Willie Lee said, approaching the elderly gentleman who was directing the work of his younger fellow Rose Club members, frequently pointing with his cane, from a lawn chair in the shade of a big elm.

"Hi there, Mister Willie Lee."

The two shook hands.

Marilee bid Winston hello, as well as his two lady boarders, Mildred and Ruthanne, who sat on either side of him. Mildred was eating jelly beans out of her purse, and occasionally Ruthanne would ask for one, throwing each orange one she received into the grass.

The Rose Club members, the eight who were retired and therefore not at jobs, were busy planting Madame Isaac Pereire rosebushes at each end of the sign and smaller polyanthas, Excellenz von Shubert, in the middle. When Winston and Vella had not been able to find the varieties at any of the local nurseries, the club had been forced to order from a grower in Texas. Aunt Vella had coerced her fellow members of the Rose Club to agree to this, mainly by bowling everyone over with her knowledge of the varieties. Just then, dressed in a lightweight, blue sprigged cotton dress, wide straw hat and purple gloves, she at once directed and got right into the dirt of the work to make certain her fellow members did the job right, which meant according to her specifications.

Marilee marveled at how her Aunt Vella did not sweat and could come away clean from digging in the ground.

"We got a late start," Aunt Vella told her, shaking dirt off her gloves. "We still have to plant the east sign, but now that everyone knows what they're doin', it ought to go faster."

Seeing how vibrant her aunt appeared caused a little panic inside Marilee, who would have preferred a little more pining for her husband on her aunt's part.

Aunt Vella said, "Winston and I are takin' Mildred and Ruthanne out to pizza tonight. We can bring some home for you, so that you don't have to cook," she added quickly, her expression so eager to please that Marilee's heart constricted.

"That will be lovely, Aunt Vella. I need to get a rough draft done up from my notes on this detention center as soon as possible." If she didn't get it down before other situations took command of her mind, she tended to forget the passionate point she wanted to make with a piece.

"Let the children stay and help us. Oh, do say yes, Marilee. We'd love to have them, and then we can take them to get pizza with us, and you can focus directly on your write-up."

"Well, I don't know. . . ." The strong reluctance to let the children out of her sight swept Marilee; she was getting to an irrational point of reluctance with this.

Her gaze went quickly to locate her little people. Willie Lee was on hands and knees helping Doris Northrupt tamp dirt around a small bush, and Munro lay sprawled a foot away in the shade of the city sign. She looked down at Corrine, who looked up at her.

"Would you like to stay and play here?"

Corrine nodded somewhat hesitantly. A smile was on her heart-shaped face, if not quite on her lips.

Taking herself in hand, Marilee kissed the children, got back behind the wheel of her Cherokee and drove away, although she looked in her rearview mirror several times. She reminded herself that they were all in the same town, that it wasn't the same as being separated by one hundred miles. And she really was very glad to have a few hours to herself. Even if it was a bit strange to be on her own.

She pulled swiftly into the driveway, went into the house, dropped her leather tote on the couch and carefully put her keys on the desk. Since Corrine wasn't there to help her find her keys, she had better keep track of them.

Pausing, she listened. There was the ticking of the small clock on her desk, a gurgle from the refrigerator.

She had not heard it this quiet in months. For the past five nights, Aunt Vella's snoring had filled the air. Heaven knew Marilee didn't want Aunt Vella to feel as if she were in the way. Aunt Vella had been trying so hard not to be an inconvenience, which was why Marilee felt like a rat wishing she could see an end to the situation of her aunt snoring every night in one of the children's beds. The snoring did not concern soundly sleeping Willie Lee, but Corrine could not sleep in the same room with Aunt Vella. After two mornings of waking up and finding Corrine on the couch, Marilee had insisted Corrine share her bed; she did not believe the couch was good support for a child's growing little body. With Corrine came Munro. As much as she had enjoyed the first nights of her niece and the dog sharing her bed, Marilee now found herself needing breathing room.

Aunt Vella meant one more adult sharing a house with only two bedrooms and one bathroom, and one coffeemaker. Marilee simply wasn't used to it. It gave her a disconcerting glimpse of how set in her ways she had become, and the adjustments that would be required if she married Parker.

She and Parker still had not settled the question of marriage. For the past five days had hardly seen each other. He had stopped in for supper several times, but had rushed out again on emergency calls. He had not made any further mention of his proposal of marriage. She was not only too hesitant to ask, but too stubborn, too.

Right this minute there was no need to think of that, she told herself, yanking open the refrigerator and staring into it, right at the latest glass pitcher of tea bestowed upon her by Tate Holloway.

The man was true to his word about returning her box of tea all made up, she thought, carrying the pitcher to the counter, where she poured herself a glass of the sweet, invigorating brew. In fact, her editor seemed to have developed the habit of popping in her back door each evening to bring her a pitcher of tea and ask if she needed his help on the new whiz-bang computer, or question her about one or another person he had met in town. Tate definitely had the journalistic quality of being curious about people.

She had not been alone with him, though, to have the opportunity to ask him what he had meant by *a woman like her,* the phrase still echoing in her mind. Although tempted, she resisted the urge to seek time alone with him. That did not seem like a good idea. Every time she came face-to-face with the man, she imagined what it would be like to kiss him, which was foolishness in the highest extreme.

She took the glass of tea—which had just the right amount of lemon; the man sure knew how to make iced tea—to her desk, where she sat with firmness and turned on the little whiz-bang computer that she had grown to appreciate . . . mostly. She had forgotten her notes, so she had to get up to get them. She sat back down and adjusted herself on the chair. Sometimes adjusting herself in the chair helped her to think.

With determination, she took up a pencil and made a hasty outline. She didn't find it an adequate outline; she couldn't seem to get things lined in her mind. She sipped the tea, thinking it would stimulate thought.

Then she realized she was staring at the photograph of Stuart. She picked it up and looked more closely at the smiling face. She did keep it for Willie Lee . . . but she supposed she kept it for herself, too.

Gazing at her ex-husband's image, she wondered where he was now.

He could be dead, for all she knew.

But she did not believe he was dead. She had felt him a lot in her heart these last weeks, for some strange reason. She wondered, in the way a woman does when remembering snapshots from the past, if he had changed radically from the dashing young man he was in the photograph—he had been thirty-eight then. He would be almost fifty-five now.

She firmly set the photograph back in place.

With a frustrated sigh, she ran her hands through her hair. She found it ridiculous that she could not keep her thoughts in place. She had a story to write. She adjusted herself in the chair again, looked over the scribbled outline, then sat staring at the computer screen.

She found it ridiculous that the house seemed too quiet.

With that uncomfortable thought, her mind went zinging back to the children and Aunt Vella. She had the sensation of being bereft, and had the very odd urge to race right down and get the children and her aunt.

Almost before realizing it, she was on her feet, taking up her keys and purse, and heading out to her car.

She did not go to get the children. She *could not* go get them; they were having a perfectly wonderful time with Aunt Vella and Winston. They would all think she had lost her mind if she went and got them.

And Marilee really wanted this time alone. That she felt a little afraid of being alone was, she concluded, to be expected, since she had not experienced the alone state in quite a while.

While thinking all of this, she homed directly like a carrier pigeon to the drugstore. Realizing this, she thought that she could have walked down and gotten out nervous energy, at the same time having an argument with herself, demanding that she go back home and get to work. She would do that, she decided, after a hot-fudge sundae.

She came to a bumping halt head-in at the curb. She got out, slammed the Cherokee door, walked swiftly into the drugstore and ordered the sundae from her cousin Belinda, who had, since her mother had left both husband and store, been working the day shift and leaving the evenings to two high school teens.

"Just go ahead and get it yourself, okay? I've been on my feet all day. I'm beat." Belinda said this from where she sat on her mother's tall stool, reading the Sunday edition of the newspaper. "Would you refill my Dr Pepper, while you're there?"

She pushed forward a glass of ice on the counter. What told Marilee that the person behind the wide-open newspaper was indeed her cousin were the pink fuzzy slippers.

Marilee snatched up the glass, thinking that it was a good thing Aunt Vella wasn't there. Aunt Vella despised her youngest child and only daughter going around in bedroom slippers.

Marilee herself often had trouble believing Belinda had come out of her aunt. Aunt Vella had once been a raven-haired beauty possessed of ten-carat diamond style, which she had still. Belinda, on the other hand, was a dishwater blonde with a style no higher than five-and-dime glass. That Belinda took after her father was the explanation in Marilee's mind, most especially as she glanced toward the pharmacy window.

She could hear the murmur of her uncle's television and imagined him back there slouched in his old chair. The thought annoyed her. She felt her uncle should not go on as if his wife of forty-five years had not up and left. She did not expect Uncle Perry to suddenly turn into a Lothario, but the least he could do was pick up the phone and call Aunt Vella.

"I left your mother a little bit ago out at the west welcome sign. She's out there with the Rose Club planting roses." Marilee plopped the refilled soft drink on the counter.

"I know," Belinda said from behind the paper. "Minnie Oakes stopped in here on her way out there to take cold drinks. She made sure to tell Daddy where Mama was."

"What did he say?" Marilee got a vintage sundae glass from the shelf.

"I don't know. I didn't hear. Jaydee is sure chewing at this detention center like a dog with a bone. I heard the mayor will probably have to have plastic surgery on his nose."

"They won't know for sure if it is broken until the swelling goes down." She fought the cellophane covering of a new box of chocolate brownies; apparently the wrapping was designed to keep the brownies safe for a century.

"Well, the detention center is comin'. Socking the mayor doesn't seem like a big help."

"Jaydee didn't really mean to sock the mayor, and it wasn't really over the detention center. He was just frustrated in general, like he can get."

Marilee felt similarly frustrated in that instant by the cellophane covering on the brownie box. She had the enormous urge to throw the package on the floor and stomp on it. And suddenly she realized that she was irrationally angry. It seemed like she had been falling into irrational anger for weeks.

"Then what was it about? I heard it was the detention center. Paper says detention center."

With deliberate calmness, Marilee got the scissors from beside the cash register. "Jaydee was pretty worked up about the detention center, but he was aiming to sock Juice Tinsley, because he made a smart remark about Jaydee's wife possibly ending up in the juvenile detention center, so it would be easy for Jaydee to visit her. Walter got socked when he stepped in to keep the peace." With careful control, she cut the cellophane at the end of the brownie box.

"Jaydee's wife?" Belinda peeked around the paper. "Did he marry that twenty-one-year-old girl he's been goin' around with?"

"Uh-huh. A week ago Sunday."

"Well . . . he's at that age for men."

Marilee frowned at the comment, which she found highly sexist. She also found Belinda highly lacking in her attitude about the situation with her parents. She was tired of being the one to shoulder all the care about all of this.

"This is pretty much of a surprise about that dead guy being Fayrene's first ex-husband, isn't it?" Belinda again peeked around the paper. "How many husbands has she had?"

"Three, I think." Marilee plopped a brownie in the dish and licked her fingers.

"Well, it sure is a good thing Fayrene read that back issue of the paper, isn't it? If she had just thrown it out, no one might ever have known about that guy bein' her ex-husband."

Marilee leaned back against the chrome cabinets. "Belinda, we need to get your father to call your mother. The longer they stay split like this, the harder it will be for them to make up."

"I don't know what we can do about it."

"What if your mother does not go home, Belinda? What if this turns out to be a permanent split?"

Belinda peered around the paper. "Well, I told Daddy that I'm gonna hire somebody to come in here to work this counter during the day. Just because he had Mama doin' it for thirty-five years, doesn't mean I'm gonna. I'll work four nights a week, like I have, and that's all." She disappeared back behind the paper.

Marilee stared at the wall of newspaper, and then her gaze went to the pharmacy window. She thought of her aunt's face whenever speaking to or about Winston Valentine. She looked down at the box of brownies, took a second one and plopped it into the dish.

Belinda said, "I knew all this about Fayrene's ex-husband. Lyle was over there at the station Friday afternoon when Fayrene came in, waving the picture of the car in the paper. He went with the sheriff to take her up to identify the body. He said when she saw the man, she went nuts, just flipped right out. I guess she had really been countin' on seein' this guy, and not dead."

Dropping an enormous scoop of vanilla ice cream atop the brownies, Marilee thought that people counted on so much in this life, such as finding a mate and staying in love. Being able to find happiness. Being able to at least know what life was about. High expectations that appeared to be a mistake.

"It sure is funny about this guy using an alias. John V. Smith . . . Wonder what that *V* was for."

"It was a made-up name," Marilee pointed out with an energetic tone she felt necessary to combat Belinda's one-way train of thought, as she scooped warm fudge over the ice cream.

"Well, that was the whole trouble with why they couldn't identify him. They were runnin' searches on a John V. Smith, not a Dan Kaplan," Belinda said, as if the fact needed stating. "Lyle said the sheriff mentioned right off that it was strange this guy just had a driver's license and no credit cards or anything. What did Fayrene say about her husband using a fake ID?" She peeked out with a raised eyebrow. "Lyle never saw her after she flipped out."

"I only talked to her a minute. She wasn't in any shape for me to ask questions." Marilee said, taking up the can of whipped cream, shaking it. "I got what's in the article from the sheriff."

She aimed whipped cream at her sundae and thought that it would be a waste of effort to talk to Belinda about her mother's probable infatuation with Winston; Belinda would not be able to bring her head out of the newspaper.

Fluffy cream spurted out, and then only a dribbling stream. "Are you all out of whipped cream?"

"I don't know."

Marilee walked to the refrigerator in the storeroom and returned shaking a fresh can of whipped cream, the ball inside clinking like a piston.

Belinda was saying, "Lyle says fake drivers' licenses are real easy to get. You can get 'em at a lot of flea markets, if you know who to see. I don't know why any of us bother to go get a real driver's license, if that is the case."

Why, indeed? The whipped cream shot out of the can with a velocity that caused her to jump.

"Well, Fayrene will be sittin' pretty," Belinda said, "if she gets the fifty thousand."

"What fifty thousand?" Marilee paused in the act of opening the jar of cherries.

Belinda peeked around the paper. "The fifty-thousand dollars that was in the guy's trunk. You didn't know about it? I thought maybe you knew but the sheriff didn't want you to put it in the article. Lyle says he wants it kept quiet right now."

"No." And if the sheriff wanted it quiet, he shouldn't have told Lyle.

"Oh, well, I guess Neville is still lookin' into it. I don't think they've even told Fayrene. Lyle just told me this mornin'. Lyle thinks Fayrene could end up gettin' it, since her ex doesn't have any relatives. But that's only if it isn't stolen. This Dan Kaplan could have just robbed a bank or something."

Belinda disappeared behind the newspaper again.

Marilee stood there with the jar of cherries, wondering if she ought to go down there and get the scoop from Neville.

But she really didn't want to. Lord knew she had a story she was supposed to be writing right that minute, and here she was making a gigantic sundae. She wanted to sit down with the sundae and eat every scrap of it. Besides, there was little need for a write-up in the newspaper; with Lyle knowing about the money, likely half the town would know by the end of the day.

She twisted the top off the jar of cherries and fished out a stem with her fingers, while Belinda commented on the sinkhole.

"Wonder where all that dirt went?" she said. "Maybe it fills up the hole where they have pumped out oil somewhere else. Holes do have to be filled."

Marilee plopped the cherry in her mouth, twirling the stem and tying it in a knot with her tongue. Stuart had taught her that trick. It took concentration and settled her mind.

Fourteen

The bell over the door rang out. It was Charlene MacCoy. She came over to the soda fountain and ordered two barbecue sandwiches and three fountain Coca-Colas to go.

"The sandwiches are for me and Oralee," she said. "Dixie doesn't touch barbecue. I wish I wouldn't," she added with a sigh.

"Marilee will make the sandwiches for you." Belinda sat where she was. "You're already workin' around, Marilee."

Marilee reached for the container of buns. While she began making the sandwiches, Imperia Brown came in to discuss another month of weekly Blaine's Drugstore ads in the newspaper with Belinda, since Vella, who usually handled the store's advertising, wasn't available.

Belinda refused to do anything about the advertising. "I'm not takin' on that job. You'll have to talk to Daddy."

Imperia, who never minced words, said, "Girl, talkin' to Perry is like talkin' to a stump." Then, "Marilee, that barbecue smells good. Would you make me one?" Imperia was a big-boned woman who deemed worrying about eating schedules and calories and cholesterol harmful to health.

Marilee got out another bun.

Imperia, who sported fire-engine-red fingernails, admired Charlene's manicure, and Charlene said that it was the work of the new nail technician who had just begun that week.

"I'm getting too old to be doin' nails," Charlene sighed. "It is a young woman's job."

"Oh, listen to you, girl," Imperia said, waving her away. "Age is a matter of mind."

"Age is a matter of eyes, too, and mine are starin' down the barrel of the far side of forty-five. You can do all sorts of things to look thirty-five forever, but there is just no way to make your eyes see like they did at thirty-five."

Imperia, who was in her mid-thirties, cast Charlene a startled look.

"I don't imagine you need to work, anyway, bein' married to Mason MacCoy now," Belinda said, not at all concealing envy.

"Well, I still have a life," Charlene pointed out. "I've gone back to school for a license in therapeutic massage. I'll do that in a dim room anyway, and we're planning to put in a salon at the retirement community. Iris is going to finance it, and Dixie and I are goin' to run it, and we're goin' to offer massages and all sorts of herbal treatments."

Marilee, who had been listening idly and who now handed Charlene her sack of sandwiches, thought how lovely Charlene was. Attitude, she concluded. Since marrying Mason, Charlene seemed to get younger every day, which was a mark in favor of marriage, Marilee thought, her gaze drifting to the mirror to check out her own appearance.

There were deeper than normal circles under her eyes, and her hair was limp. She was just about ready to fall off the vine, and then who would want her? Would she bloom, as Charlene had done, if she married Parker?

Just then Charlene said, "I got your note last week, Marilee, and I meant to call and tell you that we'll be there for Parker's birthday party on Saturday. I'll bring my sour cream dip."

The party was a casual affair that Marilee had somehow fallen into organizing each year for the past five. She had sent out the reminder notes to Parker's small group of friends at the beginning of the month and then forgotten about it. She started just a bit when Charlene mentioned it.

"I have to get the cake," she said, checking the calendar. "I forgot about it."

"How old is Parker gonna be?" Belinda wanted to know.

"Forty-three."

"Has he ever been married?"

"Once . . . for six months when he was twenty." Marilee wondered why she always answered Belinda's intimate questions.

Just then Iris MacCoy entered the store and came forward with rapid steps, even in platform shoes. She gave Charlene, her sister-in-law, a kiss on the cheek like she always did, whether she saw her once a week or three times in a day, and showed them all a poster she wanted to put in the window, announcing the grand opening of the Green Acres Senior Living Community.

"See . . . we are emphasizing the word *Living*. The chamber is putting advertisements in national magazines, too."

Going gung ho on working with her husband Adam on building a full-service retirement community, Iris had taken a position on the board of the chamber of commerce. It was widely agreed that Iris could get men to do what they had set their minds not to do. In point of fact, her husband Adam had told everyone he did not intend to build a community for retired old farts, and a week after Iris worked on him, he was contacting architects.

"Iris designed the poster herself," Charlene pointed out.

Each woman made appropriate compliments over it. Iris really had a flare for color and design. She was herself very much of an eye-catcher. Her personal style of bimbo pretty much camouflaged the fact that she had an intelligent brain. Marilee, who had known Iris moderately well for eight years, had an idea that both libertine and intellectual existed inside the woman, and she envied Iris for being able to contain such conflicting natures with apparent peace.

Marilee put Imperia's barbecue sandwich in front of her on the counter. She saw Iris, setting herself on a stool, eyeing the plate.

"Do you want one?" Marilee asked her.

"Well . . . what I'd really like is one of those hot fudge sundaes." She pointed her silvery-nailed finger in the direction of Marilee's carefully constructed sundae.

Marilee stuck a stainless-steel spoon in the ice cream, now softened just the way she liked it, and plopped the dish in front of Iris. She wondered if she might get some tips.

Belinda was up and leaning on the counter, reading aloud the list of activities for the opening. "All day buffet . . . bingo . . . pinball . . . pool tournament . . . golf tournament . . . poker . . . gospel and country music bands and dancing in the evening." She looked up. "You sure better have paramedics on-site . . . you are gonna kill these people with all this activity."

Marilee watched Iris stick a spoonful swirled with vanilla and chocolate into her mouth. Turning to the shelves, she took down another sundae dish.

Outside on the sidewalk, Tate Holloway looked up and saw Parker Lindsey approaching from the opposite direction. It was plain that both of them were headed to the drugstore.

Tate stepped up his pace, ducked into the alcove just ahead of Lindsey and got a drip on the top of his head from the air conditioner just as he pushed open the door.

"After you." Tate motioned Lindsey onward. He also got another drip, as he was standing in the correct place for it.

"After you." Lindsey stood his ground.

"No, please . . ." Tate gestured magnanimously. Lindsey kept standing there, so Tate gave in and stepped forward to enter, but Lindsey picked that second to move, too, so they ended up jostling themselves through the door.

At the bit of commotion at the door, the women at the counter quit talking, and Marilee lifted her eyes from the box of brownies to see two figures entering. With the glare from the bright light through the glass, it took her several seconds to recognize Tate Holloway. Then, with surprise, she saw Parker step out from behind Tate.

Marilee took in the two men. Tate Holloway whipped off his hat, saying, "Good afternoon, ladies," and his blue eyes met hers. She jerked her gaze downward, pulled a brownie from the box and plopped it into the sundae dish.

"Hello, gals. Havin' a conference?" Parker asked. Each of the other women said hello.

Marilee, occupied with arranging two brownies in the dish and avoiding the temptation of stuffing a third directly into her mouth, did not realize she had not offered a greeting until well after the time to do so had passed. Her lapse, however, obviously had not been noted, possibly because of the welcome so evident in the other women at the counter.

It was as if an energy swept them, each woman coming just a little bit more to life as a female will when confronted with powerful male energy, and in this case, it was two very vibrant men suddenly dropping into their midst. Even Belinda, who had been about to lower herself onto her stool, stood straight, brushed a hand through her hair and hid her slippers by tucking them beneath the front counter.

Charlene, moved by the disruption and possibly by Tate Holloway addressing her as "The most beautiful Miss Charlene," suddenly remembered that she had to return to the salon. "My gosh, Oralee wants this sandwich!"

She cast a wave. "Marilee, bring the children out to see the ponies. Parker, I'll see you on your birthday. Bye, y'all."

Tate was sprinting to open the door, and this set Imperia into motion. She jumped to her feet, leaving her half-eaten sandwich on the counter, saying for Tate's benefit, "I have customers to visit," and hurried after Charlene.

Like a knight from a storybook, Tate bowed to each woman as she went through the door. Observing, Marilee thought that there was not a single man around Valentine who behaved as Tate Holloway did. His antics had Iris laughing gaily of course. Iris laughed quite easily anyway. Men just loved the way Iris laughed, with her head lifted and her hand sometimes touching her bare neck, or them. Marilee noticed Tate wink at Iris, not that it was any of her business, and she focused on building herself another sundae.

Parker, who thought Holloway a stupid show-off, nevertheless determined to show off in his own way. He rounded the counter and went about getting himself a Coke out of the fountain machine. He wanted Holloway to see this, to see that this was Parker's place first. Parker had been here for years and years, and Holloway was a latecomer.

"Would you like somethin', Tate?" Parker wiped drips off his foaming glass.

"Thank you." Holloway had sat himself on a stool next to Iris. "I came in for the wonderful iced tea. I miss Miss Vella, but the cold tea is still good."

"Yes, it is, because it comes from the iced tea maker," Belinda told him. "It's made from packets. The only thing Mama did was put the packet in the machine."

She pushed the button that opened the cash register drawer with a ding and counted away the money Charlene and Imperia had left. Belinda liked to count money. She didn't like to make food for customers and was inclined to encourage anyone to help himself. She reminded Parker that he needed to pay for his Coke, though.

Parker scooped ice into a glass and poured the tea from the pitcher, then plunked the wet glass in front of Holloway, who said, "Thank you. I appreciate you servin' me. Pay the lady, too, will you?"

Annoyed to find himself being treated like a servant, Parker grandly told Belinda, "Put the editor's drink on my tab."

"I'm not runnin' a tab like Mama did. I'm not keepin' track of it."

He pulled a couple dollars from his pocket and passed them to her outstretched hand.

"Thank you, buddy," Holloway said with that annoying grin of his. "Could you hand me a slice of lemon there?"

Parker got the lemon slice and threw it so that it plunked with a splash into the man's glass. "Hey, I'm sorry, *buddy.*" He used Holloway's term back at him. "Let me wipe up that mess I made." Parker grabbed a cloth, lifted Holloway's glass and, with elaborate motions wiped the counter, setting up to accidently dump the glass in Holloway's lap.

The next instant, however, Holloway reached for the glass. "Thank you, sir. That's just fine now."

Parker, feeling thwarted, stepped back and sipped his Coke a couple of times, and then his eyes lit on Marilee, who was busy shaking a can of whipped cream, and thus causing her neat bottom to shake in a nice manner.

Stepping close behind her, he put both hands on her waist and bent his lips near her ear. "That sundae is lookin' awfully good. Think you could make me one?"

He was thinking: See this, Holloway. This is my place.

Marilee wriggled away from him, saying, "You are perfectly capable of gettin' it yourself."

Parker stood there, his back to those on the other side of the counter. Thank goodness Marilee had spoken in a low voice that only he could hear. *What in the hell was wrong with her?* He reached for his soft drink glass and casually turned, checking the faces of those at the counter. He was relieved to see that no one was looking his way. He looked again at Marilee, wondering what had gotten her back up. He was getting darn tired of her prickly manner.

This thought caused an uneasiness inside him, and he drank deeply of his soft drink, then ran his gaze down Marilee's profile. He found himself caught between being afraid of her breaking off with him, and being afraid she would say she wanted to marry him. He kept hoping if he left it alone, it would all work out somehow.

Marilee plopped a cherry on the top of her sundae. She wished for more, but by eating them and putting them on sundaes, she had used them all up, and she didn't want to risk this sundae by taking time to go get another jar from the storeroom. She felt certain that she had annoyed Parker—and she didn't know why she had done that, except that she didn't like him putting his hands on her in front of everyone, as if he had ownership.

Of course, surely he did have some sort of ownership, with their pending engagement. Although it might not be pending. Parker had not said one more word about it. Maybe he wanted to just forget he had ever asked, and that he did not tell her this annoyed the living daylights out of her.

The problem was that she felt guilty for not making a decision about marrying Parker and telling him one way or the other. That still hung over her, even if he had not mentioned it again.

She sprinkled pecans atop her sundae, then sprinkled a second helping. She had the feeling Tate was watching her and told herself this was foolishness on her part. She glanced up to check this out and saw him in conversation with Iris and Belinda, his eyes fully on Iris. Parker leaned over on the counter and joined in the conversation. They were talking about the merits of jogging.

Good Lord, Iris said she jogged six miles four times a week.

Again Marilee looked over at Tate, and this time his eyes came swinging around to hers.

Marilee averted her eyes and reached for a cloth to wipe her hands. The next instant, while getting a long-handled spoon from the container, she succeeded in sending two dozen stainless spoons clattering to the floor. She had to get down on her knees to gather them up. Parker helped, and she thought that was nice of him, after she had behaved so sharply to him. This fact deepened her guilt.

She saved a spoon for herself and threw the rest into the dishwasher. When she turned around, she discovered Parker was helping himself to her sundae.

Snatching it from beneath his next scoop, she sat herself on Belinda's stool and began to eat.

She had sampled one lovely taste of sweet cream and chocolate when Belinda, who had not noticed a body in her stool, backed up to sit herself down. Marilee saw it coming and let out a warning, but Belinda, intent on telling about the fifty-thousand dollars found in Fayrene's ex-husband's car, did not hear and ended up squashing the sundae all over Marilee's bosom.

It was lucky that Aunt Vella was staying at her house, Marilee thought, observing the chocolate stains on her blouse in the filmy old rest room mirror. Aunt Vella was good at getting stains out of clothing. That mirror had to be the first one hung in here, probably at least sixty years old.

With a sigh, she threw the paper towel in the trash and emerged from the rest room. Looking down the narrow hallway, she saw Tate and Parker and Belinda at the soda fountain, silhouetted by the bright light through the big front window. Iris was just leaving.

She stood there a moment, staring.

Then she looked left, at the door leading to the rear room of the pharmacy. The drone of her uncle's television came through the door. After a moment's hesitation, she quietly turned the knob and entered. She apparently wasn't going to get a sundae, but maybe she could have an influential word with her uncle.

"Uncle Perry?"

Her uncle's eyes opened, and he made a mild effort to straighten himself. He nodded at Marilee.

"Are you doin' all right?" she asked. He looked a little too pale to her, but admittedly, she had not paid her uncle any attention for quite some time.

"Yep. Fine. Somebody need a prescription?"

"No. I just wanted to say hello."

He nodded and straightened some more. His gaze moved back to the television, as if drawn there by a string.

Marilee noticed that the early edition of the news was just going off, so it was about five o'clock. She needed to get on home if she was to get anything done on her newspaper article before Aunt Vella returned with the kids. She would be embarrassed not to have any writing done.

"Uncle Perry, aren't you gonna call Aunt Vella?" Aggravation at thinking about being embarrassed had caused her to get short-tempered.

He looked at her. "I guess not," he said, his jaw getting tight.

"Why not?" Marilee pressed.

"Vella's made her decision. Don't see any need to argue with it."

"Don't you miss her?"

"Nope." He focused his eyes on the television screen.

Marilee looked at him and thought she was carrying on the stupidest conversation in the world. She saw, too, that her uncle's life had not changed one iota with her aunt not here.

Annoyed with the entire situation, Marilee said smartly, "You might want to know that while you're sittin' in here all day and half the night with the television, Aunt Vella is seein' Winston Valentine. She is serious about going off in a new direction. You can sit here if you want, but you're likely to be losin' your house and a part of this store."

While she said that, she searched his face for some reaction, no matter how small. But she did not see any. Her uncle sat there and looked like the lump Imperia had called him. An old man, as her Aunt Vella had said.

Marilee, feeling defeated, left him there and walked out, closing the door quietly behind her.

Pausing, she looked into the front of the store to see Tate and Parker and Belinda, still silhouetted against the light of the big front window.

Stepping out with purpose, Marilee glided out to the soda fountain.

"You're not wearin' a sundae anymore," Parker said.

"No, it didn't fit." She cast him a grin because she felt it rude not to, then picked up her purse from the rear, saying, "I need to go home to write. Good evenin', y'all," and was out the door almost before she realized how coolly she had breezed out.

Whew.

She paused on the sidewalk to take a good breath. The air had become quite humid and heavy, indicating coming storms.

Then her gaze fell on Munro, sitting in front of her Cherokee.

"My goodness, where did you come from?" She had left him with the children and Aunt Vella.

She glanced quickly up and down the sidewalk, looking for familiar figures, wondering if some sort of emergency had happened.

The dog was regarding her with quiet eyes, and she seemed to hear him say, *I came to keep you company.*

"Well, come on, and we'll go home," she told him and opened the door of the Cherokee for him to hop into the seat.

Munro was with her when she entered the empty house, and he curled beneath her desk, while she chewed on a fingernail and dredged up from memory the point of her article for next Sunday's edition.

An hour and a half later, in a T-shirt and sweatpants and bare feet, Marilee had a rough draft written. She had written it in spurts between glancing at the clock and out the window, looking for her family, and then forcing herself to sit in the chair and put words down for ten minutes at a time. She was exhausted and well ready for Aunt Vella and Winston and the children to blow in with the rising wind of an evening thunderstorm. She greeted everyone with happy hugs.

"Well, he *is* here," Aunt Vella said, upon seeing Munro. She stopped with the pizza box high in the air. "I was afraid I was going to have to tell you I had lost him."

"I told them Mun-ro said he need-ed to come be with you," Willie Lee said in his practical tone.

There came a knock, and Parker poked his head inside. "Anyone home?"

Marilee looked up from the computer screen to see him glancing around, still with only his head poking in the front door. His gaze found hers, and he regarded her uncertainly, no doubt because of her sharp behavior that afternoon. She felt immediately contrite.

"Come in." Marilee rose and went to greet him warmly with a smile and swift kiss, and to more or less haul him inside.

His grin grew broader. "Just passed Winston. He said maybe I could get some pizza here."

Willie Lee came racing in dog-fashion, on hands and knees, barking.

"Why is he doing that?" Parker asked.

"He's pretending to be a dog."

Willie Lee followed along, barking the entire way into the kitchen, where Marilee heated the last two pieces of pizza in the microwave.

"He's really into this, isn't he?" Parker said of Willie Lee, who was now sniffing at his shoes.

"Pretending is a normal part of childhood." Marilee liked to point that out whenever Willie Lee was being perfectly normal.

"Uh-huh." Parker raised an eyebrow and whispered, "I hope he isn't gonna pee on my leg."

Then he said to Willie Lee, "Have you had your rabies shot? I need to get Munro's shots, I can get you one, too."

Willie Lee raced away on hands and knees. This tickled Parker, and his amusement pleased Marilee. For an instant their gazes met, and the fond look in his eyes caused warmth to wash over her.

"Sit," she said, moving him to the table and setting the slices of pizza in front of him. Then she took the chair next to him and propped her chin in her hand and watched him eat. She could hear Aunt Vella in the children's bedroom, reading them a bedtime story. Parker commented that the pizza was delicious and that he would starve if it wasn't for microwave ovens and Marilee's kitchen. She accepted this compliment graciously, and passed the credit on to Aunt Vella.

"It really is nice for me, having Aunt Vella here to help with the kids and meals and things," she said.

"I'm surprised she hasn't gone back to Perry," Parker said.

"I am, too." She thought of it sadly.

"Do you think she will?"

"I don't know . . . I really don't know."

The situation confused and frightened her. If her aunt and uncle could get divorced after forty-five years of marriage, then it seemed there was no certain thing in life at all.

Possibly Parker was thinking along the same lines, as he was frowning and staring at the table. Marilee studied his face and thought how he was not only handsome but a good man who would help in a crisis, even if he had a little trouble with mundane, everyday living.

And he needed her to keep him decently fed. To give him a place to call home. A family, such as he had not had before. He needed that, even if he wasn't aware of needing it. The memory of their lovemaking once upon a time sliced through her mind and right down to her belly. Their lovemaking had been very good, and they had been close once.

Of course she should marry him. She should snatch him up. She almost popped out with, "I'll marry you, Parker," but hesitated, suddenly overcome with self-consciousness that maybe he had changed his mind.

She rose and took his hand. "Come on."

"Wha . . ." He met her gaze and dropped his last bite of pizza, letting himself be dragged out on the back stoop, going with her with a growing grin.

Marilee closed the door behind them, putting them in the dimness of the step, where the only light was reflected through the window curtains. In a bold advance, she brought Parker's head down, parting her lips in invitation to his very apparent enthusiasm.

"Parker . . ."

She whispered his name with longing and pushed her hands through the opening of his shirt at the base of his neck. His skin was warm and silky. His tongue tasted like pizza. She wrapped one leg around his.

In seconds they were all heavy breath and wet lips and tugging hands. Parker made her wild by kissing her neck and shoving a warm hand between her legs. He whispered for them to go to his truck, and she said she could not do that. In fact, in an instant her fertile imagination drew up a picture of them both, old enough to know better, getting caught right in the middle of the act by a curious neighbor coming to investigate the rocking truck. Added to that was the sudden thought that Tate could come through the back gate and catch them making out on the back step.

Both mind pictures cooled her ardor a considerable amount, and she began to pull away, but Parker held her fast and kissed her deeply, seeking to draw her back into the passion.

Just then, as if coming to her aid, a loud clap of thunder reverberated, causing Marilee to jump and just about sending Parker backward off the stoop. He recovered and attempted to get back to business but was not able to overcome the rain that suddenly came in a downpour, as if someone had unstopped a sink.

"Damn!"

"Ohmygosh, Parker, you're gettin' soaked!"

Her hand fumbled with the screen door, which proved stubborn, but then she got it open, along with the inner door, and they threw themselves inside.

"Here . . ." She tossed Parker a towel from a fresh pile atop the dryer.

He rubbed his head, and she, with her own towel, dried her face. Then, clutching the towel, she looked at him.

He looked at her.

"Parker, do you still want to get married?"

His eyebrows went up. "Yeah."

The answer was not fully satisfying.

She breathed deeply, summoning words to her tongue.

But then Willie Lee's voice calling "Ma-ma" and running footsteps approaching abruptly ended further discussion. The next instant there came a loud thump, and then a pain-filled wail.

Marilee raced into the kitchen and found Willie Lee had fallen against a kitchen chair and put his bottom teeth into his upper lip. She scooped him up, calling immediately for a cold cloth.

She sat and pressed Willie Lee, sobbing, against her, instinctively seeking to absorb her child's pain.

Parker put a cloth in her hand.

Willie Lee cuddled close and sucked on the wet cloth. After a minute, Marilee had to pry his head from her bosom and force him to allow her to examine the wound. Then the others—Parker, Aunt Vella, and even Corrine, who seemed to have a great curiosity for bloody wounds—gave Willie Lee's cut lip a thorough examination. Parker pronounced it not serious. Marilee finally concluded that Willie Lee did not need stitches, but he did need her to hold him and rock him back and forth.

She was still holding Willie Lee when Parker bent to kiss her good-night.

"Parker . . ."

He paused and looked at her. But with Willie Lee in her arms and Aunt Vella in and out of the kitchen, there was no room for privacy. "I'm glad you stopped by tonight."

He nodded. "I'll call you tomorrow."

"Yes. Do."

Then she was alone in the silent kitchen, Willie Lee dozing against her breasts, where not so long ago Parker's ministrations had been working her into wild passion.

The house was quiet. Aunt Vella was not snoring. Marilee tiptoed to the door of the bedroom and looked in, wondering if she should put a mirror underneath her aunt's nose to make certain she was alive. She did not know which she found more disconcerting, her aunt snoring like a character in an animated cartoon, or her aunt not making any noise at all.

At that particular moment, Aunt Vella let out a ragged breath, proving she was alive. With relief, Marilee glanced at Willie Lee, who was sprawled in a perfectly relaxed manner. She smiled. She might worry a great deal about his future, but his present was quite blessed. The swelling on his lip was marginal, and he had fallen back into his se-cure, easygoing ways.

She then looked into her own bedroom, where the bedside table lamp glowed dimly. Corrine, with Munro lying beside her, had fallen asleep, once again with a book lying on her chest. Under Munro's watchful eyes, Marilee removed the book and turned out the light.

"You are a good friend," she whispered to the dog and touched his head.

Still gazing at him, she wondered where the dog had come from. She wondered at how he had come into their lives seemingly at just the right moment.

Tender mercies, her mother had once explained in a particularly un-characteristic thoughtful moment. For an instant, warm memories of childhood fluttered over Marilee like a delicate butterfly. There had been good times, but the memories of these times seemed to have been clouded over with the hard, stormy ones. She wished she could find a better balance between the two.

Going into the kitchen, she got out the pitcher of tea—Tate's round pitcher that she needed to return to him. There was one full glass of tea left in it; he had not brought fresh that evening, and she wondered at this. She missed him.

No, she did not, she told herself.

Oh, she liked Tate, and that was good and natural, too. Tate was a likeable man. But she could not make more out of it than was there. There was not a "thing" between them. Parker was hers, what she needed.

Parker was what she could deal with. Tate was way beyond her ca-pabilities.

She thought this as, carrying along her glass of tea, she went to the back door, opened it and peered in the direction of her editor's house. It was perfectly black in that direction; the trees blocking any lights that might shine from his windows, if Tate was reading or doing some strange thing, like making another pitcher of iced tea in the careful manner he liked to take with it.

Inhaling the warm, humid air of coming summer through the screen door, she thought how summer edged upon them this time of year, one night humid as July and the next cool again. As if trying to sneak up on them, or accustom them to what was coming, one day at a time, un-til all their days were summer, hot and dry and so long sometimes she thought she would burn right up.

What else had her mother said? *The good news is that you can get used to anything. The bad news is that you can get used to anything.*

She paused and listened for a moment, hearing the first click of an early cicada far out beneath a tree . . . the rustle of leaves . . . light rain pattering through the leaves and onto the roof. Aunt Vella had begun to snore gently, and the refrigerator purred beneath this.

Thank you, God, after all, even for the hot and dry when it comes. Thank you for my family, for my children all safe in bed. Thank you for the safety of this house. Look after my sister, Lord. And Mama . . . yes, and dear Mama.

The gratitude came out of nowhere, and she embraced it as the precious emotion it was. This was something she could cling to. Something that anchored her and erased, for brief moments, anyway, the anxiousness that seemed to plague her soul.

She remained there at the door, as if she could keep the gratitude by not moving. As if it had come to her on the night air.

Yet then, inevitably, came a cool, swift breeze.

With a shiver, she closed the door and carried her now empty tea glass to the kitchen sink.

Glancing in the night-black window, she saw the reflection of the telephone on the wall behind her.

She turned and went to it and dialed Parker's number.

The answering service came on the line. The doctor was unavailable at the moment. If Marilee would give them the emergency message, the woman would relay it to the doctor. "He'll return your call as soon as possible."

"Oh, no, this isn't an emergency." Marilee looked at the clock. It was after eleven. Parker might already be asleep. "I'll catch him tomorrow during office hours. Thank you."

She didn't suppose saying, "I'll marry you," was something she should blurt out on the telephone, not to mention waking up Parker to do it.

Fifteen

Toss Up the Heart, See Where it Lands

Tate came out into air heavy as wet wool. The weatherman on the radio predicted high temperatures and possibly more storms that evening. It was enjoy the morning and get in out of the heat by afternoon. Summer was here.

Jogging down the porch steps, Tate felt a sense of power infuse him. This was an atmosphere with which he had full familiarity. By golly, Houston had mornings thicker than this on a dry summer day.

He went past the lilac bush fast enough to cause wet leaves to flutter. Bubba popped out from beneath it and jumped high. Tate sprinted over a puddle at the curb; when his Nikes hit the street, they seemed to be carrying him along all on their own.

Down Porter he went at a pace to warm him up. No one stirring at the James house. The young UPS man did only one quickie on the porch beam and plopped to the ground. Tate lifted a high five to him and headed on around the corner, his legs and arms and heart all picking up the pace and going with the same strong rhythm. He nodded and called "Mornin'," as he sprinted passed the walking ladies, who were strolling this morning, one fanning herself with her hat.

On Main Street, Bonita Embree was entering her bakery. As she unlocked the door, she dropped the bag in her hand, and Betty Crocker box mixes spilled out on the sidewalk five feet in front of Tate. With the grace of a ballet dancer, Tate bent and swept up the boxes, deposited them in Bonita's arms and proceeded on, having done it all with only a pause of three heartbeats.

"Please don't tell," Bonita's voice followed after him.

"Not a word," Tate tossed over his shoulder and kept on going in his groove.

There was Charlotte across the street, poking the flag in its holder out front of the *Voice*. He waved, but she was already going back in the door.

Then it was around the corner of the police station—was that a mocha aroma in the coffee this morning?—and onward up Church into the first rays of the sun breaking through the morning mist, jogging all the way and still not slowing down.

Good morning, Life! Good morning, Lord! I am ready for whatever comes this day. Thank you for that.

Woo-eee! See me now, Lindsey.

But Lindsey was nowhere in sight.

Tate slowed his pace. He jogged up his driveway and back down again, checked his watch and slowed down as his chest began to burn. He did leg-stretching exercises there at the end of his driveway, keeping an eye out up the hill.

Lindsey did not appear. Of all the mornings for Lindsey to skip jogging, this had to be one of them.

Silly to be wanting to show off, anyway, Tate thought and took himself in hand, jogging on around to his back door.

Ha! Likely Lindsey could not take the thick humidity. Whereas Tate was rather pleased to see that he thrived in it.

He sure wished Lindsey had come along to see.

Through the open door of her editor's office, Marilee saw Tate on the telephone. He was reared back in his chair, his feet up on his desk, every bit the big editor, which everyone had taken to calling him.

Intending to slip in and lay her current detention center piece on his desk and slip back out again, she moved quietly and didn't look at him, but Tate jumped up and grabbed her arm, stretching the telephone cord, which pulled the telephone along the desk at an alarming rate.

His hand was hot and firm through her sleeve.

"Well, I look forward to meetin' the congressman, too, Mayor," he said into the phone. "Sure do. Seven o'clock. I'll see you then, and we'll talk some more. Goodbye."

He let go of her arm and leaned over to drop the receiver into its cradle, causing his shirt to stretch tight over his firm shoulders.

Then he was facing her, his blue eyes dancing. "It's a delight to see you, Miss Marilee." His gaze went to her hair, in that way he had of always seeming to *observe* her.

"Hello." She held out the papers and disk. "I brought the disk with my detention center piece, and a printed copy, too."

"I like your hair up like that. It gives you a very elegant neck."

"Oh . . . I wear my hair up when it gets so humid." She was smoothing at her hair before she realized it.

"Well, you are lovely as a summer day with it like that." He slipped his rear onto the edge of his desk.

"Thank you." She felt foolishly self-conscious. Charm was Tate's way, like water from a faucet. "Well, that's all I had." She turned to leave.

"I think Lindsey must not compliment you enough."

That stopped her in her tracks. "Why do you say that?"

"Because you were surprised at me doing it. You always seem a little surprised at my compliments."

"Anyone would be surprised. You say things that almost no other man on earth says. And I really don't believe that Parker complimenting me or not complimenting me is any of your business." She was instantly ashamed at both her bold statement and tone of voice. She didn't know what got into her.

He smiled at her, though. "The secret of life . . . *one* secret of life," he corrected, "is to know when to make things my business." Without giving her time to comment on that, he added, "You could have sent the file directly to my computer from yours," and picked up the typed pages she had brought him.

"I wasted twenty minutes attempting to do that. Bringing it over seemed a whole lot easier." That was where her temper had come from; dealing with the new computer was wearing on her last nerve.

"This is just fine. No problem at all."

"Good." She nodded at him and stepped toward the door.

"Wait a minute." In a swift movement, he slipped off the desk, reached the door in two strides and surprised her by closing it.

He looked at her, and she looked at him. Was he going to kiss her? She stepped back before she realized, taken by a little panic.

Then, folding his arms, he said. "You are a lovely woman, Miss Marilee, and your hair like that gives you a definite exotic air."

She could find nothing to say to that.

He smiled a smile she had come to recognize as seductive. "I would very much like you to go to dinner with me Saturday night. I'm supposed to have dinner with the mayor and his wife, a state congressman, and a few other people I've already forgotten. Would you accompany me, so that I can have a really good time?"

His eyes were intent upon her, blue as the summer sky, and with a hint of something that caused her to hold her breath for a fraction of a second.

Then she shook her head. "I'm sorry, I can't. I already have dinner plans."

"Well now . . . there's always another night. How about Sunday night? What's your preference—steak, chicken fry or Mexican?"

"No, I don't think so." She brushed at imaginary stray hairs and looked at the door.

"I suppose this is because you have a standing date with Lindsey."

"I am dating Parker at this time, yes." Which he well knew. She moved a half step toward the door, indicating that she wanted to go.

Her editor, however, leaned his shoulder against the door, fully blocking her in with him.

"Just what is goin' on with you and Lindsey? I have it from him that you two are engaged, and I have it from you that you two are going to-gether and considering being engaged. Which is it? Engaged or not engaged?"

"Parker's and my relationship is not any of your concern." She felt trapped.

"I have the concern of being attracted to you."

She gazed at her boss, and he gazed at her. A certain glint came into his eyes.

"You've known Lindsey for many years, I take it, both of you livin' here in this small town. Since Lindsey is the one who told me you two were engaged, and you are the one who has said you're goin' together and considering engagement, I'm assuming you aren't wild about ac-ceptin' the man's proposal. It seems to me that your behavior could be considered a little on the rude side. Just how long do you intend to keep the poor man in suspense?"

"It seems to me that your training as a journalist has caused you to do a lot of supposin' into private lives that are none of your business." She reached out and took hold of the door handle.

His jaw tight now, he moved aside. She jerked the door open and left.

When she was halfway to her desk, where she had left the children with coloring pens, a loud banging came from behind her in Tate's of-fice. She, Charlotte and June, who was nearby at the copy machine, turned. Nothing could be seen through the partially opened door.

Charlotte immediately marched herself into his office and seconds later returned and said, particularly to Marilee, "He kicked his trash can across the room."

She had provoked him, she knew it very well, but was too wrought up to feel remorse. He pricked her in the wrong places. She hoped she did not get fired.

The only car in the lot of the Lindsey Veterinary Clinic was a blue Honda that belonged to Deedee, the receptionist. It had white silhou-ettes of different breeds of dogs stuck all over its rear window.

Marilee pulled to a stop beside the Honda. Munro needing shots gave her the perfect excuse to stop by. Parker had mentioned the shots from the very first day and had kept forgetting to give them to the dog.

Why would she need an excuse to stop by?

Whipping down the visor, she checked her face in the mirror to make certain she didn't have mascara smudges. *Come to supper tonight, Parker.* No, that wouldn't do. She needed to speak to him alone, which meant going out.

Her lipstick had faded, but she would not freshen it and appear so obviously after a man with Corrine looking at her. Good heavens, what was happening to her? She flipped the visor back up and grabbed her purse.

Let's go out to supper, Parker. She didn't think she should be the one to ask. She had asked him last night if he still wanted to get married. It was his turn to speak of the matter. He had said he would call her, but he hadn't. Although he might have called that morning, after they had left the house.

I'm sorry about the interruption last night. The rain wasn't her fault, though. Her son busting his mouth open and needing her attention had not been her fault, either. Why in the world did she feel so at fault?

She realized then that Corrine was out and walking to the clinic door, while Willie Lee remained sitting in the back seat. She opened his door.

"Why aren't you and Munro getting out?"

"Mun-ro doesn't want to go in there." His blue eyes blinked behind his thick glasses.

"Oh. Well, he has to, sugar. He needs to get vaccinated so he won't get sick. Parker will give him a shot, so that Munro won't get rabies. He could get rabies from a skunk that might bite him." She gazed at both her son and the dog, who sat with his chin as if permanently stuck to Willie Lee's thigh. "Besides that, honey, you and Corrine both have flea bites from Munro sleeping with you. We need to get something to help Munro with fleas . . . so he can continue to sleep with you," she added in a deliberate and measured tone.

She waited, gazing at him.

Willie Lee gave a big sigh and inched out of the seat. "Come on, Mun-ro."

Marilee followed her son and the dog to the building. *I am ready to talk about this thing, Parker. Are you?* She was ready to get this thing settled between them. *I'll marry you, Parker.*

She took hold of the glass door and they all entered; Corrine in the lead, Willie Lee trudging inside, and Munro slinking with his tail dragging.

Marilee, stepping into the waiting room that smelled of disinfectant, didn't think right this minute, in front of the children, was the place to have any sort of marriage discussion. But if she didn't, maybe neither one of them would have time to get together to get it said. Maybe she should just say it, and they could work out the details later.

"Doc's not in," Deedee told them immediately.

"Oh." She had not given this possibility a thought.

Deedee popped chewing gum. "He's out on a couple of calls." She stood and looked over the counter at Munro, who had lain down, his paws on the floor, trying his best to sink out of sight. "I can page him if this is an emergency."

"No . . . it's not an emergency. We were just going to get Munro his shots."

"I don't give shots, but I can sell them to you, and you can do it to your own. Lots of people do."

Marilee looked down at Munro, whose eyes popped wide and stared at her.

My thoughts exactly. "I think I'd better wait for Parker."

Munro got to his feet, ready to go.

Aunt Vella was asleep and snoring in the big wingback chair. Willie Lee went straight to the chair, leaned on the arm and watched her with fascination.

"Willie Lee, come away from there. Don't wake Aunt Vella."

Marilee spoke in a hushed voice, but Aunt Vella's eyes popped open. "I'm not asleep. I was just restin' my eyes."

"You were snor-ring," Willie Lee said.

"Oh, you're a little wild boy."

Willie Lee gazed at his great-aunt, judging the truth of what she said, not grinning until she poked him in the side with her finger. "I am," he said, giggling.

"Has Parker called?" Marilee asked.

"You had some phone calls, but I didn't answer them. Two came while I was hanging clothes on the line, and I wasn't about to run in here from the yard. It's a lot easier to let the answerin' machine get them. That way I won't mess up and forget to give you the message."

Marilee saw the light blinking on her machine. Three blinks. She punched the button.

"Marilee, this is Charlene. I wanted to let you know we'll be bringing my cousin Leanne to Parker's barbecue on Saturday. I don't know if you know, but she's livin' with us for a while. That's why her horses are here. Oh, Jojo will be coming, but Danny J. won't, so really we'll be the same number as expected. Leanne's makin' her salsa recipe and bringin' it. It's really good. Bye."

The machine beeped, and a deep male voice said, "This is Rick returnin' your call, Marilee. I got the steaks for Saturday. All set."

One more beep. "If you are thinking of siding your house, call Martin's Home Siding. We're runnin' a special. 555-2323."

That was the end of the messages. Nothing from Parker.

In the kitchen, Aunt Vella was making peanut butter and jelly sandwiches for the children. Marilee poured glasses of apple juice and asked Aunt Vella if she would be available to watch the children that evening.

Aunt Vella said she would love to do so, and Willie Lee, grinning, said, "You will watch me, a wild boy."

Aunt Vella poked him and got him giggling, then she asked Marilee, "Where are you going, dear?"

"I think I may have a date with Parker, if I can get ahold of him."

A couple of hours ought to be enough time to find out if Parker still wanted to get married, and to tell him that she would. She would like to be back home in time to put the children to bed.

Marilee, sitting at her desk and writing club reports on the new whiz-bang computer, cocked her head to listen to the voices float from the kitchen.

"Hello, missy."

"Hello, Mr. Tate."

Marilee's heartbeat fluttered. *Which is it—engaged or not engaged?* She recalled his blue eyes, so intense when he had asked.

He was her boss, the man who paid her salary, the man who irritated her and who she found too attractive by far.

"How are you today?" His voice could charm birds from trees.

"Fii-ine."

Marilee found herself leaning forward, as if to see around the door. Ridiculous. She got up and went to the kitchen, where her boss stood in the middle of the room. Corrine was beside him, looking at Marilee with deep, dark eyes.

"Peace." Her boss and neighbor held up offerings—a fresh pitcher of tea with one hand, and a small square bakery box with the other. "Cake . . . a double-chocolate from Miss Bonita's. She puts pure chocolate chips in them, she assured me."

She gazed at him, trying to get perspective on this thing. He wore his enticing, although at the moment reserved, grin.

Turning, she went to the counter and picked up the clean pitcher waiting there. "Here's your other pitcher. You sure have a lot of them."

"Muriel left her dishes. When she left her old life, she really left it."

He set his offerings on the table. "I apologize for my behavior this mornin', Miss Marilee. You are right—your relationship with Lindsey is not my business. I behaved rudely, and I'm sorry." He looked her in the eye.

It took her several seconds to find a response.

"Apology accepted." She took a deep breath and then went for it. "I believe I owe you an apology, as well. I perhaps have not been clear about where I stand. Parker and I have a long-standing relationship that is precious to me. It's not that I don't find you an attractive and charming man. It's that I am committed to the relationship I have with Parker." The statement, once given voice, gave her a clear focus.

"I respect your choice." His summer-sky-blue eyes met hers without wavering.

"Thank you."

Then his grin came soft and sweet, and he opened the bakery box, saying, "If you would go ahead and cut this cake, I could help y'all polish it off."

Tate Holloway not only could make an apology, he could sweep everyone along with him.

At that moment Vella and Willie Lee came to the door and spied the cake. Corrine was already leaning across the table, putting her finger in the icing.

"I have vanilla ice cream for those who want it," Marilee said.

They all sat round the kitchen table, where Tate regaled them with stories of being a boy in East Texas and eating homemade ice cream laced with overripe peaches salvaged after the pickers had finished with an orchard.

"We cut off the bad places. Mmm-mm . . . nothin' sweeter than overripe peaches. They're one secret to life." He bestowed his wonderful grin upon the children, casting a side glance to Marilee.

Marilee took a bite of rich chocolate and thought that she would not have any appetite for supper with Parker.

The television flickered black and white—the old movie channel which was showing the musical *42ⁿᵈ Street*—although Marilee was too busy obsessing about how Parker had not called her to be following the movie's story line. There really wasn't a story line, anyway, just excuses for dancing that was nice to watch.

When the telephone at her elbow rang, she jumped six inches, then snatched it up before it could ring again. The hands of the mantle clock read 10:55.

"Hello," she said, clicking off the television at the same time. Aunt Vella's snores continued with rhythm from the front bedroom.

"Hi, Marilee." It was Parker—at last.

"Hi." After all the waiting, she was now uncertain of what to say.

"I got your message, but I just got in. I've been out on calls all day."

"Oh. You must be pooped."

"I am."

A pause.

She plowed on into it. "I called because I was going to suggest we go to dinner. Aunt Vella was going to watch the children for a couple of hours." Explanation seemed in order. "We need to talk, Parker. We've kept getting interrupted, I know."

"Yeah. I'm sorry I didn't get back to you earlier."

"Oh, I understand. I know you're busy."

She wished she did not feel so annoyed at hearing him say yeah. Yeah had no sense of positiveness about it. She really needed some positiveness from Parker.

He said, "Yeah. It's been one of those weeks, I guess."

She clamped her mouth shut.

When she had not said anything for a full minute, he put forth, "Do you think you could get Vella to watch the children tomorrow night? We could go to Rodeo Rio's."

Whew. He had spoken slowly, but at least he had taken part.

"Vella has her Rose Club meeting. But I'll see if I can get Jenny. And let's go up to Michelina's. It's quieter there."

There she went, taking charge again. That was a major problem between them. But Parker simply did not think of things like atmosphere in a restaurant.

Main Street in Valentine shut up by nine o'clock on weeknights. Now, at eleven, a few flags that shop owners did not take in remained, seeming to have lost color in the lights from the old-fashioned pole lamps. Fred Grace, who had been balancing his accounts, wearily closed the door of his florist shop and got into his car and drove away, leaving a totally empty street.

Belinda, gazing out the open window of her apartment over the drugstore, watched Fred's car turn left at the Church Street stoplight. Behind her, from the bathroom, Lyle called "Ba-lin-da," in a tone that struck her as being very much like her father's. He wanted to know had she bought him any new shaving cream. She always insisted he shave before they went to bed. The one good thing she felt she had was her complexion.

Over at the newspaper, Tate turned off the light in his office. A security light in the rear of the big room cast a dim glow, illuminating his way to the front door. He stepped out onto the sidewalk and made certain the door had caught, then stood there for some seconds giving *The Valentine Voice* sign a look, before shoving his hands into his pockets and heading home.

A big red one-ton truck coming down Church rumbled to a stop at the red light at the intersection of Main. He saw the barrel-racing logo on the door and then recognized the blond woman jogger behind the wheel. He had learned her name was Leanne Overton. She turned right, heading out of town, and he crossed the street.

At the police station, light flowed out through the glass doors, and officer Dorothy Jean Riddle could be seen inside, standing at the reception desk.

Tate briefly considered stopping in and chatting. Coming back to his office and working had not been able to banish his blues. Maybe what he needed was some good conversation.

Deciding that the last thing he wanted was idle chitchat, he headed on up Church Street in long strides.

I am mad, God.

He had done the right thing in going over and apologizing to Marilee. It had sure been hard. He had thought that by now he would find apologizing a little easier, having been obligated to do it so many times in his life.

I let her go, God. I let go of this woman, but I don't seem to be able to let go of the desire for her.

He kicked at some pebbles as he crossed the alleyway running behind the row of Main Street buildings. He kept on walking and found his hands were fists in his pockets. He pulled them free and began to jog lightly.

Whatever is meant to be or not be with Marilee James is in Your hands. I give it all over to You, right along with all the other parts of my life.

There. He had done it, yes-sir. But there was no way he would like it.

The Valentine Voice

View from the Editor's Desk
by Tate Holloway

Next week, our good congressmen and women up at the state house take up a discussion about whether or not to change the law so that coffins can be purchased at places other than funeral homes. Although this idea has been kicked around for a long time in private circles, this is the first time it has made it to the state house. I predict this first official discussion will be quickly tossed aside; however, the idea is not going to go away.

As far as I know, every single person who dies is buried in a coffin purchased from the funeral home that handles the funeral. There is cremation, but discussion about that is better saved for another editorial. Now, one may call different funeral homes and shop around for price, however, the only place to get a coffin is at a funeral home. The point I am bringing forth is that what we have is a monopoly on coffin sales by funeral homes, and when there is a monopoly, higher prices are generally the result. It seems to me that corporations in this country have been broken up because of just such situations.

What if one could purchase a coffin at any number of stores? What if, say, one could shop for a coffin at Kmart or Wal-Mart? No doubt a person could save considerably on the cost of the coffin, maybe as much as half in comparison to private funeral home prices.

It is this editor's view that not only would one save quite a bit of money, but I suspect the selection would be greater should coffins be readily available in regular stores. Also, anyone who is forward-thinking would be able to watch for a sale, buy the coffin and keep it in their garage, right on hand, and save their loved ones a lot of expense and trouble when the inevitable time comes. I think this sounds like a good deal all the way around.

Send me your views on this subject, or any other matter, and I'll print them. Call up there to the state house and let your congressmen know how you feel. Participation is the key to good government.

On another note, I'm happy to report that the mayor is acting on Winston Valentine's idea of placing benches about town. He said he would use his limited power of purchasing as needed and would start with four benches. Now it has to be settled on where to put them, so call over to city hall and give them your preferences.

Don't forget, I'm handling the petition to get trees on Main Street. Come on by and see us. The coffee is always hot.

Charlotte was shocked by Tate's editorial. After she had proofed it, she had to question him about the wisdom of printing it. He thought it was fine, of course, just like he thought everything he wrote should be spotlighted with a beam from God.

"We're gonna get a lot of calls." She had to say it.

To which he replied, "Of course we are—and we're gonna sell more papers, too." He winked. That man was a caution, for sure.

"You have one hour to think about it. I'll pull it if you come to your senses." Adjusting her glasses and focusing on the computer screen, she set the piece in place in the layout, knowing he wasn't likely to change his mind.

Twenty minutes later, she picked up the phone and called over to Montgomery's Funeral Home to set up an appointment for making plans. She needed to be prepared for her mother and to take care of her own arrangements. God knew her mother wouldn't be able to handle anything, should Charlotte be the first to go.

Sixteen

Lives Unseen

Lindsey was back jogging this morning, if about five minutes late. Tate met him coming around the curve of Church and down the hill, as Tate jogged up. When he saw the figure coming toward him, Tate's chest seemed to quit burning and his legs to become iron and carry him along like a marathoner.

"Good mornin', Doc," Tate called gaily, his breath even.

"Mornin, Editor," Lindsey replied, certainly a little surprised at the sight of Tate continuing up the hill.

And possibly a little surly? Maybe missing a day's jogging caused Lindsey some discomfort.

Tate kept on jogging up the hill, halfway expecting Leanne Overton to come jogging along, or maybe riding her bike.

She did not appear, and he slowed, finally taking a glance over his shoulder to make certain he was out of sight of Lindsey. He stopped in the street and fought for breath. Lindsey had it easy, going down the hill every day.

Just then music blared out and about knocked him off his feet. It appeared to come from opposite directions—*The Star Spangled Banner* from his right and *Dixie* from his left. Winston Valentine and Everett Northrupt were raising their flags.

Tate, who had done a ten-month stint on an aircraft carrier during Viet Nam, stood straight in the middle of the street and joined the older men in patriotic salute of the flags and a new day.

Munro padded along beside his boy's sneakers through a door into a delicious-smelling place. The smell triggered the memory of the mornings he had spent with the man, when the man would give Munro warm biscuits or sometimes a sweet roll.

There was a long counter with glass that everyone was looking into, but Munro could not see. Finally he rose up, propped his paws on the glass and looked into the wondrous display, spying piles of what he knew instantly were the sweets the children sometimes shared with him. He wondered how he would let his lady know he wanted one. The next instant, however, a shriek aimed directly at him sent him down and ducking behind his boy's legs.

"Good Lord! He was up on the glass." And then, "I'm sure there are ordinances about dogs not being in places that serve food." This was said by a tall woman who stared down at Munro.

"Mun-ro goes with us ever-y-where," his boy explained.

"I'm sorry, I didn't think," his lady said. "Willie Lee . . . honey, you'll have to take Munro outside. Corrine, you and Willie Lee wait outside while I get Parker's cake ordered."

His boy dropped to hands and knees beside Munro and barked like a dog.

"Willie Lee, not now. Take Munro outside."

"I'll take 'em, Aunt Marilee. Come on, Willie Lee dog and Munro."

His boy continued on all fours right beside him to the door that his girl held open.

Munro, feeling uncertain and annoyed with the tall woman, cast her a reproachful glance and then followed behind the boy.

On the sidewalk, his girl stood near the building, while his boy got to his feet and walked to the curb. Munro felt a little torn. He liked to keep very close to his charges. Finally he went to the curb with the boy and sat where he could keep an eye on both children.

Seeing his boy, who was now hanging an arm around a pole, shade his eyes to look at a gleaming car passing slowly, Munro looked, too. A face behind the tinted window seemed to stare right at them. Munro, sensing a high curiosity from this human in the car, moved closer to the boy.

The car disappeared behind a parked truck, and the bell over the door of the store rang out.

"Here, y'all . . . sweets for my sweets. Here's a snickerdoodle for you, too, Munro."

Munro thought how wonderful it was that his lady had heard him thinking. The treat, however, caused him some difficulty in that his humans, who could eat while walking, headed on down the sidewalk, leaving Munro behind. He wolfed down the sweet food, took half a second to lick the crumbs from the sidewalk, then raced to catch up to his humans.

He reached them at the vehicle, where he looked up to see two strangers appear on the sidewalk. He saw that the gleaming car was parked right next to his lady's, and understood that these people had come from that car.

He looked at them, and he caught a whiff of familiar scent. He *knew* these humans. They had been with his former man, the one he had met in the bright-shining parking lot.

The woman, whose eyes were covered by black sunglasses, had her face and attention pointed at him.

"Come on, Mun-ro," his boy called.

Munro dove off the sidewalk and jumped through the door the boy held open. Immediately he rose up with his paws on the back of the front seat and looked through the windshield. The strangers remained on the sidewalk, side by side, with both their heads turned toward his lady's vehicle, which was backing out onto the street.

A shiver went down Munro's spine.

His boy rose up beside him and put a hand on his back. "Ma-ma . . . who are those peo-ple?"

"Who, honey?"

"That man and la-dy. They were look-ing at Munro. He does not like them, he told me."

"Oh, honey, they are strangers, and probably just lookin' at a lot of stuff. They didn't mean anything by looking at Munro. Now put on your seat belt and get Munro down on the seat with you."

"Mun-ro needs a seat-belt," his boy said.

Munro quickly got down and laid his chin on his boy's leg to show how good he was all on his own.

Tate, having just gotten the details of Deputy Lyle Midgett's apprehension early that morning of twelve suspected illegal aliens, parted with the young, proud deputy just outside the glass doors of the police department.

"The report'll be in this afternoon's edition," Tate promised. He would have to hurry to get it in there.

"I'll tell Belinda," the young man said eagerly, casting a wave and hotfooting it toward the drugstore.

Tate had heard rumors of wild passion between Belinda Blaine and Lyle Midgett; it was a concept somewhat hard to imagine, given the innocent apple-pie face of the deputy and the careless, dim demeanor of Miss Blaine. He recalled the cake mix boxes falling out of Bonita Embree's shopping bag. One never knew about the deep secrets of ordinary lives.

At that particular moment, he caught site of Marilee driving past. If she saw him, she did not indicate it but kept her eyes focused straight ahead out the windshield. He stood there on the sunlit sidewalk and watched the white Cherokee pass through the intersection, heading on to somewhere other than home, maybe to the IGA or the post office, or maybe out to Parker Lindsey's place.

Then he realized that he was still staring after her vehicle and pictured what he must look like, standing there on the sidewalk, drooling after a woman.

With a disgusted sigh, he stuffed his hands into the pockets of his khakis and turned to head on over to the newspaper, when his attention was caught by a man and woman who passed with swift steps.

No one walked that fast in Valentine without a good reason.

And these two were a type that stood out as much as the twelve Mexican men Deputy Midgett had come upon driving through town in a Ford Bronco. The man's blond hair was slicked back in the old-new style of the current sophisticate from L.A. or New York; he wore a crisp white shirt, colorful tie, dark-blue sport coat and pants, and shiny wing-tipped shoes and dark glasses. The woman wore a classy raw silk suit that neatly hugged her tight body, with the skirt a good three inches above her knees, and heels that made her legs go on forever. Her gleaming brown hair was carefully a mess, and her eyes were also hidden behind dark glasses. The pair seemed right out of a made-for-TV cops-and-robbers movie.

Tate watched over his shoulder and saw the two turn into the police station. Immediately sensing a story, he pivoted and followed. As he came through the double glass doors, the two were at the reception desk, telling Lori Wright that they wanted to speak to Sheriff Oakes.

"We're from Tell-In Technologies. He's expecting us," the tight-suited woman said.

Lori, as if blown back a step by the force emanating from the woman, said, "Just a minute," picked up the phone and punched the button for the sheriff's office ten feet away, door shut.

The man turned and looked curiously at Tate, who stuck out his hand. "Tate Holloway . . . I'm editor of *The Valentine Voice.* Can I be of any help?"

At that he found himself given a once-over by two pairs of sunglasses.

"I don't think so," the woman said and turned her back, dismissing him.

Tate, who as a journalist had plenty of experience hanging around in oddball fashion, just stood there.

The next moment the door of the sheriff's office opened, and Neville, a big man with a correctly creased uniform, filled the space. He nodded at the visitors, " 'Lo," and stood aside for them to pass through into his office. As he closed the door, his gaze met Tate's and he gave a nod that said, "I'll tell you later."

"Who are they?" Tate asked Lori when they were alone.

"That dead guy—Fayrene's first ex-husband—he worked for their company, I guess. Tell-In Technologies. He was some sort of computer genius or something."

"Hmmm. I imagine they're here about the money."

"I guess . . . but I don't know. Sheriff Oakes isn't one to talk around, and even if I knew what-all it was about, I couldn't be talkin' about it to the press without his okay," she added, as if feeling it should be stated.

The telephone on her desk rang, and in a manner indicating her complete readiness for any possible crisis, she snatched up the receiver, saying crisply, "Valentine P.D."

It apparently wasn't a crisis, though, as Tate saw her slim shoulders instantly relax. He left her helping the caller with what apparently required computer searching and wandered back to the drink machine.

He and Lori were the only ones in the rather crowded office space. Valentine only had four people on the police force: Lori, their receptionist during the day; Sheriff Neville Oakes, who had taken over when his father had retired; Deputy Lyle Midgett; and Deputy Dorothy Jean Riddle, a young woman fresh out of the police academy up in Oklahoma City, who had joined the force two months ago. Behind the wall the drink machine sat against was a single jail cell, used for rare overnight stays by drunks or disturbers of the peace. Any true criminals, who might show up once a year, were taken up to the county jail.

Tate punched the button for Orange Crush. It was in the can, not the bottle he preferred, but this was the first drink machine he had seen in years with Orange Crush in it. Orange Crush reminded him of when he was a boy.

Minutes later, the door to the sheriff's office opened, and the three people came out, Neville leading the way.

"Lori, get Fayrene on the phone, please."

"Yes-sir."

Lori immediately picked up the phone. The three people, the sheriff leaning his tall frame on the counter, waited. Tate looked at the out-of-towners, and they looked at him.

Lori spoke to Fayrene and then handed the receiver to the sheriff, who said, "Fayrene, honey, I've got those people from Tell-In here, and they'd like to talk to you. Are you feelin' up to it today?"

Tate's ears pricked at the sheriff's warm tone. He studied the man's face, and then he drank deeply from his Orange Crush. All sorts of things went on in people's lives.

"Okay, honey, thanks," the sheriff said into the phone. "We'll be over there directly."

Tate watched the three people leave through the glass double doors, then downed the last of his Orange Crush, dropped the can in the recycling barrel, and walked quickly back across the street to get Deputy Midgett's story written up in the next half hour before the deadline. He wouldn't want to disappoint the boy.

Belinda was on her knees, straightening magazines on the wide wooden shelf and reading any headline that caught her interest. It was the lull time in the morning, before the lunch crowd, which she dreaded. She kept thinking she could hang the closed sign on the door. Her father, who never came out from the pharmacy, wouldn't know. Unless someone telephoned him.

The bell above the door rang out, interrupting her. Well darn, was the first thing she thought. Knowing she was hidden by the comic book rack, she kept still, thinking maybe whoever it was would leave and she wouldn't have to wait on them. She was darn tired of waiting on people.

The footsteps and voices told her it was two people.

Just then she realized that they were arguing.

"I know that was the same dog." A woman said this. Belinda tried to place the voice but could not.

"There must be a lot of dogs like that in the world." This was a man's voice, and unfamiliar, too.

"How many dogs could there be that look exactly like that mutt Dan Kaplan picked up in the head office parking lot, and now right here, where he ended up?"

Dan Kaplan. Wasn't that the dead guy, Fayrene's first ex-husband? Belinda cocked her ear attentively.

"There have to be thousands of mutts like that in the world. And so what if it is the dog?"

"I don't know . . . but we still haven't found the chip, and we have found that dog."

"*Maybe* it's that dog. And we don't know we haven't found the chip. It's most likely in the car or the briefcase, and we'll get at those when Frank gets us the court order. At least it's all safe right now. Man, I've got a devil of a headache—I'm gonna get some Motrin and something to drink, if anyone shows up to wait on us in this hick place."

Belinda, who thought it was a hick place, too, took no offense, nor did she feel prodded to do anything about waiting on them. She peeked around the bottom of the revolving comic book rack and saw the slim, nylon-covered legs of a woman in dark pumps and the dark-trousered legs of a man in shiny loafers disappear behind one of the drugstore shelves.

She sat back on her heels, wondering about who the people were. Somebody to do with that dead guy. What dog?

The man called, "Hey, anyone back there?" and Belinda, opening a hairdo magazine, heard her daddy come out and wait on them.

A minute later her daddy called, "Baa-linda? Ba-linda, we got some people here who want somethin' to drink."

"All right, Daddy," Belinda said, pushing stiffly to her feet. Her legs were numb from sitting on them. She scrambled around to slip on her flip-flops.

The man and woman looked a little stunned to see her come out from behind the magazine rack. They ordered Cokes to go and didn't even sit while she made them. They threw the money on the counter, where she had to pick it up. She watched them walk out, and she thought of the looks the two had exchanged upon sight of her.

Well, she thought as she edged herself onto the stool and opened the hairdo magazine again, she would get it out of Lyle that night who these people were, and what it was all about with that Dan Kaplan and some chip and a dog.

Vella missed her home. She couldn't say she missed Perry. Maybe she missed who Perry used to be. Maybe that was part of old age— missing everything as it used to be. It had just seemed to slip away so fast. All those years. Where had they gone?

She pulled her champagne-colored Crown Victoria into the drive-way, shut off the ignition and looked around to see any neighbors who might witness her arrival. There was not a sign of anyone, as usual during a weekday morning in the old neighborhood. Which did not mean that Doris Northrupt wasn't peeking out from behind her win-dow curtains. Likely nosy Mildred down at Winston Valentine's house was, too, unless she was eating or watching television.

Her purse strap over her arm pressed to her middle, she walked quickly across the side yard around to the back to her rose garden, where she slowed to a stroll, enjoying whiffs of fragrance.

Pulling a pair of all-purpose scissors out of her purse, she cut blos-soms for a bouquet. Again and again she reverently touched the leaves and sniffed the wide blooms. When she was full of the scent, she walked slowly to the house and let herself in the kitchen door that had not been locked in the forty years she had lived there.

She put her bouquet in a mason jar of water and sat it on the table and admired it. Then, noticing food stuck to the table, she got a wet cloth and scrubbed it clean. Next she cleaned the coffeemaker and made a fresh pot.

The window drew her, and she looked out toward the Valentine home, wishing for Winston to come across the pasture. He had visited her at Marilee's, but they had not been alone since she had left home.

She washed the cup and glasses left in the sink and cleaned the counter that had food and coffee stains on it. She went on to wipe over everything and sweep the floor. She looked toward the Valentine house again, then sat at the table to drink her coffee. Halfway through it, she began sobbing. The suddenness and depth of the sobbing frightened her. When she managed to stop, she wiped her eyes and blew her nose.

Then, swept along on a wave of fresh desperation, she took up the telephone and dialed Winston's phone number.

Winston himself answered the phone. *A sign from God.*

"Winston, I'm over here in my kitchen. Could you come down? I'd like to talk."

After what seemed a very long moment, during which Vella worried what Winston must think, he said he would come right away.

Fairly flying around the kitchen, she got Winston's favorite blue mug from the cupboard, wiped it shining, then poured it full of coffee and set it on the table along with sugar and cream. With the roses and her cup there, the table looked inviting.

She glanced out the window and saw Winston coming across the small fenced pasture between their houses at an encouraging rate, even with his cane.

A man hurrying to her. Tears sprang to her eyes at the wondrous sight. She whirled and, with the heart of a young woman, she raced to the back door and opened it before Winston had time to make it up the few stairs.

"Are you all right, Vella? You didn't sound very good on the phone." His expression was filled with concern as he came stiffly up the stairs.

"No . . . no, I'm not all right." The words poured forth, and then she burst into tears and had to avert her face in shame.

Winston, whose ripe age and experience with women had accustomed him to tears, reached out, drew Vella against him and let her cry into his shirt. She leaned on him a bit, and he had to balance with his cane, and after about a minute, he began to worry that Vella might push him over. He didn't want to break a hip here in her kitchen and have the paramedics have to show up and everyone know he was alone with her.

"Vella . . . here, gal. Sit down and drink some coffee. That will help you feel better."

He got her sat down, and then he sat himself down and felt greatly relieved at having averted breaking his hip. Old age was a pain in the neck, as well as the hips, elbows and knees.

He poured coffee for both of them. After a few sniffs, Vella took up her coffee cup with both hands and drank. Winston drank his, and for a couple of minutes there was silence, broken only by the hum of the refrigerator and Vella's sniffs.

"This is really good coffee," Winston told her. "I've missed it."

Instantly he realized he had said a wrong thing, because she began to cry again. He decided to retreat into the safety of silence, drink his coffee, and wait her out and hope she stopped crying before Perry came home.

Keeping silent did the trick. Before he had finished his coffee, she managed to get ahold of herself and, as so many people did, slipped from sadness into anger.

"Oh, Winston," she said with some vehemence. "I miss my house, and I miss my roses."

Winston nodded, biting back the comment that she should just come home. There was no telling what might set her off again.

"I feel so foolish . . . leavin' my house and Perry like I have. At my age, Winston."

Winston nodded again.

"It's just that . . . well, I'm all confused. I don't seem to fit. It's like all the rules have changed . . . like there just aren't any rules today."

Winston said, "Things are sure different," and nodded.

"My heaven . . . even my menopause was later than most."

Ohmygod. He sure hoped she did not continue on that subject.

She didn't. She snatched up a magazine from a stack atop the microwave oven and shook it at him. "Just look at all the people they are puttin' on the cover of *Modern Maturity* these days. Movie stars. Do we all have to compare ourselves to movie stars? Do we have to have advice from people who get their faces and Lord knows what-all lifted and tucked? I can't look at the thing anymore."

With that, she tossed the magazine to the floor with force enough to send it sliding through to the dining room. Winston laid his hand firmly on the table to hold the cloth if need be.

"I look in the mirror and there's this old woman," Vella said with passion, "but I don't feel that in my heart."

Winston watched her press her hand in the middle of her very ample bosom. Something stirred inside him, a natural curiosity to see her lovely bosom. He was pleasantly surprised at his reaction.

"Perry has not touched me in so long, Winston."

Winston, who definitely did not want to go any deeper with that, said quickly, "You are a lively woman, Vella. And you are not so old. I'm old," he added, heavily.

"I'm sixty-six."

"You are still in the youth of old age," he volunteered, thinking of how he was in the old age of old age.

Vella said, "I don't look forty . . . but I don't feel sixty-six."

"You are a handsome woman, Vella."

She regarded him in a way that made him feel uncertain.

"At my age," she said, "my mother was a really old woman and didn't do anything but sit on her porch and talk about eating. She talked about what she had for breakfast and what she was going to have for lunch and for supper. Minnie Oakes talks about that, and what she plans to watch each night on television. She marks it all down in the *TV Guide*.

"The only other woman my age that I think may have my same feelings is Odessa Collier, and she's . . . well, it is understandable for Odessa to be a little wild and loose, because she has always been wild and loose. She's artistic," she added pensively.

"You're artistic," Winston volunteered. "Just look at how you grow your roses and then arrange them." He gestured at those in the mason jar.

Vella looked at the roses. Then, feeling an urge to move, she got to her feet and stepped to the counter. She now wished she had not started pouring her heart out to Winston. But since she had started, she might as well continue. She had so thoroughly tossed everything to the wind, what did she have to lose?

"I am not like Odessa. I'm just not like anyone, and being my age is not like I had imagined at all. I don't know what to do with myself. I still want to do so many things. I still *feel* so many things."

She sighed then, a sigh that hovered between exhaustion and desperation. She felt herself in a precarious balance between sobs and screams.

Winston got to his feet. He had begun to worry a little about Mildred coming down to check on him, and his bones pained him when he sat too long. He thought it time to look for an exit.

"It's a good thing to feel, Vella. It proves you are alive. And I guess being a little mixed up is a big part of livin'. It is better than the alternative," he added.

This was a phrase he had been telling himself a lot of late. He wasn't believing it so much anymore, though. Death had come to look pleasant, an end to many aches and pains and annoyances.

Vella lifted her head and looked at him. He was startled to find it was like she was aiming at him, and the very next moment she moved right up against him and kissed him. He saw it coming and couldn't do anything but stand there and take it.

"Thank you, Winston, for your kindness to me," she whispered with her lips still brushing his.

Her kiss had not been a thank-you sort of kiss. It had been an invitation, and she remained against him, looking him in the eye with that invitation that kindled a surprising feeling inside him.

He further astonished himself by encircling her with his free arm and kissing her with a passion he had not known he could summon. He wasn't dead yet.

The sun was far to the west when Vella turned the Crown Victoria into the alley at a high enough rate of speed to cause the front to bounce precariously, but without slowing, she shot on past behind the police station and came to a jarring halt at the back door to the drugstore, right behind Perry's dusty Lincoln parked in his space. She jammed the shift lever into park, left the engine running and propelled herself out from behind the steering wheel.

Rounding the hood, she stalked to the rear passenger door and pulled out two suitcases. She started dragging them on their wheels; they fell over on the gravel, and she didn't bother to right them, but dragged them on their side, until she got to the door, where she hefted them inside, making a lot of commotion in the endeavor. She was, after all, a sixty-six-year-old woman throwing around suitcases that each weighed half as much as she did. The thought brought her strength, and she threw the second case halfway across the storeroom.

Belinda appeared in the doorway from the front. "What in the world . . . ?"

"I'm bringin' your daddy's things."

"You are *what?*" Belinda took a wide stance and put her arms akimbo on her hips, as if to block Vella's entry.

"I brought your daddy's things from home," said Vella, who had righted both cases and started tugging them forward. "He is down here from dawn to dusk anyway, he might as well move on down here. I'm movin' back home."

"You *aren't!*"

"Yes, I am." Vella was heading for the rear pharmacy door. She yanked it open. "I made that home for forty years. I worked down here, too, but I'm choosing the house. Your father already chose this pharmacy years ago. Perry!"

There wasn't any need to yell his name. Her husband was struggling to get himself out of his old chair. His eyes were wide, and his mouth open.

"What in the world are you doin' now, Vella?"

"You heard me, I'm sure. Here are your things." She did her best to swing the cases forward, and in the process she almost toppled herself and had to grab the doorjamb to keep from falling. Breathing deeply, feeling her heavy breasts move up and down, she added in a more controlled manner, "I'm movin' back home. You can stay here. I'm seein' Jaydee about a formal separation."

She turned and headed out of the store, and Belinda followed, saying hysterically, "Mama . . . don't do this. Don't do this to me . . . leavin' Daddy with me!"

Vella was listening for Perry, God help her, but she listened in vain, because her husband did not call to her.

With her vision blurred by tears, she got back into her car and headed on down the alleyway, bumping out on the other end.

Seventeen

Situations Unfolding

"**M**arilee?" Vella called out as she entered the house and tossed her purse onto the couch. She breathed deeply, feeling depleted and therefore totally calm.

The house was warm. Marilee had not put on the air-conditioning. The windows were wide, and late-afternoon sunshine shone across the porch and through the front screens.

"In here."

Vella followed the sound of the voice to the back bedroom, where she found Marilee sitting on the foot of the bed, which was covered with clothing and shoe boxes and various other paraphernalia. In fact, the entire room was covered with a wide variety of paraphernalia.

"It looks like a tornado hit this room."

"What? Oh." Marilee, who had been reading something, looked around as if seeing for the first time. "I was picking out a dress to wear tonight, and then I got to lookin' for the box with my birthday stuff . . . tryin' to find the candle for Parker's birthday cake on Saturday. Pretty soon I had so much out, it seemed a good time to clean thoroughly." She paused. "I had a keep pile and a give-away pile, but now I don't remember which is which."

"You have a certain candle for Parker's cake?" Vella shifted a pile of clothing to make room on the corner of the bed, sat and slipped off her shoes. Her big toes were becoming arthritic and suffered in shoes, although it struck her now that this was the first she had thought of it all day. That seemed a good sign of how alive she felt.

"The number four," Marilee was saying. "I've been savin' the four and just buy a new number to go after it. I used it on my cake last year. We blow it out real quick, so it's like new." She twisted and reached a hand to the windowsill, bringing back the candle to show Vella. "See . . . just a little bit melted there."

"It looks fine." Vella thought that her niece could sure be thrifty.

The two sat there a minute, as if both out of breath. Vella found the room dim after the afternoon brightness outside. Golden light beams filtered through the trees and the window screen. A faint breeze brought the sound of the children's voices in the backyard and gently stirred the drapes. Watching the drapes move, Vella thought, not for the first time, that her niece showed a marked fondness for a forties look; the draperies were of a large flower pattern similar to one Vella herself had in her living room way back when. She did not care for it now.

Perhaps for a while the young got old, and then the old got young again.

Her gaze came around to her niece, as if to see herself at that age. She then noticed Marilee's disheveled appearance.

"Have you been crying?"

Vella had long ago given up expecting Marilee to be truly happy. It was a set of mind that Vella, too, had struggled with when in her forties. Maybe she was just now coming out of it, she thought.

"Oh—" Marilee wiped her eyes "—yes, and it's silly really. I just got to reading some of Stuart's old letters." She fluttered one and indicated the shoe box filled with folded papers and envelopes. "I kept them . . . heaven knows why, but I did. I just now found the box in the back of the closet."

She looked at the letter she held, and Vella did, too, recalling the tall, handsome man who had swept her niece off her feet, and for whom Vella had never cared. She had known Stuart James instantly as a childish philanderer, without an ounce of giving anywhere in him.

"We wrote a lot of letters to each other, even when we were together. We were both writers." Her niece smiled wanly, looking in that instant so very young.

"Of course you kept them. We like to go back over things like that so we can cry all over again." Then, more gently, "They are memories that are important. They deserve to be kept."

Vella thought perhaps she was speaking to herself. She automatically reached to take out a letter.

"You can't read them!" Marilee pushed Vella's hand away and gathered the box to her lap.

"Oh, I wasn't thinking. Of course I can't read them." She had simply been following curiosity, with the box right in front of her. Her escapade of the afternoon had her thoughts all awry.

"Well, some of them you could read." Marilee's expression was apologetic. "Most of them, in fact. We did a lot of discussing of theories in general, like love in general. Most of them were written when I was in college and indulging in an intellectual phase that is so far removed from reality. I was profoundly impressed with Stuart's mind. I guess I thought he knew everything there was to know about life. He'd seen so much, done so much traveling to exotic places, and he presented such a wise philosophical figure. He was like a guru. He loved that, gathering all of us admiring students around him. Look, here's a picture of our little gang."

"Where are you?" Vella pushed her glasses down her nose to sharpen the bifocals.

"I'm . . . this one, here's my head."

"Oh." She recognized her niece's face, in the rear of the picture and half-hidden by hair. Marilee in those days had been quite introverted, hiding her feelings and her entire self, if possible. She still hid her true self to a great extent, Vella thought.

"Reading the letters now, I see that I put a lot of intentions into them that were never there. I built Stuart and our love up into some great fantasy that it never was." She paused. "Maybe I didn't love him as the man he was but as a fantasy of him in my mind. Then, when he was the human man he was, I got mad at him for disappointing me."

"Oh, everyone does that when they fall in love," Vella said. "None of us would ever get married if we saw our lover as human. We have to be blinded by love and then grow to accept the reality. By the time we do, we're a little more used to it."

What had happened to her being used to Perry? Maybe she simply could only take so much reality of him.

"Well, it was a great disappointment when I could suddenly see. Stuart didn't want a wife. He wanted a perpetual cheerleader."

"Don't most men?"

Marilee laughed at that. "Yes, but most do grow out of it by the age of forty."

"Hmm, maybe." Vella, whose spirits were sinking by the minute, thought that it would be nice if Perry wanted anything more than someone to mop up after him.

Marilee stuffed the letters back in the shoe box and put the lid on it. "I'll need to go ahead and get rid of these. I doubt Parker would take very kindly to me hauling my former husband's letter along into our marriage."

"You're goin' to marry Parker, then?"

"Yes. And here's the dress I'm going to wear tonight to tell him. What do you think?"

"It's lovely."

Holding the dress before her, another one that reminded Vella of the forties, Marilee observed herself in the mirror. "I've been rude and thoughtless to Parker," she said to her aunt and to herself. "Keeping him waiting all this time. I didn't mean to be.... I just don't want to make another mistake." Marilee's eyes were dark and had that bit of worry that seemed always to be there.

"Oh, honey ... you are human, and the plain fact is humans make mistakes all over the place. Don't be so hard on yourself, and don't expect to escape making mistakes. Every mistake makes us smarter."

Marilee turned to face Vella and said, "We won't be getting married immediately. We'll have to make plans, get Parker's house ready for us ... but you can come with us, Aunt Vella. There'll always be room for you with us."

Vella had not realized that she had fallen into a thoughtful state, which Marilee had read as pensive. "Oh, honey, how very thoughtful of you." She supposed she *had* been pensive, thinking of living alone. "But I won't need to go live with you and Parker. I'm going back home."

Marilee looked startled. Then she smiled broadly. "Oh, Aunt Vella, I'm so glad. I know you've been disappointed in Uncle Perry, but you two can work this out. You should be together."

"Well, I don't know about shoulds," Vella said, touched by her niece's emotion and sorry to disappoint, "but I know what I had to do. I went to see Jaydee Mayhall and started separation proceedings. I've moved Perry out of the house, so that I can move back in."

Marilee, in a stunned state, followed her aunt into the kitchen, where Aunt Vella began opening cabinet doors and asked, "Do you have anything planned for supper for the children?"

When Marilee said she did not, Aunt Vella suggested macaroni and cheese. "I can eat with the children before I go to the Rose Club meeting, and then all Jenny has to do is get them bathed. I'll be moving back home tonight, too."

"I'm going to bathe them before I go." Marilee was following her aunt around the kitchen. "Have you really thrown Uncle Perry out? How can you do that?"

Vella said, yes, she had thrown Perry out, and it had been easy. "I just packed him two suitcases. He really doesn't have much. He can get all his televisions whenever he wants."

"How can you throw away forty-five years of marriage? Aren't they worth anything?" Marilee wanted to know.

To which Aunt Vella replied, "Yes, they are worth a lot, and I'm not throwing them away. I am honoring those years. They have made me the woman I am ... a woman who isn't so stupid that she wants to spend her remaining, relatively few, years being tied to an unfeeling dolt. Here, grate this cheese."

Marilee grated cheese and chopped up carrot and celery sticks, all the while saying in ten different ways: "Are you sure, Aunt Vella? Are you really sure? Do you not care at all for Uncle Perry anymore?"

Vella replied, "Yes, I do care for Perry. I wish him well. I want him to be happy. But the first person I love is myself. God gave me a life, and it is my responsibility to honor and live this life. My husband no longer takes part in our marriage. He doesn't even see me, so I see no reason to hang around and be ignored. I cannot live with that level of indifference.

"I also love my house," she added. "I picked it out, I decorated, I've kept it all these years, and I see no reason to give it up just because I've given up my marriage."

All of her aunt's confident explanations dried up Marilee's questions. A heavy sadness at the situation and at life in general settled over her. It appeared in that moment that life was a most uncertain and lonely business.

When Marilee gave voice to this depressing sentiment, Aunt Vella said, "Of course it is. Those who think differently are fooling themselves with unreasonable expectations. There are no hard and fast answers anywhere, except to keep moving on and trusting God to guide, trusting Him to be there with you, as well, through both wise and foolish actions."

Marilee could not seem to grasp this concept. Foolishness seemed too risky to trust even to God. When she stated this opinion, Aunt Vella said, "Why, honey, foolishness is the human condition and exactly what God handles best."

The IGA was a major place of running into neighbors and holding conversations. Tate wasn't much in the mood for holding conversations, but he didn't seem to have a choice in the matter.

Minnie Oakes came up to him in the produce aisle and told him in no uncertain terms that she would not at all appreciate walking through Wal-Mart and coming upon a bunch of caskets. "If they did stock them, I'd expect a separate room, with the door closed. That's my opinion, for the paper."

"Yes, ma'am. Thank you, Miss Minnie."

Tate noted her comments on an index card. She gave a quick nod and went off toward the bread, her tiny back ramrod straight. He turned to choosing bananas and some very aromatic nectarines, laid the bags gently in his cart and pushed on to the meat section. He hated grocery shopping.

The store was having a beef sale, and Norm Stidham had a cart full of steaks and rump roasts. "Got a passel of grandkids comin' in this weekend," Norm explained, then gave the long list of names. "Oh, and I been meanin' to give you my opinion on this casket monopoly, Editor. I think maybe we ought to have a tax and all funerals paid for by the government. Just my opinion. Do you know how to spell my name?"

Over in the condiments aisle Tate ran into the mayor's wife, Kaye Upchurch, who asked his choice for the appetizer for Saturday night's dinner party: cold artichokes or green bean vinaigrette.

"Green bean vinaigrette," he said.

"Oh, really? I was leaning toward the artichokes."

"Then artichokes are wonderful." He did not know how he would stand several hours of this woman's demanding company, on top of his disappointment over Marilee not being with him.

"Oh, and, Tate, please don't bring up the subject of coffins at the party."

"No, ma'am, I won't."

"And if anyone else brings it up, change the subject."

"Yes, ma'am." His mother had taught him well.

She gave him a quick nod and went on her way. With a deep breath, he lifted a bottle of ketchup off the shelf, then headed on around to the next aisle. As he went around the corner, he almost bumped right into an oncoming cart. It was Leanne Overton, and the first time he had seen her in other than her jogging clothes. She wore a crisp white shirt and turquoise jeans that hugged her slim shape in about the same manner as her spandex pants.

"Excuse me," he said. "They need traffic lights in here."

"Yes . . ." She smiled and headed on.

For an instant Tate thought of engaging her in further conversation. Perhaps he should open himself to other women, since he had given up on Marilee James.

He had no heart for the idea, though, and pushed on to the end of the aisle and the tea section, where he stood gazing at the array of colorful boxes of herb tea. His low mood might profit from his cutting his caffeine intake.

"Marilee is still havin' his party. Juice said that no one has canceled the order for steaks."

Tate's ears immediately pricked.

"Maybe Leanne had an emergency with one of her horses," said another voice. "Her horses have had problems lately."

The vaguely familiar voices were coming from around the corner of the aisle, from women hidden from Tate's view by the bulging end shelves of Little Debbie snack cakes and cookies.

"I imagine they have," said the first voice in a knowing fashion. "But what kind of emergency could it have been that she was comin' out of Parker's driveway at four o'clock in the mornin'?"

Whoa, buddy. Tate became very still.

The voice continued, "I had brought Juice to work, since his Jeep was in the shop, and I was goin' home to get some sleep before I had to get to the post office. Tuesday's my late mornin'. I should get a whole day off, but since Alice has been down in her back, I can't get that."

It was Julia Jenkins-Tinsley, postmistress and Juice's wife, speaking. She came pushing her cart around the corner and down the aisle, followed by a rather plump woman who Tate recognized although could not name.

After a quick glance, he focused hard on the teas, more or less trying to blend in.

"Well, I've seen 'em joggin' together in the mornin's. They come along about the time Everett raises his flag." Ah—he placed the woman now—Doris Everett. "They don't come together . . . they've been meeting up there where the path comes out in the field the other side of Blaines'. Sometimes Leanne rides her bike . . . and all the way in from MacCoys', too. That's maybe five miles. Usually when she comes back she stops at Winston's, and Charlene'll get her and take her back, or I guess she goes down to the beauty shop and has Charlene get her from there."

Tate, still focusing on the array of tea, saw in his mind's eye Lindsey and the shapely Miss Overton jogging along together.

"She come out of his driveway without her headlights on," the postmistress said. "Maybe she thought she couldn't be seen, but there's that pole lamp right there at the edge of the parking lot for the vet clinic. I mean, really, plain as day. Oh, shoot, I got to go on back and get biscuits. Mama's comin' to supper this Sunday, and she just loves those Grands biscuits."

Tate was again in the aisle alone. He snatched a box of Lipton loose-leaf black-and-orange pekoe and dropped it into his cart. He liked Grands biscuits, too, but he kept himself from continuing to eavesdrop on a conversation he could not truly qualify as having journalistic merit.

* * *

What was he going to do about this thing?

He hardly knew when he had made it to his kitchen, he was stewing so hard over the situation.

Tuesday morning, the morning Lindsey had not shown up jogging, Leanne Overton had been coming out of Parker Lindsey's driveway.

He set his grocery bags on the counter and put the kettle of water on the stove over the flame.

Leanne Overton had not shown up that morning, either.

Of course, the two had been jogging together a lot, but not every morning. Leanne Overton generally did three mornings a week, while the Doc did all five . . . until that Tuesday.

He had seen Leanne Overton's truck heading in the direction of the veterinary clinic last night. She could have been going anywhere, though. He had no way of knowing the truth. What he had heard at the grocery store was idle gossip, not fact.

Yet Julia Jenkins-Tinsley had been speaking of a firsthand sighting.

I am committed to my relationship with Parker.

There was no way he could go to her and tell her about this, he thought, spooning tea leaves into the china pot without even counting. It dawned on him that he had about five spoonfuls in the pot, and he had to empty it out and start over.

It wasn't his business. Except that he cared for her. Somehow her welfare did seem his business. Heat swept over him as he thought about Lindsey messing around on her.

Then it came to him: she had said that about her commitment to Lindsey yesterday evening. He had not spoken to her today at all. Maybe she and Parker had broken up since then.

He got rather excited about the idea for a couple of seconds. But he hadn't heard anything about it, and surely he would have heard if they had broken up. People would have been talking about it already.

Still, it was possible it had happened late in the day, and he might not have heard. He didn't hear every single thing that went on.

If Lindsey expected to keep his liaison secret, he was the biggest kind of fool.

He had to find out about this thing. That was all, just find out where Marilee stood.

Quickly, he fixed up a pitcher of tea with lemon and sugar, and ice cubes clinking around, and went across the backyard into the deepening evening shadows of the trees and through the gate.

* * *

Marilee opened the door for him. Her eyes popped wide, as if she were surprised. "Oh, hello. Come in."

Tate himself was pretty surprised. Marilee was dressed in a black slinky dinner dress, a silver bracelet on her wrist, a silver earring in one ear, and she was trying to get the other earring in the other ear.

He gave a whistle. "Goin' somewhere?"

"Yes." Her cheeks turned pink, and her gaze flitted away. "Parker and I are going out." She strode into the kitchen. "I'm sorry I don't have time to chat."

He followed, going to the refrigerator and shoving the pitcher of tea inside, which was the only thing he could think of to do at the moment.

"You don't have to keep bringing me iced tea. I'm sure you've repaid me a number of times over."

"Don't you like it?" he demanded, feeling suddenly quite annoyed.

"Oh, yes. I do, very much, it's just that I don't want you to feel obligated."

"I don't do things out of obligation." He realized his anger was out of all proportion.

"Here . . . let me help you with that." He motioned toward her earring, which she still had not gotten into her ear.

"That's okay . . . I'll go to the mirror."

"Just let me have it." He fairly snatched the earring out of her hand.

Her eyes met his, and then she leaned her head over and pulled back her hair. He focused on the pierced hole in her lobe. Her flesh was warm to his fingers.

She said, "Aunt Vella has moved back home."

He saw her blink rapidly. He couldn't see well enough to get the wire through the hole. "Let's move over to the light." He fairly dragged her by the ear. "So Vella and Perry are gettin' back together?"

"No . . . Aunt Vella threw Uncle Perry out."

"Well, dogged." He got the wire through the hole and let go of her ear. "It will be all right with Vella and Perry. Things do work out."

She gazed at him. "I don't know. I hope so."

They stood there gazing at each other. He wanted to haul her against him and kiss her senseless. Kiss her and show her what she needed.

The sound of the front door opening broke their gaze. Marilee stepped around him and away into the living room. He heard her voice welcoming Lindsey.

Tate stepped into the doorway to the living room, and at that same moment the telephone rang, drawing Marilee away from Lindsey's embrace.

Tate looked full into Lindsey's face. The veterinarian frowned at him.

"So you and Marilee are goin' out to dinner," Tate said, coming forward.

"Yes."

"That's nice." Should he bring up what he had heard?

"Yes, it is. What are you doin' here?"

"I brought some iced tea. Marilee likes my iced tea." He wanted to knock the guy's teeth down his throat.

Something in Marilee's voice had them both looking over at her.

"Yes . . . thank you for calling, Ruth. I hope Jenny gets feeling better very quickly."

She replaced the receiver. "Jenny's sick with the stomach flu. Just started throwing up twenty minutes ago. She can't come baby-sit."

She sighed, and Lindsey said, "Oh, great," in thorough disgust.

"What about Vella?" Lindsey wanted to know.

"She's already gone to get Winston. It's her Rose Club night." Then she added, "And she's moved her things back home. I don't want to disturb her."

Lindsey made an irritated sound this time.

"We can stay by ourselves," Corrine said. She had come silently, as always, to the hallway and stood there looking small but brave. "I can look after Willie Lee."

"Oh, honey, I know you can look after you and Willie Lee, but I wouldn't want you here by yourself." Marilee went to Corrine and pressed the small girl against her legs.

"You can give her my mobile number, Marilee. She could get us if she needed us."

"No."

Lindsey was a fool to think she would go for that. Not Marilee, who did not care to let the children out of her sight.

"I'll stay with the kids." Tate spoke before he even knew he was going to. Was he nuts? Why should he help Lindsey?

Marilee and Lindsey looked at Tate. Marilee's eyes were wide, Lindsey's searching.

"I think I qualify as an adult. I'll stay with them. What do ya' say, missy? You and me can handle it, okay?"

Corrine grinned at him, tentatively, and then her grin widened as Marilee looked down at her. She nodded at Marilee.

"Well, I guess that would work." Marilee spoke slowly, still uncertain. "If you're sure you wouldn't mind? You don't have plans?"

Her eyes, smoky and beautiful, were on Tate.

"No, I don't have plans. You two go on with yours." He did what he felt was required of him.

She had to make certain with Willie Lee, before agreeing to the plan. For two minutes Tate stood five feet away from Lindsey.

"You've been a busy man lately, I hear," Tate said.

"Yeah . . . a little bit."

No time to go further with it, because Marilee came back and got her purse, at the same time thanking him all over the place. She kissed the children good-night, and walked out the door on Lindsey's guiding hand, and Tate kept all of his words inside himself. He had made a pledge to God to let go.

Marilee and Lindsey returned three hours later. She had an engagement ring on her finger. Tate congratulated the couple and kissed the bride-to-be on the lips, but quickly.

He did not leave, but stood there while Marilee went to the bedroom to check her children, who were now asleep.

The instant she was out of the room, he said in a low voice, "I trust that this engagement means you have cut off your fling with Leanne Overton."

Lindsey about jumped out of his skin. "What do you mean?" he said in an equally low voice.

"You have a small problem in that Leanne was seen driving away from your house at four o'clock in the morning." He let that sit there while Lindsey stared at him about like a deer caught in headlights. "Marilee is bound to hear about it sooner or later, so I would suggest you be the one to tell her."

"There isn't anything between me and Leanne."

"Tell Marilee, don't tell me."

Marilee came back into the room. "Thank you, Tate, for watching them."

She was relaxed now, and pleased, and this pleased him. "It was my pleasure. I got to be a kid again for a while."

He would have kissed her again, but something held him back, some unnamed, fearful caution.

Then he shook Lindsey's hand, squeezing it as hard as possible.

It was not his place to tell people how to live their lives. Each one had to find his own way. He hated that. He was reminded how Lucille used to tell him that he liked to think he knew everything, that he thought he was God. He had learned a thing or two since then, one major lesson being that people did not like tale bearers. Marilee would not thank him for telling her the truth about this man she had decided to marry.

Eighteen

Rough Day

Marilee just about put her eye out with her engagement ring the following morning, when she awoke and flopped her hand backward over her eyes to shield them from the fresh light of morning spilling through the windows. She had forgotten to pull the shades.

Extending her hand, she squinted at the ring. The diamond caught the light, blinding her further, and she dropped her hand to the bed, thinking, Ohmygod.

She had been stunned when Parker had produced the ring from his jacket pocket and proceeded to put it on her finger. It had been his mother's. It looked like something his mother would wear. It slid all around on Marilee's slender finger.

Pushing herself out of bed, she shuffled her way to the kitchen, where Corrine had a pot of coffee ready and waiting.

"Bless you, my child," Marilee said, kissing Corrine, who sat at the table, already dressed and reading a book.

Marilee sipped the dark coffee from the mug she held with both hands. Where was Willie Lee?

"He's out in the garden, moving worms," Corrine informed her.

"Moving worms?"

Corrine nodded. "He wants to make certain there are lots of worms around his flowers."

Marilee looked out the window to see her small son, his pale hair spiked in all directions—a haircut was in order—digging with a trowel in the garden, in a very concentrated manner. Munro lay beside him, his head upon his paws, watching.

Just then the front door opened. "Hey . . . anybody awake?"

Parker? Well, my goodness.

"In here." Her voice came out a croak, as his footsteps came jogging through the house.

There he was, fully awake and jogging lightly into the room, wearing a muscle shirt that showed his tanned, hard frame, shorts and bright-white running shoes.

"Mornin', beautiful." He smiled and kissed her cheek, with barely a pause in jogging.

"Good morning." Her voice was still croaking like a frog. She hated chipper people first thing in the morning. Hadn't she told Parker that sometime in the past years? Surely he would have figured it out by now.

"Just thought I would drop by." Obviously. He was jogging in place now. "What do you think about me and your aunt gettin' married?" he said to Corrine.

Corrine's eyes shifted uncertainly to Marilee.

"I haven't talked to them about it yet, Parker. I just got up, and they were asleep when we came in last night."

Parker's jogging was causing the floor to vibrate. She had the sudden thought to grab the iron frying pan off the stove and smack him to get him to stop.

"Oh." He kissed her cheek again. "I'll call you later." He turned and jogged away. Marilee's eyes lingered on his hard-muscled back until he disappeared. His shoes thudded through the house, and then the front door shut with a near slam.

Marilee drank another good swallow of the thick black coffee, and then she showed Corrine her engagement ring. Corrine said it was pretty.

Marilee couldn't figure out what else she could expect Corrine to say.

She poured her coffee cup full to the brim and took it into the bathroom and a shower. Peace and quiet and aloneness for twenty minutes.

Parker was a morning person and a jogger; she was *not* a morning person, and definitely *not* a jogger. They were going to have to make some ground rules first thing.

Tate, making a good pace up from Main Street, saw a jogger come from right on Porter Street. Lindsey . . . from the direction of Marilee's cottage. Well now.

Tate slowed as he entered the intersection at the same time as the veterinarian.

"Stopped by to see Marilee this mornin'," Lindsey told him.

The man had at last begun to protect his investment, Tate thought. Giving a nod, he kept going, jogging up the hill of Church Street. He had liked participating in the raising of the flags and thought he would keep it up.

Parker, who was mildly surprised to see the editor bypass his own house and head on up the curving hill of Church Street at a fair rate of speed, took note that thus far the road coming down was empty. Relief swept him, followed by determination that gave him a fresh burst of speed, sending him along Porter and in the direction of home. He had started out early in order to miss running into Leanne. He didn't want to risk her catching up with him now.

They sat on the couch in a line: Corrine, Willie Lee and Munro. None of their feet touched the floor, and three pairs of eyes regarded Marilee, Willie Lee's large and blue behind his thick glasses, Corrine's black as drops of crude oil, and Munro's the golden-brown of a fall leaf.

The children were obviously not surprised about her announcement of impending marriage to Parker. Marilee had not expected they would be, although one could never be certain of children's thoughts, and she had been a little anxious about the matter.

Corrine appeared pleased—or as close as Corrine could ever get to pleased—but she still held her wariness, as usual. Willie Lee, quite reluctant to have been pulled away from his worm moving, had the only concern of being reassured that Munro would go with them to Parker's house.

"Of course Munro comes. We are a family. Munro, too." Munro looked relieved, and she smiled at him. "And you and Corrine will each have your own room. Parker's house is a lot bigger than this one."

She was very pleased to tell the children this fact. This marriage would be good for all of them, a bigger house, wider yard, greater financial security. She had made the right decision.

Willie Lee frowned. "I will need Mun-ro to sleep with me, if I have to sleep in my own room." He made sleeping in his own room sound like a punishment. Tilting his head, he told Corrine, "Mun-ro can go sleep with you af-ter I go to sleep, o-kay? O-kay, Mun-ro?"

Then it was, "Can I bring my worms with me to Par-ker's house?"

Marilee, who was thinking of sleeping with Parker, said, "Honey, Parker's yard will have worms in it."

She came out of her thoughts enough to see her son regarding her very seriously from behind his thick glasses. He said, "Yes . . . but I want my own worms."

"You can bring your worms, honey."

Her mind was not on worms, but on wondering how she would handle sleeping with a man, after so many years alone. This concern mounted with lightning speed. It had been many years since she had shared a mattress and covers with another adult. What if Parker snored? She did not know this about him.

There would be many adjustments to getting married. She had known this, but she had obviously not known it in the same capacity with which the knowledge now came to her on a rising tide of revelation.

She supposed they were all going to be bringing worms, of a sort, with them into this union.

As she made up her bed, she wondered if Parker liked his sheets folded over the mattress in hospital corners, or if he preferred them loose, so he could stick his feet out. He had a king-size bed, and she would like that. There would be plenty of room for Willie Lee or Corrine, if they needed to sleep with her because of a nightmare or sickness or thunderstorm.

Parker might not like the children to sleep with them.

As she got a glass from the kitchen cabinet and poured herself some cold tea from Tate's round pitcher, she thought of Parker's cabinets full of dishes. All mismatched.

She loved her dishes, which were heavily accented with cobalt blue. Hopefully Parker would be agreeable to pitching his dishes in the trash and using hers.

She would be asking Parker to make a lot of changes.

The ring would have to be sized down for her. She had said she would take care of it, and now she was vexed at herself for taking on the responsibility. Shouldn't Parker have said he would do it? It was, though, her finger that would have to be present. They should make plans to do it together. That was probably going to be one of their major adjustments, learning to do things together after each of them had lived so many years alone.

The setting on the engagement ring would also need to be worked on. It snagged in her hair, and on the rough fabric of the desk chair, and on the kitchen hand towel.

Finally she took the ring off and laid it in the little dish of paper clips on her desk. Wearing it would take some getting used to.

Just then the telephone rang. Marilee reached out to answer and then withdrew her hand.

The phone rang again, and then again, while Marilee sat there, gazing at it.

At the third ring, Corrine came in from the bedroom.

"We'll let the answerin' machine pick up this morning," Marilee told her. "I have things to do and don't want to be distracted. Unless it's Parker," she added hurriedly, as the answering machine clicked on.

Her mother's voice came through the speaker. "Just checking to see if my eldest daughter is still among the living," her mother said. "I haven't heard from you. I wanted to let you know that Carl and I are going away to a sales conference in Las Vegas this weekend. We're flying out Friday afternoon. Well . . . I guess that's it."

Marilee felt guilt wash over her for not picking up the phone. She felt more guilty because Corrine had witnessed her avoidance of speaking to her mother.

In the following moments of reflection, however, Marilee decided that she was perhaps glad to have displayed for Corrine her choice to have quiet time for herself. She had made a great leap by engaging herself to Parker. She had to catch her breath.

Parker stopped by at just after noon to give Munro his shots. Marilee had to quickly run to her desk and get the ring, then slip it on her finger, before he noticed she didn't have it on.

He shoved his chair away from his desk, refraining from putting his fist through his computer screen.

Why could he not come up with an editorial that pleased him? Where had all his brains gone?

Stalking from his office, Tate went to the coffee station to find that the coffeepot was empty, and so was the coffee can. Why hadn't someone thrown it out? Silly to have an empty can sitting in the cabinet. He tossed it into the trash and looked through the cabinets for a new can, slamming doors with increasing annoyance when he found no coffee.

When Charlotte ignored his slamming doors, he called to her, "We are all out of coffee."

"Yes?" she called back. Her brown eyes regarded him in an unconcerned manner that annoyed him.

"Who is responsible for maintaining the coffee?"

"Whoever is drinking it. Today that is you. A lot." Tate sighed. "We need to keep coffee ready to offer to visitors." He didn't want his office to seem skimpy on anything. And doggonit, he wanted a cup of coffee.

Charlotte simply looked at him.

At the moment, the only other person in the offices was June, who proceeded to keep her head down and to scribble on paper. Tate contained himself. He had learned not to raise his voice to June. She got teary.

He glanced at the closed door of their comptroller's office. Zona had her own coffeemaker, and the absurdity of his employee having her own coffeemaker and him not having one struck him. He could go in and request a cup from her, but he would have to knock on the door and wait for her to unlock it. This was definitely a deterrent.

"I appoint you in charge of purchasing coffee supplies," he said to Charlotte, as he strode back past her desk. "I want you to make certain we have cans of coffee, filters, cups, anything else we need."

Maybe he would get his own coffeemaker. He should do that as the editor-publisher. But then he would be the only one to make it, and he liked other people to make the coffee. He got tired of getting his own food all the time, which was the bane of being single.

"Who's going to brew it?" She rose and reached for her purse.

"I'll be in charge of brewing it." Since he apparently could not get anyone else to do it. "We'll rotate the weeks of who will brew it." The idea came to him, and he liked it! With rotation, he would only have to do it every six weeks or so. "But you will be fully in charge of stocking it." There, that settled it.

"Yes, *sir.* But I think in your mood the last thing you need is some more caffeine." With that, she whipped open the door and strode out in her longlegged fashion.

He was in a mood. A rare one for him, but he was in it, by golly, and that was it. He did not think having coffee was too much to ask to console him in such a mood.

The door had not fully closed behind Charlotte when Sheriff Oakes appeared through it. Tate was still standing there just outside his office door, dealing with his confusion between being in a bad mood and feeling guilty for not being able to correct himself.

"Just passed Charlotte. She said you were in, but that you were in a wicked mood."

That washed away his guilt and shoved him completely into his mood. "It's a rough day," he said, more sharply than he had intended.

"Yep. For me, too." The sheriff's drawn expression caught Tate's attention. "I came over to fill you in about these Tell-In Technologies folks."

"Come on in." Tate waved toward his office. "I'm sorry I can't offer you any coffee. I got an Orange Crush, in a can. It's hot, though." He had not gotten the six-pack into the refrigerator. What he needed was a good private assistant.

*   *   *

The sheriff, wisely declining the warm Orange Crush, lowered himself into the leather chair across the desk from Tate. He produced a toothpick from his breast pocket, stuck it in his mouth, wet it well and then began. "I got those Tell-In folks buggin' me from one side, and my wife chewin' at me from the other."

"Oh?" Curiosity swept Tate, improving his mood.

"Here it is from the start. What these Tell-In folks put forth is that this Dan Kaplan stole a computer chip he had invented for them. Something for increasing memory . . . I don't understand all this computer stuff. Anyway, he turned around and sold it to some Japanese outfit, and that's where the money comes from. Those Tell-In folks therefore claim that the money is theirs."

"That seems to be reaching a bit far." Tate found himself rather fascinated by Neville's use of a toothpick, which he chewed on even when speaking, whipping it from one side of his mouth to the other, as if to emphasize certain points.

"That's pretty much my opinion." He shifted the toothpick again and chewed rapidly. "What they're also claimin' is that this chip, or plans for it, or what-have-you, was in Dan Kaplan's possession and could still be in his things."

"I imagine it's small and hidden," Tate offered. Watching the sheriff's mouth maneuver the toothpick, he tensed, ready for action, in case the man choked. He was not certain what he would do, though; likely normal procedures would be ineffective with a toothpick that might have to be surgically removed if stuck.

"So they say. What I gather is that they had some sort of informant who leads them to believe . . . *hope* is probably a better word . . . that Kaplan had only partially been paid and was in the process of deliverin' the chip and full plans, at which time he would receive the final payment. Fayrene does say that Kaplan told her that he was supposed to meet some people in Dallas, that he was headin' there, and was stoppin' here on his way down, and wantin' Fayrene to go down with him to Dallas." He slid the toothpick to the left.

"Anyway, to my mind, just because the chip once belonged to these Tell-In folks—and they haven't really proved that part, yet—I don't see how they can lay claim to the money. And I'm sure not givin' it over to these two yahoos on just their say-so, nor am I givin' over Dan Kaplan's stuff. That's what I told 'em, too."

"I imagine they were not too happy about that."

"No . . . no, they weren't." The toothpick went back and forth at a rapid rate. "That woman offered me five hundred dollars, if I'd give over the case and the money."

"Huh." Now here was a story stirring.

"Yep, and whcn I turned that down, she offered me a thousand."

Tate, who was not surprised, shook his head. The big man shifted in his chair, broke the toothpick in half with his tongue and spat it out.

"I just about threw her butt in jail, but I didn't have a witness . . . and besides, I wanted rid of them.

"I'll tell you what . . . those people do not understand that money doesn't call the shots around here. Justice and legality call the shots, and I uphold them, as is my sworn duty. The money and the briefcase and all of Dan Kaplan's effects are evidence in my jurisdiction, and until this is all sorted out, and with them producing some proof of their claims, what I got is a man who died clean of a heart attack, no report of theft from anywhere, besides what these Tell-In people are oayin', and everything paid up and no relatives, so his ex-wife has right to inherit by virtue of she was his only wife, and he left some letters stating plainly his intention to legally marry her again."

"Will that stand up in court?"

"Well, I don't know. But that's how I see it, and I figure until some judge tells me different, I'm in charge. My sworn duty is to protect and serve the people of this town, and that means Fayrene, not some strangers from outta state."

Tate nodded. They didn't make a lot of dedicated sheriffs like the one sitting before him.

The next instant the big man's shoulders slumped. "My wife isn't happy about any of this."

"She isn't?" Another wrinkle.

The sheriff shook his head and, in an obviously nervous habit, brought another toothpick from his breast pocket, as he said, "Maybe I am goin' out on a limb for Fayrene, but she's a good friend. When I was just a kid, seventeen, Fayrene sixteen years older, she and I . . . well, she showed a boy a big part about bein' a man." A softness came over his face. "Man, I was scared for my first time, and she showed me all about it. I guess she was my first love, but there wasn't anything either of us could do about it—you know, another time, another place, maybe."

The big man's face was filled with emotion that he obviously revealed to few people. Tate felt humbled.

He also thought about how still waters hid surprising matters. And about how for some reason people had always confided in him the deeply private details of their lives. Even as a teenager, other boys and girls would seek him out and confess all this stuff that he would rather they had kept to themselves. Back in his hometown he had known whose parents beat who, who was pregnant and unmarried, who was cheating whom out of what. His mother had said it was his demeanor and that he was meant to be a preacher; his brother had said he was perfect for journalism, that all the stories would seek him out.

He recalled overhearing the women gossiping yesterday at the grocery store.

Neville jerked him out of his wandering thoughts by saying, "My relationship with Fayrene was never anything like how I love my wife, and all of it was years ago, anyway. The only way it pertains to today is my friendship for her. A man doesn't leave his friends just because he gets married."

"No, can't do that."

"My wife can't seem to see it any other way than that I'm strayin', though." Back and forth again went the toothpick. "Ever since she found out about Fayrene and me, she's been jealous, even though it happened years before she and I ever met. I've explained my head off, but nothin' I say can seem to change how she takes it." He shook his head. "I tell you, women can make a mountain out of a molehill."

Tate figured that each person viewed a molehill from a different perspective. If said molehill was in a neighbor's backyard, it was never so important as when it was popping up in your own backyard. Mighty hard to be unconcerned with your own backyard torn to pieces.

He had just seen the sheriff out the door when Charlotte came blowing in, and she looked madder than a wet hen.

Without a word, she slammed her purse on her desk and, still standing, proceeded to sort through the stack of mail she had brought with her.

Tate debated whether or not to ask her what was wrong. He did not feel up to handling another confidence or problem. He did, however, want his coffee, and he did not see that Charlotte had brought a can.

"Where's the coffee?" he asked.

"What?" She paused in her mail sorting to frown at him. "Oh, shoot. I went to the post office to get the mail first, and I got to talkin' to Julia and clean forgot I had gone out for coffee."

She had spoken to Julia Jenkins-Tinsley. He wasn't going to question that.

"I'll go get the coffee," he said and walked out the door.

He wondered if the main secret to life might be minding one's own business, and if this might not be the hardest thing in the world for a human being to do.

*   *   *

That evening Marilee experienced certainty in her decision to marry Parker. She was, in fact, finding her effort to love him worthwhile, because he was responding with equal effort to be agreeable. He got them both Coca-Colas, pouring hers into a glass, and brought the drinks to the dining room table, where together they discussed wedding plans.

Actually, it was not a discussion. Parker asked Marilee what she wanted to do about getting married. Marilee, wondering at the expression, cocked her head.

"Do you mean what to do about the wedding?"

"Yes," he said, and she noted the positive yes.

She wanted a small church wedding, with Pastor Smith officiating, and the children and her Aunt Vella present, and her mother would want to be included, of course. She got carried away with hopeful thoughts that maybe Anita would come up for the ceremony. And she would like enough time to get a new dress for herself, and new clothes for the children. And flowers.

"Whatever you want," Parker said.

"Well . . . I think it will take a couple weeks, at least, to get it together. We'll have to work around Pastor Smith's availability." She began a list, putting contacting the pastor first.

Then there was the question of a honeymoon. Marilee thought it would be a good idea for them to get away, and Parker exhibited more eagerness for this idea than for the wedding. The first question was where to go.

"Wherever you want," Parker said.

She wasn't certain where she wanted to go. "Charlene and Mason went to Cancun. They liked it." However, the prospect of distance and time between her and the children unnerved her. She did not say this, however.

"If that's where you want to go, that's where we'll go," Parker said. Then he added, "I'll have to see if Morris can come down from Lawton, or maybe get Dr. Swisher to come out of retirement. I'll let you know what week one of them can stand in for me, and we'll go anywhere you want. Your call."

Later, with the children in bed, they sat on the couch. Parker kissed her deeply and suggested that he stay the night.

Marilee pushed his hands from her breasts and told him gently, "I would rather we not go sleeping together until we are married. I think this is best for the children. We need to take one step at a time, Parker. I want to present the children with a secure environment."

Parker was quiet, and then he said, "All right."

Having focused on the children, which was easiest, Marilee said she was concerned about having to leave their garden behind. They all enjoyed it so much. It was too late to plant an entire garden in Parker's yard now, but she and the children could plant flower beds. Then there was the combining of their households to be considered.

"It'll take me time to sort through all our stuff. We can move over to your house gradually. Okay?" She was suddenly struck by a great reluctance to leave her cottage, no matter how small and cramped.

Parker said, "Sounds good."

"I'd like to buy Corrine a four-poster bed and make her room up really pretty."

Parker nodded and said, "Fine."

He kissed her and pushed her down upon the couch and began slipping his hands up beneath her shirt. Marilee felt the great confusion of desire and restraint. She wished she could explain to him how she felt about her position as a mother of small children. She could not speak to other times of her life, neither years before nor years ahead, but only to that particular time right then, when her choice was to wait. When, in fact, she felt a panic at the thought of sex. She fairly pushed him on the floor.

He did his little-boy frown, and she stroked his temple hair back around his ear with her fingernail. "I'm tired, anyway . . . and you said you were, too."

"Yep. Got a dog I need to check when I get back." He got to his feet.

She closed the door after him and went to clear away their coffee cups and clean up the sink. She paused, staring at her reflection in the night-black windows.

Parker had been most agreeable all evening. Why, then, did she feel such dissatisfaction?

She wished he wouldn't keep going after her body like a wildcatter determined to bore for oil. And that he would have been more forthcoming in making mutual decisions. He seemed unwilling to take part in planning, content to leave it all to her.

She sighed deeply, feeling as if she were a very hard woman to please.

Maybe that was the correct answer to *a woman like her.*

Marilee was just slipping into bed—and almost guiltily glad of having it all to herself again—when the telephone rang.

It was Belinda, who said, "Well, you are gonna have to do somethin' about Mama and Daddy."

"What do you mean?"

"Now I have got Daddy up here in my apartment, in front of my television, sleepin' on my sofa, and strewin' his stuff all over my bathroom. This is just not gonna work. You are gonna have to do somethin'. You have got to talk to Mama and get her to take Daddy back home."

Marilee said she had talked to Aunt Vella and had gotten nowhere. "I talked to your daddy earlier, too, and didn't get anywhere. I'm sorry, Belinda, but there doesn't seem to be anything I can do." Marilee was also thinking that Belinda should have been more concerned before everything had gotten to this point.

"Well, somebody is gonna have to do somethin'. I can't stand this," said Belinda, as distraught as Marilee had ever heard her. Then the line clicked dead.

With thinking up things to do to get her aunt and uncle back together, worrying over how the upheaval of moving from their house to Parker's would affect the children, and trying to work up enthusiasm for leaving the children to go on a honeymoon, Marilee lay awake a long time.

Nineteen

The Engagement

"Well, congratulations." It was Charlene, telephoning just before nine. "Parker was just here to worm Leanne's horses, and he told us about giving you a ring. So it is finally going to happen—you and Parker are going to get married."

"Yes."

She really could not postpone another day telling people of the news. The first one she needed to tell was her mother, and she had better catch her before she got off to Las Vegas. Right there, with her hand still on the receiver after hanging up from Charlene, Marilee dialed her mother's number.

"Hello, dear. I'm packing. . . . I had to go out and get new luggage last night. Our other set was just so old, it looked tawdry. I didn't think it would look good for Carl's store for us to be lugging that stuff around. I still need to get Carl's shirts from the cleaners. . . . He's back at the store, and I'll pick him up on the way to the airport. I'd just as soon he stayed at the store and out of the way. He just hates to travel. . . . He gets all wrought up, and there won't be any food on the short flight down to Dallas. It's that awful prop plane. I sure hope it isn't rainin' down in Dallas, when we have to change planes. I have the hotel number around here somewhere . . . we're stayin' at the Grand. Oh, you won't need us anyway. It's just the weekend." Her mother finally paused.

"Mother, Parker and I are engaged."

There was no answer. The line was silent.

"*Here* it is! Whew, what a relief. It is such a nice packet from the travel agency. The itinerary isn't quite as detailed as usual. Dotty didn't do it, she's havin' her gallbladder out, and this young girl did it. She doesn't half know what she is doin'. Here's the confirmation number for the hotel. We sure need to have that. Last time the hotel was way overbooked and they wanted to put us across town, but I had my confirmation number, and I just refused. That's what you have to do, just refuse. I have the girl's name from the travel agency, too, just in case. Now, I have to get off here, honey. I have to get this packin' done. Carl doesn't like me to keep him waiting."

Marilee said quickly, "I wanted to tell you Parker and I are engaged."

"You are? You and Parker?" She sounded as if it came as a complete surprise.

"Yes. He gave me an engagement ring. We haven't set the date, but we plan sometime next month, as soon as Parker can get a fill-in vet, and I can schedule Pastor Smith."

"Well, I'm glad you have come to your senses on this thing. You are darn lucky to get Parker. Have you called Anita to tell her?"

"No . . . not yet."

"Well . . . oh, there's another call . . . it may be Carl. You can tell me all about your plans when I get home. Goodbye, dear."

Marilee hung up and breathed deeply. She thought Parker might be a little lucky to have her, too. Except that she felt so short of temper these days. She hoped she was not turning into a shrew.

She sat there for a full two minutes with her hand on the telephone, considering telephoning her sister. Anita would be at work, but maybe she had an answering machine hooked up now. Marilee thought she would just leave a message. That seemed the easiest.

In the end she decided to telephone her sister on Sunday and tell her everything. She was just too busy with doing Parker's birthday and telling everyone in town about the engagement.

Charlotte's reaction to Marilee's news was curious. Granted, Charlotte was not an effusive woman at the best of times, but Marilee found her manner, when told of Marilee's engagement, quite lacking.

Everyone at the newspaper was happy for her, of course. She made her announcement, and they all, except Charlotte, gathered round and repeatedly oohed and aahed at her ring. June began to cry, and Reggie went into that really annoying bit of making an announcement into a pen and then singing "There Is Love." She tugged Leo to his feet and danced him around. They really were a handsome couple. Tammy poured canned cola into paper cups and proposed a toast. Imperia thought to go call Zona to come out to see Marilee's ring and join them in celebration. The small accountant came forward and said, "I hope you two will be very happy, Marilee," in her amazingly sweet voice, lifted a paper cup of soft drink in good wishes, and then turned around and slipped right back to her office.

Marilee kept glancing at Tate's open office door. He was not at his desk, and she concluded he was not in at all. Disappointment swept over her, which was totally silly, of course. It was so much easier for her without him present.

Charlotte had quickly returned to her desk and focused on her computer screen. Marilee was a little taken aback by this distant behavior. Of everyone at the paper, Charlotte was her closest friend. She and Charlotte had worked there the longest, watching many others come and go. Both she and Charlotte knew the workings of the paper and could do everyone else's job, too, and they had done it all on numerous occasions. This expertise gave them a certain camaraderie born of facing crises together. So many times getting the *Voice* out had hung by a thread that Marilee and Charlotte had knitted up together.

It struck Marilee that perhaps the woman was jealous. Marilee's heart swelled with feeling. Charlotte was thirty-six and had never been married; she read scads of romance novels, saw every romance movie, and had displayed quiet crushes on a number of men passing through her life, Leo, Sr. being only the latest, yet as far as Marilee knew, Charlotte had not even had a date in ages. There were few single men in town who met with her approval, not to mention her height, which tended to scare men away.

Marilee sauntered over to Charlotte's desk and said in a low voice, "We're just going to have a tiny ceremony, no fancy dressing and not a lot of guests, just Mama and the children, but I was hoping you would stand up with me . . . be my matron of honor."

Charlotte regarded her solemnly from behind her thick glasses. "Okay. What day? Don't forget the grand opening of Green Acres on the first weekend of the month. We'll have to cover that, and I have a dental appointment the next Friday—on the ninth."

Marilee absorbed this rather halfhearted reply. "We haven't set a day yet," she said. "I'll work around those dates."

Across the street at the soda fountain of Blaine's Drugstore, Deputy Lyle Midgett enjoyed a Coca-Cola and barbecue sandwich made by Nadine, the new girl Belinda had hired, and told Belinda all about the goings-on down at the police station, where the people from Tell-In had returned with a third person, a thin, silent man who was some sort of search expert. Armed with a court order that gave them access to the dead man's effects, although not possession, they began an immediate and thorough search of Kaplan's luggage, briefcase and car. Lori was given custody of the fifty thousand dollars, stuck in a paper sack that she put under her desk at her feet.

"Judge Watkins signed the court order. They can't take nothin', but they can search it right here, and they sure are doin' it," Lyle told Belinda, his voice muffled by a full bite of barbecue sandwich. "This is good." He smiled at Nadine, and Belinda did not like that much. She shifted herself to be right in front of him.

"Have they said how big the chip is?" Belinda already knew all about Kaplan being the inventor of the chip and having stolen it, as she had gotten the full account out of Lyle days ago. "Do they need a magnifyin' glass to see it?"

"Shush," Lyle whispered. Glancing around furtively, he lowered his voice. "I heard them say it is about the size of a dime, I think. Or maybe it was a nickel. Somethin' like that. I said he could have mailed it to the Russians, since it wasn't no bigger than that. I don't know why he wouldn't have done that."

"Russians? What would they want with it?" Lyle did not keep up with commerce, whereas Belinda read a lot of magazines. She read *Today's Money* just about every month. "Maybe you mean the Microsoft people."

Lyle shook his head and said it was some foreign country, only he couldn't remember which one. China, he finally decided, after thinking hard on the matter.

"I don't think anyone ever sends stuff like that through the mail," Belinda offered. "But I don't know why not. Maybe they do, and they just don't make movies about it, because that would be boring. I wonder where the dog fits into this."

"I haven't heard anything about any dog." Lyle shook his head.

"I told you about the dog," she reminded him, and he said he knew that. "You said there was a dog dish in Kaplan's car."

"Maybe it was a dog dish, but there wasn't any dog food or anything. Might have just been some old dish." And Lyle had not been about to ask the sheriff about the dog, either, because questions might reveal to the sheriff that he told Belinda a lot of stuff he wasn't supposed to be telling her. He didn't know why he told her. Somehow he just found himself doing it. She was the first woman to ever really listen to him, for one thing.

The bell over the door rang, and Marilee and her children came in. Marilee called over for the children to be given whatever they wanted. "I'll be there in a minute. I'd like a chocolate shake."

Belinda, watching Marilee disappear behind one of the shelves of the pharmacy, wondered how Marilee could keep drinking chocolate shakes like she did and not ever get any fatter. Probably it was that Marilee was too nervous most of the time. Marilee was always doing or planning something. Belinda had observed that having kids tended to do this to a woman, which was why she had no desire for any. People were all the time asking her when she and Lyle were going to get married and have children. She replied that she knew when she was well off and could read an entire magazine when she wanted.

Her gaze flowed over the two small figures approaching the counter and lit upon the dog walking at Willie Lee's heels. A multicolored dog, with spots.

The children came and sat on stools to Lyle's right. Lyle, upon seeing the dog said, "I'm not sure dogs are supposed to be in an eating establishment. I think there's an ordinance."

Belinda, who came around the counter to get a better look at the dog, told Lyle, "Don't look, then."

Corrine twisted her stool back and forth and stared up at the lighted menu, obviously trying to make up her mind. Willie Lee wanted an ice-cream cone, one scoop of vanilla on a sugar cone. Belinda had found that Willie Lee generally knew exactly what he wanted.

"Mun-ro wants a dish of water, please," said Willie Lee, who always knew what his dog wanted, too.

Marilee came over with a gift box set of men's aftershave and cologne. It was the expensive brand Belinda's mother ordered from Germany, and she had managed to get a good business going with it among a number of the women seeking to spruce up their husbands. Belinda preferred regular stuff on Lyle; she saw no need to waste money.

Lyle told Marilee that he thought there might be a fine for bringing a dog into an eating establishment.

Marilee replied that they would leave, just as soon as they got done with their refreshments. "I'd like to buy a gallon of the vanilla ice cream, too, Belinda—for Parker's birthday tomorrow."

"You can get it out of the freezer before you leave," Belinda said and added, "It's gone up to seven and a quarter." If the ice cream was so special that Marilee wanted to buy it, she might as well pay well for it.

While Belinda rang up Marilee's charges, Marilee introduced herself to Nadine, who said, "Hiya' " and instantly turned around to wipe up all around. Nadine was proving a hard worker, who did not care to talk and cared even less to eat. Belinda was pleased.

As Marilee wrote out her check, Belinda saw the ring on her finger. "Is that an engagement ring?"

"Yes. Parker and I got engaged."

"Huh. Nice ring. When's the wedding?"

"We haven't set the date yet. Next month, though."

Belinda's attention was distracted from any comment on the matter, however, when the bell over the door chimed and in came the tall blond man—one of the Tell-In people. He stood there with the door open a moment, the air conditioner dripping behind him, all straight in clothes crisp and shiny, as he removed his sunglasses and seemed to scan the store. Then he came forward to the soda counter.

"I'll take a packet of the Motrin," he said, speaking to Belinda and motioning with his hand. "And a Coke, to go."

"You should try the headache powders," Lyle offered.

The man's head spun as if on a pivot, and his eyes observed Lyle, who added that headache powders went to work a lot faster. Lyle could be overly friendly, and Belinda could understand the man's frown, while Lyle just kept on. "It's 'cause they don't have to dissolve like a pill."

The man, not replying to Lyle's recommendation, paid Belinda with exact change. She put the money in the cash drawer and closed it with a snap. As she turned back to the counter, movement caught her eye, and she saw Nadine bending down . . . she was petting the dog that had slipped behind the counter.

The man walked out of the store, with his Motrin and Coca-Cola, without a word of polite goodbye.

Nadine said, "I would guess that guy is not from around here."

"He's one of those Tell-In people, and he has headaches," Belinda said, informing Marilee that she knew things. "The sun probably gets to him. They're down there searchin' that Dave Kaplan's car out back of the police station, lookin' for a computer chip."

"Belinda . . . you aren't supposed to go tellin' ever'body," Lyle objected.

"I'm not tellin' everybody. Just Marilee, and I think she probably should know, bein' a member of the press . . . and she is my cousin."

"What computer chip?" Marilee glanced from Belinda to Lyle and back.

"That ex of Fayrene's stole a computer chip from his company. He invented it, but that doesn't matter, it was still the company's chip, and he took it to sell to the Chinese. That's where he got the fifty thousand. But his company hopes he didn't have time to get it to the Chinese, and they came today with a court order to search his stuff. The sheriff hasn't told you any of this?" She leaned forward on the counter.

Marilee shook her head. "Tate is probably doing the story. All I did was speak with Fayrene and do the initial write-up."

Belinda did not think Marilee was sufficiently impressed with what Belinda was telling her. "They're takin' that Mercedes apart. They must figure that chip is hidden in there somewhere, or in that brief-case. A computer chip isn't very big. This is computer espionage."

Marilee, getting the children up from their stools, said she would make certain Tate knew to investigate for a possible story. Lyle asked her not to say where she heard about the matter.

As Marilee went out the door, Belinda looked at the dog walking behind Willie Lee's feet. It sure seemed that dog had made certain the Tell-In guy had not seen him.

"You are gonna get me into trouble, tellin' everything all over," Lyle said in a dispirited voice.

Belinda, ignoring the comment, leaned across the counter and said, "Parker is havin' an affair with Leanne Overton."

Lyle blinked. "But didn't Marilee just say she and Parker were en-gaged?"

"Yes."

"I guess Marilee must not know about Leanne, then," he said.

Belinda sighed. "Well, of course not." Lyle could be so dense.

After a minute, Lyle said, "How do you know about Parker and Leanne?" as if she couldn't possibly know anything and had gone and made up the story.

"That Julia Jenkins-Tinsley saw them," said Belinda in a what-for manner. "And she is tellin' it all over. She is such a gossip."

Fred Grace had installed a mechanical pony ride out front of the florist, sandwiched in between racks holding buckets of bouquets be-neath his awning. Willie Lee saw it instantly when Marilee headed to the florist to get flowers for the party.

Marilee thought the ride a fine ploy to draw more mothers and grandmothers to the store.

"You aren't too big to ride yet, are you, Corrine?"

Corrine smiled shyly in answer. Marilee put a quarter in each child's hand and allowed them to remain outside and ride the pony while she went inside to get a table arrangement.

Corrine said, "I'll watch Willie Lee," as if to earn the quarter.

"I know you will, honey. Thank you."

Marilee entered the florist and stood for a minute to let her eyes ad-just to the much dimmer interior. The first thing she saw clearly was Tate Holloway standing back at the counter. She heard his familiar voice, too.

"Have it delivered this afternoon," he said to Fred Grace.

Marilee had a little panic about seeing him, one that she did not understand at all. She couldn't just turn around and go out, though, and she wondered who he was having flowers delivered to.

She went toward the counter, and Fred Grace saw her and greeted her, and then Tate turned her way.

"Hello, Miss Marilee."

"Hello."

"I hear you and Parker are finally gonna tie the knot," Fred Grace said. The adam's apple in his thin neck bobbed whenever he spoke.

"Yes, we are. Next month sometime." She really needed to get a date set; she was getting tired of saying *sometime.*

Fred Grace, holding up an order paper, said, "I'll be right with you, Marilee . . . let me get Tate's order in the works," and disappeared through the rear curtain, leaving Marilee and Tate standing there, alone.

It was perfectly silly for her to feel nervous about being alone with Tate. She launched immediately into telling him about the articles she had left with Charlotte, and the entire time she spoke, she tried to figure a casual way to ask about who was to receive Tate's flowers.

Willie Lee rode the pony first, and he laughed and laughed. Corrine liked watching him. She felt excited and happy about playing with the electric pony. This was a feeling she did not fully trust. Her past experience had been that she could not trust having fun. Somehow she usually had to pay for it.

As if to prove this point, suddenly here came the school principal, Mrs. Blankenship. "Hello, children."

Corrine said hello, and Willie Lee did, too.

Then, right there in front of Corrine's wide eyes, the principal said, "Here, let me treat you to another ride," and immediately she put a quarter in the slot for Willie Lee, and then gave Corrine a coin, holding it out until Corrine took it. With a smile and a nod, the principal disappeared inside the florist's store.

Corrine stared at the glass door and figured that the principal was in a good mood because school was out. Willie Lee was laughing and saying, "Yeee-haaa," and Corrine found she could begin breathing again.

It came Corrine's turn, and she rode, feeling a little self-conscious, since she was eleven years old. With her second coin, she said, "Willie Lee, ride with me." That way, if any classmates from school should come along and see her, it would look like she was helping Willie Lee.

"O-kay!"

He scrambled up behind her and put his hands around her waist.

She quickly put the coin into the slot, and beneath them the metal pony began to gyrate. Wille Lee called out, "Yeee-haaa!"

Corrine had to laugh.

But then there was Munro in the middle of the sidewalk, backing up and wrinkling his nose with a growl.

Corrine blinked, taking in everything that was happening. It was the man who had come into the drugstore earlier—the man Belinda had said was a Tell-In man and had headaches—and a woman was with him. It came suddenly to Corrine that these were the two people who had stared at them on the sidewalk earlier that week, and they were heading for Munro.

The woman was saying, "Here, doggy."

"That is *my* dog," Willie Lee said, speaking with alarm.

Corrine felt Willie Lee let go of her waist. She reached back to grab him, to keep him from falling off the pony that was still bouncing.

"He looks like the dog that belonged to a friend of ours," the woman said.

"He is *my* dog," Willie stated again.

Corrine wished the pony would stop.

"How long have you had him?" the woman said, even as she moved toward Munro.

Just then the man jumped at Munro, to grab him, but Munro quick as a flash scooted under the front bumper of a parked car.

Willie Lee launched himself off the pony, yelling, "That is *my* dog!"

Corrine scrambled off the bouncing horse, toppling onto the concrete.

The next thing she saw was the man and the woman running into the street, and Willie Lee after them. Somehow she got to her feet and ran after Willie Lee, catching him right in the middle of the street and dragging him back to the sidewalk, her heart pounding clean out of her chest. There had been only one car far down the street, but it could have reached Willie Lee. And she was supposed to look after him.

Willie Lee was crying. Corrine put her arm around him and tried to think of something to say.

But then suddenly Munro appeared from behind the stand of flower buckets.

"Mun-ro!" Willie Lee went to the dog, while Corrine looked over her shoulder to see the two strangers going down the opposite side of the street.

"Shush!" She grabbed Willie Lee, and shoved him and the dog back against the stand of flower buckets, crouching there herself.

"I am go-ing to tell Ma-ma." Willie Lee made a move toward the florist.

"No," said Corrine, who believed it better to never tell anything. "If they do own Munro, your mother will make us give him back."

Willie Lee gazed at her from behind his thick glasses.

Just then Marilee came out of the florist shop, and Mr. Tate was with her. Right behind them came Principal Blankenship. Because the grown-ups were all talking, no one noticed that Willie Lee was sniffing. Corrine shook her head at him, and he pressed his lips together.

Aunt Marilee bid goodbye to Principal Blankenship, and Mr. Tate walked them along to the Cherokee, which was only a few yards down the sidewalk. Corrine kept an eye out for the two strangers but didn't see them. It was hard to see over the cars, though.

They got into the Cherokee, and Munro lay down with his head on Willie Lee's leg. Corrine and Willie Lee remained perfectly quiet while Aunt Marilee talked with Mr. Tate some more through the driver window.

As Aunt Marilee headed the Cherokee home, Corrine caught a glance of the man and woman at their dark car in front of the police station. She squished down in the seat.

"Corrine? Honey, what's wrong? You feel okay?"

"Yes, ma'am . . . I'm just a little tired. I think I want a nap. Willie Lee does, too."

"I will not tell, Cor-rine," Willie Lee said from over in his bed, where he lay with Munro.

"I won't, either," Corrine said. "And we'll have to watch out for a while, make sure we don't see those people again."

After a minute, Willie Lee asked, "Why?"

"Because they may be the real owners of Munro. They will take him." Corrine was puzzled about this entire thing, but she did not see anything to do but hide. In her experience, grown-ups rarely cared what little kids wanted.

Marilee turned off the whiz-bang computer, where she had written two small pieces for the paper, and rubbed her eyes. She should see about glasses.

Her gaze fell on Stuart's photograph. Should she put it away? Willie had long ago quit asking about his father. She had explained that Stuart traveled away, finally ending that he was gone from their lives. Willie Lee was such an accepting person. She wished she could be so, she thought, finally tucking the picture into the top drawer of her desk.

Rising, she turned out the lamps and walked softly to peer at the children on her way to bed. The light from the hall lamp fell softly into the room. Her gaze fell on Willie Lee, asleep all spread out, and then onto Corrine, who was facedown into her pillow, with Munro pressed to her side.

Corrine was crying softly. "Oh, honey, what is it?" Marilee pulled her niece up into her arms.

"I . . . I had . . . a bad dream."

"Oh, it was only a dream. You are okay." After another minute, "Come on and sleep with me." She took Corrine's hand. Munro hopped from the bed and up beside sleeping Willie Lee.

Marilee snuggled Corrine into bed, got into her own gown and slipped in beside her niece, whose hands were formed into balls.

"I'm sorry, Aunt Marilee," Corrine whispered.

"Whatever for, honey?"

"Because I know you like to have the bed to yourself."

"Oh, sweetheart . . . yes, I do," she said, knowing honesty was in order. "But I also like to have you come in here sometimes, and Willie Lee, too. I like to hold you both close. You are a comfort to me, too."

Gradually she felt her niece relax, and gradually Marilee relaxed, too.

Some time before dawn, Marilee awoke to find Corrine on one side of her, Willie Lee on the other, and Munro at her feet. It occurred to her that it was quite possible that Parker would object to such crowded sleeping arrangements.

In that moment, however, thus surrounded by her children, with Corrine's hand knotted in Marilee's hair and Willie Lee breathing upon her chest, Marilee was supremely contented and fell immediately back into a deep, lovely sleep.

Twenty

Nick of Time

Marilee got up early, squeezing carefully out from between the children and the dog, succeeding in not awakening them. She went to the kitchen, made coffee as strong as Corrine's, and set about throwing her mind into the accomplishment of Parker's birthday party.

Sometime between the first and second cups of strong coffee, she began to go at it in an all-consuming manner that fully occupied her mind and kept her from perturbing thoughts about her pending marriage. She would deal with those concerns later, after she had finished with Parker's party.

She had the children's breakfast made when they came into the kitchen; Corrine was quite surprised, of course.

Leaving them eating and dawdling, she dashed around, gathering everything to take to Parker's house. She got herself into a chambray shorts sunsuit she had been saving for the occasion and that showed her bare shoulders to good advantange, applied her face in the thorough manner of the unmadeup look, and carefully pinned up her hair to appear careless.

While tying on canvas wedge sandals, she caught a glimpse of herself in the long mirror. She stood and observed her appearance and decided that she had made her decision about marrying Parker in the nick of time, while she still had something to offer and a man would even consider her. Her breath seemed to grow shallow with these thoughts, and she strode out the door and onward into the day.

At ten-thirty, they were each carrying boxes and bags out to the Cherokee; Marilee was somewhat surprised at the amount of the supplies, now that she tried to fit them all into the rear of her vehicle. As she was going about this, Tate came driving past, the top down on his car, his pale hair catching the sunlight. He stopped in the street and wished them a good day.

Marilee called back, "Good day to you, too," and the next instant, she turned, slammed the rear door closed, headed for the driver's seat and told the children to get in. Slipping behind the wheel, she wrenched the rearview mirror around, as if to look at herself, but really to watch Tate drive on.

She breathed a sigh of relief as his car disappeared, and then felt perversely annoyed.

Jerking the shift lever into reverse, she backed out into the street and then took off with the windows open. Willie Lee and Munro stuck their heads out their window, their faces to the wind for the drive to Parker's house. Willie Lee began singing "Happy Birthday," and Corrine and Marilee joined in. They were singing "Happy Birthday" when they rolled down Parker's long driveway.

She was a bit startled to note the neglected landscape. The house could be deserted, in fact, with no other attention than mowed grass. She thought it odd that she had never noticed the lack of care before. Surely it had not been that way when she had last visited, which had been all the way last fall.

Parker came out the front door, and they all tumbled out of the car, yelling, "Happy Birthday!"

His smile was like that of a delighted boy. It made Marilee's heart ache and fill at the same time. "Here . . . you can take this helium bottle and this box," she said, pressing him into service to help empty the Cherokee of all the party paraphernalia.

"Wow!" Parker said when he saw his cake.

Marilee, very pleased, shifted the cake out of its box and onto the middle of the breakfast bar. She stuck in the candles, while Parker snitched a fingerful of icing and the children laughed as Marilee shoved him away.

Marilee saw immediately that she had not anticipated correctly the work necessary to have the house in order for a party. She was a little shocked at Parker's house, again pointing up the fact that she had not been there in some time.

While Parker was generally clean, he exhibited no thought to the finer points of home decoration. The house looked as if it was a stopping off place and nothing more, and his every-other-week housekeeper was obviously less than dedicated. This was the week that the housekeeper did not come.

The job of readying the house for the party was an endeavor that properly required days, but Marilee dove right in to accomplish the task in two hours. Like a veteran general, she gave everyone their assignments, setting Parker to work filling balloons with helium and Willie Lee to helping him. She gave Corrine the duty of arranging the patio furniture, table and dishes, and directing the males on how to hang the ribbons and balloons.

Tying an apron over her sunsuit, an addition that made her feel like a pinup girl, and armed with a basket for collecting strewn items, a bag for trash, several sizes of dusters and the vacuum cleaner, Marilee swept through the house in the manner of a guerrilla single-handedly reclaiming lost territory.

She first attacked the kitchen, the room that would receive the most use during the party, and had it in acceptable order, if still lacking in identity, in forty-five minutes, with numerous detours to answer questions from the crew on the patio. In a similar manner of pointed concentration, she proceeded on into the dining room, through the living room, and into the rear of the house and the two bathrooms and master bedroom. Pacing herself, she broke into only a light sweat; she had turned the air-conditioning thermostat down to an extravagant level.

All the while she cleaned, Marilee made mental notes of necessary decorating changes for when she and the children moved in. The carpet throughout would have to be changed from a deep blue that didn't go with anything. The bathrooms required new wallpaper and total decoration; the walls were currently some off-orange, and there was not one stick of pleasantry in them. She had never noticed that Parker had no taste in home decor colors. Marilee pictured towels of complementary colors, rather than selected at random, as Parker's appeared to be. She wanted linens in colors to match the towels, too, and she preferred the muted, earthy colors of sea green, lilac and blue that she employed in her own home. This would mean brand-new sheets for Parker's king-size bed, so enormous in comparison to her own standard double. Spreading up the covers, she wondered how Parker slept on such sheets—bright yellow and orange and green stripes. Surely such colors would tend to keep one awake.

Pausing, she stared at the bed, and then she sat down on it, testing the mattress by bouncing lightly. She quite liked it, although she would prefer to move it to the opposite wall, where there would be more room and the bathroom door would not keep hitting the left nightstand.

Parker liked mints and threw the wrappers on the nightstand, along with various brochures about animal medications, pairs of socks, a spare key, his pocket knife and loose coins. Marilee opened the drawer to brush the stray items inside, all except the socks. She snatched them up to toss into the basket of dirty clothes.

Something dropped to the floor.

An earring.

Picking it up from the carpet, she looked at it closely—a dangling earring of silver and turquoise and black onyx. And there, on the night stand, lay a matching earring, underneath where the socks had been.

Placing them in her palm, she gazed at them, then looked at the pillow right beside the nightstand, and then back again to the earrings, while all manner of thoughts twirled in her head, all of them on the same theme: what woman had been in this room?

"Marilee?" Parker poked his head in the doorway.

She jumped. "Yes?"

"Are you 'bout ready? Rick and Vickie just got here. . . . Rick's firin' up the grill." Parker looked happy and expectant, and very handsome.

"I'm coming."

She slipped the earrings into the pocket of her sun-suit, picked up her cleaning supplies and hurried to the kitchen. Parker was there getting cold drinks. She told him she wanted a Coca-Cola, and while he got it for her, she put her wrists beneath the faucet of cold water.

Of course, there could be any number of reasons why the earrings that were not hers were on Parker's nightstand.

He could have found them somewhere. This was the most reasonable explanation. Maybe the owner of one of his patients had left them at the clinic. This line of thought presented the image of some lunatic woman who took off expensive handmade earrings, maybe bored while awaiting her appointment, and just threw them on the floor or over the counter. Maybe she was hysterical because her pet died, so she ripped them out of her ears and tossed them down, and Parker had not yet discovered to which owner of which deceased pet the earrings belonged. He'd had a few deaths recently.

Marilee realized her imagination was running wild. There were, in fact, a lot of indecipherable thoughts running around in her head, which she kept shoving aside and which kept popping back at her, so much so that she found herself going to the kitchen to get a basting brush for Rick and ended up staring into the refrigerator, picking a grape tomato out of the big bowl of salad and eating it. What she really wanted was a piece of chocolate. The birthday cake caught her eye, and she had to resist the urge to cut herself a piece; it was rich chocolate underneath the vanilla icing.

Why did she not simply ask Parker where the earrings came from?

That was out, with Parker standing at the grill with Rick and the doorbell giving out a chime.

*   *   *

Ted and Wendy Oakes came without their three children. "I need a break," Wendy said, putting her hand on her round belly. "I'm trying to get all the rest I can before this one gets here. Here's Parker's present. It's a . . . oh, my gosh, is that an engagement ring on your finger?"

Marilee told her it was and ushered her out to the patio, where the big bowl of chips and guacamole caught the very pregnant woman's attention.

Ray Horn, who was recently divorced, brought his new girlfriend, Heather. Everyone was polite and didn't stare at her. She was a dark-haired, dark-eyed knockout, and looked at least fifteen years younger than Ray. She had brought her son, Bobby, a very pretty, shy dark-haired boy who was determined to remain on her lap. The two really were a lovely sight.

The Macombs, Jerry and Mary Lynn and their daughter Sarah, drove up in their minivan, followed immediately by Charlene, Mason, Jojo and Leanne Overton in a brand-new Suburban. The people came pouring out of the vehicles, laughing and talking and bearing gifts and covered dishes. Charlene had cut her hair again; she looked stunning, walking beside Mason. The two's happiness was breathtaking. Mary Lynn, always in a hurry, was urging Jerry, who probably couldn't hurry from a fire, to get up to the house.

Marilee led the way to the patio, directed where to set dishes and offered cold drinks.

Charlene grabbed Marilee's hand and took a look at the engagement ring. "My heaven, that is a gorgeous ring. Congratulations, Parker!" she called across the patio to Parker, who apparently had taken up residence next to the grill with Rick. Parker, giving a shy grin, raised his beer in acknowledgment.

The women oohed and aahed appropriately at the engagement ring, each taking hold of Marilee's hand. She glanced over to observe Parker.

"Oh, you two haven't met," Charlene was saying. "This is my cousin, Leanne . . . Leanne, this is Marilee, Parker's fiancée and the official hostess of the annual Parker Day barbecue."

Leanne was pretty. "Hello." She stuck out her hand.

"Hello."

Marilee shook the woman's hand. Good blond frosting job, polished silver earrings, the makeup of a fashion model and bright smile . . . and a necklace crafted of fine silver and turquoise and black onyx.

"It's nice to meet you." Her gaze stuck on the necklace.

"You, too. I've heard so much about you."

"Oh?" The earrings burned a hole in her pocket. She refrained from whipping them out and asking the woman to lean over so she could compare.

Charlene, dipping a large corn chip into a red mixture, said, "Leanne brought her simply-to-die-for salsa. You have to try this, Marilee."

Marilee complied. "Oh, yes, it is good, really good."

"I want some," said Wendy, who came armed with a chip in each hand. "Vitamins A and C and almost no fat. I need to eat a lot of it."

"Go for it," Marilee said, then turned away. "I'll get more ice."

She took up the ice bucket that was still half-filled and retreated to the kitchen, where she stood for a moment gazing at nothing. Then she went to the window that looked out at the patio of people—Heather was whispering something in her son's ear. The two girls, Jojo and Sarah had commandeered the glider and were swinging. Corrine sat alone, watching them. Was Willie Lee still okay? Yes, there he was beneath the rose of Sharon, digging for worms.

There was Leanne, her profile turned toward Marilee. Marilee realized the younger woman had her blond hair pinned up in almost the same way Marilee did. Parker was over in the male knot beside the grill, as if this were their domain. She watched him tilt his head in the manner he used when listening, this time to Ted, who seemed to be telling a joke.

Marilee fished the earrings out of her pocket and gazed at them.

Returning them to her pocket, she then filled the ice bucket and returned to the patio to smile and serve as the gracious hostess.

Things might not be as she thought. She should not jump to conclusions.

The moment came, totally unplanned.

Marilee was loading the dishwasher with the first load, Parker was filling the ice bucket from the freezer, and Leanne appeared, bearing an armload of dirty dishes.

"Here's the last of them, I think." Leanne set the dishes on the counter and wiped her hands on her shorts.

"Thank you."

There they were, just the three of them.

"Oh, Leanne . . . I think I have something that belongs to you." Marilee reached into her pocket.

Leanne, who had already turned to leave, paused and cast Marilee a curious look.

Marilee held out the earrings on her palm.

"Oh," Leanne said. Her face lit with recognition, and her hand reached out, then stopped in midair, as her eyes cut to Parker.

Parker, who had turned to look, averted his eyes.

"I found them on Parker's bedside table. I believe they match your necklace, Leanne."

She knew the truth of it, the same as if it had been stated aloud, although no one said a thing.

Leanne's pale eyes studied Marilee, and Parker looked at the floor. She wondered if she had expected him to say anything. Surely she knew him better than to expect him to take his part.

Laying the earrings on the counter, she stepped past Leanne and went out to the patio to gather the tablecloth off the table that Ted and Ray were moving, in order to have room to dance.

Marilee and Parker danced and mingled and gave no indication there was a problem between them, other than that they did not say a direct word to each other, a fact no one seemed to notice. Leanne kept to herself, but no one seemed to notice that, either. A good time was had by all.

Afterward, after everyone had left, traipsing out to their respective vehicles and going away down the gravel drive in a cloud of dust rising in the evening heat, Marilee gave Parker back his ring.

He said, "It didn't mean anything, Marilee . . . it just happened, and you and I weren't engaged then. You wouldn't even sleep with me. Leanne doesn't mean anything to me. Don't take it like this."

She said, "It isn't because of you and Leanne. I understand . . . I know it wasn't anything. It is just that I suddenly realize we are not suited. I apologize that I just now see this. I should have seen it from the beginning. We are great as friends, but not as mates. We'll kill each other in six months, if we live that close. I can't stand it that you put up with mismatched colors."

He was staring at her, possibly, she thought, because she had never dared speak so directly to him. She had never dared to speak so directly to herself.

Gathering her purse and the last bag of her stuff to take home, she headed for the door. He followed close behind her.

"Marilee, let's talk about this."

She was running away, she realized, but did not stop. "Let's talk later, when we've thought this all out," she tossed over her shoulder. That would have to do.

She strode out the door and down the walk to the Cherokee, where Corrine, given the keys, had the engine and air-conditioning running. She got behind the wheel, took a last look at Parker, standing there at his front door, and then turned the car and drove away.

Great emotion welled up in her. It was a great epiphany that seemed to ring out from above and wash all over her.

The incident had given her an out, she realized, experiencing relief. This was followed closely by seeping guilt, because she had basically led Parker on. She had led herself on. She had allowed the fear of loneliness, the desire for physical and financial ease, as well as desire for her mother's approval, plus who knew what-all other motives, to make a fantasy out of a relationship that could be only what it was: friendship. Nothing more.

She had been trying to make herself fit where she was not going to fit, and further, she had been trying to make Parker fit into her image of what she wanted.

She caught sight of his neglected yard in her rearview mirror.

In the nick of time, she thought. In the nick of time.

It was dusk. Marilee walked with Aunt Vella in her aunt's rose garden, where lights stuck in the ground emitted a soft glow. The children chased the first fireflies of the season across the lawn.

"I'm so ashamed," Marilee told her aunt. "I was making my relationship with Parker into something it just couldn't ever be. I was trying to make him how I wanted him to be." She shook her head. "I just saw myself getting older, and I didn't want to be alone, I guess."

"Ah, honey, I know." Aunt Vella put her arm around Marilee and squeezed her tight. "There is nothing to be ashamed of. You had to go through this experience to learn. . . . That's what these things are for. We learn, and we press on ahead, without looking back.

"And as for being alone, well, we all are really, for all of our days on this earth. We are all in this alone together."

Moths were batting around streetlights when Marilee loaded the children and Munro into the Cherokee and headed down the street and around the corner to home.

The Porter house—Holloway house—was dark, the portico where Tate parked empty. He had his dinner with the mayor, she remembered.

And then she was turning into her own driveway. Home. Her porch light shone warmly. She unlocked the door and thought that she could never again enter her house and not be glad to be home. It might be small, but it was so very pleasant, and all the colors matched.

The Valentine Voice

Sunday, May 20

Today's Highlights:

—More people spending their money at home. City sales tax revenue up by 3 percent. Debate as to how to spend money. Story on page 1.

—Tuesday election for city council seat vote. Overview of two candidates: Mayhall versus Tinsley. Story page 1.

—Sinkhole on First Street causes dilemma for City Works Department. Story page 4.

—Majority of Valentine citizens want easier purchase of caskets, but not at discount department stores. Your views on page 3.

Twenty-One

Filling in the Holes

Tate waited until nine o'clock to telephone Charlotte. He was afraid he would either catch her too early and wake her up, or miss her if she went to church. He felt relief when she answered on the second ring, her voice as competent as ever.

"No, it isn't too early. I do sleep in on Sunday mornings, don't get up until seven."

Tate could imagine. "I'm going out of town," he told her. "Down to Houston to see some folks, and then on to Galveston to visit my mother. I'll be back Friday or Saturday at the latest. I finished up my editorials for the next two editions, plus a couple extra pieces, and left them on my desk. I'll be in touch by phone and e-mail. Oh, and tell Marilee not to worry about feeding the cat. I'm takin' him with me."

There wasn't much to that, he thought, as he hung up and finished packing.

He threw his two bags in the back seat of the BMW, with its top down. Then he got Bubba and put him in a cat carrier he had found in the laundry room, and put the carrier in the front seat.

Bubba wasn't happy. He growled. Continually.

A man and his cat. It appeared it had come to this, Tate thought, throwing a towel over Bubba, who then quit growling.

He turned the key, backed out of his drive and started away, thinking that his mother was probably at some healing revival or bridge tournament, and he would end up alone with Bubba, lying in her spare bed with a ceiling fan to look at for the next three days.

No matter. He needed a long drive. He could not stay and see Marilee engaged. Maybe getting away would give him a better perspective. He would come to accept what he could not change.

The sun was bright and warm when Marilee and the children and Munro walked to church. Out front of the parsonage, the sinkhole was still cordoned off with the yellow City Works tape. Holding securely to both children's hands, Marilee took them over to join the small knot of observers. The hole had grown; the engineer at City Works was still working out the best way to deal with it.

Marilee looked at the hole and thought of her life. Munro accompanied them up the steps and into church and into the back pew. He was accepted as routine now.

Marilee, sitting there gazing at the light playing on the altar and determinedly keeping to her no-worry status, was suddenly jerked to awareness by whispers. People were whispering and looking at the group who had just passed Marilee's pew.

It was Winston, with Ruthanne and Mildred on his arms, and Aunt Vella following them, sashaying in a bright floral dress and an enormous sweeping hat. Ramona Stidham, who sat with Norm and an entire pew of grandchildren in front of Marilee, turned and said, "Marilee, I don't care what people say, Vella has sure gotten a life since she and Perry split up."

Getting a life was an apt phrase, Marilee thought, watching her aunt's filmy dress sway as she slipped into the pew beside Winston Valentine. The poor man was somewhat squished, with Mildred leaning toward him on one side, and Aunt Vella smacking him with her hat on the other every time she turned her head.

They stood for the opening hymn. Willie Lee, standing on the pew, leaned on Marilee's arm, his eyes on the hymnal while he tried to sing along as if reading the words. Corrine stood straight, holding open her own hymnal, singing in a faint voice. " 'His eye is on the sparrow . . .' "

Tears of gratitude filled Marilee's eyes. She looked with her blurry vision at the cross on the altar. *I'm sorry, Lord, for all this mess with Parker. I behaved poorly with him. Running on fear, not faith. Show me the way, Lord. I can't do it on my own.*

Just as Pastor Smith was giving the closing blessing, there came the sound of a crash from outside. Before he had properly finished, people were exiting the building, intent to see what had happened. Marilee guarded Corrine and Willie Lee, to keep them from being trampled.

"Well, look at that."

"My Lord."

"Marilee, you'd better get over here for a story."

The pastor's wife's little green Toyota, which had been parked several yards distant from the sinkhole, was now sitting very nearly nose first in the hole that had widened in all directions.

"This is good," said Winston, causing people to look at him. "This thing has probably hit bottom, so there's nowhere to go with it but up."

*   *   *

It was a daunting thought that now she would have to go tell every-one that she and Parker were not getting married after all. She man-aged to get away from church without one person asking her about it, and her Sunday was spent blissfully alone with the children, but on Monday, the prospect loomed over her head.

"I do not want to go down-town," Willie Lee stated, when she told him they were going down to the *Voice* offices.

"You don't?" she said, surprised. Willie Lee was always so agree-able. "I need to take some articles to the paper, honey, and afterward I will take you to get ice cream. Wouldn't you like that?"

"Yes. I like ice cream."

"Then come on. Let's get your shoes on."

Willie Lee shook his head. "Mun-ro and I want to stay home." He climbed on the couch and sat there, looking at her from behind his thick glasses.

"Are you sick, honey?" She felt his forehead. It felt fine.

He looked at her. "No. I am not sick. I want to stay home."

Marilee looked over at Corrine, who sat in the big chair with a book. "I want to stay home, too," Corrine said.

Marilee called Aunt Vella, who readily and eagerly agreed to come stay with the children. "They are probably tired of you draggin' them around everywhere with you," Aunt Vella said.

Likely this was true, Marilee reflected. She needed to find a way to get them interacting with other children.

She decided to walk downtown, and along the way she rehearsed several ways of nonchalantly telling Tate, "Parker and I are not en-gaged. We have called it off."

She had seen Tate only once since the night she and Parker had got-ten officially engaged, when he had taken care of Willie Lee and Cor-rine. He had kissed her quickly, in congratulations. She was disap-pointed that he had not come to her house with a pitcher of iced tea since then. Perhaps he had found some other woman upon whom to bestow his tea. And of course that was just fine. She did not want any-thing special to do with Tate Holloway. In fact, thinking of it further, she was torn between wanting to tell him that the engagement with Parker was off and being quite reluctant to admit it. Tate had been the one to be adamant that Parker was not the one for her. Now she would have to admit he had been right.

Tate's office door was closed, she saw first thing upon coming into the newspaper offices. She had not seen the door closed in some time.

Perhaps he was having a private meeting, maybe with Leo, who was the only one not in evidence.

She went to her desk, plopped down her tote and purse, and stated in a loud voice, to get it over in one fell swoop, "Parker and I are not getting married. We have called it off."

There were the expected surprise and condolences. Reggie, bless her heart, came over and hugged Marilee hard and long.

"I'm here, if you want to talk," Reggie said.

"Thank you, Regg." Her heart warmed. Reggie gave her another quick hug, Imperia kissed her cheek, and June laid a handful of Hershey's chocolate Kisses on her desk.

She looked at the closed door to Zona's office; she did not want to leave the woman out of the goingson, so she went over and knocked.

When Zona's faint, "Come in," sounded, Marilee poked her head in the door and said, "I just wanted to let you know I won't be marrying Parker after all."

"Oh." Zona blinked behind her glasses.

Marilee withdrew and was closing the door, when Zona said, "I'm sorry for your disappointment, Marilee."

She put her head back in again. "I'm okay."

"Good."

Marilee withdrew again, and Zona said, "Maybe you had better leave the door open . . . just a crack."

"Oh, okay. How's that?"

"That's fine. Thank you."

Marilee stood there looking at the crack in Zona's door, the crack in her secure wall.

Then she went back to her desk. Well, she had dispensed with a necessary responsibility, and everyone was back to work at their desks, evidence that her private life had little effect on others.

Her editor's door was still closed. She debated about whether to go knock on it.

She took the update on the sinkhole and the obituary write-ups to Charlotte's desk and said in an offhand manner, "His door is closed. Is he in some sort of meeting?"

Charlotte shook her head. "Nope. Gone for the week, be back Friday or Saturday."

"Oh."

When she recovered enough from this surprise to speak, she said to Charlotte, "I guess you're off the hook for standin' up with me at my wedding."

"I never felt on the hook. I just wasn't too thrilled about you marrying Parker." Charlotte sat back and turned her computer screen to the side.

Marilee looked into the woman's dark eyes. "You knew about him and Leanne."

"Yes."

"Does everyone know?"

"Not everyone, but enough people. Julia Jenkins-Tinsley knows and told."

Marilee let out a large sigh.

"I didn't think it was my place to tell you," Charlotte said, looking apologetic. "Telling just never seems to make anything . . . well, work out."

Marilee nodded, at once touched by Charlotte's caring, and hurt that the woman had held such a secret about her life.

"I never thought you two were suited. You don't match. You are a woman who . . ." Charlotte paused, as if thinking.

"A woman who what?" *A woman like you.*

Charlotte shrugged. "A woman who needs someone different than Parker."

That did not at all satisfy, but Marilee decided she would rather let the subject drop. "I guess I'll go over to the post office and let Julia know the engagement is off. If I tell her and Belinda, I won't have to tell another soul."

"Well, you're probably right there," Charlotte said. Then, as Marilee went out the door, she called, "Oh . . . you don't have to feed Tate's cat. He took it with him."

"Well, my goodness, he must have gotten fond of it."

"A man and his cat," Charlotte said, casting a wave and picking up her glasses to again focus on her computer screen. It was wearing to be involved in people's private lives; she preferred books that she could put down at will.

The phone on her desk rang. Without taking her gaze off the computer screen, she reached to answer. It was her boss.

"Hi, is Marilee there? I just called her house and Vella said she was down there."

"She's already gone . . . just this minute." Charlotte spoke loudly; there was a lot of noise coming across the line.

"Oh." Pause. "Well, how is everything there?"

"The same as always . . . too much for the few of us to do but none of it earthshaking. Oh, except I suppose the sinkhole is earthshaking— it just about ate the pastor's wife's car yesterday morning." She was again raising her voice over background noise on her editor's end, and this made her peevish. "Where are you? What's all that noise?" People should know trying to talk and listen over noise was impolite.

"That's just some friends . . . we're at a bar for lunch."

Now Tate had raised his voice, and Charlotte's mind went into visions that caused some disapproval, and worry. Maybe, because of all the strain of changing the *Voice* around, their editor was going to stray into all manner of irresponsible behavior. He'd just up and left on this trip, like he was running off.

The noise abated. "There, that's better," he said. "Put Reggie on the sinkhole. Tell her just to take a picture and write a caption. No need for an article. We'll begin following it with pictures."

"Marilee took care of it."

"Oh, okay." Pause. "Then everyone is fine."

"Yes, everything is going along fine." Then, because he sounded a little disappointed and she wanted him to feel responsibility, she added, "But you've only been gone a day. You never can tell what emergency might happen. You'd better stay ready."

The visit to Julia Jenkins-Tinsley was short. Marilee poked her head in the door, saw Julia at the counter and said, "Julia, Parker and I have broken off our engagement."

Julia's eyes went round. She opened her mouth, but Marilee pulled her head back out of the doorway and headed down the sidewalk for the drugstore. She required an enormous chocolate sundae.

Just as she entered the store, the door opened and there came Winston, being hustled out the door by Uncle Perry. Marilee had to back up.

"I'll thank you to go use the new Rexall out on the highway," said Uncle Perry, who then shut the door.

Winston straightened himself, smoothing his shirt and adjusting his belt.

"Are you all right, Winston?"

"Yes." He smiled quite happily. "Yes, I am. I stirred him." With a nod and "Good day" to her, he smacked his cane on the concrete and started away.

Marilee went in and checked on her uncle, who she found sitting in his chair, like always, although his face had color in it for the first time in years. She asked him if he was okay, and he said, "I am as okay as any man could be who has been thrown out of his home by his wife gone insane and havin' an affair, and who has a daughter who doesn't want him, either."

For a moment Marilee worked on finding some positive comment to refute the statements. At least she should contradict the accusation of Aunt Vella having an affair. But could she?

What came out was, "I'm sorry, Uncle Perry," and by the look he gave her, she knew she had fallen far short.

She made a retreat to the soda fountain, where the new girl, Nadine, looked at her over the counter.

"I'll have a chocolate . . ." She paused, reconsidering. "I'd like a glass of iced tea," she said. She was ready for a change.

"Sweetened or unsweetened?" Nadine asked.

"Sweetened." She watched the girl turn to fill the order. She had to stand on tiptoe to get the glass. "Where is my cousin this morning?" she asked.

"Upstairs . . . said she was goin' to put a cold cloth on her head."

"Oh." Marilee sat there, her eyes coming around to see her image in the long mirror on the wall.

Nadine set the tall glass, with a slice of lemon on the rim, in front of Marilee and plunked down a spoon beside it, then turned back to her compulsion of wiping every bit of stainless steel in sight.

Marilee sipped the tea and occasionally looked at herself in the long mirror on the wall. She made no effort to figure out anyone's life, not even her own. For those minutes she sat and relished the cold sweet tea in a tall glass, and it was enough.

When she finished, she put the money on the counter and said to Nadine, "Please give Belinda a message for me. Tell her that her cousin Marilee and Parker Lindsey broke off their engagement."

Then she left and walked home, thoroughly refreshed.

It needed to be done. A full apology and explanation were in order. If he did not want to speak to her, he could say so.

She telephoned Parker and asked if he was free to come by that evening.

He said, "Yeah . . . I guess I can."

It was dusk when he arrived. She met him on the front porch. "The children are watching a movie on television. Let's sit on the steps."

They sat side by side. Parker didn't say anything; he sat rubbing his hands together as he often did when uncertain. Marilee reminded herself that she was the one who had requested the meeting. She had rehearsed what she was going to say and still had great difficulty getting the words to her tongue. "I'm sorry, Parker, for how I've treated you."

He looked surprised, but said nothing.

She took a breath and went on to say that she had been attempting to make more out of their relationship than was there all along. She had done this by having the wrong motives, and said she had not seen the reason she kept putting off sleeping with him was that she was not as committed to the relationship as she believed. She explained that she was just not ready to be married. Finally she quit talking, because she doubted that Parker got any of it anyway. She doubted she had made a lot of sense out of something that even she did not fully understand.

"I do hope we can be friends. We always were good friends," she ended.

She wondered about Parker's motive for wanting to marry her, but decided not to ask. If he said he loved her, she doubted she would believe it. She suspected he had wanted to marry her simply to get her into bed again, which seemed really strange, so perhaps it was that added to someone to keep house and cook for him. Parker did seem to need taking care of.

The extent of what Parker said was, "Yeah . . . I guess we're pretty good friends."

Marilee looked out at the streetlight where it pooled on the sidewalk. Yep, nick of time.

Twenty-Two

Family Matters

Corrine was reading in the big chair when she heard a car pull up in the driveway. Her Aunt Marilee was working at her desk. She sat there staring at the computer, with her chin propped on her hand, looking like she did when she was frustrated. Willie Lee and Munro were watching cartoons on the television.

Corrine, as if her antenna were tuned to any change, rose up enough to see out the window. The car, sleek and dark, was unfamiliar; an unfamiliar man was getting out from the driver's side.

With a gulp, Corrine slipped down beside Willie Lee and whispered in his ear, "Somebody's here. Take Munro in the bedroom."

He cast her a puzzled frown, and she made wide eyes at him. "Hurry up . . . they might be here for Munro." Ever since that day when the two people downtown had tried to get Munro, she had been on the lookout and ready.

Willie Lee scrambled to his feet, causing Aunt Marilee to look over from the computer. Corrine heard voices coming up the walk and shook her head at Willie Lee, to tell him to keep his mouth shut. He and Munro went on to the bedroom, and Corrine looked at the door. Someone knocked.

Corrine went to the door and slowly opened it, peering around it with half an idea that she could shut it again if need be.

It was her mother standing there. Her mother with a smiling face.

"Hello, hon. Are you gonna let me in?"

"Mama!"

Marilee, in something of a daze, walked across the room to greet her sister, taking in the man standing behind Anita with a cursory glance, before her gaze fell totally on her sister's head bent against Corrine's. Two dark heads together, two at last.

Then Anita looked up at Marilee, her expression so hesitant and doubtful of her welcome, that Marilee instantly opened her arms, and the two of them fell together, embracing and crying, "Ohmygosh, it is good to see you!"

It was strange how the burst of warm closeness could quickly fade to one of caution.

Marliee made coffee for her sister, who had come, out of the blue, not even calling first, taking for granted, of course, that Marilee would be right here where she always was—good ol' Marilee—just waiting to see Anita and entertain her and the man who had brought her, Louis Alvarez, a man so handsome and full of sex appeal that he could probably get women to drop their pants with one glance of his smoldering eyes.

Marilee, after the initial surprise, told herself she had been awaiting such a visit. Anita was given to showing up when she felt like it. Listening to Anita's and Corrine's voices, softly talking, coming from the dining room, she felt a stab of fear. *Was Anita going to take Corrine away?*

Parker had been so right; she had not wanted to deal with this happening. For an instant she felt as if her brain were sizzling and she might just go all to pieces.

With a deep breath, she straightened her shoulders and put the hot pot of coffee on a tray, with cups and saucers, cream and sugar, glasses of juice for the children, and her best cloth napkins. She carried it all in to the table.

"I'm sorry I don't have a coffee cake or anything. I planned to go shopping this evenin'." It was lunchtime. She could not feed them peanut butter and jelly, which she had planned for her and the children. "Would you two like pizza? I could order it in."

"Oh, we don't need anything, Marilee. Don't fuss." Anita flashed a smile bright as a camera bulb. Anita was as beautiful as ever, thoroughly and expertly made up, hair shining, clothes as if they came from Neiman-Marcus, which she had always managed, even when unemployed. She laughed gaily. "Louis doesn't eat sweets anyway."

Louis, who drove a Jaguar and wore a large diamond ring on his little finger, looked like nothing softer than well-done steak ever entered his mouth.

Marilee passed out the cups of coffee and tried to ignore that her hair was pulled back in a band, and she wore a T-shirt and sweatpants.

"My car would never have made this trip," Anita said. "But I wanted to see my baby—" she stroked Corrine's hair "—so Louis said he would bring me. We can't stay . . . just this afternoon, and we have to get back. Louis has a court case tomorrow, and I've got to be back at work."

No mention of taking Corrine with her.

Marilee studied her sister's face, then looked over to see Corrine's dark eyes moving anxiously back and forth from Anita to the dark-haired, totally impassive Louis.

Willie Lee came and showed his Aunt Anita his dog and his fresh bucket of worms dug just that morning. When she asked how he kept the worms alive, he told her he let them go every night in the garden. "But I keep Mun-ro with me. He sleeps with me. He is my dog. Some peo-ple tried to take him away, but they did not get him."

"Well . . . that's good," Anita said.

"Who tried to take Munro, Willie Lee?" Marilee asked, puzzled about the comment. She could not recall any such incident.

"Oh, it was the dogcatcher came by," Corrine put in, "while you were in the florist . . . remember? We told them that Munro was our dog."

"Yes, they were try-ing to catch my dog," Willie Lee said.

"I'm hungry," Corrine said, sliding off her chair. "I'm going to make us sandwiches, okay, Aunt Marilee? Willie Lee can help me. You all stay there and talk."

She and Willie Lee, followed by Munro, went into the kitchen. Marilee saw Anita leaning over, following her daughter with her eyes, until the swinging door came swinging closed. Then Anita and her Louis and Marilee all looked at each other, in the manner of wondering what in the world to talk about now that they were left on their own.

Marilee picked up the pot of coffee. It was still warm; she had made it strong, and now it was thick as sludge, but Louis pushed his cup forward. He did not use cream or sugar. He had yet to say a full sentence, she realized.

"So you are an attorney, Louis?" Marilee asked, surveying him, wondering what sort of bad habits were hidden beneath his fine clothes and appearance.

"Yes," he said, his eyes coming up and meeting hers in a surprisingly straightforward manner. "I work for the county prosecutor's office."

"Ah. Sounds interesting." She experienced a sort of attack of liking for the man. It came from his steady gaze and steady tone of voice.

"You're not wearing a ring," Anita said, as Marilee spooned sugar into her warm coffee.

At Marilee's look, Anita said, "Mama called me last Friday and

said you and Parker are gettin' married. Where's your ring? Didn't
Parker give you a ring?"

Bingo. This was the reason for the sudden visit, and for hauling up
here with her Mr. Stud-man.

"Parker and I called it off," Marilee said.

Anita looked startled. "Called it off? But didn't you just get engaged last Thursday?"

"Wednesday. And we called it off Saturday, after his birthday party.
We realized our error quickly." She did not know what possessed her,
but she looked straight at Louis and said, "So, Louis, are you and
Anita getting married?"

He shook his head, and it was his turn to surprise her, when he said,
"I'm already married."

Marilee, who had just sipped her coffee, almost spat it out.

They had long been separated by Anita's bent for the "high life,"
and Marilee's bent for the quiet side. Anita, in anger, went her way,
and Marilee, in anger, went hers, and every once in a while, when
Anita needed Marilee, the two got together. Why was it Anita never
seemed to think that maybe sometimes Marilee needed her? Maybe
she did think it and didn't care, and this caused Marilee's stomach to
knot.

She was not surprised that Anita intended to leave Corrine with her
indefinitely. She *was* a little surprised that Anita was moving with
Louis to New Orleans.

"He's takin' a position there with a private law firm . . . a big, important firm," she said, and reached up to break a leaf off a low-hanging branch of the elm tree.

They were out in the yard, walking around the garden, just the two
of them alone. Standing there, with a slice of late-afternoon sun playing on her dark hair, there was about Anita the air of a woman on the
edge. Marilee could not put her finger on it. Her sister had always
been too much, she thought. Too beautiful, too sensitive, too wild and
passionate, all too much for her small body and unstable spirit.

"And what will you do?" Marilee wanted to shake Anita. "You're
going to up and leave your good job at the courthouse?"

"Louis will see if I can get on at the firm." Anita, withdrawing from
Marilee's annoyance, played the leaf around in the air. "I have experience now in the legal field, and offices always need experienced secretaries. If the firm doesn't want me, there'll be somewhere I can work."

"You are not going to marry him, but you are going to base your
life on his. So, where does his wife fit in?"

"Oh, don't be so righteous, Marilee. His wife has left him but doesn't want a divorce and will make it real nasty if he tries it. Is your life any better? Stuck here in this one-horse town, workin' like a dog to keep this little cottage. Lordy."

"This little cottage is apparently good enough for your daughter."

Anita's eyes flashed at her. "I'm not you, Marilee, and I never will be."

"Thank God" hung in the air.

Anita's eyes were pinpoints. "I need a man in my life, Marilee. I don't want to be a woman alone. I don't see any future at all in that. At least, not a future worth livin'."

Marilee, gazing into her sister's sultry countenance, thought that she agreed a lot with the sentiment, if not fully, but that it would do no good to discuss her views.

In an instant Anita turned all sweetness, as if turning on a faucet, and went on about how the cottage and Valentine really were most suited to raising children, and how Marilee was a much better mother than she herself could be. Marilee realized that whenever anyone wanted her to do something, they would praise her as being so much better at it than themselves.

"I need time to catch up," Anita said. "I'm going to keep saving, and in another nine months or so, maybe I can have a proper home in New Orleans for Corrine. Until then, I'm so grateful to you, Marilee. I know Corrine is well taken care of . . . much better off than she would be with me trying to get my life established."

Marilee, who had been doing some figuring of her own, said, "*You* tell Corrine your plans."

"Oh, won't you? You are so much better at it than I am." She cast her sweet, little-girl smile.

"No." She did not feel guilty for her stance, either.

Anita and Corrine went for a walk to have a talk; Willie Lee went out back to put his worms to bed in the garden. This left Marilee to entertain Louis. Neither of them knew what to say to the other, although this did not seem to bother Louis. Possibly not much at all could bother Louis.

Just then there came the sound of the ice cream truck. Marilee said, "Would you like a fudge Popsicle from the ice-cream man?"

A look of delight bloomed on the man's chiseled face. "Yeah . . . I haven't had one of those in years."

Marilee grabbed her purse and ran outside to wave down the colorful, slow-moving van that came along sounding its gay tune. It occurred to her that her world was beginning to revolve around food. It did seem to soothe the savage beast.

When she came back in the house, Louis stood at her desk, the telephone to his ear. He thrust the receiver at her. "It's for you."

"Thank you." She handed him his fudge Popsicle, said into the phone, "Just a minute," and went to put the other Popsicles she had purchased into the freezer.

Back again at the phone, she was startled to hear Tate's low drawl come across the line. "Hi, Miss Marilee, this is Tate. Who was that who answered the phone? He said his name was Louis."

"Yes. Louis." She had the perverse inclination to not explain.

"Who is Louis?"

She was being silly. "My sister's boyfriend." She looked over to see Louis licking his fudge Popsicle like a little boy. It was an arresting sight. For an instant Marilee could clearly see Anita's point about wanting a man.

"Oh. So your sister is visitin'?"

"Yes. She came up for the day."

He paused. She thought to say: *Parker and I are no longer engaged.*

Good grief, she could not say it straight out. And why should she tell him? She would feel the biggest fool. He had told her that Parker was not for her. She hated to admit that he had been right.

"How is the city council election coverage coming?" he asked.

"Tammy is doing the coverage today, and I have interviews with both candidates in the morning, after the firm results. We'll get it in the Wednesday afternoon edition. Are you having a nice vacation?"

"Of sorts." He did not seem thrilled. She was glad, and felt silly.

He said, "So everything is goin' along all right up there—no hitches?"

"None that I know of." She supposed her called-off engagement was a hitch in things going along. At least a change of direction. She could slip it in now.

She didn't.

She never did say anything about it. She and Tate, both obviously at a loss for words, said goodbye and hung up. That she had not told him about her canceled engagement was annoying. It really was not so big a deal, though. Why would he care?

But she did think he would care. She hoped he would care, and this hope made her quite annoyed.

Louis was over at the table eating his fudge Popsicle with great concentration, probably in the same manner he would grill a defendant, or perhaps lick a woman.

She went and called Willie Lee and got their Popsicles and joined Louis, all three sitting there having a pretty grand time licking when Anita and Corrine came in the door. Corrine did not want her Popsicle. Anita ate only a bite of hers before giving hers over to Louis, who licked it like a boy.

Standing at the bottom of the porch steps, Corrine watched her mother drive away. Aunt Marilee stood beside her, with a hand on her shoulder. Her mother called from the car, "Love you, honey," and waved and acted like she was about to cry. Corrine stood there and did not cry. She would not cry about it.

When the car was gone, she felt her Aunt Marilee looking at her. She hated her aunt looking, and she hated everybody.

"Come on, Willie Lee." She did not hate Willie Lee. Willie Lee was the one person on earth she loved, and in that minute it was like every bit of love she had inside focused on him to such a degree she just about lost her breath. "We'll finish putting your worms to bed."

She turned and went straight through the house and out the back door, with Willie Lee and Munro following behind. She got down on her knees in the dirt. Put her hands in it. It was just about too dark to see any worms, but she wanted to dig. She could feel Aunt Marilee come to look out at them every now and then.

It was understandable that her mother would leave her here with Aunt Marilee. Her mother said she wanted to get them a nice house in New Orleans. Her mother was moving very far this time; usually it was just across town, leaving because she couldn't pay the rent, or was embarrassed because of one of her boyfriends. Corrine wanted to stay with Aunt Marilee; she liked it here. It was okay what her mother did. She didn't care. It didn't matter.

Marilee was at the kitchen table, jotting a grocery list; actually, making up a grocery list was something to do to let her sit at the table and do nothing. Her energy seemed at a low ebb. It was as if Anita had taken it all away. She kept trying to figure out what she should say to Corrine, if anything. Corrine seemed perfectly contained, not upset at all. Perhaps Marilee was blowing things all out of proportion.

Corrine, all bathed and in fresh pajamas, came into the kitchen and asked if she could have a juice drink from the refrigerator.

"Sure, honey." Marilee, trying not to appear to stare, noticed Corrine had dark circles under her eyes.

Corrine got the juice, uncapped the bottle and threw the lid in the trash. Marilee went back to trying to make a grocery list.

Then, "Aunt Marilee, why doesn't my mother want me?"

Marilee's head came up to see Corrine standing there, her bottom lip trembling.

In an instant Marilee had Corrine in her arms, and she held Corrine, until Corrine pushed away, choking somewhat and gasping for breath. Possibly, Marilee thought, she had been holding her niece way too tight, in her great urge to absorb the child's pain and make everything all right with a hug.

Wiping the tears away, Corrine turned and took up her juice. "I'm sorry . . . it doesn't matter."

"Oh, yes, it does matter." Marilee spoke so forcefully that she startled both herself and Corrine.

All right, God, tell me what to say.

She took Corrine's hand. "It is not that your mother does not want you. That's not it at all. As a single woman, your mother is in a diffi cult position. She does not have the skills to earn a salary that can support you and her at an adequate level."

Corrine's dark eyes were on her.

Marilee closed her mouth and searched for elusive honesty. "Corrine, it isn't about wanting you or not wanting you. It is about your mother being your mother. None of it is about you. It is about your mother and her needs, and what happens is that you are caught in that. You have not caused your mother to make this choice, and you cannot change it.

"And really, your mother is making a decision that benefits all of us. God knew I wanted more children, and this is His way of letting me have a daughter. It is perfect. Your mother wants you to have a good solid home, and I want you to be here with me. I'm so glad you are here, Corrine."

She tugged her niece to her again and attempted to hug everything right, but trying not to do so with quite as much force. Corrine accepted this.

Feeling as if she had yet not gotten everything said that needed saying, just before Corrine went to bed, Marilee gave it another go.

"I want to tell you something important, and that is that every feeling you have matters. When you are angry, it matters. When you feel hurt, it matters, the same as when you are happy. We matter because we are human beings who are children of God. You matter, I matter, Willie Lee matters, Mr. Tate matters . . . each person on earth." Suddenly, with startling clarity, Marilee knew that she was saying this to herself, to the little girl who still lived inside and who had to hear the words. "Don't ever again say that you, or how you feel, does not matter."

"Yes, Aunt Marilee." Corrine's dark eyes blinked impassively.

Marilee, persistent for her own need as much as for what she thought her niece needed, again hugged Corrine, and after a brief hesitation, Corrine hugged her back.

Later Marilee thought of how upset Parker would have been at the turn of events. And how happy she was at it. She felt a little guilty, for it meant she was glad Anita had abdicated her role as mother. That was the truth of it, Lord. Forgive me. I am glad.

It had to be done. Marilee had put it off as long as she could. She telephoned her mother to tell her that she and Parker would not be getting married after all.

"Hi, Mom. How was your trip to Las Vegas?"

"Wore me out. We had a good time, but it wore me out. We didn't get home until noon yesterday. We decided to stay over Sunday night, because Carl and Charlie Linford got to playing slot machines, and Carl got on a roll. He just started winnin' and winnin'. I played, too, and I won three hundred dollars, but Carl won two thousand, so he told me to go change our plane reservations. I didn't want to do it, but I did, and when I came back, Carl had won another five thousand dollars, at the slot machine. His machine hit some premium number. When that happens a light goes off on your machine, and a guy will come over and give you a ticket for the money. When I got there, a crowd was all around where Carl had been playing, and I thought at first that he'd had a heart attack."

When her mother paused for a breath, Marilee, quite impressed, said, "That is just wonderful, Mom."

"Well, you know Carl had to keep on then. He gave me five hundred of it, and he took the rest. I played the machines for a while, but then just went up to bed, and Carl played way into the night, until they wouldn't let him play anymore, because he'd had too much to drink. He had won another four thousand, though."

Marilee was amazed. "Carl won eleven thousand dollars?"

"Yes, he did. He didn't know how much he had won by the time he came up to the room. He had a bucket, but he had chips stuck all in his coat and pants pockets. I pulled one out of each of his shoes, even. Heaven knows what he was thinking, but he had tucked them in his shoes.

"I took all of those out of his clothes, and I went downstairs and cashed them in. There was nearly fifteen hundred dollars from just in his clothes. He never knew when he woke up. He just remembered about the bucketful. And then, while we were waitin' for our cab, he went in there and lost that entire bucket at the blackjack table."

"Oh."

"I never did tell him about that fifteen hundred dollars I got out of his clothes. He remembered the five hundred he'd given me and wanted that, but I wouldn't give it to him. I told him I had paid it on his drink bill." Her mother's voice dropped. "I want you to help me get it into the bank down there in Valentine. Carl won't know about it there. I want you to help me choose a CD."

Marilee sat there a minute. Then she said, "The bank will help you choose a CD. I wanted to tell you that Parker and I are not getting married."

She did not know why every conversation with her mother seemed as if they each spoke a foreign language.

Twenty-Three

Seize the Day

He spilled his guts to his mother, in her kitchen at 6:00 a.m., over morning coffee. His mother had already had her meditation and yoga workout, and having slept very little, he had lain in his bed, listening to her stir.

He had, he realized, come running to her just as he always had, despite being a man of a certain age. He was also quite amazed at his level of heartache. He simply had not known what was going on inside him until he had arrived at his mother's house and found he didn't want to bathe or shave.

Now that he had poured out his difficulty of wanting a woman he could not have, he didn't feel any better, either. If anything, he felt worse.

His mother's response was not a great deal of help. When he had finished with his sad tale of love rejected, she said, "So she got engaged, and you ran off."

Tate did not appreciate this take on the situation. "I let go. I quit tryin' to make it be my way. She's made her choice. I'm not going to beat my head against a brick wall to change things I cannot change."

"Oh, pshaw . . . all she did was get engaged." She sipped her ginseng tea. "You can let go but still stay around to see what happens and see if things are eventually going to go your way. What you did was more like giving up. Two different things entirely."

Tate was stung. He had not expected this criticism.

"People often change their minds, most especially about being engaged," his mother continued. "You don't know that she might not have changed her mind the next day. You were too busy runnin' off because of your hurt pride."

As Tate saw it, a man did have his pride.

"You're down here, so you aren't goin' to know what is goin' on up there. You say this Parker fella isn't right for your Marilee. Well, it may take time for her to realize this. What if she realizes it while you're down here pitying yourself?"

"I am not pitying myself." Tate did not appreciate the picture his mother painted of him. He smoothed his hair and got up to refill his coffee, real coffee, not some health-nut stuff his mother wanted to palm off on him.

Grudgingly, he could admit to slogging around in a bit of pity. Maybe ankle deep.

"You wanted my opinion, and I'm givin' it. Get back up there and see what develops."

"I didn't ask for your opinion," he clarified. "I just wanted you to listen . . . and to make me feel better." He was disappointed and annoyed, and felt very childish.

His mother got up and came over, kissed him and hugged him hard. "There you go."

Just before noon, the door opened and Charlotte looked up to see a man enter. Young, in his twenties, thin as a rail, and wearing his slacks high at his waist. Her mother would have told him to jerk his trousers down where they belonged. It was, however, his great height that arrested her attention; she found herself looking at his thighs, and then her gaze moved upward, higher and higher, to six and a half feet at the very least.

"Hello. I'm Sandy Conroy."

"Hello . . . Mr. Conroy," Charlotte said, as she slowly stood, until she was straight as a rod. Finally, at long last, she was looking upward at a man. "Can I help you?"

"I'm here to see Mr. Holloway."

"I'm sorry. Mr. Holloway is out of town. Was he expecting you?"

"Well, no . . . well, yes, ma'am, but he was expectin' me next week. He's hired me to do layout. I was supposed to be in next week, but I decided to come on down."

Charlotte saw his blush and instantly drew the conclusion that there was a story behind his coming early. The most likely scenario would be a breakup with his girlfriend.

"I should have called, I guess." He looked at a loss.

"I can show you to your desk," Charlotte said so quickly that he blinked. She suddenly was not going to take a chance on him leaving.

"Oh, I'm Charlotte Nation. I'm the receptionist and general do-all person."

She put out her hand, and he shook it with some eagerness. "Glad to meet you, ma'am." At his touch Charlotte thought something happened to her. She seemed to lose coherent thought.

Seeking to regain her poise, she strode firmly back to the office cubicle that had belonged to their former layout artist, gesturing along the way at the empty desks—"The paper is put to bed, so everyone sort of scatters, and Leo has taken the disks to the printer . . . he'll see to the deliveries later."—and Zona's office, telling him the names of his new colleagues. She was thrilled to be walking beside a man who stood a full head taller than herself.

She had to knock dust off the desk. Only then did she notice he carried a bulging case with him, likely a portable computer. "This space hasn't been used much since we lost our layout man, several months ago now. June uses the long table some."

He placed his case on the desk and looked around. He was shy, and quite suddenly Charlotte felt very shy. It was such a foreign emotion that she didn't know how to handle it. She had no idea of where to lay her eyes, because she found she could not meet his gaze.

"There's the coffee machine," she said gesturing. "Oh, only there isn't any coffee made, since the editor is out. But you can help yourself to the cold drinks in the refrigerator . . . if there are any. I don't know. I haven't looked today. I like mixed juice drinks, but I haven't brought any down this week. Sometimes the editor puts Orange Crush in there. Do you like that?"

She was rattling and just came out with the question, while what she was really thinking as she gazed into his soft brown eyes was: Are you free and open to an older woman, and would you possibly like Chinese food, which is my favorite?

"Yes, I like Orange Crush," he said, seeming a little surprised at the question.

"Well, help yourself. Look around. I'll leave you to settling in." She was backing up. "If you need anything, let me know."

She beat a retreat to her desk, sat herself squarely, and sought to find her familiar composed, even cool, self. Goodness. She was shy. This was quite a surprise. It had never happened to her before. She did not care for the feeling.

As she struggled to bring herself into some order, she attempted to focus on her computer screen, while her eyes were repeatedly drawn back to the young man moving around in his glass cubicle. The ringing of the phone was a welcome interruption.

"Charlotte?" It was the editor.

"Yes. It's a good thing you called."

"It didn't sound like you. Why? What's happened? Is there trouble with the Wednesday edition?"

She was a little surprised at his rapid-fire questions. Her boss did not usually speak so fast. He sounded almost as if he wanted trouble. "No trouble with the paper. It's a light edition, already gone to the printer. But the layout artist you hired—Sandy Conroy—has shown up."

"I wasn't expecting him until next week."

"That's what he said."

"Well, make him welcome. You can show him his desk and stuff."

"I did." Did he think she'd thrown him out? "He's at his desk now. Do you want to speak to him?"

Her editor said he did want to talk to the "young man." Charlotte called back, "Mr. Conroy, the editor is on the phone for you," and punched the button.

Sandy Conroy was looking wide-eyed at her through his window. Then his phone rang, and he answered it. Charlotte sat there thinking that he wasn't all that young. He had just taken a responsible position at a newspaper.

The two men conversed for some minutes, and then Sandy Conroy lifted his head right over his cubicle window and hollered, "He wants to talk to you again, Miss Charlotte."

She snatched up the phone and pressed the button. Her editor told her the young man was starting immediately and to have Zona cut him a check for a week's pay. He then wanted to know who won the council seat, and she told him it was Jaydee Mayhall by a landslide. "He was embarrassing going on about it, and then him and Juice got into it so bad that Sheriff Oakes hauled them in for disorderly conduct last night. Marilee interviewed them both at the jailhouse, right after they were let out. Reggie got a picture, too."

"I've missed some excitement," he said. "Where is Marilee? I called her house, but no one answered. She didn't go get married today, did she?"

"Oh, no. Marilee and Parker broke up."

"They broke up?"

Her editor fairly yelled, and this got her attention. She had been concentrating so hard on an unobtrusive way to ask about Sandy Conroy's age that she had not fully processed his question, which, now that she thought of it, was a very telling one.

"When?" he demanded.

"Well . . . they were broke up on Monday." She had not asked Marilee when, and she didn't think it really mattered, although she clearly saw the situation now.

"Why didn't anyone tell me?"

"You weren't here, and I did not know you particularly wanted to know." Okay, that dealt with, she said in a hoarse whisper, "How old is Sandy Conroy?"

"Uh . . . twenty-five. And, Miss Charlotte, don't let Marilee get back engaged to that idiot before I get there."

"I don't think I can do anything about what Marilee does." Her editor was getting carried away.

"I put you in charge of it—and in charge of helping Sandy Conroy find a place to live, so you owe me. I'll be there tonight." And the line clicked dead.

She sat there, wondering how she could have been so blind to her editor's inclinations toward Marilee, but then her gaze slipped over, and she was looking through the window of Sandy Conroy's office again. It was only an eleven-year difference. That wasn't so much. And he was taller than she was. He was so tall that she could once again wear high heels.

What she thought was something along the lines of: Seize the day. She had spent too long mooning after Leo, Sr., and many others before him, men who were too short to be fully satisfying, and usually married or otherwise beyond her reach. She had done this because she was afraid to reach out. Now, here before her, was a real chance, and she was going to go forward and take it.

She pushed her chair away from her desk, took up her purse and walked back toward the young man's office. On the way she poked her head inside Zona's cracked door and said, "Zona, Editor says cut a week's check for Sandy Conroy. We'll pick it up later. I'm leaving for the day. You are now in charge."

She proceeded onward so quickly that she caught the barest glimpse of Zona's shocked expression.

"The editor said for me to help you find an apartment. Would you like to go check out some places, and then possibly have supper?" She was no longer shy. She knew what she wanted. Her ship had come in.

"Well . . . yes, thank you." His grin was shy but wide.

As she walked beside him out the door, she dared to slip her arm through his, and she stood straight and tall.

After some minutes, Zona came to her door and peeked her head out, looking around at the huge empty room. Slowly she opened her door wider and left it that way. Everyone was getting too lax in the workings of this paper, and the responsibility to hold the fort apparently had fallen to her. She could do this, for Ms. Porter.

Tate told his mother, "Okay, you were right."

She did not ask what about but said simply, "I won't ever say I told you so."

In twenty minutes he had his bags packed, Bubba stuffed into his carrier, and was loading his car. His mother brought him a mason jar of cold tea with lots of ice, just like the ones she would pack in the old days, for working in the cotton fields. For an instant, memory of how cool and sweet the tea would be on his tongue and going down his hot throat washed over him.

"Thanks, Mom," he said and kissed her cheek.

"You're welcome, and now remember: everything will turn out how it is supposed to, and in its own time."

"That isn't what you were saying this mornin'."

"I could not say it then, because you were running away, upsetting the flow of life. Go back up there and get into the flow."

She was standing in her little yard, watching after him, as he drove away with the salty air of the Gulf blowing around his windshield. He gauged that he could get to Valentine in less than seven hours. And he supposed he had within his reach the best secrets of life: cold sweet tea and a high heart.

When Perry came driving down the street, Vella was sitting on the front porch, drinking iced tea flavored with her own mint leaves. She had not wanted to start sitting on her porch; that was something her mother and other old ladies did. However, she had been taken with a new set of wicker furniture on sale up at the Home Depot, really pretty, newfangled wicker that went through anything and never molded, so the brochure said.

Her front porch was beautiful with it, and once she had sat down in the chair, she found it rather relaxing, sitting there, gazing out at the street, watching the birds and rabbits, a blue jay harass a cat. Certainly it wasn't as bad as she had anticipated. She didn't feel any older or more depressed sitting on the front porch than she did sitting anywhere else. In fact, it did seem to soothe her.

Sitting there, she was quite surprised to see Perry's black Lincoln approaching in the middle of the morning. She did not think she had ever seen him go anywhere outside the pharmacy before five o'clock in the afternoon, not in a decade, since they had buried his brother in a morning service. She felt a flicker of anticipation. Of hope, and it ran along the lines of her husband dashing up in the driveway and saying he had come to be the man she had married.

Watching the black Lincoln more or less crawl along the street at an incredibly slow pace, however, she squashed that fantasy down in the manner of swatting a fly. Get real, Vella. The black Lincoln turned into the driveway so slowly that it looked like it might just roll back out again. Vella found herself tensing, as if trying to give the car a helping hand. Somebody needed to tell Perry that if he couldn't drive with more conviction, he needed to get off the road.

When he got out of the car, he hitched up his pants and gave a look around, then started up the walk. About halfway along, his head came up and he saw her for the first time. He sort of jumped, his eyes widening.

"It's me," she said. Who in the world did he expect to find here?

He did not reply, and she might have known he would not.

He came up the walk and stopped at the foot of the stairs. Lord, he looked awful. Her gaze moved back and forth from her husband to his car, which she noticed had stuff piled inside it at the same time that she took note that his shirt looked as if he had deliberately squashed it into a ball before putting it on. He needed a haircut, and his pants were sagging. He looked generally wrung out. How would anyone confidently accept a prescription filled by this man?

"My television took out down at the store." He squinted at her. "I came for the one in the kitchen." He squinted at her.

"It isn't in the kitchen anymore. I put it in the closet under the stairs. You're welcome to it."

He stood there a moment more, then started up the stairs, holding to the handrail, his head bent, as if to watch carefully his footsteps that trudged.

Oh, Lord, oh, Lord. Vella felt emotions, like bubbles, erupt from deep within her and move upward: pity, resentment, regret, guilt.

She sat very still. Perry opened the door and went inside. The storm door closed after him. Shifting her gaze to his car, she saw shirts hanging at the back window. It looked like clothes were lying over the front seat. Panic mounted. Was he living in his car? Had he come to this? Whatever would she do?

She was not responsible for him; he was a man grown. If he could not take the initiative to go to a motel or do his laundry, so be it. She was not his mother. She picked up her glass of tea, drank deeply and wrestled with her demons, trying to bring out her better self, but uncertain as to just what that entailed. She had been uncertain about this for some time. *Lord, help!*

Perry, standing with the door of the closet open, cocked his head, listening for his wife to come inside. He wished she would come inside and start a conversation.

Moving slowly, still listening, he bent into the closet and hefted out the television; it was a little heavier than he had anticipated. He wondered at Vella having hauled it into the closet. He felt like a wimp, and he jerked it up, got it out of the closet, and then he felt stuck with a kink in his back. He had the fleeting thought that maybe in carrying it he would suffer a heart attack. Vella would not be able to boot him out then.

Pretending to be ill had been Winston's suggestion, as if that were the only way he could get his foot back in his own house. Truth was, he had been thinking along the same lines, and then Winston had gone and suggested it, which made Perry furious. He could not go and follow a suggestion from Winston.

It did not appear that Vella was going to come in to see what was taking him so long, and the television was getting heavy, just standing there holding it. He went to the door and realized he could not open it and carry the television at the same time. He banged on the door.

"All you had to do was ask," Vella said, opening the door for him. "You don't have to bang down the house."

"Open the dang door wider, then."

He got out on the front porch and with sudden decision veered over to the porch rail, where he set the television. He pulled a handkerchief out of his pocket to mop his face.

"How did you get this dang thing in the closet?" he had to ask.

"I put it on the towel it was sittin' on and dragged it in there. I couldn't carry it."

He felt silly. Of course, he wouldn't have been able to drag it across the living room carpet. And he felt good that he had carried it.

"Are you livin' in your car?" Vella asked.

"My wife threw me out of my house." She ought to know what she was putting him through. "And there ain't room at Belinda's for my clothes."

"Don't you know how to go on out to the Motel 6 and get yourself a room? Don't you know how to find an apartment?"

"Maybe I don't want to." That answer did not suffice. He felt he had never been clever with words.

He had sat down before he knew he was going to. Suddenly his legs would not carry him farther. The thought of leaving the porch made him feel that all would be lost.

And unless he asked Vella to go down there ahead of him and open the door, he would have to go down there, set the television on the hood, open the door and scoot clothes out of the way to make room for it. If she did go down there and open the door, she would see the mess of his car, and she would have a great comment on that. He did not think he could stand up under her comments.

Vella sat down in the other chair, on the other side of the door. She kept looking at the car and feeling guilty, mad at herself for it, and mad at Perry.

"Where's your boyfriend?" Perry asked. "I thought you two were a hot combo?"

"If you mean Winston, he is where he is every afternoon, at home takin' a nap. And no, we are not a hot combo . . . except maybe compared to you and I. Two dead people are a hot combo compared to us. And Winston and I do converse. We have not burned our brains away with the television."

The truth was that Winston had proved a disappointment to Vella. She had gotten carried away with a fantasy there. Winston was not up to her fantasy. It could very well be that *she* was not up to her fantasy.

Just then, at the same instant, they each let out great sighs. Vella looked over at Perry, and he looked over at her.

"I'm not up to this, Vella."

That his words so closely mirrored her thoughts startled her.

"I'll help you carry the television," she told him, and slid to the edge of the wicker chair.

"No, I don't mean that . . . I mean startin' a new life somewheres besides here. I'm not up to gettin' out there by myself, and I don't think I'm up to anything you want from me, either." His voice cracked, bless his heart. And then he said in a worn-out tone, "I think the only thing I am up to is sittin' on this porch."

The idea came to him that he was going to sit on the porch and not leave. Vella would have to call the police, and they would have to forcibly remove him. Sitting still was one thing he could darn well do.

He realized just then that the chair was brand-new. "I like this chair." He had always found fancy outdoor chairs lacking in strength to hold his big frame, but this one felt solid.

"I bought it this week up at Home Depot."

"Well, I like it. I could enjoy sittin' here."

"You always enjoyed sittin'," she said, then added, "but I'm not havin' a television on my porch."

"I don't think I'd need one here. It's nice just to watch the street and things around."

They sat there in silence, Perry halfway waiting for Vella to tell him to leave. He was a little disappointed that she did not, and that it was unlikely the police would be called to break him out of his sit-in. The entire idea had enthused him, and now, knowing it wouldn't happen, he dipped deeper into discouragement.

After about fifteen minutes, Perry said he could use a glass of something cold to drink.

"Go get it, then," Vella told him. He needed to realize that she was not his maid. "There's Coke and iced tea in the refrigerator."

After a minute, he got up. He extended his hand, and she wondered what in the world.

He said, "Would you like me to freshen yours?"

Could have knocked her over with a feather, but she refused to let on. "Yes, thank you." She handed up her glass.

He went inside and was gone so long that she was just about to go in and see what had happened when he came out with two full glasses. He handed her one and sat back down in his chair.

Vella thought how it really didn't matter whether he was in the house or not. She did not need to kick him out to have her life. The only thing stopping her from having the life she chose was her own choices. She could only find another man without Perry hanging on to her, but maybe the most startling thing she had come to know was that any man her own age would be unable to keep up with her, and she did not have the constitution, nor the opportunity, to take up a man fifteen years younger.

"Could you look at me in the mornings and thank me for your coffee?" she asked, without looking at him.

"I could do that." His voice cracked, and he cleared his throat. "And I could take you out to dinner once a week."

Knock her over again.

"No more television in the kitchen. We will talk while we eat."

There was a long pause, and Vella felt her fury rising. She was just about to whip around and give Perry a what-for about the television when suddenly he was on his feet, and he leaned over and gave the television a shove off the railing. It landed on the ground with a loud crash.

Vella, who had involuntarily gotten to her feet, stared at him. Slowly, stunned, she moved backward and sat down.

"I still want my one in the living room, though," said Perry, who was pleased to have shocked her as she had shocked him the day she had left him with half her clothes hanging open.

He sat back down and mused, in the silence between them, that knowing he had shocked her really seemed to get his blood pumping, and he had the most surprising thoughts to follow. Thoughts of a sensual nature.

Vella, after some twenty minutes of silence, said, "I guess we'd better get your clothes inside. I'm not doin' them all up, though. We can send them to the laundry. I have lots of other things I want to do."

The sun shone far from the west, casting long shadows, when Marilee looked up from the book she was reading about learning disabled children to see it was past their normal supper time. Then her gaze fell on a clay giraffe Willie Lee had fashioned. She picked it up and looked at it, marveling at the craftsmanship. There was a part of Willie Lee that excelled.

The children's shouts and laughter floated in from the backyard. She got up from her desk and went to the back door, looking through the screen. Corrine and Willie Lee were playing tag with Munro again. The dog would chase them, pulling on their shorts, tripping them, and children and dog rolled across the grass.

Since her mother's visit, Corrine had been withdrawn again, no laughter, nor even much of a smile. Now, thanks to the dog, Corrine was running and jumping and laughing. Surely the dog was a gift from God, healing the child where Marilee could not.

Both children were sprawled in the grass now, exhausted. Marilee opened the door and hollered for them to come help her with supper. In they came, running again, Munro bringing up the rear. It was fruit drinks for the children and a fresh bowl of water for the dog.

It was pleasant, all of them in the kitchen together. While she put spaghetti noodles and canned sauce on the stove, Corrine and Willie Lee set the table.

"Summertime, and the livin' is easy," Marilee began to sing, and the children joined in. They repeated the verse over and over, as it was all any of them knew.

The doorbell rang out, loudly, as if someone might have pushed it more than once before they could hear it over their rather raucous singing. Corrine went to see who it was, and when Marilee turned around again, there stood Parker in the kitchen doorway, looking both hesitant and hopeful.

"Hello, Parker."

"Hi." And then, "I wondered if there might be a place for a friend for supper."

Marilee smiled. "Set another place, Corrine."

Parker went to the sink to wash his hands. He said with feeling, "A person can get tired of eating out, or cookin' just for himself."

Twenty-Four

Opening Doors

Tate came hauling down the state highway past the Welcome to Valentine sign, and suddenly he saw red blinking lights behind him. As he pulled off the road, he recognized Lyle Midgett's wide-brimmed hat behind the windshield of the patrol car.

"You need to slow down, Editor."

"Well, yes, I guess I do. I'm a little anxious to get home." Sitting at the top of a hill, he saw Valentine in the valley, washed in the golden glow of a setting sun.

"I thought I'd missed seein' you around." The deputy propped himself on the windshield frame. "Where you been?"

"Galveston. I went down to see my mother for a couple days."

"Your mother lives there? My uncle lives in Galveston. Isn't that a coincidence? I haven't seen my uncle in years, since he moved down there." The young man wanted to chat. Tate, one hand on the wheel, one on the stick shift, kept himself from running out from beneath him.

The deputy was saying, "The fartherest I've been from Valentine is up to Oklahoma City and down to Dallas. Ever'body goes to Dallas. I'm thinkin' about goin' over to Tunica for my vacation this fall, though. You know, to those gambling casinos. The sheriff and his wife go over there least once a year. He says you don't have to pay for any food."

"It's good seein' you, Deputy," Tate stuck in, "but I need to get home. This cat has had about all the travelin' he wants."

"Oh . . . sure. He is startin' to growl pretty loud, isn't he?"

"Do you want to give me a ticket?"

"What? Oh, naw. Just don't you be—"

But Tate was already away, and the deputy's words were snatched by the wind.

He came down Main Street and then turned up First and onto Porter, to pass by Marilee's house.

Right there in her driveway sat Parker Lindsey's blue pickup truck, big as life on a bad day.

She had just served up four plates of spaghetti and sauce when the back door opened and in came Tate.

"Hi, I'm back," he said immediately.

Marilee was so surprised that she stood there holding the empty saucepan in one hand and the spoon in the other. She was alone in the room, the others having gone to watch television until she served.

He came forward. "I've brought iced tea." Ice cubes clinked as he lifted the colorful pitcher.

"Uh . . . thank you."

Then they were face-to-face, Tate having come along the counter and set the pitcher down next to the lineup of glasses. Marilee set the pan and spoon aside.

"I heard that you and Lindsey were no longer engaged." He spoke in a manner she did not quite appreciate.

"Yes." She was annoyed at herself. He did not need to know her business. But she wanted him to know.

"Yes, you are not, or yes, you are?"

"Yes, we have broken our engagement, if it is necessary for you to know," said Marilee, who thought he just had to twist everything that was said.

"Good."

She did not respond to that. In fact, her attention was tuned to the other room and listening for footsteps coming this way. For some reason she felt acutely self-conscious at the thought that at any moment the children or Parker could walk in.

"Parker is here, but just for supper." She felt the need to tell him that, and the inclination annoyed her.

"I'd sure like supper, too. I've been drivin' all day. I'm starved."

He gave her a provocative look. How could she have forgotten how luminous his eyes were?

"I guess I could stretch it," she said. She looked at the plates wondering how in the world she would do that, and at the same time knowing she was darn well going to accomplish it.

"Great. I'll fill the glasses."

It was only supper, she told herself, as she stole part of Parker's spaghetti. This made her think of her mother, stealing money from Carl's pockets. Not the same, she told herself, and took some from her own plate, and then a little from Willie Lee's. He never ate all of his. And she could make more garlic bread; she had another small loaf in the freezer. Only supper. That was all. No need to make a big deal out of it.

Parker came in, and immediately Tate said, "Hey, buddy, how are you tonight?" There never was anything subdued about Tate Holloway.

"Hey, Editor," Parker responded in a flat tone of voice.

Tate said an effusive hello to the children, who responded in kind.

Willie Lee said a very curious thing. "I am glad you are not the dogcatcher."

"I'm glad, too." Tate said, setting himself down at the place Parker usually took at the table. "Why would you think I was the dogcatcher?"

"You might be," Willie Lee said, quite logically. "But you are not."

Parker stared down at the plate she put in front of him. She had tried to disguise stealing from it, but her efforts could not fully be concealed.

"Here's the Italian bread," she said, setting the basket on the table. "There'll be more in a few minutes.

She saw Parker looking from his plate to Tate's.

Marilee said, "Shall we bow our heads for grace?"

"I like the end of Italian bread," said Tate, taking up the end slice.

"A lot of people use the ends of the loaf to feed the birds, or as fish bait," said Parker, taking a slice from the middle.

"Then I'm easily caught," Tate said, "because these hard ends suit me."

"I guess I have a taste for the finer things in life." Parker smiled as he tore his bread in half.

Marilee, her gaze going back and forth between the two men, felt a food fight might be imminent. Further, Corrine was closely observing both men.

"Does anyone need a refill of tea?" Marilee asked, getting to her feet, which seemed to be required. She felt more in command on her feet. And, in fact, the two men looked up at her, and she gave them her best stop-it-this-instant-you-are-not-fooling-anyone expression.

As she sat down, it occurred to her that she should be flattered, two men fighting over her. Although, on second, deeper thought, it had little to do with her and was about the men themselves. When the two came together, it was like flint hitting a rock.

Willie Lee, who was busy passing pieces of bread underneath the table, said, "Mun-ro likes the end *and* the middle."

"Well-rounded dog," Tate commented. He was a man to have the last word.

He was more the rock, Marilee thought.

Tate found himself left with Parker. That was how he thought of it, as if left with a difficulty. Marilee was getting the children bathed and ready for bed. In his estimation, she had thrown herself into that activity to avoid him and Lindsey. He wasn't certain what he had expected when he got back to town, but he had not expected to drive six hours and have Marilee avoid him. The least she could have done was tell Lindsey to go home.

"You had your meal," he said to Lindsey, who had taken root on the sofa, remote control in hand, watching the news. "You can go on home now."

Lindsey looked up at him. "*You* can go on home. Don't let me stop you."

Realizing then that he was the one on his feet and therefore in a less-rooted position, Tate went over and sat himself at Marilee's desk, definitely a more solid position than Lindsey on the sofa. He looked over her desk, which was neat as always. There was a small clay giraffe. He picked it up and looked it over, and then looked over at the stack of books to the side, all which appeared to be on children and learning disabilities. Hmmm.

His gaze slipped to the telephone, and he looked from it to Lindsey, who was staring at the nightly news. He experienced possibly the greatest idea of his life, and he got so enthused in thinking of it that he had to force himself not to chuckle out loud.

"Well, I need something to drink," he said, speaking a little loudly and toning himself down. "Would you like something—tea or cola?"

Lindsey looked over with a frown. "I'm fine, thank you."

Tate shrugged and went into the kitchen. Immediately through the door, he slipped to the side and over to the phone on the wall. His heart beat rapidly. Did Marilee have the number on her speed dial? There it was. Yes! Thank you, God!

He experienced an instant where he questioned God's part in this, but quickly put the thought aside, punched the number and listened to the ringing come over the line.

"Lindsey Veterinary Clinic. This is the answering service."

Answering service. Hallelujah! He cupped the speaker. "Hey, this is Sheriff Oakes, and we got an emergency out here. A horse has been hit by a car—out on Highway Six, a mile north of Rodeo Rio's. Tell the doc to get out here pronto and I think we can save him." Tate thought he imitated the sheriff quite well.

"Can you give me your number, Sheriff?"

"I got a situation here. Just tell the doc to get out here."

He hung up and moved quickly from the phone. He should be ashamed of being so pleased. But he wasn't.

As he poured his glass of tea, he heard Lindsey's mobile phone go off. He heard the veterinarian's terse tone, if not the exact words.

Tate, seeing Marilee's reflection in the kitchen window as she entered the living room, went to the doorway. Lindsey was on his feet and talking into the telephone.

"Yeah, I got it. I'm on my way."

He snapped off his phone and told Marilee, "I got an emergency. Horse hit by a car on Highway Six."

"Oh . . . my."

He kissed her cheek and thanked her for supper, and headed for the door.

Marilee followed and called after him, "I hope it goes well."

She shut the door and turned to look at Tate across the low-lit room. She looked so worried that he felt a stab of guilt.

"I hope the horse isn't hurt too badly," she said and then continued on about how Parker had such a hard time whenever he lost a patient. "And it is even worse on him when he has to put one down."

"Ah . . ." He wrestled with his conscience. "There isn't really an injured horse."

"What?" She cocked her head to the side, regarding him.

He felt quicksand beneath his feet. "Well, I put in the call to his answering service. I pretended to be the sheriff and said there was a horse . . . hit by a car," he finished slowly as he saw his own image reflected in her incredulous expression.

"How could you do that? Parker—" she was getting wrought up and gestured with her arm swinging out "—is fully committed to saving animals' lives. He is racin' out there now, committed to doing all that he can to save a horse. He could be in a wreck because he's hurryin' out there to save a horse that isn't even there!"

Tate had no answer to that. The full import of his actions came to him, although he did not see them in quite the disreputable light Marilee painted. Obviously she believed he had crossed over the line of integrity.

"I wanted time with you," he said. "Lindsey is a big boy, and he will deal with this."

Marilee heard what he said but could not absorb it. She was too

taken up with hurt for Parker. She felt horribly guilty, knowing she
was the cause of him being falsely called out.

"He can't stand to see an animal die," she told Tate, as she went to
the phone on her desk and snatched up the receiver. "He will go to
great lengths to prevent that." In her mind, she saw him colliding with
another vehicle in his race to get out to find and save the injured horse.

"Marilee—" he took hold of her forearm "—he will get there and
realize what happened. He does not need you to be his mother."

She looked at him. "You have sent him off on a fool's errand. I
can't let him be drivin' all over creation, lookin' for a horse that isn't
there. He'll feel a fool when he realizes what you've done."

"That's it." Suddenly she was facing Tate's fury. "Focus on Parker,
mother Parker, because you can't face your own life as a woman.
When I found out you had broken off with Parker, I came drivin' up
here at breakneck speed for six hours to see you. I don't see you getting all worked up about my welfare. I'm tired and lonely and wearin'
my heart on my sleeve here. What are you gonna do about that? About
this man—" he jabbed his chest "—not a boy, who is crazy about
you."

Marilee stared at him and felt a type of paralysis come over her
emotions and her body. She could not seem to put down the phone.
She could not seem to stop her course, even if she wanted to.

"I have to call him. You don't know how these things hurt." She did
not think she could bear the consequences of not calling Parker, not
that she knew what those consequences would be, just that she needed
to cling to making the call. She felt compelled to cling to the course
she knew, because to abandon it would mean she would be lost.

"Do you think he is too stupid to figure out what happened when he
gets out there and there isn't any horse, nor any police cars?" He flung
her arm away in disgust. "Do you have such a low opinion of his coping powers? He'll figure it out, and he'll be mad as hell, but he'll be
wiser, and someday he'll use this same little trick on somebody else.
That's how I learned it—it was played on me, to get me out of the way
of somewhere I never belonged in the first place."

"I can't," she said, anger flaring because he was pressing her for
something she did not feel capable of giving.

"I'm not going to stand here and beg for your attention. I wouldn't
want to interrupt your motherin' of Parker. Apparently you need that
more than you can appreciate some attention from a man."

He stalked off to the kitchen, and she called after him, "Go ahead. I
never asked you to come around here . . . and that is what men do—

they leave. Better sooner than later." She shut her mouth then, afraid she might have awakened the children.

The sound of the back door shutting caused her to just about double over, as if from a blow.

What Tate said was true, she realized, her spirit sinking to depths so dark she ached with despair. She simply could never seem to get herself out of mother mode. She had always been a mother, from the age of nine, when she'd had to be a mother to Anita, and on to becoming a mother to her own mother. It was all she knew.

Likely she attracted men who needed her to mother them—like Stuart and Parker—and repelled men, like Tate, who did not require her mothering talents but wanted her to be a full woman and mate, which was something she could not seem to grasp. She could not be a woman to a man, because she did not know how. Probably she did not have some sort of gene required to be a woman to a man. It was as if she were learning disabled in this area, the same as her Willie Lee was in the rest of life.

A voice came from the receiver: "If you'd like to make a call, please hang up and dial again."

She was still standing there, holding the receiver. She stretched a finger to depress the button and start again, but her inclination to call Parker had faded. Suddenly she did not think she could speak, she was so totally discouraged. Likely Parker was close to figuring out that there was no emergency with a horse, anyway. Surely another ten minutes and he would know this. He would be furious and feel the fool, and she did not feel up to taking on his emotions.

Tate, at the back gate, stopped in his tracks. It was as if a hand had come down on his shoulder and turned him around, and he distinctly heard a command to get back in there.

He had come too far to give up now. And he wouldn't leave her his tea, in any case. By golly, he was not wasting any more tea on the woman. He would just march right in there and get his pitcher. He went up the stairs and burst in the doorway.

Marilee, hearing the back door open, threw the receiver onto the hook and hurried to the kitchen doorway, from which she saw Tate stalking across the room toward the counter.

"I forgot my tea." His tone and manner were furious. He snatched up the pitcher sitting there. "I'm takin' it back." He had lost his mind, he thought.

Marilee, standing with her hand on the door frame, tried to drag herself from her odd paralysis of emotion, a course she had seemingly been on all her life. *He had driven six hours for her . . . for a woman like her.*

The phone rang, and this jarred her into motion. Two steps and she lifted the receiver.

But then Tate was there, taking hold of her and jerking the receiver from her hand. He said into it, "Go away," then let it drop, where it bobbed and banged against the wall, while Tate took her by her shoulders and looked deep into her eyes.

"Let me in, Marilee. Open up and let me in."

His eyes entreated her; his voice commanded her.

"I can't. . . . I don't know how." Crying, shaking her head, trying to avoid his lips, but still he went to kissing her cheeks and her eyes. She hit his chest with her balled fists. "I don't want to be married . . . I can't go there again . . . it hurts too bad . . . I don't know how."

He found her mouth and stopped her words with his kiss, which caused an immediate and enormous response from deep inside of her. Quite suddenly she found herself kissing him in return, with the passion of a woman come to life, full of desire that burned away the fear. They became all hot breath and pounding blood and passionate bodies. When finally Tate lifted his head, so that she could see his luminous grey eyes, she could not stand up and had to hold on to him.

"That's how," he whispered against her lips, and then kissed her again, having to hold her up against him to do it.

When at last the kiss ended and she was staring up at him through dazed eyes, she said what popped into her mind. "I've wanted to know what it would be like to kiss you from the moment I saw you."

"I've wanted to know, too," said Tate, with a ragged chuckle. Then, "Let's do it again."

And he kissed her again.

When at last he raised his head, she gasped for breath. "I won't," she managed to say, meaning she would not sleep with him, she would not marry him, she would not go any further.

He merely chuckled again and gave her yet another kiss, deeply and expertly, making her know in that minute that she would follow the delicious passion wherever it led. He kissed her, and she kissed him, until they were both about to burst into flame.

She had never in all her life been so thoroughly kissed, so that she felt it in every cell in her body.

"Now, what were you sayin'?" he whispered in her ear, his breath warm and moist upon her tender skin.

"I can't remember." She felt helpless. Never had she felt helpless with a man. She did not know if she liked the feeling.

* * *

"The phone's still off the hook." The recording was speaking about hanging up.

"Leave it."

"Okay." She could not think a coherent thought.

Tate scooped her up into his arms and carried her through to the living room, where he sat in the big chair, holding her across his lap.

"Why not the sofa?" she asked, as getting down into the chair proved to take some doing.

"You and Parker used to be on the sofa."

"Oh." She laid her head on his shoulder and nuzzled into his neck. "I cannot have sex with you. I have two children in the other room."

"Quit blaming it all on the children. I'll wait until you are ready." He stroked her head, and she felt ready.

"I want to marry you," he said. "That's what I want."

She realized that Tate was a little struck silly by passion, too. "I don't know if I can marry you. I don't think we should even try to think about it right now." Heaven knew she could not think.

She added after a moment, "I don't know if I can ever marry anyone."

"I'll wait for you to find out."

"I don't know how to be a wife. I'm a good mother, but I am awful at being a woman with a man."

She began to cry. She could not figure out her emotions. They were no longer paralyzed but now felt as if they were fighting to go in all directions. She cried harder, so hard that she soaked his shirt, while he held her to him and kissed her hair and murmured that she was just the sort of woman he needed.

"What sort is that?" she asked, sniffing. "What did you mean—a woman like me?"

It seemed a very long time before he answered. She pulled back and looked at him. He looked puzzled, and at last he said, "That you are a full and passionate woman who demands that a man stand up on equal footing. I have to be a better man when I'm around you. I have to be all the man I can be."

"Oh, Tate." Had ever a woman been so complimented? Her heart felt as if it had cracked in two. She kissed him full and hard.

After that kiss, he said, "Will you be my girl?"

"Yes." At first the word would only come in a whisper. She tried again. "Yes, I'll be your girl. But I am not making any further promises."

She lay back in his arms then, and he kissed her softly, and then held her. They sat there, and it was both sensual and comfortable. She listened to his heart beating and inhaled his scent, imprinting it on her mind, imprinting the feel of his body through their clothing. He stroked her leg, and it was in such a tender and worshipful manner that she began to cry again.

Tate did not say so, but he had a feeling that Marilee had never known a man to truly make love to her. Obviously she had experienced sex, but quite possibly never experienced having a man make love to her as a woman enjoyed by a man. This thought excited him, but it made him a little nervous, too. He hoped he would be up to the job. It would take a hell of a man to give Marilee what she needed. Maybe he would need to study books or something.

He was thinking so hard on this matter, that it was some minutes before he realized she had fallen asleep. He sat there, for that space of time, as if he had opened wide the door and was staring into the full secret of life in his heart.

Twenty-Five

Life is Good

The night lifted, and the light of a new day dawned on the roofs and trees of town and across the land, west to where a long, white limousine turned off the Interstate and onto the state highway, gliding past the sign that read: Valentine, 10 miles. The driver, commanded by his employer, who did not like speed, went at a slow pace.

In town, garbage trucks started their run, the City Works crew were gathering to make another attack on the sinkhole, and Winston Valentine, putting on his glasses, looked out the kitchen window at the thermometer; the needle pointed already at eighty degrees.

"Summer's here," he said, and turned, heading through the long hall, where he took up his flags from the hall table and went out the front door. He was early, and this seemed prudent, with the heat coming. Everett had apparently made the same decision; he was just coming out his door, too.

As Winston went to his flagpole, his gaze focused in the distance at the Blaines' driveway across the meadow, and Perry's black Lincoln sitting there, still. That seemed a promising sign. Vella had called Winston last night to say that Perry had moved back in. He would go down there later and see how things had gone. He had not felt up to being all Vella wanted of him, but he was a little sad to lose her attention. Oh, well, aggravating Perry would give him something worthwhile to do.

Down on Porter, Tate, minus Bubba, who was sulking, jogged past Marilee's cottage; it was quiet. He knew better than to stop in, because he knew Marilee was not a morning person.

At the house on the corner, the young UPS man was coming down his front walk. He had a black eye.

"Woo-ee, that's a beaut," Tate said, admiring, but not breaking stride.

"You should see the other guy." The young man grinned and then winced.

Tate, sweat already beginning to wet his hair, turned left instead of right on First, and jogged down to where a burly City Works employee was guiding a concrete truck into position some feet away from the sinkhole site. Apparently they were going to run a tube from the truck, so as to not take a chance of getting the truck stuck in the hole.

Tate took a second look at the big elm tree in the front yard of the Methodist Church parsonage; it seemed to be leaning toward the sinkhole.

"We got a handle on this thing now, Editor," the burly City Works worker told him. "We are fixin' to pump thirty-five yards of concrete into this sucker. That's gotta stop it."

Tate gave the worker Reggie's phone number and requested the man call her immediately on his cell phone, so she could get a shot for the Sunday paper. Then he headed back along to Main Street, waving at Bonita Embree through the bakery window. The flag was not yet flying at the *Voice;* Charlotte was much later than usual this morning. He wondered what that was about. Turning the corner at the police station, he headed up Church, keeping an eye out in the distance.

There came Lindsey down the hill.

They met at the intersection. Tate was prepared to defend himself. He had not had a fight in a long time, so he hoped he could come out of it in decent shape.

Lindsey stopped to stretch his legs, and Tate followed suit.

"Guess you think you're pretty funny, don't you, Editor."

"*Clever* is the better word. Actually, I think it could be considered outmaneuvering." He was warming to the descriptions, yet still keeping a watchful eye on Lindsey's demeanor.

At that moment, there came Leanne Overton, flying down the hill on her bicycle. She cast a nod directed at both men as she zipped between them and curved around to Porter heading east, the cheeks of her lovely derriere moving in rhythm as she pedaled.

"If you hurry, maybe you could catch up with her," Tate suggested, a little puzzled at how Lindsey was just standing there, as if out of energy.

Lindsey shook his head. "Her looks hide some other stuff. You know?"

"Ah, well, that's not too good." Tate felt a twinge of pity for the guy.

But suddenly Lindsey straightened his shoulders and looked straight at Tate. "I'm goin' to get you back, Editor. It may take me a while, but I'm goin' to pay you back for last night."

It was a firm promise, and with that, the veterinarian swung into motion, heading away east on Porter at an easy jog with his powerful tanned legs.

Tate decided to cut his jog short and went on around, entering through the back door. The phone was ringing.

"Would you like to come to breakfast?" It was Marilee!

"Do you know your voice is very sexy first thing in the morning?" he said. "And I'll be over in fifteen minutes."

Life is good, he thought as he hurried upstairs to shower. He had a woman who liked to cook, and who had a sexy voice, too.

He ran his shower quite cold.

The long white limousine glided to a stop in front of the James house. The neighbor across the street saw it and kneeled on her couch to get a better look out her front window.

Marilee was putting homemade biscuits in the oven when the doorbell rang. Corrine was setting the table.

"Now, who could that be so early in the morning?" It was too quick for it to be Tate.

Marilee brushed her hair back from her face, and then realized her hands were coated with flour. She asked Corrine to go see who was at the door. She was annoyed for being interrupted in cooking biscuits and gravy. She had not cooked both from scratch in a long time, and the effort required all her concentration.

The doorbell rang again. Corrine, skipping through the living room, saw a head peering in the front window.

"It is the dog-catch-ers!" said Willie Lee, who had come from the hallway and had his shirt buttoned crooked over his pajama pants. He raced back into the bedroom, calling Munro with him, and slammed the door.

"What in the world?" Aunt Marilee came from the kitchen. "Who is it, Corrine?"

Corrine, who had made it to the door but was hesitant to open it, gazed at Marilee and blinked her deep-brown eyes.

Marilee went to open the front door herself. A man with a shock of thick and rather long white hair, and dressed in a crisp, pale-blue suit, smiled at her.

"Hello. Do I have the pleasure of addressing Mrs. James?"

"Yes."

"Do you have a little boy who has a rather splotchy type of dog, an Australian shepherd, I believe?"

"Well, yes . . . what is this about?"

She did not know the man, but she recognized the tall, slick blond man, the one Belinda had said was from Tell-In Technologies. He stood behind one of the white-haired man's shoulders, while a very sophisticated woman stood behind the other shoulder. All three were gazing at her.

"I'm Thomas Gerard, president of the Tell-In Technologies. May I have a few minutes of your time? If you would not mind, I would like to come in and sit down, and explain in detail."

The man and woman behind him were now peering around his shoulders, as if looking at something behind Marilee.

"Well, okay." She opened the door for them to step inside.

Quite slowly, the man went to sit on her sofa. Marilee wondered how old he was. His face was not old, but he was stooped. Corrine, who was stuck to Marilee like glue, squeezed herself down in the big chair beside Marilee, and Marilee put an arm around her niece. Glancing downward, she saw she had streaks of flour on her dress.

"You are familiar with the facts of our case?" The man spoke slowly and in a very gentle manner. "That a former Tell-In employee died of a heart attack just outside of town?"

Marilee said she was familiar with the incident, and that the former employee apparently had some sort of company property.

"Yes." The man nodded. "We believe your son now possesses a dog that belonged to that former employee, and we have reason to believe this dog may be the key to us locating . . . something . . . our former employee stole from our company. Could you please tell us—was the dog wearing a collar when your son found him?"

"Yes. It had his name on it."

"And is he still wearing that collar?"

"Well . . . yes."

The man nodded some more and said, "We need to see that collar. It is possible that what we are looking for is in the collar, or may even be implanted in the dog itself."

"Implanted in the dog?" Marilee repeated. She looked at Corrine, as if to make note of the child in order to be certain she was not imagining this conversation.

"Yes, possibly," said Mr. Gerard in his distinctive manner. "Could we see your son's dog? I promise that we mean the dog no harm. We do not want to take the dog, only to examine him."

When Marilee sat there, thinking and gazing at the three sitting on her couch, he added, "This means a great deal to my company, Mrs. James."

"I have no doubt. As my son means a great deal to me, and for some reason, he is afraid of you." She added, "Let me speak to my son."

Marilee went to Willie Lee's bedroom door. It was locked. "Willie Lee? Honey, I need to talk to you."

Corrine was right beside her. "He thinks they want to take Munro." At Marilee's questioning gaze, she said, "They tried to, one day in town. Munro ran away. He does not like them," she added in a pointed manner.

Marilee called to Willie Lee again, but there was no answer.

Then Tate came from the kitchen. "What's going on over here? Willie Lee said the dogcatchers are in his house." He looked from Marilee in the hallway to the people on the couch and back at Marilee.

"You've seen Willie Lee?" She looked back at the door and realized her son must have gone out the window.

"Yes, but I told him I wouldn't tell where he and Munro are." He turned a questioning eye on the three strangers, who were now getting to their feet.

"Ah," Tate said to the younger man and woman. "I believe we have met . . . in the police station. You were waiting to talk to the sheriff. I'm the editor of *The Valentine Voice,* who you said couldn't help you. I might be able to now, it seems."

Tate went out to talk to Willie Lee.

Corrine stood guarding the closed swinging kitchen door, while Marilee, watching through the window, saw Tate go across the yard to the tree containing Willie Lee's tree house. He looked upward, speaking, and there was an exchange for some minutes, after which an object came dropping out of the tree. Munro's collar, which Tate brought back in to the people sitting on Marilee's couch.

The blond man reached for the collar, and all three on the couch bent their heads to look at it. Marilee and Tate and Corrine hovered, trying to see, too.

"There it is," the blond man said with triumph. "Oh, and here's the—"

Whatever it was, was gone from sight in an instant, as the blond man pocketed the collar.

Thomas Gerard, getting to his feet, said, "I would like to thank your son personally. I owe him my company's future. I'd like to give him a reward."

Willie Lee, assured that Munro was still safely his dog, came back inside and into the living room and right up to Thomas Gerard, holding up his hand for a shake. "Hel-lo, Mr. Ger-aard," he said very carefully when introduced.

"Hello, Mr. James. I thank you for taking such good care of this dog."

"He takes care of me, and Cor-rine, and Ma-ma," Willie Lee interrupted.

"Ah, so he does." The man's pale eyes fell on the dog sitting at Willie Lee's legs. "I had a dog such as this once, when I was a boy. A long time ago. I wish so much to have another."

"Ask God. That is what I did."

"Ah . . . I shall." Thomas Gerard pulled a paper from his inner suit pocket. "Here you are, Mr. James. Please accept this with my gratitude for returning to me something very important. Good day to you all."

Marilee saw the three people to the door and watched a moment as the white-haired gentleman went carefully down her porch steps. There was no rushing or excess of movement in Mr. Gerard.

When she turned around, she saw Tate examining the paper the Tell-In president had given Willie Lee. "Stock," he told Marilee. "Looks like Thomas Gerard just gave Willie Lee thirty-thousand dollars worth of stock."

Marilee had to sit down. She looked at Willie Lee. *He will have something for when I'm gone.* Tears came into her eyes. *Thank you, God.*

Suddenly the smoke detector started going off, and all of them raced to the kitchen to see smoke rolling out of the oven. Her biscuits had burned right up.

Tate told her. "Well, get yourselves fixed up. I'm takin' us all down to the Main Street Café for breakfast. I'd like to start showin' everyone that you're my girl."

She jerked her head up and looked at him, and his luminous eyes smiled a deep smile at her. Slowly she returned the smile. Maybe she could be a woman to him.

Maybe for her to be the right sort of woman for a man, she needed the right sort of man to bring her out. And maybe she had at last found him.

The Valentine Voice

Sunday, August 6
View from the Editor's Desk
by Tate Holloway

Tomorrow another school year begins, so be on the lookout for children darting in the road as you are driving around. The Valentine School Board finds enrollment up again this year. This growth in population is becoming a serious concern for the school board.

Principal of our elementary school, Gwen Blankenship, has reported that this year she has some classes with over thirty students. Classes this large are a difficulty for both students and teachers. Folks, we are looking at the definite need to expand our schools and increase the number of teachers.

My hat is off to the school board for hiring two more assistant librarians. Our libraries are our greatest resource. This brings me to the proposition that if there is an increase in tax revenue this coming year, we need to establish a town library. I want to hear your views on this. Drop by the offices, or stop me on the street.

My hat is also off to the school board for establishing for the first time in the Valentine schools a program for the learning disabled. We have a lot of promise in these young folks, and it is to our own benefit to provide the best education for them we can. You can thank our own Marilee James, who worked hard all summer to bring this program into our schools, and who saw to getting a teacher with the right requirements. You can read a profile of this class on page 4.

And lastly, Norm Stidham caught me on the street and took me to task for not writing about anything controversial for several weeks. Norm, I'll work on it, and I'll be happy to take suggestions. Come on in and visit.

Charlotte was still not happy with Tate's bent for inviting all and sundry in to visit them. She deleted the last sentence, thinking Tate would not notice.

"Put that back in there," he told her, just before she sent the disks to the printer.

Twenty-Six

Moving On

"Tate's here," Corrine called.

Marilee grabbed her purse and her tote. "Okay, let's get movin'."

"We are mov-ing, Ma-ma," Willie Lee said, as he walked with deliberate motion out the door ahead of her, Munro at his heels.

They piled into Tate's car and drove to school, where children were pouring out of buses and cars, and streaming across the yard and up the walks. Marilee kissed Willie Lee, who then walked away with Tate, Munro walking right along with them, to his classroom. Then she walked Corrine to her classroom.

Outside the door, Marilee said, "Do not hesitate to call me if you need me."

"I won't."

"I'll miss you."

"I know . . . but you will be all right."

Marilee breathed a deep breath, wondering at who mothered whom. She kissed her niece, who, her shoulders straight and stride easy, went into the classroom. Corrine had grown taller, and her grace of movement was arresting. Marilee, still gazing in the doorway, saw a number of boys turn their eyes to her dark-haired niece. Oh boy, more hurdles. Corrine would be equally as beautiful as Anita.

It was so hard, leaving them. As she walked out of the school, she felt she left her heart behind.

"How'd he do?" she asked Tate when they met back at the car. She had resisted the urge to go peek into Willie Lee's classroom, afraid she might be spotted, afraid she might go in there and jerk Willie Lee back out.

"Very well. He seemed to accept that Munro is show and tell just for today."

Tate directed the car from the curb, and Marilee sat there, looking straight ahead. She breathed deeply. She would be okay. As long as her children were okay, she would be okay.

Tate drove to the *Voice* offices, parked at his space in the rear, and gave her a quick kiss before getting out of the car. They went inside together, Tate into his office and Marilee to her desk, where she worked for two hours, her eyes repeatedly checking the clock and thinking the day so very long.

Finally, almost not realizing she was doing so, she took up her purse and tote and headed out the door, telling Charlotte, "I need to go home for some things that are on my computer there."

She walked out the door into the hot August day, across the street and up the long block of Church. She was wet with perspiration by the time she got to the corner of Porter. Her pace picked up, though, heading for home. She went into her house and shut the door and leaned against it, listening to the quiet.

She hated the quiet.

Pushing herself away from the door, she went to her computer on the desk, sat down and turned it on.

She wished Munro were there, at least.

This would not do. She had to get ahold of herself and her swirling thoughts.

She went to the back door, more or less just aimlessly moving. The sunlight made speckles through the trees on the back steps. She went out and sat down.

This was where Tate found her. He drove over to check on her when he had found her gone from her desk. It was a little absurd, but he had been worried since they had let the children off at school. He knew it was hard on her, and she had seemed too calm to him.

He got in a little panic when he went in the front door of her house and didn't find her. The house was stone quiet, and he had the thought that maybe she had been abducted. She never did lock her doors. Things could and did happen, even in small towns.

"Oh, here you are," he said, speaking with some relief when he got to the back door and found her sitting there.

"Well, yes."

She moved over to let him out to come sit beside her.

"Someday I shall get new lawn furniture," she said.

"I like sitting on the step."

"I do, too."

They grinned at each other.

She looked away quickly, suddenly sad and afraid to reveal herself. Then she dared to say, "I miss them."

"I do, too."

"I'm really glad for the summer we had. They came so far this summer. I think Willie Lee has real talent with sculpting, and we wouldn't have known that if I hadn't started tutoring him."

"He really does. No tellin' what can happen there."

"And Corrine's had time to get confidence. She's really growing up. She's becoming a young lady."

"Yes. A lovely young lady."

The entire time Marilee was thinking and chatting of these things, she was becoming more and more aware of Tate's strong thigh touching hers. More aware of the fact that they were there alone, for the first time in months. Her brain seemed to whirl, bouncing between her awareness of Tate and her sadness at missing the children that had by now caused a lump in her throat and the need to cry, which she really did not want to do.

"They don't need me like they used to," she said. "Oh, they'll always need me, but it's changing. I feel like there's a sinkhole right underneath me, the sand just runnin' out." Tears began to roll down her cheeks. "I'm so tired of adjusting. You know that's what life is, adjusting time after time, and sometimes I just don't want to adjust any more."

"I know." Tate put his hand on the back of her neck and pulled her against his chest. "I sure miss them, too."

"You do, don't you?" This fact somewhat amazed her. Tate had so fully involved himself in the children's lives.

"Yes. Makes me feel old without them."

"Oh, you're not old." She tried for a smile for him and to dry her eyes, but then a fresh wave of discouragement came over her. "I feel old, too. My babies are growin' up. What will I do?"

With that she went to sobbing against him. He rubbed her back and whispered soothing whispers. Gradually she became very aware of his hand caressing her back, of his strong chest, of the scent of him.

Then he was nuzzling her neck and said, "Let me make you feel better . . . let me . . ."

She lifted her head and met his kiss, eagerly and completely.

Tate's response to this kiss, when he lifted his head, was to say, "Good golly!"

They made love in her bed, slowly and without nervousness. They had been together for months now and discovered, with delight, that they knew each other very well.

He was a miracle, Marilee thought, pressing her cheek against his chest and hearing the beating of his heart.

"Nothing is awkward with you," she said.

"Don't know why it should be," he replied. "This is most natural between a man and a woman who are attracted to each other."

He kissed her in places all over her body, and he caressed her with abandoned pleasure, and he made her laugh, and made her cry, and made her shout his name with searing ecstasy.

Afterward, they lay in each other's arms and talked as they had not talked in the past two months.

"I guess when two people have done this," she said blushing, "it is easier to say some things."

He grinned at her and kissed her and whispered that she sure did something to him that was great.

She told him she was afraid, and then she told him something about when she had grown up, how she realized where she got the mothering talent. "I'm afraid I won't be able to be a woman as a wife. I've messed it up for two relationships now."

"But you've learned. We learn from our mistakes. And I'm not the same as Stuart and Parker."

"No, you aren't."

He told her about his growing up, about a father who drank until he got run over by a train, and his mother, whom he described as beautiful and with quite strong spiritual ideas, as he put it. Marilee liked watching the light in his eyes as he spoke. He told of his failed marriage, and how he had not been able to be married, had not really wanted to be.

Then he said, "But I want to be married now. And I want to marry you. Will you?"

Immediately all sorts of questions popped into her mind. Fears.

"Yes," she managed to get out at last.

He laughed aloud. "It is sure a good thing I'm a secure man."

Then he kissed her in the way every woman wants to be kissed and only a few get to experience.

They went to pick up the children together, as they had taken them to school. Marilee could not wait, and they were in Tate's car at the curb in front of the school ten minutes before the children were let out.

Marilee jumped out and went to meet them and kiss them both. "Oh, I missed you so much!"

Willie Lee said school was okay, but that Munro did not want to go anymore.

Corrine said she would like a special planner notebook. "In lavender, if I can," she added.

Tate said, "We need to celebrate today," and cast Marilee a private smile. "Let's go down to Blaine's."

They were greeted by Aunt Vella, who was once again manning the soda fountain, but only four days a week, with Fridays off. She said, "How are my shugahs today?" and kissed each of them, even Tate.

Willie Lee wanted a cherry ice-cream cone, and, "Mun-ro wants a dish of van-il-la, please."

Corrine, after much deliberation, chose a dish of pecan ice cream.

Tate ordered a glass of iced tea, and Marilee, who had been about to get a chocolate shake, changed her mind. "I'll take iced tea, too."

The bell above the door rang out, and Parker entered. Tate welcomed him over. "Let me buy you a cold drink, buddy."

Parker went behind the counter and got his own drink, then leaned on the counter to visit with all of them, the children telling about school, Parker telling about one of his patients, Aunt Vella talking about her latest rose catalog. Soon here came Uncle Perry and Winston from back in the pharmacy. The two, to everyone's amazement, had taken up playing chess. They sat in chairs with glasses of lemonade and discussed the television channel that featured a chess instruction program.

Marilee's eyes chanced to look up in the long mirror on the wall. She saw herself and Tate, sitting side by side, in the midst of her family and friends.

Quite suddenly she realized she was looking at today, herself as a full woman, the haunting of yesterday's child nearly faded clear away.

Tate's gaze met hers in the mirror. He leaned over and gave her a kiss, then said, "Good company, good tea . . . it doesn't get any better than this."

The Valentine Voice

Wednesday, August 23
Local Boy Struck By Fortune
By Tammy Crawford
Staff Writer

Willie Lee James woke up to find himself rich this morning, when the stock he owns in the Tell-In Technologies Corporation split two for one late yesterday afternoon.

It was reported early last week that Tell-In Technologies Corporation, a computer firm, had released a revolutionary new computer containing a more accurate and faster processor, in part powered by a chip developed within the company. Since that time, the corporation's stock has been climbing in value.

Last spring, Tell-In suffered a theft of the new chip that enables their revolutionary processor. Willie Lee James was instrumental in finding the chip, and the president of Tell-In, Mr. Thomas Gerard, personally rewarded the boy with a gift of stock.

In the past weeks, beginning with rumors of the new computer, the young James found his stock already nearing triple its original value. With this split, and as of this report, his stock's value is in excess of $115,000. The stock is expected to keep rising for some months to come.

When asked for comment, Mr. Willie Lee James said, "I am going to buy Munro a new collar. A gold one."

Young James's mother said they did plan to sell some of the stock and begin a trust fund for her son, as well as endow a learning-disabled program for the Valentine school district.

Tell-In president, Thomas Gerard, has said he is going to join in spirit with Ms. James by establishing an endowment for the learning-disabled nationwide.

Tate, upon making his normal rounds of town that afternoon, made certain everyone saw the article on Willie Lee. He said, "Just when you think it doesn't get any better, by golly, it always can!"

AT THE CORNER
of LOVE AND
HEARTACHE

The Valentine Voice, Wednesday, February 21

Publisher and Associate Editor to Wed
James, Holloway Announce Engagement

Tate Briggs Holloway, publisher of *The Valentine Voice,* and Marilee Roe James, associate editor, announce their engagement and plans to marry March 21, 11:00 a.m., at the First Street Methodist Church, with Pastor Stanley Smith officiating.

Ms. James is the daughter of Norma Cooper of Lawton, formerly of Valentine, and the late Frank Justus of Valentine, and the niece of Vella and Perry Blaine, of Valentine. She has served on the staff of *The Valentine Voice* for over eight years, and is the founder and director of Angel Gifts, a nonprofit organization that provides educational assistance for special-needs children to small schools.

The prospective groom is the son of Franny Holloway of Galveston, Texas, and first cousin to Muriel Porter-Abercrombie, formerly of Valentine and from whom he purchased *The Valentine Voice* last spring.

The couple will make their home in Valentine, with Ms. James's son, Willie Lee, and niece, Corrine Pendley.

New York City, 6:15 a.m.

Stuart James sat in the dim glow of a single desk lamp in his room at the Algonquin Hotel. The sounds beyond his room were becoming more frequent, footsteps in the hallway, the whoosh of the elevator, horns on the streets below, as the city awoke.

Stuart, in a navy sweatshirt, plaid flannel lounge pants and worn kid leather moccasins bought years ago while on a photo shoot on a Navaho reservation, was reared back in the chair with his feet up on the desk and a notebook computer open in his lap. He rarely slept more than four hours a night, and had been awake since three and occupying himself by surfing the Internet.

Peering at the luminous screen through half glasses, he read the headline that appeared. He became still, as if even the blood stopped in his veins.

Movement returned, first with his eyes, which ran along the lines of text that announced the upcoming marriage of his ex-wife. Then his hand came from behind his head, and his feet dropped to the floor, while he stared for long seconds at the text, his mind assimilating the news.

Then he reached for the two medication vials sitting nearby. Popping off the lids, he shook one pill from each vial, tossed both into his mouth and downed them with water from a glass that was ready and waiting.

Carefully, breathing deeply, he set the computer on the desk, his eyes drawn again to the text, which he reread.

His hand shot out and took up the receiver of the phone. But he halted the action in midair, then slowly replaced the receiver, sitting for a long minute with his hand resting there, as his mind swept back, touching on memories out of time.

In a motion more swift than he had achieved for some months, he rose and reached for his slacks thrown across a chair. Pulling his wallet from the back pocket, he opened it to the picture he had kept of her and held it into the circle cast by the lamp.

Marilee's image was there beneath the cloudy plastic. Not smiling, but fiery. He smiled softly, remembering. He had taken the picture himself, and it was the best of her possible. Marilee had never been one to take a very good picture. She posed too hard. But this one he had caught her unawares, and angry. What had it been that time? Oh, yes, it had been when he had left her a whole day, waiting at that old grocery in the Tennessee mountains.

He supposed his main mistake had been leaving her too often.

Rubbing the stubble on his cheeks, he again read the text on the computer screen and felt such emotion as made him turn away. It was just a podunk newspaper in a podunk town, he thought, and that was why the announcement appeared on the front page.

Marilee had been floating around in his mind so much for the past six months. That was why he had come back to the States, why he had found the *Voice* on the Internet and looked there every few days for the past month. He had been resisting the urge to run to her. His urge was stupid. Why couldn't he let it go?

He shook his head, and then he caught sight of himself in the mirror on the wall. Always thin, his face was bony now. In the low-lighted room, his image appeared colorless, lifeless. Fear swept down his spine and sent him turning from the sight.

He looked again at the telephone for a long minute, before going to the closet, pulling out his bags and beginning packing. He would not call her. He wouldn't give her an opportunity to tell him not to come. If he just showed up on her doorstep, she would see him then. And he doubted she would send him, the father of her child come at last, away.

One

Today—the first day of the rest of your life.
Valentine, Oklahoma, 5:30 a.m.

Streetlights twinkled through the trees, and here and there kitchen lights were popping on, as the earliest risers, or those who were just coming home, began to make morning coffee.

Up on Church Street, Winston Valentine didn't have to make coffee. His niece, Leanne, had moved in two weeks earlier and brought her fancy coffee machine with its automatic timer. She set it to come on around the time Winston awoke each morning and checked to make certain he was alive. At eighty-eight, he thought it prudent to check his vital signs each morning. He took being able to smell the aroma of the coffee as a main indication that he remained among the living.

Rising, he looked out the window, saw the frost on the porch roof and thought it a good choice that he and his neighbor, Everett Northrupt, had decided that during the winter months they would push their flag-raising time until one half hour after sunrise.

He dressed, caught up his breath and his cane, and headed downstairs, passing the closed door of the room his niece occupied and stopping to peek in the room of his elderly friend and boarder, Mildred Covington, who snored lightly with her mouth wide-open. He liked to make certain Mildred was still alive, too, since the death of his former elderly boarder, Ruthanne Bell, who, just after Christmas, had passed away sitting in a chair and they all thought she was asleep for half a day.

In the kitchen, he swallowed two aspirin, slipped into his old wool coat, poured a mugful of coffee and took it to the front porch. There he eased himself into a rocker, watched for daybreak and talked to God. He thought it best to be on speaking terms with God, since each day he came closer to kicking the bucket.

Down at the intersection of Main and Church Streets, a spotlight shone on two flags, the Oklahoma state flag and the Valentine city flag, faintly fluttering in front of City Hall. To the west, the buildings of

Main Street stretched in shades of grey at this hour, the color broken on the south side by the fluorescent blue and yellow of the old Blaines' Drugstore sign.

The stray black cat that had taken up at Blaines', where Belinda Blaine fed it milk out the back door, walked across the street and disappeared beneath the only parked car on the street, a Grand Am belonging to Charlotte Nation, who was inside *The Valentine Voice* building. Light shone around the closed blinds covering the plate glass windows of the *Voice*. Charlotte, receptionist and general girl Friday, sat in front of her computer, where she had been since the early hours of the morning.

Charlotte's mother had suffered a stroke back in January, and in an effort to escape the sound of her mother's labored breathing in the other room, she often left her in the care of the night nurse and came down to her office computer, where she worked on the *Voice*'s Web site, or boosted herself with e-mail from support lists, such as Exec-Secs, for executive secretaries, and MomofMom, for daughters caretaking their mothers, and RealWomen, for women with younger lovers.

A knock at the front door jarred Charlotte's attention from her computer.

"It's me, honey."

It was Sandy Conroy, layout man for the *Voice*. Charlotte threw off her glasses and raced to the door, where Sandy stood with a bag of cinnamon rolls from the IGA bakery.

"I know you're beat. I'll make us some coffee," he told her.

No one had ever considered that staunch Charlotte might need some care; it had always been Charlotte looking after everyone else. Until Sandy.

Touched to the core in that instant, Charlotte pulled him inside and into her strong embrace, kissing him ardently.

"Marry me, Charlotte," he whispered when he dragged his lips free.

Her answer was to kiss him again, so as not to have to tell him, yet once more, that no, she could not. She was almost thirty-seven, and Sandy was just barely twenty-six, and she had an invalid mother to care for. It was too much—for both of them.

Over on Porter Street, in the rear bedroom of a bungalow with a deep front porch, Marilee James came awake from a vivid dream. The dream was a repeat of one she had had earlier in the week. While not exactly the same dream, it was close enough to be a little disturbing and cause her to turn on her bedside lamp.

It was what came from listening to Julia Jenkins-Tinsley, the postmistress, who knew everyone's business and told it every chance she got. This time Julia had been telling about how Kaye Upchurch had met her husband at the door wearing nothing but a fur coat, which she flashed open to bare her altogether, as Julia put it. Julia did not know if Kaye had succeeded in heating up her husband with this stunt, but she did know that he was now receiving *Men's Health* magazine and vitamins through the mail.

Since hearing about this, Marilee had been toying with the idea of doing something similar to Tate. She thought of it now, her gaze falling to the new engagement ring sparkling on her finger. She shined it on the bedspread and admired it again.

Of course the idea was preposterous. Marilee was not the sort who did such things. She did not *want* to be that sort to do such a silly thing.

Except that Tate told her she was way too serious, and she wanted to show him that she was not. And she felt the need to stir him up, get him to take command of their intimate lives. Well, sort of.

Marilee wasn't certain exactly what need she was experiencing, except that there was a craving deep inside causing her to feel frustrated and wild.

She slipped out of bed and went to open her lingerie drawer, pulling out a long, silk, flaming red nightgown that she had, in a fit of reckless intentions, ordered from Victoria's Secret.

Two

In the front bedroom of the bungalow, Little Willie Lee, as he was generally known by bigger kids at school, opened his eyes and saw the fuzzy first grey light of morning around the edges of the window blinds. The entire room looked fuzzy. He found his glasses on his bedside table and put them on in the careful, almost reverent manner he always used, because his glasses enabled him to see.

There was just enough light for him to make out his shiny red cape lying at the end of his bed. He had loved the cape since his mother had made it for him to be Superman on Halloween.

He looked over at his cousin, Corrine, peering hard through the gloom. The room was yet so shadowy that he could barely identify a lump under her covers. Corrine, who liked a pile of blankets—Aunt Vella said it was because she was so skinny—slept with the covers over her head.

He held his finger to his lips at Munro, who remained with his head on his paws, although his eyes blinked. Munro knew the plan, and to be quiet.

Slipping from the bed, Willie Lee knew how to step so that he missed the places where the floor would creak. The wood was cool through his socks.

His shoes waited in the dark corner. He had to sit to slip them on, but he did not have to tie them, because he had learned to remove them without untying the laces. He took his coat from the hook on the door and put it on over his flannel pajamas. Concentrating as hard as he could, he got it zipped up.

Just as he was reaching for his cape, floorboards creaked. *Mama! Coming from her room.*

For an instant Willie Lee stared wide-eyed at Munro, who sat up on the bed and was also wide-eyed, and then he dived for the bed just as a slice of light came shining in from the hall. He scrambled to get himself, his cape clutched in his hands, and his bulky coat, hidden beneath the covers. Munro lay back down, up close against his legs.

There came the swish of his mother's robe and the creak of the floor as she came to the bedroom door. He saw her in his mind's eye, in her long pink robe, her hair billowy, her eyes that often searched him; he could even smell her sweet scent.

It was strange for his mother to be up this early. His mother did not like mornings. No one liked mornings the way Willie Lee did.

He heard his mother go back to her bedroom and shut the door. He peeked out from the covers and saw the empty doorway, hall light out now.

Slipping again from bed, he stood contemplating his problem. His mother might hear him go out the window. His mother seemed to have a certain knowledge about him. She might already know about him going out the window on the previous mornings.

He looked at Munro and heard clearly, *"Better not this morning."*

But Willie Lee whispered, "I have to."

He pushed his pillow and blankets until they looked like how Corrine did in her bed. He got his cape snapped around his neck and shook it out behind him so that it fell properly. Then, on his knees on his bed, with Munro twitching beside him, he raised the window blinds. He had long ago figured out how to do it with almost no noise. The window needed a tug, and then it whooshed up silently, as if with angels' help.

Fresh cold air hit his hands and face.

"Me first!" Munro jumped through the window from which Willie Lee had removed the screen a week ago. No one had noticed.

Willie Lee carefully lowered the blinds back into position, then glanced over his shoulder at Corrine. She was still beneath her covers.

There was no way to be silent in trying to get on the other side of the blinds. He did the best he could. Nothing was going to stop him now, anyway. He got his feet out the window and his rear end positioned on the windowsill, holding to the frame on either side with a hard grip. Munro was sitting on the ground, looking up expectantly. *"Come on!"*

Willie Lee braced his feet against the outside wall. Then he put his arms out in front, the way Superman did, took a breath, closed his eyes and imagined . . . *jump!*

For an instant he was hurtling through the air, with his cape flying out behind him.

His feet hit the ground with a hard jolt, then his knees—something sharp stabbed his left knee—and he caught himself instinctively with his hands, only to lose balance and go rolling across the cold, wet ground.

He found himself staring at the brick foundation three feet from his face. Munro came over to lick his face. "I am o-kay," he told his dog.

He sat up. Everything looked funny. Oh, his glasses. He straightened them on his face. He got to his feet and rubbed his hands on his coat. He had almost flown, he felt sure. Almost. Yes, his cape was okay.

Turning, he looked up into the bare branches of the elm tree that stretched over toward the corner of the house. He looked at Munro. "May-be I need to be high-er . . . up in the tree."

Munro looked up at the tree and then at Willie Lee. *"I don't think so."*

Willie Lee went over to the tree and walked around on the lumps of roots spreading out at the base. He felt the rough bark. He pressed his ear against the trunk, hearing the life running through the tree the same way he could sometimes hear it in the wind or in the ground.

He looked upward again for a long minute. He raised both arms out in front and upward, hands together, closed his eyes and stood there, imagining, feeling himself begin to soar.

But when he opened his eyes, he was still on the ground.

Just then a door opened next door.

Willie Lee dropped his arms and squished himself against the tree trunk. Munro moved close.

Trash cans banged. Mr. Purvis putting out his garbage.

Next came a small meow and then Mr. Purvis saying, "Git . . . git outta here!"

Willie Lee risked peeking around the tree. He saw Mr. Purvis stamp one of his big boots at a small grey kitten, as if trying to smash it.

The kitten scampered under the hedges that divided Mr. Purvis's driveway from Willie Lee's front yard.

Mr. Purvis went back into his house.

Willie Lee, crouching, went along the hedge, until he saw the little kitten.

"Do you know him, Mun-ro?"

"No."

Willie Lee said, "Here, kit-ty."

The kitten, frightened of everything, scampered farther along through the branches of the hedge. Munro went ahead and tried to speak with the kitten, while Willie Lee held back and watched. But the kitten just hissed at Munro.

"Stupid cat." Munro retreated.

Then Mr. Purvis came back out to start his pickup, and at the roar of the engine—which Willie Lee's mother and just about everyone else in their neighborhood complained of—the kitten zipped through the hedge, and then it was as if it shot out and up into the air, right out into the road, unfortunately at the exact moment that a little car came speeding past.

Thud!

Willie Lee saw and heard it. It looked as if the kitten hit the car and not the other way around.

The next instant the car was gone, and the kitten lay in the road, like a dirty rag.

Munro took off like a bullet for the street, and Willie Lee, forgetting to remain hidden, hurried as fast as he could after the dog.

He stopped at the curb. He was not allowed in the street. But the kitten was only a little way into the street. Munro was sniffing it gingerly.

Carefully Willie Lee stepped off the curb and over to the lifeless grey-striped form. Pushing his glasses up on his nose, he crouched with his hands on his knees for a closer look.

"Road-kill," Munro said.

"Well, by golly, Willie Lee, is that your kitten that got run over there?" It was Mr. Purvis, looking over from scraping frost off his windshield. Puffs of white came out of his mouth, about like the dark puffs coming out of the tailpipe of his rumbling truck.

"No, sir."

"Well, son, you had better get out of the street before a car comes and runs over you. I'm fixin' to back out."

Mr. Purvis reached for the door handle.

Willie Lee watched with alarm, and Munro pranced. *"Pick him up, quick . . . hold him."*

Willie Lee reached down to gather up the kitten's limp body. His knuckles scraped the pavement. He always had such a hard time moving fast. He could never move as fast as everyone wanted him to.

Then, holding the kitten close against his chest, he carried it up into his yard, stumbling on the curbing. He walked beneath the massive bare branches of the elm tree and stood there, feeling the kitten warm in his arms. He closed his eyes and imagined himself flying, and as Mr. Purvis's pickup truck roared out of the driveway, he could feel himself lifting.

Inside the house, Marilee had her face jutted toward her dresser mirror and, in the impossibly low light of the little crystal lamp, was applying lipstick, when Leon Purvis's hot-rod pickup roared in the driveway next door. She jumped and shot red toward her cheek.

Dang that man! Somebody ought to shoot him. She threw down the lipstick and headed for the bedroom door. Hearing her boot heels connect with the floor, she went up on tiptoe, lifting up the red silk nightgown as she raced across the short hallway to the children's bedroom.

She stood there, hearing her neighbor's hot-rod truck fade away down the street and holding her breath as she studied the forms in the beds.

The forms did not move. A bomb going off outside would not wake Willie Lee unless he wanted to wake, but Corrine could be awakened at times by the least thing.

It occurred to Marilee that she would feel pretty foolish should her niece wake up and find her standing there in the sexy red negligee and tall taupe cowboy boots.

She tiptoed back into her bedroom, where she stood for a moment, listening with the door cracked. Silence. No one stirred. She reassured herself that one could generally count on children sleeping more soundly on school days.

Back again in front of the mirror, she took a tissue to the smudged lipstick, then reapplied it. A last study of her image, then she dropped the lipstick and strode to the closet, where the door sat open with clothes hung all over it, got out her long trench coat and put it on. She hadn't worn it in years, usually opting for her practical and comfortable Pendleton barn coat.

Standing in front of the full-length mirror, she tied the coat around her, leaving the buttons undone. It would be much easier to whip open the coat if it were just tied.

She gave it a try, jerked the belt loose and flung open the coat and struck a provocative pose. Plunging neckline, skin shadowy beneath the filmy gown, high-heeled cowboy boots. Well. That was a picture to get attention, she would think.

Sucking in a breath, she folded the coat closed and retied the belt. Taking advantage of a sudden leap of faith, she opened the bedroom door, tiptoed again to the door of the children's room. The lumps remained still in the beds.

Turning, she tiptoed through the house and out the back door into the cold morning, and hurried across the frosty yard shadowed by the trees. She was still on tiptoe, she realized, and let her feet down.

The latch on the old back gate was frozen in place. She jiggled it, and it opened with a small squeak. She hurried through the gate and the line of cedars at the back of Tate's yard, across the expanse of lawn and up the back steps. She felt like some sort of criminal sneaking through the neighborhood.

The doorknob was cold beneath her hand. The door that had not been locked since Tate moved in opened quietly.

She stuck her head through and peered into the room. A light burned above the sink, but there was no aroma of coffee. Her nose twitched, detecting the acrid scent of old moldy wood.

Listening carefully, she thought she detected water running through pipes. Maybe so, maybe not.

She stepped into the kitchen and closed the door quietly behind her, leaned against it, catching her breath. Then she was struck with the boldness of her following through with her idea, and that the idea was actually rolling along.

Pushing from the door with a bit of eagerness now, she went to the coffeemaker, pulled it forward on the counter, then looked at the cabinets, guessing the location of the coffee and opening the door directly above.

She and Tate had been dating since last fall, and she had not spent enough time in his kitchen to know for certain the location of his coffee. This fact seemed to speak about a definite hole in their relationship. She didn't know where his coffee was kept, and she had only made love with him four times. Four rather furtive times, stolen moments that had much more to do with passionate need than commitment, which they had now made.

At the thought of her commitment, Marilee's mind did a sharp jog back to the preparation of coffee. Just to be ready in case Tate appeared, she untied the belt of her coat and did a quick practice seductive flash. Okay, that would do.

The next instant the back door swung inward.

Marilee whirled around. She had thought Tate was upstairs. What was he doing coming in the back door? *Grab the edges of her coat, pose and flash.*

She had her coat whipped open when she realized the figure stepping into the kitchen was not Tate but . . . a woman.

Yes, a woman coming in the door. A small woman, in a bright pink-and-purple silk jogging suit, who gazed at Marilee with equal surprise.

Marilee wrapped her coat closed.

The woman said, "Oh, honey, I'm sorry to startle you. I guess you weren't expectin' me." She laughed. "And I wasn't you, either."

Who was this woman?

As if in answer to the unspoken question, the woman said, "I'm Tate's mother, Franny. I got in late last night." Lowering her voice, she leaned forward and held up a pack of Virginia Slims. "I took my smoke outside, before Tate got up. He will take me to task if he finds out I still smoke a cigarette on occasion. I *do* take care of myself, and one little cigarette isn't going to kill me, and I like to have it while I do my mornin' meditations. But I thought it best to go outside. . . . I don't want to do anything to make Tate start up again." She put a hand over her heart. "Heaven knows he had such a hard time quittin'. And I do not want to be any temptation in the wrong direction for my son."

The entire time the woman spoke, Marilee stood frozen, holding her coat around her and taking in the woman's bright green eyes, pixie-styled, carrot-red hair, dangling earrings and bangle bracelets that tingled, noticing that her features greatly resembled Tate's, although surely she was too young to be his mother, and she looked not at all like her picture on his office wall. Her accent, too, was very much like his; she said the word *direction* with a long *i,* and there was a brightness about her that was arresting, as if she glowed.

Then the woman said, "You're Marilee, aren't you? If you're not, Tate has a lot more problems than startin' up smokin' again." She gave a throaty chuckle.

"Oh, yes, I'm Marilee." Clutching her coat together with one hand, she extended the other. "Hello."

"Hello, my dear." The woman took Marilee's hand, but instead of a shake, she came forward and pressed her cheek against Marilee's in a warm manner. "It is a delight to at last meet the love of my son's life."

Then she drew back and was again assessing Marilee, who said, "I . . . I was just . . . well, I thought I'd make Tate some coffee this mornin'."

"Ahh . . ." The woman's gaze traveled up and down Marilee, and then she turned to reach into a cabinet for a mug, which she stuck beneath the water faucet. "I always have a cup of hot water before my coffee. I don't make very good coffee, so I'm awfully glad you can." Popping the cup into the microwave, she pushed buttons.

Marilee decided she had to get out of there.

"I need to be getting back home. The children are alone. I just left them for a few minutes." She didn't want Tate's mother to think her careless as a parent. No doubt the woman was already having plenty of skeptical thoughts about her. She moved toward the door, remembering at last to tie her belt and not keep clutching her coat together like an insane woman.

"But, honey, you haven't seen Tate."

"I'll see him later." She opened the door.

"Now, I don't want to be an interruption to you and Tate and y'all's routine. I'm takin' my hot water right up to my room and leavin' you two alone to do . . . whatever."

"We don't have a routine," Marilee said instantly, taking the woman's "whatever" to be something like making mad, passionate love on the floor. "I just . . . well, I have to get back."

At that minute Tate entered. He was pulling a T-shirt over his head. Marilee saw his bare chest, blue flannel lounge pants and bare feet. When her gaze came up from his feet, she found his head out of his shirt and his eyes staring at her in surprise.

"Marilee?"

"Good mornin', dear," his mother said as the microwave oven beeped. "I think Marilee has a surprise for you." And then, bearing her cup of hot water, the woman swept out of the room in a swish of her silk jogging suit.

Tate looked at Marilee, who said, "I just came to make your coffee. See you later."

Turning, she left him there with his confused expression, going out without so much as a kiss on the cheek, closing the door to the aroma of coffee, descending down the steps with the cold crisp air blowing up her coat and gown, a painful reminder of her foolish, audacious actions. As she hurried across the frosty grass that crunched under her feet, she listened for Tate to follow. But he did not. Bitter disappointment brought tears to her eyes.

She should have known better than to try something silly. She had never been very good at silly.

In the bathroom, Corrine heard a noise and opened the door a crack, peeking out. Light poured in the living-room windows now. She heard her aunt Marilee's steps through the house, coming from the kitchen. The question of where her aunt had been so early in the morning flitted through Corrine's mind but was pushed out by the immediacy of her situation.

Her aunt, just entering the hallway, stopped on sight of Corrine, who said, "I . . . I started," and thrust her panties out through the cracked door.

"What?" Aunt Marilee looked puzzled.

Corrine closed her eyes and shook the panties, which Aunt Marilee took and looked at. Corrine opened her eyes to check her aunt's response.

Aunt Marilee's bottom lip quivered, and her eyes went all soft and warm, and Corrine could breathe again.

"Oh, sugar," Aunt Marilee said, pushing open the door and pulling

Corrine out. She pressed Corrine against her, saying again, "Oh, sweetheart," and Corrine had to turn her head to the side to keep from being smothered. Aunt Marilee led them into her room and sat on her big bed, all the while saying how Corrine had taken a big step into womanhood.

"Remember all I told you? All we learned?" her aunt asked.

In her dedicated effort to school Corrine and Willie Lee at home last summer, Aunt Marilee had taught Corrine all about the human body. Aunt Marilee had done such a thorough job that when her teacher this year at school had addressed a lot of the same facts, Corrine had felt she could have taught the class.

Corrine nodded that she did remember.

"Do you have any questions?" asked Aunt Marilee, who had tears flowing down her cheeks even while she smiled.

Corrine didn't think the smile reached her aunt's eyes. She wondered what her aunt was really thinking, but she was not about to ask.

Then Aunt Marilee was stroking Corrine's hair. "I wish sometimes that I could keep you from growin' up. . . . Life just gets more complicated from here," her aunt said in a sighing voice.

Corrine thought life was pretty complicated now, but she was glad to be growing up, and it couldn't happen soon enough for her. She believed that when she grew up she would know all that she needed to know, and that she would never act as stupid as all the adults she saw.

Just then Aunt Marilee got to her feet. "We need to call your mother, and you can tell her. She'll want to share this time with you. Wouldn't you like to tell her of your big day?"

Corrine read the assumption on her aunt's face and said the expected "Yes." She watched as her aunt reached for the telephone on the nightstand. Her stomach tightened, and uncertainty tumbled over her body. Apparently Aunt Marilee had forgotten that early mornings were not a good time to call her mother, who was never, even when not hung over, in a good mood first thing in the morning. When Corrine had lived at home, she had learned not to wake her mother and in the mornings to make coffee so that her mother could have a cup as soon as possible upon awaking. One never spoke to Corrine's mother before she had her coffee. And one generally didn't speak of private things at all with her mother, who did not like to speak of bodily functions.

"Oh, this phone doesn't have your mother's number," Aunt Marilee said, and Corrine felt an instant of relief, but then Aunt Marilee was heading for the phone on her desk in the living room.

Corrine followed, for the first time noting that her aunt had on a long coat she had not before seen, and boots. Curiosity over her aunt's dress and where her aunt had been so early in the morning flitted through her mind but was replaced by wondering if she should remind her aunt that morning was not a good time to call her mother.

She threw herself into the big chair, to hide, but then she poked up on her knees and said in a sudden, hurried whisper, "You tell her, Aunt Marilee."

Aunt Marilee cupped Corrine's chin with her hand, which was cool and smooth.

A moment later Aunt Marilee was saying into the phone, "Anita, this is Marilee. Call up here this evenin', okay? Corrine has something to tell you." She paused and added, "We love you, Anita."

Aunt Marilee put down the phone. "Your mother's probably still sleepin', but she'll call us back this evenin'."

Corrine looked into her aunt's eyes and saw the eagerness to please there. She smiled, trying to give her aunt what she wanted, while inside she felt relieved not to have to hear her mother's groggy morning voice. Guilt came with the relief.

Aunt Marilee hugged Corrine in that way she had of trying to make everything right.

Just then the front doorbell rang, causing both of them to jump, and Aunt Marilee to let out an "Oh!"

Aunt Marilee moved to answer, and Corrine hurried to stand beside her, to be ready in case. She did not know in case of what, but Corrine always felt the need to be ready for dire happenings.

It was Willie Lee and Munro standing there.

Willie Lee was in his coat and Superman cape, and holding on to a little kitten squirming in his arms.

"I have been out-side." He stated the obvious as he came forward. "And I have a new kitten."

Corrine thought of Willie Lee's bed, of the lump she had thought was him.

"Oh, Willie Lee, not another one," Aunt Marilee said.

Just then the kitten managed to spring out of Willie Lee's grasp, bolted over his shoulder and across the porch. Willie Lee turned to call to it, but it disappeared beneath the house.

Aunt Marilee tugged Willie Lee inside and told him that he could have the kitten if it showed up again. She wanted to know what he had been doing outside.

"I have been learn-ing to fly," he said.

Three

Officially engaged . . .

Tate came driving up in his yellow BMW just as Marilee was herd-ing the children out to her Cherokee. Tate had been taking them to school each day since the beginning of the school year, but he was late today, and Marilee had assumed that he had decided to skip this morn-ing because of his mother's presence. She had thought him rude for not calling to tell her so, too, and now she felt silly for jumping to con-clusions.

"Sorry I'm late," he said, leaning over and opening the passenger door.

"I just figured you were spending the morning with your mother." Marilee stood looking in the door at him. She felt sharp and was an-noyed with herself because of it.

"My mother generally amuses herself in the mornin'. Come on, kids." He beckoned to Willie Lee and Corrine, who were already eas-ing past Marilee and into the back seat.

Marilee slipped into the passenger seat, keeping her eyes averted as she buckled herself in.

"Thank you for the coffee," Tate said as he shifted into Reverse. She looked over to see his blue eyes warm upon her.

"You're welcome," she answered, thinking how nice he was being, and of how he had not followed her out the door that morning. Shift-ing her gaze to Willie Lee, she made certain he had fastened his seat belt.

On the short drive to the school, Tate told them that his mother had arrived in the middle of the night. He used the phrase, "She landed in about one o'clock." This caused a bit of discussion.

"Did she land on the roof?" Willie Lee wanted to know.

"Uh, no . . . she stopped in the driveway."

"You said she land-ed."

"I meant she arrived at one o'clock," Tate corrected. "She drove

into the driveway at one o'clock . . . and stopped." One had to be spe-
cific with Willie Lee.

"Oh. You do not mean your mo-ther can fly?"

"I guess she could, but Valentine doesn't have an airport, Willie
Lee."

"I know that. I thought may-be your mo-ther could fly by her-self."
Willie Lee's voice echoed with disappointment.

Understanding dawned on Tate's face. Then he shook his head.
"No, son. My mother has a number of supreme abilities, but flyin' is
not one of 'em."

Marilee wondered about his mother, who did seem somewhat
unique.

He went on to tell Marilee that his mother had not even telephoned
him that she was coming until she was one hour outside of town, when
she called for directions. When Marilee commented on her youthful
appearance, he said that his mother had turned seventy years old, and
that youthful appearance was a family trait.

Marilee, looking at his profile and at the way his pale hair curled
slightly behind his ear, said she saw it in him.

Tate stopped the BMW at the curb in front of the school, where
Marilee got out and lifted the back of the seat to let the children out. In
the manner of many a single mother carrying sole responsibility and
occasionally being a little manic about it, Marilee adjusted Willie
Lee's backpack to the proper position and then made certain Corrine
had the coins she had given her for a pay phone, in case of emergency
use.

"I could always use the office phone," Corrine said, even as she
showed Marilee the coins.

"I just like you to have options. You can call me anytime, and I'll
come get you, if you don't feel well." She wanted Corrine to know it
was okay to come home, if she wanted. She wanted things to be different for Corrine than they had been for herself. For an instant in memory, she recalled being at school and feeling the blood run out between
her legs, afraid of shaming herself and not having anyone to turn to.

"I'm okay," Corrine said in a low voice, shooting a cautioning
glance toward the car and Tate.

Marilee got the message to shut up. "Okay. Love you."

She kissed them both quickly and then stood there, holding the car
door, resisting the urge to stuff them back inside and race home with
them, to keep them there with her, safe from the hard world.

She watched them walk away up the sidewalk, falling in beside
other children, yet seeming to stand out, different, marching to a drum

unheard by others. Corrine, always protective, took Willie Lee's hand. Her niece possessed a fierce heart in a thin, fragile body.

And Willie Lee . . . Marilee's eyes lingered on her son, on his spiky blond hair that nothing could tame, almost like Willie Lee himself, different from others and going at his own pace in a world that hated different and slow and kept pressing him to be customary and fast. But he was Willie Lee, who had been denied oxygen at birth, or some such thing she had never fully understood and felt vaguely guilty at possibly causing. His brain could not comprehend as a standard brain and would never be able to go beyond the understanding of what it was right now, a five-year-old brain in a nine-year-old body.

And what did it matter? Her son was happy, and Marilee did her best to encourage him to be exactly who he was, while at the same time trying to help him to learn to live in the world in which he had to live.

It would no doubt be easier for him in the long run. As Willie Lee's body matured, his handicaps would be more and more obvious, and the world made allowances for handicaps that could be seen.

Not so for Corrine. Her handicaps were wounded emotions, invisible and considered shameful, if considered at all. The world was frightened of wounded emotions, because everyone had a bit of their own. To admit them meant admitting to weakness, and the world had little tolerance for weakness.

Marilee slipped back into the car.

"They are fine," Tate said, and squeezed her knee.

She glanced over and saw the look of understanding on his face. She wished she could believe him. There was such a faith in life about Tate Holloway.

With this thought came a jumble of emotions, admiration, gratitude, desire, all coming in a flood so strong that she flushed warmly and put her hand atop his, entwining her fingers with his. Quite suddenly her mind filled with the image of throwing herself onto Tate and doing it right there in the school parking lot, or, conversely, jumping out of the car, which was now exiting the lot, and running far, far away.

She let go his hand and turned her head toward the window, seeing the bare-branched trees against a clear blue sky, the empty playground, and the buses pulling into the garages. To say she was in a confused emotional state probably put it mildly.

"The announcement will be in the paper today," he said, and the comment drew her head around; his expression was pleased as all getout.

"Yes, it will," she said, putting a pleased smile on her face for him. And she *was* pleased. Of course she was pleased.

"It's already on the Web site."

There was no need to tell him that she had not looked. She felt a little guilty for possibly not paying sufficient attention to their official engagement announcement.

Tate was saying, "Charlotte must not have been able to sleep last night. She got the entire front page updated already."

"Charlotte has become something of a computer maven. She put the announcement on the front page?" She found this vaguely disconcerting. Marilee did not like to stand out.

Tate nodded happily. "We thought that appropriate. After all, I am the publisher. You are marryin' big-time, darlin'." Tate *did* like to stand out. He enjoyed attention as much as he generally liked to give it.

They had come to the corner of Main and Church Streets. *The Valentine Voice* building sat like a stanchion on the north corner.

"Take me home," Marilee said, giving the building a glance. "I'll work at home today."

He looked at her, questioning.

"I just need the quiet. I need to concentrate to finish the piece on the teachers' proposed pay raise."

Up Church Street, a right turn onto Porter, and then they were pulling into her driveway behind her white Cherokee. Munro, waiting on the porch, got to his feet. From next to him came a flash of fur.

"Oh," she said. "I think that was the kitten Willie Lee wants slipping underneath the porch. I'm so tired of all these strays. We have finally gotten down to two rabbits, the mice and the goldfish."

"Animals are his talent."

Marilee agreed with a sigh. "Remember, all these animals will be living with you soon."

"There's plenty of room over at the Big House," he said, using the new term he had for his house. "And I'll build him cages in the backyard, if we have to. We could have a budding veterinarian on our hands."

"No, we don't. We have Willie Lee." Sometimes Tate, who could be as imaginative as a little boy, needed reminding that this was the real world.

He said, "Yes, it is Willie Lee, but no doubt his talent with animals will be profitable in some way."

At that, Marilee had to put her hand on his cheek. "I do love you, Tate Holloway." She did not say it often. Even now, the words came as if propelled past her reasoning mind, which could hardly believe in love between a man and a woman.

Then she was looking at his lips and bending toward him, and the next instant they had melted together in a deep kiss, causing her to put her hand to the back of his neck and hold him when he would have lifted his head. She went to kissing him for all she was worth, and he responded, and soon they were slipping down in the car seat. Marilee heard the caution in the back of her brain and pushed it away. She thought of the house, now empty of children, of her bed that she had not even made that morning.

Ask him . . . tell him how you feel . . . ask him inside . . . no, don't you dare do that.

Then Tate was pulling away. "Well . . . I guess we'd better remember where we are."

Marilee was quite limp and breathless. She saw his face all hot with passion, and she let him see clearly how she felt. Or she attempted to do this, but his response was to sit up straight and say that he needed to get on over to the office.

"I'd best check and make sure everything is on its way to being ready for deadline." His sky-blue eyes flitted up to her hair, then down to her lips, and then up again to meet hers.

"Yes," she said. "I need to get to work, too." She scooted out of the seat, taking up her purse as she moved.

"I'll call you later."

"Okay. Have a good day."

She shut the car door and gave him a wave, then headed in long strides for the porch, thinking that they were behaving as though they were very good friends, which of course they were. Marilee was always good friends with the men in her life. She knew how to be a friend. It was being a lover that she found problematic.

She turned the knob on the unlocked front door. The old wooden door stuck, and she shoved it, realizing with a suddenness how very angry she felt.

The door swung inward, all the way back to bang against the wall. Munro, coming into the house at her feet, skittered out of the way at the sound, then shot her an accusing look.

Marilee took a deep breath and carefully closed the door. She leaned against it for a moment, then pushed herself away and went to her desk, took up the phone and punched the automatic dial for her aunt Vella, tucked the receiver into her neck and picked up a fingernail file as she listened to the slow rings across the line. Just when she thought her aunt was not going to pick up, she heard a click.

"Aunt Vella? Hello?"

"Yes, I'm here, sugar." Aunt Vella's voice came with static across the line. "I'm on my cell phone . . . calls forwarded . . . I'm . . . way . . . sale . . . Home De . . ."

"Aunt Vella? You're breakin' up. I'll call you later."

Hearing her aunt's acknowledgment, Marilee hung up and sat there, thinking of her situation, which was that here she was, marrying a man to whom she could not talk about her deep need for closeness. Who she could not manage to get alone for any length of time—in fact, with whom being alone seemed to frighten her.

Her record in previous situations of this type was not a good one. Here she was, now officially engaged to a man, the third one in her lifetime, although she and Stuart hadn't really had an engagement of any longer than it took to get a marriage license and get married, and thinking that maybe she was, yet again, making a terrible mistake.

Four

One picture is worth a thousand words. . . .

The clock on his desk read one-fifty when Charlotte called out from her reception desk, "Paper's here."

He popped out of his swivel chair, and was out of his office in three swift strides and heading through the tall-ceilinged main room at a pace just shy of running. He jerked open the heavy steel door into what had once, during the *Voice*'s heyday, been the printing press area and was now the loading garage.

The large overhead door was up and the opening filled with the back end of the printer's delivery truck. Diesel exhaust hung like a cloud, mingling with the scents of musty wood and brick and newspaper ink, bringing to Tate's mind faint memories of his boyhood, when he delivered papers at the crack of dawn.

"Yo, Editor!" Burly Chet Harmon, their circulation manager, and two of his helpers were busy unloading the bundled newspapers, stacking them on the dock, then loading them into the *Voice* van that sat nearby. Chet pulled a rolled paper from his back pocket and tossed it to Tate. "Here ya' go, boss. One picture is worth a thousand words, so they say." He grinned widely.

Newsprint ink wafted up to Tate as he unrolled the paper and saw the announcement right there on the front page. He gazed on Marilee's face smiling out from the paper. She had agreed to marry him, Tate Holloway, who was fifty-two years old and just now getting a start on a home and family. That he was seeing his dream come to reality was almost more than he could take in.

"Congratulations, Editor," called one of the men—Durham, who did the store route.

Tate grinned broadly. "Thanks!" He shot a wave to all, then turned, slammed the door closed and strode back through the main room, waving the newspaper at their reclusive comptroller, Zona, through her opened door, "It's here!" and to Sandy at the layout counter, who grinned his young, good ol' boy grin.

When he reached Charlotte's desk, he smacked the paper over her monitor screen. "Here it is."

"I've seen it."

"Yeah, well—" he dropped the paper so she had to grab it "—look at it now. *Published.*"

Heading on to his office, he ducked behind the door and snatched his brown suede jacket from the hook, slipping it on as he returned. "You know, they say if you see it in the *Voice,* it's the truth."

"You stole that." She was on her feet and holding the paper out to him. Charlotte was tall, and today, in heels, she seemed to look down on him.

"I only *borrow* the true statements." He adjusted his shirt collar over his jacket. "It's announced now . . . to everyone."

"Yes, it is." She pushed her glasses up over her thick dark hair and regarded him with her dark eyes.

He finished straightening his collar and met her gaze for a moment, savoring an accomplishment.

Charlotte gave him one of her rare smiles. "Congratulations. You two are perfect for each other."

"Thank you. I think so." He couldn't seem to stop grinning. "I'm off for an hour."

"Show-off," she said with a shake of her head.

"You bet." And he was out the door into the bright winter sunlight and crisp, fresh breeze.

He slipped into his car and backed out onto the street. There was one person he had to show first. He owed it to Parker Lindsey. They had become friends, of a sort. They had shared a rivalry for Marilee— which Tate had won—and they shared the same hour in the morning for jogging, where Parker by far proved the more hearty runner. These things were ties enough. It seemed the honorable thing to do, to tell Lindsey in person, and the reason Tate hadn't told him straight away, after settling things with Marilee on Sunday, was that Lindsey had been off at a convention down in Houston and had returned only yesterday.

Guilt nagged at him that he had not gone over to speak to Lindsey last night. He didn't want the man to hear the news from someone else. But last night he'd been full of Marilee's good stew and biscuits, and crawling into bed before he thought of it. He hadn't even mentioned about Lindsey to Marilee.

Possibly Marilee had broken the news to her former fiancé that morning. But that did not take care of Tate's sense of responsibility. Okay, might as well admit that a great deal of pride was involved.

Such an attitude seemed small on his part. Oh, well, such was he and such was life, he thought, grinning just a bit as he pulled into the gravel lot of the Lindsey Veterinary Clinic.

"Doc's out back, workin' on a cow," the young girl at the desk told him. She was new to him; she had dyed black hair, spiked. "You can go on back through here."

Tate, tapping the newspaper against his thigh, went through the main lab room and opened another door, stepping into the large rear room with two stalls. Parker was coming out of one.

"Hey, Editor," Parker said, peeling off a soiled glove that covered his arm to his shoulder.

"Hey, Doc." Eyeing the plastic glove, Tate said, "I admire your courage, putting your hand deep into parts unknown."

Parker grinned. "Always interesting. Found a Wal-Mart bag this time."

"Empty?" Tate asked.

"Not exactly."

Just then another figure stepped out from the stall, carefully closing the gate behind her. It was a woman. Slim, blond hair, good-looking. She had on a medical smock. Parker often had interns in training, and he seemed to manage to get the pretty females.

Parker introduced them. "Amy, this is the illustrious editor of *The Valentine Voice,* Tate Holloway. We all just call him Editor," he said to the girl. "Editor, this is Amy Lawrence, my new partner."

Partner?

Amy was a no-nonsense sort and stuck out her hand for a firm shake. "I'm Amy Lindsey now."

Tate took that with surprise, looking from the woman to Lindsey, who blushed and rubbed his nose.

"He isn't used to it yet," the young woman said, flashing a grin. "I guess I'll have to make him practice saying it: Mrs. Amy Lindsey."

Lindsey put his now clean arm around her. "Yes, that's right. Editor, please meet my wife . . . Mrs. Amy Lindsey."

The two were about the same height and coloring. And they were clearly two people in love.

Tate recovered his senses. "Well, congratulations!" he said and stuck out his hand to shake Lindsey's. "This is . . . quite a surprise. You go away to a veterinarians' convention and return with a wife." The man had upstaged him.

"Yeah, well . . ." said Lindsey, whose eyes returned warmly to the woman at his side.

"It came as a surprise to us, too," she said with a laugh.

Tate said, "So, you have captured our proverbial bachelor. You must be awfully special." He looked her over. She was younger than Parker, possibly as much as fifteen years younger, he would guess. The difference was probably a good match.

And she was a talker, was Amy Lawrence Lindsey. An up-front, straight talker, who quite quickly imparted the information that she and Lindsey had met over two years ago and renewed acquaintances at the convention. "I make up my mind pretty quickly, and Parker figured he wasn't getting any younger."

She draped herself there against her husband. They were in love. It was fantastic.

Probably won't last, Tate thought, and then purposely swept that bit of uncharitable negativity out of his mind.

He was so stunned by this turn of events that he almost forgot his own news, and in fact when Lindsey asked why he had come by, he felt a little defeated. Then he held out the newspaper and showed his announcement to the man who had been Marilee's former lover and almost husband.

"Well, that's fine," Lindsey said slowly after long seconds of looking at the photograph. His eyes came up to meet Tate's. "I'm really glad for both of you, Tate. You're good for Marilee." He meant it.

"Thank you. I think I am, and I know she is good for me. And I was hopin' you would be willin' to stand up with me as my best man." He was aware asking was a tall order, but he didn't have a close friend, and he meant it as an honor to Lindsey, too.

"I'd be glad to, Tate. Thank you." The man spoke sincerely.

"You bet." Well, he'd said what he had come to say. He shook Lindsey's hand and wished the two newlyweds a good future, then walked back out into the late winter sunshine, fighting off a very foolish annoyance at Lindsey for having upstaged his news. As he got back in his car, he figured his general attitude of Parker Lindsey being a childish sort was the pot calling the kettle black.

Then his gaze fell to the newspaper lying on the seat beside him, to his and Marilee's picture. Happiness took over, for Lindsey who he no longer had to feel guilty about leaving odd man out, and for himself, because he was getting the woman of his dreams, and for the whole dang world.

He caught a glimpse of himself in the rearview mirror and saw he was smiling broadly. He was a pretty handsome fella.

Coming back into town, stopping at the light at Main and Church Streets, he saw Mayor Upchurch, a bucket of fried chicken under his arm, crossing the street from the Quick Shop to City Hall.

"Hey, Walter!" Tate hollered, and waved the paper out the window while turning to slip up to the curb in front of City Hall.

Just then a horn blared and brakes squealed. It was a brown UPS truck taking the same space while Tate had been looking at the mayor. He squeezed on past and pulled to the curb haphazardly in front of the truck.

"Hey, Editor!" It was Buddy Wyatt, his young neighbor from the far end of Porter Street, popping out of the UPS truck with a large box.

"Sorry I about ran into you," Tate said, "but I'm engaged!" Tate thrust the newspaper at him, and the young man peered at the front page, then slid his gaze to Tate. The boy probably thought Tate beyond such a thing as newlywed bliss; Buddy wasn't but about twenty-five, lived at home with his mother and had as a main ambition to sport the biceps of Atlas.

"Hey, that's cool, Editor. But you'd better be more careful watching where you're goin'. Don't think your fi-an-cée would be too happy should you get run over." He gave the box he carried a bit of a toss, flexing his biceps, which showed beneath the short sleeves he sported, even in the winter, and then went through the door that Mayor Up-church held open.

Tate showed the mayor the announcement as the two of them entered the building. Walter Upchurch handed him the warm bucket of chicken and took the paper, reading the announcement aloud; he slapped Tate on the back, and together they showed all the clerks, and the mayor's wife, who stopped by, caught her husband with the greasy fried chicken and scolded him severely for setting himself up for a heart attack and leaving her a lonely widow.

Tate thanked God for giving him a partner like his Marilee and not a harpy like Kaye Upchurch.

From City Hall, he went down to the Main Street Café, where he showed everyone in there his great news and bought a round of coffee. After that he continued up and down Main Street, with its shops sporting fluttering flags of various sentiments and its sidewalks newly planted with redbud trees, for which Tate had led the fund drive. He stopped in the shops and met people on the sidewalk, and spread the news that he and Marilee were formally engaged and had set the date for their nuptials. He wanted to make certain everyone knew, and he wasn't trusting to the newspaper or gossip to get the job done.

At the Sweetie Cakes bakery, he ordered a double chocolate cake for that evening, a surprise and celebration of the official announcement. "Marilee loves her chocolate," Bonita Embree said knowingly.

"I know how to keep my girl happy," Tate said.

Bonita, laughing gaily, said, "Better than sex."

Tate ducked out on that and headed down to Grace Florist, where he ordered a mixed spring bouquet.

"It's still winter. May snow, the weatherman says," said Fred Grace.

"All the more reason for a spring-looking bouquet. Deliver it this afternoon, will ya'?"

He wrote on the card to go with the flowers: *Thank you for agreeing to be my wife . . . with love from the happiest man in the world.* Lay it on thick.

Why did he feel vaguely guilty? He hadn't known she was coming at the crack of dawn to make him coffee. She had hurried away, like she didn't want him to bother her. And he hadn't thought she seemed as if she wanted him to ask about her unusual actions. Marilee could get real touchy about some stuff.

Probably it was her way of celebrating this special day, and he wanted to show her that he felt the same.

Outside of the florist he ran into Norm Stidham, owner of the Texaco, married for thirty-five years and father of eight. "Well, you've been a bachelor for quite a while, Editor," Stidham said in his direct manner. "Do you know full well what you are gettin' into?"

To which Tate replied, "Yes, sir, I do. I'm more than ready to take me a wife and her children."

It was with this swelling thought that he entered Blaines' Drugstore and showed the announcement to Vella Blaine, Marilee's aunt and the most influential person in her life.

Vella was handling the soda counter by herself, it being a quiet time of day at the drugstore. She met him with her normal warm smile and reached to take the newspaper out of his hand. "Marilee called me this morning, but I was on my way to the Home Depot and haven't had time to call her back. Perry!" she shouted. "Come out and see Tate and Marilee's engagement in the paper. Tate's brought it hot off the press."

Tate watched the older woman's face as she peered through her bifocals, reading the announcement. For the first time he noted a bit of resemblance between the older woman and Marilee. It was there in the concentrated expression.

He felt a little disconcerted with the realization. Although he admired Vella's intelligence, grace and liveliness—in fact, he often encouraged Marilee to loosen up and be more lively—in that moment the thought sliced through him that if Marilee adopted some of the attitudes that Vella had of late, he would not care for it at all. Vella could get out of hand. She could be a demanding woman.

He had this thought as Perry came out from the pharmacy, smoothing his hair down as if he were about to face a judging. "What is it, Vella? I couldn't hear you." His gaze came to Tate. "'Lo, Tate, how are ya?"

With a raised voice, Tate said, "I'm an officially engaged man."

"It's Marilee's and Tate's engagement announcement in the paper," Vella told her husband. Perry had been getting progressively harder of hearing and was resisting a hearing aid. His resisting annoyed his wife, but Tate could understand the man's point of view. Some things were hard for a man to accept.

"I read it. I read the paper online this mornin'." Perry was definitely a video man; he loved his television and had recently gotten hooked up to the Internet through cable.

Vella said with aggravation, "Tate brought the paper especially to show us. You need to read the announcement printed on real paper." Vella was not a fan of television or computers.

Perry nodded and took the newspaper his wife shoved at him and began to read, while Vella asked Tate if he wanted cold tea or hot coffee. Tate chose the coffee.

When Vella set it in front of him, she said, "Marriage to Marilee isn't goin' to be one long picnic. You'd better be ready goin' in."

He blinked. "Yes, ma'am. I don't believe any marriage is any picnic."

"You got that right. Just remember that Marilee is your gift from God and you are her gift from God. Know that deep down, and then, when disagreements come, you can stand them."

She cast Perry a glance of rare adoration, and this surprised Tate, who averted his gaze to his coffee and pondered what he and Marilee would be like at their age.

He would wear a hearing aid, he decided.

When Tate got up to leave, Perry slapped a hand on his shoulder and walked him to the door, leaning close to his ear to say, "If you decide you want any of that Viagra, I can give you a discount, since you'll be family. You let me know."

Tate managed to reply, "Okay . . . bye now," and got himself out on the sidewalk, where he stood for a few seconds in a daze, then spied Sheriff Oakes stepping out of the police station next door and turning in Tate's direction.

"Hi there, Neville. Have you seen the paper yet?"

Tate waved the paper at the big man, who was a good head taller and twice as big around, and who took the newspaper and read the headline, saying, "Well, well," even as he moved the toothpick he invariably kept in his mouth from one side to the other.

Tate, watching the toothpick, reassured himself that the big man had not, in the year that Tate had known him, come near choking.

The sliver of wood disappeared into the sheriff's mouth, where the sheriff broke it in two before he leaned to the side and spat it out. "Well," the sheriff said again, "I congratulate you, but I really think you should give this another thought. You don't know when you are well-off. Here you are at middle-age . . ."

Tate sort of jumped at that. Middle-age? It was true, but he didn't like the sound of it.

". . . with a fancy car and a house of your own. You are set, man. She'll make you get rid of that car, and take my advice and don't be fallin' for that 'honesty in everything, so we can be closer' stuff. My wife still won't let me forget about what I told her about when I was seventeen. And just a minute ago she called to tell me she is haulin' my butt off on one of those Caribbean cruises. Says we have to relate. She gets that on *Oprah*."

The sheriff pulled out a fresh toothpick and jabbed it in the air toward Tate. "We got three kids. Wouldn't you say that's relating?"

Tate said he thought it was.

"Well, I gotta get on down to the bank and see about a loan for this romantic Caribbean getaway. Maybe go see about a vasectomy, too, because I don't want to end up with another tax deduction from this trip, either. Take my advice and don't encourage Marilee for any more children."

He headed on down the sidewalk, leaving Tate standing there, blinking and drawing in a good breath, struggling to hoist his enthusiasm back up from the ditch that had momentarily swallowed it. This was hard work, as now his thoughts were running with questions. Surely Marilee wouldn't want any more children.

What if she did, and he couldn't provide them? He didn't know about that, not having any of his own. And he was middle-aged. Uncle Perry's voice offering the stimulating virility drug echoed in memory.

Was he up to all that was going to be required of him?

Five

A Chocolate Day . . .

Charlotte called and told her, "Leo, Jr.'s on his way over with five copies of the paper. That way you'll have some clippings for your mother. I know she'll want to show them around."

"Oh, yes. Thanks so much, Charlotte. I had forgotten." Marilee raked back her hair and thought how Charlotte was good at remembering these details. Charlotte took loving care of her invalid mother; she bought Mrs. Nation an ice-cream cone almost every day and fed it to her.

"I'll laminate two clippings," Charlotte said crisply. "That way you'll have one, and one for your mother. Permanent copies."

Laminate? The announcement could end up outlasting the marriage.

Replacing the receiver, she scolded herself for such negative thoughts. One could not go into a marriage with such an attitude.

Oh, maybe it was normal to have fears. Life certainly was not a secure proposition.

Of late, painful memories of the past seemed to be weighing on Marilee's shoulders. Neither herself, her sister Anita, nor their mother had thus far succeeded in what could be called a good and lasting relationship with a man. Her grandmother, her mother's mother, had had three husbands, one had embezzled and run off, one had just run off, and another had stayed while having a continual affair with a neighbor woman.

Maybe it was some disorder of the female side of the family, like something lacking in the blood, causing them not to choose well, or to drive men to drink, to dire actions, or to simply run away.

With thoughts of her own mother, Marilee opened the center drawer on her desk and took out a chocolate Hershey's Kiss. It was the last one in the little dish. She unwrapped it and popped it on her tongue. Then she sighed.

She had always felt herself to be one more disappointment in a lifetime of disappointments to her mother. Right off the bat, Marilee had been a girl instead of the boy that Norma had been set on as a first child. Her mother had counted on a son to take care of her, since she had already discovered her weak husband was not going to do that to her satisfaction. Second, Marilee had not come to be the great beauty that won the "Little Miss" contest in grade school nor the homecoming queen title in high school. A shy and studious girl, she had refused to even enter those contests, no matter how her mother had coerced, pleaded, threatened.

Then Marilee had run off to college, leaving her mother alone to cope with a failing husband and high-spirited younger daughter. Marilee had married Stuart, who was, to his credit, a semifamous and successful man, and who had proceeded to take Marilee off even further to see the world, while her mother was back home dealing with a husband who had the disgrace to choke to death while drunk and leave his wife, a victim of leftover Victorian mores, desperately seeking another man to support her.

When Marilee had returned home, she had divorced Stuart—her mother had not divorced her father, no matter what—so therefore she gave her mother a divorced daughter with an embarrassing grandchild who was disabled. Furthermore, Marilee had had an affair, which the entire town knew of, with Parker Lindsey, a very eligible bachelor and upstanding veterinarian, but had not gotten him to the altar.

That Marilee had turned down the altar because she had grown to see many errors in her ways, primarily that she and Parker were not at all a suitable match, was not how her mother saw it. In her mother's eyes, her daughter had failed to snatch up a good thing and become a well-to-do woman of society, such as it was in Valentine.

Now, at last, Marilee was doing something right in her mother's eyes. "Well, I'm so glad you are showing some sense, Marilee. I won't have to worry about your future," her mother had said upon receiving the news of the engagement.

Leo Pahdocony, Jr., riding his fancy bicycle right up the stairs to her front door, brought five copies of the newspaper. Leo, Jr. was set to join the Olympic cycle team when he went to Rice in the fall. Reggie, his mother, was set on her son *not* following in his father's footsteps and kept him on track for an education that would bring him fortune and keep him too busy to look at girls, who were obviously looking at him and his steel-hard body. Marilee didn't think Reggie needed to worry about the girls. Leo, Jr.'s first love was bikes.

"Thanks, Leo." She left off the junior out of respect that seemed his due.

"You bet." With strong arms, he flipped his bike around and rode off down the steps, going off like a rocket on the walkway.

Marilee went into the kitchen and laid the newspapers on the table. There at the bottom of the front page was her and Tate's picture.

Gosh, it looked good, it really did. Tate was handsome as all get-out. His warmth shone out. And she didn't look so bad . . . looked pretty, actually.

Marilee read the headline: Publisher And Associate Editor To Wed.

No matter what happened from here, *this* would please her mother.

"Mama, I have the copies of the announcement. If you're going to be home, I'll get the children from school, and we'll come up with the paper."

"What announcement?"

"The engagement announcement—it's in the *Voice* today."

"Oh, yes, dear, bring it . . . and will you stop and get a quart of milk, a loaf of bread and a pair of panty hose? It's turned so cold, I don't want to go out."

After ascertaining the correct color of panty hose, Marilee hung up, then went to her bedroom to put on shoes and lipstick and a comfortable old barn coat. Seeing her trench coat caused her to blush. She pushed it out of sight.

She checked her nightstand drawer for a piece of chocolate and found a lone Hershey's Kiss, which she ate, but it did not satisfy the craving that had come over her, so she checked the kitchen cabinet, where she liked to keep chocolate in various forms. There was only powdered cocoa. Her purse was empty of chocolate, too.

Taking up the copies of the *Voice,* she said, "Come on, Munro," to the dog, and headed out the door.

Driving at a rapid rate, she pulled the Cherokee into the Quick Shop and got a chocolate bar and two small packages of Hershey's Kisses. The Kisses went into her purse, while she ate the chocolate bar as she drove to school. She had to eat fast, as it was only a couple minutes' drive. Seeing Munro eyeing her, she put a small bite down for him. "You can't have any more. Chocolate can kill a dog."

At the rate she was consuming it, chocolate might kill her, too.

When she pulled into the waiting area for parents, she jammed the last of the bar into her mouth and chewed it while she wiped chocolate smears off the steering wheel with a tissue. The end-of-school bell pierced the air, and instantly children came pouring out of the building. She jerked the rearview mirror around, checked her mouth, wiped it with a tissue and applied lipstick, then tucked the chocolate-smeared tissues deep into her purse.

Should any woman with such a chocolate addiction consider herself sane enough to get married?

Getting out of the truck, she stood beside it, where Corrine and Willie Lee would be sure and see her. They had the past days been walking home from school in the balmy weather.

Munro saw the children first and started off to meet them with his tail wagging. There was Corrine; her bright red sweater shone out. Corrine was clearly going to be willowy and beautiful, like her mother, Marilee thought with a pang. Anita had so many problems that seemed to stem from possessing a beauty that she could not manage to handle.

Willie Lee, dragging his book bag and with one tennis shoe untied, came running forward to fall on his knees and hug his dog and be kissed all over the face.

Munro was such a blessing, Marilee thought with gratefulness to God for sending the dog, one more stray that Willie Lee had attracted. It was because of the dog coming into their lives and bringing an important computer chip in his collar that Willie Lee could receive a reward and now be financially set for life. It was a miracle that even now she found hard to believe.

"I didn't know you were coming to get us." Corrine eyed Marilee in the way she had of summing up a situation.

"I think you deserve a treat today, Missy," Marilee said sweetly and hugged her niece. "And we're goin' up to Grandma's." She noted that Corrine's expression turned carefully blank.

"Hey, Ma-ma." Willie Lee grinned up at her from behind his thick glasses.

"Hey, sweetheart." She kissed him.

"You smell like choc-o-late," he told her.

It took twenty-five minutes to get to Lawton and her mother's house in a neighborhood of upscale twenty-year-old residences with sweeping lawns. Marilee pulled to a stop in the concrete driveway.

Munro had to wait in the car. A dog was not allowed in Grama's house, where there was pristine white carpeting. Willie Lee wanted to wait with Munro, but Marilee told him, "Honey, it's gotten too cold." The wind was cutting through her coat. "Munro is okay. He has a winter coat. You do not. Come on inside with me and Corrine."

She felt compelled to add to Munro, who gazed at her with sad eyes, "We won't be long."

Corrine carried the stack of newspapers, and Marilee hoisted the sack of groceries. They hurried, heads down, through the cold wind to the back door, which turned out to be locked.

Marilee pounded on the storm door.

The inside door opened. "Well, goodness knows . . . don't break the glass." Her mother stood back, gesturing. "Come in so we can get this door closed. You're letting in the cold."

The door got closed. Marilee took a good breath.

"Hello, Mother." She bent to kiss her mother's cheek. Her mother was a petite woman, and Marilee often felt awkward next to her.

And then she noticed her mother's chic black dress and pumps—stepping-out clothes. "You're looking pretty." Her mother was looking lovely these days, having lost weight and gotten very stylish since she had become a patron of the local *art league.*

"Oh . . ." Her mother smoothed her dress. "I was out at a meeting today and some shopping . . . but I got tired and thought I'd just not bother to get these things. But Carl likes the milk for his coffee . . . he just won't stop to get it."

Marilee set the bag of groceries on the counter, thinking of Carl not being inconvenienced, and how she wished she had not dragged the children into the store.

Her mother smiled brightly. "Here, you children sit at the table. I have apple juice for you." She looked questioningly at Marilee. "I didn't know if they liked this kind, but it's all I have."

"They love apple juice, thanks, Mom. Here, y'all take off your coats." Marilee helped Willie Lee, wanting to circumvent any possibility of him knocking over his apple juice.

"Marilee, this isn't the kind of panty hose I wanted." Frowning, her mother stared at the package.

"It was all they had. It's nude, like you wanted, and that's your size, right?"

"Well, yes, but I don't know if I'll like this kind." Her mother sighed. "Oh, well, I'm sure I can return them."

Marilee thought perhaps she should offer to return them.

The teakettle whistled on the stove. "I'm making us tea," her mother said, brightening. "Isn't this a day for tea? It's so seldom that you all come up to see me, and I have some exciting news."

"You do?"

"Yes. I found out just a few minutes ago, when Carl called. We're . . . oh dear, I don't have any Earl Grey." She raised her head from the container and looked at Marilee with doleful eyes.

"That's okay, Mom. I like regular best, anyway."

"Well, Earl Grey is my favorite . . . and it seems to settle my stomach." She pressed a hand over her abdomen. "I wish I had known I was out of it. I would have asked you to get some at the store." She stared forlornly at the teapot.

Marilee had the brief fantasy of calling Homeland and asking if they could deliver a box of Earl Grey in five minutes.

Popping to her feet, she looked in the refrigerator, thrilled to find a lemon. "Here's a lemon, Mom. It is wonderful in tea, and good for the stomach."

"Oh. Well, okay. Will you slice it, dear?"

As Marilee went to the counter, she glanced over to see Corrine's deep brown eyes watching her.

She cut several slices from the lemon and brought them to the table. Her mother followed with the teapot and cups on a tray, sliding the newspapers aside to make room. Marilee's gaze glided over the papers, and she asked, "What is your exciting news, Mom?"

"Oh!" Her mother slid into a chair and pressed her hands together. "Carl and I are going on a cruise."

"You are?"

Her mother and Carl, who was the owner of Cooper's Appliance Mart, had in the past year taken to traveling often to sales conventions. Her mother launched into explaining how she had just last night been telling Carl she was tired of winter, and how he had called to tell her there was a small convention of appliance salespeople taking place on a cruise out of Miami to the Caribbean.

"We can fly directly to Miami. I am so excited! Margaret Springer from the League went on a cruise last fall and said she had the best time. There's all this food and dancing . . . of course, Carl won't dance, but he likes to eat, and there's lots of card playing, too."

"What is a cruuze, please?" Willie Lee asked.

Marilee, struck by a difficulty with the description, said, "It is a trip that people take sailing in a big ship on the ocean. Some trips are sailing across the ocean and some are sailing from island to island."

"They are trips for people to relax and have a good time out on the ocean," her mother said to him, speaking slowly and in the loud tone she always employed with Willie Lee, as if he were deaf. "People dress up in their prettiest clothes and talk and dance, and they can shop, too, right on the ship."

Marilee noticed Corrine tapping the stack of newspapers back toward the center of the table. Her niece regarded her pointedly.

"Oh, Mom . . . here's the announcement."

"The announcement?"

"The engagement announcement in the *Voice*."

Marilee passed a copy to her mother, who said, "Oh, yes," shot her a smile and then dropped her gaze to the page.

"Why, honey, this is a really good picture of you and Tate," she said with surprise. "What a couple you two make." Her tone held a warmth that Marilee felt all over. "You really look lovely here, dear, and Tate looks so handsome."

She had made her mother happy.

Then, "Oh, dear."

"What is it?" Where did the happiness go?

"Well . . ." Her mother's eyes came up slowly from the paper, and she gazed at Marilee with anguish. "That's the very week of our cruise."

Marilee, who distinctly remembered telling her mother the wedding date, looked at her mother, and her mother looked back with eyes just like Munro's. *People forget . . . people make mistakes.*

"I just can't cancel on Carl."

Marilee shifted her gaze and said, "Mother, don't worry about it. It's okay. Our wedding is just going to be small and short, not a big ceremony."

Hearing herself, she clamped her mouth shut.

"Well, my being at your wedding really isn't all that important," her mother allowed. "The important thing is Tate being there."

Marilee smiled at this truth. She was a woman grown. She did not need to impress her mother. She would never be able to impress her mother. And God knew she did not need at this late date for her mother to stand by her side.

Twenty minutes later, noticing that Willie Lee was falling asleep on Corrine, Marilee put him into his coat and lifted him into her arms. He was gaining weight; she did not know how much longer she would be able to carry him when he fell asleep. She would do it as long as she could, she thought, shifting his body, holding him so tightly that he gave a little grunt. She relaxed her hold.

At the door, her mother said, "I hope you understand about the cruise. It will be so good for Carl to get away. He stays under so much pressure."

"It's okay, Mom." She found the words came easily.

As they went out the door, she spied the package of panty hose on the counter. "Corrine, honey, get those hose. I'll return them for you, Mom."

Her mother thanked her profusely.

* * *

Willie Lee and Munro lay together on the back seat, beneath a wool throw Marilee kept in the Cherokee. The faint snoring was Munro's.

"You wanted to return the panty hose," Corrine reminded her as they went past Homeland.

"No, I don't feel like it now," said Marilee, watching the rush hour traffic. There was not such a thing as rush hour in Valentine. All the traffic made her feel a little insecure, and she felt the obligation to be alert, as her windshield kept misting over. She was always more cautious when she had the children with her.

"I'll do it for you, Aunt Marilee."

Marilee, stopped at a light, looked over to see Corrine's heart-shaped face with an eager-to-please expression. Experiencing a warm rush of emotion, she gave her niece's arm a squeeze. "You are about the sweetest thing on earth, you know that?" Corrine ducked her head, as she always did at compliments. "But I would much rather you stay warm and dry in the car. Let's just get ourselves home."

Her own home, with her children around her. There was no better place.

And in that instant, focusing her eyes on the wet pavement ahead, she knew the truest fact to be that these two children were her world. She needed them, maybe far more than they did her. It was a need that she could understand and that her heart expanded to accept.

She was not certain that she could do the same for Tate. Or any man. To allow herself to need a man made her so painfully vulnerable.

When they got home, the Grace Florist van was at the curb. Tiffany, the delivery girl, met them at the foot of the steps with an enormous bouquet of bright flowers in a basket.

"Miz James . . . these are for you."

"Oh! My goodness. Thank you," Marilee instinctively said, staring, stunned, at the bouquet.

"You'd better get them in out of the cold, Aunt Marilee."

Yes, indeed. Marilee stepped quickly, anxious to protect the delicate iris petals. But, oh, she had forgotten to tip Tiffany! Too late now.

She followed Corrine through the front door and received another surprise—delicious aromas and the sound of voices in the kitchen. She and Corrine looked at each other with questioning eyes.

Then through the house and the swinging door, pushing it wide to behold Tate's mother, Franny, sitting at the kitchen table, her feet propped up on another chair, paperback book in hand and a coffee cup in front of her. And there was Tate at the stove, a dish towel tucked around his waist, blue shirtsleeves rolled on his strong forearms.

Seeing his bare forearms always affected Marilee, and her gaze lingered there a long second, before Tate's holding up a wooden spoon jarred her thoughts back to the moment.

"Welcome home, sweetheart. We're havin' chicken and noodles, brussels sprouts, fresh, and tossed salad with sesame seed dressing."

All her favorites.

"I made sugared carrots for those of us who do not favor brussels sprouts." He winked at Corrine, and then his blue eyes came to Marilee's, and he gazed at her in an intense manner that caused her breath to catch in her throat.

"Look what I got on the way in," she said, finding her voice.

"Well, my golly. Do you think they're for you?" That was Tate, always kidding.

"The delivery girl said they were for a *Miz* James, but it could have been another." She set the bouquet on the table. "Hello . . . Franny." She was uncertain as to exactly how to address the woman.

Apparently she had chosen correctly. The woman smiled. "Hello, dear." Marilee took note again of the woman's loveliness. Surely that shade of carrot-red hair could not be natural, but no matter, it was a perfect choice.

"There's chocolate, Aunt Marilee." Corrine, at the counter, pointed to a cake.

"Well, my goodness."

Tate came toward her with a cup of something hot. Mocha, she caught by the aroma flashing past her nose.

He said, "I told you, this is a celebration. Sit and relax. I'm taking care of everything." He set the cup on the table and motioned her into a chair. "Where's Willie Lee?"

"Oh, my goodness, we left him in the car."

Marilee was instantly pushing to her feet, but Tate, pressing a hand on her shoulder, said he would get Willie Lee. "He's gettin' too heavy for you to carry around."

She sat there, with the leftover pressure of his warm hand on her shoulder, gazing after him, even after he had disappeared through the kitchen doorway. She heard the front door open and close.

Then she looked at Franny. "I don't know what I did to deserve finding such a man."

"Divine selection," the woman replied, and then motioned at the flowers, "Open the card. Is the bouquet from Tate?"

"Well, I assumed they were from him."

"Don't ever assume, dear. You can miss out on so many surprises."

Marilee, now wondering who the flowers could be from, if not from

Tate, plucked the envelope out of the bouquet and opened it to pull out the card.

She immediately recognized the handwriting. "Oh, yes, they're from Tate," she said, happiness coming like little flashes of fireworks.

She read, and upon coming to *the happiest man in the world,* she burst into tears so strong that she had to put her arm around her middle, as if to hold herself together.

Corrine came over and patted her shoulder. Quite quickly in control, Marilee smiled and snatched a tissue from the box nearby and blew her nose. She hated acting so silly in front of Franny, who already must have a skewed opinion of her after that business of the morning. And heaven knew Corrine did not need to see one more emotionally confused woman.

"Flowers can do that to a woman," Franny said quite sensibly.

Marilee looked at her. "Yes . . . yes, they can. It's just that this is so sweet." But she couldn't show anyone. She involuntarily held the card to her chest.

"My son is quite a guy."

"Yes, he is." A sense of unworthiness flowed over her. It seemed fantastic that Tate could truly love her, Marilee.

Seeing Franny and Corrine turn their heads toward the doorway, Marilee twisted in her chair, prepared to thank Tate for the flowers. But, his expression . . . what had happened?

"We have a guest," he said, in a low voice because of Willie Lee's sleeping head against his chest.

A guest?

Then Tate had withdrawn and another man took the doorway.

"Hello, Marilee."

She took in the bright white shirt standing out against the growing dimness of the rooms behind him, a figure so tall that he seemed to have to duck.

"Ohmygod," she said, recognition dawning, slowly, like a foggy morning.

"Not exactly." He cocked his head and smiled.

"Stuart?" It could not be him.

"Yes. Surprise, sweetheart."

In a smooth, graceful movement, he stepped into the room and over to brush her lips with his.

Six

Lost in the Grand Canyon of life . . .

They had a guest, her ex-husband, who she had not heard from in almost two years, and who, having come right at suppertime, was asked to join them.

"We're havin' our engagement celebration. Please join us," Tate said to Stuart, while Marilee was still busy thinking: *ohmygod.*

She tried to regain coherent thought by busying herself with spreading the linen tablecloth on the big dining table, upon which Corrine placed the gold-trimmed china that would accommodate the down-home chicken and noodles. Tate, getting thoroughly carried away, lit candles.

Sitting with her ex-husband at her right hand, she shifted her gaze to look down the length of the candlelit table and into the handsome, smiling face of her fiancé and, returning his smile, wondered how the disconcerting situation had possibly come about.

Franny, who had brought a bottle of champagne, raised her glass and led them in a toast. "To Tate and Marilee and the vast possibilities stretching ahead of them."

Vast possibilities. It sounded like the Grand Canyon, far too wide to traverse.

Feeling Stuart's gaze on her, Marilee concentrated on getting her napkin spread in her lap, and next to seeing that dishes were passed. And keeping a smile on her lips and her eyes not lighting any one place.

Then here came Willie Lee, accompanied by Munro, padding in his sock feet from the bedroom. "I am hun-gry."

Marilee and everyone, having momentarily forgotten his existence and the ramifications, sat staring at him as he went to the chair where he normally sat at the dining table, which was at this moment occupied by Stuart.

"Who are you?" he asked Stuart in his forthright manner.

Marilee said, "Willie Lee, honey, this is your daddy. He has come to see you." Suddenly her vision was blurry. She blinked, seeing Willie Lee's eyebrows go up. "It is a surprise," she added, feeling totally inadequate to explanations.

"You are my dad-dy?" he asked Stuart.

"Yes. I am . . . Willie Lee."

He spoke as if uncertain of his son's name. No doubt he had forgotten the existence of a son, as well he had intended to do.

"Hel-lo," said Willie Lee and stuck out his hand for a shake, as so often he and Tate did with each other.

Stuart's eyebrows rose, and, hesitantly, he took the small hand, shaking it. "Hello."

"This is Mun-ro. He is my dog."

"Ah . . . hello, Munro."

"You are sit-ting in my chair, but I will sit over here," Willie Lee said as he rounded the table to the chair beside Corrine, and at Tate's right. "You can see me from there," he added in his very literal fashion.

Marilee had the urge to grab her son to her and hug him and tell him he truly was the most magnificent soul on earth.

Stuart said, "Ah . . . thank you."

"I'll get your plate, honey." She started to rise, but Tate was already on his feet and reaching for a china plate and silverware.

"Here ya' go, buddy."

"Thank you." His thick glasses reflected the candlelight as he looked across at Stuart. "I like chic-ken and noo-dles. Do you?"

"Yes." Stuart looked down at his plate. "I haven't had it in a long time, but yes, I believe I do." His eyes came up to Marilee, and an expression crossed his face that she could not define and did not care to try.

In the midst of Stuart's telling about a trip to Scotland to photograph and report on castles, the telephone rang.

Marilee instantly threw down her napkin. "I'll get it," and she dashed through the swinging kitchen door to answer the phone on the wall.

Alone in the kitchen, thank you, God.

"Hello, Marilee. This is Parker."

Parker.

She pressed her fingers to her lips. Caught up in her inner turmoil, she had forgotten him. Guilt fell all over her. She always experienced a great deal of guilt about Parker; she always seemed to forget about him.

"Oh, Parker, I'm so glad you called. I've wanted to speak with you." Moving her palm to her cheek, she searched for words to tell the man she'd almost married some six months previously that she was about to marry another. Of course, her and Tate's engagement could not be a surprise to him.

"Well, I just got back in town yesterday," he said. "I stayed at the convention a couple of days longer . . . because I got married."

Marilee pressed her back against the wall. "You got married?"

"Yes. And Tate was by here today . . . telling me that you two are gettin' married next month."

"Yes, yes we are." Her mind was spinning. She had the sense of being in *The Twilight Zone*.

Tate had not told her he'd seen Parker, but there had not been time for Tate to tell her anything. She pressed harder against the wall, holding herself up.

"I look forward to meeting your wife." Her voice dropped. "I'd like you both to come, Parker . . . to our wedding."

"I'm going to be Tate's best man. . . . Amy and I will both be there," he said with a warmth that went to her bones.

"Oh, good." Then, "You sound happy, Parker. Really happy."

"I am." The two words rang with joy. "I'm a lucky guy, and I can't wait for you to meet Amy."

Amy, a feminine name, perfect for a woman for Parker.

"I look forward to that. And, Parker—I'm glad for you." They had been much better friends than lovers.

"Thanks, Marilee. Me, too, you."

They bid goodbye, and she slowly replaced the receiver, standing with her hand on it. There were just too many things happening one right after another. All she could do was hang on until everything eventually stopped. Things did eventually come to an end, of some sort.

Tate was poking at a flickering fire in the fireplace. He liked to start fires, liked to have something to poke at, Marilee thought, watching him.

Franny had long gone, the children were in bed, and Marilee was ready to follow them. She was ready to crawl into bed, eat a package of Hershey's Kisses and pull the covers over her head.

She was composing phrases to ease the men out of the house when Tate, carefully setting aside the poker, asked Stuart where he was staying.

"Uh, I meant to ask if there was a hotel in town," Stuart answered, slowly uncrossing his long legs and sitting forward in the big chair.

"You passed it on your way in," said Tate. He returned to his seat on the couch, draping his arm along the back behind Marilee, his hand brushing her shoulder in a proprietary gesture. "The Goodnight, out on the west highway."

"I did? I don't remember it."

"Well, you did. Vintage place. Has small duplex cabins. Gives you privacy."

"Ah, yes, but does it provide running water?"

"I think you'd find a comfortable place up in Lawton," Marilee put in and scooted to the edge of the couch. "It has really grown since you were here. And now I'm ready to call it a night. The children will be up for school in the morning."

So much for subtlety. "We've enjoyed your visit so much, Stuart, and we look forward to seeing you tomorrow, I hope. I know Willie Lee wants to get more time with his father. We want you to visit as much as you can while you're here."

She made the best attempt she could at softening her abruptness, even as she rose and went to the door, gave him a quick hug and ushered him out.

As soon as she had shut the front door after Stuart, she turned to Tate and told him, in a manner she wished was not blunt but was, that she was too tired to talk anymore. It was as if she had come to the end of her energy and there was absolutely nothing left; she had gone bone-dry in the emotion department.

Tate responded to this by saying instantly, "Go to bed." He gave her a quick kiss, the touch of his warm lips on hers, and then, in long, totally unhesitating strides, he headed for the back door, where he paused only long enough to say, "Sleep late. I'll get the kids ready for school."

She closed the door and stood looking through the glass, watching him be swallowed up by the darkened backyard and thinking that there was nothing more a woman could want in a man than agreeability.

Then she went to the bathroom, stripped in two seconds and stood beneath the hot shower spray, letting the water pummel all thought right out of her head.

When Willie Lee heard the water running in the bathroom, he rose up, slipped from under the covers and went to the deep dark by the closet. He felt for and pushed on the closet light switch; there was enough glow through the cracks around the door for him to locate his shoes, which he put on, and then his coat and his cape.

On his knees on his bed, he pulled the string for the blinds, raising them as quietly as possible, and then lifted the window.

"What are you doin'?"

Corrine's loud whisper caused him to jump.

"I am learn-ing to fly. Go on, Mun-ro." Being a very good dog, Munro disappeared out the window.

"You're what?" Corrine came scrambling across his bed.

Willie continued on his course, sticking his feet out the window and getting himself sat down on the windowsill. He was trying to get out before the water stopped running in the bathroom. Once his mother told him not to do something, he would not be able to. So far, she had not ever told him not to go out his window.

"Willie Lee, you get back in your bed." Corrine grabbed hold of his coat.

He prepared to tell her that she was not his boss, when, quite suddenly, the running water sound stopped in the bathroom. Willie Lee looked at Corrine, and she looked back at him.

The next minute low music sounded through the wall. His mother had turned on the little radio in there. That meant she would be there a while, probably painting her toenails. His mother sometimes liked to paint her toenails and eat chocolate bars.

Also, at that same moment of hearing the radio, Corrine relaxed her grip on his coat. Willie stuck out his hands, closed his eyes, and jumped.

He landed with a thud, falling over on his side onto the cold, wet ground.

Well, he *almost* flew.

"Willie Lee?" Corrine's head poked out the window.

"I am go-ing to my tree-house," he called up to her.

"No!"

He continued, running as best he could, following Munro, who was ahead of him.

Just then, at the corner of the house, Munro darted to the back steps, through the yellow glow cast by the porch light and disappeared into the darkness beneath the house.

Willie Lee heard hissing and snarling. Munro yelped and popped out, then ran back again into the darkness. Willie Lee followed and got down on his hands and knees, entering the dark area beneath the steps.

Light filtered through cracks in the steps. He saw a big cat and something smaller. *His kitten!* He just knew it was his kitten—and the big cat was Bubba, *Mr. Tate's big old yellow cat. Bubba was beating up his kitten!*

"No, Bub-ba!" Willie Lee reached out and shoved the big cat, but the big cat just hopped sideways, out of reach. With ears flattened and growling in his throat, he advanced against the kitten, whose small shadow could just be seen, crouching against the inside of the bottom step.

Willie Lee tried to crawl closer. "Here, kit-ty, kit-ty."

Munro darted in, but Bubba got his nose, and Munro jumped back with a yelp.

Then here came Corrine. "What are you doin'? Aunt Marilee's gonna hear."

"Bub-ba is be-ing mean to my kit-ten." He was about to pound on the door and get his mother-who-saved to come to the rescue, but he could not leave his kitten. Bubba would eat him up. "Cor-rine?"

"Oh . . . sheesh." Corrine picked up a dirt clod of substantial proportion and threw it at the big yellow cat, saying at the same time, "Get him, Munro." The clod hit Bubba in the side, and Munro, sufficiently supported now, made another dart. The big cat, seeing he was outnumbered, went running away into the deep dark beneath the house, or as near running as a tub of lard can go.

Despite Corrine warning him about snakes, Willie Lee scrambled forward until he could grab the kitten. It scratched his hands, but he held on, pulling it out from beneath the steps.

On his knees outside the foundation, Willie Lee cuddled the kitten close. It was shaking. "He got hit by a car this morn-ing and got dead-ed," he said, sniffing back tears, "but I picked him up, and he got okay. He needs me to take care of him."

Corrine petted the kitten. "You mean he got knocked out and woke up."

Willie Lee did not see any point in correcting Corrine. He pressed his cold nose into the kitten's warm fur. The kitten smelled like cold dirt.

"It's okay, Willie Lee. You have the kitten now."

"Why was Bub-ba so mean to him?"

"Well . . ." She paused, and he waited. "It is what grown boy cats do. Bubba was just bein' a boy cat and protecting his territory. But when this kitten is grown, Bubba won't do it, or this kitten will whip Bubba's tail."

"I do not like that. I want them to be frie-ends."

"Yeah, well, we all want a lot of things. Come on. We gotta get back in before Aunt Marilee finds out we are out, or we're gonna get it."

Willie Lee thought that Corrine would know just how to get back inside, and he was very happy to be taking his kitten. Only he had not practiced learning to fly, and this made him sad.

Then Corrine said, "Let's go back by the fence, where it's dark, and see if we can see the stars."

To his great surprise, she was already dashing off across the yard, with Munro at her heels. Willie Lee, holding his kitten close to his chest, took off after them with his ever-clumsy run.

He wished so much that he could run like other boys. Feeling his cape flutter behind him, he thought, someday I will fly.

The decor of the cottage room at the Goodnight Motel contained every god-awful ugly style of the fifties, sixties and seventies, starting with the giant rose-printed curtains and going on to the green shag carpeting.

After his first look, Stuart turned off the glaring overhead light and switched on the bedside lamp, putting most of the room in shadow. Then he sank down to the edge of the mattress. He felt queasy, as he often did when exhaustion overtook him. He had been too exhausted to drive up to Lawton and a decent hotel, and determined to show Tate Holloway that he did not require pampering. It had taken almost twenty minutes to get registered by the chatty old man who was hard of hearing and was watching a television turned up to shouting level. Only one other cottage in the strip appeared occupied; it had two cars parked in front of it, indicating the probability of a tryst. The No-Tell Motel was what Stuart would have named the place.

Just then he noticed the brown metal box sitting on the bedside table. The bed had a vibrating machine.

After several long seconds of staring at the box, he dug into his slacks pocket, came up with a quarter and stuck it in the slot. The bed began to vibrate. The thing actually worked.

Stuart lay back gingerly, wondering if it would make him more nauseous. It did not. In fact, he began to relax.

His mind slipped into memories of a time he and Marilee had stayed at one of those once-modern economy motels that sported a vibrating bed, which by that time had passed the summit of popularity but were still frequently found. He recalled her youthful delight in putting in the quarters and laughing with the sensation.

And he recalled what she had felt like beneath him, giving him all she had, while the bed rocked underneath and he rocked on top.

He ached right that moment to reach back in time and touch her as she had been. To have her fill him up, as she had then, with the life of her.

Pained, he threw his forearm over his eyes. He had hardly thought of Marilee since the day he had left her, but these days the memories came repeatedly, plaguing him with a relentlessness, now that he was dying.

Damn Stuart James anyway. His showing up right at this time was no coincidence. No, sir. James professed no knowledge of the engagement, but Tate was as certain as he had spit in his mouth that the man had read about the engagement on the *Voice* Web page. He judged the man a liar and a taker. While he could admit to being on the prejudiced side, Tate had a good ability to call people as they were, and he had called this man correct, by golly.

There was no sleeping. Middle of the night, and Tate got up, got dressed in sweatpants and shirt and Nikes. Passing his mother's closed door on the landing, he saw light showing beneath. His mother never seemed to sleep, although since he did not hear a sound within, perhaps she slept with the light on.

Down the stairs with light steps, out the front door and across the porch into a cold, misty night. His big tomcat, Bubba, popped out from beneath the porch and came bouncing behind him to the street, where the animal stopped. Bubba had gotten too fat and old to even go halfway down the street.

Tate pushed himself to pick up the pace, heading along Porter and, despite good intentions, slowing to see if Marilee's bedroom light was on. Yes, it was.

He stood for a moment, gazing at the light and imagining going in her back door and into her bedroom and taking her into his arms to remind her that she was his.

Quite quickly his imagination went headlong into seeing them naked and tangled in the sheets. This picture propelled him jogging again, fast. Down Porter, up First to Main and, with no letup in his steady pace, down Main, crossing over to *The Valentine Voice* building, where the blinds were raised, so Charlotte was not there, at least not yet, thank heaven. Breathing heavily, he let himself in with his key.

The low glow of night-lights, plus streetlights shining through the plate-glass windows, lit his way to his office, where a poster-size print of Marilyn Monroe in her sexy skirt-blowing pose watched over his desk. He turned on his computer, shut the door and spent thirty minutes surfing the Internet to find out what he could about one Stuart James, photo-journalist. With the information he found, he formed a picture of a man who had been gung-ho on reporting on the hot situations and people of the world, making a name for himself, until the past years, when his pieces—all about exotic and comfortable places—had been for slick travel magazines and *National Geographic*. Three separate pieces alone had been about gothic estates in Switzerland, England and Scotland, glorious photographs showing the magnificent structures and grounds, all well within a town that provided equally glorious accommodation.

A man gets older and doesn't want to be bedding down in some dive or a tent or looking into the faces of endless struggle and pain. Tate could not blame James. He himself had given up tough stories long ago, finding living his own life tough and painful enough. He quit trying to make sense of life's struggles, because his finite earthly brain couldn't make sense of it.

Perhaps that was what James had discovered. Maybe that was why he had suddenly turned up—to see what he could salvage from what he had lost.

Salvaging the results of some poor choices was exactly what had brought Tate himself to Valentine, where he was making a new life for himself.

And Tate wasn't going to let James take what he had found, either.

He shut down his computer and locked the front door after himself. Setting off jogging once again, although not as fast, he headed up Church Street toward home.

Marilee loved him. He knew this. Yet he also knew her loyalty to others in her life. It was a trait he admired greatly in her. But he did not want to see that trait come to life for Stuart James.

Seven

It's about time . . .

You knew about Parker getting married? You told him about our
coming wedding? What did he say, how did he look, what's his new
wife like? What do you think about Stuart showing up like this? What
about *us?*

There had been no time to talk, of course. Tate had come in and
given her a quick kiss, then out he went with the children, while she
stood waving from the front door, a mother in her pink terry bathrobe
sending off her family.

Closing the door, she turned and leaned against it, feeling a sense of
flowing from one part of her life and ever onward to more, as her eye
traveled the room, seeing all that she needed to get done.

There was an old wisdom that said life was made up of time, dirt
and money. Marilee heartily agreed with that estimate, most especially
when one had children. With children, one was always sweeping out
dirt and wildly trying to bring in money.

At best, life was a messy affair.

She pushed herself away from the door and went through the room,
picking up strewn clothes—Willie Lee's pajamas, which, curiously,
had dirt on the knees, Corrine's discarded sweater, her own socks.

Perhaps everything came down to time. Time to clean away dirt,
and time to earn money, so that one could purchase soap to clean dirt.
One purchased time, too, with each breath.

There was a kitten sleeping atop the clothes dryer, in a shaft of sunlight falling through the window of the back door.

"Oh, good grief, you are back." The grey kitten opened its narrow
eyes a crack, yawned and closed its eyes again.

Her son's doing, of course. She looked at his pajamas with the
soiled knees.

There were a lot of things she did not see her son do. Likely she
was glad of that, she thought, tossing the pajamas into the nearby basket of dirty clothes.

She stroked the kitten's silky head. The kitten purred loudly. Oh, dang it anyway, but she would not put it out. She filled a small dish with milk and placed it on the floor beside the washer; it would have to do until she could get to the IGA for cat food. Picking up the kitten, she set him . . . yes, definitely a him . . . in front of the bowl. He went to licking, while she dug into the storage closet, brought out a kitty litter pan and litter, which were left over from the last feline, fixed it for the kitten and pointed at it. "There. That is for you."

Willie Lee brought them in, and she got a new pet.

Taking her precious second cup of coffee to the bedroom, she deliberately slowed her motions as she got out her clothes. She was always moving so fast. Hurry, hurry in this world. She always felt as if she could not do enough fast enough. As if she were always behind, lacking in some manner.

As she sat to work on her panty hose, Marilee thought of her front porch. She had not sat in her porch swing for at least . . . why, not for three weeks. She was startled at the swift passage of time. Her life was passing her by, and she hardly realized.

The telephone rang, and, thinking of Stuart, who nagged at the edges of her mind like a pesky mosquito, she paused to prepare herself.

"Hey, sweet darlin'." It was Tate. His precious drawl vibrated through her body, causing an instant smile to bloom up and out. "Kids are safe at school," he told her, "and I'm safe at the office. How's your mornin'?"

"Good. I think I shall walk to work." She quite suddenly felt grand. The result of a few extra minutes, a second cup of coffee and a warm call from a warm man. "Thank you for takin' the kids this mornin'." She mentally threw herself into his arms.

"I enjoy takin' them." She imagined he winked, as was his habit. "Well . . . see you when you get down here."

All sorts of thoughts flew through her mind, too quickly to grasp. There was more she wanted to say but that she could not get out. "Yes . . . see you in a bit."

Holding onto the receiver, she heard it click on the other end. *We have to talk, Tate. I have to share some things with you.*

Slowly she replaced the receiver into its cradle, her thoughts spinning back in time to when she had finally given in to exploring a relationship with Tate. Oh, my, how he had courted her, until she had come around. She smiled with the memory that was tucked into a sacred place in her heart.

Once she had admitted her strong attraction to him, she had relished the wonderful discovery that she could say some things to Tate that she had not ever been able to speak of to anyone else. Things about her life growing up, her difficulties with her mother and with her sister, her fear of her weaknesses, her fears for the children, and her dearest desires for them. Tate listened. He had much in common with her. What a miracle that was, finding someone who understood. And, mostly, Tate did not tell her not to have fears.

When had being able to talk to Tate changed for her?

Everything had gotten so hectic, with the Christmas holidays and many things to do for the children. They had sort of lost touch with each other, and it seemed difficult to get back together.

Perhaps she had quit being able to talk so easily when she had become fully aware of how deeply she had fallen in love with him. In the past, that had been her first big error: falling in love with a man.

Marilee walked along the sidewalk with her hands jammed into the deep pockets of her barn coat, buttons unfastened. Munro followed directly at her heels. The bright sun was warm on her head, promising a balmy day, and indeed the air was rich with the scent of verdant ground getting ready for growing things and the melody of songbirds calling to their mates.

It was what was called a moment out of time, she thought, where she could walk easy and wave to friends who drove past, such as Charlene MacCoy, who she had known just about all her life, and who waved and hollered out the window of her Suburban. "Hey, Marilee!"

"Hey, Charlene!"

Charlene perpetually drove at the pace of a woman with somewhere to go and no time to waste. The Suburban roared through the intersection of Main and Church, bouncing where the road humped.

Then, as Marilee and Munro approached the intersection, here came Aunt Vella in her new Land Rover that she had purchased in order to more conveniently haul roses, fertilizer and all the landscaping items for which she had developed a passion.

The truck stopped, and the tinted window came down. "I'm sorry I didn't get back to you yesterday. Tate came by the store and showed us the announcement. I meant to call you then, but Mrs. Andresen's dance class came in for sundaes, and last night was the first meeting of the rose club this year—I'll call you this afternoon with the report for the paper. Did you need somethin' in particular?"

Hollering from vehicle to sidewalk did not seem conducive to adequate conversation. Marilee shook her head. "I'll call you tonight."

"Okay, sugar." Aunt Vella waved, the tinted window went back up, and the Land Rover slid away, crossing the intersection and heading on north, possibly again up to Lawton and the Home Depot, where her aunt spent an inordinate amount of time perusing the wares, usually coming home to deliberate, giving her another excuse to drive up and look again.

Marilee stood on the corner, waiting for the light to change, and realized that she stood on concrete that she had traveled as a child, walking, running, riding her bicycle. Main Street stretching west and east had changed very little. When she had been a child, there had been trees along it; they had seemed big trees then, since she had been so small. When she visited from college, the trees had been gone, as the town went through a drought and a phase of modern, no-frills improvement. Five years ago the phase of returning to the original look of the town had swept through, and modern facades had been torn down to reveal the authentic rural town fronts beneath. Thanks to Tate's efforts, the trees, planted last November, had returned, as well.

Cars, head-in, lined the edges of the wide street or drove slowly up and down. Flags flew gaily from storefronts. Fred Grace was once more putting out bins of fresh flowers in front of the florist, and the Main Street Café sported a spanking new green awning. Fayrene Gardner, who had bought the café with the money she received at the death of her ex-husband, was updating the entire building. She planned to renovate the upstairs into a luxury apartment.

In that minute, Marilee experienced a soaring of her spirits. *Thank you, God, for letting me live in such a good, peaceful town.* There was absolutely nowhere else on earth she would want to live.

Full of gratitude and feeling as if she walked on sunshine, she sashayed across the street, down the sidewalk and through the *Voice* doors, where she was met by the sight of Sandy Conroy bending his long tall frame over Charlotte's shoulder, taking the opportunity to press extra close as they studied something on Charlotte's computer monitor.

"Hi, y'all."

"Hi," the two responded in unity. Charlotte automatically straightened and put on an ultraproper expression, but Sandy did not pull away from her.

"When are you going to talk this woman into marryin' you, Sandy?"

"It isn't like I don't try," Sandy said, and gave his slow, innocent grin.

Charlotte frowned, and it was the sort of painful frown that made

Marilee feel a bit guilty for having brought up what she knew was a sore subject.

She headed on to her desk and dropped her portfolio and purse atop the mess of papers and files. Then, with the lingering of uplifted spirits, she strode eagerly to Tate's office. He saw her, got up from his desk, pulled her close and shoved his office door closed at the same time. She heard it slam shut as his lips took hers. Wrapping her arms around his neck, she let herself sink into the passion.

"Well . . ." He took a breath and eased away. "Good mornin'."

"Good morning." Was he embarrassed now? Why did he keep backing away? Oh, she was imagining all sorts of things.

The telephone rang, and he stepped quickly to the desk to answer it. "Yes, Charlotte. Oh?" His eyes met Marilee's, and she knew who it was even before he said, "Hello, Stuart. How are you?"

She turned her back, while her ears remained tuned to each word and inflection.

"You did?" A bit of surprise. "No, we haven't done a story on it, but it probably would be a good idea. Can't afford your pictures, though." Tate came up behind her and grabbed her hand. "Well, now, that's generous of you. We'd give you title credit." And then, "Yes, here she is. Right here with me." He spoke the last very deliberately, devoid of his pleasant drawl.

He handed over the receiver, whispering, "He stayed at the Goodnight."

He did? "Hello, Stuart."

"Good morning."

Marilee tried to phrase her questions: okay, why have you shown up now? What do you want?

"I thank you for dinner last night." His tone was truly appreciative.

"You're welcome. Tate said you are stayin' out at the Goodnight." She had trouble picturing this.

"Yes. If you stick to the bedside lamp, it isn't a bad place."

"It reminds me of a more peaceful time."

"Oh, yeah . . . so when did you stay here?" he asked with high curiosity. She heard a clicking and remembered that Stuart used to talk on the phone and click pictures at the same time. He could never seem to pay direct attention to her. Or to others, for that matter.

"Year or so ago, when I had our house fumigated."

"Oh. Since both you and Tate are so familiar with the place, I thought maybe you two were regulars out here."

She understood the inference then. "No. We're grown-ups."

"Well, you might ask Tate. He's the one who suggested the place."

She did not reply to this, refusing to continue the juvenile line of thought. She glanced at Tate, who perched on the corner of his desk and made no pretense whatsoever not to be listening.

"Listen." The clicking stopped. "I'd like the opportunity to return the favor of dinner last night by taking you out. Tonight, if that isn't too short notice."

She responded immediately that school nights were not available for going out. "The children have homework, and I have their clothes to get ready. There're just a lot of things to do."

Of course he didn't understand about busy school nights. He had run out on his child. She could almost taste the resentment on her tongue. It took her by surprise, and brought guilt.

"If you came to see Willie Lee, you're certainly welcome to visit him, Stuart. Why don't you come to the house again this evening, say around seven?"

Silence from Stuart's end, while Marilee, on hers, was wondering at her choice of words: *if* you came to see Willie Lee. Realizing her tight grip on the telephone receiver, she relaxed her fingers.

Stuart said, "I could pick him up from school. Him and Corrine."

"No. No, you couldn't," Marilee responded flatly. "Willie Lee and Corrine don't know you. And I don't know you." Was she being paranoid? Rather that than sorry.

Another pause, and then, "I'm hoping you will give me a chance to change that, Marilee."

She absorbed his words, his earnest tone. Stuart could always use earnestness well. "We need to talk, Stuart."

"O-kay."

That was vaguely unsatisfactory. "Would you like to come to supper again tonight? Nothing fancy. I'll get some baked hens from the deli. We eat at six, and you can come early, around four-thirty."

He agreed, and they bid goodbye.

"He's still here," she said to Tate, when she hung up.

"Did you think he wouldn't be?" He cast her an amused glance and then drank deeply from his coffee cup.

She felt annoyed, at what, she was uncertain. She just did not appreciate his attitude.

"I don't know exactly what I thought," she said. "He just dropped in. No advance warning. No nothin'. At least back when he left, he said he was going." Although there had not been but about an hour, time enough to pack, between him saying he was leaving and then walking out the door.

She recalled her feeling of confusion from the previous evening, the sense of powerlessness in the face of seeing Stuart standing there in the kitchen doorway. Had he not considered that he might be intruding in her life? "And you invited him to supper."

Tate's eyes widened. "*You* just invited him."

"No, I mean last night."

"What was I supposed to do? Tell him, 'Sorry, but we are about to eat and would rather you leave'?"

"Well, no, of course not." How silly of her. His inviting Stuart had been the right thing, and actually the best thing, in that Marilee and Willie Lee had not been alone to face Stuart. She realized suddenly how glad she had been for Tate's presence. Not only had she faced her ex-husband as a desirable and engaged woman, but Tate could smooth any awkward situation. He had been there for her.

"Besides," he was saying, "I thought maybe you would want to visit with him."

"Oh?" She looked at him, at his silky hair curling neatly behind his ear. What in the world was he thinking about this?

Then, before she could explore the subject further, the telephone rang and a knock sounded at the door.

Tate picked up the telephone, and Marilee opened the door.

Leo Pahdocony, Sr., their sports and agri-business reporter, who looked like a model out of one of the western wear catalogs, stuck his head in the office. "I need to see Editor a minute."

Marilee sighed deeply. "There he is," she said and left, conceding to time, which decreed an end to conversation and a moving on. With brisk steps, she returned to her desk, slipped on glasses and went to work, an exchange of time for the wherewithal to keep her life going along at a relatively clean pace.

Eight

Right out of the blue . . .

If Stuart had come to try to make up for what his absence—totally dropping out of their lives—had caused, a check in the mail for somewhere around $30,000, roughly figuring child support for the past four years, would have been a good starting point. Although, from the start of their divorce eight years ago, Stuart had never once paid anywhere near what had been agreed upon.

In thinking of it, Marilee supposed that since her marriage had not turned out exactly as she had expected, she should have known that her divorce would not meet her expectations, either. The trouble all began when one got carried away with expectations.

Marilee had met Stuart when she was barely twenty and attending her second year at the University of Oklahoma. At that time her expectations had settled around the idea of finding happiness by escaping her family and years of growing up invisible in a chaotic home environment with an alcoholic father and a mother who coped by pretending nothing at all was wrong.

She had thought to escape the dark chaos of her family's home life when she went away to college on a full scholarship, but she was to learn that blood and attitude followed. She continued to feel safer when invisible, until she had met Stuart, a thirty-five-year-old visiting professor. She had laid eyes on Stuart and his savoir faire, thrown away her weak glasses and fluffed her vibrant hair, and stepped out of the shadows. She could thank Stuart for that—he had drawn her out.

Miracle of miracles was Stuart noticing her, although now she understood that each of their needs had been like lock and key. She had needed Stuart's mature attention, and he had needed her naive hero worship. They had been perfect for each other.

Things had continued along thus, in such a perfect vein, for the first years, in which Marilee gave up her education and any tiny budding dreams of her own and tagged happily after Stuart, worshiping him, keeping his shirts clean, starched and ironed, no matter where they might be—crowded streets of Calcutta, thick Tennessee backwoods, concrete canyons of Chicago—as he pursued his photojournalistic career.

Then, as she gradually grew up, she began to notice that Stuart didn't so much notice her as use her for his purposes, which generally were to attend to him. He required a *lot* of clean shirts, light starch. Funny how, even today, she could still recall exactly how he liked his shirts.

As countless women before her, she thought perhaps a child would bring them fulfillment and togetherness. Also, there had been that continual ticking of her biological clock. Time again, dictating life. One day she was pregnant. She did not think she had done it on purpose, but she sure meant to enjoy her dream of a child, a family, mommy and daddy and baby makes three, and it would all be perfect in the way it never had been when she was a child.

But Stuart had said, in his most affable fashion, "I don't want to be a father, Marilee. I don't want any part of it. I don't particularly want to be a husband."

The bald truth was that Stuart had never felt the need to pretend to be anything other than what he was, which was a man emotionally sufficient unto himself. He took her as his wife, as long as she tagged along, like an agreeable traveling companion, to give him some pleasure in bed and keep his life organized. He was exactly correct—he never had fit into the mold of husband and mate.

From the beginning, it had been Marilee's own illusions that had blinded her to who Stuart really was. In her need, she had tried to make him fit those illusions. How painful it had been when she had been forced to see that she had been the author of her own mistakes with Stuart. He had not hurt her; her own illusions had caused her pain.

But now, here he was, having shown up out of the blue, at his own pleasing, Stuart being Stuart. She felt like smacking him.

Just then she came out of her memories, blinking as she saw an enormous vase of roses floating toward her. Long-stemmed deep red roses in a tall green glass vase.

"Miz James, flower delivery for you."

"For me?"

Tiffany poked her face around the flowers. "Yes . . . I need to set them down, they're heavy."

Grabbing files and papers, Marilee made a space on the corner of her desk.

"Whew." Tiffany stepped back. "Got my workout for the day. There's two dozen of those beauties there."

From bottom to top, the arrangement was over three feet high, at least.

"Oh, wait a minute. Let me . . ." She dug into her purse and brought out enough tip money for yesterday's delivery, too.

"Thanks! I sure hope you stay popular."

Her fellow workers crowded around her desk.

"Let me get your picture with them," said Reggie, pointing her camera.

"Whoo-ee, honey, this guy has more money than sense," said Leo Sr., shaking his head.

"They look too perfect to be real," said June.

"Don't touch the petals, June. You'll bruise them." This last was Charlotte giving orders. She also plucked the envelope from its holder and passed it to Marliee.

Marilee opened the envelope. Leo was right: Tate was spending foolishly, buying her flowers as if he was a millionaire.

She pulled out the card. *For all the years gone past, my apologies. With love, Stuart.*

With love? Her first thought was that the roses might have been expensive, but they didn't make a dent in past-due child support payments, not to mention nights spent rocking a colicky baby and worrying about the future and making decisions alone.

She looked up and saw Tate staring at the bouquet.

"I'm going on. I have to run by the IGA and pick up dinner."

They met on the sidewalk. Marilee, with Munro at her heels, was just coming out the doors of the *Voice* building, and Tate was returning from a Chamber of Commerce luncheon.

"You are joinin' us for supper, aren't you?"

"I thought I would, unless you want to be alone with Stuart."

For heaven's sake. "I am seeing Stuart to talk with him before supper. That is enough. I'll plan on your mother, too, just in case. Is there anything you particularly want me to get at the store?"

"Can't think of anything." He stood at least three feet away.

"Okay. Well, we'll eat about six." She stepped toward him and went up on tiptoe to give him a quick kiss.

"Hey, here." He threw her his keys. "Take my car, and you can go past the IGA on your way home. I'll walk home later."

She opened the door for Munro to hop in; then she slipped behind the wheel and buckled up. Both hands on the steering wheel, she was gathering concentration.

She always experienced a disconcerting conflict when driving Tate's BMW. She adored driving it—sporty and powerful—but she worried about wrecking it.

With extreme care, she backed it out from its space. If she ever did wreck the car, she wanted it to be the other driver's fault. Heading down Main, keeping an eye out for some idiot who might pull out in front of her, she stopped at the light. She ran her hand over the leather steering wheel and wiggled her rear in the seat that was sun-warmed. Or was that heat lingering from Tate's rear?

Had Tate seemed unusually distant? As if he were angry at her about something. The flowers, of course, although that had not been her fault, nor anything to feel guilty over.

But she had sensed the distance earlier, in his office. That was why she had felt annoyance at him, she realized. But maybe she was imagining things.

A horn honked behind her, causing her to jump. "Oh!" The grill of an enormous truck took up the rearview mirror.

Pressing the accelerator and turning the steering wheel, she sent the BMW zipping around the corner onto First Street going north. Another glance in the rearview mirror, and she sighed with relief at being out of the gun-sight of the big truck, which had continued heading straight.

She deposited the grocery bags on the counter, then turned to gaze at the colorful bouquet of flowers Tate had given her yesterday. She liked these ever so much more than the roses, she thought as she added a bit of water to the vase. The roses were extravagant. Larger than life. This bouquet was lovely, warm and real. It fit her, and Tate knew it.

A knock sounded at the back door. Marilee opened the door to Franny, with her shiny carrot-red hair and radiant face, and wearing an ivory knit layered outfit that seemed to flow around her.

"Hi, darlin'." She gave an impish grin. "I've been shoppin' and wanted to bring over my goodies."

"Oh?"

"Yes. Are the kids home?"

"Not yet." Marilee checked the clock. "It'll be probably another ten minutes. They could make it in twenty minutes, easily, but they like to dawdle, you know."

Marilee looked curiously at the bags, and Franny said she would just have to show what she had. She could not wait.

There was an ant farm, quite an elaborate setup, for Willie Lee. "I asked the man if he had a worm farm. I understand Willie Lee likes worms, but the man didn't have a worm farm."

"Thank goodness," Marilee said, and they both laughed.

There was a set of four books of the American Girls series for Corrine, plus a young girl's journal and pen that lit up. "For writing in the dark. See." Franny demonstrated.

It was all lovely, each thing perfect for the children. How had she known?

"Oh, I just let God speak to me when I'm shopping. I got a great buy on a pair of brown leather jeans for myself. I heard distinctly to go to a certain store and down a certain aisle, and there they were, less than half price. I have wanted a pair all winter."

Leather? Marilee quickly surveyed her future mother-in-law and thought the woman could pull it off.

"And here's for you."

"Oh! Thank you." A small pink gift bag. She pulled out a small bottle of perfumed bath beads and a packet of something that looked like tea.

"Herbal," Franny told her. "My own blend. It relaxes, opens the sinuses to air and the mind to understanding. I thought you and Stuart might enjoy it, when he comes."

Tate must have told her.

Franny motioned. "I'll set your kitchen table for tea, and I'll keep the kids busy when they come in, so that you and Stuart can have a nice chat. You go on now and get yourself dolled up."

"Well . . ."

"Darlin', your ex-husband is coming over. A woman always feels confident when she looks her best. You want to look like dynamite."

She did. It had been her plan all along, but she had not faced what seemed a foolish, prideful notion. Now, with Franny giving it an okay, Marilee laughed aloud.

"Yes, I do."

"Then, dear, go get to it." She shooed at Marilee with her graceful hands. "And choose something teal."

Choose something teal?

Marilee got out her favorite sweater, soft teal. Franny seemed to know things.

If Stuart thought he was just going to pop back in here, just as if he had not deserted them, he might as well think again.

She peered at her image in the mirror. She didn't need very much blush, that was for sure. She applied lipstick, then carefully set the tube down, backed up and sank down on the side of the bed.

God, help me here. Surely you can help me, if you shop for Franny. I don't understand myself. And I can't imagine why, now, Stuart has to come and make more complications. Help me to see what I'm supposed to see. And give me understanding . . . and . . . oh, this one was hard. *Please soften my heart to let go of the past hurt that no longer matters.*

Heaven knew she had enough to understand about today without hauling the past around with her. But she did think that removing the resentment she felt against Stuart was a lot bigger job than directing someone to leather pants.

A knock sounded at the door, and Franny poked her head in the room. "There's a problem."

Hadn't she just prayed to God for help? This did not seem like help. *He works in mysterious ways, his wonders to perform.*

A skunk. Marilee could smell the odor through the back door.

She opened the door and looked down on Willie Lee, a forlorn figure sitting on the bottom step. "Willie Lee, honey."

He twisted around and peered up at her, blinking behind his thick glasses. "He need-ed me to help him, Ma-ma."

Corrine and Munro stood far out in the middle of the yard, looking on.

"Everyone stay right where you are. Corrine, don't you let Munro near Willie Lee."

She closed the door again, told Franny they would have to get Willie Lee undressed outside, and raced away to gather a towel and blankets. On her way past the phone, she called Parker. Valentine had a part-time animal control officer, but she knew Parker's mobile phone number by heart.

"Willie Lee got sprayed by a skunk in the daylight," she told him. "Corrine can show you where it is . . . or was."

Franny and Corrine, keeping their heads turned in a vain attempt to escape the odor, held blankets for privacy. Marilee had to be in the thick of it, in the middle of the blankets with Willie Lee, helping him with his buttons, tossing his clothes up over the blankets and out into the grass as far as possible. Munro watched from over by the fence.

"I told him not to go after that skunk," Corrine said, with disgust. "Even Munro was smart enough not to do that."

Willie Lee had begun crying now.

"A lesson actively learned sticks best," Franny said softly.

Her future mother-in-law, out on the lawn in ivory cashmere, exposed to skunk odor. Giving a big sigh, Marilee caught a heaping dose of stink and ended up coughing.

Then she was shepherding Willie Lee through the house, trailing a cloud of skunk odor, into the tub of water scented with the new bath beads. The odor changed to skunk plus sweet jasmine, with skunk odor dominating.

"He need-ed me to make him bet-ter, Mama. I tri-ied to tell him."

She gazed into her son's teary eyes. "Was the skunk sick, honey?"

Willie Lee nodded.

"How do you know?"

"He told-ed me."

Her heartbeat thudded. "Did you touch him, Willie Lee? I mean at all. Did you touch the skunk?"

Willie Lee gazed at her and shook his head. "No, Ma-ma."

Willie Lee never lied. Thank you, God, for keeping my little boy safe.

Shampoo his hair. The odor became one of skunk mixed with herbal fragrance. Skunk was still winning.

The door opened; Parker Lindsey's head appeared around it. "How is it in here?"

"He's okay. He never touched the skunk. It just sprayed him."

"I'll say." And the door closed again.

Marilee, on her knees in her best skirt and teal sweater, rinsed Willie Lee and prepared to soap him up again.

Out front, Stuart was just stepping up on Marilee's porch when the door opened and out came Corrine, followed by a man. Stuart and the man stared at each other with surprise.

Corrine said, "Hey, Mr. James . . . this is Parker Lindsey, our vet. Parker, this is Stuart James, Aunt Marilee's old husband."

The girl made him sound like a discarded shoe. "That's *ex*-husband," he clarified and stuck out his hand.

The man shook his hand quickly. "Hello. I'm her old boyfriend, Parker. Sorry to rush, but we're off to find a skunk."

Perplexed, Stuart watched the two go down the steps and over to the blue truck sitting in the driveway.

Stuart stepped through the door that had been left open, then closed it behind him. He was a little early.

"Marilee?" What was that smell? *We're off to find a skunk.* Was that skunk odor?

A figure came through the swinging door of the kitchen—Franny Holloway, who took time to prop open the door. "Whew, better to let the air flow. I'm afraid there is an upset to the schedule, Mr. James. Willie Lee has met with an unfortunate accident, and Marilee is occupied with bathing him. I'm making you some tea, though."

Just then Marilee appeared out of the bathroom. "Oh, Stuart. Good. Would you go to the grocery store and get some big cans of tomato juice? Three quarts, at least." With that, she disappeared back into the bathroom.

He looked at Franny Holloway, who said, "Tea will be waiting when you get back."

Turning, he went back out the front door, where he met Tate Holloway coming up the walk. There were certainly men coming and going from his ex-wife's house.

"Going for tomato juice," he told Holloway and got a kick out of the man's surprised expression. At least Holloway knew less than he did, he thought with satisfaction.

Parker and Corrine returned, and Parker, poking his head in the front door, as if in too much of a hurry to come all the way inside, told Marilee, "No sign of it anywhere. Morley Lund said he saw a skunk wandering down the ditch out back of his yard, and he got his gun, but when he came back, it was gone."

"Does it mean it's rabid, since it's wandering around in the day?"

Parker shrugged. "Could be, or it could simply have been rousted out of its hole by something. Morley says he's shot five skunks this winter. They're livin' under those old cars of his out beside his shop, and they keep eating his cats' food, gettin' into it with the cats and sprayin'."

"Well, why doesn't he move those cars?"

"Easier to shoot the skunks, I guess."

"Well, for heaven's sake."

He shrugged, gave her a quick kiss on the cheek, then left.

Marilee, standing there with the feel of his lips on her cheek, felt a smile in her heart.

Tate, who had come up behind her, said, "He's a good friend."

"Yes," she said, smiling at him. "He is." And she put her hand into his.

Everyone who needed to be gone was gone, and those who needed to be in bed were in bed. Whew.

They sat together in the porch swing, in the dark, where the beams of the streetlight did not reach. Marilee, in jeans and a thick sweater, was cocooned in a quilt. She snuggled up against Tate, who wore his suede jacket and refused to cocoon with her.

Why was it that men could not abide wrapping in a quilt? It was cozy, two wrapped together.

"Makes me feel tangled," Tate said. "If somethin' happened—the house caught on fire, or an attacker came up—I'd have to get unwrapped from the quilt before I could defend us."

And men said women had great imaginations. "Remember bundling?" she asked.

"Way before my time," he replied, and gently rocked the swing, causing a slight squeak with each sway.

Squeak, squeak, squeak. She really needed to grease the porch swing chain.

After a moment, she said, "I believe tonight Stuart got a taste of the rigors of parenthood."

"Huh? What did he do?"

Good question. "I guess he got to observe it all. The time and energy it takes to clean up unexpected messes."

"That's about it. He observes well and gets fed in the bargain."

She thought she detected a note of deprecation in his voice and found it satisfying. No woman ever wanted her man to be patient with an old lover. It had been gratifying that he and Parker had been rivals. Their rivalry had distressed her, but it had also given her satisfaction, she thought, being totally honest with herself. Although, seeing their friendship now, she felt pleased. It was odd how feelings could change.

Probably she should be appreciative of Tate's patience in many matters, and she *was* appreciative, but at the same time his patience could get on her nerves. In her estimation, Tate could be too patient at times. For one thing, his level of patience very often showed hers to a disadvantage, and it got tiring to always be the one to lose patience first.

Squeak, squeak, squeak.

She had lost a bit of patience with the tomato juice. It had seemed to go everywhere. Willie Lee had seen her exasperation and cried, "I am sor-ry to make you mad, Ma-ma." He could never stand for her to be angry. Corrine had helped her to clean up the tomato juice. Dear, precious Corrine.

"I never, ever want to have to deal with skunk smell again," she said.

"Oh, I imagine your chances of that are slim, livin' in town. Although on the other hand, this is a rural town and in the South . . . and you are the mother of a growin' boy."

Her situation sounded precarious.

Squeak, squeak, squeak.

"Willie Lee said the skunk told him it was sick." She let that sit there a second and then added, "It could have rabies, Tate, and it is still out there."

"Yes, that is so," Tate agreed slowly. "But there are a lot of skunks out there, and I imagine there are a lot of skunks with rabies, and yet few people—or even dogs, for that matter—are bitten or even get around one, so I don't think we need to worry over it a whole lot." His arm tightened around her. "Willie Lee's okay, Marilee. He's safe in that bed in there. And clean, too."

Yes, her son was safe and clean. Closing her eyes, she laid her head back again on Tate's firm shoulder. She could not recall anyone she ever knew being bitten by a rabid animal. Maybe she would speak to Parker about the danger, though. This made her recall that Parker was married.

"What's Parker's wife like?"

"Amy? Oh . . . she's tall. . . . She's a vet, too. Real nice. Nice smile. Nice eyes. Real nice."

Squeak, squeak, squeak.

"She's a knockout, isn't she?"

"Yep."

Marilee wondered if she could get time tomorrow to go see Parker to get his view on this skunk problem and her own view of his wife.

"Well, I'm glad for him." She realized with a suddenness that she was purely delighted for Parker.

"Me, too."

She sighed deeply, feeling the weight she had not even known she carried roll off her shoulders. Even though she knew she had done the right thing, there had remained a bit of guilt for calling off her marriage to Parker and leaving him in his lonely life, not to mention the mismatched colors of his home. She had felt responsible for Parker for so long that she didn't know how to stop, and now she could. Another woman had taken over the job. Quite swiftly this relief was followed by gratitude for the man in her life, and she squeezed Tate.

"Now, if we could just get Stuart settled." It pained her to see Stuart. So alone, he seemed.

"Stuart is not your responsibility to settle."

"I know that." The censure in his tone pricked her. "What I mean is that his dropping in out of the blue to—*develop* an acquaintance with

Willie Lee at this late date encompasses so much more than I care to be involved with right now." How did one make up for nine years of lost fatherhood?

"So don't be involved," Tate said. "Stuart is a fairly capable sort. I think he can manage to make friends with Willie Lee, even make a stab at being a father to him, without you having much to do with it. Don't meddle in it."

"I don't think being concerned for my son's welfare is meddling," she said, and then shut her mouth, pulling away from him, if only inwardly.

His accusation hurt. And the idea of no involvement frightened her. Someone needed to see that things went along in a safe fashion and make certain Stuart didn't do something foolish with Willie Lee. What exactly this foolishness might entail, she could not have named. She only knew that she had to be involved to keep the situation from getting out of control somehow. Stuart had no idea of how to be a parent. She felt obligated to do her best to show him.

She did feel responsible for Stuart, she realized. He seemed like a lost soul, and he had once been her husband, and now here he was again, plopped down in front of her.

All of which she could not say to Tate, who more than once had voiced the opinion that she had the overwhelming tendency to mother everyone. He had been verbal in his view that her part in the relationship with Parker had been one of mothering, had even gone so far as to say she had not allowed Parker to be a man.

Well, she did not think a woman could stop a man from being a man. There was no question but that she was a mothering sort, but she thought it going too far to say that she had stopped Parker from being a man. Parker was the sort who gave himself over to be looked after and doted on and led around so that he didn't have to make decisions. Possibly he found that it took all his strength to be a veterinarian and looking after animals all the time, so he wanted a woman to look after him.

No one could stop Tate from being a man, that was for sure. Tate never let her mother him. Tate was the type who might enjoy her ministrations but never her directions.

She became aware, quite suddenly, that he was pressing his lips to the top of her head. And that his hand was kneading her arm through the blanket.

Tate whispered, "You smell so good."

"Citrus shampoo." She had felt compelled to wash from head to toe, too.

She twisted to look up at him. Even though it was too dark to see his eyes, she knew their blueness and how he looked at her. She brought her hand free of the quilt and pressed it to the back of his neck, at the same time lifting her lips to meet his.

They kissed and kissed and kissed in a way that caused them both to gasp for breath and then go at it again. Tate claimed her lips in the thrilling manner of urgency and demand that made her pulse throb in intimate parts of her body. The passion went even higher because of their position, there on the swing, a place suitable for necking but not suitable for sex.

He kissed her until she thought she would fly to pieces with wanting.

"Oh, Tate . . . Tate," she whispered when his lips at last let hers go.

"Marilee . . ."

He trailed moist kisses down the tender skin of her neck. She put her hand into his open collar and felt the warmth of his skin.

Then, abruptly, he broke away. "I've got to go home, Marilee."

He got up so fast that she fell over.

"I'll be here in the mornin'. Same time," he said, as he hot-footed it across the yard, not looking back.

Well, for heaven's sake.

Squeak, squeak, squeak.

Marilee wrestled herself free of the quilt and strode inside, where she stripped out of her clothes, including panties quite damp, put on flannel pajamas, took three aspirin and went to bed with the pillow over her head. Even so, she thought she caught a whiff of skunk.

Nine

In the eye of the beholder . . .

Winston was a little disconcerted to find Mildred out of bed before sunup. Seeing the shut bathroom door, he figured she was in there, and that he could slip down and get his coffee in peace.

Unfortunately, when he came into the kitchen, there was Mildred at the table, in her orange turban and bright green print robe, with what had been a package of a dozen cinnamon rolls but was now down to six in front of her on the table.

"Leanne brought us a treat," she said. White sugar icing smudged her lips.

"If it was for us, then you might have left more."

Apparently Leanne had set the packaged sweet rolls out the night before. Winston blamed himself for not telling her that she couldn't set out things like that in front of Mildred, who had developed diabetes, the worst thing in the world for someone who was addicted to food.

"You know what the doctor said about eatin' like this, Mildred." He moved the remaining cinnamon rolls to the counter, threw a towel over them and wet a paper napkin with which he wiped Mildred's face, while she complained that the doctor didn't know how hungry she got.

"I was so hungry that I woke up," she said in a small voice.

Now she was tuning up to cry, and Winston knew it would do no good to scold her. She was growing more like a child every day, and she simply couldn't leave food alone. She had always carried it around in her purse, but now she was hiding it around the house. Yesterday he had found dried-up bacon in with the towels.

He put a hand on her shoulder, then noticed that she had not fully buttoned her robe over her humongous breasts, so he did that for her, telling her, "Why don't you have that Jell-O in the refrigerator? It ought to tide you over until we have us some breakfast." It was the artificial sugar variety, made the previous afternoon by their day help, Marie.

Mildred, brightening, got up more quickly than he would have imagined anyone of her considerable rotundness could move.

Feeling tired and annoyed at having his early morning time invaded, he turned to get himself a cup of coffee. He decided on a cinnamon roll, too, but felt guilty about eating it in front of Mildred. He gave in to the urge, keeping his back turned while he munched on it. It seemed a sad state to not be able to eat a cinnamon roll in his own home. Perhaps that was how Mildred felt, too.

Facing the window, he moved the curtain and peered out at the corral and the mare there with her filly, a pretty sight in first light. It lifted his spirits to see the horses, at the same time making him think sadly of days gone by, when his wife always had a horse or two out there. Coweta had been gone now almost four years.

Life was difficult for a man of his advancing years and still in his right mind, and not doing too poorly physically, either. It was as if people blamed him for his unusual stamina, at the same time resenting that he did not have stamina enough.

As if seeking comfort, he shifted his gaze to look across the small meadow at the Blaines' house. There was a glow in the kitchen window.

Full sadness fell over him. Days with Vella were pretty much gone, too, and he missed them. It had been pleasant to have a woman serve him morning coffee, put on lipstick for him and be capable of stimulating conversation.

But last fall, when it had gotten too cold to sit outside, he had quit having morning coffee with her. Since she had taken Perry back, Winston didn't think it fitting that he be alone with her inside the house. Not that there was anything Winston could really do of an untoward nature, but he was still a man, no matter how society discounted him as being old, and it was not proper to be alone in the company of another man's wife.

He knew he had proved a disappointment to Vella. He had kissed her one time, but the passion that erupted proved to be of a short-lived nature, with nothing whatsoever coming behind it. He himself had been pretty disappointed, although he didn't know what either of them had expected at his age. That she, a woman considerably younger than he, had actually been interested and anticipated anything else on his part had been a pleasant experience, though.

Then Perry had ended up doing enough to get Vella to take him back, and to keep himself there. The stick-in-the-mud had actually gotten up the gumption to give that Vi-ra-grow, or whatever it was called, a try. Perry had reported considerable improvement and delight, but there was one thing Perry would never have, and that was spark. One could not get spark from a pill. At any rate, Perry's liveliness had proved as short-lived as Winston's passion, and he had returned to his dull ways and his television. Vella had turned her considerable energy to home improvement and landscaping ideas.

And Winston was alone. Again.

"'Mornin', y'all."

He turned to see Leanne, all sleepy-eyed and scratching her hair, which looked like birds had nested in it overnight. It was the going style for young women, and there was no accounting it. He had to admit, even with the hair, Leanne was a looker; she was from his wife's side of the family—Overtons, known for beautiful women.

"Good mornin'," he said.

She came over to get a mug out of the cabinet and pour her coffee. Winston watched her graceful movements. Not too many women moved like Leanne, like a lazy female cat, despite she had on men's insulated overalls with suspenders that went over a silk undershirt so thin that he could see clearly she did not bother with a bra. And she was a fully developed woman, too.

"In a little bit here, I'm gonna go feed my horses and then go up to MacCoy's for grain." She sipped her coffee. "Do either of you need me to pick up anything while I'm out?"

Mildred said, "I would like some ice cream. . . . Can I have ice cream, Winston? And some chocolate pudding."

"She needs anything low carb and sugar free," he told his niece.

He said he didn't need anything, then added, "But there is one thing I would like, and that is the courtesy of you coverin' up your body. I'm sayin' this to the both of you. I may be old and on my last leg, but I am deservin' of the respect due a man."

With that, he took his coffee and went through the house, put on his coat, tucked the flags under his arm, and went out on the front porch, with the certain attitude of sending back anyone who tried to come out with him.

As he lowered himself into the rocker, he glanced out at the street and saw a figure, a rather small woman, walking past, heading east at a smart pace, swinging her arms. He followed her with his gaze, trying to figure out if he knew her. The first golden glow of the morning sun hit her, and he saw she had copper-penny hair.

Just then the "Star Spangled Banner" blared out from a speaker at the base of Everett Northrupt's flag pole across the street. Winston jumped and sloshed his coffee.

There was Everett, coming to the edge of the porch.

Annoyed at being behind—apparently Everett had decided winter rules were off—Winston fumbled to get out the remote control, kept ready in his coat pocket, and point it through the window. He succeeded, and the strains of "Dixie" filled the air, coming from speakers up underneath the eaves, as he hurried to the pole to raise his flag. He stood as straight as possible and saluted. Then he saw that the woman in the street was standing at attention.

He liked her immediately.

And, to his immense surprise, when the last strains of the two patriotic songs died, here she came striding across his yard.

"Good mornin'," she said, sticking out her hand. "You must be Winston Valentine. I've heard so much about you from my son. I'm Franny Holloway."

Her voice was smooth and her accent in no hurry. Silver-and-bead earrings swayed from her ears, and her deep green eyes sparkled.

Winston, mesmerized, stared at her for a full three seconds before managing to gather his wits to shake her hand. *Thank you, God, I guess I'm glad to be alive after all.*

Charlotte was hanging the flags when Sandy pulled up out front. He had a small bag from the IGA deli.

"How early this morning?" he asked her, coming inside and pulling her into his arms.

"Not so early . . . around five." She rose slightly on tiptoe to kiss him. It was nice that she had to stretch to reach him, rather than bend down, as she had for every man in her life until Sandy, who was over six feet six inches in his boots.

The kiss revived her, as did his lean, hard body against her.

He had brought bagels this morning, and cups of rich mocha. And then he pulled something out of his pocket, a small box.

"I want you to marry me, Charlotte." His jaw muscle worked with unusual firmness as he opened the box, revealing a beautiful diamond solitaire. "I want to marry you . . . for you to be my wife and for me to be your husband. I want to sleep with you. I want to be there with you. I want us to be together. Let me help you with your mother. I want to do that."

Charlotte, who never let anyone help her with anything, looked into his face. Into his dear, sweet, wholesome brown eyes. She brought her palm to touch his cheek.

"I can't." Her words came out hoarse and yet poured forth, painfully, all on the order of: I'm too old for you; you can have so much more with a woman your own age; maybe I can't have children;

and I have the burden of my mother. She said all this, but not what really burned in her mind, what Sandy already knew, which was that she loved him as she had never loved any other person in her whole life. And because she loved him, she wanted the world for him. She did not want to be a burden to him; she did not want to face a day when he became sorry he had married a woman eleven years his senior.

Sandy reached for her, but, overwhelmed, she turned and ran out the front door.

She ran, in her heeled pumps, all the way, four and a half blocks, to her house. A number of people saw her, recognized Charlotte Nation, the really tall girl who worked at the *Voice,* running and wondered what might be the matter downtown. A few people called around. The telephone down at the *Voice* rang, but Sandy, still alone, was uncertain about answering. He had never answered the phone at the office before. Hardly anyone did, except Charlotte. Charlotte got a little mad if anyone else answered the phone, and especially if they didn't do it exactly right.

He stood there, with the phone ringing, trying to figure out what to do, wondering if he should go after Charlotte or let her have the time alone. He sure didn't want to press her so hard that she threw him completely out of her life.

At home, where she had thrown herself across her bed, Charlotte cried until she felt herself go almost into a faint. She had not slept but three hours the night before, and she had not had anything to eat since a small supper that hadn't set well; however, she struggled up from her state and got the telephone to call Marilee and tell her she was taking the day off. She felt terribly irresponsible taking time off and would not have been able to stand being so irresponsible as not to alert someone who could take over.

Ten

Her mother's little girl . . .

Miss Charlotte had a broken heart. Corrine heard Aunt Marilee on the phone to her, and saw her aunt pacing with her long strides, like she did whenever she was upset. "Honey . . . oh, honey," Aunt Marilee said, and when she finally hung up and saw Corrine, who never liked for her aunt Marilee to get upset, looking at her, she breathed deeply and said, "Miss Charlotte is okay. No one dies from a heartbreak." Then, as she headed for her bedroom, she added, "They just feel like they will."

It wasn't good that Miss Charlotte had called before Aunt Marilee had finished a whole cup of coffee. She never did get to finish her coffee, though, because she needed to get down to the newspaper office early to take Miss Charlotte's place, and as usual she was running about fifteen minutes late. Aunt Vella said that when it was time for Aunt Marilee to be born, they made her mama wait for the doctor, who was not yet at the hospital, for fifteen minutes, so ever since then, Aunt Marilee stayed the same course. You could set a watch by her lateness.

Aunt Marilee rushed around, telling them to hurry up. Corrine, who was always ready early, didn't need to hurry; she focused on helping Willie Lee, who was incapable of hurrying. Aunt Marilee had forgotten that she had thrown away his skunkified shoes. Corrine dug his good Sunday shoes out of the closet.

The telephone rang. Corrine jammed the shoes at Willie Lee and called out, "I'll get it," and Aunt Marilee called back, "Bless you, honey," in the way that made Corrine know that she was a big help to her aunt.

She raced into the living room, then came to a dead stop and stared at the phone on her aunt's desk. She knew suddenly that it was her mother calling. Whenever Aunt Marilee left a message on her mother's answering machine, it was always two or three days until her mother would call. Corrine was fairly certain her mother did this on purpose. She could not have explained her reasoning, just that this was her mother's manner.

Willie Lee, who had come in the room, walked past Corrine and went to pick up the phone. "Hello?" He listened. "Yes, this is Wil-lie Lee. Hel-lo, Aunt A-ni-ta."

Corrine breathed deeply.

He giggled. "Yes, this is Wil-lie Lee, but I am grow-ing."

She realized her mother had said something funny to Willie Lee. Her mother always made an effort to make Willie Lee smile. Her mother was beautiful when she made an effort to make someone smile.

"Cor-rine is right here."

She took the receiver he held out to her. "Hello, Mama."

"Corrine? Corrine, is that my baby?" At the sound of her mother's high-pitched tone, she pictured her mother on the other end of the line, as she was when she was in a energetic mood, walking around as she spoke, puffing on a cigarette, every part of her in motion.

"Yes."

"Well, what is it you have to tell me, honey? Your Aunt Marilee sounded like there was a surprise."

She didn't want to say it aloud. She checked and saw that Willie Lee was over on the couch, trying to get his shoes on. She cupped the receiver with her hand. "I started my period."

"What, honey? I didn't hear you."

Corrine repeated it.

Her mother let out a squeal that stabbed Corrine's ears. "You started your period? Oh my goodness!"

Corrine wished to drop through the floor. "Yes," she croaked. She wondered if her mother's boyfriend, Louis, was right there with her mother.

"I cannot believe you have started so young. Surely I am not old enough to be your mother."

Corrine experienced a stab of guilt at doing something wrong.

"Well, honey, I'm sending you a present. I'm puttin' it in the mail today."

"You are?" Sometimes her mother sent presents, but except for a jewelry box with a wind-up ballerina that she had sent at Christmas, the things were all for younger girls: pop-beads, several stuffed toys, books for young readers. Corrine had found out that it had been her mother's boyfriend, Louis, who had chosen the jewelry box.

"Don't ask me what it is. I want it to be a surprise."

"Okay." Corrine wondered if she should want to ask.

. "Oh, honey, I wish I could be there with you," her mother was saying. "I miss you so much."

"I miss you, too, Mama."

Then there was silence, and Corrine had a small panic in trying to think of something more to say.

Thankfully her mother spoke. "We're thinkin' of comin' up there next month. Grama says Aunt Marilee and Tate have set the date for their weddin'."

"Yes, they have."

"Well . . . honey, let me talk to your aunt just a minute."

"Okay. She's gettin' dressed." She put her hand over the receiver and called out for Aunt Marilee, who was just then coming into the room. "It's Mama."

Aunt Marilee took the phone. "Hey, Anita." Then she bit her lip. "Yes she sure is growin' up," she said after a moment.

Corrine went to the couch to help Willie Lee tie his shoes. He told her to let him do it, so she just sat there on her knees, one ear tuned to her aunt's conversation. Aunt Marilee had turned her back and was mostly listening. When she spoke, it was with that clipped tone that meant something her mother was saying annoyed her, but she would not let on.

Then Aunt Marilee was holding the receiver out to her. "She wants to say goodbye."

Corrine took the phone and bid goodbye to her mother, who said, "Love you, honey," and made a smooching sound.

In answer, Corrine said, "You, too." She could not make the smooching sound, and she felt guilty for this lapse that seemed mean.

Corrine could not tell her mother that she loved her; she could not say the words. One time on the phone her mother had pressed her.

"Don't you love your mother, sugar?"

"Yes, I do, Mama."

Thankfully her mother had let it drop, and Corrine had never had to actually say the words.

She felt guilty for not being able to say the words. She knew she loved her mother, but what confused her was how much she sometimes hated her, too. It was a secret that lay like a stain on her heart. She always felt that she needed to tell her mother she was sorry— sorry for being so mean, sorry for being a nuisance, sorry for ever being born.

Corrine knew she loved Aunt Marilee, but she never could have told her aunt with the words, either. This seemed okay, maybe because

Aunt Marilee didn't say the words. Still, Corrine felt her aunt loved her. Aunt Marilee would smile at her in a way that made her feel warm and full, and sometimes Aunt Marilee would hug her right out of the blue, or would say that Corrine was sweet, or neat, or smart, or pretty as a picture. Maybe what was best was that Aunt Marilee seemed to like her to be around. Sometimes Corrine felt so grateful to her aunt Marilee, but she couldn't say that, either. She would lay her head against Aunt Marilee, hoping her aunt could feel how she felt.

Corrine was mostly grateful to Aunt Marilee for sharing Willie Lee, who was the one person Corrine knew for certain she loved totally, completely. With Willie Lee, Corrine shared two important life factors: the lack, at least until now, of a flesh and blood father, and the sense of being different from everyone in the world.

The details Corrine's mother had told her about her father were few. At the times her mother spoke of her father, her mother would cry, sending mascara running down her cheeks, and tell her all about a man named Scott Pendley, a sweet ranch boy from some burg over near Odessa, who had been a roustabout on the oil rigs, then fallen off one and died three short weeks after they had married. But if her Scotty had only lived, he would have taken good care of her and Corrine, and they would have had everything in the world.

Her mother had described her Scotty as having blue eyes and curly blond hair, and her mother had light brown hair and green eyes. But Corrine's own eyes were the color of crude oil and her hair all but black. And why was there no picture of this man? Why were there no grandparents from her father?

Once, piecing together rumors, speculation about her parentage, she had told her mother that she did not believe her mother had ever been married. Her mother had produced a marriage certificate. "I was married. You are not a bastard child. I made sure of that."

The event that brought Corrine to live with Aunt Marilee and Willie Lee was her mother being beaten up by her latest boyfriend. Corrine did not see this violence, although it might have been better to see it than what her vivid imagination drew up when she arrived home, a small, skinny girl bearing a bag of items from the 7-Eleven at the corner, stepping through the door to find two enormous policemen questioning her mother in a living room where the television was kicked out and lamps broken, and her mother's face all cut and bruised.

Her mother went into the bathroom and had Corrine help her put little butterfly bandages on the worst of the broken skin. Later, lying awake and worrying that the violent man might return, or that something else equally horrible was about to happen at any minute, she overheard her mother on the telephone to Aunt Marilee, crying, "They'll take her away from me, Marilee."

Aunt Marilee came flying down the highway and arrived early the next morning, coming into the house with the firm strides that she employed when she meant business. She took one look at Corrine's mother draped dramatically on the couch, her face all black and blue, another at Corrine, who was frantically cleaning the house instead of in school, then looked in the refrigerator, staring for a long minute at the basic contents of a half a quart of milk, a six-pack of beer, jars of grape jelly and mayonnaise, and a package of bologna. Slamming closed the refrigerator, Aunt Marilee strode out back and looked in the trash can, and then slammed that closed, too. With each slam, Corrine's mother winced.

Aunt Marilee came marching back inside, got Corrine and took her out to the back step, pulled a Hershey chocolate bar from her purse and gave it to Corrine, saying, "Sit here." Corrine sat; no one in their right mind crossed Aunt Marilee when she meant business.

While Corrine broke off squares of the Hershey bar and put them into her mouth and looked up at the blue, blue sky and wished she were a bird that could fly away, the two women inside went at each other. Corrine wondered vaguely if some neighbor would again call the police.

Aunt Marilee screamed at Corrine's mother for being so stupid as to waste her life with booze and men. "Anita, didn't you have enough of that with Daddy and Mama? What do you want to do? Kill yourself with it, like Daddy did?"

And her mother alternately sobbed and screamed back that it was her life to do with as she pleased. "Get off your high horse, Marilee. You tried a man, and it didn't work out any better. Now you're afraid to have a life."

Gradually the women's voices subsided, and eventually Corrine was summoned back inside. Both women's eyes were red and swollen.

Her mother got down on her knees, her swollen face level with Corrine's. "I want you to go stay with your aunt Marilee for a while, honey. Just till I get a good job and can save up for a good place to live, okay? It will only be for a few months. Aunt Marilee can take care of you real well."

The few months had turned into almost two years. Her mother had visited a total of four times; the telephone calls and cards were coming more infrequently.

On the last visit, her mother had been beautiful and as happy as Corrine had ever seen her. She had brought a new boyfriend—Louis, who looked like a movie star and drove a fancy car. Corrine thought he was the nicest boyfriend her mother had ever had. That afternoon her mother had made her feel special, and Louis had actually seemed to like her. She had begun to think maybe it would be okay to go with her mother, that maybe now she would have a real mother and father and home.

But her mother and Louis had gone off to live in New Orleans, her mother promising, "I'll get us a wonderful place in New Orleans, honey, and then you can come live with me." That had been last fall.

Corrine no longer believed her mother would ever have a place for her. And she felt terribly guilty, because she no longer wanted to go live with her mother.

She had arrived at her aunt Marilee's house with all her stuff in a large plaid suitcase and four liquor boxes. Since then, Aunt Marilee had bought her a brand-new mattress and box spring, and a violet sprigged comforter and matching sheets. She had gotten Corrine all new clothes and toys, and three shelves of books. When Aunt Marilee and Mr. Tate were married, and they all moved over to Mr. Tate's house, Aunt Marilee said Corrine would have her own room, the one with an east window.

All in all, Corrine had begun to feel that her life might be okay after all. Until Willie Lee's father had shown up.

The first worry she had was that Willie Lee's father had come to take him away. That had happened to a kid—Frankie Ramundo—who had lived next door to her in Fort Worth; his father had shown up one day in a suit and shiny car and taken Frankie off with him, while Frankie's mother screamed and pulled her hair out in the driveway.

With further consideration, however, Corrine sincerely doubted anyone could take Willie Lee from Aunt Marilee, not even a police squad breaking in with machine guns, like on television.

On Friday night Mr. Tate and Aunt Marilee and Miss Franny, who had explained, "After a certain age, dear, we women turn back to Miss again," were visiting in the kitchen, while Mr. Tate made supper. Corrine was happily reading one of her books, and Willie Lee was on the floor, observing his ant farm, all of them just like it was supposed to be, when the doorbell rang. It was Mr. James, coming in and ruining it all.

"Hello, Corrine . . . may I come in?"

She reluctantly stepped back. "They're in the kitchen. We're about to eat supper."

"I'm just in time, then. I brought pie and ice cream." He had bags in his hand. One was from the dairy store. Apparently he had figured out quick to bring food. She said, "We have chocolate cake."

"Well, the ice cream is vanilla and will go with that." He held out a bag for her. "And here is something for you . . . and something for Willie Lee."

Slowly she took the bag he offered. To not take it would be too rude. "Thank you," she remembered to add.

"You're welcome." His eyes lingered on her briefly, flitting over her face like a searchlight. She looked away to the bag she now held.

When he stepped away toward Willie Lee, she lifted her eyes and watched him. He gave Willie Lee his bag, and Willie Lee showed him the ant farm. Mr. James gave it a glance and made a comment, then strode on into the kitchen with his long legs.

Corrine sat in the big chair and peered carefully into the shopping bag, one of the fancy kind, with twine handles. She really wished Mr. James hadn't bought her anything. She felt obligated to him now. But it wasn't like a real present, not like Miss Franny's gifts.

Mr. James's present was like what her mother's boyfriends used to bring her mother, to get her to go out with them, or make up after a fight. The boyfriends brought her mother flowers and candy and jewelry, and even a microwave oven and a television. One time one of the boyfriends gave her mother a pair of diamond earrings, and the next week, when they got in a fight, he jerked them out of her ears and left. Another time, after the boyfriend was gone and they needed money, her mother pawned the microwave he had given her. "This was my investment," her mother told her as they walked along the hot sidewalk to the pawnshop. "You make sure a man gives you a decent gift, so you can get some money from it when he leaves you."

Mr. James's gift was a really fancy doll. The sort you don't play with but set up somewhere to look at. A blond girl doll, with a beautiful china face. Cost bucks, she thought, examining it.

She put it back in the bag and moved to see Willie Lee's gift. It was a truck that ran on batteries.

Willie Lee, chin in his hand and eyes intently on the ant farm, said, "I can-not play with it now. I am watch-ing this ant . . . ev-cry-where he goes."

She went to the kitchen and through it to the laundry room, where she folded towels clean from the dryer. Aunt Marilee had begun giving her five dollars a week for allowance, and Corrine liked to be of help, plus at that minute she could listen and watch the adults in the kitchen, without them noticing her. She had learned long ago how to be invisible.

She continued watching the adults throughout the evening. She saw how Mr. James kept looking at Aunt Marilee. Saw how whenever he spoke, like when answering Miss Franny's questions about Scotland, he kept looking at Aunt Marilee. And when he took Willie Lee on his lap and observed the ant farm with him, he kept lifting his head to look at Aunt Marilee. It was sort of a sad look. But that did not make Corrine feel soft toward him.

Corrine had an uneasy feeling about the entire situation. In her experience, sooner or later bad was bound to happen, and it sure seemed that the arrival of Mr. James meant trouble.

"Hey, Corrine!"

It was Ricky Dale Oakes, pedaling past on his bicycle, with a black dog running alongside. Ricky Dale did a quick stop, hopped off and wheeled his bike up the walk to the porch, where Corrine and Willie Lee were playing with Willie Lee's kitten and his new battery-powered truck.

Corrine said, "Hey," but did not want to act overly interested. Ricky Dale was in her grade at school, in Mrs. Noble's class. He was the sheriff's son, but he wasn't stuck-up about it. All the girls thought he was cute, and Corrine did, too, but she wasn't about to admit it.

The next instant here came that black dog, a big puppy, running up on the porch, knocking over the truck and chasing the kitten. The kitten screeched, Willie Lee tried to grab him but missed, and Munro went after the intruding dog, while Ricky Dale and Corrine both tried to get hold of the big canine. It was so much commotion as to cause Aunt Marilee to poke her head out the door.

"What's goin' on?"

"Just my dog went after the cat, Miz James. I'm sorry. He's just a pup."

"Well . . ." Aunt Marilee's eyes swept them. "Y'all look okay. . . . Nice to see you, Ricky Dale. How's your mama doin'?"

"Fine, I guess. She doesn't really tell me, though."

Aunt Marilee chuckled at that and went back in the house. She was working on an article and had that absentminded look she wore when trying to figure out her writing.

Ricky Dale dragged his puppy to the foot of the stairs and held on to him. Willie Lee, with his arm around Munro, sat on the top step. Corrine leaned against the post. She was glad she had on the pair of good denim overalls and a tanned turtleneck sweater that Aunt Marilee had bought her from The Gap.

"I live down Porter two blocks," Ricky Dale said, inclining his head in the direction from where he'd come.

"Oh," Corrine said. She had little experience in talking to boys, or girls, either, for that matter.

He said, "I'm goin' up to Mr. Valentine's to take care of a couple of horses."

"You are?" This from Willie Lee, whose eyes popped wide.

"When did Mr. Winston get horses?" Corrine asked. She had a disappointing moment when she wondered if Ricky Dale was just a faker.

"Oh, they ain't his. They're Leanne Overton's—she's his niece. She moved in there a couple of weeks ago. Mr. Valentine's friend, Ms. Bell, died last Christmas, and his family thinks him and that other old lady that lives with him need somebody to kinda keep an eye on them. Miz Overton needed to separate her mare and its filly from her others out there at the MacCoys', and Mr. Valentine has that good horse place. His wife used to be a barrel racer."

Ricky Dale seemed like he knew a lot about people and goings-on.

"Miz Overton hired me to look out for 'em. Fifteen dollars for the week, and an extra five dollars when I come on Saturdays. I'll groom and exercise 'em, just work with them, so they have people attention. That's important with baby horses, like that filly."

Corrine wondered if he really knew this much about what he was saying, or if he liked to pretend he knew so much. She wondered if he was big enough to handle horses; he wasn't but just a bit taller than she was, maybe ten pounds heavier. Probably what he would do mostly was clean the stalls, and that wasn't exactly handling horses, but she saw no need to say this.

He continued on to say that he had been riding horses since he was three years old, that his grandfather, who used to be the sheriff for years, had taught him. He had even herded cattle with his grandfather.

"But he had to sell out his place and move into MacCoy Acres for old farts."

Corrine wished she could think of something to say.

Willie Lee did. "Do you have a horse?"

"No. I did have. Mason MacCoy gave me his Old Buck to ride, but he died."

Corrine could not speak to that horribly sad thing.

"I am sorry," Willie Lee said. "That is sad."

"Yeah, well, it happens. Buck was real old." He looked downward as he spoke, then lifted his head. "My grandfather's gonna help me buy another horse. A young one that I can train. I'm gonna save my money from this job."

"That will be nice," Corrine said, wishing she could come up with a better comment.

Then Ricky Dale asked, "You guys want to come up to Mr. Winston's and see the horses? You'd like the baby horse, Willie Lee."

Corrine stared at him. She was at once impressed that he spoke equally to Willie Lee and amazed at the invitation.

"Yes, I want to come," Willie Lee said instantly.

Corrine, always more cautious, said, "We have to ask Aunt Marilee."

"Okay," Ricky Dale said.

Willie Lee went racing inside. Corrine followed more slowly behind. Her mind was skimming over all sorts of reasons why going with Ricky Dale could turn out to be a bad idea. She was afraid she might do or say something stupid, and she really didn't want to find out something stupid about him.

But Willie Lee threw himself upon Aunt Marilee's lap. "Ma-ma, can we go to see hors-es up at Mr. Win-ston's with Ric . . . Ric-ky Dale?"

Corrine's faint hope that Aunt Marilee would disapprove was squashed when her aunt said, "Why, that sounds like a fine idea for a Saturday mornin'." Aunt Marilee apparently considered Ricky Dale in a good light.

Mr. Winston's corral was at the rear of his deep backyard, partially shaded by large pecan trees. The mare was a black-and-white paint, a "high-dollar" kind, Ricky Dale said. Her baby, a two-month-old filly, was the same, with a large black spot on one hip and black on each ear, as if someone had painted them.

When he saw the horses, the black dog, Beau, went racing forward, barking, ducked under the fence and chased after the horses, that went all over the corral. Ricky Dale ran after him, yelling until the dog, tongue hanging out, stopped and obeyed his master's call. Corrine, standing with Willie Lee and Munro outside the corral, looking on, figured it was more that the dog had stopped to get his breath.

Ricky Dale parked Beau outside the fence and called Corrine and Willie Lee inside. Munro followed. The filly poked her head beneath the mare's neck, watching them with sharp curiosity.

In that moment of looking at the mare and her baby, looking into the deep, dark eyes, Corrine fell totally in love with another being other than Willie Lee. In that instant she was lost forever to an adoration of horses.

"Come here, Pretty Girl," Ricky Dale coaxed, then instructed Corrine and Willie Lee not to move, nor look the horse right in the eyes.

The next instant the filly was slipping beneath the mother's neck and coming forward, straight for Willie Lee. The mare moved, putting herself next to the baby, who stretched her neck and nose toward Willie Lee.

"Breathe into her nose, Willie Lee," said Ricky Dale.

Willie Lee touched his nose to the filly's nose. The filly drew back and then put her nose out again. Corrine thought it was about the neatest thing she'd ever seen, and she was glad when she got a chance to do it, too.

They all eventually got to pet the filly and the mare. Corrine decided she liked the mare best. She liked the way the mare let her lean against her and put her cheek against her strong shoulder. She could have stayed there with the mare forever.

But Ricky Dale had come to do a job. He found two rakes, and Corrine and Willie Lee took turns helping to clean the large stall. Corrine figured Ricky Dale wasn't a fool; he'd gotten help for the job.

Willie Lee was not much help, but Ricky Dale told him that he was.

They were putting fresh pine shavings into the stall when Ricky Dale's dog started chasing the horses again. Ricky Dale ran out into the corral. "Beau! Beau! You stop that!"

Beau looked at Ricky Dale, and the mare at that instant kicked the fire out of the dog. Kicked him hard enough to cause a loud thud and to send the dog flying backward. Corrine, watching, experienced a slice of horror and unreality. The dog got immediately up from the ground, then stood with all four legs splayed, as if for balance. Ricky Dale went toward him, and the dog started toward Ricky Dale, and then he just keeled over.

Ricky Dale reached the dog and went down on his knees. "Beau?"

Corrine, having followed after Ricky Dale, saw that the dog's eyes were closed, and its blackish tongue hung out of its mouth, but it wasn't panting. It lay still as death, a term she had heard one of the women in her old neighborhood down in Fort Worth use.

Panic rose inside her, and she looked over to the Valentine house, wondering if she should go get someone.

Then there was Willie Lee getting on his knees and pulling the dog's head onto his lap. Corrine went to tell him to stop that disgusting action of touching a dead dog, but something, some odd prickling at the back of her neck, stopped the words. Slowly she fell on her knees beside him.

"Willie Lee?"

He didn't answer. His arms were around the dog's neck, his cheek pressed against the dog's fur. His eyes were closed, and there was this strange look on his face. It was the sunlight, she thought, and looked up, seeing the beams slanting through the bare branches and shining on Willie Lee, making his pale hair glow. Corrine blinked, looking at it. She saw Munro pressed against Willie Lee; the dog's eyes were slits, as if things were bright for him, too. All was still as death.

Then she looked across at Ricky Dale, who looked at her. For whatever reason, neither of them pulled Willie Lee away.

And then Willie Lee's eyes came open, and he straightened back up. "He is o-kay."

"What?" Ricky Dale said.

Then the black dog's eyes opened up. Corrine looked harder. Yes, his eyes opened and his tongue went back in his mouth. He lifted his head.

Ricky Dale said, "Beau?"

The dog got up, sort of drunk like, and licked Ricky Dale in the face.

"Beau is bet-ter now. Right, Mun-ro?" Willie Lee smiled.

Corrine told Willie Lee to go to the backyard ahead of her. "Start feeding the rabbits, and I'll help you in a minute," she said, and hung back to say goodbye to Ricky Dale, who was getting his bike. His black dog waited a few feet away, watching with his stupid-puppy-looking expression. The kick hadn't made him any smarter.

"Thanks for takin' us along to see the horses," Corrine said.

"Yeah."

She thought he was looking at her as oddly as he had Willie Lee.

"I'm glad your Beau was just knocked out," she said, watching his face closely.

He looked down at his bike. "Yeah. Me, too." Then his eyes came up—they were very green, looked like cat's-eye marbles. "I think maybe he wasn't just knocked out, Corrine. I think maybe he was dead, and that maybe Willie Lee brought him back to life."

Corrine chose her words. "Well, I don't know about that." She regarded him with a raised eyebrow, the way Aunt Marilee could do to someone. "But I do know that if we tell that story, everyone will think we made it up. And they'll think we're crazy. Some people already look down on Willie Lee as being half-crazy."

His shoulders dropped, and his eyes shifted, thoughtful like, to the ground.

"Don't tell anyone about what happened, Ricky Dale. Just don't tell." She started it as a plea, but then she added firmly, "I won't back you up, if you tell. I'll say you're lyin'."

She gazed at him in a way to let him know she meant business. In that moment, she felt exactly like she imagined her aunt Marilee did, which was knowing and doing whatever it took to protect Willie Lee.

Ricky Dale wet his lips, but she couldn't read his expression. Then he nodded and turned his bike toward the street. Halfway along the walk, he stopped and looked over his shoulder. "I don't think Willie Lee is crazy."

She didn't reply, and he got on his bike.

She turned then and went up the steps, pausing at the top to hang on to the porch post and watch Ricky Dale pedal off down the street, with the black dog running behind him.

Eleven

Off with the old, on with the new . . .

What was wrong? He and Marilee were to be married. They were getting along fine. No arguing. Comfortable.

The problem was the word "comfortable." *It* was not comfortable.

It was like there were questions buzzing around their heads now when they were together.

It was as if she were saying things that he could not hear.

They hadn't made love since before Christmas.

It wasn't required, he argued with himself. He had never considered sex the proof of love. Hadn't he loved Barbara Ann Jewel in senior high, and he hadn't had sex with her, simply *because* he had loved her so much. Plus, he had been terrified of the consequences, he admitted. In those days a person went straight to hell for even touching his own private parts, not to mention a woman's. Kissing was okay, but keep the tongue out of it, too, or you went to hell.

Of course, he had by the age of sixteen dared all of it, and he hadn't gone to hell. He'd gone to heaven. Well, until later, when there would be all sorts of squirmy feelings and complications. Growing up meant hard lessons, but he was far from that now. What was going on with him about this thing? He was an adult man; he should be able to understand. But that was a pitiful joke played on humankind. Did anyone ever come to understand enough?

He thought of how he had felt with Marilee in the porch swing, that last time they had been alone. Why in the world had he acted like such a fool?

He had wanted her so badly right then. Every part of him had longed and clamored to bury himself in her sweet warmth. To take succor in her rich womanliness. In fact, he swelled at this very moment with the memory and desire, as his mind quickly took off with images of their hot and sweating bodies entangled in sheets made damp by their lovemaking.

A chill swept him. The desire scared him afresh, as it had then. The wanting, the need, seemed not to have an end. It was like looking into an endless black pit that threatened to swallow him should he get one step closer.

And Marilee was backing away from him. There was no evidence in her manner of this, he argued with himself. Yet he could feel it.

Stuart James did not help matters. Not that Tate felt actually threatened by the man, but he did not at all like the way James kept looking at Marilee, as if he was about to scoop her up and run off. Tate kept having the urge to punch the man.

At least that urge he could understand, he thought with a loud sigh.

"What are you sighing about?"

His mother had come into the kitchen, quietly, in her soft-soled ballerina slippers that she wore when doing her yoga.

"Oh, nothin'." He didn't want to resent his mother being in the house. He loved his mother. But sometimes she made him feel like a child again. Would that ever end? "I've been working on an editorial. Havin' trouble comin' up with something interesting." He hid his face in his cup, draining the last of the coffee.

"They don't all have to be Pulitzer prize winners." She put a cup of water in the microwave and pushed the buttons. "Maybe you need to skip an edition or two. You know, your readers might more appreciate your column after a bit of absence."

He frowned, not liking the thought at all. What if his readers decided they didn't miss his column? It was his paper; he wanted his name in it. Besides, use it or lose it, so the saying went.

This thought was like a splinter into his mind.

He had not done well at being a husband the first time around. And since his divorce, he had not had a long-term relationship with a woman. He could count on three fingers the number of women he had slept with in the over fifteen years since his divorce. He always wondered if men exaggerated this part of their lives.

Once again alone, he sat himself at the kitchen table and his notebook computer. Put his fingers on the keys. Writing, he knew, did not depend on inspiration. Writing came from application. Just write, and the ideas would then begin, not the other way around.

Was this the answer to his relationship with Marilee, too? And to his fears? He faced the fear of writing by the doing. Would this work with the black hole of uncertainty that sucked at him?

He wondered this as he typed out what came to mind, a garbled sentence, but within ten words, he was forming ideas and putting them on the page.

Half an hour later, as he finished up his editorial, his mother came through lugging a white plastic trash bag. She informed him that she had cleaned out the towel closet and the medicine cabinet.

The medicine cabinet? He hoped his shaving cream and razors and aspirin were not in the trash bag.

"Do you know, I found Milk of Magnesia bottles in the bathroom closet, with a fifteen-year-old date? Muriel had some definite problems with keeping house."

He had seen the blue bottles in the far back of the deep closet. He hadn't thought they were bothering anything.

With some amazement, he watched as she simply opened the back door, threw the bag out, then closed the door again, turned and immediately demanded of him: "Why have you not done anything around here?"

"I haven't even been here a full year," he said, feeling the odd need to defend himself. "And I did have a newspaper to get on its feet."

She likely didn't understand the magnitude of the job he had taken on.

"Between Marilee and the newspaper, Mom, I've been fully occupied."

His thoughts followed with: And it was easier to spend most of his time over at Marilee's. He *liked* being over at her house.

Quite suddenly he was seeing the dreary old house through his mother's eyes. The only rooms he had used at all were his bedroom, the bathroom and the kitchen. He had an aversion to the other rooms, he realized.

The big old Porter house had previously belonged to his cousin, Muriel Porter, who had also owned the paper. She had sold both to Tate and left town, and when Muriel had left town, she had carried away with her only her clothes, and no more of those than she could fit into two full-size suitcases and an over-nighter. When Tate had arrived the previous spring, the closets had been crowded with clothes that looked to have belonged to at least two generations, the rooms filled with heavy furniture that possibly dated from the early part of the century, and the walls decorated with wallpaper not much newer, and aged photographs and memorabilia from a bygone era.

He realized his mother was speaking.

"There wasn't room for Muriel in this house. There was too much of her father and mother and stepmother in here. God knows they were a brooding bunch. E. G. Porter clung to every last dollar and possession of his pitiful life, until he lost it." She rubbed her shoulders and cast a disdaining eye around the kitchen.

Tate, following her gaze, saw wallpaper peeling in the corner and the dingy paint on all the woodwork.

"It is hard to breathe in this house," his mother said. "Muriel was chokin' to death here. And now all you've done since you came is bring old junk from your old life and add it all in. There is no room for new life, because of all the old dead hanging around."

His mother could get some far-out ideas.

His mother looked at him in that way she had that indicated she saw things inside him.

"I never had a house before," he said.

Maybe what he meant was that he had never made such a commitment before, not to a house, nor to creating a family life.

"Are you here to stay?"

"Yes," he said with some aggravation. "Marilee and I have talked about the house." Yes, they had. "There are lots of changes we'll be making. We're goin' to have another bathroom installed down here under the stairs, get everything painted."

He left off, unable to recall what exactly they had spoken of. Their discussions had been the sort of talk people indulge in when they're dreaming out loud.

"Life is a flow, Tate. When you hang on to things, you dam up the flow. Discard what is no longer used . . . what no longer *suits*," she said in an emphatic manner, "and you make way for the new and better and perfectly suitable to enter. Do you really need an antique refrigerator?" she asked, putting her hand on the old Kelvinator.

Without waiting for an answer, which Tate was trying to come up with, she came toward him and touched his arm.

"Let go of the old life and start with the new, Tate. Simply begin."

After several long seconds, he said, "Yes, you're right," and bent and kissed her cheek.

He started out of the room, then paused at the doorway. "What will I do when you are gone?" he asked her, struck suddenly to the core with the horrendous thought.

"What makes you think I'm goin' first?" she snapped at him, adding her saucy grin.

He shook his head and walked out, his eyes misting over, thinking about the foolish assumption that there came a day a man got too old to listen to his mother. He had not reached that stage. Maybe because his mother kept one step ahead of him at all times. One step ahead of just about everybody, really.

In his bedroom, from the top drawer of his dresser, he brought out the black velvet ring box. He opened it and looked at the band inside that matched the diamond ring on Marilee's finger.

With this ring, I thee wed. That was what he had thought when he slipped the engagement ring on her finger. He had, somewhere in the past days, forgotten that. He had made his commitment to her, and then gotten sidetracked.

Possibly commitments had to be reconfirmed each day.

Replacing the ring in the drawer, he stood looking around for a full minute, assessing the situation with the eye of a man of renewed conviction.

Then, moving in long strides, he went to the bedside table and pulled out a well-worn leather address book, flipping through it until he found the number for the travel agent he used most often. Guy, down in Houston. He dialed, and when Guy came on the line, he told him to put together a vacation at Disney World for two adults and two children. "The best rooms, the best wine, the best . . . well, you get it. This is a trip for a lifetime," he told the young man. He was already in debt; going deeper didn't seem a problem.

As he said goodbye, his eye dropped down the short page of the worn address book and stopped on his ex-wife's address and number. He had not used it in some ten years. Yesterday, dead and gone. He ripped out the address and tore it into small pieces, then tossed it into the trash basket.

Again he surveyed the room. Somewhere he had read that the bedroom set the tone for the marriage. Should start off on the right foot— make this an incredible room, since he hoped what went on in here would be pretty incredible. A room for lovers.

A room for his fair love, for the heart of his heart, for the wife he would love as he loved himself.

But, and here was a daunting dilemma, he had no idea how to bring about such a room, or quite what Marilee would find suitable for incredible happenings.

A knock sounded at the door, and his mother poked her head inside. "Here, dear. I knew I saved this card for a reason. It's the card of an interior decorator in Dallas. I used to go to yoga class with her mother. Delightful lady. Liked colors. I imagine her daughter will be equally adept at colors and such."

"I was just thinking about a decorator," Tate said, slowly taking the card.

"Oh, I'm sure you were. The memory of that card just popped into my mind." She glanced around the room. "God knows we need some help here." She swept out in her usual sweeping manner.

The name printed on the card, in iridescent turquoise, was Honey Moon. "Specializing in personal expression and harmony in environments."

Sounded really New Age.

Taking a deep breath, he picked up the telephone. Never let it be said that he wasn't ready to move right along with the modern era.

He went through several assistants, but stuck to his guns in his intention to go to the top and speak to Honey Moon herself. If nothing else, he wanted to know what a woman with such a name sounded like.

"Yes, this is Honey Moon." Her tone made him think of moonlit nights in the bayou, just the type of interior decorator he suspected he needed.

He explained his need, and, much to his surprise, she told him she could do all the work from Dallas. "I have clients all over the country. I will have everything delivered and set up by emissaries."

Emissaries? Sounded expensive. He had good credit, thus far.

She said, "I will e-mail you a questionnaire. Fill it out, skip no questions. Make a drawing of your bedroom, and include the directions north, south, etcetera. Send that and a picture of you and your intended bride. Don't fax those. Send them FedEx."

He didn't think he would have been surprised if she had requested a lock of Marilee's hair.

A shrill buzzing split the air, followed by what sounded and felt like a wrecking ball slamming into the house.

Marilee, reacting in the fashion of someone deeply in thought, as she was with the article she was writing about rabies in the state, jumped and let out a "Yaaa!"

Abandoning her chair, she raced into the laundry room, where the washer was halfway across the floor and into takeoff position. She threw herself atop it in an attempt to hold it down, while pulling out the knob. It halted abruptly, as if shot dead.

Whew. Catching her breath, she glared at the machine, wondering how it could barely wash clothes but could manage to walk a good two feet.

It probably was due to the strength of the quilt from Willie Lee's bed. She should have taken it to the laundry but had not wanted to take the time, so she had stuffed it into her large-capacity, but not large enough for quilts, fifteen-year-old model that she had purchased from her neighbor Leon Purvis when, in an effort to bribe his wife into not leaving him, he had bought her a brand-new and sparkling Kenmore washer and dryer set. His wife had been appeased—indeed, had sang Leon's praises for about a year—but eventually she had left him anyway to become a cross-country truck driver who apparently never had to bother doing her own laundry but used drop-off service.

She thought longingly of the washer she had seen in the latest *Better Homes and Gardens* magazine. It loaded from the front, like a commercial washer, and handled quilts and bedspreads with ease, so the advertising stated. It cost a mint.

She could buy one when she married Tate, came the whisper into her mind, followed closely by the question: Would Tate mind her spending so much money on a washer?

Was she marrying Tate for a washer?

This dismaying and guilty thought sliced through her and was followed immediately by another: Would marrying him be in vain, if he wouldn't let her buy a washer?

She did not like to think of herself as a woman who married for appliances. Of course that wasn't why she was marrying Tate.

Although she would have to concede that it was a hard world, and women had married for less convenience than an appliance, she thought, just as the children burst in the back door, Willie Lee saying, "We are back from Mis-ter Win-ston's, Ma-ma."

"I can see that. Did you have a good time?"

"Yes."

"Take your shoes off, Willie Lee," said Corrine, always neat. "We fed the rabbits and cleaned their cages before we came in."

"You two have been busy this mornin'." Marilee shoved at the washer, and Corrine, familiar with the machine's idiosyncrasies, stepped beside her to help move it back into proper position. Marilee jumping on one corner was required to get it level again.

"Hors-es have long necks," Willie Lee said. "I pet-ted the baby. She lik-ed me. The mo-ther lik-ed me, too, but not too much."

Marilee repositioned the quilt and started the washer; it wobbled like a chair that had lost a leg, but it ran okay. She went to make the children peanut butter and jelly sandwiches and to listen to tales of their experience with the horses. Talking of horses made her think of what Parker had told her about there being more cases of rabies in horses and cattle than in dogs or cats. She couldn't find a pencil to jot down the thought.

"It's in your hair," said Corrine, the ever-helpful.

She jotted the thought on a napkin, stuck the pencil back in her hair for future notations and went back to being a mother, passing bread to the children. "Go on. What else?"

Willie Lee cocked his head and said, "They smell-ed like sun-shine. They poop a lot, but it does not stink so much like dog poop. And the mo-ther is grumpy."

"She is?" She thought proudly that Willie Lee was doing good these days spreading his peanut butter on the bread.

"Yes. She kick-ed Beau. Hard."

"She did? Who's Beau? Is he hurt?" Becoming alarmed, she looked to Corrine for explanation.

"Just Ricky Dale's dog . . . stupid puppy. He was annoyin' the mare. He's okay."

"Oh, well, good." She had the distressing thought that perhaps she had been negligent in allowing the children to go alone to see the horses. Some horses could be dangerous, and she had not even considered this, being preoccupied with laundry and writing to earn a living.

"He got dead-ed, but he is o-kay."

He got deaded?

The doorbell rang. "Hey . . . anyone home?"

It was Stuart's voice. He came into the kitchen at the same instant the washer had another fit. Marilee and Corrine raced into the laundry room and threw themselves on the washer to hold it down, Marilee fumbling to turn it off.

Into the resulting quiet came Stuart's voice. "What's wrong with it?"

"Overload," Marilee said.

She doubted that the man had ever operated a washing machine in his life. At least not a private one.

There he stood, her debonair ex-husband, with his hands casually slipped into the pockets of his slacks, not a hair out of place, and wearing a perfectly starched cotton shirt and sharply creased chinos, done up at some hot, steamy laundry out of his view. He could have stepped out of a glossy catalog for high-priced travel clothes, while she, leaning desperately on a washer, with sweat curling her hair that she was not certain she had combed that morning, and wearing a worn T-shirt and jogging pants, felt she could be cited as justification as to why men ran off with their secretaries.

The pencil fell out of her hair and clattered to the floor.

Stuart bent to retrieve it. She saw the silky, shiny silver hairs at the top of his head as he did so. As he handed her the pencil, he chuckled and suggested that she was no match for a washing machine. This comment and accompanying laugh struck her in a fateful, wounded place.

She said, "I'm going to take a hot bath. Children, you can take naps

or watch television. Stuart . . ." She grabbed the basket filled with
clean clothes and jammed it at him. "You can fold clothes. And when I
get out of my bath, we're going to have a talk."

She strode past him, leaving the fumes of her anger in the passing,
and leaving Stuart, thoroughly bewildered as to what he had said
wrong, holding the basket.

He looked into it. There were lacy panties on the top. And bras.
How did one fold a bra? He did not do his own laundry, except for
washing out underwear and a shirt now and again while on a shoot in
some wild yonder, and it had been years since he had been out in the
wild yonder.

He looked down to see the girl, Corrine, staring up at him. He often
found her watching him with her eyes deep and dark as those of the
old witchy-women back in the Cajun bayou where he had spent his
childhood, then escaped. Gave him the willies.

"How about I give you, say—" he checked his pocket "—three
bucks, and you fold these things?"

He thought for a surprising instant that she was going to refuse, but
then she said, "Okay," and reached to take the basket. It was a load for
her, but she seemed adept. She took it to the kitchen table, then turned
to him and held out her hand.

"You fold them first."

She shook her head and kept the hand out. He put dollar bills in it.
"Smart girl."

Some minutes later he had sat himself on the couch, idly watching
cartoon figures that Willie Lee liked on television and wondering exactly what he should reveal to Marilee when they talked. He had
hoped to make better inroads into her good graces before he had to reveal the state of his health. Or ill health, as was the case.

He had sent her roses, but she hadn't brought them home from the
office. He had been trying for a romantic candlelit dinner for two, but
he couldn't seem to get her away from a crowd of people. He had begun to think of a picnic, which was to have been his proposal this afternoon.

Then her voice echoed in his thoughts: "We're going to have a
talk."

He began to feel a little panicked. He wasn't ready for any deep,
calling-to-account conversation. He just wanted to make up to her,
somehow, to have things okay between them, so that she would feel
kindly toward him when he told her the truth of his situation.

The girl appeared in front of him, stuck an opened magazine toward him and tapped it with her finger. "Aunt Marilee would like one of thesc."

He stared at her a moment, then took the magazine and looked at what she showed him, an advertisement for a washing machine. "This one?"

"Yes. And you might want to get the dryer, too."

Although Corrine could not name the desire that drove her, she felt a longing to take care of her aunt Marilee, if she could possibly do so, in the same manner that she looked after Willie Lee. In some general way she had the idea that they would all be better, no matter what happened, to get a washing machine while the getting was good.

She was pleased when Mr. James poked his head in the kitchen, where she folded clothes at the table, and said in a very rushed manner, "Tell your aunt Marilee that I'll be back later." He winked. "I'm going to get her a surprise."

Marilee slathered on her best face lotion, blew her hair dry and billowy, and whipped on her makeup, doing the full job. Lastly she chose Sahara Sunset Red lipstick. With all this, she was putting on every bit of confidence she could rake up. She had a few things to say to Mr. Stuart James, and she would do best to look competent when she spoke.

Dashing in her robe from the bathroom to her bedroom, she slipped into soft jeans and a deep blue sweater with a draping boat-neck neckline. Sultry, but not too much. She spritzed White Shoulders on her neck and remembered how Tate always told her she smelled delicious when she wore it.

What was she trying to do?

She looked at her reflection in the mirror. She did not want to be a woman a man left, as Stuart had left her. She could not abide appearing like that.

That was yesterday. Let go of the resentment. Deal with today.

She tried, as if heaving an enormous rock from the middle of her soul. The feeling would not budge. And *today* she still did not want to be the sort of woman a man ran from. She did not want to be ashamed.

Straightening her shoulders, she stepped out into the living room, where she found Willie Lee and Munro asleep upon the rug in front of the television, and Corrine slouched in the big chair, reading.

"Where's Stuart?" she asked, casting a glance toward the kitchen.

"Oh, he left for a little bit," Corrine told her. "But he said to tell you that he'd be back later."

"How much later?"

"He didn't say. But I think he went to get you something."

"What? What did he say?"

"Oh, I don't know. He just said he was going out to get you a surprise."

Stuart had never once given her what she needed, Marilee thought, which was his undivided attention.

Twelve

Of love, women and washing machines . . .

Aunt Vella called. "Is now a good time to come over? I have some bridal magazines for you, and I want to talk to you." Vella had learned, most especially in the last year, to say things straight out.

"I guess so. What do you want to talk about?"

Holding the telephone between her shoulder and her chin, Marilee dipped a peppermint tea bag into a cup of steaming water. She could only stomach herb tea when the lowest of moods came on her. Those moods were beyond even the ministrations of chocolate. Stuart's inclination to keep leaving her, which had gone on throughout their entire marriage, when he had frequently left her places—stranded at hotels waiting for him; stranded out at back-country groceries, waiting for him; and even once stranded at an airport overnight, waiting for him—until one day he told her he was going and would not return, so there was no need to wait, seemed to overwhelm her, as fresh as when she had been married to him.

"Well, about Stuart being here, for one thing. I had to hear about that from Julia J.T., who also told me that Tate's mother has come up from Texas." Her aunt's voice betrayed hurt.

"We've all been busy," Marilee said, then thought to ask, "Who's Julia J.T.?"

"Our postmistress and self-appointed society reporter, Julia Jenkins-Tinsley. I get so tired of saying that entire name. Why doesn't she pick one or the other and stick with it? Julia says Frank Goode told her Stuart has paid for a month out at the Goodnight."

"He has?" So there was a strong possibility that he truly would be back. The knowledge, curiously, did not lighten her mood.

"You didn't know?"

"He hasn't said. We haven't had time to talk, either." The peppermint tea burned her tongue.

"Well, that's what Julia says, and Julia is usually accurate. I'll be there in five minutes."

Marilee hung up and wondered if she ought to go ask Julia just where Stuart had gone that afternoon, and when he would return.

Vella Blaine had seen her niece only a scant few brief times in the past month, as they had both been very involved with their own business. Vella's business had constituted what she thought of as getting a life. This endeavor had begun last summer, when she had thrown her husband Perry out of the house. Since their reuniting had not proved fulfilling, she had worked to accept the marriage as it was and gone on to make a life she could possibly stand to live, while remaining as Perry's wife. She could not bear to throw him out again. That was too much upheaval for both of them, having been married for forty-six years. The guilt was too much for her to bear, because she recognized her fault in causing Perry to become dependent on her in the ways of everyday living. He had no idea what to do on his own, couldn't even keep his clothes clean. And she did love him. That remained, despite being bored to death by him.

Yet living with him and having so little in common, most especially no sexual relations at all, was killing her. She sought expression for the more lively side of her nature in the venue of classes in gardening and landscape design, researching healthy cooking, and encouraging herself into the new woman she longed to be.

That was why, when Marilee saw her, her eyes widened. "You got your hair cut."

"Oh, yes. Like it?" Vella touched the back of her smoky-colored hair. Always short, it was now very, very short and enhanced with hair gel in the modern manner. And today she wore painter's jeans and a large cotton sweater. Being a big-boned woman, she had rarely ever worn pants. She always felt too prominent in them. But she decided it was okay to be prominent, and she liked the loose jeans.

Her niece was gazing at her, taking it all in. "Yes. It looks wonderful on you . . . but I'm glad you didn't dye it," she said of the hair. In fact, Marilee thought she might not be able to stand it if her aunt showed up with bright black or orange hair.

"Oh, no . . . I don't have time for that stuff. Here are the bridal magazines. Belinda snatched them from the magazine deliveryman." She liked to point out whenever her daughter did something thoughtful for someone, as usually Belinda did not stir herself on anyone's account but her own. "He regularly only leaves two different ones at the store, but she got you all he carried on his truck—five in all. There ought to be some good ideas in them."

As she spoke, Vella sat herself down. She observed her niece and

saw the tea bag in the saucer. "Are you drinking herb tea?" Her observation turned sharper; things were deep if Marilee was past chocolate.

"Yes," Marilee answered in a tired voice.

"What's wrong?" Vella knew her niece well; she had been more of
a mother to Marilee than her own mother. Heaven knew her sister-in-
law had tried, but, as a mother, Norma Cooper had always been a
square peg trying to fit into a round hole. She had never grown up herself. Some people simply were not cut out for parenthood, and it was
too bad those people could not figure that out before they had children.

"Oh, nothing."

Vella sat there.

Marilee's gaze came up and met Vella's. "Stuart comin' back seems
to have dredged up some annoying old feelings."

"That's usually the way of it."

"Well, it's silly. I got past this years ago. I was a little surprised
when he showed up. Here I had not had a word from him in almost
two years, and he shows up. Now, of all times."

"A bit rude to be so startling," Vella put in. "What if you hadn't
been at home? What if it had been your wedding day, or you were off
on your honeymoon?"

"I don't imagine that would have bothered him. And I wish I *had*
been gone. Then I would not have to go through this now." Anger vibrated in her voice, and she lowered her eyes. "You know, I am wantin' him to have regrets for what he gave up . . . wanting him to want
me now that I don't want him and he can't have me, and I'm feeling
the hurt of him leaving me all over again, and worryin' that he needs
somethin' from me . . . and I don't have it to give. It is just plain nuts,"
Marilee added emphatically.

"But it *is* human." Vella had grown to the age where she was generally surprised when human beings *did* make sense. "Feelings are feelings, sugar. They are not good or bad or rational, they just *are*. And
they are indicators of things going on within us that need to be dealt
with."

Marilee sighed. "I know."

Vella didn't think her niece did know. People were all the time saying they knew, when they really didn't.

"It is wearing. I do not have time for this." Marilee raked her hand
through her hair with agitation.

Vella observed her, then asked, "Where's Tate today?" and glanced
at the door, as if he might appear any minute. In fact, Tate Holloway
had been in this house most times whenever Vella had stopped by in

the past months. He had pursued Marilee with an uncommon single-mindedness possessed by few men when it came to a woman.

"He was working when he called this mornin'. We both were. I don't know about this afternoon." She turned her eyes to the clock. "I suppose he and Franny will call about supper. I have no idea what to have for supper."

"Franny—that's his mother, right? I guess she came up to get a look at you. Julia says she is from Texas and is very artsy."

"She is . . . and quite pretty, and very nice."

Vella noted the warmth in her niece's voice and experienced a prick of pique, which she found highly annoying. She was a grown woman, and certainly too adult to be touched by such a shallow thing as jealousy of another woman.

She said, "I'll have to meet her. I heard she had coffee with Winston the other mornin'." Ah, there was the needle poking again, just with the telling. But Vella's relationship with Winston was over . . . over before it had become anything, because it never could.

"Oh, really?"

Vella changed the subject. "What about Stuart?"

Marilee played with the earring in her lobe in an absent manner. "He hasn't changed all that much. He's thinner. Older. But it's sort of like time has not touched him."

"Hmm . . . that sounds like Stuart." Vella had never thought there was much inside Stuart that time could touch. "How'd it go between him and Tate?"

Marilee shrugged. "Tate was cordial. You know Tate."

"No one can be as cordial as Tate when he makes up his mind to be. Sometimes it's annoying. He makes everyone else look petty." And it made Tate appear untouchable at times, she thought. "Nothing like a good foolish blowup to make a person be real and alive."

Marilee didn't appear to be listening. They each fell silent for some moments.

Then Vella asked about how arrangements were going for the wedding. She noted that Marilee looked almost surprised at the question.

"Well . . . we have an appointment with Pastor Smith on—" her gaze went to the calendar hanging by the telephone "—oh, tomorrow afternoon. I'd forgotten. Do you suppose you could baby-sit? Maybe Franny could stay with the kids."

Her niece was definitely distracted about the matter, Vella thought.

"I have an appointment," Vella said, feeling vaguely guilty, but not guilty enough to call off her appointment—the tall, thick-shouldered image of a man filled her mind—about which she did not intend to elaborate, but Marilee didn't ask, anyway.

"What about the invitations?" she asked. "I'll be glad to help you address them."

"I haven't gotten them yet."

Vella did not think this adequate. "Have you made a list of those you want to invite?"

"Well . . . there isn't a long list. You and Uncle Perry. The kids, of course. Everyone at the paper. Charlotte's going to stand up with me, and Parker is Tate's best man. Mama and Carl are going to be out of town—"

"They are?" Vella cut in.

Marilee nodded. "They're goin' on a Caribbean cruise. It's all set."

Vella didn't think she should criticize Marilee's mother to her face, and, in fact, she didn't think Norma would add all that much but demands if she did attend the wedding.

"Oh. And where are you and Tate plannin' on goin' for your honeymoon?"

"I don't know. We haven't decided."

There was simply too much undecided to suit Vella. She wondered if she should point out that Marilee was not giving this wedding anywhere near sufficient attention. It was going to be an important milestone in her life—entering a second marriage, the second chance of a lifetime, and she wasn't likely to get another at her age, not to mention that half the town would be coming to the ceremony, formally invited or not. Tate had been going around inviting people at the same time he had been showing off the engagement announcement. This was Tate's manner. And so many people loved Tate and Marilee and would want to celebrate with them. Marilee could not see this. Marilee rarely saw how beloved she was by many people, who remembered her from childhood, and who had read her writings in the newspaper each week for years and thought of her as their very own Marilee.

The next instant Vella realized she herself had not been giving sufficient attention to the moment, when Marilee's expression crumbled like a clay figurine shot with a BB gun, and she dropped her head to her arms on the table and sobbed.

Vella quickly pushed the swinging door closed, not wanting to awaken Willie Lee and Corrine, who had fallen asleep with her book on her chest. She filled a glass of water for Marilee, then on second thought she drank it herself and ran another for her niece.

Her niece cried for quite an amazing amount of time. When she seemed to be drying up, Vella said, "Here, sugar, have a glass of water and a tissue, and tell me what this is all about."

Marilee blew her nose fully. "Oh, my mascara is probably all over my face." She got up and looked in the mirror and moaned.

"Marilee," Vella said firmly, "quit worryin' about your looks and tell me what is going on with you. You are about to be married to a wonderful man and start a wonderful new life, and here you haven't made one arrangement and you're cryin' your head off."

Her niece sighed and sat down heavily, dropping her hands between her legs. "I don't know where to begin with this wedding. Stuart and I were married by a justice of the peace. I have never been involved with a wedding."

"That is easily solved. I will help you. Most of it we can contract out." Vella's time at landscaping classes had her using terms like contract out. "What else is the matter?"

Then Marilee shook her head. "I'm so angry at Stuart. I hate feeling so angry. It was all so long ago. It's just stupid, and Tate and I . . ." She shook her head. "Oh, I don't know what's wrong. Just nerves, I guess."

Vella regarded her with an expectant eye. "Nerves, you guess?"

Her niece shook her head and bit her bottom lip, looking teary again.

It came out from her then, haltingly and in great confusion, something about how Tate didn't seem interested in making love, or they didn't have time, but as far as Vella could gather, Marilee was very interested. Or maybe not. Vella got so annoyed at the confusion of messages she was getting that she said, "Which is it? You want sex, or you don't?"

Her tone was rather sharp, and she instantly regretted it. She herself knew very well what confusion a person could get into over the many facets of a relationship with a man.

Marilee looked startled. "Oh, I do." Her gaze wandered again. "I want Tate badly, but . . . well, we *are* busy, and Tate doesn't seem all that interested. Well, if he were, wouldn't he insist on us finding time? Of course the children . . . and then, well, Stuart has shown up."

There were too many wells in there to suit Vella. "You are having jitters, Marilee. And questions. It is to be expected in your situation."

"Yes, I am afraid, and I should have learned something from the past."

Vella saw they were at last getting to the heart of the matter.

"What if I'm makin' another mistake?" her niece wanted to know. "What if I'm not a person who can be married? I am quite good as a mother, but I just seem to mess up with tryin' to be a wife . . . a lover to a man. Why, I can't even attract my own ex-husband to stay and have a conversation with me."

"Stuart is not attracted to anything other than his own desires. Did Tate seem dissatisfied with you, when you have made love?"

Marilee reddened. "Well, no. But that was months ago. And it isn't the same as being married to a person. He just seems, well, far too accommodating without sex."

Vella, who noted the well, had her own experiences with and without sex; either could be trying and confusing.

She laid her hand atop that of her niece. "Sugar, you need to talk this all over with Tate. You are afraid because of old fears. Get them out where you can look at them, and they won't seem nearly so daunting."

Marilee's gaze slipped sideways.

Vella shifted in her chair, getting a firmer seat. This matter required conviction of attitude. "I have learned that one thing paramount in this life is to accept your feelings and speak them honestly aloud. Feelings are given to us by God. There's no need for shame over a one of them, not a one. Don't let them pile up inside, but deal with them as they come. Take them to God and confess them to Him, and you'll feel better immediately. Then deal with them with this man with whom you intend to spend the rest of your life. Start out straight and honest with exactly who you are.

"This is important, Marilee. Don't form the habit of hiding yourself from Tate, because you think what you feel is wrong, or because you don't want to hurt him. It isn't that you don't want to hurt him so much as you are afraid of yourself."

Marilee's eyes came up then, sparking. Vella was encouraged.

"Talk to Tate," she said again.

Marilee breathed deeply. "Yes, I will."

"Ohhh!"

Marilee had been rather listlessly going through the bridal magazines with her aunt, who was making a schedule of what they would need to accomplish, and when, for the wedding, when her eyes lit on a dress that caused that certain leap inside of her that happens when a woman recognizes the perfect outfit.

It was a wedding dress with a wide sweep of a neckline, cutting across the shoulders, much in the manner of the sweater she wore at that minute. Marilee adored tops that showed her shoulders, which she thought were one of her better features. The sleeves of the dress were long and slim, and the dress skimmed the body, then fell in a soft swirl just above the ankles.

"Now that's a dress for a *woman*." Aunt Vella's eyes shone with approval. "It is perfect for you."

"But not in white." Marilee had certain convictions about her wedding. "How do you think it would look in . . ." Eyes glued on the image, she tried various colors. "Dusty blue?"

"Hmmm . . ." Aunt Vella looked at Marilee, then looked at the photograph on the page. "Apricot. Deep, warm apricot."

"Oh, yes." Certainty and pleasure washed over her.

"And we'll take this picture down the street to Margaret Wyatt and get her to make it up. Doesn't look too hard."

"I didn't know she made gowns."

"Uh-huh . . . Margaret made the costumes for the senior play this year, and the gowns for each of Ramona Stidham's daughters' weddings. She is excellent. Then we will be able to tell Fred Grace that we want all apricot roses. He'll handle that."

Marilee studied the dress on the glossy page, picturing her hair done up and herself wearing the dress, in apricot. Her heartbeat picked up a delighted tempo as it does in any woman who sees herself happily beautiful in a dress, all saucy and swirling around her ankles that swept up from strappy heels, smiling and gracious, and indeed capable of any endeavor required of her.

At that particular moment there came a rapping at the back door, and it opened, with Tate poking his head inside. "Hello . . . is my bride-to-be home?" He came inside, followed by Franny.

Marilee, still affected by seeing herself in the beautiful dress, went instantly to Tate, totally oblivious to Franny, and wrapped her arms around his neck and kissed him. She had meant it to be a simple kiss, but he held her fast and went all out.

"Well, don't mind us," said Franny, who went forward to Vella to hold out her hand and introduce herself.

Marilee, coming back to earth, pushed away from Tate, wondering what in the world had gotten into her.

There was no time to recover or smooth over, because just then the kitchen door swung inward, with Corrine following and announcing in a breathless manner, "There's a big truck comin' in the driveway!"

En masse, like a tidal flow, they all exited the kitchen and went through to the front windows to see what Corrine was talking about. It was a truck, the side emblazoned with Cooper's Appliances, the appliance store owned by Marilee's stepfather. Stuart was there speaking to the driver.

Marilee went to the door Tate had already opened and followed him out onto the porch to greet Stuart, who said quite grandly, "Make way for the new washing machine."

Well, mercy.

"It's the latest technology," James said to Tate. "Loads from the front. Won't go off balance. Can handle blankets and quilts."

"I see that," said Tate, who stood beside him, looking on from a safe distance so as to avoid being mowed over by female enthusiasm. The women were oohing and aahing and swarming over the washer and dryer like bees feeding on ripe honeysuckle.

"Marilee had her heart set on it," the man said of the washer. He was clearly pleased with himself.

Tate kept his mouth shut and his arms folded in front of him, although he was fairly certain that no one would condemn him for socking the guy who was attempting to seduce his fiancée with appliances.

"I can fit," Willie Lee said. He had crawled into the washing machine.

"Oh, you wild boy," Vella said. "Get out of there. What if it started?"

"I would get wet."

"It can't start without pushin' these buttons," said Corrine, who indicated the buttons, then put her face back into the instruction manual.

"Why don't you try it out, Marilee, while the appliance men are still here?" proposed his mother, who Tate would have thought would not have been in there, getting carried away. He considered his mother's enthusiasm very near betrayal.

"Good idea. Let's rewash Willie Lee's quilt."

Watching the women, Tate was put in mind of hens clucking over a new baby chick. He wished he could have gotten something back from Guy about the honeymoon arrangements. Surely a grand honeymoon would top a washer and dryer, although, observing the excitement, he wasn't certain that even carte blanche to Walt Disney World and breakfast in bed for a week could top this deal.

Marilee, her face glowing with pure rapture—yes, it was rapture, Tate saw—whirled around. "Oh, Stuart." This was her fourth *Oh, Stuart,* at least. "I've been wanting this very washer. How did you know?"

"A little bird told me," Stuart answered and winked at Corrine, whose expression also showed traces of admiration.

Stuart, who had little experience in buying presents, was thoroughly glad he'd gone all out with the washer and the matching dryer, too. Apparently two dozen long-stemmed roses didn't cut ice here in this country of motherhood and home-ownership.

He had a sense of a glimpse into a foreign world and was reminded of how Marilee had been during her first trip to Europe with him. She had looked at everything from the giant plane to the first-class accommodations to every bit of the foreign land with great wonder, and upon Stuart as a prince among men for giving her the world.

He had forgotten how it felt to be a prince among men, he realized. Each time Marilee's eyes lit on him, he experienced a sort of expansion of his entire being.

She kept saying, "Oh, Stuart," and regarding him with wonder and delight, and he kept expanding. He had the thought that maybe he had found the cure for his illness, that maybe he had gone into instant healing. At the very least, in that moment his sickness held no meaning for him at all.

When Tate announced, "I'm takin' everyone out to celebrate the new washer and dryer," Marilee instantly came out of her ecstasy over the new washing machine and realized the situation.

Tate was jealous. Always a man who liked to shine, he had stood back this entire time, while she had neglected him in her thrill over the washing machine. She felt immediately ashamed that an inanimate object could have gotten her so off track as to make her forget him, one of the most thoughtful men in the world and one who certainly didn't deserve being forgotten for a washing machine, no matter how wonderful.

She went to him, and quick thinking came to her aid, when she said the perfect thing. "Oh, thank you, sweetheart. What a wonderful idea. That way we can go out and celebrate this lovely wedding present Stuart has given us."

She beamed at Stuart, and he blinked.

Tate, instantly jumping onto Marilee's train of thought, said, "That's right. A present like this needs celebrating. Let us show our thanks, Stuart. Valentine's choice of restaurants certainly won't come up to those you've enjoyed throughout the world, but the Main Street Café does the best it can."

The idea met with enthusiasm from Aunt Vella and Franny, who appeared to have become friends on first sight. The friendship was stimulated by both women discovering they each liked onion burgers.

"I'll drive," Aunt Vella said, and directed everyone where to sit.

Willie Lee and Munro went back into the cargo area, while Corrine sat between Franny and Vella up front, and Marilee found herself crammed between Tate and Stuart in the back seat. Tate put his hand around her shoulders, while he leaned forward and tossed comments to Stuart, and Stuart batted them back, about like a tennis match going on in front of her face.

"So, how long are you goin' to be able to stay, Stuart?"

"I don't really have any schedule."

Marilee thought of what Aunt Vella had said about him paying for a month at the Goodnight. She didn't want to get into that, though.

"No assignment waiting?" Tate asked.

"No . . . I am working on the one about vintage motels. When I get enough together, I'll let you see if you want bits on ones in this area."

"I know we will. Maybe you'll want to stretch your stay until next month and come to our wedding."

Marilee listened carefully.

"I might be here."

In her robe and slippers, Marilee went through the dimly lit rooms, checking the front door, putting final dirty dishes into the dishwasher, checking the back door, all the while savoring the quiet of the house. Just her and the children, sleeping now, alone, at last.

If she was this relieved to be alone with the children, how would she manage when she married and Tate was present all the time? The thought was disturbing.

They would be over at his house, she thought, with an instinctive glance through the back door window glass, in the direction of the big Porter-Holloway house, which could not be seen through the rows of cedars.

Which was it—she could hear Aunt Vella's voice—Porter or Holloway?

Holloway, she thought firmly, and tried the name on for size: Marilee Holloway.

The girl, Marilee Justus, had been left so far behind that she sometimes could barely remember her. Marilee James, who had been married to Stuart, no longer existed, so it was right that the name passed on. It seemed there ought to have been a name between Marilee James and Marilee Holloway. Perhaps it was the right time, after all, for Stuart's visit, in order that she might, in a manner of speaking, hand him back his name.

Just then her gaze fell on the new washer and dryer. Smiling with pleasure, she ran her hand along the cool, smooth enamel surface of the washer, and remembered Stuart and how happy he had seemed at giving her this present.

She was deeply touched. Surely this was his attempt to make amends for his past neglect.

It would take a lot more than a washer and dryer to make up for nine years of abandonment.

Perhaps there was no way to make up for the hurt. Perhaps there was only moving past it. With forgiveness.

Thirteen

Where love comes great, so comes fear . . .

"**Y**our mother has a date with Winston?"

Tate nodded. "They're attending a play up at the senior center in Lawton."

"A play? What is it?"

"*Kiss Me Kate,* I believe."

She tried to picture this. Yes, she could see it, wigs, costumes and big bosoms.

Tate added, "And afterward they're havin' dinner at Christopher's. Mom was dolled up for the occasion. Wore her diamond earrings."

"Your mother seems to me to always be dolled up. She's drivin', I take it?" This would be nice for Winston, who wasn't allowed to drive himself anymore. Then she pictured Franny's sports car. "The MG?"

"I lent her the BMW. It's easier on Winston . . . who looked like a cool cat, too. His best Stetson, dark coat and string tie. Looked ten years younger."

Aunt Vella was busy, and Franny was off on her date. This meant the children would have to go with them to their consultation with Pastor Smith.

"What about Jenny?" Tate asked. Jenny was the teenager who had baby-sat for the children on a number of occasions.

"It's too short notice to call her," Marilee said.

There was a question in Tate's expression. She could almost hear him thinking: Why hadn't she reserved Jenny days earlier? Why had she not prepared for this meeting? In that annoying instant of clarity that one gets when facing oneself, she knew she had kept putting off any plans concerning this meeting with Pastor Smith.

"Where's Stuart?" Tate asked. "He's been here every day, and now he's not? Why don't we call him to come stay with the kids?"

Marilee didn't like the idea.

"Why not?" Tate observed her. "He's Willie Lee's father, Marilee.

And if he was going to *abscond* with Willie Lee, I imagine he would have done so before now."

Marilee did not care for the sarcasm in his voice.

Before she could whip out a reply, however, Willie Lee appeared in the kitchen doorway. "What is ab-ab-s-con-d?"

"Tate was just teasing, honey. Ab-scond. It means to carry away. Now, sugar, go get your jacket. We are all goin' to see Pastor Smith . . . yes, Munro, too, but he'll have to wait outside."

She shot Tate a pointedly raised eyebrow while waiting for Willie Lee to be out of earshot, after which she said, "No, I don't think Stuart wants to take off with Willie Lee, but neither do I feel confident that he could handle any crisis that might arise. Crises do arise at the most inopportune times, like when mothers are absent.

"And I am not telephoning him—" she spoke with careful diction, enunciating every one of her *g*'s, as was her habit when seeking to make a point "—because I do not consider him at my beck and call for baby-sitting . . . and because I cannot tell you of the countless times during our marriage when I would be waiting for him and would telephone him to find out where he was and when he was going to come, only to get no answer, or to have him say one thing and do another. I had not heard a word from him in two years before he decided to drop in. I am not calling him now."

Tate was staring at her, his eyes widening as her feelings tumbled out, unchecked, like so much water breaking a dam.

Immediately she turned her back, awash with self-consciousness. She had not known she felt any of it and was quite dismayed to have to look at her anger fresh, as if her intentions of forgiveness last night had never been.

"Come here," Tate said in a gruff manner, and then he had grabbed her arm, turned her and was hauling her against him. "The man should be horse-whipped," he said, his tone and words a soothing balm to her wounded spirit. And then he was kissing her in a way that caused her to slip her arms around his neck and kiss him ardently in return.

She gasped for breath when they broke apart, and her head spun, and she blinked back silly tears.

Tate whispered, "I am not such a fool as to ever set you aside, Marilee. I love you, and I won't ever let you doubt it."

"Oh, Tate."

She looked into his eyes, which were intent upon her, so dear and blue and hot as a day in midsummer. Words tumbled over themselves and jammed in her throat. She pressed her hand to his cheek.

Then a movement, a footfall, some motion, drew their attention to the doorway. Stuart stood there.

"Sorry to interrupt."

There he was, her ex-husband dropping in at will again.

Stuart's eyes moved from Marilee to Tate and back again. "Willie Lee asked me—if I understood him correctly—if I was going to abscond with him." He paused, gazing directly at Marilee. "I told him I hadn't planned on it."

Tate said promptly, "Well, good. Would you stay with the kids while we go to see the pastor about the wedding plans? Make yourself at home. There's a fresh pitcher of ice tea in the refrigerator."

Marilee found Stuart's reply of, "Uh . . . okay," far from reassuring.

"That's great," Tate said. "Thanks a lot, buddy. We won't be but an hour or so." He had hold of Marilee's hand and was leading her toward the door.

Tugging away, she insisted on jotting down the phone numbers for the parsonage and Tate's cell phone. "Just in case anything should happen."

Tate appeared with her coat, and as she slipped into it, she thought Stuart's expression was still a little hesitant and uncertain. He actually looked a little ill.

But then Corrine was there and saying, "I know Tate's cell phone number by heart, Aunt Marilee," with a logic and confidence that caused Marilee to smile and bend over to kiss her niece's cheek.

Tate took her hand again and hurried her through the living room, saying as they went out the door, "It's a beautiful day. Let's walk." He entwined his fingers in hers and smiled a smile that touched deep into her middle. What a bug she was for her moodiness of late. She so wished she could get a handle on that.

Corrine, who had followed, hung on the porch post and watched her aunt and Tate walk down the brick path to the sidewalk. Her gaze lingered on the adults, seeing Aunt Marilee's soft wool coat swing jauntily with her steps and how her aunt leaned her head briefly against Mr. Tate's shoulder. A great sense of satisfaction engulfed her. Somehow, whenever her aunt seemed happy, Corrine felt happy.

For another full minute she clung to the porch post, listening to birds chirp, looking up through the bare tree branches to the cloudless sky and feeling the warmth that promised spring was just around the corner. She went over and sat herself in the porch swing, at the edge, so that her feet would touch the floor; she pushed back and forth and prayed that she would never have to leave her aunt and Willie Lee.

Her imagination, given rare rein to visit the positive side, formed lovely pictures of life for all of them together, with Aunt Marilee as her mother and Mr. Tate as her daddy, and Willie Lee there needing her to look after him, flowers on the breakfast table, saying grace at meals. And having her own room, with a four-poster bed, like the one she had seen in *Southern Living* magazine.

Maybe she could even have a horse. Maybe they would move to a house out in the country. She pictured moving Mr. Tate's big house out in the country, and there was a red barn and a wooden corral, and inside it a horse for her, a painted pony, and a littler one for Willie Lee. And big trees surrounding the house, hovering over it as if stalwart protectors. It was all so beautiful and filled her heart so much that her breathing was squeezed.

Just then, a sound—a bicycle rattle—popped her eyes open. Here came Ricky Dale Oakes, speeding into the driveway, veering from the rear bumper of Mr. James's car and coming across the grass, braking at the foot of the porch steps. Corrine felt a flash of delight.

The way he said, "Hey, Corrine," in a hushed voice, like he had a secret, caused her wonder what was up. He parked his bike and took the steps two at a time. "I got—"

His words were cut off when his stupid black puppy, tongue lolling out of the side of his mouth, came pushing up past him and over to slobber on Corrine.

"Eww . . . get away from me, dog."

"Oh . . . here, hold this." Ricky Dale pulled a box from inside his jacket and shoved it at her. It was a big matchbox. Then he took his rowdy dog by the collar and led him off the porch, making him lie down at the foot of the steps.

Corrine looked at the matchbox. There was something inside, and it did not feel like matches.

Ricky Dale hopped back up on the porch and took the box, saying, "Look at this."

He pushed open the box. Why, there was a little bird inside. Its head came popping up.

"It's just a baby," Ricky Dale said in a hushed tone.

Corrine looked more closely. The little bird blinked its eyes and shook its little self, then fell over.

"I found it over at Mr. Winston's. I think it's wing is broken."

"Oh," Corrine said sadly. Then, "Why are you whisperin'?"

"Look, get Willie Lee out here and see if he can fix it."

Corrine stared at him. Then she shook her head. "No."

"Come on, Corrine. Let's just see what happens. Maybe it was coincidence that Beau got up after bein' kicked . . . but maybe Willie Lee did do somethin'. Let's just see what happens. I won't tell. I promise I won't."

She glared at him. She didn't think she could like him now, and this made her really mad at him, because she had begun to count on liking him and having him for a friend.

"Don't you want to see if Willie Lee can do it?" Ricky Dale said pointedly.

Her gaze, which had dropped again to the little bird in the box, flew upward to his eyes. They were the cat's-eye marbles again.

"We need to see, Corrine."

She did want to see, although she could not say that, so she just said, "Okay. You go on around back. I'll bring him out there." The backyard seemed a lot more private.

She slipped quietly through the front door. Willie Lee, with Munro lying against him, was watching his ant farm, over on the rug in front of the television. The action of explosions on the television arrested her briefly. It was a movie. On Pay-for-View. They almost never got to watch movies on Pay-for-View. Aunt Marilee considered most of them unfit for children's consumption. Apparently Mr. James found them fit for him.

But he wasn't in sight, and she wondered where he was. She pushed the front door closed and went to look in the kitchen, but upon passing the hall, she saw that the bathroom door was shut. Maybe she could get Willie Lee before he came out.

She raced on tiptoe over to Willie Lee, who she saw wore his red cape. "Willie Lee—" she knelt down and spoke in a hushed voice "—come on outside a minute."

"I am watch-ing my ants."

"I know, but you can come back and watch 'em. Come outside a minute. Ricky Dale has somethin' he wants to show you." She tugged at his cape.

"O-kaayy. Come on, Mun-ro."

They had reached the kitchen doorway when Mr. James's voice came from behind them. "Where are you kids goin'?"

Corrine turned to see him wiping his face with a washcloth, which struck her as curious, although her mind went on quickly to thinking up what to say. "Just out in the backyard. One of our friends is here."

"Well, don't be goin' off. I don't think Marilee would want you go-ing anywhere when she isn't here."

"We aren't." Corrine had Willie Lee by the hand and pulled him on through the kitchen and out the back door.

Ricky Dale, sitting on the bottom step, hopped up. "Hey, Willie Lee."

"Hel-lo."

Corrine saw with a little worry that Ricky Dale had closed the big matchbox again; she hoped the little bird wasn't smothered or squished.

This worry was relieved when Ricky Dale opened the matchbox, and the little creature fluffed itself up. It was amazing how much smaller the already small thing could become.

"A bird," Willie Lee said with delight, blinking rapidly behind his glasses.

The bird fluttered and fell over.

Ricky Dale said, "I think it has a broken wing. Can you fix it, Willie Lee?"

Willie Lee tilted his head, and his eyes went from Ricky Dale to Corrine. Then he looked back at the bird.

"Maayy-be."

Corrine noticed how small her cousin's hands were when they gently took the little bird. He showed it to Munro. "Lo-ok, Mun-ro, a little bird. Oh, it is ok-ay lit-tle bird-y. Do not be a-fraid. Mun-ro won't hurt you. He likes birds."

Corrine had a sudden worry about disease. She had heard that birds could spread disease, by lice or something. She hoped Willie Lee didn't catch something. It would be all her fault, if he did.

Willie Lee, holding the small creature in one hand, stroked its head with one of his fingers. Corrine watched his hand and finger, but then she noticed it seemed like the sun was shining on him. She looked upward. The sky was clear, but she couldn't see any particular shafts of sunlight.

She looked again at Willie Lee, and her skin prickled as she saw that his pale hair seemed so bright, and that his glasses had glare on them.

Just then Ricky Dale's stupid puppy let out a woof and lunged up on Ricky Dale, knocking him off-kilter. Munro, who obviously didn't want any excess woofing around Willie Lee, turned on the bigger dog and growled his displeasure.

"Be quiet, Beau. Sit!" Ricky Dale ordered, but the dog had already lain down.

Corrine, who had been distracted by Ricky Dale and his dog, found Willie Lee was opening his hand and giggling.

"It tick-les," he said. "Mun-ro, it tickles."

The bird was fluffing in Willie Lee's lightly cupped hands.

"Can it fly?" Ricky Dale asked breathlessly.

"I think so. Maayy-be."

Willie Lee opened his hands and lifted them. The bird fluttered, and then the wing that had before been bent, came out to match the other, once, twice, and then the little bird flew up in the air. Corrine, her heart in her throat, watched it fly, little wings batting the air as it made a short trip to the clothesline pole, where it perched, tilting its little head back and forth at them.

Munro gave a yip at the bird.

"It flew," Ricky Dale said.

Corrine breathed deeply and gazed at the bird. Then a movement, something, caused her to glance at the back door, and she thought she caught sight of what could have been Mr. James's white shirt.

They had formed the basic plan for the wedding ceremony and were at a lull when Marilee felt the hair on the back of her neck prickle. It was the sensation she had whenever she sensed, usually correctly, that her children were up to something or needed her aid. She told herself to not react foolishly, as her gaze went to the telephone on the pastor's walnut desk. The telephone, however, picked that fateful moment to ring.

Marilee jumped and looked expectantly at the pastor, who said nonchalantly, "Naomi will get it," and shifted in his chair, leaning forward with his forearms on his thighs.

Marilee, who had sufficient experience with synchronicity, had to restrain herself from snatching up the phone when it rang a second time.

Pastor Smith continued, "Well, then, now that we've got the actual wedding itself ironed out, I want to talk to you both about marriage in general." He held up his hands. "Now, I know that you two are adults well experienced with life and the problems that can come up. You both probably know far more than I do about living, but I don't see that as an excuse to give you two a cut-rate job." He grinned in a hopeful manner.

Marilee thought of how he was younger than herself by four years; he did seem happily married, however, with normally happy children. Five of them. How did he stay sane? Maybe he wasn't.

A knock at the door, and Naomi poked her head inside. "You need to take this call, dear."

Marilee watched the small, compact man go out, rather than take the phone right there at his desk, and, like a fast train south, her mind went from approving his forward thinking about the possible need for privacy to anticipating that the call concerned her children, that possibly something dire had happened.

Her thoughts were jerked from this vein by Tate, rising from beside her on the love seat and stepping over to the large potted fern at the window, where he poured the contents of his china cup. This action, which she had only seen on comedies, astounded her.

"Naomi makes the worst coffee I have ever tasted," he said in a hushed voice, returning beside her on the couch and setting his cup back in its saucer. "I don't like to disappoint her, though. She always seems so eager to please."

"I know. If she gives a choice, I usually ask for a cold drink." She gazed at her own half-finished cup and was considering getting up and tossing it in the fern, too, although there was the question of possibly killing the plant. She had waited too long, though, because Pastor Smith appeared back through the door.

At his smile, Marilee, remembering her concern for the children minutes before, felt reassured.

"Sorry for that interruption." Easing his khaki trousers, he resumed his seat in the chair across the coffee table from them. He gestured at their cups. "Would you two like more coffee?"

"Oh, no, one cup is just fine for me," Tate said instantly. "Keeps me awake."

The pastor regarded them. "Well, now, where was I?"

"Something about marriage," Marilee prompted. She had begun to feel the need to move things along in order to get done and get back to the children.

"Oh, yes. I thought I'd go over some of the points I like to make to couples getting married. Probably this is old hat to you both, like I said, but I like to do my job." He rubbed his hands together, as if warming himself up to the task. "Let me begin with the trickiest subject." A brief pause. "Sex."

Tate said, "Well, sir, that's always an attention-getter."

Marilee hoped she wasn't about to learn something about Pastor Smith that she would find either annoying or distasteful.

"Yes, it is . . . my point exactly," said the pastor, clearly satisfied that his point was appreciated. "Sex," he said, and rather loudly, his gaze moving from her to Tate, "has proven a good barometer for the state of a marital union. Falling in love is thrilling, but staying in love can be tiresome, and it requires attention. This is what commitment is about—paying attention.

The pastor was a man who talked with his hands, and now he swept the air with one. "Pay attention, and commitment naturally follows. If two people are interested in their sex life, paying attention to it, then likely the marriage is a happy one, based on honesty and openness with each other in all areas. If not, then the trouble is not in the bedroom, it just appears there, and it generally appears there earlier than people recognize, starting with inattention."

He took a breath and pointed with his finger. "Think about this, when either of you let yourselves get too distracted to pay open attention to each other, or quit being honest about your feelings. Don't deny your feelings, pay attention to them and speak of them."

Marilee experienced this curious crawling sensation up her spine at the word feelings.

"If you will pay attention and be totally honest in this one area of your life, likely you will be honest in all other things. It is sort of like me speaking of it first. Now that we've spoken of sex, I've got your attention, and we can go on much more easily to other things, can't we?"

Marilee, who realized that she had been anticipating some real revelations that hadn't materialized on the sex subject, found herself preoccupied with ideas of a sensual nature. She wondered what other subjects could successfully follow that of sex and still be heard. She caught more about honesty of feelings, and experienced that crawling sensation again, and the admonition to make actions match words, and about how marriage could on occasion be a grind . . . something in there about wheat kernels being ground to useable soft flour.

He ended by saying, "Read Psalm four. It's a good one. Now, let's have a word of prayer."

He put Marilee's and Tate's right hands together between his own and said, "God, bless these two hearts in union, and carry them through the next hectic weeks of bringing together a wedding. Amen."

What everyone appreciated about Pastor Smith's prayers was that he got to the point.

Fourteen

A picture is worth a thousand words. . . .

They had visited with Pastor Smith for barely an hour, but when she stepped out the front door of the parsonage, it almost seemed like another day to Marilee. The sky had become hazy, and a breeze had come up. She pulled the collar of her coat closed. Tate put his arm around her shoulders and gave her a squeeze. He looked like he was about to speak, but he did not.

She wished he would speak whatever was on his mind. That she couldn't seem to speak her own thoughts did not keep her from blaming him for not speaking his.

Oh, Lord, keep me from shrewishness.

They crossed the street in front of the church, and suddenly Marilee said, "Let's go inside."

The double doors of the sanctuary were unlocked. Marilee thought Pastor Smith unlocked them each morning and locked up each night. He had started the practice of opening the sanctuary every day shortly after he had gone away to a pastoral retreat and returned with a beard and to introduce guitar music into the services. The beard was short-lived, but the guitar music and open welcome to the sanctuary had remained.

Once a hobo had been found living in the sanctuary; he had been there for three days in the middle of the week. He had been extremely neat. Upon discovery, he said that he had come in for a retreat and felt much refreshed. The congregation had rallied to provide the man with assistance and a place to live, but the man, Hot-foot John, he called himself, said he was not a vagrant but a hobo and wanted to be on his way. The congregation outfitted him with brand-new clothes, a top-of-the-line backpack, food and fifty dollars in cash. After he had left, there had been discussion of keeping the sanctuary locked, but Pastor Smith had stood firm.

Marilee told Tate all this standing there in the vestibule, gazing into the sanctuary that was bathed in ethereal sepia tones from the hazy af-

ternoon light coming through the tall, gold glass at the top of the pic-
torial windows. When she had finished her tale, she realized she had
not said as much to him in weeks. Maybe she had never told him such
a lengthy narrative, and she could not imagine why she had done so
now. He gazed at her, as if questioning this, too.

Turning from him, she went into the sanctuary. He followed. Their
feet made no sound on the thick carpeting. She slipped into the back
pew, their regular place on Sunday. Tate slipped in beside her.

Her gaze was drawn to the front and the dark wood of the altar.
Everything was peaceful, empty of voices and movement.

"It's beautiful," she said.

"Yes."

They sat in silence for some minutes in which Tate began to bounce
his knee.

"Tate," she began, then stopped.

He took her hand in his and squeezed it.

Finally Marilee said, "I'm scared." She paused to search for a complete and understandable explanation of her feelings, in order to share
them as the pastor, and even Aunt Vella, had advised.

Before she could come up with this explanation, however, Tate
broke in, saying, "Well, me, too. I think only a numbskull would *not*
be scared. I've been a bachelor for most of my life, and here I am,
marryin' a woman who is ten years younger than myself."

Marilee, who had experienced a slice of annoyance at being interrupted, was surprised. "I don't even think about our age difference."

She realized she had held the expectation that Tate would soothe
her fears, and here he was putting more out there. She was irritated
with him for doing this, and irritated at herself for being irritated at
him. She also thought his concern a little petty.

"Ten years is not a great age difference," she said. "Lots of people
are ten years apart. Once people get to a certain age, a few years don't
mean anything."

"I don't want you to look around one day and realize that you're
married to an old man."

"I will be."

His eyebrows shot up.

"You will be old, Tate. Someday. And so will I. We can only hope
this proves the case, anyway."

Tate's expression turned reflective. "I believe you're right there."

Marilee's mind moved on to the fact that she was actually eleven
years younger than Tate. Odd how he took it as ten. Maybe, being

honest, she was somewhat glad to be a number of years younger, although speaking of this did not seem uplifting, so she let it go.

"I don't face being old very well," he said.

"I don't think any of us do, but I don't see the need to get all worked up over how things will be twenty years from now. Today is enough to handle."

Marilee spoke more sharply than she had intended, and her conscience pricked. She should apologize, but she did not, and sat there staring at the altar far in the front. Be honest with your feelings, the pastor had said. She would be—if she wasn't so confused about them.

"I want to marry you, Tate, and I'm scared to death, too." She turned to face him, and having said that much, continued to push the words from her mouth. "And I need contact with you, Tate. But whenever I've initiated contact with you, you always have to run off somewhere."

He blinked twice, as if he had no clue about this. She wondered how in the world he could not have a clue.

"We hardly have a minute to ourselves, Marilee," he said.

His frown bothered her. "We had quite a few minutes the other night in the swing, and you just up and ran off. The term is 'running.' That is what you did."

"We couldn't do anything in the swing. I thought it best not to let things get out of hand. There's no sense in gettin' tied in a knot."

"There's a lot people can do in a swing, underneath a blanket," Marilee said, surprising herself. Her cheeks burned. But she thought of what Pastor Smith had said about honesty. She wanted to be honest about what she thought. This thing needed attention.

"You simply didn't want to be . . . well, intimate with me. You wouldn't even get wrapped in the blanket with me. And before that, there was Wednesday morning in your car. You could have come in. We had the house to ourselves."

"I had things waiting for me at the paper . . . and you had work, too. You said that. You said you wanted to work."

"Don't you want to make love with me? Maybe we already have the intimacy problem the pastor was talking about. It is already showing up in the bedroom."

"We don't have a bedroom."

"We could have gone to your house . . . before your mother came. We could go off to a motel—to the Goodnight."

"Would you do that? Do you want it like that? Sneaking around?"

"Well, maybe not . . . I don't know." She could not nail down the difference between sneaking time alone in her house or sneaking it at the Goodnight but somehow there *was* a difference. She did not like the basic idea of sneaking.

"I don't care if we decide not to do anything about it, but I would like you to suggest sex, at least. To show me that you want me. If you wanted me, I think you would make certain that you showed me. I think every moment you got me alone, you would be kissing my socks off."

There. It was out. And she felt quite silly. But she did feel honest, and the honesty seemed to ride a wave of courage.

"You know what I've always liked about you, Tate? That you are a man who takes initiative. I don't want you to command me, but there are some things that I feel are important for you to do, and one of those things is for you to take the initiative in this situation." Fair or not, that was what she thought.

He gazed at her. She couldn't read his expression. The next instant, however, he took her face in his hands, saying in a husky voice, "So you want some kissin' that will knock your socks off?"

She saw the raw intent in his eyes just before he kissed her.

It was a thoroughly alluring kiss that turned red-hot in an instant. They broke for air and then went back for more, all greedy and devouring.

"Marilee . . ." His voice was hoarse and breathless when he lifted his head. There was pain and yearning so profound in his blue eyes that she could hardly bear it.

"Oh, Tate." She touched the side of his face. His dear face.

"Marilee . . . Marilee, I . . ."

Her flinging her arms around his neck and kissing him yet again stopped his voice but not the words that echoed in her mind. It was more than his words, it was the love and raw desire pouring out of his eyes and through his lips and eager tongue that kissed a hot, tantalizing trail down her neck.

Eyes squeezed against tears, she pressed her cheek to his.

"Oh, Marilee, I've felt so far away."

"Oh, Tate, so have I. I just didn't know how to get past it all and get back to you. . . . Tate . . ."

Then he was kissing her again, her mouth, her cheeks, her eyes, eating her up with his lips and his hands that pressed her to him, heating her body until the hard, cold knot that had been inside gave way in a sudden burst, and love, like sweet heated honey, poured throughout her being. She savored the taste and scent of him, the sense of love swirling around them like a dust devil on a hot day, a magic blessing not to be missed.

"Marilee, I want you. I do." His voice was ragged and breathless in a manner that made her feel like a woman blessed and powerful, as he trailed kisses down the other side of her neck. "Oh, Marilee . . ."

"Tate . . . Tate, my darling." She kissed him, his lips, his cheeks, his neck, wanting to soak him up, all of him.

"Daddy, there's someone in the church."

The young voice echoed through the tall-ceilinged sanctuary and seemed to flow down upon them, like cold rain.

Ohmygod.

She and Tate sprang apart. Straightening her spine, and her clothing, trying as best she could to appear sane, although she felt far too shaky to be doing a very good job of it. Thank goodness for Tate's supporting hand on her elbow.

Pastor Smith appeared, and right beside him were his three sons. "Ah . . . I'm sorry to interrupt, ah, your prayer together." He grinned a knowing grin. "Good thing to start, too, right at the very first." His grin widened. "We came over to get ready for Sunday night services. The children make certain the sanctuary's straightened up for me."

"We're done with our time alone . . . after your powerful sharin' with us, we needed to contemplate it together," Tate said, giving way to his tendency for exposition as he and Marilee edged toward the front door.

"Well, good. Start out right. And come back for tonight's services. We'll be glad to see you!"

The pastor's voice rang out behind them as they raced hand in hand and choking back laughter, out the vestibule and down the wide concrete steps and along the sidewalk, like children fleeing their mischief, flying on exuberance. The cool air on her hot, damp skin felt sensual and delicious. She saw the damp hair that fell across Tate's forehead, his merry eyes and bright teeth as he laughed.

Oh, he was so handsome!

Just past the church parking lot and beneath the still-bare branches of a crepe myrtle arching over the sidewalk, they fell together in laughter.

Brushing back her hair with his fingers, Tate cupped the side of her head. "Ah, Marilee . . . I do want you, darlin' . . . I do."

He kissed her tenderly, and then, for the barest touch, they pressed their foreheads together. The feelings that ran through her were profound, real and true and precious, like the first sight of a brand-new morning.

He put his arm around her shoulders, squeezed her against him, and they began the stroll homeward.

Hugging close to him, her arm around his waist, Marilee felt joy almost too much to contain. She realized that the fears of only moments ago were gone. She had gotten them out into the light, and had seen how distorted and unreal they really were. In an instant of clarity, she looked into her feelings, like Willie Lee looking into his ant farm, and saw that she had not wanted sex so much as this that she now experienced with Tate. This feeling—it was everything—a sense of being with him totally, having his total attention and giving him hers.

"I'm not very good at expressing my feelings," she said, in that moment of understanding. "Most of the time it seems easier not to pay them any attention."

"Hmmm."

"I can't very well express them, when so often I don't know what they are." She regarded him earnestly. This seemed an important revelation.

He nodded in a most gratifying manner. "I'm not too good with speakin' of feelings, either," he said. "I haven't had much experience with it," he added, and she thought this a splendid effort on his part.

"Well, we have that in common." She again nestled into his shoulder, thinking of this, delighted to remain connected to him.

After a moment, Tate said, "We'll just have to learn, won't we?"

"Yes. Yes, we will." What a dear, rare man he was.

She laughed, and he laughed, and then, right there in plain sight, he kissed her socks off again.

When a carload of teens went past and blew their horn, they jumped apart.

"We're gonna get arrested before we get home," Marilee said.

"It'll be worth it. . . . We'll get the sheriff to put us in the same cell." He cast her a lascivious grin as again his arm went around her shoulder, and they fell into a comfortable stroll.

"In the Valentine jail, we would be in plain view of everyone . . . and you know who Pastor Smith reminds me of? A short version of Andy Griffith."

"Yeah, he does. Especially his accent when he was yelling for us to come back tonight. I expected to hear him say, 'Y'all come on back now, y'hear?'"

They laughed again, and Marilee thought what she appreciated most in Tate was his sense of humor about everything, from the smallest to the largest incidents. She told him this, and he said what he admired in her was that she encouraged everyone to have humor.

They walked along, casting smiles at each other, their hearts communicating without words. The fears, unacknowledged and unspoken, had built a wall, Marilee thought.

"We will need to remember times like this," she said.

"Yes." And after a minute, he said, "Let's have a secret signal to remind us."

"A signal?"

"Yes, maybe a tug on the ear, like this."

"You do that all the time anyway, when you're thinking."

"I do?"

"Yes, you do. How 'bout wetting the lips." She showed him.

"I don't know. Other women might think I'm comin' on to them."

"Then . . . tongue in cheek."

He shook his head. "Here, wiggle the eyebrows. Just a bit."

She tried it. "Okay. I can do that."

"That's it, then. Our private secret signal to remind us we are connected."

Oh, it was lovely. Lovely walking home with his arm around her and the warm, sparkling feelings in her heart.

Then, at the corner of Porter Street, Tate said suddenly, "We need to talk a little bit more," and glancing around, he then started across the street, tugging her along.

"Where . . . ?"

"Here."

Marilee was startled. "Buddy's Mustang?"

"He won't mind," Tate said, rounding the front of the red Mustang that sat parked in its usual place at the curb in front of the white house on the corner where Buddy Wyatt, the young UPS deliveryman, lived with his mother, Margaret.

Opening the passenger door, Tate helped her into the seat, slammed the door, then went back around and got in on the driver side.

Marilee admired Tate's audacity—surely no one could be as charmingly audacious as Tate, and this always attracted her—yet she was concerned about overstepping respectable behavior by making themselves at home in another person's private vehicle.

"Oh, Buddy and I are friends," Tate said, when she brought up the concern. "I showed him our engagement picture in the paper the other day, and he wished us well. Besides, he isn't usin' his car right now."

True enough.

Tate twisted to face her. "Let's make a pact right now. We will be honest with each other from here on out."

"I didn't know I wasn't being honest about my feelings, Tate. Did you? Did you deliberately not tell me that you were worried about your age, or about not having time alone?" She wasn't certain he had admitted to being worried about not having time alone with her, but she believed he had indicated this.

He blinked. "Well, no. I didn't deliberately not talk about it, but I was reluctant to talk of it, and I knew this. I somehow thought . . . well, that things would just work themselves out, but now I know that is not necessarily so, and that the best policy is to bring things out into the open. Even if I feel I might be misunderstood, it is best to speak what's on my mind."

"Did you think I wouldn't understand you?" She had always considered herself a rather understanding person.

"Of course not." Tate stared at her, then tugged on his ear. "But some things are hard to speak of, Marilee, and that may be the clue to the need to do just that."

"Yes, now we know. But we didn't before, so that was not dishonesty. That was lack of knowledge." This was distinctly different to her, and she wanted that understood.

Tate opened his mouth, closed it, then said, "Okay, let's make a pact to talk out our fears. From right here and now, for the rest of our lives. We'll talk each night before bed. Or any time we need to. We won't hold back. We'll speak any concerns, honestly and openly."

"I agree. Let's shake on it."

They did, and kissed on it, too. Then Marilee was startled by a tapping at her window glass. It was Buddy Wyatt, hands in his tight jeans pockets. She rolled down the window.

"Hi, Buddy," Marilee said, a little embarrassed.

Tate leaned across the console. "We needed a place to talk privately. I didn't think you'd mind."

"Oh, no. I don't mind, Editor . . . but are you two about finished? I have a date. You can use my mom's car under the carport, if you want. She's busy watchin' *The African Queen* on the television."

They thanked the young man, declining his kind offer, got out of the car and headed on home to Marilee's house, again hand in hand.

Stuart was in the kitchen, gazing out the window. "The kids have a wild bird," he told them.

Marilee and Tate went out to the tree house to get the details.

Yes, they were told, Willie Lee had tamed a wild bird. Corrine explained something about it being pushed out of its own nest over at Mr. Winston's, and that Ricky Dale had brought it to Willie Lee.

"Of course," Marilee said.

Willie Lee jutted his arm over the tree house railing, displaying a small bird perched on his finger. The small bird took off in a fluttering manner, flying over to the clothesline pole. Tate said it was a titmouse and generally not afraid of humans.

"I was a Boy Scout for a brief time," Tate explained, at her raised eyebrow.

"Where did you get the birdhouse?" Marilee asked, returning her attention upward to Corrine and Ricky Dale, who were fastening a basket birdhouse to a thick branch in the tree.

"Mr. James made it," Corrine said.

For heaven's sake. Marilee squinted, trying to get a better view of the birdhouse.

Corrine said, "I found the basket in the laundry closet, Aunt Marilee. I didn't think you would mind."

"No, honey, of course I don't mind." She saw that Stuart had cut and rewoven the basket quite neatly.

Stuart, still watching from the kitchen window, saw Marilee turn and look his way. No doubt she was surprised about him making the birdhouse. He had surprised himself in the action.

He watched the bird fly back to the tree house and land on a branch very near his son's head. He recalled seeing the bird in his son's hand.

Then his gaze passed over Marilee standing beside Tate, who slung his arm easily over her shoulder. Holloway said something, and Marilee and the kids laughed. He felt left out. Totally alone.

Turning from the window, Stuart walked slowly to the kitchen table, where he sank down into a chair. He was so tired. Dread, like a stormy sea, washed over him. He saw stretched in front of him the great horror of his life all alone, and his heart squeezed with such intensity, he felt as if he could not get his breath. If he could change many decisions from his past, maybe he would now. But he could not.

A tremor went through him. He couldn't face his future alone. He just didn't think he could.

Raising his head, he looked through the open kitchen door, through the living room to the big front door, in his mind getting up and walking out, getting in his car and driving away. He had no idea where he would go. Likely there wasn't one person on earth who would miss him. Who would look one minute for him.

He could not seem to make himself move.

Just then the back door opened. Instinctively Stuart straightened his spine, gathering himself and what dignity he could muster. In came Willie Lee, running in his clumsy gait, straight to Stuart and saying the most amazing thing.

"Fa-ther . . . Fa-ther, come and see."

Hearing the boy call him Father was startling enough, and then Willie Lee threw himself onto Stuart's thigh, where Stuart had to grab him to keep him from falling.

"My bird went in the nest you made. He likes it. Come see." The boy's eyes were large behind his thick glasses. He tilted his head, regarding Stuart in a disconcertingly probing fashion.

Then there was Marilee in the doorway. She regarded him, and he regarded her. "Go on and see the result of your handiwork. I'm going to make us some sandwiches."

Her tone was warm, and so was her smile.

Stuart, a lump coming into his throat, nodded. "Okay, kid," he said to Willie Lee. "Let's go see this bird of yours in his house."

Willie Lee surprised him by taking his hand. "I will show you."

Marilee watched them go out; then she peered through the window, seeing her small son leading the tall man across the yard.

The sight of Stuart, sitting all alone at the table when they entered, the stark loneliness she had glimpsed on his features, cut deep into her heart.

Willie Lee scrambled up into bed, and Marilee tucked him in. Kissing his cheek, she was reminded by the fresh-washed scent of him of the horrible encounter with the skunk. Give thanks for small blessings, she thought.

"Ma-ma?"

"What, sugar?"

"I think my fa-ther is sick."

She paused in smoothing his blankets. "Why do you think that?"

"I just do."

"Well . . . maybe he just isn't feeling well today. Maybe tomorrow he will feel fine."

Her son's expression cleared. "Okay." And he turned over, snuggling into the covers, where he would be asleep in seconds.

Marilee kissed his unruly hair and whispered, "God bless and keep Willie Lee."

Fifteen

Age is only a matter of mind. . . .

There he was, Winston Valentine, sitting at a candlelit table with a beautiful woman, in a fancy-schmancy restaurant, eating a piece of chocolate cake rich enough to provoke an instant heart attack in a man of his age.

"I'll be poppin' Tums after this," he said, gazing at the lovely face across from him.

"But it's worth it, isn't it?" she said, as sultry as any woman could possibly be.

Winston wondered at what had come into his life in the form of Franny Holloway.

She had said, "Winston, I believe we need to go out. How 'bout it?" Tongues would be wagging over this, her sitting on the front porch with him, and then showing up, dressed in what looked like a whole bunch of silk scarves, with a neckline that dipped to show the creamy flesh of her small breasts.

She took hold of his arm when they walked, too, and she looked at him when he spoke. She listened to him as if what he said was of great interest. She seemed especially interested in what Valentine was like in the early days, and he delighted in telling her about how the train used to stop there, and the way the town filled up on Saturday nights in the summer, and the long lines of cotton wagons in the fall. Where she had grown up in Texas had been much the same.

And she didn't laugh or even look mildly bored when he told her about the visits, that first year, from his dead wife, Coweta.

"The flesh is temporary, but the spirit lives on," she said with warm understanding. "I've seen a number of dead people—any that I had a close attachment to. I loved my daddy dearly, and I saw him shortly after he died from a kick in the head by a mule. Only one time. He went right on to the other side, and I never saw him again. My mother told me I imagined it and gave me a teaspoon of cod liver oil. Believe you me, I certainly was not quick to tell her when I saw my aunt get up out of her casket and go looking at everyone. I never saw Mama, but then Mama liked my sister best."

Winston, who at first was relieved to know she had some experience in seeing spirits, began to feel uneasy. He sure hoped she wasn't a nut. Although, what other type of woman who looked like her would go out to a restaurant like this with him?

"You must have loved your wife very much, and she you," she said.

Something struck him hard. He nodded, averting his eyes. "We had ups and downs . . . some humdingers, too . . . but we both saw it through. I miss her."

Franny stretched out her arm and laid her hand on his. "You were very blessed, Winston. Better to have known the love, even with the hurt, than not to know it at all."

He felt the need to ask her about her life, but he shied from this. What if she told him secret feelings? That would just wear him out.

She said then, "Excuse me, darlin'," and slid back her chair. "I need to go powder my nose, and I think I'll call Tate to let him know we're all right. No tellin' when we might show up at home." She winked.

Yep, that Franny was something, Winston thought.

He felt a little regret at his cowardice in not asking about her husband. He knew she was a widow. She had said that much. Maybe he could bring himself around to asking when she came back.

He took several deep breaths and stretched his shoulders. He sure didn't want to be some old man who fell asleep in his chair in a public restaurant. It wasn't yet seven o'clock, either.

Glancing around, checking out the other occupants of the restaurant, he felt his spirit sink. He was the oldest in the place by far. He got tired of being the oldest.

Just then he recognized the woman at a table across the room.

Vella?

Naw. That wasn't Perry across from her. It was some guy with dark, steely-colored hair. Wore a turtleneck with his sport coat. Fashion plate.

He looked again at the woman. Sure looked like Vella. That was Vella's exact new haircut.

Certainty hit him hard. It *was* Vella.

Just then, he watched the man reach over and take Vella's hand.

And, possibly because he was staring at her, Vella's head came around, and she saw him. She looked surprised. He wished he had looked away earlier, but since he had not, he gave her a nod.

It might not be at all what it looked like, he told himself, taking a sip from his water glass to give himself something to do. And even if it was, it wasn't any of his business. But Vella had to be a durn fool if she thought just because she was up here in Lawton, someone from Valentine wouldn't see her. He sure wished it hadn't been him.

He had drunk half his glass of water before he realized.

Franny returned. "Tate must be at Marilee's. . . . I left a message. No need to disturb them. Those two don't hardly get a minute to themselves. Would you mind if we took time for coffee? I hardly ever drink it, but I do like this mocha."

He said fine. He was trying not to look in Vella's direction.

But then here she came, making a bead on their table. She came head-on in that long stride of hers, with her escort coming right behind her.

Winston stared at her when she stopped and said, "Hello, Winston . . . Franny." Then she proceeded to introduce the man as a Lawrence Somebody—Winston didn't clearly catch the last name. "Lawrence is landscaping my backyard. I'm havin' raised beds, a flagstone patio with a pergola, and a pond."

"That sounds right grand, Vella," Winston said, while observing that the Lawrence fella had his hand on Vella's elbow, like she was his. He wasn't a day over fifty-five, either.

That Vella and Franny were apparently quite good friends surprised Winston, who understood that Franny had only been in town since Tuesday night. She and Vella chatted a bit about the new washer and dryer that Marilee had received from her ex-husband. The ex-husband being around was news to Winston, who began to feel he was missing a whole lot. That was what happened when a man got old. He either missed things, or people overlooked telling him.

When Vella and her man friend left, Winston said, "Vella's married."

"I gathered that," Franny said, and smiled blandly. "One would think you are jealous, Winston."

Startled, he found himself gazing into her twinkling green eyes. "No, ma'am. I'm enjoyin' the company of a beautiful woman right this minute, and I'm smart enough to know when I'm in tall cotton."

She laughed gaily and asked if he would like to go home by way of the lake, which she had heard about. "Perhaps you could direct me, darlin'?"

Good heavens, she was flirting with him.

Eighty-eight years old, but he wasn't dead yet. And if he got excited so much by Franny that he had a heart attack, he would die happy.

The headlights of Lawrence's Cadillac spotlighted Vella's Land Rover, which was parked in the black-topped lot outside his shop.

"Thank you for a lovely evening, Lawrence," she said, even as she opened the door to slide out of the seat. She had to hold herself back from running to her vehicle, jumping in and racing off. She was acting like a fool.

But Lawrence got out quickly and walked her to the Land Rover, took the keys from her hand and opened the door. He was such a gentleman.

"I thank *you* for your company tonight, Vella."

Before she knew what he was about, he bent and brushed her lips with his.

"Oh." She started to duck into her vehicle, then paused and turned back to him. There were moments in the life of a woman her age that weren't likely to come around again.

She lifted her lips, and his met hers. It was a full, deep kiss, and when they parted, her eyes opened reluctantly and she swayed just ever so slightly.

Placing a steadying hand on his chest, she leaned over and whispered her age into his ear.

His acceptance of the knowledge with such equanimity—a mere soft smile and murmur that she was a very attractive woman—caused Vella to wonder if he was actually that unconcerned, or if she looked every inch her age, so he had not been fooled from the beginning.

Trembling, she quickly averted her face and slipped behind the wheel of her vehicle.

"I'll be down in the afternoon. Two o'clock," Lawrence said, before shutting the door firmly.

Allowing herself only the barest glance at him out of the corner of her eye, she drove the Land Rover out of his parking lot and back to Valentine, driving with both hands on the steering wheel, praying with fervor, although her prayer came out something like: ohmygod, ohmygod.

Thinking that she had to speak to someone, she drove to Marilee's house. It wasn't very late, barely eight-thirty. She could always talk to her niece. Marilee had been there for her last year, when she had gotten all messed up and left Perry flat. She did not want anyone to solve the confusion for her, but she just wanted to talk to Marilee. Probably Marilee would be shocked. Maybe she shouldn't tell Marilee about a possible lover. Leaving Perry was mild compared to the thought of getting into an affair. Marilee could really be strict about such things.

No, she could not tell her, Vella decided, as she pulled to a stop in front of Marilee's cottage, where warm light glowed from the front windows.

She gazed at the house for some moments, debating about going in at all. Loneliness fell over her like the darkness outside, and she thought of how simply touching Marilee always brought comfort. It always had, she reflected, hooking the strap of her patent leather purse over her arm and striding up the walkway. Perhaps that was why so many people seemed to come to Marilee and lean on her. And now here she, Vella, the elder and usually strong one, was coming to do the same thing.

Jerking her shoulders up straight, she told herself sternly that she would simply have tea and discuss the wedding arrangements some more. That would give her time to get her emotions straight before she had to go home and sleep beside Perry.

Then, just as her hand went to the knob, something—some sound, some change in light—arrested the action. She looked left and saw the light from the window had dropped. Faint strains of music . . . sultry . . . George Strait singing a love song . . . reached her.

She stepped to the window and peered through the glass to see Tate and Marilee at the far end of the room, silhouettes lit from behind by light falling through the kitchen doorway. They danced, moving slowly, intimately.

They kissed.

Vella stared for a long moment, her throat growing thick and her chest filling with longing. Once upon a time, so many years ago, she had done the same with Perry.

And dear God, she longed for such a time with a man again, she thought as she turned from the window.

Would this longing never end? She had tried to have a relationship with Perry, but he had locked most of himself away for forty-five years and could not open up to her. She understood this and did not blame him, yet she so wanted a man with whom to share her heart . . . her being.

She would not intrude on Tate and Marilee's precious time. This was the sort of times a couple needed to have and to build on in order to open themselves to each other. If she had understood that reality forty years ago—even thirty years ago—and acted upon it, maybe she would have something with Perry now.

Or maybe not. Perry was such a lump, she thought, without rancor, as she went quictly down the porch steps.

Just then, here came a black Cadillac pulling into the driveway, swinging in wildly, stopping short behind Marilee's Cherokee. Norma Cooper, her small head sticking up behind the steering wheel.

Vella knew instantly that some crisis had befallen Marilee's mother; Norma never came down, and most definitely not at night, unless she needed something from Marilee.

Stepping out with determination, Vella headed for the Cadillac and met Norma struggling to get out of the seat.

"Marilee is busy right now, Norma. She and Tate are finally havin' some time alone." Vella was tall enough to look down at the top of her ex-sister-in-law's head.

"I need to talk to my daughter." Norma slammed the car door.

Vella, who noted with a bit of surprise that Norma appeared very stylishly dressed, blocked the woman's path. "Your daughter is busy with her husband-to-be. Don't go in there and interrupt them with whatever you have on your plate this time. Is it Carl?" No wild guess; Norma's problems always revolved around Carl.

The petite woman stretched herself as tall as possible, looking up at Vella. "It is none of your business. This is something I need to discuss with Marilee."

She moved to step around Vella, who sidestepped and blocked her way.

"Norma, if you go in there and bother them, I will tell Marilee about all the men you slept with after her daddy killed himself. I will tell her of the clarinet player you ran off to Dallas with."

She saw this was not fully getting the effect she wished. In fact, Norma said, "What have you been drinkin' Vella? You are nuts. Get out of my way."

The woman shot out a hand to push Vella aside. Vella held her ground as hard as any lineman. "I'll tell Carl about your private account in the Citizens Community Bank. I believe it's up to fifteen thousand dollars now. At least it was last month. Where did you get all that?"

Norma stopped, her mouth flying open. "How do you know about that?"

"Oh, Norma, nothin' in Valentine is secret."

Norma reached a hand out to the Cadillac fender. "I've got to talk to Marilee. Carl got arrested for public drunkeness. I don't know how to get him out. Marilee always helps me with this." Her voice broke.

Vella, experiencing only the slightest twinge of pity at the woman's distress, nevertheless closed her mouth against the initial comment that as many times as Carl had been bailed out of jail for drunkenness, Norma ought to have the procedure down pat. Instead she looked at the facts—Norma never had been able to do a darn thing for herself; it was too much to expect miracles now.

"I'll help you, Norma. All we have to do is call a bail bondsman.

Come on. I'll follow you up to your house, and we can make the call
from there."

· She made certain Norma was in her car and headed in the right direction before getting into the Land Rover and following. Once more
on the road, both hands on the wheel, it occurred to Vella that she had
taken a rather distorted tack about being so protective of Marilee.

It had been about herself, she realized. In that moment of looking in
the window at Marilee, she had looked back at herself and seen clearly
all her mistakes and regrets at things left undone. It did not seem the
wrong things done that caused such regret, but more the opportunities
and desires that had gone *un*done.

She had no right to criticize Norma for her silliness, she decided,
keeping her eyes focused on the red taillights of the black Cadillac.
First get the beam out of her own eye.

Vella, always confident about handling details, took care of secur-
ing Carl Cooper's release all by telephone from his own kitchen.
"He'll be out and headed home in half an hour," she told Norma when
she replaced the receiver.

"Will it be in the newspaper report?"

"Carl is not some state senator or somethin'. There's no way to stop
him being listed along with all the others."

"Oh."

Wearily Vella took up her patent leather purse once more, wondering at how, only a few short hours earlier, she had been dining with a
most handsome and charming gentleman who was not her husband. A
woman of her age. She felt every inch her years right at that moment.

"Well . . ." Norma rubbed her arms, trying to bring herself to say
thank you to this woman, her dead husband's sister, who had always
been a royal pain in her side. Amenities were required. And when it
came to the choice of humbling herself to either her daughter or Vella,
she found it easier with Vella, who had, after all, blackmailed her into
this, so Vella owed her the effort to get Carl released.

Norma opened the back door and said the required, "I appreciate
your efforts, Vella." She wanted Vella gone now. She just wanted
everything to be over.

Unfortunately, in that instant, Vella took note of Norma's tone of
voice, which was not at all thankful. She looked at Norma and had a
vague recollection that she could not name, but that prompted her to
say, "Norma, you have treated Marilee as if she were responsible for
you from the day she was born, as if you were the child instead of the
mother. Stop it. Let her have her life now, with Tate."

"Well, I never . . ."

"I know you haven't, and it is time you did. Grow up."

Leaving the woman looking as if she wanted to hit her, Vella walked out into the night, to her invincible Land Rover, which always gave her a sense of power to drive. In fact, for an instant, when she turned on the headlights and saw Norma's Cadillac in front of her, she had to resist the strong urge to drive right over the black car.

What had happened to her, Lord? Why had she turned so mean? She tried to feel remorse and ask forgiveness, but did not succeed. She might regret speaking frankly to Norma in the morning, but she thought not.

She sighed deeply, having the inner knowing that this confrontation with Norma had not come on suddenly. She had wanted to say what she had to the woman for at least thirty years, ever since she saw Marilee living an uncertain childhood.

Then a deeper knowing came on her. Norma had reminded her of her own mother. Vella had been mother to her own mother, to her brothers and sisters, onward to two daughters, one who had not left home until the age of thirty, when Vella had pushed her out, and even then, Belinda had gone only as far as the apartment over the drugstore.

And, somehow, to her own husband, Perry, God love him, she had also become mother, rather than wife. After forty-five years, this was ingrained and unchangeable, leaving her feeling a hole in her being, where a full woman should be.

Maybe some things needed to be said, she decided. Maybe hard things had to be said by tough people. She could not change things for herself, but maybe what she said would help Marilee . . . and Norma, too.

At home, Vella found Perry asleep in his recliner in front of the television. She regarded him and felt a sense of tenderness, for which she was very glad.

She touched his shoulder gently. "Perry . . . come on up to bed. You'll get a backache if you sleep here. Here, sugar, let me help you up . . . there you go."

There was nothing like realizing one was not perfect to bring on the peace of true humbleness. Vella spent a long time that night, propped against her rose-print covered pillows, watching the moonlight make a pattern on the walls, listening to Perry snore beside her and apologizing for her sins.

She was not, however, one bit sorry for what she had said to Norma Cooper.

Sixteen

State of grace . . .

Marilee awoke with traces of a lingering dream that she could not fully remember, but that reignited her desire to surprise Tate by appearing in his kitchen, in the Victoria's Secret nightgown, first thing in the morning.

She had regretted ever since the previous week her botched intentions in this endeavor and kept feeling the urge to give it another try. It was an inner struggle, one voice urging her to open wide and risk, the other voice advising her to keep to the narrow way of caution.

This moment the voice of daring dominated, however, and she flung back the covers with a sense of purpose. She needed to follow romantic desires, she thought, in order to practice being a romantic woman. She really felt she would forever regret it if she did not follow through.

Quite quickly, she splashed water on her face, brushed her teeth, creamed up, added a dash of lipstick and pinned up her hair in an alluring disarrayed manner.

As she was getting into the nightgown, the roar of her neighbor's truck blasted through the early-morning silence.

If the roar awoke her children, then that would be an indication from God that her endeavor was foolhardy, she thought, as she tiptoed past the children's door—although what good was it to tiptoe, after that roaring blast that was still fading down the street?

Munro and the new kitten were curled on Willie Lee's bed. Neither moved, nor did the lumps beneath the covers of the two beds, for the long seconds that Marilee watched.

Fully encouraged, she went back to her bedroom, slipped quickly into her trench coat and tall cowboy boots, and, as an afterthought, hung long silver earrings at her lobes. Long dangling earrings always made her feel sexy. A cautionary voice hissed in her mind, and she shoved it in a closet and glided through the house and out the back door, then across the yard to the gate that seemed to open magically with her first touch. In fact, it swung open with such ease and quietness that she had to wonder about it and looked around her for evidence of angel beings.

Perhaps the gate had been affected by her confidence, her new thrill and delight at allowing a self deeply denied and buried to come out and shine forth.

If Franny were in the kitchen, she thought, she would simply say, "Excuse me, I've come to make Tate's coffee and entice him a little bit." Or something equally as bold.

Tate's kitchen was empty. She was relieved.

She listened. No sounds. She went to the cabinet, located the tin of coffee, and prepared the coffeemaker. As it gurgled, she again listened closely to hear if someone might be stirring upstairs. All was silent.

This was perturbing. Her gaze located the clock on the wall; it was old and yellowed, displaying the time as ten after six.

She couldn't stay here long, waiting for Tate to appear. Her motherly instincts were beginning to tug, haranguing her for having left the children unattended and coming up with all sorts of dire predictions of what could happen should she not be her normal vigilant self.

The coffeemaker gurgled its final gurgle. Marilee prepared Tate a cup with cream and sugar, as he liked it, took a deep breath and started down the hallway and up the steps, heading for Tate's bedroom. Each step in her boots seemed to echo on the oak flooring.

She paused at the top of the steps, again cocking her head. All the doors were closed; the hall landing was shadowy, lit only by the first light of dawn coming in the window at the end. She thought she caught a sound, and she walked on tiptoe, stopping at the bathroom door to listen.

Just then the sound of water running on the other side of the door caused her to jump slightly. Tate, or his mother?

Knowing the bathroom also had a door into the master bedroom, she continued on to Tate's bedroom, which she had seen only twice ever—and thinking of this, she felt firmer determination to become familiar with the house of the man she would be marrying, so she walked more firmly.

At the closed door, however, she did not burst in but slowly opened it and peeked around. "Tate?"

The lamp on the nightstand was on, showing the empty, rumpled bed. The door to the bathroom was ajar, light spilling through.

Shy about seeing him naked, and curious at the same time, she at first averted her head as she stepped into the center of the room. It went totally against her nature to come into a person's privacy like this.

She was going to marry this man, for heaven's sake.

She had been single so long that sharing someone's privacy and giving of her own seemed exceedingly foreign to her.

As she thought this, she leaned over to see exactly what she could see through the crack. A virile figure, bare skin, plaid pajama pants.

The sight caused a pleasant throbbing deep inside of her.

Just then the door swung open, and Tate, wiping a towel over his face, stepped out.

Marilee jerked up straight, sloshing the coffee, and Tate jumped back upon sight of her, sending the towel flying.

And then he was laughing. "You scared me."

She held out the cup and saucer. "I brought your mornin' coffee."

"You did?" Surprise was quickly followed by delight. "Well, thank you."

She smiled as she handed it to him, and then she opened wide her coat, saying in as sexy a voice as she could find, "I also brought you a sight to stir your senses."

His eyebrows arched upward on a grand scale, and he stared at her, his mouth parting in a manner that Marilee found quite satisfying. Watching expressions pass over his face, she experienced her power as a woman. It came over her with such force as to amaze her.

Thus encouraged, and still holding the coat wide, she sauntered forward until her face was inches from his, her eyes locked on his. "Good mornin', Editor." She lifted her lips to kiss him.

Tate broke away. "Oh, lady . . . let me set this coffee down."

Almost in one movement, he set the cup and saucer on the nearby chest of drawers, then took her to him and kissed her in a manner so thoroughly consuming as to leave Marilee breathless and panting.

"Tate . . . I . . . have to go back. . . . The children are alone."

"Hmmm . . ." He kissed her again, moving his hands beneath her coat and caressing the bare flesh of her back.

She sighed against him, with passion flowing in delicious waves over her body as she felt his warm, hard skin, and his scent filled her nostrils. She had the thought that perhaps she was more surprised than he.

More firmly, she got hold of herself. "I really do have to go back. I just wanted to practice gettin' into the habit of being a lover."

"Well, I like it, lady. You goin' to do this every mornin'?" He grinned wickedly.

"If you're good . . . very, very good."

He reached for her, and, giggling, she eluded him and raced on tip-toe out the door, wrapping her coat closed, mindful of running into Franny.

He came after her, down the length of landing, and caught her at the top of the stairs, pushing her up against the wall as both of them laughed breathlessly.

"Tate . . . your mother will hear."

"So? I need to kiss your socks off."

And he did.

When he broke away, she cupped the sides of his head and gazed into his dear, luminous eyes only inches from her own. "I didn't know," she said in a breathless whisper of wonder. "I thought it was sex I wanted. Oh, and I do . . . but it really is this that I wanted. This closeness with you."

It was a miracle to her, and she took in the virile scent of him, the salty taste of him on her tongue, the warm, erotic glaze in his eyes.

He said, "I know." And she saw the truth of his understanding in his eyes.

She nodded, biting her bottom lip, then bringing forth, "Let's wait . . . for sex. I don't want it to be something sandwiched in . . . something grabbed without thought. There's so much, with the wedding, Stuart here, the children. Let's wait until our wedding night."

Would he understand? Where were her words to say that she rather liked this precious getting to know each other?

He regarded her, then pushed himself against her, pinning her to the wall and rubbing her pelvis with his groin, which was clearly aroused, and the realization caused an immediate reaction inside of her.

"I think that's a fine idea, Miz James," he drawled in a tone that rippled through her body. "I can practice kissin' your socks off—" he kissed her eyes, then bent and kissed the bare skin at the swell of her breasts, sending tremors down her legs "—and anticipate making love to my wife. Anticipation is sweet, don't you think?"

"Yes . . . yes, I . . . think." Actually she could not think at all.

"Ah-hem."

At the sound of the voice, she and Tate first froze, looked wide-eyed at each other, and then turned of one accord and looked down the stairs to see Franny standing at the foot.

"I am sorry to interrupt. I really am. But I need to go to the bath-room, Tate, and there is only one of those in this old house, so excuse me."

She came sweeping up the stairs as she spoke, in her flowing dress, throwing her scarf over her shoulders. Her pumps dangled from two fingers.

"Are you just gettin' in?" Tate asked, incredulous.

"Yes, dear. I had a wonderful night. Simply lovely."

"And Winston is still alive, I hope?"

"Oh, yes, dear, quite. Old people don't sleep as much and are used to odd hours," she tossed over her shoulder as she passed by and headed for the bathroom.

Just as she opened the door, she turned to them and said, "You know, the sexiest organ in the body is the mind. Winston still has all his mental capacities."

Then she disappeared.

Marilee and Tate stared at each other, and then burst out laughing. "Go," Marilee said, pushing him toward his bedroom. "Have the coffee before it is stone-cold . . . and don't you jog in the mornings?"

She hurried down the stairs, and he called over the railing to her, "You bet I'm joggin'. I've got to work this frustration off somehow."

"Tate Holloway!" She was mortified to think of his mother hearing him.

She raced out of the house and across their backyards, and when, halfway, she threw back her head, a joyous laugh erupted from her lips.

How had she been so blind as to not understand what she was truly seeking? How had she been so blind as not to know about this beautiful, magnificent sense of oneness with a man?

She was in love. She really was. Did she glow? She looked at her arms and body as she fairly floated through the gate in the magical dreamy state of grace of a woman in love.

"Good morn-ing, Ma-ma."

Startled, she pressed a hand to her chest and jerked her head upward. "Willie Lee, what are you doin'?"

"I am in my tree house," he said in his usual factual fashion.

"I see that, honey. *What* are you doing in your tree house so early in the morning?" She hoped he didn't ask her what she was doing in the yard so early in the morning.

"I am teach-ing Whis-kers to like Bir-dy." He lifted the kitten to show her.

Only Willie Lee could do such things.

She allowed him his freedom, saying only that she would call him when breakfast was ready.

Pausing at the back door, she looked back into the big elm tree and the small basket birdhouse there, remembering Stuart and what Willie Lee had said about him being sick.

Willie Lee was only a little boy, she reminded herself. Not burdened with intellect, he had a unique way of seeing the truth of things, however; he was still only a little boy who could misinterpret what he saw in his literal take on things. He might have picked up some sense of distress on Stuart's part, but it likely meant that Stuart had suffered a headache and had been tired of his lengthy and unaccustomed exposure to the children.

Tate came out whistling and paused at the edge of the porch to inhale deeply. By golly, he could smell the sweet freshness of spring!

Again whistling, he jogged down the steps and broke into a run, whizzing past the twiggy lilac bush that was beginning to swell with leaf buds. The orange cat, Bubba, jumped out and followed him down the street but gave up after several yards and plopped down near the curb to clean his fat belly.

As Tate came to the Wyatt house on the corner, Buddy, who was doing his morning pull-ups on the porch beam, called, "You sure are full of energy this morning, Editor!"

"Yes, indeed," Tate called back. Passion did not belong only to young men with biceps, he thought.

He made it around to Main and was still going at a good clip. Being ten minutes earlier than usual, he found the street quiet. Bonita Embree of Sweetie Cakes Bakery had not yet opened up, nor had Grace Florist. Charlotte's car was the only one on the street, parked out front of the *Voice,* and the flags fluttered on either side of the door, further indication of her presence.

Tate was relieved. Charlotte's absence on Friday had given him great appreciation for the scope of her work at the paper. She virtually ran the place, although he wouldn't want to admit that to her. She already had an exalted sense of importance. In fact, she could overwhelm him.

Maybe he should go over and tell her how much he appreciated her, he thought, slowing his stride. Holding on to his pride so often got him into trouble.

Just then, however, the door of the *Voice* opened, and a tall man strode out. Sandy, walking with swift, angry strides to the corner, where he vehemently tossed a brown bag into the green mesh trash can. Then he headed on across Church Street and beyond, in the direction of his apartment.

Watching the young man, Tate's spirit took a nosedive. This seemed a definitely disheartening sign that Sandy and Charlotte had not made up. He came to a full stop, gazing across the street to the *Voice* windows, which were still covered by the closed blinds. He sighed, considered going to talk to Charlotte, but a certain trepidation at facing the woman, plus the desire to hold to the joy filling his life right that minute, propelled him once more into a jog. This morning was too special and precious to get weighed down by things that by rights were not any of his business.

Spirit rising once more, he hit the corner and turned up the hill of Church Street at an energetic stride.

Then here came Parker down the hill, approaching the intersection from the opposite direction.

"Looks like you are tryin' to wear yourself out," the younger man said with a knowing grin.

"Yep," Tate said, grinning broadly.

Life was good.

Vella, dressed smartly and sensibly for an active day, went to the kitchen phone and dialed the private office number for Waller Landscaping. Lawrence's voice, his recorded voice mail, came over the line, as she had expected at this early hour.

"Lawrence, this is Vella Blaine," she said in a businesslike tone. "I will not be home this afternoon. I am occupied with producing a wedding, however, I leave the backyard in your capable hands. I will be in touch."

And that was the end of that, she thought, giving, upon returning the receiver to its hook, a large, deep sigh, which was a mixture of regret and relief.

She had made her choice to direct her considerable energies into the preparations for Marilee's wedding, rather than get lost in an impossible affair. She had distinctly heard a direction from God to get out of herself and her carnal desires and focus on helping see that Marilee got married. Since she had developed such a strong controlling streak over the years, she might as well put it to good use.

Just as the sun became a fiery ball on the horizon, she stepped out her front door, carrying a notebook that bulged with magazine articles and lists of things to do. She backed her Land Rover out of the driveway in a purposeful manner and headed down the street.

Everett Northrupt was out in his yard, standing at attention and saluting his flags. "The Star Spangled Banner" was blaring from his house. Vella's gaze shifted over to the Valentine house. But there was no sign of Winston, not in his yard nor on his porch.

Tapping the brake pedal, she slowed the Land Rover, her eyes searching the porch. No, no stooped figure bringing himself to attention.

She slammed on her brakes in the middle of the road between the two houses and their flagpoles, lowered the passenger window and cocked her head. She did not hear "Dixie" playing. The house was silent.

Ohmygod, he's died!

In a state of shock, she veered over to the curb, jammed the gearshift into Park and hopped out just as the strains of "The Star Spangled Banner" faded away. A man did not raise a flag for all these years, every morning that the sun came up, and suddenly quit. The only time Winston had missed was when he'd had his stroke. She looked again at Winston's yard and front porch, thinking her eyes must have failed her. She had known this day would come, only she could not bear it now. She simply could not.

She looked across to Everett, who did not seem as concerned as he should be. "Where's Winston?"

She was already heading around the front of the Land Rover when Everett said, "He's in bed."

"What?" She stopped. Had he said in bed or dead?

"He's in bed. Doris saw him come in just about thirty minutes ago. That fancy woman—the Editor's mother—brought him. Looked like they'd been out *allll* night."

All night?

The image of Winston and Franny and their intimate camaraderie at the restaurant passed across Vella's memory, coming like a blow to her chest.

Everett shook his head. "Gonna kill himself, but I guess no one wants to live forever."

Vella slowly walked back around to get into her Land Rover, automatically shifting it into gear and pressing the accelerator, heading along the street in something of a numb state.

Winston wasn't dead. He hadn't had another stroke. Thank you, God.

Oh, she missed Winston. She squeezed the steering wheel with fervor.

But she was a married woman, and Franny was not. She was not jealous, and this surprised her. She would not, after all, change her decision to remain married to Perry. She had once thought maybe she would, but she would not. She was growing to accept her life, and with this acceptance, she could see her many blessings. Her heart filled with gladness for Winston, a dear old friend, and for Franny, a promising new friend.

Just then she realized that she had come to a stop at the intersection of Porter and Church. She noticed an early blooming forsythia on the opposite corner. The weather was warming early this year. The forsythia blossoms would be perfect for Marilee's wedding. If they were done blooming around Valentine before the wedding, she could drive north and still get some.

The wedding was only three weeks away!

Seventeen

Destiny of a small, intimate wedding . . .

Vella, toting a heavy-looking notebook, came blowing into his office. "Marilee has okayed this invitation style, but she wants your okay on it."

"She called me earlier. I was told to be at your disposal." Tate had not known he had been concerned about the wedding preparations until Marilee had told him that Vella was taking charge. With Vella in charge, things would go smoothly.

She whipped out the card and held it before him.

"Okay." He was quite pleased to have accommodated her.

She sat herself in the chair next to his desk, saying as she put on her reading glasses, "Now, let me have your invitation list. I'm just gettin' a head-count now. I'll get addresses later." She unfolded a notepad and poised a pencil.

"Well . . . everyone here at the paper, of course. That'll be fifteen. Here's a list, and the addresses, too," he said, pulling two sheets of paper out of a desk drawer and passing them to her. "Parker Lindsey's my best man—that's Mr. and Mrs. now. His wife's name is Amy."

"They came in the store the other day. She got prenatal vitamins, said she was planning for the future. I need to tell Marilee."

Tate found this startling. It made him think of his own position, as a soon-to-be new husband. And it seemed life was moving on at too quick a pace.

Vella prodded him to continue with his list.

"Okay . . . there's Sheriff Oakes and his family, and everyone over there at the sheriff's office. I guess we should invite the mayor and everyone on the City Council . . . and their families, too, of course."

"That's just one invitation per family, though." Vella was writing furiously.

"Put Fayrene Gardner down. I think I've already invited her. And Norm Stidham and Ramona. Fred Grace and his family, of course."

Vella lowered her pad and gazed at him. "How about if I just invite everyone who is a member of the Chamber of Commerce?"

He nodded. "That will probably cover it. And you'd better get an extra ten invitations, at least, to allow for those we think of at the last minute."

"You know, Tate, this *is* about the last minute."

Marilee was finishing up the final edits on her piece on rabies and her "Voices of Valentine" column, both of which she would proudly be turning in by the deadline time of noon, when the telephone rang at the edge of her desk.

It was her mother. "Hello, dear . . . I won't bother you but a minute."

"You aren't botherin' me, Mom. What is it?" Marilee tucked the receiver in her neck and proceeded to save her documents to a separate disk.

Her mother was saying, "Well, it won't take me but a few minutes. I know you are busy. Vella called up here this morning to get my list of people to invite to the wedding."

Vella had called her mother? Oh dear. Marilee stopped her endeavors with the computer and took hold of the receiver.

She had not thought about Vella possibly contacting her mother. Not that she had meant to hide the fact that her aunt Vella was organizing the wedding; she just hadn't intended to purposely tell her mother. Marilee experienced a panic, having the sudden vision of her mother and Aunt Vella vying over control of the wedding plans, something along the lines of World War III breaking out between the women. This scenario included yelling, spitting and hair-pulling.

"Vella told me she was helping you with the wedding." That sat there.

"Yes." She couldn't think of anything else to say.

The line hummed for some seconds. "Well, I told her to be sure and invite the Mathesons and Cora Smith, who I used to live next door to down there. And my pastor and his wife, and of course everyone from Carl's store."

Marilee closed her eyes. "We're just having a small wedding, Mom. Just immediate family and close friends."

"Betty Matheson has been my best friend for fifteen years now. And I've known Cora Smith since I was ten years old. She knew Mama. She'll be hurt if she doesn't get an invitation. There are manners, Marilee. Probably hardly anyone from the store will come, but it's rude not to invite them. It would make Carl look bad. And Vella did ask me. I tell you what, that is my list, just do what you want to."

"We'll be keeping it down, Mom, but I'll make sure and invite the Mathesons, and Cora."

"You can't invite the Mathesons and not Pastor Ames. The Mathesons are members of our church. And Carl will feel badly if you don't invite the people from his store. I guess if you want to not invite people, don't invite Cora and the Mathesons, but do include Pastor Ames. And you have to invite Carl's manager, Roger Gaither.

"No, on second thought, invite the Mathesons, Roger Gaither, and Cora and Pastor, but you know Cora won't come—she hardly gets out anymore—so you'll still have only the others."

Marilee swallowed. "We'll invite them all, Mom. We'll need you to provide addresses, though."

"I told Vella I'd have them to her by tomorrow. I wish she would have told me earlier."

Marilee wondered if she and Tate could elope. They had considered it briefly. Maybe they should reconsider.

"Well, the other thing I wanted to speak to you about is your wedding present," her mother said in a more forceful tone.

"What about my wedding present?" was all she could think to ask. It seemed a little greedy to expect a present, and a little ungrateful to say she did not want one. Oh, this wedding was becoming a thorough nuisance. She had experience with being engaged and calling it off, but no experience with weddings.

"Carl and I have decided we want to pay for your wedding."

Marilee sucked in a breath. "Pay for the wedding? Oh, Mom, I don't think that is necessary."

"Of course it isn't necessary, Marilee. This is what we *want* to do. And this way you don't have to worry about expenses or trying so hard to keep it small."

"It isn't the money, Mom. I want a small, intimate wedding." Crowds had always made her nervous.

"How much did you plan on spending?"

"I don't know." She felt silly, not having thought this through. "I'm having Margaret Wyatt make my dress, and then Corrine will have to have a dress, and Willie Lee a suit." Quite suddenly she began to see that she did need to make a budget. She grabbed a pad and began making notes to consult with Vella.

"What about your bridesmaids' dresses?"

"I'm just having one—Charlotte is standing up with me." But maybe it was required that Marilee purchase a dress for Charlotte.

Her mother answered that. "Dear, it is the bride's part to pay for the dress of her attendant . . . and there are invitations, and the flowers and the photographer."

Yikes! Marilee hadn't thought at all of the photographer. Maybe Reggie would do it as a favor.

"There's the reception hall," said her mother. "And you could really enjoy a live band. Betty's daughter had a band at her wedding. It really adds to everything."

"A band?" Good heavens. "No, Mom, we aren't having that elaborate an affair. Just cake and punch. It's going to be simple and small, like I said, and we're havin' the whole thing at the church. We are using china and crystal, though," she added, knowing her mother would appreciate that.

"How about if you just send me your bills?"

"Oh, no. No, I can't do that." She imagined her mother poring over every receipt and shaking her head. "How about if you pay for my dress? I'd really like that, Mom."

At that particular moment, Vella breezed in the front door. Marilee waved at her, while trying to keep her mind on the conversation with her mother, who was saying maybe she would have her bank simply transfer money into Marilee's account.

"Mother, you don't need to do that. My dress is not terribly fancy. The material is a little expensive, but there isn't any beading or anything. I'll find out a cost on it and let you know."

"Marilee," her mother said with unaccustomed firmness, "I *want* to pay for the entire wedding, just like Vella wants to help you with all she is doing. I want to help, and this is my way. It is what I can do."

Her words and tone struck deep into Marilee, who, after a minute got out, "Okay, Mom. I would appreciate it very much."

"Good." She heard the pleasure in her mother's voice. "I think, then, dear, since you say it will be small, I will have the bank transfer five thousand into your account. That is our present to you. Use it how you will, and if you go over, I'll send down another two thousand."

Marilee sucked in a breath. "Mom, that is way too much."

Vella was hovering. "How much?"

There was a pause on the line, and then, "Dear, I *want* to do this. Please let me do this for my daughter."

Her mother's sincere tone brought tears to her eyes. "Thank you, Mom."

"You're very welcome." Her mother was happy again. "And get lots of pictures for me to see when I come back from the cruise."

"I will."

The two made their goodbyes, and, breathing deeply, Marilee hung up.

Vella, who had plopped herself on the end of the couch and was kicking off her shoes, said, "However much she is giving you, she can afford it. So how much is it?"

Marilee, who was considering exactly what to reveal to Vella about her mother's rivalry, told her.

"Oh, good. Now we can get a live band."

Marilee looked at her.

"It was your mother's idea, and I told her that would be a little costly. Isn't it nice that she took the hint?"

"Vella!"

"Marilee, your mother wanted instantly to help, and her way is to give you money. You can use it. Let her do this."

Aunt Vella eyed her. "It makes her feel good about herself, sugar. You hardly let your mother do anything for you. You hardly ever let *anyone* do for you. That is false pride. It is how you keep people from getting close to you."

Marilee gazed at her aunt, whose eyes did not waver.

"Now lay that pride aside. Take this gift from your mother graciously, thank her heartily, and enjoy it. You will be giving her the gift of a part in your life . . . of being helpful to you for a change."

The wedding preparations were well and truly under way. Marilee took twenty minutes to confer with Vella at the kitchen table.

"Margaret is set to do the dress and will search out the fabric and bring us samples. I gave Fred Grace a bare-bones idea of what we wanted in the way of vases and flowers, and he's working up an estimate. Bonita Embree will do the cake—white, with chocolate chips," Vella said.

"Tate okayed the invitations, and I've ordered them," she went on. "They will be ready on Thursday. I'm going to ask Belinda to address the envelopes. She has beautiful handwriting." She tapped her pencil on her lips. "We've got to get them in the mail before the end of the week. On second thought, you and I will have to do the addressing. Belinda is too slow."

"How many people did Tate come up with?"

"Oh, with couples, I figure about fifty-five or sixty, give or take a few."

Marilee stared at her.

"With your mother's list, that brings us to seventy-five, give or take a few. And you do know it is the custom to invite the entire church?

We don't have to send out invitations, though. We simply have an announcement put in the bulletin."

Vella made a note on her pad, then looked up to see Marilee staring at her.

"Sugar, don't worry. Only about half of these people will actually show up. And these will be the ones who love you."

Leaning forward, she laid her hand over Marilee's. "I think you should realize that you and Tate do have a certain standing in the town. And these people really care about you. They are happy for you and want to rejoice with you, sugar.

"You have never let yourself be fully happy. Do so now. Let yourself be happy and celebrate this time, Marilee."

It was sprinkling, so she drove to the paper, and just as she pulled into a space at the front sidewalk, it became a downpour. Impatient and determined to make the noon deadline—Marilee was habitually late and frequently taken to task for this by Charlotte—she raced through the rain and in the door, calling out to Charlotte, "I am on time this Monday."

Ever since Vella had spoken about allowing herself to be fully happy, she had been trying to see what that felt like. She smiled at Charlotte and produced her computer disk, as well as the folder with the paper copies. She could have sent the files directly from her computer, but she was not as yet comfortable with this. She always had an odd feeling, as if her articles were going off into outer space. She preferred to hand them personally to Charlotte and Tate.

Charlotte did not look up from her computer monitor.

"I'm on time," Marilee repeated as she laid the file folder and disk on the counter in front of Charlotte's desk.

"Yep," Charlotte said. That was all.

"How are you today, Charlotte?"

Charlotte glanced at her over her glasses. "In a hurry. It is deadline day."

"Yes, it is. I'll take these on into Tate." Marilee picked up the disk and folder again, then hurried off to Tate's office.

"I brought my pieces." She went to put the disk on his desk, which she saw was covered with black-and-white photographs. Before she could see what they were, however, he was up, shutting the door, taking her into his arms and kissing her.

Afterward, she laid her head on his chest. Just for a few seconds. She felt a thorough happiness for those seconds, too. Maybe that was how happiness came, in seconds, and one had to take note or one missed them.

She looked down to the photographs again. Stuart's, she thought, her eyes falling on a shot of the Goodnight's neon sign.

There were shots of the local motel's exterior and interior, and pictures of three other motels that appeared to date from the forties and fifties and were still in operation over on State Highway 81, Tate told her. Each had the explanatory text in Stuart's precise printing.

"He's captured the lingering glory under the shabbiness," Tate said, admiration in his voice. "He's good at what he does."

"He always was."

"He's lettin' us have these for nothing, except his byline."

"That's generous of him."

"Well, it isn't likely that printing them in a small local paper will keep one of the big magazines from buying his complete article. He's going down to get some shots from some places in Texas. He's decided to concentrate on towns along Highway 81—the Meridian Highway. Route 66 has been done to death.

"Oh, by the way, he wanted me to tell you that he's goin' down to Texas for the next couple of days, so don't look for him."

"He's left town?" She was surprised.

"Yes. He said he'll be back Wednesday evening." Tate studied her, and she averted her gaze downward again, at the photographs.

Why hadn't Stuart called her himself? She opened her mouth to ask Tate, but closed it. There was no need to question Tate about her ex-husband's motives. Of course, there was no particular reason for Stuart to speak directly to her, no need for her to be overly sensitive. Likely he would return, and in any case, it wouldn't matter if he did not.

"When are you going to print these?" she asked of the photographs.

"Starting them on Sunday. Gonna run a series of three. Put them in their own pullout insert," he said, eager and proud as a boy with a new toy.

It came as something of a surprise to experience a quiet evening. The children were in bed early, and she and Tate were alone. There was nothing like a good rain to slow things down. There came a pleasant pattering on the windows and roof, while they sat together on the sofa in front of a crackling fire.

Tate, kneeling and poking at the fire, said, "Do you realize we've barely been alone since my mother and your ex-husband arrived last week?"

"Yes. So don't waste time frittering with that fire, when you can sit here and fritter with me." She was really becoming bold in her honesty.

His smile thrilled her. He positioned himself next to her and pulled her into the curve of his shoulder.

"Oh, this is so nice," she said, sighing deeply and nestling close.

He nuzzled her ear and whispered, "Mmm, yes, ma'am, it is."

After a few minutes, she said, "What do you think of eloping?" She twisted and looked at him.

"Eloping?" His eyebrows went up, and the firelight reflected in his wide eyes.

"Yes. We could elope and not bother with a wedding." She again laid her head on his shoulder. He wore a cotton flannel shirt that was worn soft and carried his scent.

"I will do whatever you want to do, Marilee. The wedding will be nice, but it isn't essential. But we would have to face Vella, and now your mother." She had told him about her mother's gift of the wedding costs. "I don't know about that. I guess it depends on how badly you want to elope."

She sighed and thought of Corrine's face that evening, when told she would be the flower girl, which was Vella's idea.

"I just want it to be peaceful, like right now. This wedding—" she twisted to look at him "—there's more to it than I had imagined. It's like when a woman buys a dress. A new dress means one must have new shoes, and the new shoes have to have a bag to match, and sometimes one must have a sweater or coat to match all that. It all just grows."

"We should have just eloped the day we decided to get married." She flopped back against him.

He said, "We could elope, get it over with and still have the wedding."

"What would that accomplish? We would still be having the wedding."

They fell quiet.

"Maybe I should tell you," he said.

"Tell me what?"

"No, I don't think I should tell you. Spoil the surprise."

"You have to tell me now." Again she twisted to look at him.

"No, I don't."

"Yes, you do."

"Nah . . . you can wait."

"I won't leave you alone unless you tell me." She began nibbling on his ear and slipping her hand seductively inside his shirt.

"I can take it," he said, smiling broadly and showing how much he enjoyed her caresses.

"Oh, tell me, Tate. There, now I've begged."

He grinned. "Okay. I have a honeymoon booked at Walt Disney World. I don't have everything finalized, but we're gonna have the luxury suite, with the kids right across the sitting room from us, and a room for the nanny."

"A nanny?"

"Yes, ma'am. Fully qualified, with references. It's sleeping late, breakfast in bed, champagne with dinner. Top of the line all the way . . . if that is agreeable with you. It is all contingent on you accepting the idea, too."

"Oh, Tate." She stared at him. "You planned for the children to come on our honeymoon?" What manner of man was she about to marry?

"I want their mother's undivided attention. I'm no fool. And since we're startin' this thing out as a family, we might as well get used to the concept."

She laughed and hugged him so hard that he had to caution her not to break his neck or wake up the children with her excitement.

"Boy, I sure wish the wedding date would hurry up and get here." She was ready to get on with the honeymoon.

"Anticipation, remember?" he said, with a wicked gleam in his eye, as he pulled her across his lap.

A while later they broke apart, both breathless and perspiring, gazing longingly at each other.

"I do want the wedding," she said in a soft voice, as if hesitant at admitting too great a desire. "I do," she said more firmly and daringly. "I want to celebrate this that we've found, Tate."

She could not express what she felt she had found. The single word, love, seemed not to cover it. It was so precious, so far beyond her understanding.

"I want to honor our marriage, and to share the joy with our friends." She had wanted this all along but had been afraid to speak of it, as if, once spoken, the powers that were always ready to snatch away dreams would surely snatch this one.

"We'll do it," he said with conviction.

She sighed and laid her head against him, staring into the fire. Why did she always feel the other shoe was about to fall? Why could she not simply accept the happiness, without feeling guilty or anxious, and that she was in some way going to have to pay dearly for it?

Eighteen

Change begets change. . . .

It was warmer in Dallas than it had been up in Valentine. Stuart felt the morning sun through the pale blue shirt he wore. Even sheltered by sunglasses, his eyes squinted slightly in the glare from all the sun-bright concrete of the hospital complex.

Having always traveled, he was adept at confidently finding his way to where he wanted to go in an unfamiliar setting. There was the sign: Cancer Center. All one had to do when going anywhere, he mused, was follow the signs. It would have been better if there were such direct signs on the journey through life. Turn here for the Walk of Fame . . . take this road for Relationship Success.

Although he could not say that he would have done things differently, he did so much wish things had turned out different. Wished that he had formed true friendships. But he had always found them binding in some way and had simply not been able to do so. That was the fact. No need to wish for what was not. No need to let it hurt.

Standing just outside the automatic doors was a frail-looking woman wearing a green turban, with oxygen tubes attached to her nose. Her husband—or a man Stuart took to be her husband—stood beside her, his hand on the handle of the wheeled oxygen bottle.

Stuart turned his eyes from the pair and focused on the darkly tinted doors as they slid open.

Just inside the doors, his gaze fell on a boy in a wheelchair. The boy's pallor and shaved head bore witness to sickness. Stuart's gaze slid sideways and fell on a woman, probably the boy's mother, who stood nearby, conferring with a hospital person, identified by a pleasant blue smock and a name tag bearing the hospital insignia. Hospital personnel were like soldiers, he thought.

He skirted the information booth, went around a corner and then turned, taking the camera he more often than not carried slung over his shoulder, unsnapping the case and checking the light. Quickly, in one motion and all on instinct, not a designed purpose, he stepped out from the corner, focused on the boy in the wheelchair and clicked. Then he pressed his back against the wall and snapped the cover in place.

He remained pressed against the wall for several seconds, feeling a little dizzy and out of breath. When that settled, he went back to the information booth, where he was given directions to the lab by a woman far too perky to be appreciated in such a place.

He went down the hall and made the turns, passing hospital personnel chatting, an elderly man being wheeled by an equally elderly woman—he held the double doors open for them—and a big man with his head bandaged, who seemed disoriented and had to be led along by his wife and a male nurse.

At the window of the lab, he was directed to fill out some papers by a pleasant woman who appeared so young as to give him an urge to ask for her ID. He refrained from the joke, which she might find in poor taste. Besides, he wanted it all done, with as little chatting as possible.

He knew the routine, had provided everything beforehand by the miracle of fax and computer, but they needed the information again, the young woman told him in a patient manner. He was reminded of how everyone in Texas always seemed rather happy and never in a hurry, except when driving on the interstate—where vehicles flew rather than drove.

He filled out the form and returned it to the young woman, who told him to have a seat.

Several minutes later the double doors swung open, and through them came a man in a wheelchair. Stuart took him in—he could have been anywhere from fifty to eighty, pale complexion, shoulders slumped, eyes vacant, being pushed by a burly male nurse, who said, "Wait right here for a minute, Mr. W—"

Stuart did not catch the man's name, and he quickly overted his attention and gaze to the wall, where a big print of three Navaho women hung. It was a semi-abstract. He thought of his father, dead now some forty-three years. Where had the years gone? He never liked to think about his father and felt a foolish anger at the old man in the wheelchair for reminding him.

Another turn of his head and he saw his faint reflection in a glass partition. He jerked his gaze away, looking at magazines on a nearby table but not having the inclination to browse. He'd seen most of them already anyway.

Ten minutes ticked by, and no one came for the man in the wheelchair. Stuart, who glanced surreptitiously at the man, began to worry, as it looked as if the man was listing to one side. Another five minutes, and still no one came.

Stuart, who was checking his watch every minute or so by then, began to hope his name was not called for the lab tests, because he wanted to make certain someone came for the sick man, who was definitely listing to one side. He began to worry all sorts of worries about the man's needs that no one was seeing to. What if the man had been forgotten, overlooked? What if he sat there and died, and no one knew? Stuart kept glancing at the woman at the desk, to see if she paid any attention; he debated speaking to her about the sick man.

A glance around the waiting room, but he saw no one else who seemed concerned. They were all either talking or had their nose in a magazine, or simply stared at their shoes. Mostly definitely no one looked at each other, as if they could not bear to see more sickness.

In an automatic manner born of his lifetime's work, Stuart unsnapped his camera cover and quickly focused, snapping the man's picture without anyone in the waiting room knowing what he did. And then he took another of the room of people.

"Stuart James?" A young woman in the hospital uniform and holding an official-looking clipboard stood at the double doors.

He got up and followed her, leaving the sick old man still sitting in his wheelchair. He was about to ask the young woman about the man when she directed him through another door, leaving him standing alone, awaiting further instruction.

When his tests where done, he returned to the waiting room to find that the sick man in the wheelchair was gone. He was greatly relieved.

Although the appliance store—his future wife's stepfather's store—agreed, for a handsome extra fee, to same-day delivery, they absolutely refused to haul away the old appliances. "Not our job. We deliver. That's it."

Tate thought this was pretty tacky, considering the small fortune he had just dropped in their store. Stuart James wasn't the only one who could splurge on the latest in home technology.

Asking for help had always been difficult for him. He mentally went through the list of men who might be willing to lend a hand. Short list. Finally he sucked up his pride and put in a call to Parker Lindsey. "Hey, does a best man help move out old appliances?"

Lindsey said he didn't know about best man rules, but he would help. He could come over around noon in his old pickup truck that he kept for those times he might have to haul around a hog or dogs or equipment. The man's ready willingness made it easier for Tate to breathe.

They tackled the old curved-top Kelvinator first. They wrestled it out the door and onto the top step and then across onto the opened tailgate of Lindsey's old pickup. Next they hauled out the stove, vintage seventies' gold, and then the dishwasher from around the same time period. Part of the floor came up with the dishwasher.

"Watch it, don't drop that corner on your toe."

"Just yank it up."

"If we scoot it around this way, it'll go through the door."

"In your dreams."

"Be careful . . . don't . . . You okay?"

It was work from which friendships grew.

"Thanks, buddy. I'll do the same for you sometime," he told Lindsey, puffing a little when they closed the pickup tailgate.

It was a new experience for him, having a friend to help him like this. He grabbed Lindsey's hand and shook it with feeling.

Lindsey grinned. "You'll be following up on that payback sooner than you realize. Amy is makin' her plans to redo my whole house. You know, you might have wanted to let Marilee do this herself. Women are a little funny about gettin' things in the house how they want them."

"Oh, I intend to leave her plenty to work on, but I didn't want her to have to put up with too much old stuff right off. Don't want to frighten her away."

He waved Lindsey off and watched the truck head out into the street, carrying the old appliances away to join all the other decades of used up and discarded appliances at the landfill. One day the planet would likely be made of such things, he thought.

The delivery truck arrived. He raced outside and directed it through the portico and around the back. It would be more convenient to bring the things through the back door, plus he didn't want to take any chances of Marilee spotting the truck. He thought it might be too much to hope that his neighbor across the street wasn't keeping a watch out her window.

Two bulky young men did the job of bringing in the appliances and setting them in place. Tate stood back and watched. Young muscles and experience made bringing the new in seem a lot easier than it had been taking the old out.

"You don't have a hookup for the ice maker," the young man told him, looking a little perplexed at not finding a water hose connection.

"Is that a requirement for the refrigerator to work?" Tate asked, feeling definitely behind the times.

"Oh . . . no. But your ice delivery in the door won't work . . . and neither will the cold water. It's inconvenient," he added, still holding the perplexed expression.

"I'll have a pipe put in." Tate made a note on an index card to locate a plumber.

In came the stove. The trim at the end of the counter had to be broken off for the stove to fit. Tate had mismeasured. He made another notation for a carpenter. After getting the gas pipe hooked up, the young man told him very seriously that he needed to have a new gas pipe run. "I did the best I could, but this here hookup is old, and it's leaking. Smell it?"

"I don't smell anything."

"Then you're the one in a hundred who can't smell it. I'd have a repairman come, if I was you. You might wake up dead one mornin'."

"I can smell it," said his mother, who came over sniffing. She added, "I'm one of the few who is able to smell carbon dioxide, too." The young man gave her a respectful look.

The dishwasher fit exactly. "Can't stop this water leak, though," the young man told him. "You'll have to get the repairman. You need a new connection. I think you might need a whole new pipe comin' in here. And some floorin'."

Tate made more notes on the index card. He wondered if he was going to end up having the entire house replumbed and rewired. He might have to sell the house in order to raise the money for all the remodeling that was going to be required.

Then he remembered the look on Marilee's face when she had received her washer and dryer. It was worth any amount of money to see her face when she beheld these new appliances. He had topped Stuart James, yes, sir.

It sure brought a man high to be able to please his woman, he thought, waving off the appliance deliverymen.

He went back inside and saw his mother caressing the new stove with great reverence. "I'll make some fresh bread," she said with enthusiasm. "We must make certain it works correctly."

"Don't tell Marilee," he cautioned her, afraid she would get carried away and let the cat out of the bag.

He glanced around the room and thought that he'd better have painters in, too, at least for the kitchen. The gleaming brand-new appliances made the walls and cabinets look twice as shabby. Knock out the wall to the old laundry-storage room and do it up right with new linoleum and refinished woodwork. Maybe even new windows.

It was like Marilee had said, get one thing, and then another was required, and another and another. Change begat change, he thought, and found that revelation as disconcerting as it was exciting.

As fate would have it, Honey Moon, his decorator with the outlandish name, telephoned him that very afternoon to say that her emissaries were set to come the following day to begin work on the bedroom walls.

"We are doing a texture on the walls. Apricot sunset."

"O-kay." Tate tried to let go the urge to question and direct.

"You'll love it," the woman told him in her sultry voice. "Trust me."

He almost asked her if she could handle repainting the kitchen, then decided that he needed some control somewhere. He would find his own painters and choose his own colors, too. White. Basic white appeared to be back in favor.

"By the way," said Honey Moon, "you'll have to move out of the bedroom."

Even though it was cool and breezy, Aunt Marilee wasn't there after school to pick them up, and they got to walk home. When they reached the corner of their block, Corrine saw Aunt Vella's Land Rover parked out front. Ricky Dale, who had walked with them, pushing his bicycle, got on it and pedaled on home, calling to her, "I'll be back pretty quick."

While Willie Lee rolled around with Munro in the yard, Corrine raced up on the porch. She pulled over the little stool, stood on it, stuck her hand in the mailbox on the wall and fished around inside, bringing out three envelopes and an IGA flyer.

Her spirit drooped with disappointment. There was no package from her mother. It was awfully early for the present her mother had promised to come. Her mother would put off mailing things for days. She might even forget she had said she would send a surprise, Corrine reminded herself. There was no need to keep hoping, because she might be disappointed.

She went on inside, where Aunt Marilee, Aunt Vella and a woman she recognized as living in the house on the corner were sitting at the dining-room table.

"Come here, honey," Aunt Marilee said, "We need you to choose a dress for the wedding. Mrs. Wyatt is going to make it."

On her way across the room, Corrine dropped her backpack on the sofa and placed the mail on her aunt's desk. Then her aunt introduced her to Mrs. Wyatt, who was a pleasant-looking woman. Corrine stayed plastered to Aunt Marilee's side.

Her aunt showed her two patterns. "Do you like either of these?"

Corrine studied the drawings, tilting her head this way and that, trying to imagine. "This one, I think." She watched her aunt carefully.

She knew she had chosen correctly when Aunt Marilee smiled. "That's the one Vella and I like best, too." Corrine felt relieved.

It took Mrs. Wyatt only about three minutes to measure Corrine, who did her best to be still. Then, finally, it seemed okay for her to leave. She slipped away to change her clothes and was just tying her play sneakers when she heard the front door open and close, and Willie Lee call out, "I'll get her."

"Well, hello, Ricky Dale," said Aunt Marilee. Corrine, coming out of the bedroom, almost ran into Willie Lee. "Ric-ky Dale is here. He wants us to come with him to see his grand-moth-er."

Corrine went into the living room and heard Ricky Dale saying, "It won't take long, Miz James. After I see my grama, then we can go to take care of the horses. I'll take real good care of Willie Lee."

"I know you will, Ricky Dale," Aunt Marilee said. She had a thorough liking for Ricky Dale. "At five o'clock you come on home," she said to Corrine. "I'll be expectin' you by five-fifteen."

"Yes, ma'am."

"And you all mind that horses kick."

"Yes, we will." Corrine saw that her aunt was getting that worried expression and feared she might change her mind about allowing them to go, so she edged toward the door, tugging Willie Lee along.

Then Aunt Vella asked, "How is Minnie doin', Ricky Dale? Is her eye still giving her trouble?"

"Yeah. She still has to wear a patch." Corrine had the door open and implored him with eyes.

"You tell Minnie I said hello, and I'll stop by tomorrow," Aunt Vella called as they slipped out the door.

Corrine closed the door and whispered to Ricky Dale: "What's this about your grandmother?" She wanted to get over to see the horses and didn't appreciate being dragged around the neighborhood.

Ricky Dale motioned for them to come off the porch. His stupid dog, Beau, was on the walkway acting goofy, and Munro growled at him. Beau sat and panted.

"My grama found out today that her old cat has liver disease. It's been sick for months, and Doc Lindsey told her he has done all he can." Ricky Dale looked from Corrine to Willie Lee. "My grama really loves this cat, and Mama is afraid she is goin' to give up livin' when the cat dies."

Corrine looked at Willie Lee, who looked back at them.

"Grama has to rest her eye at this time of day, so she's layin' down listenin' to *Lake Woebegone* on the radio. We can go in the back door, Willie Lee can touch the cat, and no one will know."

Ricky Dale's grandmother, Minnie, lived over on First Street, two houses before the pastor's house.

"How are you gonna get the cat?" Corrine wanted to know as they went down the side yard to the back. "You're gonna have to find it. What if your grama hears you?"

They came to the back door, and Corrine stopped, waiting for an answer to this question before she would move another inch. She took hold of Willie Lee's hand and held him, too. She liked to have a plan.

Ricky Dale had to come back to them. "She isn't gonna hear me, but if she does, I'll just tell her that I'm showin' Willie Lee the cat."

"Why would you show Willie Lee a sick cat?"

"Who cares? You guys wait here, and I'll bring it out."

He went up the brick steps, opened the screen door and then the big door without hardly a sound, and disappeared inside. Willie Lee sat himself on the bottom brick step, and Munro sat beside him. Corrine stood with her arms crossed, and Ricky Dale's black dog lay beside her feet, thankfully quiet for once. Perhaps Munro was training him.

A few minutes later Ricky Dale came out, quickly and quietly, with a big old grey fluffy cat. A Persian. He handed the cat to Willie Lee. Fur went everywhere.

"It's losin' its hair," Ricky Dale whispered. Indeed, it did seem like it was getting patchy, Corrine thought. Other than that, it was just an old cat.

Ricky Dale took hold of Beau, who wanted to sniff the cat. Munro pressed up close to Willie Lee, who said hello to the cat and then showed the cat to Munro. The cat seemed too sick to be worried about the dogs. He just lay in Willie Lee's arms. Ricky Dale said it hadn't eaten in two days.

Corrine watched her cousin pet the animal. Willie Lee's eyes looked closed, but she wasn't certain. She looked carefully to see if he glowed, but the sun was very bright, and she thought it might just be the sun shining on him.

"Are you done, Willie Lee?" Ricky Dale asked after what seemed a long time, and Willie Lee was still petting the cat.

"O-kay," Willie Lee said, looking upward with a smile. "He is a nice cat."

"Did you make him better?" Ricky Dale asked.

"May-be." Willie Lee shrugged.

Ricky Dale took the cat back inside, and then they went over to Mr. Winston's to see the horses. Ricky Dale led the way on a path that cut through yards. Corrine had a daring feeling, as if she were entering a new part of her life, beginning to learn about the neighborhood, where she had lived for over two years and yet had not before ventured beyond her aunt's and Mr. Tate's houses.

Taking hold of Willie Lee's hand, she told Ricky Dale to take the other, and they began to run, lifting Willie Lee, who giggled in delight, off the ground. They ran until they fell, all at once in a heap and laughing, then got up, lifted Willie Lee, and ran again.

When her gaze lit on the horses, Corrine hurried on ahead of the boys, forgetting about Willie Lee in a rare moment of rapture. The mare came slowly forward, put down her nose, and Corrine exchanged breaths with her.

The recent rain had caused the three-sided stall to be overly wet. Totally disgusting to Corrine, who did not like messy, and she would not have had anything to do with it, but Ricky Dale was her friend. Loyalty, which Corrine possessed in abundance, compelled her to help.

They worked side by side, shoveling the old urine- and rain-soaked shavings and manure into a wheelbarrow, which Ricky Dale, the biceps of his skinny arms bulging, would then push outside to a compost pile. He was thorough and intent on pleasing his employer, whom he said was very particular about her horses having a clean stall with fresh pine shavings. Corrine wanted to please both the horses and her innate desire for neatness.

Just then, hearing Willie Lee's laugh, she looked up to see him atop the mare. Her heart leaped in her throat. Throwing down her manure rake, she hurried forward, but Ricky Dale grabbed her arm.

"He's okay. Let him be. Don't scare the mare."

She held her breath as she watched. If anything happened to Willie Lee, Aunt Marilee would die. Corrine was supposed to look out for him. She would die, too, if anything happened to him.

Her eyes fastened on to Willie Lee, she watched him be carried around by the mare, who walked in a lazy manner, while Willie Lee gripped her mane and grinned happily. The filly, prancing, followed at the mare's hip.

Willie Lee looked over and saw them. "Look at me," he said, proud as could be.

Winston, inside at the kitchen sink, glanced out the window and saw the small boy atop the big paint mare. "I thought you said that mare was barely green broke," he said to his niece, who was at the table, painting her fingernails.

"She is. She's only been ridden maybe twice."

"Well, it's three times now." Winston watched Willie Lee in the act of getting the mare to move over beside the rail fence, while Corrine climbed up to get on behind him.

"Ohmygod! She'll kill them," said Leanne, who had come to peer beside him. "I told Ricky Dale . . . I told him not to try to ride her."

"Well, apparently no one told Willie Lee," Winston said. Seeing the stricken expression on his niece's face, he added, "Honey, there ain't nothin' you can do but trust God right this minute. And it looks like it's all okay," he added, returning his gaze to the corral and watching the two figures, the small boy and the taller girl, be carried around by the big horse in a perfectly gentle manner. He was not so amazed as Leanne, who, he noticed, stood there with a baffled expression, still carefully holding her fingernails out, as if doing some sort of Chinese Kung Fu stance. He was older and had seen his dead wife reappear, so he didn't think anything could surprise him.

"That mare might want to throw *you* off," he told her, "but she knows those are kids. She'll take care of 'em. Kids and animals are closer together. They're closer to the Lord in their innocence."

Still watching the children in the sunlight, he remembered back in time to his own children, who had ridden in that same corral. "Not much prettier than kids and horses, is there?" he said.

He didn't think Leanne heard him, though, as she was through the back door before he finished. He watched her stride toward the corral, checking her pace as she neared, mindful of not scaring the mare.

"Corrine!" Aunt Marilee called. "Telephone for you. It's Ricky Dale." She raised an amused eyebrow.

Corrine took the telephone. "Hello." She had never spoken to a friend on the phone. And Ricky Dale was a boy.

"I wanted to tell you that my grama just called and said that her ol' cat ate half a can of food tonight. Grama's real excited."

"Well, good." She breathed easier because her aunt Marilee moved away.

"Maybe it will live."

"Maybe. I hope so," she added, wanting to let him know that she hoped the best for his grandmother and her cat.

"Well, guess that's it. Tell Willie Lee."

"Okay."

"See you tomorrow at school. Want to do the horses with me again?"

"Oh, yes. If I can."

They said goodbye, and Corrine happily replaced the receiver.

When Aunt Marilee tucked them into bed, Willie Lee said, "I ride-ed a horse to-day."

Corrine held her breath. Thus far, in telling the story of his ride, Willie Lee had not slipped up and revealed that they had ridden without permission, and that Leanne Overton had forbidden them to ride anymore. Likely her aunt would worry and not let them go to the corral.

"Yes, you did," her aunt said with a smile and kissed Willie Lee.

"I guess I can-not fly, but I can ride a horse."

"That's right, honey. A boy cannot fly, but a boy can ride a horse."

Thankfully Willie Lee just said, "I am glad I am a boy," and turned over.

Aunt Marilee said she was glad Willie Lee was *her* boy, kissed him, and then came over to hear Corrine's prayers. She said, tucking the covers around Corrine, "A girl can ride, too."

Corrine nodded, careful not to say anything. That was the best way not to slip up with a wrong word.

Her aunt turned out the light and left the room. Corrine listened to her aunt's footsteps go away into the kitchen, then she whispered a fresh caution to Willie Lee not to talk a bunch about riding the horse. "Aunt Marilee won't let us go over there if she finds out we rode the mare without askin'."

After a minute Willie Lee whispered back, "I rided, Cor-rine, just like a nor-mal boy."

Corrine blinked and knotted her hand in the covers. "You sure did. You were good, too."

A rage took hold deep inside of her. People thought because Willie Lee was a little backward that he couldn't understand that they made fun of him. That he didn't hurt like everyone else. Anytime Willie Lee suffered, she did, too, because of her immense desire to protect him and her frustration at not being able to do so. She wanted to beat up the entire mean world.

Nineteen

Family ties . . .

Moving out of the bedroom was not too hard. Presuming he could leave his clothes in the closet, he took himself off to sleep in the third bedroom down the hall. The bed was old and lumpy but would suffice. His mother brought him the Pledge and a dust rag, both of which he used on the nightstand, leaving everything else untouched.

Tate's definite dilemma, however, was how to keep Marilee away from his house and from seeing the work being done. He didn't want her to see anything until it was finished. He wanted it to be a great surprise. What if she decided to repeat her fanciful effort of bringing him morning coffee?

There was nothing else to do but head off all possibility of her coming to him by going to her first. Just before daybreak, he went hotfooting it across the backyards, bearing two bags from Juice's bakery at the IGA, where he had gotten the best French roast coffee and sweet rolls.

He crept in the back door and was instantly met by Munro, who blocked his way into the dimly lit kitchen. "It's me, Munro."

The dog wagged his stub of a tail.

Tate got Marilee's favorite mug and one for himself from the cabinet, and emptied the steaming contents of the foam cups into them. He arranged the sweet rolls on two plates.

Seeing Munro sitting there, gazing up at him, Tate broke off a bit from one roll and gave it to the dog.

He left one plate of sweet rolls on the table for the kids, put the other on a tray, along with the coffee, and headed through to Marilee's room. Outside it was growing lighter at a rapid rate. There was enough light coming in the windows for him to clearly see Marilee's tousled dark head of hair on her pale pillow. She did a little wuffling snore.

Standing there, gazing down at her creamy cheek, Tate's heart swelled with so much feeling as to bring a lump to his throat and cause him to forget himself and begin to sit on the side of the bed.

Just in time, he froze in midsit, as he remembered that Marilee didn't much care for mornings. He feared she would get aggravated at him for waking her.

Looking around, he quickly reviewed his options, which seemed few. Simply leaving his offerings might not keep her away from his house.

He decided to sit in the small chair and wait a few minutes. Maybe he would be lucky, and she would wake up on her own, he thought. He took a chance to edge the tray onto the table underneath the window, the tabletop already crowded with photographs, fancy glass bottles, books, and other odds and ends. He just about knocked over a bottle but caught it before it clattered.

Setting the bottle on the floor seemed the best choice.

Marilee snored loudly, and he practically jumped. He had to move some clothes draped on the chair in order to sit. He looked over the room, seeing the dresser top crowded with paraphernalia. Clothes, on hangers and off, hung over the closet door, and shoes were scattered about.

It was instructive, looking over her bedroom. He noted that rose was a repeated color. He would have to tell that to Honey Moon.

He was a neat person about clothes. He liked to put all his shirts of one color together in the closet. His mother had shaken her head at this. He said it was easier to get dressed with his clothes in such order. He wondered what Marilee would think of this habit. Separate closets appeared a must, another thing to mention to Honey Moon.

This room was all woman. It was frilly. It even smelled like a woman.

He liked the smell.

His gaze returned to Marilee. She was doing that little wuffling sound again.

He leaned back in the little chair, carefully, because it seemed dainty and perhaps could collapse under his weight. He watched the steam spiral up from the cups in the fresh light falling through the open window blinds.

Tate did not realize he had fallen asleep until he opened his eyes and saw three pairs of eyes staring at him.

"Good mornin', Tate," Marilee said, a slow, sultry smile playing across her lips. Sitting cross-legged on the bed, she sipped coffee and ate a sweet roll.

"Mis-ter Tate, you snore." Willie Lee was peering right at Tate's nose.

"So does your mother." He took up his coffee, which was no longer steaming, rose and went around the bed and climbed in, positioning himself against the propped up pillow.

Marilee and Corrine were staring at him as if he were some apparition.

"I do not snore," Marilee said.

"Yes, you do, and sweetly, too."

"You snore a little bit, Aunt Marilee," Corrine said, and then, apparently deciding retreat was in order, headed for the door, saying, "I'm goin' to get us some milk, Willie Lee."

They all ate together in the bed.

"I can get used to this," Tate said happily. Marilee gazed at him, as if wondering if he told the truth.

Tate ushered the children out the door to his BMW, leaving Marilee gathering her purse, keys and tote, as usual.

"Look, can you kids keep a secret?"

Corrine nodded, and Willie Lee said, "Mun-ro will, too."

"Okay. I need your help. I'm havin' a bunch of work done over at my house as a surprise for Marilee, for her wedding present. I don't want her to see any of it until it's done. Now, I need you two to either head her off or call me, if you find out she's about to come over to my house. Just for the next couple of weeks or so. Do you think you can help me out here?"

Corrine, bottom lip caught between her teeth, nodded eagerly, her dark eyes holding a rare sparkle.

"I will try, Mis-ter Tate," Willie Lee said in an elaborate whisper.

"How about you just callin' me Tate? Would that be all right with you?" This did not seem quite right, but it was all he could think of.

The boy blinked his eyes behind his thick glasses. "Yes. That is all right."

Then, as they got into the car and Marilee was joining them, Willie Lee asked from the back seat, "Ta-ate, you are go-ing to mar-ry my mo-ther, right?"

"Yep."

"But you will not be my fa-ther."

"No, son. Stuart is your father." Tate looked at Willie Lee in the rearview mirror, then glanced at Marilee. He felt on uncertain ground.

"Tate will be like your father, though, honey," Marilee said. "You will have two fathers. Why don't you call Mr. Tate Pa?" She seemed quite happy, as if having been very clever to think of this.

Tate wasn't certain he liked the sound of Pa. It seemed like that was a name for an old man.

Corrine piped up to ask, "What am I going to call you?"

What indeed?

"Why don't you call him Pa, too?" Marilee suggested. She was definitely pleased.

He glanced in the rearview mirror and saw Corrine's mouth moving, practicing the word. They were all going to sound like a family from the backwoods addressing their grandfather.

"How about Papa Tate," he said. It was marginally better, somehow. As he repeated it to himself, he found it had a certain ring to it, rather reminiscent of Papa Hemingway.

The discussion of the morning of what to call Tate got Marilee to thinking. She was Willie Lee's mother, but aunt to Corrine. Tate would be Willie Lee's stepfather but Corrine's . . . what? Stepuncle? Neither title carried any legal responsibilities.

Corrine, she thought, was like a little raft, adrift, having neither father nor mother. Certainly Marilee had no legal standing at all. This concern had passed across her mind so many times since the day she had brought Corrine home from Anita's. Not having a solid idea of how to cope with the fact, she kept putting off doing anything at all.

In an instant her mind had drawn up the distressing picture of having to bar the front door of the bungalow, holding off state officials with chiseled faces, but knowing she was doomed because the state, total strangers, had more rights than she did. The next instant, she saw the bungalow empty, lifeless, because she had moved away to Tate's big house and Corrine had been taken away.

The hard facts remained, as true today as the day Anita had given her Corrine's care—Anita could come at any time and take Corrine away, or they could be faced with a health catastrophe, because Corrine, not being Marilee's legal daughter, was not covered under Marilee's health insurance, and Anita did not have any health insurance at all.

When Marilee married Tate, likely she would go under his health insurance policy, as his wife, but this left Corrine and Willie Lee, no legal relations at all, out, drifting on their little raft.

Something had to be done.

"No, I won't accept your resignation."

Tate's loud voice jerked Marilee out of her troubling thoughts. She looked over to see him standing in the doorway of his office and shaking a paper at Charlotte, who strode to her desk.

"You can quit," he said, "but I won't accept it."

Marilee had never heard Tate yell. She had heard him annoyed with Charlotte and arguing with her, but never yelling.

Tate disappeared back into his office. There came a somewhat familiar clanging sound. He had kicked his trash can. Tate did not yell, until now, and he did not slam doors, but he had been known to kick his trash can.

Marilee's gaze swung over to Charlotte, sitting at her desk in the bright light falling through the plate-glass window.

Charlotte quitting? She had been with the *Voice* longer than any of them, for fifteen years, since she finished junior college and decided she liked working at the paper more than anything else and would not go on to higher education.

Marilee pushed up from her chair and hurried forward to her friend's desk. "You aren't quitting the paper?"

"Yes." Charlotte's mouth was an implacable line. "I'm going to head Molly Hayes's office. She's expanding her tax service."

"Charlotte." She stared at her friend, who finally raised her eyes. They were red-rimmed, Marilee saw. "Oh, Charlotte, don't do this."

"I have to," Charlotte said in a faint voice.

"No," Marilee said, quite suddenly angry. "You *choose* to."

Just then, as she walked away, she saw Sandy turning from the doorway of his glass cubicle. He was slumped as if someone had shot him.

They went to lunch at the Main Street Café.

"I'm not all that hungry," Tate said, as they slipped into one of the newly covered green vinyl booths.

Fayrene Gardner, with the passion of new ownership, was updating the café, and green was her favorite color. She had gone with a breezy and soothing fern-leaf-sprigged paper for the walls.

"I'm starved," Marilee said. She felt a little piqued over Tate's poor humor. She felt responsible for lifting him up, only she didn't know what to do for him.

She gazed across the table at him, and sympathy, and quite a bit of curiosity swept her. She had never seen him so angry. He was clearly wrought. This was gratifying, as it illuminated the fact that he was as human and shakable as the rest of them.

Perhaps she did recognize the scowl, she thought, remembering having seen it when she had been adamant about not entering into a relationship with him. He had reacted in the same fashion, she remembered. Feelings from that time, when she had so badly wanted to give in to her own desires for him and yet kept holding herself away out of fear, came flowing over her. She had treated him quite ruthlessly in her fear, and now here Charlotte was doing the same. How senselessly humans behaved.

Swamped with the urge to wipe away his hurt, she put her hand atop his. He gave her a smile, but it did not reach his eyes.

Fayrene, thoroughly familiar with serving them, came with glasses of ice tea. "Meat loaf is good today, Editor."

Marilee thought that it was a good thing she did not mind being second banana to Tate.

"Okay," he said, then withdrew his hand from Marilee's and rubbed his knuckles.

"I'll have a BLT," Marilee ordered. "And a piece of chocolate cake," she added, feeling in need of bolstering.

"Uh-huh." Fayrene jotted on her pad, gave them a speculative eye, then went away with their orders.

"I couldn't get her to see reason," Tate said, still rubbing his knuckles.

"There's no gettin' Charlotte to do anything she doesn't want to."

"I offered her a raise."

"It isn't the money, darlin'."

"I know that. It's her stupid pride. She thinks she's God. That she has to take care of her mother and make Sandy's decisions for him. That's what I told her, too."

Marilee nodded. She was dumping sugar into her ice tea and realized that she likely had enough.

"You've got to try and talk her out of it. We can't operate without her." His gaze was intense.

"Tate, when has anyone ever been able to talk Charlotte into or out of anything?" Even as she said this, she was mentally composing what she could say to Charlotte; all of it was angry, so better left unsaid. Why in the world was she so angry at Charlotte? Didn't the woman have a right to do whatever she wished? None of it was Marilee's problem.

Just then Franny came in, and, spying them, she swept over and slid in beside Marilee, who scooted over to make room. "We may have a band for the wedding," she said with some excitement.

Marilee gazed at her with surprise, and Franny explained that she had been alerted by Vella as to the need for a band.

"And then there I was at the post office, gettin' a post office box, and somehow out of my mouth came the information that we were lookin' for a band for your wedding, and Julia Jenkins-Tinsley told me about her brother's band."

Marilee wondered about Franny getting a post office box, but this question went unasked, because Franny continued to explain that the band was called the Swing Boys, and that they played both country swing and jazz.

This seemed a curious stretch of ability.

"Now, I haven't heard them, so I'm going on Julia Jenkins-Tinsley's opinion right now, and she is related to the band leader. They are playin' this Friday night over at the VFW club, so Winston and I are goin' over there to check them out."

Marilee regarded her, imagining her and Winston out on the dance floor. She wondered if she should add a word of caution.

Fayrene brought Tate's and Marilee's orders, and, assuming rightly, an ice tea for Franny, who ordered a large serving of guacomole and chips, based on Winston's recommendation that Fayrene's cook made the best guacomole in the state.

Then Franny wanted to know what was wrong, because Tate had the volcano expression. Tate eyed his mother, and Marilee explained about the crisis with Charlotte quitting, and all the whys and wherefores. By the time she finished, she had begun to worry that possibly this meant Charlotte would not be her bridesmaid.

"She probably won't want to have anything to do with a wedding. And Sandy will be there. We can't not invite him, especially since he'll still be workin' for the paper."

Thinking of Charlotte not working for the paper, she got overwhelmed and started in eating her chocolate cake before she finished all of her sandwich. In fact, she held the sandwich in one hand, while she forked the cake with the other.

"She is caught up in 'should living,'" Franny said. "Bless her heart. Oh, my, this guacomole looks wonderful!"

Realizing she had food in both hands, Marilee decided to go with the cake and laid the remaining bit of sandwich back on the plate.

Out on the bright sidewalk, heading back to the *Voice* offices, Marilee said, "Tate, we need to talk about some legalities with Willie Lee and Corrine."

"What legalities?" He appeared still preoccupied.

"We will need to consider where we stand in regards to legal guardianship. We have to do that for health insurance, and if anything else should come up where the children need a legal guardian. Like, what if something were to happen to me? Willie Lee wouldn't legally be your son, and Stuart could take him off to who knows where, and Corrine would be left hanging, too."

Actually, this disconcerting thought had just come to her.

"We have to discuss all this, Tate, and get straight what all we need to do to see that the children are secure."

"You're right," he said, glancing at his watch. "But I can't do it right this minute, because I have a meeting with the Downtown Improvement Alliance this afternoon, and before that I need to consult with Monahan about the insert for Sunday's edition." He opened the door to the building.

"How about tonight?" She was mentally checking what she had to do that evening. Stuart might show up. She probably should not begin a discussion with him until she and Tate had ironed things out.

Tate shook his head. "I'm coverin' the County Republican Party monthly meeting. The state chairman is gonna be there. In fact, it's a dinner meetin'."

"Tate, we have to get this straight." All sorts of concerns about the children were racing through her mind.

"I know, darlin'. We'll do it Thursday. How's that look for you?"

She thought it was okay.

"We'll take off in the afternoon, if we can, and spend some time together." He wiggled his eyebrows in their secret sign, kissed her cheek and headed away to his office, passing Charlotte's reception desk like a bullet.

Marilee looked at Charlotte, who kept her gaze on her computer monitor. She went on to her own desk, where she plopped down and opened her planner, seeing the notation for the following evening—invitations.

She sat there for some minutes, listening to time marching on.

Twenty

Letting go of yesterday . . .

In the late afternoon, with several windows thrown wide to the warming spring, and the radio playing country music, Marilee went searching through bureau drawers and closets for the topaz earrings that she and Anita had bought years ago at an antique shop in Dallas. She wanted them to go with the something new, which would be the dress, and the something borrowed, which would be her aunt Vella's vintage hair comb, and something blue, the garter, of course, to wear for her wedding.

In the course of the search, Marilee began dragging out long forgotten items, so many things that she had started to clean out the previous year, when she had been about to marry Parker. Then she had aborted both her marriage to Parker and the cleaning out, as well.

One of the things that she dragged out now was the ridiculous velvet robe with the fur collar that her mother had given her as a present. Evidence of her mother's love.

She slipped it on, surveyed herself in the mirror, laughed, and strode over to the table beneath the window to get her glass of ice tea, doing an impersonation of Bette Davis, letting the length of robe sweep grandly behind her.

That was how Stuart found her. "I knocked, but no one answered. I thought I heard the radio, and the door was unlocked." He was chuckling.

He had come back. He had said he would return, and he had followed through.

"Drama Queen at your disposal," she said grandly, presenting the back of her hand.

He strode forward, kissed her hand and whipped a bright bouquet of flowers from behind his back. "For my queen," he said.

"Oh, Stuart."

A lump formed in her throat. These were not roses. These were evidence of his thinking of her at an odd and tender moment. The gladness she felt amazed her, and, feeling the need to hide her emotions, she buried her face in the flowers, as if to inhale their fragrance.

Then she saw him whipping forth his camera.

"Oh, no, Stuart!" Seeing that she could not jerk the robe off in time, she then posed there in the fuzzy light falling through the screened windows.

"Enough." She removed the robe, even as he kept clicking shots.

Trying to ignore his action, and making faces into the camera at the same time, she strode to the kitchen to put the flowers into a vase, telling him along the way that the children were over helping a friend—"Ricky Dale, you remember him, don't you?"—look after some horses.

"Would you like to go see them?" she asked then, seizing the idea quite suddenly. "You should see Willie Lee, Stuart. He's so excited over the horses. They're just a little over a block away, an easy walk."

Struck with the idea of encouraging him to get to know his son, as well as the excuse to cut short their time alone, she barely gave him the opportunity to decline, plunked the flowers into a quart mason jar, and was leading the way out the back door, taking a shortcut across Tate's backyard, all the while chatting about Willie Lee's and Corrine's newfound love of horses.

To her own amazement, she brought forth an idea that had been percolating in the back of her mind that a horse might be a particularly good learning tool for Willie Lee, to help build his sense of self-confidence, as well as something that could be employed in the specialty classes for the learning disabled children that she helped develop for the local school.

Stuart walked along beside her, ducking under several low-hanging tree branches, his hands easy in the pockets of his slacks, his head tilted in a manner that indicated he was actually listening intently.

"The mare ain't gonna come over this way, 'cause y'all are strangers," Ricky Dale informed them. He stood there at the fence with them, the short sleeves of his T-shirt rolled up on his skinny arms in the manner of thirteen going on seventeen, while they watched Willie Lee and Corrine pet the big horse and her baby.

Stuart clicked shot after shot with his camera. There was a curious intensity to his expression. Marilee supposed that he had always been intense with his photography, and that this quality had simply grown stronger with his age.

Willie Lee demonstrated how he could call the filly, and Ricky Dale said, as if he were proud, "That filly'll follow Willie Lee anywhere."

Marilee and Stuart applauded, while Willie Lee beamed and said, "She likes me."

"Well, of course," said Marilee, with motherly pride.

"We can-not ride the mare. Miss-uss Over-ton said not to," Willie Lee told them.

"She did?" Marilee said, puzzled.

"She wants to be here with us," Corrine said. "Can we bring them carrots tomorrow, Aunt Marilee? They like carrots and apples."

As they walked back through the yard, Winston came outside and visited with them for a few minutes. He shook first Stuart's hand and then Willie Lee's, in the familiar way the two had developed long ago. He bragged on the children's care of the horses in a way that was good for children to hear.

Then they walked home, by way of the sidewalk this time. At one point Willie Lee took hold of Stuart's hand. Impatient with the slower elders, Corrine and Ricky Dale began a game of tag and enticed Willie Lee to join in with them, adapting themselves to his slower movements.

Watching, Marilee gave thanks at being able to provide a carefree sort of childhood for Willie Lee and Corrine.

"We don't appreciate our childhood until we're far beyond it," Stuart said, apparently having some of Marilee's same thoughts. "At least I didn't."

Marilee nodded. She often felt she'd never had a childhood, but let this thought go unspoken.

Stuart took several shots of the children, and then said, "I didn't appreciate what I had with you, either, until it was gone. My excuse is that it took me a long time to grow up. I guess a person has to get beyond some things to really see what they were. I regret that, Marilee. Please accept my apology."

She stared at him, speechless, searching his face for sincerity. "I accept," she said, and swallowed. "It was a long time ago. It's water under the bridge now."

Feelings that she didn't want to deal with tumbled over her.

After another minute, as she watched the children running and laughing in the street, she added, "I apologize for ever blaming you, Stuart. And you know, I do believe that everything works out for the best. It's been best for me on my own. I had a lot of growing up to do, too. And I've had a good life here, and so has Willie Lee."

Looking at Stuart then, she saw him nod and avert his gaze downward. He looks so old, she thought suddenly. And tired, and sad. She was struck deeply.

"Today is what matters, Stuart. I'm glad you've come." She took his hand and squeezed it.

His response was surprise, then a smile. Marilee hoped he didn't misinterpret her overture and think she wanted more than she did. But she was glad for what she had said. It was as if a burden had been lifted from her shoulders.

When they reached the front porch, Stuart asked, "Where's Tate this evening?"

"He has to cover a political meeting."

He nodded.

"Are you stayin' for supper?" She very much wanted him to.

"I can, Miz James," Ricky Dale put in. "But I gotta call my mom."

"Then do so . . . but your dog cannot come in the house." Chuckling, she looked at Stuart with a raised eyebrow.

"Are you making spaghetti?" he asked, and she was relieved to see his playful humor had returned. "I always liked your spaghetti."

"You did? I didn't know that."

"I did," he said adamantly, and as they all went into the house, he told the children how Marilee had managed to make spaghetti on a hot plate in a number of hotels.

Although she had not fully discussed things with Tate, the quiet evening with Stuart seemed the golden opportunity to broach the matter of Willie Lee's present precarious legal situation and the possibility of Tate adopting him. Surely Stuart would not take offense, but would see that the best interest of his son was at stake.

Help me, God. Give me the words.

All through the meal, the conversation carried mostly by the children, she watched her ex-husband and mentally composed ways of opening the subject of Willie Lee.

She came out from tucking the children into bed to find Stuart had made coffee and brought the pot and mugs on a tray into the living room. He had the stereo playing soft music.

"May I have this dance?" he said in a grand manner.

She went loosely into his arms, keeping a proper distance as they waltzed around the room. Stuart had always possessed a litheness and grace that made dancing with him a special experience.

Inhaling his scent, feeling the crisp cotton of his shirt beneath her fingertips, feeling the movements of their bodies to the music and his hand warm on her back, it occurred to Marilee that the three men she had loved each had a certain grace and smoothness about them. Educated men, all, and lovers of fine things, even fine moments.

She looked into his face then. He smiled at her, that winsome, endearing smile.

The music ended, and Stuart released her, saying, "Shall we have our coffee before it gets cold?"

He sat on the sofa. She picked up her mug and, feeling the need of distance, sat in the big armchair, kicking off her shoes and curling one leg beneath her. She felt uncertain of the intimacy between them, and glad for it, too.

"Your coffee is very good," she told him, breaking the silence.

"I learned on my own." Again that self-deprecating smile.

There was another silence, and then Stuart said, "You've done a really good job with Willie Lee."

She chuckled. "I think Willie Lee is the one who does a good job with everyone else."

They fell quite naturally to speaking about their son then. She got up, retrieved Willie Lee's baby book from the shelf and brought it to the couch, where she sat beside him and showed him the pages with some eagerness to share with him what he had mistakenly given up.

Closing the book, she sat with it on her knees. "Stuart . . ."

He gazed at her with a raised eyebrow.

"I have been thinking that it would be best if Tate adopted Willie Lee. He never intends to take your place with Willie Lee, but there are legal considerations, such as insurance, and to have Willie Lee provided for if anything should happen to me."

Stuart looked down at his hands.

"Willie Lee will always need care. He'll always need to be provided for. These are things that must be planned for long-term."

Stuart nodded in a manner that allowed Marilee to quit holding her breath. He leaned forward, his forearms on his thighs. "I think . . ." His voice was hoarse, and he cleared his throat. "It is the prudent course. I have no objections."

"Thank you, Stuart." She was so grateful she had not given in to her spiteful feelings of days before. She had misjudged him, and was glad not to have revealed it.

"I want to help provide for Willie Lee," he said. "I know I haven't done anything regular. And I'm pretty ashamed of the amount of money I've gone through. But I do have some savings and some stock investments. I want to turn it all over to him."

Marilee didn't think it would be very nice to say that Willie Lee had money. She reached over and took his hand. "Be here in his life, Stuart, whenever you can. We welcome you."

Stuart looked at her, and then stared at the floor. "I guess that's still the one thing I can't do, any more than I ever could. You see, I don't have long to live."

Marilee wondered if she had heard correctly. Surely not.

He was looking at her.

"What?" She drew her hand from his.

"I'm dying, Marilee. I have maybe six weeks to three months."

He gazed at her for some moments, in which she stared at him, having no idea of what to say; in fact, a certain roaring began in the back of her brain and spread to her ears, so that she heard his voice just above it, as he told her that he had an incurable cancer, already spread to his liver and other places, and that even if he could have been offered treatment, he wouldn't have taken it, because what sort of life would he be given?

Of all the things he might have said to her, of all the things she had imagined, such as him walking out without a word and not returning, or him going crazy and running off with Willie Lee—only she had never really believed this, simply thought it up in angry moments—or getting a phone call to tell her he had dropped dead out on some photo-shoot in the far reaches of Tibet or glitzy Monaco, this was one thing she had not imagined.

So why had he come back? She listened as he told her, in a roundabout fashion. She listened, and she looked at the coffeepot and cups on the tray he had brought in, and she thought of the colorful bouquet that sat now on the kitchen table, and the brand-new washer and dryer, which she was using almost maniacally, and the giant vase of roses. And the way he had danced with her.

Thinking of all these things, the roaring grew louder in her ears and her hands knotted into fists in her lap.

"My father died of cancer," he told her, his face drawn and his eyes on the coffee table. "In a nursing home. I went to see him. He was in a bed pushed against a wall."

He looked at her. "I didn't understand anything then. I didn't understand that the way I lived was the same way he had lived, not forming any attachments, and that then in the end, there isn't anyone. I don't know how I'll face that. I don't know how I'll face any of this."

So he had come to her. And brought presents.

He gazed at the coffee table.

"What do you want from me?" said Marilee, who sat with her spine ramrod straight, her hands in fists in her lap.

His head came up. He frowned and ran a hand over his face. "I don't know. I just thought that I wanted to see you . . . and Willie Lee."

He looked at her, at her hands. "I know I don't deserve anything from you, Marilee. God knows, I know I'm asking a lot, but . . . I was hoping to just be with you, as much as I can."

"You are hoping to be with me."

An uncertain expression passed over his features.

"I am getting married, Stuart. In one month."

He nodded, again looking pitiful. "I know," he said in a hoarse, low tone. Then he chuckled. "If I could have, I would have had better timing."

She counted to ten, but the words came out anyway. "We are divorced, Stuart. We have been divorced for nine years. I am marrying another man. I am going to be his wife. I don't quite know how I can say to him, 'Oh, by the way, my ex-husband needs me to be with him for the first months of our marriage.' "

It was sarcasm, and it cut like a knife. She saw him wince, as if from a blow. She hated herself for allowing her anger to have control. Compassion fought for a place, but so did the urge to lift the sofa cushion and beat the living daylights out of him.

"I have Willie Lee and Tate and Corrine to think of. And my own life, Stuart. I'm not putting all of us aside for you. I'm not doing it."

She was on her feet and speaking loudly with the last of it. Totally at a loss, she turned and strode around the couch and into her bedroom, where she managed to keep herself from slamming the door, at the last minute thinking of the children.

She plopped down on the bed; then after a minute, she got up and checked the drawer of her bedside table for some chocolate. Finding none, she slammed the drawer closed.

She paced for some minutes; then, turning out the light, she lay back on the bed and stared up at the ceiling. She thought she heard the front door open and close, but she wasn't certain, and wasn't about to open the door and look and possibly have to face him again. She felt imprisoned in her own bedroom. She felt as if she could hardly breathe, and as if she, too, were fighting for her life.

She tossed and turned and cried into the pillow. She reached for the phone half a dozen times but did not call Tate. She didn't want to wake him. She wondered at him not calling when he came in, but likely he had come in late, figured she would be asleep and decided not to wake her.

Her not calling him was more than not wanting to wake him. It was shame at her attitude. Shame at showing her anger at a dying man. Surely Tate would think her heartless. Or else he would be outraged at Stuart, and she couldn't bear that.

Stuart did not mean that he wanted to be with her. What he meant was that he didn't want to be alone. He had come to her to take care of him, as he had always done. To use her. And his presents had been bribes, not presents at all.

He was dying.

What concern was it of hers? She was getting married. She had a new life ahead of her with a wonderful man who didn't deserve to be put second.

But Stuart was the father of her son. He was a fellow human who needed help in a horrible trial. He had no one else.

What about Tate and Willie Lee and Corrine? What about their lives? Was everyone simply to put their own lives on hold for this man who had never cared about anyone or anything but himself?

What about my own life?

The pillowcase and bed sheet were damp with her tears and sweat. She dragged herself up and slid down on her knees beside the bed. Folding her hands together, she rested her forehead on them and prayed, "Help me, God. Help me to know what to do, and to do it."

Crawling on hands and knees, she got back into the bed and slept at last.

Twenty-One

Life lessons . . .

She awoke and lay there for timeless moments, staring at the grey first light filtering through the window blinds. Then, like one awakening from the dead, she drew herself up from the warm bed, turned on the bedside lamp, and slid her feet into slippers and her body into her robe. She looked at her reflection in the mirror over the dresser. Even in the dim light she could see that her eyes looked like slits in a cantaloupe.

She was at the kitchen table, sitting with a steaming mug of coffee in two hands, when Tate came in the back door. He stopped in the laundry room doorway, regarding her with surprise.

"You're up."

"Yes," Marilee croaked in a hoarse voice. She had to admire that Tate was made of stern stuff to smile at her, with her looking like the wrath of God.

He came over, bringing with him the aromas of mocha and sweet rolls—two bags from the IGA deli. Setting the bags on the table, he kissed her quickly. "I can't stay. I've got the Methodist men's breakfast meeting this mornin'. I forgot all about it, until Pastor Smith called me to remind me that I was speakin'."

She nodded. She caught the warm, adoring light in his eyes and had to look away.

"I'll see you down at the paper later," he said, in a gently lowered voice, as if respectful that she was not fully awake. He knew her well. He tenderly kissed her forehead and left, closing the back door softly behind him.

In her mind, she raced to the door to call him back and to pour out her situation to him. In reality, she sat, knowing, for one thing, that she was incapable of fast movement.

Oh, she wished she had been able to tell him about Stuart. At the same time, she was relieved not to have to speak of it just yet.

Such thinking was too much for so early in the morning. She tossed the rest of her coffee down the sink, poured the mocha from the deli's foam cup into her blue earthenware one and carried the sweet brew into the bath.

She ate a Hershey's Kiss and opened another while she looked up the number for the Goodnight Motel and dialed. A craggy voice answered.

"May I have Stuart James's room, please?" She had no idea at all of what she would say to him. Some sort of apology seemed in order, although she was feeling a rising urge to beat him with the telephone receiver.

"Whats'zat?"

She raised her voice. "Stuart James's room, please."

"Wait a minute."

She waited.

A woman's voice came on the line. "Can I help you?"

"I'd like to speak to Stuart James's room, please." That sounded silly. She wanted him, not the room. She really didn't want him. Possibly she wouldn't get him.

"I'm sorry, he's not here."

She gripped the receiver. "Do you know when he'll be back? Can I leave a message for him?"

"He isn't comin' back. He checked out this mornin'."

"Oh. Did he leave a forwarding address . . . a number where he can be reached?" Speaking to him had become imperative to her.

"No. There's no reason for him to do that, I don't guess. Is this Marilee James?"

"Yes."

"Well, honey, your ex's done gone. I'm sorry. But I want to tell you how much we enjoy your pieces in the paper. That series you did on detention centers was real interestin'. Our nephew is out here in this one that just opened. He goes home on the weekends."

"Thank you . . . thank you very much." Just as she replaced the receiver, she realized the woman had still been talking. She felt so rude.

She only realized she had been sitting for some moments at her desk when Corrine came up beside her and said in a small voice, "Are you all right, Aunt Marilee?"

She saw that Corrine had the anxious expression she had so often worn during the first months upon coming to live with them, and which could on occasion still crop up. No child should have so much nameless anxiety.

"I'm just fine, honey." She put her arm around Corrine and hugged her. Then, knowing security came only from honesty, she said, "I have a problem, but it isn't anything you can help with, sweetheart, and it is not life-threatening."

She saw the anxiety ease on the child's heart-shaped face. "Is it one of those life-lessons, like Aunt Vella sometimes says?"

"Yes, dear . . . yes, it is." Marilee chuckled.

"Maybe you should let God handle it," Corrine said in a helpful manner.

Marilee hugged the dear child again. "I'm trying, honey. I'm tryin'."

Being with the children always made her feel stronger. Perhaps this was because she determined to appear courageous and not worry them; she was, she thought, as she rounded up children, backpacks, purse, keys and cheerfulness for the drive to school, a good enough actress to win an Oscar.

The children were deposited at school, and that left Marilee alone with her own thoughts, which quickly generated regrets and fears. As she drove to the newspaper, her spirits sank to her toes.

She had been cruel to Stuart. Oh, not in her decision that she could not change her life to suit his, but in her much less than sympathetic response. An angry response, understandable, but not acceptable.

She *had* to speak to him. The urge came over her so strongly that she realized her eyes kept searching for him along her way, as if she could find him right there on the corner of the IGA parking lot. *Oh, God, please let me have the opportunity to make things right.* Just how she would accomplish this feat, she wasn't certain. She only knew that she had to speak to him. To show him that she did care. To right a wrong she had committed.

The hopeful idea popped into her mind as she approached the *Voice* building that Stuart might have left a message there. She zipped into a space head-in to the curb and strode inside, on the short walk from her Cherokee having come by the absolute certainty that she would find a message from him, because this made perfect sense. Surely he would leave her a message and not just run out on her again.

Now why would she think that? He'd run out before. Running was what he did.

It was earlier than she ever arrived, and Charlotte was the only one present.

"Do I have messages?" Marilee stopped in front of the reception desk.

Charlotte, without a word, handed Marilee one slip of paper. The message was from yesterday afternoon, from Iris out at the MacCoy

Green Acres Senior Living Center, who said she would fax in the up-coming report for the March activities.

"Stuart didn't call this morning?"

Charlotte looked up and blinked. "No." She looked curious. "What's the matter?"

Marilee, starting to speak, felt tears well into her eyes, and the lump in her throat choked any words. This amazed her, even as she saw Charlotte's eyes pop wide. Marilee James never cried, at least not in public.

With Charlotte staring at her, Marilee blinked and swallowed and tried to get herself together.

Then Charlotte was on her feet, saying, "Marilee, I have to quit. . . . I just can't stay here around Sandy. I just *can't.*" With the last, Charlotte's face crumpled, and she went into tears, too.

The mention of Charlotte quitting, combined with the sadness over Stuart, caused Marilee's mind to produce a heavy dark blanket of sad-ness about the entire state of life on earth, and she burst into full-fledged sobbing. Words came then, on the order of, "Oh, Char-looottte . . ."

She started around the reception desk, where Charlotte met her, and the two women fell together, sobbing.

Sheriff Neville was coming out of the Main Street Café just as Tate parked head-in to the sidewalk, right beside Marilee's Cherokee.

"Hey, Editor. How-you this mornin'?" Sheriff Neville shifted the toothpick sticking out from his lips from one corner of his mouth to the other.

"Too good," said Tate, watching the toothpick. "I'm a man gettin' married—weddin' is still on for March 21."

"Well, we'll see." The sheriff grinned, and the toothpick stayed right in the corner of his lips. "Maybe you'll come to your senses."

"Any news for the paper?"

The sheriff shook his head. "Things are right quiet. Oh, tell Marilee that Morley Lund got those skunks cleaned out around his place. We had to go over there yesterd'y and get him to stop usin' his firearm in the city limits. He misaimed and shot out his neighbor's garage win-dow and like to have got the man in the behind, too. But before we got there, Morley had sent those skunks runnin', two of 'em straight to heaven. The vet's new wife came with humane traps and said she'd see to roundin' up any more that happened along. She got Mrs. Lund's prize Pekingese right off the bat."

By the time he finished, the sheriff, who enjoyed playing the small-town hick to the hilt, was grinning widely.

"Have you ever considered writing up these tales, Neville?"

"I believe that's your job . . . but maybe I could help you out on occasion." Giving a wink, he added, "Adios," and headed on along the sidewalk, while Tate strode into the *Voice,* his steps quickened by the sudden, gleaming idea of writing a book based on characters drawn from Valentine. In a flash he had imagined the book and its outstanding cover, and seen himself autographing it for lines miles long. The networks would even come to cover the event.

The fantasy vanished from his mind in the manner of being shot clean to smithereens, however, when he stepped through the glass door and saw Marilee and Charlotte, clinging to each other and crying to beat the band.

The sight of any two women in such behavior would be startling, but with these two usually reserved females, it was immensely unnerving. All sorts of horrible scenarios required to work up this emotional display passed through his imagination.

God, don't let it be any of the children. The thought caused a weakening in his knees.

Tate closed the door with enough force to get the women's attention.

Upon seeing him, they made visible efforts to get hold of themselves. When he finally spoke, he asked in a careful tone, "This isn't about something happenin' with one of the children . . . or your mother, Charlotte?" Better Charlotte's mother than the children, truth be known; he was a practical man.

Both women shook their heads. Marilee, sniffing, said, "It's . . . it's . . . oh . . ." She got two tissues from the box on Charlotte's desk, handing one to Charlotte.

Feeling a firm hand was needed, he said, "Let's go into my office and have some coffee." He took Marilee's elbow. She was shaking.

Charlotte hung back, so he said, "Charlotte, how about you, too?"

Thankfully she did not argue. Perhaps she was too worn-out from crying.

Tate got three cups of coffee from the pot that Charlotte had already brewed. He was surprised that his hands shook. It was a heck of a note that these women had been able to upset him so much—he, a seasoned journalist who had covered and dealt with all manner of crises, from murders and fatal accidents and riots.

Although, on his own, in his solitary life, he had never been as vulnerable as he was now, as a man who loved a woman and children and friends. Love and connection made a man vulnerable.

He returned to his office. The women sat on each end of the leather couch, dabbing at their eyes with a tissue. As he passed them their coffee, he heard voices entering the City Room. Stepping to his door, he saw June, Imperia and Reggie coming in the rear entrance from the alley. He called to Reggie to please handle the reception desk and phone. "Charlotte's in conference in here. I don't want to be disturbed."

Reggie's eyes widened, and then she nodded. He shut his door and pulled the visitor chair around to face the couch.

"Now, let's talk out what is goin' on here," he said. "Marilee, why don't you go first?" He was closer with Marilee and felt he could respond to her easier. He would have to work up to Miss Charlotte.

"Stuart is dying," Marilee said.

"What?" said Tate, feeling hit out of left field.

"What?" said Charlotte, clearly feeling the same. Apparently her crying was not about the same thing that Marilee's was.

"Stuart told me last night that he is dying." She began tearing up and took deep breaths. "I was so thoughtless in how I responded, and then I came in here and looked at Charlotte, and thought about her leaving . . ." She looked down at the tissue in her hand and began tearing it to pieces. "I haven't done well in either circumstance. I haven't said straight to Charlotte that I don't want her to leave."

She leaned toward Charlotte. "I haven't been there for you. I'm so sorry, Charlotte. I have been so caught up in my own life. I've been racin' around, trying to avoid so many feelings and doubts, that I simply couldn't be there for you. I haven't been there for you to talk things over, like a friend does for another. I should have been willing to step in and speak to you about this situation with Sandy and your mother, and to say that I understand—but you do need to open your mind to other options," she added, more like the normal Marilee.

"I have not seen any of this. I have just felt like I had more than I could handle, dealing with myself," she went on. Her shoulders and her tone dropped, and she pressed the shredded tissue to her breast. "And then last night Stuart told me about . . . his situation, and I saw how he needed me, and I was so awful to him. I was angry at him for needing me."

She began to tear up again as she turned to Tate. "Oh, Tate, we have to find him."

Tate's mind was still trying to catch up to all she had been saying.

This was one of those horrible times in life when reality seemed totally unreal.

"Stuart told you he is dying?" Maybe he had misunderstood.

But Marilee nodded. "Yes." She swallowed and breathed deeply. "He told me that he has cancer of a fast and consuming variety, nontreatable. He probably has only a couple more months. That's why he came here. Because he has nowhere else to go, and he doesn't want to be alone."

It was sinking into Tate with the full force of a sledgehammer. All the pieces being pounded into place.

He watched Marilee's magnificent struggle to keep from sobbing. "He wants me to be there for him," she said, reaching over and squeezing Charlotte's hand. "Like Charlotte is for her mother."

A cold shiver of understanding went down Tate's back.

Then Marilee added, her voice rising, "But now he's gone off, and I can't let him leave like that. I have to speak to him."

"Stuart's gone off?" His mind was now separating and dissecting the matter.

"Yes. I called the Goodnight earlier, and they said he had checked out. He's just run off again, like he always does."

Tate was somewhat glad to see her flash of anger.

"We have to find him, Tate. We have to."

Tate and Charlotte looked at each other in a moment of coming together as one mind, knowing what must be done.

"We'll find him, Marilee." Then, to Charlotte, he said, "He was drivin' a Hertz rental car. You take that end, and I'll make some calls."

Instantly Charlotte was on her feet and striding out the door on her long, purposeful legs.

Tate went to his desk and took up the phone, punching in the numbers for the sheriff's office. He looked over at Marilee.

"We'll find him," he said, thinking about how he had wanted to beat out the guy with all his new appliances, and all the time the guy was dying. *Maybe.* Maybe the guy was working another angle. Tate didn't think he should overlook that possibility until he knew for sure.

Marilee came over, put her arms around his waist and laid her head on his shoulder. He held her against him, feeling the need now to hold on tight to keep her from slipping away.

"The rental car has not been turned back in to Hertz," Charlotte reported to him an hour later.

"It's early yet. He hasn't had time to get back down to Dallas . . . if that was where he was goin'." He mused that James could take the rental car anywhere. Still, Dallas seemed the best bet. He did not think James would go very far from good comfort, whether truly dying or not.

"I'll check back with them in a couple of hours," Charlotte said. "I don't want to wait for another shift. I told the girl I was from the sheriff's office. She bought it, so I want to try to get her again."

He breathed deeply. "Well, Sheriff Neville has made some calls to request friends to keep a lookout, but he won't put out any all-points. James has only been gone a few hours and hasn't committed any crime. We'll just have to wait and see what turns up. I called a buddy down in Houston who knows how to find people."

Charlotte began going through a stack of papers and files on the corner of his desk.

"What are you looking for?"

"My resignation. I'm retracting it."

Waa-hoo!

"I tore it up," he admitted.

"You tore up my resignation?" She regarded him with indignant eyes from behind her dark-rimmed glasses.

He felt mildly ashamed. "Yes," he said, falling back on the strength of honesty. "I told you I would not accept it."

She turned on her heel and strode away, saying, "A person does not get the respect due around here."

He jumped up from his chair and hurried after her, catching up with her just before she got to her desk and grabbing her to him in a big hug.

"How's that for respect? I'm darn glad you've changed your mind, Miss Charlotte. . . . So glad that I'm willin' to make a fool of myself and get slapped for it. This paper can't run without you. That's it, plain and simple. I'm indebted to you for stayin'." There, he couldn't be more humble than that.

Applause came from the other desks in the big room, getting louder and louder, until Charlotte's coworkers were on their feet. Sandy Conroy's long, tall frame came out from his glass cubicle and into the middle of the big room, where, clapping, he called out, "Yee-ha!"

Charlotte, her face flushed, swept her gaze from Tate to everyone, then primly sat herself at her desk and went to work on her computer.

"Charlotte!"

Marilee ran to catch up to the tall woman, who was walking home to check on her mother during her lunch hour. The two walked together along the older sidewalks that led into the neighborhood of small clapboard boxlike houses dating from a brief boom in the fifties. Most were painted white, many needing repainting. Some had been fortunate not only to have been kept up, but to have received improvements along the lines of vinyl siding, picture windows and enclosed porches. The limbs of great elm trees stretched above yards where one was neatly tended and daffodils poked forth, and another had worn patches in the grass and was littered with plastic toys.

"Thank you for trying to find Stuart," Marilee said, annoyed at herself for finding conversation so difficult.

"Mmm." Charlotte nodded.

They walked in silence for a long minute, while Marilee formed what she wanted to say.

Finally she came out with, "I don't have many friends. Oh, I know a lot of people, but I don't think of them as friends. I just never have been able to open up and let other people into my life much."

She found understanding on Charlotte's face.

"I think of you as about my best friend, and I'm so glad you aren't leaving the paper. Thank you for being there for all of us. I don't think you know what you do, but everyone there relies on you. And I really want you to stand up for me at my wedding. It means a lot to me."

Despite feeling that she sounded a little incoherent, Marilee felt a sense of freedom coming over her at the effort to speak her heart.

"I think of you as my only real friend," Charlotte said slowly, without looking at Marilee. "And I'm looking forward to being your bridesmaid. I have never been a bridesmaid."

They smiled at each other, shyly, and then they began to speak of the wedding, deciding to have a shopping spree for choosing a new dress for Charlotte. Marilee, who had never in her life been shopping with a woman friend, wondered what the experience would be like. She dared to say as much, and Charlotte replied that she, too, had not ever been shopping with another woman, besides her mother. "And that was years ago," she added.

"We have led inhibited lives," Marilee observed.

Charlotte chuckled at that. "I've been having an affair with a younger man. That does not seem so inhibited . . . but you are right," she added, breathing a deep breath. "My life has been quite inhibited. I don't know how it happened. Just one day I woke up and here I was in this place, thirty-five, having tended Mama for nigh on ten years, and with day following day of always saying, 'tomorrow.' "

Marilee nodded. "I know what you mean."

At that, for some reason, Charlotte laughed more gaily than Marilee had heard her laugh in a long time.

Charlotte's house had not undergone any grand remodeling from its original state, but it was kept nicely, a small white cottage with a climbing rosebush, bare yet, but promising to climb up a trellis onto the porch. It was a picture out of a children's book, thoroughly feminine, having been inhabited only by Charlotte and her mother for some twenty years.

The inside continued with the same cottage atmosphere, with chintz curtains and flouncy pillows, everything in shades of pink, mauve and blue. The decor seemed too cute for Charlotte, not to mention long, tall Sandy. It was the reflection of Mrs. Nation, who was as small as Charlotte was tall. Obviously Charlotte took after her father, who, it was reported, had been tall and robust and had run off when Charlotte had been in grade school.

Marilee said hello to Mrs. Nation from the bedroom door; the tiny room was so crowded with frills as to discourage entering. In any case, Mrs. Nation, a shrunken figure in the hospital bed, simply looked at her with rather vacant eyes. Although she nodded, it was the day nurse who said brightly, "Mrs. Nation is havin' a good day today."

Marilee followed Charlotte with her gaze, watched her friend tenderly kiss her mother's pasty cheek, fluff the pillow upon which she reclined, touch her lifeless hand, all very quickly, one motion and seeming to go ever faster, so that she was in the room and then out of it again and on into the kitchen, where she made Marilee and herself glasses of ice tea with sprigs of mint from a pot on the sill.

The thought sprang into Marilee's mind: run through life, busy, busy, busy, and then we don't have to stop and face the hungry lions.

"Tate and I can come and sit with your mother sometimes," she said, taken by impulse. "I don't really have experience, but I think Tate and I together can handle it. Tate is quite good at such things. You should see him with the children."

Gazing at Charlotte, who did not sit down, but stood at the kitchen sink, one arm across her middle and the other clutching her glass of cold tea, Marilee felt shame in not offering months ago. She, like everyone, considered Charlotte able to handle everything. Just as everyone had always thought about Marilee herself. Both of them hid their weaknesses quite well.

Charlotte observed her.

"Let Sandy help you, Charlotte. I'm learning how much Tate can help me. I'm always amazed, how much he wants to do. I simply never knew there were such men." The faint shadow of her distant father crossed her heart. "It isn't often a woman finds a man who's willing to help with things like mothers and children. Don't let this opportunity pass you by just because of a silly few years' difference in your ages. Tate was worried about growing old the other day. I told him we had enough worries to think about today, without projecting so far into the future."

She thought of Stuart and how he would not grow old. He only had today.

Charlotte said only, "If you're ready, we should head back," and set her glass in the sink.

Twenty-Two

Smoothing the knots in the skein of time . . .

When they came home from school, Willie Lee headed straight around the house to the backyard, to see his bird. Corrine went up on the front porch, drew over the stool and climbed up to stick her hand in the mailbox and fish around.

She brought out a phone bill, a sale postcard for JCPenney's, and a Victoria's Secret catalog. There was no small box addressed to herself. Likely her mother was not going to send the present. Likely she had forgotten. There had not been a card from her in weeks.

Corrine went over to sit on the swing for some minutes, not wanting to face her aunt or anyone when she felt so close to tears. What was wrong with her? Why did her mother not care about her?

Then her gaze was diverted by the Victoria's Secret catalog and the almost naked woman on the front cover. The women in the catalog fascinated her. Corrine had lately been examining her chest and finding she had breasts growing. She wasn't sure she wanted them. She always wondered how the women in the catalog got shaped as they were, since she had never seen any women like them in real life. She would have asked Aunt Marilee about this, but she was too embarrassed to speak of such private things as the shape of a body.

Maybe she *would* ask, she thought, feeling a flicker of daring as she gathered up the mail and her and Willie Lee's backpacks and went inside.

She was a little surprised to find Aunt Marilee and Mr. Tate—Papa Tate—sitting close together on the couch. They turned and looked at her, quite suddenly smiling at her in that way grown-ups smiled when wanting to hide their discussion.

"Hey, pumpkin, how was school?" said Mr. Tate.

"Okay, Papa Tate," Corrine replied. She had been making an effort to try out the new name, to see how everything set with it.

Mr. Tate seemed pleased.

All evening, Corrine did her best to please while she listened carefully to the adults and caught snatches of whispers but not what was going on that they did not want to talk about in front of her and Willie Lee. Aunt Vella came after supper, and she and Aunt Marilee and Papa Tate—the name was growing on Corrine—sat at the dining-room table and wrote out the invitations. Aunt Vella was told whatever was going on. Corrine caught Aunt Vella saying Stuart's name on several occasions, and she decided whatever it was, was something to do with him. She came to the conclusion that he was not there, and he was supposed to be there.

She was a little relieved to be satisfied that whatever the trouble was, her mother had not caused it, for once.

And she had known Mr. James would be the cause of trouble. She took it as a good sign that her aunt Marilee was making out the wedding invitations; surely this meant the marriage was to take place. Still, Corrine had learned a long time ago not to count on something too much, or it would not come about.

She thought Papa Tate looked especially worried, even if he did still smile a lot like normal. She brought him a glass of fresh ice tea, hoping to make it all better.

Stuart checked out of the hotel room he had only hours before checked into. He went down the elevator and out into the starlit night. The wind coming off the plain and whipping around the tall buildings of the city tugged at his hair, and he shivered in the falling temperatures. Halfway across the narrow lot, he dropped his duffel bag, his grip seeming to give way. In the process of trying to pick it up, he dropped one of his camera cases. A man coming from a pickup truck helped him pick up his bags.

"Thanks."

"You bet."

Stuart went on to his rental car, threw the bags inside, got behind the wheel and headed off, directing the vehicle west on the interstate, heading back to Valentine.

Marilee and his son were the only loose ends of his life, one carefully lived without ties. Now, suddenly, he didn't want to be without ties. It would be as if he had never lived at all, and that was too hard to take. Somehow, some way, he wanted to tie up the loose ends, so there would be a knot on the skein of time with the name of Stuart James written on it. The only way to do that was not to run out on Marilee in the end. It was now the single purpose for him.

* * *

Charlotte debated about telephoning Sandy all evening. She actually picked up the telephone twice but did not dial.

Then, like a gift from heaven, she heard his TransAm pull up out front. Instantly she flew to the front door and out of it into the soft, cool night. She stood on the edge of the porch and watched him round the hood of his powerful car. He carried a bouquet of flowers. He walked head down, as usual, and did not see her standing there until he was halfway up the walk.

The streetlight fell on his face, showing his surprise, which was followed quickly by determination in the quickening of his long strides.

"I brought you these." He jutted the flowers at her, as if daring her to refuse.

She found his unusual sense of firmness very attractive. "Thank you, Sandy," she said softly, reaching for the flowers.

"Can we just start seein' each other again?" he asked. She had always appreciated how simply he spoke.

"Come inside. The night nurse will be here in another hour, and then we can go off and talk." She took his hand. It was warm and moist in her own.

Just before entering, there in the deep darkness of the porch, she paused and kissed him, and was rewarded by his answering passion.

She led him into the kitchen, where she put the flowers into a vase. He stood over by the refrigerator, watching and definitely ill at ease, a long, tall hunk of a man in a dainty kitchen.

"Do you still want to marry me?" she asked, pausing to look at him.

He swallowed and tucked his hands up under his armpits. "Yes, I do."

She arranged the flowers in the vase.

"I don't have much money," he said, "but I think together we could rent a house big enough to accommodate you, me and your mother. I've looked at several."

He had been looking at houses!

She finished getting the flowers correct to please her and brought the vase to set in the middle of the table. "There. They sure are pretty."

She looked across at him. He was a patient man, never rushing her to hurry up and speak.

"I have saved, in the bank and investments, about one hundred thousand dollars. How about if we buy a house?" She was very good at investing.

His eyes went round as saucers, and his mouth fell open.

Then he began shaking his head and saying, "No . . . no, I can't be lettin' you buy our home. I . . ."

She went to him, enjoying as always being able to look slightly upward into his eyes. "Darlin', if I can bear with being eleven years older than you, I believe you can bear with using my money for a house."

And then he kissed her just as she wanted.

Vella had gone, the children were in bed, and Tate was alone with Marilee at last. He dimmed the lights, put a George Strait CD into the stereo and turned the volume low, then pulled her into his arms. Feet sliding over the smooth oak floor in the wide area behind the couch, his thighs pushed on hers, his belly to her belly, her breasts against his chest. She laid her head on his shoulder and gave a pleasurable sigh as he caressed her back.

He wanted her right then, and he knew she wanted him, and it felt good, the wanting to bond together. It was the specter of death that propelled them, he knew. It was death making them aware of how precious were their lives together.

The question before them all evening had been of Stuart James. They could not disregard him by saying he was not their problem.

"He's Willie Lee's father," Marilee said.

"Yes, he is."

"He was once my husband. He isn't anymore . . . but he is someone to me."

"Yes, he is."

At last she believed that he was in full agreement, that he was going to stand there with her.

"I'm asking so much of you, I know," she said.

"I am to be your husband. We'll get through it together," he said.

And in their dancing, bodies and hearts touched and melded together. It was stimulating and heady. He swept her one way and then another, and he savored the motions, the scent of her, the feel of her skin that already belonged to him, and which he could at any moment, he knew, take for his own.

Marilee raised her head and looked at him. "I don't want this to change our plans. We've made our plans, everything perfect for us. It's important, this time for us to anticipate our coming together as one. I don't want to give it up. I want all we've planned, Tate. This time will never come again. We don't want to let it pass by."

Even in the dimness, he saw the heat in her eyes and plain on her face.

He kissed her neck and heard her sharp intake of breath.

"We won't let it," he whispered into her ear, kissing her lobe and then down her neck, feeling her tremble against him.

Then he kissed her, and she kissed him.

"Oh, Tate."

She breathed the words against his neck. He held her tight against him, cherishing her more than he had ever cherished anything in his life.

They danced for some time, necking as they did and not daring to sit down, until both were hot and forced to break apart. They giggled like teens. It was heady, like some sort of drug, Tate thought, calming himself as Marilee went to get them coffee.

They sat long on the couch, talking about options for when they did find Stuart.

"You know, Marilee, we can make all these plans, but Stuart may not want any of them."

She said she knew that, but he didn't think she did.

Willie Lee didn't think his mother would hear him. She and Papa Tate had music playing in the living room. He tucked his pillows under his covers, then got behind his blinds and got the window open without Corrine hearing.

Munro hopped out, and Willie Lee positioned himself on the windowsill. He did not wear his cape, because he knew now that he could not fly. But he could jump, and it felt like flying.

He put his hands out and jumped.

He landed with a hard thump and went rolling on the damp, moist ground. Munro licked his face, and then Willie Lee was pushing to his feet and adjusting his glasses. He had not bothered with coat and shoes, and his feet felt really cold. It was very dark, but he could follow the wall of the house to the backyard, where he and Munro ran to where they could clearly see the stars.

He loved this time, when he could simply be. It was okay if he could not fly. He didn't have to. There were many other things he could learn to do.

Tate felt it safe to sleep in an extra half hour on Saturday morning, yet he still got up anxious to head off the possibility of Marilee coming over to his house and finding all the remodeling going on.

Finished shaving, he threw aside his towel, opened the bathroom door and saw his passage blocked by an enormous oak bedstead passing by. A man on the back end—one of Honey Moon's three emissaries—said, "Mornin'."

He was followed by another emissary, who said, "Your mother let us in. She's made prune muffins." He held one up in his callused hand.

It wasn't yet seven o'clock in the morning. His mother had been out with Winston until the small hours of the morning—and now she was up and baking?

Tate followed the men and what turned out to be the oak headboard of the bed Honey Moon had sent up from Dallas. The men propped it against the wall in the master bedroom. Tate went over to examine it.

A sleigh bed! He loved a sleigh bed!

"Like it?" asked the emissary who was in charge of the crew.

"Yes . . . yes, I do," Tate said, running a hand over the smooth rolled wood.

"Honey knew you would."

Tate's confidence that Honey Moon knew her stuff was rising. He glanced around at the walls. The dreary wallpaper was gone, replaced by something Honey Moon called texturing. Paint with sand thrown in it, Tate thought, but he liked the effect. The color was Sahara, so the head emissary had told him. It did give a warm glow. Intimate.

He was quite pleasantly surprised, as he had been preparing himself for something on the order of purples and leopard prints from Honey Moon.

Remembering then that he didn't want Marilee happening over to see any of this, he hotfooted down the stairs, with the intent of getting over to the IGA and the mocha machine. Sweet bread aroma mixed with the faint odor of paint met him, leading him into the kitchen, where he just about tripped on a tarp still spread on the floor.

There didn't seem to be enough painting being done in the kitchen to justify a tarp, he thought. Not only was the crew he had hired slower than molasses in January, but they kept coming across rotted wooden places that had to be replaced. Tate regretted that he had not turned the kitchen job over to Honey Moon, as well, rather than Joe's Paint Job crew. He had been misled by so reliable-sounding a name.

"Good mornin'," his mother said. She looked as fresh as if she had slept ten hours and had a leisurely bath.

"You didn't come in until almost two o'clock," he said, not really knowing why he had to speak of it.

"Winston and I had a grand time. And the band is booked." She handed him a basket. "Here, take these to Marilee this mornin'. So many of those commercial bakery items are not good for anyone. And here's your mocha, too."

Mocha, too?

At his obviously amazed expression, his mother said, "I bought you and Marilee a new coffee machine. Does all this fancy stuff . . . see? You needed it for your new kitchen. I saw a toaster I really liked, too.

They're makin' them like back in the fifties again, and they are so cute. I'm going to get it, and if Marilee doesn't like it, I'll keep it with me. I think I'm going to move in with Winston."

"Oh."

He watched her filling foam cups with the steaming brew.

"You mean you're goin' to stay up here in Valentine?"

"Yes. I want to be around my son and his family."

He digested that. "I'm glad, Mom."

They smiled at each other.

Then he looked around. They had new appliances, but the kitchen where they were seemed more to be coming apart than together.

"I'll get these boys goin' on this kitchen today," his mother said, as if reading his mind. "I'm goin' to ride them until they'd rather finish than deal with me. You take care of Marilee and finding Stuart." She handed him the cups set in a small box.

Finding Stuart.

Tate thought of this problem on his way out the back door. He had a sense of wanting to yell at the world. He felt a little guilty about the part of the motive he had held to upstage Stuart. For one thing, the endeavor was both petty and fruitless, especially considering that Stuart was dying. *If* he was dying, and more guilt came on him because he had doubts.

The point to all he was doing, though, was to please the woman he loved. Yes, by golly, that was the heart of his intentions, and those were good. Only good could come from a good motive. He wanted to give pleasure to Marilee and make all their lives easier in the bargain. Winners all the way around!

He would do well to keep his focus on heading toward the wedding. He wasn't letting anything stop it.

Tate found Corrine in the kitchen, standing on a chair and preparing the coffeemaker. Her tiny toenails were red on her bare feet. Such a little fragile doll, she was. He wanted to protect her from all the life that lay ahead. A sense of futility swept him; then he bolstered himself and said brightly, "You're up early, pumpkin. Is your aunt Marilee awake yet?"

"She's on the phone with my mama," Corrine said, as she carefully measured the coffee into the basket.

"Oh." He watched her get down from the chair to go over to the sink to fill the glass pot with water. "I brought your aunt a cup of mocha, but she'll want coffee, too. Would you like me to help you with that?" He indicated the pot of water that seemed a lot for her skinny arms and wrists.

"No."

"Okay." He backed off, emptied the foam cups of mocha his mother had provided into stoneware cups and fixed a plate of three muffins, telling Corrine that his mother had made them and to help herself.

He put the cups and plate on a tray and carried it all into Marilee's bedroom, where he found her sitting on the edge of the bed with the telephone pressed to her ear. She gave him a glance and a wave, but she was definitely distracted. Marilee always got distracted when talking to her sister.

He set the tray on the table by the window, easing it onto the edge, then sat beside her and kissed the silky skin of her bare shoulder where her nightgown strap had slipped away. He was instantly aroused to the point of forgetting himself and began slipping his hand to her breasts.

Marilee was so intent on speaking to her sister, who had alarmed her with the information that she was going out of town on Monday, to Buenos Aires with Louis for a week, that she pushed Tate's caresses aside. She needed all her attention focused on the conversation at hand. Marilee decided that with Anita going out of the country, now was the imperative time to speak to her sister about the question of Corrine's security.

"Anita, we need to talk about Corrine's medical insurance. There are things to consider." She might have added: now that you've pretty much left your daughter, but she bit her tongue on that bit of factual criticism.

"I'm not offered any insurance, Marilee," Anita said. "I'm still only workin' at Louis's firm part-time."

"Honey . . ." She reached for Tate's hand and hung on to him while she searched for as gentle a choice of words as possible. "Corrine needs health insurance. She isn't my daughter, so I can't put her on my policy."

"Corrine's young. If she has to go to the doctor, I'll send you some money. Louis has plenty, and he adored Corrine when he met her."

Louis had met Corrine once, the previous summer, when he and Anita had come up for a visit before moving off to New Orleans. Anita had not seen her daughter since, and the cards and calls were becoming less frequent. How did Marilee address all this? She felt as if she were walking through a minefield. What if she angered Anita? She could crush her sister with what she felt needed to be done.

She said, "Corrine could get something serious that required hospitalization. I don't know what all, Anita, but we have to look at the situation." Deep breath. "We need to make me and Tate her legal guardians. If Tate and I adopt her, she can have full medical benefits and anything else she needs."

There, she had said it.

The line hummed for long seconds. "You always wanted this, didn't you, Marilee?" Anita began to cry. "You've always wanted to take my baby from me."

"Anita, that's not how I mean it. I'm thinking of Corrine's security. She needs health insurance, and she needs to be provided for if anything should happen to me . . . or to you. Do you want her only living relatives to be Mama and Carl? She'd end up with them, if something happened to me. Or the state could come in here and put her in a foster home."

"I'll come get her," Anita said after a moment. "Give me a few weeks, and I'll come get her."

She had known this was coming. "Can you do that? Can you provide for her, with only a part-time job and no insurance?" Marilee toughened her heart. "I won't let you take her, Anita, unless you can provide for her better than you have in the past."

Anita screamed into the phone, "You can't do this! You can't!" And then she began to sob.

"Honey . . . honey, listen to me. I am not trying to hurt you. I love you. I don't want to hurt you, but we need to do what is best for Corrine. You'll always be her mother. I'm not taking that away. She knows who her mother is and always will."

Anita cried some more, and Marilee sat there squeezing Tate's hand and wondering what else to say.

Then Anita said, "I just can't talk about this anymore right now. I'll call you back later."

The line clicked dead.

Twenty-Three

Hallelujah! Shopping day . . .

Destination: the biggest shopping mall in Oklahoma City. Marilee drove, stopping to pick up Charlotte, who came running out of her house like a young girl.

Windows down! An oldies' station playing on the radio! Happy hopes of shopping till they dropped!

"I want to get somethin' to get Winston's blood pumping," Franny said.

Charlotte cast a look of alarm over the seat. "I imagine you are doin' that already, Franny. You might kill him if you increase it."

"Yes, well . . . good way to go," the older woman answered smartly.

"You *are* joking, right Granny Franny?" Corrine asked, wanting to smile, but not quite certain.

"Yes, dear. It is a truth that is so true it is funny. And I love you, darlin'." Franny kissed Corrine, whose eyes showed both pleasure and uncertainty of someone who could say I love you so easily.

They arrived at the turnoff for the mall, and then there it was before them: shopping Mecca. All in the car, small-town girls used to small-town stores, stared and gaped like hicks from the backwoods, all except Franny, who was never overly impressed by anything.

There was a host of angels singing in the heavens, Marilee thought, gripping the steering wheel and having a sense of seeing something on the order of the great pyramids, the structure being sandy in color and standing brightly against the clear blue sky. And being Saturday, the traffic, which surrounded them on all sides, flowed toward the enormous structure like the flow of pilgrims to their holy place.

Walking across the parking lot, they were all so excited with the shopping potential that awaited them, they forgot Corrine and her shorter legs. Marilee looked around and saw Corrine craning her neck upward, lost in wonder. "Y'all slow up!" she said to the others and raced back to take Corrine's hand. Quite suddenly she recognized pos-

sible dangers. "Help me keep an eye on her," she whispered to Charlotte and Franny.

From store to store, rack to rack.
"Oh, look at this!"
"Aunt Marilee, can I try this on?"
"Oh, that is perfect for you!"
"Not your color, Marilee."
"Ohmygosh, who would possibly wear this?"
"Well, I would, darlin'."
"Does this make my behind look big?"
"Sugar, don't look at that." Hands over Corrine's eyes.
"Oh! In this dress, my ship will come in!"
"A ship? Honey, you'll bring in the entire fleet with that."

Marilee came upon Corrine gazing at a mannequin wearing a hot
pink T-shirt and fashionably faded jeans. *Oh, dear Lord, she is grow-
ing up so fast.*
"Would you like to try that outfit on, sugar?"
Corrine looked at her with wide eyes, then nodded.
They went into the store for teens—flashing lights that caused Mar-
ilee's eyes to squint—and chose the proper sizes. Corrine disappeared
into the dressing room, and when she reappeared, Franny and Char-
lotte had joined Marilee.
"Perfect for you!" Franny said instantly.
"You are not a little girl anymore," Charlotte said.
"You are so lovely," Marilee said, and kissed her niece's cheek.
Then, "I'll go see if they have that shirt in yellow, too."
"Oh, thank you, Aunt Marilee!"

Three hours later, tired bones lugged shopping bags to the food
court and plopped into chairs at one of the few vacant tables.
"We should have paced ourselves," observed Charlotte, who removed her shoes.
"I never realized shopping could be such hard work," said Marilee,
who had not yet found an outfit for wearing on the flight to the fabu-
lous Walt Disney World honeymoon.
"There's just too many people around here for me," said Corrine in
a rare, candid moment.
"Perk up, y'all," said Franny, who looked as fresh as she had at the
beginning. "We have just gotten started. Charlotte doesn't have her

bridesmaid dress, and Corrine still needs a swimsuit. Marilee, you must get more than bras, and I have to find my drop-dead gorgeous dress."

"You have found three drop-dead gorgeous dresses."

"Yes, but not *the* dress."

With all they had purchased, none of it was what they had come after. Marilee said, "Franny, sometimes perky doesn't sit well."

"Oh, darlin', I love you." Franny gave her a hug, then went off to order a pita-bread sandwich.

The three others looked at each other.

Then Marilee, dragging herself off the chair, said, "Begin with action and the spirit will follow. Come on, y'all."

The three of them slumped over to join Franny in purchasing food, and quite quickly, upon eating and a bit of rest, hopeful shopping spirits soared once more.

They split up: Corrine and Franny went to several stores on the lower level, and Charlotte and Marilee went to several on the second level.

"Let's focus on gettin' you a bridesmaid dress first," Marilee said. "I sure don't want to go home without the main thing we came for."

"I'm keeping an eye out for a wedding dress, too," Charlotte said. "What do you think about this one?"

Marilee observed the dress, then realized what Charlotte had said. "A wedding dress, as in you and Sandy have decided to get married?"

"Yes," Charlotte said in a breezy manner.

"Ohmygosh!" Marilee let out a whoop, and several ladies gave her an eye. "This is wonderful, Charlotte."

"So while we're at it," Charlotte said, "you'd better get a bridesmaid dress for my wedding. Something in blue. That's going to be my theme color."

Marilee hauled off and hugged the taller woman, an action that somewhat surprised her and definitely surprised Charlotte. Self-conscious, Marilee went to draw back, but then Charlotte gave her a quick hug in return.

"We shouldn't have waited so long," Marilee said, the words popping from her mouth as tears blurred her vision.

Charlotte cast her a quizzical look.

"To be friends," Marilee said. "I'm so glad for being friends."

"Me, too." A smile quivered on Charlotte's lips, and then she quickly averted her eyes, taking dresses off the rack and slinging them over her arm. "It would have been nice if you were a little taller, though, so we could share clothes."

Marilee burst out laughing.

*   *   *

On the drive home, Marilee's thoughts turned to Stuart. Maybe there would be a message waiting at home from him. She started to use the cell phone to call and ask Tate, then decided doing that would not make her get home any sooner.

The streetlights had come on when Marilee pulled the Cherokee into her own driveway, having dropped Charlotte at her house first. She turned off the key, then looked around into the back seat to see Franny and Corrine leaning together, asleep. She gazed at them for long seconds.

Now, she thought, relief falling over her, Corrine will have another woman to help her along, to teach her things. Franny could teach Corrine so much that Marilee herself did not know.

Thank you, God . . . for today, for Franny, for my dear friend Charlotte.

And then here came Tate, stepping off the porch. On sight of him, her heart jumped, and she slipped out of the Cherokee and raced through the cool, moist night to fling herself into his arms.

His response was to lift her clear off the ground. "Ah, woman, home from the hunt."

"Oh, Tate." She hugged him fiercely and then kissed him, and all the while her heart was singing, *Oh, Tate . . . thank God for you . . . for all of the beloved people in my life.*

He set her down. "I take it you had fun and success in bagging the proper new outfits and baubles for the occasions ahead."

Only Tate would talk in such a grand manner!

"Yes, we had a delightful time. So much so that you might need to carry your mother into the house."

His eyes went wide, and then he bent to peer into the back seat. "Let's wait and see if she wakes up," he said, as if he had taken her words quite literally.

"Has there been any news?" she asked then.

He looked confused.

"About Stuart?" His expression had already told her what she needed to know, and her spirit dipped as he shook his head.

"We will find him, Marilee. It's only been a few days. He's gonna turn up any minute."

She nodded and moved to the rear of the Cherokee. He followed and helped her to unload, trooping behind her like a bellman lugging packages into the house. Her heart warmed to step into the cheery glow of home, where Willie Lee was already put to bed and coffee awaited in the kitchen.

She dropped her bags and turned to throw her arms around Tate again and to kiss him passionately.

"Hey, let's go out and come back in again," he said, continuing to hold her tightly.

The telephone rang, and Marilee moved quickly from his embrace to answer, her thoughts running straight to Stuart.

Tate put a hand on her arm. "Your sister called about an hour ago. She was pretty drunk."

Marilee looked at the telephone, ringing a second time. She went to her desk in the living room and checked the caller ID. "It's Mother." She lifted the receiver; it felt very heavy.

"Marilee?"

Her mother spoke in a sharp tone. Marilee instantly wished she had not answered. "Yes, Mother?" She met Tate's gaze, finding strength there. He moved to massage her shoulders.

"Anita just called here. She is all upset. She says you are taking Corrine from her, that you and Tate are going to adopt her away from Anita."

Marilee breathed deeply. "Yes, I have approached Anita with the idea. We need to take care of Corrine, Mom. We need to get her some health insurance and to make certain to safeguard her future. She needs to be provided for, and Anita can't do that."

As she said the last, the front door opened, and Franny and Corrine came straggling inside.

"Well, you have upset her no end. You are sayin' she isn't a fit mother. You can't do this to her. She is out of her mind about it. There is no telling what she might do."

Marilee breathed deeply and moved into her bedroom for privacy. "I am not doing anything to Anita. I am trying to take care of Corrine. And Anita *is* out of her mind. She is an alcoholic."

Marilee could not believe she had said the word flat-out to her mother.

Her mother gasped, then said, "Anita is not an alcoholic. She has a bit of a drinking problem, but she is not like your daddy."

Marilee had no words for this. "You are drivin' her to this drinking, too," her mother added. "You have gotten her so upset."

"I can't talk to you about this now, Mother. I am tired, and I have to get Corrine to bed. And I don't want her to hear any of this conversation. I'll call you about this soon. Goodbye."

Well, she didn't think she would get points in heaven for hanging up on her mother, but she believed she would be understood.

She went out and plopped herself in the big armchair, where Corrine came and cuddled against her, and Tate brought a cup of coffee thick with sugar and cream for her, and a cup of hot chocolate for Corrine. Then he sat himself on the coffee table and listened to the female "shop-till-they-dropped" tales, nodding and laughing at all the right places.

Marilee watched the way his eyes crinkled, the way he winked at Corrine, the way his sleeves were rolled up on his forearms.

She watched Corrine, who described the wondrous shopping mall and even went to dig out the clothes she had gotten and show them to Tate, holding them up with her tired skinny little arms.

Anita's image swept her mind, and her chest squeezed. She never had been able to help Anita. God knew she had tried—and failed. But she could take care of this child and help her to have a good child-hood. The sort of childhood she and Anita had missed.

She got into bed and reclined there on the cool pillows for a few minutes, gazing at nothing. Finally she turned out the light and slipped down beneath the warm covers. The temperature had fallen drastically into the thirties.

Extremes of spring trying to come and winter still holding on with strong fingers, she thought.

That was how she felt, too. She was both extremely happy and ex-tremely sad. Tears welled in her eyes, as she thought of the wonderful day she had experienced with loved ones, and the dear, wonderful man she was to marry in a wedding for which she longed with all her heart. She thought of her mother's distress, of her sister's self-destruction, and of Stuart. She felt she had failed them all, and yet, what else could she have done?

She wished she had spoken more kindly. She wished she had had answers for everyone.

The tears ran down her cheeks, and she felt hardly able to breathe. She slipped out of bed, to her knees, folding her hands in prayer. Thank you, God, for the wonderful day we all enjoyed . . . for finding that perfect dress to wear on the plane . . . that Corrine was so happy with the things she bought . . . that Charlotte is saying yes to love. Thank you for Tate.

Precious gratitude washed over her, like a healing potion.

Help me to give whatever I can to Tate, my gift of a partner that you have given me. Look after my mother . . . and my dear sister, Anita . . . and Stuart, wherever he is. I give them to You. I know I can't handle all their needs. Thank you for watching over all of us.

She climbed back into bed and cuddled beneath the comforter. The next instant she was startled by a plop on her bed.

Oh, it was Munro. He came up and pressed close to her side.

"How did you know?" she whispered, putting out a hand to pet his fur. She had become accustomed to Munro appearing at certain key times.

"Thank you, Munro." Curling around him, she drifted off to sleep.

Tate was enjoying a Sunday afternoon siesta on his porch when the call came from his detective friend. Stuart James had been located. "In the hospital. Police brought him in. He'd collapsed at a gas station Thursday night. Word is that he's due to be released tomorrow morning."

"They found Stuart?" asked his mother, who had appeared in the doorway.

"Yes." Tate got to his feet, then stood there a moment, gathering his breath in preparation for telling Marilee. He didn't quite understand the great reluctance that came over him.

"You don't have to tell her," his mother said, watching him closely.

That had occurred to him. What if he didn't tell Marilee where Stuart was? There was a big chance this would mean no more Stuart James in their lives. Problem gone.

"Yes, I do," he said.

"Yes, you do," his mother agreed with a gentle smile. "But let her decide for herself what she wants to do."

He knew that, he thought impatiently, as he went down the porch steps and across the backyards and through Marilee's back door, calling out her name.

"Just a minute!" came her answer, in a curiously panicked tone.

Corrine appeared, barring the swinging door. "You can't come in here. Aunt Marilee is in her weddin' dress. . . . She's havin' alterations."

Here was a perfect excuse to just turn around and walk back home. Perhaps during a delay in telling her, James would disappear again.

He went to the refrigerator and drew out a pitcher of cold tea, pouring himself a glass, keeping his back to the swinging door and thinking of walking out the back door.

A minute later he heard the swinging door open. He slowly turned to see Marilee tying her robe around her. She asked the instant their eyes met, "Has Stuart been found?"

He felt a flash of anger at the dying man.

"He's in a hospital down in Wichita Falls." And he had better really be dying, or Tate might kill him.

Twenty-Four

Getting through to new beginnings . . .

At the last minute, before heading out the door with Tate, it occurred to Marilee that she had to explain to the children about Stuart. She sat with them on the porch, on the top step.

"I have to tell you two something about Willie Lee's father."

Two pairs of eyes regarded her. Corrine's dark eyes were wary; Willie Lee's were soft and wide. *Give me the right words, Lord.*

Willie Lee said, "My fa-ther is sick."

Marilee, more relieved than surprised, nodded. "Yes, he is. And he needs somewhere to stay where he isn't alone . . . where people can take care of him, so Tate and I are going to go get him and bring him here to stay with us.

"Well, with you and Tate," she said, her gaze moving from Willie Lee to Corrine. "Corrine and I are going to move over to Papa Tate's house, and he will move over here, with Willie Lee and his daddy. That way your daddy can have my room."

The two pairs of eyes blinked.

"This house will be for the guys." With the thought of leaving Willie Lee at night, she reached over to touch him. "And Papa Tate's house will be for the girls. Just until the wedding. After that we'll all live together over at Mr . . . .Papa Tate's house, and Stuart can have this house, so we can still be nearby to take care of him."

That about covered it, as much as she felt she needed to cover it. If the children had questions, they kept them to themselves, and Marilee wasn't going to encourage the asking. She left them with instructions to go inside and help Aunt Vella and Franny get things ready.

Tate drove, and as he backed out of the driveway, Marilee said, "I don't know how I will leave Willie Lee at night."

Tate said, "I'll be with him, Marilee. I promise."

"I know. . . . I trust that, or I'd never do this."

* * *

"I forgot to tell Franny where the sheets for my bed are kept." It was the third thing to pop into her mind that she had forgotten.

"Corrine will show her."

"I don't know if Corrine knows. And my mattress requires those deep pocket sheets."

"Corrine knows everything, and besides, your house isn't that big. I'm sure they'll find them."

She nodded, blinking back sudden tears. "I love your mother, Tate." She was overwhelmed at the situation, and her heart seemed raw with feelings rushing through it at incredible speeds. "What would we have done had she not come up?" She was still amazed at how things seem to fit; Franny had hospice training and experience, and Stuart needed someone to take care of him.

Tate reached over and took her hand. "All this is right up Mom's alley. And she was planning on stayin' anyway. . . . I forgot to tell you. She told me she was movin' in with Winston."

Marilee took that in, and guilt fell over her. "Oh, I'm sorry we have waylaid her plans."

"Postponed. She doesn't mind. She just wants to be up here with us now." He rubbed her hand with his thumb, as if trying to impart strength.

"Well, I'm sure glad of that. She's so good for Corrine . . . good for all of us."

They had reached the outskirts of Wichita Falls. She took up the paper with the sketched directions to the hospital that she'd gotten when she had called to make certain a Stuart James was still a patient there.

"Marilee . . . you know that Stuart may not fall in with the idea of comin' back with us. Just because you've decided this, doesn't mean that he will."

"I know."

She squeezed Tate's hand and imagined him in Corrine's narrow bed. He had assured her it would be fine, although he would appreciate just blankets and not the floral bedspread.

The floor station was busy. Finally a nurse responded to their inquiry. "Yes, let's see . . . Mr. Stuart James . . . he's to be released in the morning." She pointed down the hall. "Third door on the right. It's a double room, but he's in there alone."

Marilee looked at Tate.

"I'll wait there," he said, indicating a nearby alcove with chairs and a sofa.

They kissed quickly, and she turned and left him, walking along the hallway alone, experiencing the rising urge to tiptoe. The door to Stuart's room was ajar. Was it the right one? Mistakes were made in hospitals. Yes, there was his name in one of the two slots beside the door. The other slot was empty.

The door was ajar, and there came the sound of the television. She peered inside through the narrow opening. The first bed was unoccupied, and the dividing curtain hid most of the bed on the far side next to the window.

All she could see was feet beneath the white covers. She stared at them. She could not ever recall Stuart lying in bed; he had always gotten up first thing upon opening his eyes and never gotten back in bed until he was ready for sleep at night.

She hoped she didn't give him a heart attack, appearing like this.

Knocking lightly, she went in. His eyes popped wide when he saw her. Words escaped her. She went to him and flung her arms around him.

He shook his head as she talked. "I don't need your pity."

"Oh, yes, you do," she said, startling him. "Stuart, don't be a martyr. Do what is good for all of us . . . for Willie Lee, for me—and for yourself."

He looked at her. "Let me get dressed. I can't discuss this wearing a hospital gown."

When she did not move from the side of the bed, he motioned with his hand, as if sweeping her off. She was heartened to see that he appeared stronger than when she had first laid eyes on him.

She got up, went to the edge of the curtain and stood with her back turned, continuing to explain the perfection of the plan, speaking all the while she heard drawers opened and closed, and throughout her assistance in getting his shirt and slacks from the closet on the wall.

Stuart's discharge from the hospital was obtained that very afternoon. The nurse appeared quite relieved that the patient had a family to go to, and that the hospital would not be responsible for letting him go driving off by himself.

Marilee, feeling her job for the moment was done upon getting him to go along with them, encouraged him into the front seat and left him and Tate to each other. Men, being men, they talked immediately of sports and vehicles and the journalism they both so loved, leaving Marilee to relax in the back seat, where she observed the two males. Both were in a hard place and handling it amazingly well.

Whatever lay ahead, they would all get through. *You always have gotten through, haven't you?* she heard in a whisper from the recesses of her brain.

The next thing she knew, they were driving down Main Street. She knew it was Main because she opened her eyes and saw the neon Blaines' Drugstore sign.

"Marilee . . . honey, we're almost home." Tate's voice.

She sat up. It was twilight. Streetlights had not yet come on. The buildings and trees and bushes were bathed in the ethereal glow of a sun now set but casting light upward. It had grown cold.

Stuart pressed the button to lower his window. He did it automatically, his hand moving there as if avoiding the door handle and the wild impulse that came over him to open the door and throw himself out before reaching Marilee's house, where he didn't think he could bear to walk inside. Somehow he had been confident and comfortable on the drive—he was, after all, most at home while traveling.

But now the trip was ending. He was reaching his destination, and suddenly he did not want to reach it. Trips he understood. Trips were in between times, when there were no expectations, nothing much required of him but to be carried along.

That was why he had always traveled, he saw in an instant of clarity. To avoid destinations, or to at least keep them to a minimum. There were things one had to do, accomplish, complete, upon reaching one's destination. Destinations always involved some sort of commitment.

The car came to a stop in Marilee's driveway, and when the engine died, Stuart felt like his energy did, too. He forced himself to move and get out, however, determined to keep his shoulders straight. The pity he was certain he would receive would be bad enough without his appearing pitiful. He wished angrily that he had never considered the idea of coming back here. It was a stupid idea. He didn't think he could take it.

He went to the rear of the vehicle to load himself with his own bags, camera cases around his neck, small duffel bag on one shoulder, a big one in hand. Tate took the other; he would look foolish to protest.

He was following Marilee up the walk—thank goodness she wasn't talking, saying something soothing—when he looked up and saw Willie Lee coming to meet him. He wondered what Marilee had told the boy about him.

"Hel-lo, Fa-ther." Willie Lee lifted a hand and took Stuart's and walked along beside him into the house, stepping across the threshold into his destination.

It was warm, inviting, comfortable. He was surprised, and relieved.

For just then, he would let himself rest. He could think of facts later. For right now, he would be grateful to have come to a place that wasn't a hospital and where he wasn't alone.

Franny and Corrine had cooked a pot roast, vegetables, rolls and apple pie, and they ate the meal in the dining room beneath the warm glow of the hanging lamp, in the manner of a family, as indeed they were, Marilee reminded herself.

Afterward Tate said, "Well, Marilee, let me take you over and show you my surprise."

"A surprise?"

"Come on . . . no questions, just come along."

She ran her gaze around all the faces at the table, wondering if anyone knew what Tate was talking about. Franny and Corrine's expressions showed that they did.

Tate, having rounded the table, took her hand, drawing her up after him, leading her through the kitchen and out the back door into the night. She told him they probably should have gotten coats. Were they going far? Excitement washed over her at the anticipation of a surprise.

"Not far." Tate led her through the back gate and over to his house, where he paused at the top of the back step to tell her to close her eyes.

She obliged. Her heart had begun to beat hard, and she held tight to Tate's hand, a little fearful of tripping over the threshold. She thought she smelled a familiar odor. Paint?

"Wait until I tell you to open your eyes." The light was flipped on. "Okay, you can open them now."

Marilee opened her eyes.

Where was she? Tate's kitchen? Yes, but it was different. It was painted, although the doors were off the cabinets and sitting against the wall, and the countertop was partially ripped off.

"It isn't all finished." Tate said. "But we've begun."

"Oh, Tate." There was a new refrigerator, a new dishwasher, a new stove, and a new sink, too. He watched her look at all of it, and she did her best at oohing and aahing. She was impressed, but mostly she wanted to make certain her admiration matched his expectations.

Hc had done it for her. Tears filled her eyes.

"Don't go tearing up yet." He took her hand and led her through the house, up the stairs and down the landing to his bedroom, stopping in front of the closed door.

"You cannot go in this room until our wedding night," he told her.

"You cannot open the door. In the next week, you will see men coming and going from this room, but you cannot go in there."

Men would be coming and going?

"Not even a peek?" she asked.

"Not even a peek, unless you want to spoil your surprise."

"I don't want to do that." She knew that if she spoiled her surprise, it would spoil it more for him.

"Good."

She threw her arms around his neck and brought her lips to his in a fierce and ardent kiss, until they both were out of breath. When she could speak, her voice came in a husky whisper.

"Tate Holloway, there is no other man like you on earth. I shall love you till the day I die."

When the telephone rang, Corrine was drying a pan and keeping an eye out the back window for Aunt Marilee and Papa Tate. She moved to the phone on the wall and answered, her mind immediately anticipating either her mother or her grandmother, and in either case she was wary.

"Hey, Corrine. It's me—Ricky Dale."

Her eyes popped wide. She looked over at Granny Franny, who seemed intent on cramming leftovers into the refrigerator. "Hey," she said.

There were long seconds of silence in which Corrine figured Ricky Dale had called her, so it was up to him to carry the conversation.

"Look, I got somethin' bad to tell you."

"You do?" She gripped the receiver.

"My grama's cat died."

"Oh." Then she thought to say, "I'm sorry, Ricky Dale. Is your grama real upset?"

"Mom says she's not. Mom just got back from over there. She said Grama seemed to be accepting everything now. She said Grama said the cat had ate real good, and then the next thing Grama found it dead. No sufferin'," he added.

"Well . . . good."

"I guess Willie Lee didn't cure it."

"Guess not."

Silence again.

"Are you gonna tell him . . . about my grama's cat?"

"Yeah, I'd better, or one of us might slip up, and then he'll find out anyway." She was a little irritated at Ricky Dale for letting the job fall to her.

Ricky Dale said, "Do you think it was just coincidence with Beau and the bird?"

"I don't know." She did not think it was coincidence with the dog and the bird, but she settled for saying, "Maybe he just can't do it all the time."

"Yeah, maybe."

Another silence.

Then Corrine said, "Hey, I'm movin' over to Tate's with Aunt Marilee. It's because Willie Lee's dad is goin' to live here for a while. He's sick and needs to be looked out for. You can call me over there, if I'm not here."

That sounded a little confusing, but Ricky Dale said, "Okay. My dad's got the number written right here on the wall."

After Corrine had hung up, she wondered if he had meant Tate's number was written on a piece of paper or actually on the wall. She could never bring herself to write on a wall.

She thought that maybe Willie Lee would be asleep. He had gotten his bath before supper. If he was asleep, she could wait to tell him about the cat. If he was asleep, she wasn't supposed to tell him, was the way she figured it.

But he wasn't asleep. He was on his bed, looking at his picture book of dogs, with Munro.

Corrine stopped in the doorway and looked across into her aunt Marilee's room. The light was on in there, where Mr. James was puttering around, putting away his things. Curious as to what the room looked like with him in it, she stepped back and peered cautiously. Mr. James was sitting on the end of the bed now. Just sitting there. Corrine didn't think the man was only sick. She thought he was dying, but no one wanted to say that.

Going on into her and Willie Lee's room, she quietly closed the door. Then she went over to his bed and told Willie Lee about the cat.

Willie Lee's bottom lip quivered, but he didn't cry. "It was a real-ly old cat," he said. "Real-ly, real-ly old."

"Yeah." Corrine chewed her bottom lip, then said, "Is that why you couldn't fix it, Willie Lee? Because it was so old?"

"May-be. I do not know. Mun-ro just told me may-be."

"Oh. Well, it was nice of you to try. Ricky Dale said his grandmother was not too upset."

She got up and retrieved her book bag, shoving favorite books into it, and her mother's picture, then looked around to see if there was anything else she wanted to make sure to take with her this first night. Her gaze lit on Willie Lee. She wished she could take him. She didn't like leaving him over here, out of her sight. Willie Lee had hardly been out of her sight since she had come. The more she thought of this, the more she disliked leaving him.

"Willie Lee, don't go out the window while I'm over there at Papa Tate's house, okay?"

He looked at her and blinked.

"Promise me, Willie Lee."

"I am one of the guys now, Cor-rine. I am a boy and can do some things."

"I know that, but I'm still your *older* cousin, and I'm supposed to look out for you. Just don't go out the window. You'll probably get Papa Tate all upset if you go out the window."

Willie Lee's eyebrows went together for a thoughtful moment, and then he told her in a factual manner, "No. Pa-pa Tate does not get upset."

Sometimes Willie Lee could be really smart.

Twenty-Five

Moving on . . .

Marilee, which had come "sneaking in," as Tate put it, showed its true colors and began to roar in its first full week. The temperature bounced back and forth from cold to warm, sometimes changing twenty degrees in one day. Storms rolled from the high plains, bringing tornado conditions, winds that whipped tree branches beginning to bud with leaves, and a total of almost three inches of rain. This was quite normal for the season in Oklahoma, so no one was overly shaken up. The tornado sirens went off twice, which sent more people outside to watch the sky than to take shelter.

Tate, Stuart, Willie Lee and Munro were among these sky watchers all the way out in the yard, near the curb, for the best view, while Marilee went back and forth from the television reports to the front door, trying to keep an eye on both the TV and her loved ones, anticipating when she would have to run out there and grab Willie Lee to race him to shelter. The men were on their own. Franny and Corrine, and Vella when she was there, stood in between, on the porch.

Marilee caught sight of yellow forsythia bushes that had burst into bloom, and she began to be concerned that none would be found still blooming by her wedding date. She watched each bush she found, telling herself that forsythia bushes surely were not a life-and-death matter.

Marilee's mother, who took the tack of brushing off Marilee's attempt to talk about the situation concerning Corrine and Anita, pretending, as she always had, that there was no problem, assured Marilee that she had a friend who lived half an hour farther north and who had plenty of forsythia that should bloom at exactly the correct time. "I will cut them for you," her mother said, quite amazing Marilee, who wondered how her mother would be able to accomplish this task at the same time as being on her Caribbean cruise but decided not to pursue this question and to accept the generous offer in the spirit in which it was given.

"Thank you, Mother. I would so appreciate it."

Why was it, when there were so many true worries she could think of—wedding preparations, Stuart's sickness, Anita's self-destructiveness, mothering children, becoming a wife, setting up a new household—that she had to dwell on insignificant things like the availability of forsythia?

Thinking of forsythia was so much easier, she decided; all the rest of her concerns could be, and very often were, overwhelming.

Despite a constant sense that she might be overlooking something, the wedding preparations appeared to be thoroughly on track, complete with the country-swing band of which Winston and Franny—and Vella, too, who had accompanied them to the VFW hall—approved. The three older people had become something of a trio.

Margaret Wyatt was making the final nips and tucks on Marilee's and Corrine's dresses, and Tate's and Parker's suits were approved.

"We don't have to wear tuxedos, do we?" Tate had asked anxiously at the beginning of planning. "I'd really rather not."

"No, dear, we'll keep to an informal wedding. Your grey suit will be perfect. You look so handsome in it. And Parker has a sharp-looking blue one he bought for his mother's wedding a couple of years ago."

"It's pretty convenient that you are familiar with Parker's wardrobe," Tate observed.

A little uncertain as to the exact nature of Tate's attitude, Marilee responded forthrightly, "It does make life easier, doesn't it?"

She had wanted a cozy, informal wedding, and she would get the informal, but cozy was another matter. The replies were coming in for the reception; it appeared everyone they had invited intended to come, even just about all the employees of Cooper's Appliances. The refreshment order had been increased twice. Marilee was adamant, though, on using china serving dishes. She was not going paper-plate informal.

Franny and Vella were industriously making bows for the pews and reception table and anywhere else they could think to put them; anyone who passed by during a critical bow-making procedure was asked to be of assistance and put forth his or her finger. Once Marilee came upon the surprising sight of Stuart with one index finger toward Franny and the other toward Vella. He looked quite disconcerted, a man who had managed to avoid intimate ties finally all tied up.

It appeared, very much to Marilee's amazement, that Stuart coming into their midst was proving to be a success in ways no one had imagined. A path began to be worn across the backyards, with all the coming and going from early morning into the night between Tate's and Marilee's houses.

There was constantly something forgotten in one house that was necessary in the other. Within the first two days of Stuart's arrival, Marilee's closet was empty of her many things and Stuart's belongings had taken their place. All the clutter on the table beneath her bedroom window and the nightstands was now in the bedroom she used at the big old house, as well as being scattered about other rooms there. In this gentle fashion Marilee's and Corrine's clothes and personal items, their very lives, were eased over to the big Holloway house.

To keep his things at his own house and not be hauling them back and forth, Tate returned home for major showering and dressing. He liked seeing Marilee's things living beside his own. He got excited when he saw her brush on the bathroom vanity. Once he stopped on the landing and inhaled deeply. His mother coming out of her room asked what he was doing.

"I'm soakin' up Marilee's essence," he said.

Because of the ever-increasing remodeling and repairs proceeding in the kitchen of the big house—and now a new bathroom begun beneath the stairway—meals were either cooked at Marilee's house and eaten in her dining area, or brought from the Main Street Café or the IGA delicatessen.

Franny discovered that Stuart liked espresso, so she bought an espresso machine and took up drinking it with him along about midmorning, when Stuart would arise. Within two days of this, Winston and Vella joined them, coming down Church Street and cutting through the backyards, adding to the traffic on the path.

On her second morning in Tate's house, Marilee stepped out of the bathroom and encountered three strange men passing by on the landing. Each said a polite, "Hello, ma'am," slipped into the master bedroom and shut the door. Down in the kitchen, where Tate joined her with mocha and rolls from the IGA, she could hear faint thuds from the master bedroom.

She gazed at Tate, looked at the ceiling and again at Tate, who smiled and said, "Don't spoil your surprise."

When she came back from getting the children to school, two men were working in the kitchen, and Franny was checking out their progress. Two of the bedroom workmen came through the back door, bringing a large king-size mattress. Marilee thought it big enough to accommodate their entire family.

The next day, as she was clearing out worn and faded towels from the bathroom closet, she caught the sound of hammering in the bedroom on the other side of the door. She pressed her ear against the door, then carefully laid her hand on the knob.

Drawing herself up straight, she let go of the knob and firmly left the room.

Tuesday afternoon, at her own home, when Corrine brought her the mail, Marilee found two envelopes addressed to Stuart. They were fan letters from the first part of his photo article on fifties' motels that had run in the Sunday edition of *The Valentine Voice*. Both had been sent to the *Voice* offices, but Julia Jenkins-Tinsley had forwarded them to Marilee's house. That explained how word of Stuart's presence and situation got around town so quickly.

Friends and neighbors, both sympathetic and curious, began to drop by to visit, often bringing food, and since there was so much food, people felt comfortable to stay quite a long time. A bridge game started up one afternoon, in which Stuart did not participate but took pictures with the aim of doing a study on the face of vanishing small-town America.

He began to take pictures all over the place. It seemed as if every time she turned around, Marilee heard the clicking of a camera shutter. Stuart took up going for walks around town and taking pictures that Tate began planning to run in special Sunday edition inserts. Charlotte searched the files for old photographs, which Tate paired with Stuart's new ones, resulting in the first insert to be entitled: "Valentine Then and Now."

"Small-town America isn't vanishing," stated Mayor Upchurch, who dropped by one evening and sat on the front porch with everyone. "It's just changing. Life moves on here, same as anywhere, except maybe a little slower."

As soon as the words came out of his mouth, the mayor had the idea of a brand-new slogan for the town, that it was time to leave behind their current slogan of Flag Town of America—people were letting their flags get ragged and not replacing them—and become the Small Town on the Move.

The debate about town then became: small town on the move to where? Everyone had different ideas. Tate did an editorial on the subject and invited people to drop by the offices to give their opinions, which he would then publish in the paper.

Charlotte, who hated this practice of open invitation to all and sundry, put up a sign in front of her desk that read: For All Opinions, See The Editor. Beneath it was an arrow pointing to Tate's office. She told Tate not to even think of asking her to get anyone coffee.

"I wouldn't think of it, Miss Charlotte," he said.

There was something else that went on in the town that Marilee, after hearing of the third occurrence, realized was a result of the situation with Stuart.

The first occurrence was Fayrene Gardner down at the Main Street Café telling Marilee that she had telephoned her mother, from whom she had been estranged for fifteen years.

Fayrene said, "I did not want to drop dead, like my Dave did last year, and meet St. Peter and have to explain to him why I was not speakin' to my mother." She added, "It was bad enough that Dave and I didn't get back together when we had the chance. We kept puttin' it off. It doesn't pay to put off."

The next, and quite amazing, thing to happen was Leo Pahdocony, Sr. booking a trip to Cancún for his and Reggie's upcoming twentieth anniversary. When Reggie found out that her husband had not only come up with the idea but had himself done the entire work of making the arrangements and all she had to do was pack her bags, she had gone white as a sheet and sunk into her chair. Charlotte, always alert, had made her put her head between her legs.

While Reggie was down there, she whispered to Charlotte, "He must have a lover . . . or maybe some horrible disease."

Charlotte said with all practicality, "So what if it's both? Take the chance for this celebration while you have it, Reg."

The third happening Marilee heard about was the return of her neighbor's wife. Julia Jenkins-Tinsley told the tale when Marilee went into the post office to pick up a parcel for Franny.

"Oh, hey, Marilee." Julia was hanging up the phone. "I was just talkin' to your cousin Belinda. I was tellin' her about your neighbor Leon Purvis and his wife gettin' back together. Did you know that Stella's come home?"

Julia leaned on the counter and told all about how Leon Purvis had located his wife on her trucking route and begged her to come home to try their marriage again. Stella Purvis admitted that part of it had been Leon suffering a backache, but that on the telephone he had cried and said he didn't want to die with regret about their marriage. Stella had gotten home within six hours and said she was tired of the open road anyway.

"Stella was in here this mornin' fillin' out change of address forms and told me all about it herself," said Julia. "She started cryin', even."

Marilee had found the parcel slip in her purse and handed it across the counter. Julia picked it up but didn't quit talking.

"I asked her if Leon had told her about your Stuart, and she said no, so I told her about how you've taken in your sick ex-husband, right into your home. I tell you, hon, I am so touched, and so are a lot of other people. It is sure makin' people do some thinking. I'll bet that whole thing is why Leon called Stella. Did you hear about Fayrene and her mother?"

"That Fayrene called her mother over in Childress'?"

"Yep. Her mother's comin' over here at the end of the month. She didn't even come last year when Fayrene had that setback about her ex-husband, but she is comin' now.

"I think you are a saint for takin' in your ex, but there's some around that can't imagine how you could have brought him into your house after all this time and how he treated you and Willie Lee. And there's a few sayin' it all has to do with Stuart being a big-time journalist and leaving you and Willie Lee a lot of money." She cast Marilee a curious glance.

"Would you get Franny's parcel? I need to go get the children from school."

"Oh, yes. It's right here." Julia stepped aside, looking over some shelves, then reached in and pulled out a large padded envelope that she passed across the counter. "Well, you are a rare woman, Marilee. Tate and Stuart are lucky men." She gestured at the parcel. "It's from Frederick's of Hollywood. How old is Tate's mother?"

"Old enough to shop where she wants," said Marilee. "Thanks, Julia."

She turned and went out into the muggy air of a spring day and started down the sidewalk. She got out of sight of the post office window before checking the package for verification that it really was from Frederick's of Hollywood.

It was. Well. So many things were not what they appeared.

Take her own life, for instance. For her part, Marilee knew there was a lot of talk around town about the situation with her and Tate and Stuart, and there of course was a lot of rehashing as to how she had been engaged the previous fall to Parker.

My goodness, how could she end up looking like a vamp, when she had hardly had any love life for her entire existence?

She herself did not quite understand her own actions concerning Stuart. She was neither a saint nor a sinner, and the idea that some people would consider her in either light made her uncomfortable.

She knew she had simply done what she must. It was tied up in her desire to give Willie Lee every chance to know his father, and his father a chance at knowing his son. And yet, it was more than that. She knew that to not do what she could to help Stuart, who truly was all alone, somehow denied herself, who and what she was. She believed, rightly or wrongly, that she would want someone to help her if the situation were reversed. Certainly, truth be told, she was benefiting from Stuart's presence as much as was everyone else, and it had not cost her anything out of her life but a little time and a house that would have been going empty anyway.

It was, too, as if something needed finishing, and this was the way to do it.

Still, Marilee had a little difficulty with how smoothly everything was going. She had expected more problems concerning Stuart, and she felt uneasy about the wedding preparations seemingly going on without a hitch. In her experience, when life ran this smoothly, something dire was about to happen. Fully aware that this was a negative attitude, she tried to shake it but did not quite succeed.

The truth that came floating up in her mind at that moment was her concern over the possibility that Stuart might drop dead right on the eve of the wedding.

There, she had admitted it. So much for her supposed altruism.

She had, in fact, been observing her ex-husband closely, trying to gauge his waning energy. It didn't seem to be particularly waning. Yes, he took an hour or two's nap in the evening, but this could be attributed to his walking all over town each day. He had even gotten a bit of a tan. He'd always been skinny, so his current gauntness was not any particular indication of a lack of health. Tate reported that he and Stuart—*her ex-husband,* she seemed to have to remind her intended—sat up nights talking about the ever-expanding photo article on Valentine and small-town America in general. Stuart had contacted two national magazines, and both were interested in his photographs and the concept.

Marilee hoped very much that he would live at least until after the wedding and honeymoon. She really hoped they did not get a nasty surprise and find him dead on the eve of the wedding . . . or maybe *during* the wedding.

God knew she was doing the best she could. She would trust God to handle everything and know all would work out for the best, no matter what happened, and she would take it as it came. Yes, she would.

Whatever else was there to do?

Franny showed Marilee and Corrine what she had ordered from Frederick's of Hollywood—a bright floral kimono robe and a padded girdle. Inspecting the girdle quite thoroughly, Corrine said, "Granny Franny, why does it have these little pillowy things?" The pillowy things were the padding on the derriere.

"Because I have a bony behind, and I wanted to see if this would make sitting on the church pews more comfortable."

When Marilee pointed out that the church pews were padded, Franny promptly replied, "Not enough."

Then she brought forward one more thing she had purchased from Frederick's—a shimmering white stretch satin and lace strapless teddy, a gift for Marilee.

When Marilee eyed it uncertainly, Franny said, "It is just the thing for underneath your wedding dress. It is for you alone, no one else will see, and wearing it will make you feel one-hundred-percent woman. Remember that, Corrine," she told the young girl. "God made you a woman, and that is something to respect and honor."

The way Franny put it, it would be sacrilegious not to wear the sexy thing.

Marilee donned the teddy. It was amazingly comfortable. And it did make her feel very much of a woman. "I didn't know I could look like this," she said, beholding herself and her breasts, which had become voluptuous, in the mirror on the chifforobe.

"Honey, those catalog models don't have all their endowments naturally, you know," said Franny quite practically. "They simply know how to make the best of what they have by squeezin' it all around."

Marilee slipped into her wedding dress. It felt wonderful on her skin. Seeing her reflection in the mirror, she drew in a breath.

"You look beautiful, Aunt Marilee."

Corrine's tone reflected the awe Marilee felt. She touched her bare skin above the scooped neckline, then smoothed the soft, flowing skirt that fell to just above her ankles.

"You will do my son and your mother proud," said Franny.

"I would like to move my desk to your house." She handed Tate his morning coffee. "To the alcove in your living room. It's so perfect. It's so much bigger than my living room. And I just love the area, with the windows. I was thinking that maybe we could move your small desk from the dining room and have ours side by side."

"In the living room . . . well, okay. What do we do about the stuff that's already there?"

"I called Albert's Antiques out on the highway. They'll buy them, if you are agreeable."

His eyebrows went up. "Oh." The eyebrows went down. "Fine. Then your desk is the first thing we'll move." He leaned over and kissed her, as he always did when seeking to please.

"I'd like to do it today."

"You would? Today?"

She nodded. "We could ask Parker to help, to bring his old pickup truck."

"Are we in a hurry?"

She felt a little silly and had to get courage to speak honestly. "Not a hurry, but I want it done. It just seems that moving my desk over to your house will make certain that the wedding will happen on schedule. Like putting a firm nail into the plan." She felt more confident; it all made sense to her. "Like believing and acting on the belief."

"Okay, darlin'," he said instantly. "You got it."

Early that afternoon, Parker came with his old pickup truck, and he and Tate hauled over the desk, while Marilee, Stuart, Franny and the children came along the path with the computer, lamp, pictures and whatnots. Marilee had chairs and tables moved from the alcove and directed the placing of her desk, then the moving of Tate's desk from where it was stuck in the dining-room corner. It was a small desk, but he said he liked it.

"Didn't I give you this?" asked Stuart, picking up a blue china vase and regarding it closely.

"Yes . . . and I love it." She took it and placed it correctly.

"I gave her this," Parker piped up, waving a letter opener.

"I gave her the living-room nook," said Tate quite happily.

The antique chairs and crooked walnut table now sitting in the middle of the living room were carried out the front door and loaded into Parker's truck, which sat at the foot of the steps.

Marilee stood on the front porch of the big old house and watched the truck drive away, in the front seat all four of the important men in her life: Tate, Parker, Stuart, and Willie Lee, who had said, "I am one of the gu-uys," and climbed in on top of Stuart's lap.

Franny came up beside her. "There go the men who have contributed to the woman you are. You are blessed."

"Yes," Marilee said, her vision blurring as a surge of gratitude flooded her heart. "Yes, I am."

All the hurts from her past were fading away, she realized. Life flowing on like a river, always. Pain and joy mingling. Now was a time of healing. Now was a time of forgiveness. Now was a time for letting go of the past and moving on with her new life.

She wondered why, although she felt herself moving on, she also felt a foot dragging.

Twenty-Six

Unexpected surprises . . .

Papa Tate was given a surprise bachelor party, and Aunt Marilee was given a surprise wedding shower, and each knew about the other's party but not about their own.

In fact, Aunt Marilee had told everyone that she didn't want a party, but Aunt Vella said, "That's not acceptable on her part. She'll have to bear up," and Granny Franny and Charlotte agreed; the three of them got both parties going, putting Parker and Mr. James in charge of Papa Tate's party, but pretty much telling them everything to do.

There was one thing Corrine noticed that Mr. James did all on his own, or at least started all on his own, and that was to fix up a poster of pictures of Aunt Marilee from when she was a kid on through the time of their marriage to display for Papa Tate. Aunt Vella jumped in to help him, and searched through albums belonging to Aunt Marilee in order to get some of the pictures; even though he was a photographer, he didn't have but a couple of pictures of Marilee. Corrine had seen him take one out of his wallet and put on the poster board, right in the middle.

Granny Franny liked the idea, so she gave Mr. James pictures of Papa Tate and had him make up a second poster board. It was decided that the poster of Papa Tate would go to Aunt Marilee's party, and the poster of Aunt Marilee would go to Papa Tate's party.

Corrine and Willie Lee were included on all the secret plans and admonished half a dozen times not to tell. Corrine knew neither she nor Willie Lee would tell, but she wasn't so certain about all the grown-ups, especially Aunt Vella's daughter, Belinda. She heard Aunt Vella tell Granny Franny that she wasn't inviting Julia Jenkins-Tinsley until Friday evening, to minimize the possibility of Julia letting everything slip.

It was decided to have Aunt Marilee's party down at Aunt Vella's house, where she had a big front porch and her flagstone patio was now finished, even if the landscaper had fallen off on a quality job—

Aunt Vella's description—and the party could flow inside and out, if the weather was really nice.

Papa Tate's party would be at his own house, where he would least expect it. Aunt Vella said that men didn't care about a house being partially torn up for renovation.

After church, Papa Tate and Aunt Marilee took each other to the IGA. Each one thought they were keeping the other busy. As a further diversion, Granny Franny gave them a list of groceries she herself wanted, saying that she and Winston were giving the rose club a little party on Tuesday.

Willie Lee, when Granny Franny tried to take him down to Aunt Vella's, insisted on staying at Papa Tate's house for the bachelor party. "Me and Munro are gu-uys," he said, standing firm, with arms crossed, Munro right beside him.

Corrine regarded her cousin with concern. She felt caught between taking up for him against the adults and leaving him at a place that she found questionable. She had seen Parker bring in a case of beer, and this did not set well with her. She did not know what went on at bachelor parties, but she had caught snatches of comments that led her to suspect them. Ricky Dale had told her that his older brother had described to him a bachelor party, and that such a party entailed a lot of drinking, nude women and pornographic movies. This sounded like what had gone on at a house down the street from Corrine in Fort Worth, which had been filled with unsavory characters and to which the police had often been called. Corrine, who could not imagine Papa Tate drunk or with a nude woman, had told Ricky Dale that she figured Papa Tate's party would be the NASCAR race that he liked to watch on Sundays, and talking about sports and what those nuts up in Washington were doing. Privately, though, she was not completely certain of this assessment.

Then Mr. James said, "Of course Willie Lee stays with us. I'll watch out for him."

As far as Corrine had seen, Mr. James had never watched out for Willie Lee, but there he stood, with his hand on Willie Lee's shoulder. She eyed him and recalled him placing the picture of Aunt Marilee from his wallet so very carefully in the middle of the poster.

Granny Franny agreed to letting Willie Lee stay. Corrine slowly followed the older woman out to the little MG, with the top down, and slipped into the passenger seat, where Granny Franny set the cake from Sweetie Cakes bakery—a big sheet of double chocolate, with white icing—into her lap, and they headed off to Aunt Vella's house up the hill.

The guys did not have cake, but submarine sandwiches and pickles and chips and jalapeño dip, and stuff like that that went with beer and Coke and root beer and ice tea. And farting, Ricky Dale said.

This was the first ladies' party Corrine, who had only school experience with parties, anyway, had ever been to. She slipped into being invisible and passed around the crystal dishes of mints and refreshed cups of punch, while taking in all the expressions and actions and comments made by the ladies. She was amazed by how Reggie Pahdocony jumped up in front of all the ladies and pretended to sing into a spoon, sounding just like Reba McEntire. Tammy Crawford liked to say, "I don't think so," in a smart way, and she wasn't careful where she put her sweaty tea glass. She set it right on Aunt Vella's polished mahogancy end table, but Corrine wiped the water up quickly. The general consensus was great surprise that Zona Porter came. The small grey woman sat quietly in a corner with a smile on her face. Miss Charlene—Papa Tate always called her Miss Charlene—was unusually vivacious. Corrine heard her grama Norma use this word. Miss Charlene hugged just everyone; she smelled of fresh perfume that Corrine liked.

Aunt Marilee's face was flushed, and she was smiling very big and laughing with delight each time she opened a gift. A few of the gifts were very lacy bras and panties. Corrine couldn't wait to get a closer view of these; she was beginning to understand that those women in the Victoria's Secret catalog weren't shaped like they seemed at all, but made themselves that way with underwear. This seemed a lot of trouble and silliness to Corrine. She didn't ever intend to do it but to wear jeans and T-shirts all her life.

"Little girl, could you get me some more mints?" Miss Mildred, the old lady who lived with Mr. Winston, held one of the crystal dishes toward Corrine.

"Yes, ma'am," said Corrine, who eyed the dish with some amazement, then looked at the big purse the older woman clutched on her lap. Corrine did not think it her place to be rude and question.

She went through the dining room, passing Grama Norma, who was speaking to Charlotte. "I wish Anita was here for this. It has been forever since I had my girls together. Did Vella call her, do you know?"

"Vella tried to reach Anita all week, Norma," said Charlotte. "She left messages, but Anita hasn't returned them. Marilee told me she'd tried to call Anita, too."

"Well, she might not be back from South America yet. Her

boyfriend, Louis, has a lot of business down in South America, you know."

Corrine moved on through to the kitchen, where Aunt Vella and Granny Franny were cutting the cake and putting the pieces on Aunt Vella's fine china.

"It's good for Willie Lee to be with the men," Granny Franny was saying.

"Stuart really is a surprise with this, isn't he?" Aunt Vella said.

And Granny replied, "People can rise to occasions when given the chance."

Corrine filled the dish with mints, and, laying an eye on her as if seeing her for the first time, Granny Franny asked her to start handing out the cake.

"I'll be back. . . . I'm takin' these mints to Miss Mildred. She wanted some more."

"Oh, no! We don't do that!" said Aunt Vella, throwing up her hands. "Mildred is filling her purse. . . . She can't have this much candy. Just take her this bitty piece of cake. Thank you, sugar."

As Corrine passed back through the rooms, she heard that Reggie Pahdocony thought she might be going into early menopause, and Julia Jenkins-Tinsley had an overactive thyroid, and Imperia Brown whispered something about an overactive mouth.

Miss Mildred, upon sight of the cake, seemed not to remember she had asked for the mints. "Oh, thank you, little girl."

Corrine stepped aside, casting furtive looks at the older woman, wondering if she would stuff the cake into her purse, but she sat and ate it with a smile.

Someone asked Aunt Marilee what something old she would be wearing for the wedding, and Aunt Marilee replied that she would wear earrings that she and Anita had bought down in Fort Worth a long time ago. Corrine saw a shadow pass across Aunt Marilee's face. Probably no one else noticed it, but Corrine did.

"Honey, why don't you wear my pearl necklace and earrings?" Grama Norma said. "They would be lovely."

"I want to wear the earrings Anita and I bought," Aunt Marilee said.

Grama Norma wasn't going to let it go, though, and kept saying how she thought the pearls would be more refined than costume jewelry. Corrine saw how her aunt got the straight back and small but determined smile, and all of a sudden for some reason she was thinking of her mother with great longing.

She had tried and tried to hold the feelings off, but now, because everyone had mentioned her mother's name, the feelings were coming over her in a flood. She could imagine her aunt Marilee and her mother buying the earrings. Her mother loved dangling earrings.

Corrine slipped unnoticed back into the kitchen and out the back door. She sat on the steps. Aunt Vella didn't have a back porch.

Corrine could see down to the corrals behind Mr. Winston's house. The horses stood at the wooden fence, swishing their tails.

A tiny fly lit on her arm; it was the first one that year to plague her. She noticed then how still and heavy the air had become. She gazed up at the sky that was covered by solid grey cloud. It was almost the same color as the stones in Aunt Vella's new flagstone patio.

Then she was lost in her imagination as she saw the image of her mother sweeping along toward her, smiling in the beautiful manner she did whenever she was having a good day. Oh, Corrine loved those days when her mother was having a good day! In her imagination, she hopped up and ran to her mother, who hugged her, and then produced a gold box with a gold ribbon and said to Corrine, "Oh, honey, I didn't forget you. I just had to find the exact right thing, and then the exact right box to put it in, and to bring it to you myself."

Corrine, whose eyes had filled with tears, was brought out of the daydream by a blaring noise. Puzzled, she listened to the sound. A siren, she realized at the same moment of noticing a rising breeze.

The tornado siren!

Instantly on her feet and filled with panic, she tried to get in the back door, but couldn't get the knob to turn. Behind her, the screen door banged against her back. Then, at last, she burst into the kitchen. It was empty.

"Corrine! Corrine!" That was Aunt Marilee.

"I'm here!" she called, even as she raced through the dining room, where women were on their feet and peering out the north windows and jabbering so that the siren could hardly be heard.

In the living room, Aunt Marilee took hold of her and headed for the front door.

Aunt Vella, standing at the door, stopped them and barked orders. "You can't go down there now. Those men will take care of Willie Lee. You see to Corrine. You two get in the cellar."

Corrine saw the hesitation on Aunt Marilee's face.

"It's comin' out of the west, right at us," said Reggie, who had turned on the television for the weather warning.

Then Aunt Marilee said to Corrine, "Come on. We're gettin' in the shelter."

"There's only room for six in the shelter," Aunt Vella said, raising her voice to everyone. "Four of you follow Marilee and Corrine, and you others come over here and help me make room in the closet under the stairs. Mildred, sugar, you come over here with me."

As Aunt Marilee jerked her along, Corrine caught sight of Miss Mildred crying and waddling toward Aunt Vella.

The wind was high out the back door. Granny Franny was there ahead of them and trying to get the cellar door open, but her tiny size was no match for the door in the wind that jerked it out of her hands. Corrine and Aunt Marilee took hold to help, and then Aunt Marilee was stuffing Corrine down into a cinderblock cubbyhole in the ground. Corrine looked back up for Aunt Marilee, but there was Reggie Pahdocony coming in.

"Aunt Marilee!" Corrine screamed.

"Shush . . . she's comin' honey," Reggie told her, pulling her back to the rear of the cubbyhole, where Corrine waited with a thumping heart, until she could maneuver herself to sit beside Aunt Marilee, after her aunt had closed the cellar door.

She found herself surrounded by five other women, all of them squished together and panting hard and smelling like perfume and fear. Aunt Marilee, who had miraculously produced a flashlight, pointed the beam downward, and it sent an eerie glow on their faces.

Granny Franny had not come down, Corrine saw with distress.

"Good Lord, just listen to that wind," said Imperia Brown.

They all listened. Corrine sure hoped Granny Franny wasn't blowing away. She wasn't very big. Corrine imagined Granny Franny flying through the sky, like the witch in the movie *The Wizard of Oz,* only Granny Franny was pretty and would be smiling.

"It might be just a good windstorm," Grama Norma said. "Might not have been a tornado at all."

"It's a tornado," Charlene said.

Aunt Marilee took hold of Corrine's right hand, smoothed it out of a fist and held it in her own.

Just then something thunked against the cellar doors, causing them all to jump, and Belinda to let out a little scream.

Twenty-Seven

When the going gets tough . . .

Marilee, her heart pumping with both trepidation and curiosity, first peeked out, then led the way up out of the cellar.

Well, for heaven's sake.

She stood there, blinking in the remarkable bright light shafting through thick dark clouds, and looking around at a quite normal world. The stone patio was wet from a heavy downpour, and water trickled from the eaves, but the rain fell softly now. The rain and the few limbs scattered about gave proof of a storm, and here a roof shingle, there quite a big limb, and over yonder what looked like a twisted piece of siding. But the house stood right there, seemingly undamaged.

The world was intact, the trees, Aunt Vella's rose garden, the concrete benches on the new stone patio. Perhaps it *had* been nothing more than a strong windstorm.

The other women came snaking around her, led by her mother making a beeline inside the back door. Marilee, being brought back to the present, took Corrine's hand and followed, her thoughts now racing to Willie Lee and Tate and finding out what had happened.

In the living room, women were gathering their purses and streaming out the door, although Granny Franny was at the door and telling everyone to please stay for a bit, for safety's sake. All wrought up, no one listened. They just went running out to their vehicles, while Aunt Vella, on the porch, yelled warnings about possible downed electric lines. Although scattered with small limbs, the street looked clear to Marilee. She pointed this out.

"Well, we don't know what the other streets are like," replied Aunt Vella.

"Do you think it was a tornado?" Marilee asked. She still had hold of Corrine, she realized, and she didn't let go.

"It was a good windstorm," Aunt Vella said, striding back into the house. "We don't have any electricity, so something's down some-where."

Mildred Covington had two plates of half-eaten pieces of cake bal-anced on her knees and was eating out of both.

Marilee's mother was on the couch. She looked as white as a sheet and was breathing deeply.

"Mother, are you all right?"

"Well . . . I'm shaken up."

Marilee hoped her mother was okay, because Marilee needed to leave her and get down to Tate and Willie Lee. Phone, perhaps she could phone, she thought, wishing that she had Tate's cell phone, but then he wouldn't have one. It might be quicker just to run down the street; it would only take a few minutes. While her mind was going a mile a minute in this distorted fashion, she turned to find that Belinda was at the telephone ahead of her.

"It's dead," Belinda said, dropping the receiver into the cradle.

"Aunt Vella, don't you have a cell phone?" Marilee finally let go of Corrine. Corrine stayed close beside her.

"Well, yes," said Aunt Vella in a manner as if just then thinking of it. She had to find her purse and dig into it. "Now let's see. Oh, dear, the battery's low, but it should still work." She punched in the number for the drugstore. "It's ringing," she told Marilee, who stood watching her aunt impatiently.

"No answer," Aunt Vella said after a long minute. Her eyes were round and worried as she passed the little phone to Marilee.

"Oh, Mama, Daddy's probably still sittin' there watchin' a war pic-ture on TBS," said Belinda.

"There isn't any electricity, Belinda."

"Not here, but we don't know about Main Street," Belinda pointed out.

During this exchange, Marilee dialed Tate's house and listened first to a long silence and finally to ringing . . . and ringing. "No answer," she said.

"The phones could be out, but they'll still ring," Belinda said.

Marilee thought to try Tate's cell phone, but for the life of her, she couldn't remember the number. Her brain had gone into a spin, pictur-ing the rest of the town, which they could not see, wiped off the face of the map.

Her gaze fell on her mother as she considered her options; she would have to leave her mother, who sat on Aunt Vella's couch, fan-ning herself with a magazine.

"Mom, I have to go check on Tate and Willie Lee. You sit here and rest." She grabbed Corrine's hand, giving only passing thought to leaving the child in her mother's care. She knew it would be Corrine taking care of her mother, not the other way around, and besides, the child was stuck to Marilee like glue.

"Be careful, dear," her mother called after her.

She realized she had not driven, that Tate had brought her.

"I don't think we should take the cars . . . we might get cars stuck all over," said Franny, who came beside them as they started down the front porch steps.

"I sure hope Perry had sense enough to get in the closet," said Aunt Vella, who followed.

Just then Dixie Love came out her door across the street. She hollered that she had no damage, and Aunt Vella hollered back, asking if she had electricity. Dixie said no.

The rain had stopped. Marilee, Corrine beside her, hopped over the water running thinly down the gutter, while the street was already showing dry patches.

"Nothing looks damaged around here," Marilee said, finding the fact of all the houses intact extremely reassuring.

"Mr. Winston's flags are tore up . . . so's Mr. Northrupt's," Corrine said, pointing.

Just as they passed the Northrupt house, Mr. Northrupt came out his front door and hailed them. "We're okay here!"

"Good!" Marilee called back.

She broke into a jog as they came around the curve going downhill. There was a big elm split right in two, and the part that lay out in the road blocked the view of Tate's house. Corrine went surging ahead.

"Oh, Aunt Marilee!" she called back over her shoulder in a way that sent alarm racing through Marilee.

Then she got her first sight of Tate's house.

Her stride faltered. The roof and half the top floor were gone. The bedroom that had been Franny's was totally exposed; the bedspread flopped in the breeze. The wonderful old magnolia that had stood beside the house was broken off over the portico, under which the tail-end of the BMW could be seen.

"Oh my God," Marilee said.

"Yes, Father, help us bear up," Franny said. Corrine was running ahead. "Come around the front!" she hollered back to them.

Marilee and Franny headed for the house, and Aunt Vella called that she was going on to the drugstore. Marilee hesitated, looking at her dear aunt, who was running faster than was wise for a woman of her age.

"Be careful, Aunt Vella!" Then Marilee followed Franny, and both of them started calling, "Tate! Willie Lee! Is everyone okay?"

Every dark thought that could be raced through Marilee's mind, and she saw pictures of Willie Lee, Tate and Stuart being sucked up and swirling in a tornado, and the telephone and Munro, too.

Then, just as she reached the bottom of the front steps, she looked, and there was Tate coming out the front door, with Willie Lee beside him, and Stuart's taller frame coming behind.

Oh, thank God.

Corrine reached them first and threw her arms around Willie Lee.

Marilee stood there staring, then sank down to the steps because her legs gave out.

Word of the general safety of the town and just what had happened came by way of Sheriff Oakes and Deputy Lyle Midgett, who drove past in their canvas of the town, and various neighbors living near the corner of Porter and Church Streets, who came to see the damage to the Editor's house, commiserate and tell their own stories.

The tornado had been small and had come in from the west like a bouncing ball gone astray. It had bounced its way along what used to be an alleyway running behind the houses on Porter Street, a distance of some three long blocks, snapping power lines along the way. The passage of the tornado behind their house had been witnessed by Leon and Stella Purvis, who saw it all from the window of their kitchen; the two had been working on Leon's hot rod truck and had not heard the siren because of the roar of the engine.

"Stella said that the light looked funny, and I turned off the truck engine and heard the siren about the same time I caught the roar of the dad-blamed tornado," said Leon, who had hotfooted it over to the big house to see if anyone had been injured.

Stella, who had come with him and who was puffing hard on a cigarette, said, "We saw it from our kitchen window. There wasn't any time to take shelter anywhere else—Leon had the closet so full of stuff, it could have killed us. That thing snaked down to the alleyway right behind the yard. Looked like somethin' out of the movies. Just like some animation, I swear. It danced back upward past Marilee's yard and then just disappeared into the trees behind your house, Editor. Then stuff was flyin' ever' which'er way through the sky. I knew the house'd been hit."

It was theorized that the big Holloway house had been what turned the tornado off course and sent it angling southeast. This was surely a blessing, or it might have gone right on down and demolished the school.

The way Marilee saw it, the school would not have been occupied, and Tate's house was, so that had not been much of a blessing, although she did not think she should complain, since her dear family was safe, as, it appeared, were all those in the surrounding neighborhood. From all of the early reports, it seemed that the big Holloway house was the only house in Valentine that had been touched.

The tornado had gone on across the street, taken a lick at the Fletchers' garage, then stayed on the ground for several hundred yards, where it demolished a doghouse—vacant—fences, bushes and trees, and a telephone connector box, explaining the lack of telephones all the way down Church Street. When it went into the back part of Winston's deep yard, it apparently lifted off, destroying one of the big elms in the process. As if thus satisfied, the tornado had disappeared into the clouds.

"I don't think it would have dared touch Coweta's roses," Winston said. He did not go immediately to look at his place, because he had to sit down and catch his breath from all the excitement, but Everett Northrupt had come down to tell him that his house was still there. Everett was a little miffed at not having been invited to the bachelor party.

Marilee remembered Aunt Vella. She asked for Tate's cell phone, and he told her it was in his car, which was now underneath the portico that was underneath the magnolia. He had the idea to try the telephone in the living room, which Marilee did not think for a minute could be working.

"I called down here from Aunt Vella's cell phone, but no one answered."

"Oh, I thought I heard it ring, but we were busy with everyone leavin' in such a hurry. We didn't even think about the phone."

He dialed the number for the drugstore, while Marilee waited for him to tell her the phone wasn't working, but then he surprised her by talking to Aunt Vella. She had to contain herself to keep from snatching the phone out of his hands.

"They're okay." He handed the phone to Marilee.

"Aunt Vella?"

"Yes, sugar, we are fine . . . just fine."

At the precious sound of Aunt Vella's voice, Marilee squeezed her eyes closed. It seemed odd to be speaking on the telephone in a room where everything was perfectly intact and to know that above her head the house was blown away. Opening her eyes, she saw Tate mounting the stairs. Going up to see the great wound to the house.

Aunt Vella was saying, "Your uncle Perry thought to get in the pharmacy closet. If that tornado had hit, he would have been pilled to death. I told him that's what he would have gotten for being so wedded to this place and television that he wasn't up there at Tate's party, the old stick in the mud." Profound affection echoed in her voice. "Anyway, it doesn't look like any real damage on Main Street, except for a couple of forgotten flags, and Fayrene's pretty new green awnings over at the café and her apartment are ripped to shreds. Bless her heart. She's awfully upset about it. Already asked Perry for a sedative. Oh, and our electric's out. . . . Funny the phones are working, but Perry says the wires are mostly underground."

Aunt Vella said she and Uncle Perry would be coming back quickly in Perry's car, since the roads were open, and they hung up.

Marilee stood there with her hand on the phone, thinking of Tate upstairs, but knowing she had to call Charlotte first.

Charlotte picked up on the second ring. Yes, her friend had found her mother and house all fine. Some wind had come through, but not damaging, although they, too, were without electricity.

"Isn't it funny we have a phone?" she said. Marilee started to tell her about the wires being in the ground, but Charlotte said Sandy had just driven up, she had to go, bye.

Marilee stood there with her hand on the receiver, going through a mental list of who she needed to check on.

Just then the phone rang, causing her to jump.

"Marilee?" It was Parker. "You and everyone else over there okay?"

Parker had left before she and Corrine had gotten to the house. She told him they were fine and asked about his house. She knew Amy was okay, because she was down in Dallas visiting her sister, who had a new baby.

"There wasn't any damage here at all," he told her. "All the animals made it through, and I even have electricity. I'm headin' out west of town now, though. Fella out that way has a couple of cows cut up from flying debris. Heard a radio report that said there were a couple of little tornadoes sighted touching down."

Marilee reminded him to call Amy first and let her know he was okay. He had not even thought of that, of course. As she hung up, she scolded herself; she really needed to quit trying to take care of Parker. Let his wife do the job.

Closing her eyes, she gave thanks that those nearest and dearest, and even those she didn't even know, were all safe from the storm.

What did damaged houses matter? she thought, and she headed for the stairs.

Glancing through the opened front door, she saw Stuart sitting on the front porch, his head resting back, eyes closed. Willie Lee lay leaning against him, and had fallen asleep, and next to him, Munro had curled. Corrine and Franny sat on the steps with Winston, speaking with Leon and Stella. All safe.

Quite suddenly Marilee needed to be with Tate and to touch him. She went rapidly to the steps, paused a moment with her hand on the newel post, then started up.

Hearing the creaking of the stairs, Tate looked over the landing. "Don't come up . . . the stairs may be weakened."

He didn't want her to come upstairs. He worried about the stability of the house, and he just didn't want her to come up.

But Marilee responded with all logic, "You're up there," and kept on coming. "Is my wedding dress okay?"

He told her it was fine, that her room had not been touched, hoping that might stop her, which was a useless hope, of course. She kept on up the stairs and went straight to the back bedroom she had been using, to the closet to check her dress.

He turned again to walk back into what was left of the bedroom he had intended to share with her, her voice, filled with relief and delight, floating after him. "Oh, yes, it's fine. Thank you, God!"

Tate was thankful, but he was also angry. Standing there in the midst of the wreckage, the anger was winning.

Marilee appeared behind his shoulder, wrapping her arms around his waist from the back. He supposed it didn't matter now that she saw the room; it was all ruined, his surprise, his hope for starting out on the right foot.

"Oh, Tate, the bed is beautiful!" Marilee said, then hurried over to it, hopping over fallen roof joists to get there. "My gosh, where did you get such a bed?" She gazed at him with wonderment.

"The bedroom is gone," he said, just in case she had not noticed.

With sudden, painful clarity, he realized that he had wanted to be the big man in giving her this room. He didn't want to look at that notion, and he tried to push it away, but the knowledge washed over him again, and he knew that he had wanted to be to her all that Stuart had not been, just to make sure that he proved to be a better husband.

"You planned a skylight for us," she said, sitting down on the plaster- and debris-covered mattress and looking upward.

He stared at her, at her calm face. Her positive outlook was salt in his wound. He wanted her to be as hurt and outraged as he was.

Unable to speak of his anger, he kicked a board, and it clattered, but not enough.

She said, "We're all okay, Tate. If we're together, that's all we need."

He did not need her censure, he thought, even as the truth of her words seeped into him.

He had to tell her. God knew that he could hardly face himself, much less her, but he had to tell her.

"Marilee, the house isn't insured."

Her eyes rested on him.

"I put everything into getting the paper off the ground. I've been balancin' money all over, trying to get the *Voice* goin' good, and the house insurance has come last. I let it lapse."

He had been a fool, and now she would know. She would know he was irresponsible, like Stuart, not taking care of their home. She would be disappointed in him. He was disappointed in himself. He had been reaching further than he could truly and safely reach. Trying to appear bigger and smarter than he was. How could he have let something like this go? He had thought he could gamble for six months, that everything would be fine.

Suddenly he was so tired. He'd been working and planning and balancing to get his newspaper off the ground, to keep all the staff employed and receiving paychecks, and he could no longer keep up the juggling pace.

Then she was there in front of him, attempting to put her arms around him. That made him angrier. He didn't want her pity or consolation.

"We don't have a house to move to after the wedding."

"So what?" she shot back at him.

He shook his head. "We will probably need to postpone the wedding until I can get us a place to live."

Her eyebrow arched. "Until *you* can find us a place? I thought we were together?"

"Okay, until *we* can find a place." He closed his mouth against the anger that wanted to spew out.

"We can rent somewhere, Tate. We can pitch a tent in your backyard and cook in your kitchen, if nothing else."

He thought her attitude far from realistic. "Be serious. This is Valentine, Marilee. . . . Empty houses aren't just waitin' around, even for rent, and I'm pretty well flat broke."

The last echoed inside of him. He had credit, which was already so stretched it was likely to snap back at him. He wanted to knock his head against a wall. He wanted to hit something.

"I have some money set back. Enough to rent something for a month or so. We'll find a place. There is no reason to postpone the wedding just because things are not perfect." She spoke in that reasonable tone again, and he couldn't stand it.

"I'm not usin' your money."

"Why not?"

"I'm just not. And you're not touchin' Willie Lee's money."

"I would never in this world think of touchin' Willie Lee's money. And don't you point that finger at me, Tate Holloway."

He drew back the offending finger and raked a hand through his hair, finally bringing himself to say, "I'm sorry, Marilee. I'm angry at myself, not you. I'm just tryin' to figure out what in the hell we're gonna do, since I've screwed up so badly."

Now she did that chuckling thing and looked at him as if he were a child. She reached for him, taking his face in her hands and gazing into his eyes with her own the pure blue of a clear summer sky.

"Honey," she said, speaking slowly, "we're goin' to do the best we can. That's what we're goin' to do."

He felt himself melting into her eyes.

"My dearest darlin'," she said with sweet lips turning upward, "sometimes we humans make choices that don't quite work out as we planned, because life interferes. I'm sorry to tell you, Mr. Editor, but you are as human as the rest of us. And you are the human man I love. It is not this house I love, but you. I love you and Willie Lee and Corrine, and we are all okay. It is you I want to marry, and you who Willie Lee and Corrine need for a father. We could all live in a tent. Where has your good sense gone to?"

She loved him. He heard it in her voice, felt it in her hands on his face and saw it in her eyes. It washed over him like a warm wave.

He wrapped his arms around her then, holding her as if his life depended on it. It seemed to, in that minute. "Oh, lady, you are always a surprise to me," he said, when he could speak.

She drew back and looked him in the eye. "I am repeating back to you what you have taught me."

And, although it seemed a little egotistical, he knew that was the truth. He chuckled and kissed her neck, savoring the feel and scent of her, and knowing that the biggest mistake he had made in the past minutes was in overlooking that she was on this earth and with him.

She pushed back and arched an eyebrow. "Is the bed paid for?"

"No," he said sadly. "On credit."

Curtiss Ann Matlock

"Well, let's try to pay for it before anything else."

He threw back his head and laughed hard, and the next instant the skies above opened up and rain poured down.

Startled, he looked at Marilee, and she looked at him. Her eyes were as lights from her face, shining out through rain that dribbled onto her eyelashes and down her cheeks. He felt it sliding down his face, too.

There seemed only one thing to do.

Giving her a courtly bow, then taking her loosely in his arms, he waltzed her around the small space in which they stood, atop the crumbled plaster and between the collapsed boards, to music that only he and Marilee could hear, together.

Twenty-Eight

Wonders never cease . . .

The rain was short-lived, and sunlight sliced through billowing purple clouds. To the west the dry line was approaching, showing blue sky.

As the phone at Aunt Vella's house was out, Marilee and Tate were preparing to walk up to tell her mother the roads were clear and everything was all right. Marilee had begun to worry about her mother, who she thought could have had a heart attack or something because of being so upset by the storm.

But then here came her mother's car, Belinda at the wheel, pulling to a halt at the curb. At the same time, from the opposite direction, Aunt Vella and Uncle Perry arrived in Uncle Perry's big black Cadillac.

Belinda got out of the car, slammed the door and came across the yard, leaving Marilee's mother to help Mildred out of the back seat. Marilee hurried out to assist both women. Her mother had on heels that sank in the rain-soaked lawn.

"Marilee, I've got to have some ibuprofen . . . extra strength," said her mother, rubbing her head. "I can't drive home like this. Perry, you do not have any ibuprofen in your cabinets. You don't hardly have anything at all at your house, and here you are a pharmacist."

Perry, whose arms were full with three tubs of ice cream, responded, "I have aspirin. It's a good medicine."

"She was wantin' a Valium," Belinda said under her breath. "I could use one." She took one of the gallons of ice cream from her father and proceeded straight into the house.

"We have ice cream for everyone," said Aunt Vella, putting forth two shopping bags full of gallon tubs. "I called the electric company but couldn't get an answer. There's no need to let this ice cream ruin. Let's have a celebration that we're all still here!"

Marilee, Aunt Vella and Franny took the ice cream to the kitchen to dish up. Belinda was at the table, eating straight from the container. Looked like Rocky Road.

The kitchen, too, was as if nothing at all had occurred upstairs or in the neighborhood, except for the lack of electricity. Marilee kept switching on the light switches by habit, which illustrated how dependent she was upon light. Aunt Vella told how when she was a girl, they used only daylight in the houses, because their form of lighting was the kerosene lamp, and no one would be using that during the day. Franny echoed the same sentiments and tales.

Listening to the women's voices, Marilee again felt gratitude fill her heart. She hoped that when everything got back to normal, she would not forget the lesson of what was truly important in this world, although, she probably would from time to time, and have to be reminded. She sure hoped that it wouldn't take a crisis to remind her, though, Lord. Just a gentle whisper would be fine.

"Here, Mama . . . I thought strawberry was your favorite," she said when she returned to the porch, handing her mother the bowl.

Her mother's eyes jumped, and for a moment their eyes met. "Why, yes, thank you, dear," said her mother, who sat a little straighter in the porch chair and smiled.

She handed Stuart a bowl of the vanilla and raised a questioning eyebrow.

He gave her a wink. "Still my favorite," he said and their eyes held each other's for a brief instant.

"Do you want a pillow?" she asked, concerned about his bony body sitting on the porch floor.

"Don't baby me, Marilee," he said, averting his eyes and spooning the softening ice cream.

As she headed back through the screen door, she heard her mother say, "My, this just hits the spot, Vella. Thank you for bringing this ice cream. The best thing in a crisis is to do something very normal and even festive."

Wonders never cease, Marilee thought, so startled by her mother's compliment to her aunt that she paused in midstride. A tornado did a lot of damage to material things, but perhaps it unleashed true good feelings inside people.

In the kitchen, Belinda was still sitting with her gallon of ice cream, and she had found the chocolate syrup in the cabinet. She offered some to Marilee. "I imagine you could use this," she said.

Marilee was overcome with tender feelings and hugged Belinda, saying, "I'm so glad we're all here."

"Me, too," Belinda said, holding the syrup can up to Marilee.

"I am here."

Marilee turned to see her son, with Munro beside him, gazing at her with sleepy eyes. She scooped him up, something she had not done in a long time, as he was growing so heavy, and danced around the room until he giggled. "Yes, you are here, and I am so glad," she said.

"We want ice cream," he said. "I want cher-ry, and Mun-ro wants van-i-lla, please."

"And you shall have it, my prince."

She sent him back out to the porch with a dish of cherry for himself and a dish of vanilla for Munro. Then she proceeded to spoon Rocky Road for herself from Belinda's container, and to spoon the syrup in hefty measure over it.

"Come join us outside, Belinda."

Belinda looked startled at the invitation, then came along.

The voices of those gathered on the porch floated to her as she walked the length of the hallway. It was a comforting sound. She wondered vaguely where she would sleep that night, but the fact did not seem very important. Nothing seemed too important next to seeing Tate's eyes meet hers and Willie Lee's head bent over his ice cream and Corrine licking her spoon.

Just then she heard a young voice calling, "Willie Lee! Willie Lee!"

It was Ricky Dale, pedaling hard on his bike, up the curb and across the yard, with his black dog bounding behind him.

He stopped on the walkway and beheld everyone sitting around the front porch and on the steps. "Willie Lee, you . . . got t' come." That was all he could get out, because he was gasping for breath.

Observing him, his wide eyes and tear-streaked face, Marilee panicked, thinking perhaps the boy's entire family had been killed in the tornado and this tragedy was just now coming to light.

"What is it, Ricky Dale?" asked Tate in a calm voice.

"The horses . . . the . . . the baby is hurt." His eyes shifted to Willie Lee. "She's cut bad. . . . You gotta come, Willie Lee."

Tate was on his feet. "We need to get Parker over there."

"Parker's out on a call," Marilee said, setting her bowl of ice cream on the porch rail, watching Willie Lee and Munro head down the steps, and Corrine go right behind them.

"Willie Lee?" Tate said with puzzlement.

"Is Leanne over there?" Winston asked, but the children were heading across the yard. Marilee watched, her mind going ninety miles an hour: the horse is hurt, Ricky Dale thinks Willie Lee can do something. What is going on? Should I stop them? I'll go, too.

She was already heading down the steps, slipping past Tate and

Leon Purvis and seeing Ricky Dale hit the street, his legs pumping the pedals of his bicycle. Corrine had hold of Willie Lee's hand, and they were running as fast as Willie Lee was capable. Marilee broke into a jog to catch up with them and took Willie Lee's other hand.

They were halfway up the hill when a black car slid alongside— Uncle Perry's car, with Aunt Vella at the wheel. Tate, in the back seat, said through the opened window, "Get in. We'll drive you."

He already had the back door open and was reaching for Willie Lee. Munro and Corrine scrambled into the car behind him, and Marilee threw herself inside, coming to rest against Franny and Corrine, as Aunt Vella punched the accelerator.

"Vella, don't kill us," said Uncle Perry who sat squished in the middle of the front seat, with Winston next to him.

Marilee had to take hold of the door to keep from being flung atop Tate and Willie Lee as Aunt Vella turned into the driveway of the Valentine home. Up ahead, Ricky Dale disappeared around the garage, following the overgrown gravel track that led to the rear of the acreage.

Aunt Vella followed, scraping against green budding lilac branches. Thankfully she slowed and negotiated neatly around the limbs of the demolished elm tree, coming to a stop behind Leanne's pickup truck at the corral.

The tornado had taken out not only the big elm nearby but had torn and twisted the tin horse shed, and splintered a section of the wooden corral. Pieces of tin and split boards were scattered about.

On the far side of the corral, the mare was tied to a fence post. Nearby Leanne and Ricky Dale were crouched beside the filly on the ground.

Marilee opened the car door and was hurried along in getting out by Willie Lee pushing from behind.

Willie Lee tried to run and stumbled. Corrine reached him first and helped him up, then they ran on.

A noise made Marilee look over her shoulder to see the dismaying sight of her mother's car coming up the driveway, and then she hurried on with the others toward Leanne and Ricky Dale, who was urging, "Come on, Willie Lee."

At the first sight of Leanne, Marilee instinctively reached for Tate's hand. The woman had so much blood all over her that she looked like she'd been through a battle. The explanation for this lay on the ground in front of the young woman, who had her hands wrapped around a towel that was wrapped around the filly's ankle.

"Flyin' tin got her. I can't get the bleeding stopped," Leanne said, her voice so desperate that Marilee immediately went down on a knee and put her hand to the young woman's back, as if to hold her up.

"Leanne, honey . . ." This was Winston, coming up on her other side.

Then Willie Lee was on his knees and scooting close to the filly's head. Her eyes were glazed. Marilee started to speak a word of caution to her son, but then she saw Munro pressed close, and Corrine and Ricky Dale right behind him. Something stopped the words in her mouth.

"Help her, Willie Lee . . . please help her," Ricky Dale sobbed.

Marilee kept her eyes on her son's face. No one else said anything. Willie Lee caressed the filly and laid his head down on her. All seemed quiet.

Don't let this horse die, God, Marilee prayed, but all of a sudden she experienced a great fear for her son. She moved to reach for him, but Tate held her back and whispered, "Shush," in her ear.

She leaned against his hard chest, gripped his strong hand and watched her son's pale head.

After what seemed a long minute, Willie Lee rose off the horse and looked at them all from behind his thick glasses. "I think she will be bet-ter now."

Everyone looked at the filly.

She blinked, and blinked again. Her eyes had cleared.

Next she moved, making an effort to get up.

"No . . . no, Baby Girl, lie there," Leanne said. "Ricky Dale hold her head."

This time, though, it was Corrine who took the animal's head and caressed her neck, speaking soothingly.

"There, pon-y . . . lay still," said Willie Lee, who patted her neck. The filly relaxed against Corrine.

Marilee became aware of a clicking sound. She looked over to see Stuart taking a picture. He had obviously already taken several, moving even then to a different angle.

"Stuart," she said in a low tone.

He either did not hear or ignored her.

Then Aunt Vella was there with a towel she handed to Leanne. "Here's a fresh one. It's clean enough."

Leanne slowly and carefully unwrapped the bloody towel. "Ohmygod, the bleeding's stopped," she said in a breathless tone.

"Praise God," Winston and Franny said at once. Marilee saw and heard, then looked over and saw Stuart was clicking another picture.

She was about to step over to make him quit when Tate went before her. She did not know what Tate said, but Stuart put away his camera.

"Marilee . . . Marilee." Her mother walked toward her, her arms out for balance as her spike heels sank into the dirt. "Why did that boy want Willie Lee to come down here? What is this about Willie Lee healing that horse?" Her mother's eyes were anxious.

"I don't know. . . . I guess it was because the horse especially likes Willie Lee."

"It does? Well, I don't think Willie Lee or any of those children need to see all this gore."

"Mama, you look wrung-out. Let me help you get set down in the car."

"I need something for my nerves." Then, "I could really use a cold drink, honey. Do you suppose you could see if Winston has something in his refrigerator?"

"I'll see."

Belinda was in Winston's kitchen; she had a small Coke. She told Marilee there were a couple more bottles in the refrigerator.

"Is Willie Lee some sort of healer?" Belinda asked, raising a curious eyebrow.

"The horse likes him," Marilee said, as she pulled a small bottle of Coca-Cola from the refrigerator.

"I heard Ricky Dale say he knew Willie Lee could heal the horse."

"I'm sure that Willie Lee's love helped the horse. And, Belinda, I really don't think it would be good for Willie Lee for the rumor to go around that he can heal."

Belinda's speculative gaze rested on Marilee. "Oh."

"Is the little horse gonna be all right, Marilee?"

"I hope so, Leon."

"I was just tellin' Stella that one day last month I saw Willie Lee pick up a dead cat out of the street and now he's got it over there with y'all. I've seen him playing with it."

"It couldn't have been dead, then, could it?"

"It looked dead. And now he come over here and healed this horse."

"The horse likes Willie Lee. They have a special bond."

That was her story, and she was sticking to it.

"That horse is darned lucky," Parker told her, in a private moment after he had sewed up the filly's leg. Sweat wetted his hair, even though the cool front had passed and temperatures had dropped. It had been a job to stitch the animal's deep wounds.

Marilee glanced over at the children, who were helping Leanne and Tate make a clean, safe stall. "Yes, it is." She returned her gaze to Parker. "I'm grateful that you could get here so quickly."

"It wasn't anything I did that saved that filly. I just mopped up." He leveled a gaze at her. "What's this Leanne told me about Willie Lee stopping the bleeding? 'Spoke the Word,' is the term she used."

Marilee breathed deeply. "I don't think Willie Lee spoke any word other than loving ones. I don't know, Parker. I really don't know." The honest answer came out. She had known Parker a long time. Then she added, "The horse really likes Willie Lee. Probably that helped to give her a will to live."

He regarded her thoughtfully. "Maybe."

Franny came forward, passing him a glass of the cold tea that she had made up in Winston's kitchen and now bore around on a tray, serving everyone, as if it were an afternoon lawn party, which indeed it seemed to be, Marilee thought, looking around at knots of neighbors who had gathered.

Soon the word would be all over town, added to with all manner of embellishments, of course, as to Willie Lee's role in saving the filly.

"Marilee, your mother has fainted," Franny informed her, hurrying past with a glass of water and a wet cloth.

Marilee followed and found her mother reclining on the back seat of her car. Perry was there, bending over the door, telling her mother that he couldn't give her a sedative without a prescription. "I got aspirin." He pulled a little tin from his pocket.

Franny put the cloth on her mother's head, then passed her the aspirin, which her mother at first refused, then consented to take.

After swallowing the pills, her mother cast her a weak look and said, "I can't drive home. I just can't."

Marilee patted her mother's hand. "You won't have to, Mother."

She went into Winston's house and used the phone in the kitchen to call Carl, who had not shown up at the bachelor party, and who no one had expected anyway. He picked up on the third ring.

He had not heard of the tornado. "We've been watchin' wrestlin' on cable," he told her. She heard voices in the background and pictured her mother's husband and his friends, sitting around swilling beers and eating pretzels and cheese dip. He sounded fairly sober, however. She would trust that he was.

"Mama can't drive home," she told him, raising her voice to be heard over the television and the other voices.

"Did her car get damaged?" he asked, after a moment.

"No, Carl. Her car is fine. But mother is sixty years old and upset by this whole thing, and she is in no shape to drive. She needs taking care of, and I'm too busy down here, since my roof has been blown from my head, and I can't be running her home. You will have to come get her. Now," she added, in case he was considering waiting for his wrestling show to be over.

"O-kay," he said, as if knowing he had better not say anything else.

Marilee hung up and returned to her mother.

"Carl's comin' to get you, Mother."

"Oh, he is?" Her mother's eyes went wide.

"Yes. He hadn't heard about the tornado, and when I told him, he said he was coming right down to get you, and not to worry about your car. He will have one of his men come get it this week."

"He did?"

"Yes," Marilee lied blatantly, patting her mother's hand. She considered that Carl might tell her mother the truth, but quickly tossed off any worry over it. She was fairly certain that if she put her mind to it, she could outlie Carl Cooper any day of the week.

Marilee declined Aunt Vella's invitation for them to stay at her house. "Thank you, Aunt Vella, but I think we'll just go stay out at the Goodnight." She was intent on finding a cave and crawling in, with her loved ones around her.

Twenty-Nine

So many things we carry with us . . .

It was dark when Tate pulled the Cherokee beneath the yellow fluorescent lights at the old motel. Through the picture window, Mr. Goode could be seen watching television.

"Just sit here," Tate told her, squeezing her knee, and slipped out the driver door.

Marilee's eyes followed him as he entered through the glass door and crossed in front of the picture window. He had donned a faded denim shirt that stretched across his thick shoulders.

She twisted around to check the children in the back seat. Willie Lee was asleep in Corrine's lap, and Munro lay against him. Corrine, whose spine was straight against the seat back, regarded Marilee with anxious dark eyes so reminiscent of when she had first come to live with them.

Marilee sent her an encouraging smile. "Franny sent us hot chocolate packets and the electric kettle. We'll make some when we get our pajamas on, okay?"

Corrine nodded. The anxious light remained in her eyes.

"We'll sure have a story to tell your mother, won't we?"

Corrine nodded again and tried for a smile, but it didn't reach her eyes. Marilee wished the seat was not between them. She longed to hug the child back into feeling safe and secure. Of course, perhaps the hugging would be as reassuring to Marilee herself.

Tate came back, slipped behind the wheel, and tossed her a key.

"Largest cabin they got. Two double beds and a set-tee," he said, imitating Mr. Goodnight's accent.

Marilee looked at the key. One room. She looked at his profile, then turned forward, a soft smile brimming up and out. She had not known, but this was what she wanted. She wanted her loved ones close around her. And Tate had known this. And perhaps he shared the feeling.

She and Corrine gathered bags, while Tate gathered Willie Lee, carried him inside and laid him on the bed closest to the door. "Boys will bunk over here," he said.

Munro jumped up beside Willie Lee and lay down as if having an invisible tether to the boy.

Tate brought in the rest of their things, while Marilee got Corrine going in the shower and promised to have hot chocolate for her afterward. Coming out, she closed the door and stood for a moment.

Tate was typing away on his portable computer set up on the rickety table.

The sight surprised her a little, and brought a niggle of irritation. She reminded herself that Tate was a dedicated journalist.

She gazed at him for a long minute in which she beat back the annoyance. Hadn't he given everything to her and the children all day? Now was his time to see to his needs, and the needs of the paper. Many times that day, while helping others, he had also been jotting down notes on the cards he kept handy. He had already contacted Reggie and Leo, Tammy Crawford and Charlotte, about assignments for Wednesday's *Voice*. Now he was far away, deep into writing his own account for the paper. Possibly it would be picked up by the wire. This would be. good for the paper, and his enthusiasm for journalism was what made him the special man that he was.

She dug into a duffel bag and brought out the electric teapot and packets of instant hot chocolate. The water heated quickly, and Marilee made two hot chocolates and an instant coffee for Tate, setting it beside him on the rickety table.

When he did not say anything, she pointed out the coffee.

"Thank you, darlin'." But he didn't stop or look up.

Holding her steaming cup with both hands, she stood beside him. He was oblivious to her. Oh, how his mind was moving, and his fingers on the keyboard were keeping up the pace.

That was a major difference between herself and Tate. He was a born journalist. He would have an entire idea and bring it to the paper. She had simply fallen into writing, and would have to think and think, because generally at least half her mind was focused always on her role as a mother and those whom she loved. The needs and desires of her children, and now Tate, took precedence. There was little left of her afterward to focus on writing anything factual, unless, of course, it pertained to her love of family.

Her gaze fell on Willie Lee, who lay sprawled on his back, arms wide, face like an angel. Her dear, precious, Willie Lee, who had saved a horse. She thought about that for some minutes, and then she looked back at Tate, who was still typing away.

She wished he would stop typing.

She moved to read over his shoulder. The title was: "Tornado Comes To Town."

Tate had the ability to personalize even a tornado.

Her eyes scanned rapidly downward, and her heart picked up tempo. He was telling the story of how neighbors came together in a time of crisis.

"Tate?"

"Hmmm?"

"Tate . . . you aren't going to tell about the horse being injured and Willie Lee's part in it, are you?"

"Hmmm?"

She bent around him and looked him in the face. "You aren't going to tell about Willie Lee and that filly, are you?"

"Uh . . . yes, I was plannin' to tell about the horse . . . how Willie Lee and all the neighbors came over to help." He looked confused.

"You can't do that." She sat on the corner of the bed, facing Tate firmly.

"Why not?"

"Because it is likely that Willie Lee got that horse to stop bleeding to death." She felt like closing the computer on his hands, which remained poised over the keys, as if he could barely take an instant of distraction from his task.

Tate, who felt lost at the direction Marilee was taking but noticed her staring at his hands, felt compelled to withdraw them from their position. He turned his chair to face her fully. "Well, I think it is likely. Our Willie Lee most definitely has a way with animals."

He did not understand why this was a problem, although he did understand that something was going on with Marilee. It obviously was some woman-thing, and a voice in the back of his mind told him to go carefully. He kept a patient tone, even though he was very impatient to get back to his writing.

"That's part of the human interest story. People love to hear about animals being saved, and they especially like it when it is kids doing the saving, the way Ricky Dale came seeking help for his beloved horse, and how his friends Willie Lee and Corrine responded unselfishly in the time of need."

It was a great story. He had plans of selling it to his old Houston newspaper and hopefully some magazines.

Marilee watched Tate's face and knew exactly that he was carried away with anticipating the sale and publication of his wonderful story.

"Yes, our Willie Lee has a way with animals," she said, "and by ten o'clock tomorrow morning the information is going to be all over town that Willie Lee James is a healer. Your story will broadcast it to everyone and his cousin across the country."

She thought to calm her voice, but she got to her feet and leaned toward him. "His life is already hard enough. People treat him as if he's an imbecile, or they're afraid of him, as if he might contaminate them. I don't want . . . well, I don't want people getting crazy ideas and looking at him all the time, and making pilgrimages to our door with their dying dogs and canaries." She saw the frightening prospect in rapid but clear images crossing her mind.

"Darlin', don't you think you might be gettin' a little carried away with that?"

This comment struck Marilee like a slap across the face, and she stared at him for several seconds, before saying a definite, "No, I do not."

Tate knew he had misspoken.

Marilee sought to keep a firm hold on her emotions. She knew she could get overwrought, and say and do things that later she regretted. She had lived this many times, only to wish later she had contained herself. She always promised to contain herself, but one problem with this was an equal fear that she might contain herself too much and be sorry that she had. When it came to Willie Lee, she figured she would rather have to deal with regrets at actions taken rather than not taken.

She said in a hoarse whisper, "I saw a similar thing once, in Tennessee. Stuart did a story about it. A three-parter, in fact. It was reported that this little girl could heal people, and my gosh, for a month, people were streaming to her door. The poor thing could not go anywhere hardly. People just hounded her. When she wasn't able to help them, they called her and her parents charlatans, and other people, who said she had healed them from everything from ingrown toenails to skin cancer, said she was the Virgin Mary. The little girl was lost in all of it."

Tate, not wanting to put his foot in it again, tried to think of a way to show support for her position but not encourage what seemed to him making a mountain out of a molehill.

"Now, I grant you, sweetheart, that sometimes things get sensationalized. But in Willie Lee's case, I don't think we are looking at him being proclaimed a healer. In the first place, what Willie Lee did is not something new. He laid hands on a horse he cares for, and that cares for him. The horse's wound did not magically heal up before our eyes. The horse simply came back around. I've seen my own mother use laying on of hands. Sometimes a person is helped. It was said around our neighborhood that Mama could cure headaches, neuralgia, lumbago, and once she cured my hives. But she sure didn't succeed every time. Science is even recognizing the energy fields involved in this now."

He saw by her expression that he had not calmed her fears.

"Your mother is an adult who can understand," she told him. "Willie Lee might not understand, and he sure might get worn out, trying to heal every Tom and Spot. And what if he can't heal every animal? What then? He will be so hurt. You know how he loves animals. We're liable to have a zoo in our backyard."

"We don't have a backyard at the moment," he interjected, before he thought.

Marilee's reply to that was, "I am being serious here, Tate. And we do so have a backyard, we have just lost half your house."

Her voice rose again, and they both looked at the closed bathroom door.

Then Tate said, "Darlin', I know we've had a hell of a day in which our world has been blown to pieces. I know you are worried over this thing. I promise you that I will not mention Willie Lee, okay? I'll just tell about the filly, and how everyone went over to help as best they could. I'll report the heroic human capability for compassion."

He paused a moment, and then a few more thoughts occurred to him. "If reports on healings of this nature were done in a rational style, people would not make mountains out of them but take them as a matter of the normal course of loving each other."

This idea sat very well with him; he thought how he would employ this line of reasoning in his article. Maybe it would require another article. He could certainly get a good editorial out of it.

His eyes slid over to his humming computer. He didn't want to waste time arguing; he wanted to get back at his writing.

"Honey, I have a real good chance of sellin' this story to a friend of mine down at my old Houston paper. I spoke to him earlier, and he's waitin' for me to send my first piece tonight."

Marilee, who had ceased to hear, was suddenly picturing her ex-husband and his own laptop computer. "Stuart is likely writing this story up right now."

"Well, I imagine he's workin' on something," Tate agreed, and he wanted even more to be working on his own story.

"I've got to get over there and stop him."

"You what?"

"I've got to stop him. He's got access to top magazines. He's got pictures."

Marilee was having a panic now. She did not want anything reported about Willie Lee. Already he was a target, an innocent child
who had been reported in the press last year as having gained a considerable fortune in stock, given to him as a reward for finding an important computer chip for the Tell-In Technology Corporation. After
that came out in papers nationwide, Marilee became more vigilant
than ever over her son, worrying about him being kidnapped.

Tate was telling her to calm down, but she told him to look after the
children as she hunted around for her purse and keys.

At that point the bathroom door opened, and Corrine, with wet hair
and pajamas hastily donned, came out, her eyes wide. "I heard thunder. It's lightning outside."

Marilee stopped in her tracks.

There came the unmistakeable sound of a rumble, which she and
Tate had not heard because of their argument.

Tate opened the cabin door. Lightning shot across the black sky,
giving evidence of an approaching storm.

Marilee set aside her purse. "It's okay, honey. We'll turn on the
television and see if there's a report. Come on, climb into bed."

The television screen showed a local weatherman reporting the
build up of severe storms once again. Their county was under a tornado watch, and the thunder outside became louder.

"Where will we go if there is another tornado?" Corrine asked.

"Well . . . Tate, did you see a storm shelter near the office?"

Tate, who had sat again at his computer and was typing, nevertheless warmed her heart by hearing her and saying, "Yes, there is," and
he went so far as to rip himself from his writing and take Corrine to
the window, where he pulled back the drapes and pointed to the hump
of the shelter that could just be seen near the office.

Tate returned to his computer and typing, and Corrine returned to
bed and sipping her hot chocolate. Marilee slipped off her shoes,
curled next to Corrine and put her arm around her niece, whose thin
body felt so fragile. Marilee had a sense that she would beat back the
tornado with her very fists, should it try to zoom in on them again, and
at the same time, she thought of Stuart, in her bungalow, typing away
on his computer in the same manner to which Tate had returned.

Both of them two peas in a pod—journalists, and as such, it was the
story that counted. Stuart had a special talent for sensationalism.

"Excuse me a minute, honey," she told Corrine, at a time when the
thunder had abated. She snugged the covers around the child. "Tate
. . . can I have a word with you?"

It took him several seconds to look up, and several more seconds to tear his hands and body away from his keyboard. She beckoned him outside and closed the door behind them. The concrete stoop was cool on her bare feet, and the strong humid wind whipped around them, tugging at their hair and causing her to fold her arms close.

"I want you to go talk to Stuart and tell him not to write about Willie Lee."

Tate's brows came together and then rose in unison. "Darlin', we don't know that he's doin' a story about Willie Lee."

She disliked his patent placating and ignored it. "We had best catch him before he does. I can't leave Corrine, but you can go."

"Marilee, I don't think it is my place to tell another journalist what he can and cannot cover, and I have my own story in there to write. I've got a chance at a sale, but I've got to get it down to Skip in Houston tonight. If they don't use it there, they'll at least forward it to a string of smaller papers they own over in West Texas, and with his recommendation, it will be sold. It needs to be to those papers by tomorrow morning. News is only news for a day. Things move on."

"I think Willie Lee is a little more important than selling a news story."

That comment stood in the air a moment, while Tate ran his hand over his hair, giving her a long look. "I do, too, Marilee, but I think you are wrought up . . . and that is understandable after the day we have had. But Stuart is not only a journalist—he is Willie Lee's father. What he does in that capacity is up to him. I don't believe I need to be tellin' him one way or the other. And this is somethin' that needs discussing in a rational manner, not by me rushin' over there and tellin' the man what he should or should not do."

Marilee did not know what to say to his words and entire stubborn attitude. She swallowed, pain slicing into her chest. She had relied on him to help, to see how she felt and do what she needed him to do. But he would not. He was disappointing her.

"All right, then," she said and turned.

"Marilee, don't take it like that."

She did not reply to him, did not look at him, but kept going inside, where she pasted what she hoped passed for a calm expression on her face, because Corrine's gaze fastened onto her like a magnet. "There's more storms," Corrine said, indicating the television.

"There are? Well, we're snug here in this bed." Again Marilee curled around her niece. She looked over to check Willie Lee, only just then realizing she had not gotten him out of his clothes. She enlisted Corrine's help to do so; this diverted the child from the sound of the thunder once more getting louder.

Just as they tucked Willie Lee beneath the covers, Tate got to his feet, saying, "I'll go over, Marilee. I don't know what I'll say to him, but I'll go over."

Marilee regarded him in surprise, as well as doubt. Perhaps he was just trying to soothe her, and she did not want to be soothed now, since he had already displayed his true colors in disappointing her.

Tate strode to the door, yanked it open and strode out into the night, closing the door behind him.

Marilee stared at it for long seconds, and then she raced to it, jerked it open and threw herself outside.

"Tate!" she called, raising her voice over the rising wind and thunder. "Tate!"

In bare feet, she ran almost mindlessly over the gravel, to the door of the Cherokee, taking hold of it and stopping him from closing it.

"Don't go. You're right. . . . It's too late tonight . . . the storms . . . Don't go." She could not, in that minute, bear for him to leave. To be away from them.

She gazed into his eyes, and he looked back at her as she struggled to find the honesty. "I'm afraid, Tate. I don't know why, I just am." It was the best she could do.

His expression softened with blessed understanding. Slipping out of the vehicle, he put his arm around her and hugged her close as they went back into the cabin, where Corrine waited in the open doorway.

When the door closed, the storm was shut outside. Although he would have fussed over her, Marilee sent Tate back to his writing. She would not think of any of it, she told herself. *God, please handle it.*

She focused on getting herself into her pajamas, then joined Corrine in bed, where they watched the weather reports on the television, while there came the rhythmic clicking of Tate's typing. Marilee found it comforting and fell asleep.

Just before closing down his computer, Tate checked his e-mail. There were two messages. One from Stuart: *Here you go, Editor. No charge. Several other papers are paying.*

Stuart had sent pictures of Tate's damaged house, along with the damaged garage, and the tree and horse corral in the rear of Winston's property. The most striking shots, however, were of people's faces. Stuart James was very good at capturing drama.

How had he gotten the pictures developed?

Ah—Stuart had one of those newfangled digital cameras! Of course he would have, being the renowned photojournalist that he was.

The second message was from his old friend on the Houston paper: *You made a sale, buddy. Check will be in the mail tomorrow. Am forwarding these on to our affiliates out west.*

By golly, it paid to have friends! And the Internet! These were the good ol' days.

The Houston paper would run his article in tomorrow's edition, and he would run it in the *Voice* on Wednesday. It darn sure paid to own one's own newspaper, too. He felt sweet satisfaction. Pouring all his energy and finances into the newspaper had been the right thing. He had stretched his finances to the limit in order to update the *Voice* into the computer age, but he was surely now reaping the benefits. He would have done well to get Reggie one of those digital cameras, and he would, as soon as he could afford it.

For a brief moment he closed his eyes and gave thanks. Then he turned off the computer and stretched, realizing he was darn tired. He looked across the room for the first time in hours. His gaze fell first on the bed where he would sleep with Willie Lee.

Only Willie Lee wasn't there—the bed was empty.

His gaze skittered to the far bed, which was full. Sometime while Tate worked on his piece for the papers, Willie Lee had gotten up and crawled into bed with his mother, and now Marilee was tangled with the children. Even with Munro, who lay at the foot of the bed.

Tate gazed at the sight for a long minute, feeling a mixture of gratitude and guilt. He had not meant to get so busy as to shut them out.

His ex-wife's admonitions came to mind; Lucille had said over and over, "You are a newspaperman, not a husband."

This time he wanted to be a husband. He didn't want to let Marilee down, like he felt he had let Lucille down.

He had seen that he had let Marilee down in her eyes, when he had refused to go to speak to Stuart.

He thought of Stuart's pictures and winced inwardly. What had seemed a far-fetched, overwrought worry on Marilee's part began to seem quite possible. With growing unease, he wondered if he had pushed her worries aside too easily, and that maybe he had done so because he was focused on his own desires of the moment.

His desire was to provide for his family. He was supposed to work for his family, wasn't he?

In any case, there was nothing to be done about it tonight. He washed up in the vintage bathroom, where he felt very much at home, and donned pajama bottoms, which he felt necessary because of Corrine—man, there was a lot to think about for a man who had been a bachelor as long as he had. Wearily he crawled into bed.

It was lonely.

He looked over at the bed filled with bodies and had the urge to either wake one of them up or crawl in with them, if there had been room.

Just then Munro hopped off that bed and hopped up with Tate.

"Thanks, fella. I appreciate it greatly."

He would be glad when he got to sleep with Marilee, although he had a sad suspicion that, even married to her, their intimate time alone might be scant for many years.

Stuart sat with his notebook computer open on the dining-room table in Marilee's bungalow and typed onto the e-mail message screen: *Hey, Troy. I may be on to a story here. Pictures and commentary in the three attachments. I'll check into it further. Get back to me about any publications you know of that might be doing healer stories.*

He read the black words on the white screen and sat there staring at them, hesitating about sending the message. At last he hit the send button.

Over the years he had encountered various people who, it was claimed, healed. Stuart had thought it all hogwash, either delusion or deliberate conning. From one, though, a young girl in the Tennessee hills, he had gotten a good spread in *Life* magazine. People did not care if it was truth; they wanted to believe it, and they wanted to hear about it. The pictures he took had slanted to the belief side. It was what paid.

A certain anger came over him, and he rose. His left leg almost gave way, and a pain seemed to go through every bone in his body. Surprised, he grabbed hold of the table.

He had forgotten to take his pills. He shook as he went to the bedroom to get them from the dresser drawer. There was water in the pitcher there; Franny saw to that. He downed the pills, looked at the painkillers, and took another, then lay back on the bed, closing his eyes, and seeing his son hold a bird that looked dead, and then had fluffed and flown. Stuart had thought he had not seen correctly, but perhaps he had.

He had seen the same as everyone at the corral that day—that horse had been dying, and then it hadn't been.

Wouldn't it turn out ironic if years ago he had turned his back and walked away from a really great story just waiting to be told, as well as the one person who could help him now?

Thirty

The best we can . . .

Marilee had been sitting for some time on the front stoop of the cabin, watching the sun rise, when Tate stepped out behind her.

"Here you are," he said, as if both surprised and relieved.

"Where did you think I was?"

"Well, you weren't inside," he said, sounding a little put out as he lowered himself to sit beside her. "You could have been anywhere."

"I wouldn't have gone far."

"No, you wouldn't." He grinned that boyish and charming grin she so loved and scratched his head. "I'm just a little mixed up this mornin', wakin' up with a dog in bed with me, and those bedspreads and curtains that are at war with each other. I thought maybe I was ten years old again."

She gazed at him, wondering how he could think so much first thing in the morning. "Are the children still asleep?"

"Yes, ma'am, they are, so we have a few minutes alone." He put his arm around her shoulders and faced the golden glow shining on the horizon. "Another day in paradise."

"It *is* paradise here, isn't it?" she said, running her eyes over the land that stretched in rolling hills and green pastures on the other side of the black-topped highway. It was something like a mystical drawing. "It's a good place to be."

"Hmmm . . . sure is."

He nuzzled her neck, sending little jolts of electricity through her body. She wanted to give in to the feeling but was frightened by the force of it. They were in no position to go anywhere with the passion, and she didn't feel up to dealing with it.

Her mind was distracted by her concerns over Willie Lee and finding a new place to live that would ease Tate's worries and helping the children deal with the trauma of the tornado. That was a lot to be concerned with.

Then Tate said, "I sold the article last night to the Houston paper. Good money."

"I'm glad for you."

"It's for us." He sounded a little hurt.

"I know, and I'm proud of you . . . and I'm grateful that you are looking out for us, too." She smoothed her hand on his, bringing her attention fully to him. "Why do men always get so excited about making money?"

Tate, who always had a logical answer for everything, replied, "It's the provider instinct. Togetherness, peace and love are good, but it is also nice to eat in this real world."

A sudden and very immense appreciation for him swept her. She smiled at him, and he hugged her happily. It seemed to take so little to make Tate happy. She should apologize to him for her erratic behavior the previous night, but while she was thinking of doing this, he spoke.

"You're beautiful in the morning," he told her.

"I'm sleepy in the morning," she said.

"And sexy as hell with it, too. If the children were not in the bed in there, I would drag you in there and show you how you make me feel. I guess I'll settle for a kiss right now."

The next thing she knew he kissed her in a way that made her feel hot and cold at the same time, and caused her to go limp against him.

"There. Did that knock your socks off?"

"Do it again," she whispered, and did not wait for him to move, but pressed her lips hard to his, seeking to give back the passion he had imparted to her.

When they finally broke apart, he told her that they had better slow down. "I won't be able to go in there in my condition. I don't think I'll be able to stand up."

The apology was still on her lips but wouldn't come out. She closed her eyes and felt herself safe in his arms, the scent of him around her and the warmth of the sun dawning on her face.

Then she said, "Willie Lee wants so much to be like other boys. I want to give him that, as much as I can. I want him to have a normal life. That's why I don't want people to think he's a healer." She needed to explain.

"You're doin' great at giving him a normal life, darlin'," he said, "but I think we need to face that what will be a normal life for Willie Lee isn't going to be exactly like that of other boys. He's an extraordinary boy. Maybe he is some sort of special healer, or maybe he is simply so pure with love that that horse felt it and took hold of the will to live. This is not the first healing heard of in the world, and it won't be the last. And if Willie Lee is a healer, I don't think there's anything we can do about it. But I can tell you what a really wise woman who talked to me yesterday told me."

She twisted around to look at him.

"She said to me that what we would do is the best we can."

Tate had not known he was going to say all that until the words came out. He was amazed to find that the advice was quite sound. He liked it.

He watched her sigh and accept, at least in some measure. He felt satisfied at having said the right thing.

But then she was frowning again.

"What about Stuart?" she asked. "What if he asks Willie Lee to heal him? That's fine, if it works, but what if it doesn't? What if it's as you say, just somehow Willie Lee's friendly presence helped that horse but won't be enough for a man dying of cancer? How will Willie Lee feel then?"

Tate saw immediately that his future wife could think of all possible contingencies. He felt a little foolish not to have thought of this one. In fact, this entire thing about the healing had not struck him as all that big a deal, but now, seen in the light of Stuart and the problems Marilee kept bringing up, he could understand how emotions could run deep on this.

He said slowly, "Well, I guess we're all just going to have to have a talk about this thing. An honest talk with Stuart and with Willie Lee."

Marilee gazed at him, then looked away.

The sun was now almost totally up. Gazing at it, he thought: another day in paradise, in which anything could happen. Tornados came, even to paradise. In an instant life changed. What person among them knew if he would be alive that night? Mostly what they had all been doing was ignoring the fact of Stuart's impending death. Death was embarrassing to people. It was like digestion problems. Messy. No one wanted to talk about constipation, diarrhea or dying, all basic and common difficulties in life; they were whispered about as if they were some secret sin.

He could get a good editorial from this. He needed his notepaper.

"Tate." Marilee entwined her hand with his. "I'm sorry about the way I acted last night . . . getting so upset and wanting you to stop what you needed to do in order to go speak to Stuart. I'm sorry I got so crazy." Her blue eyes were large and watery in her pale face. "I wish I could promise that I won't get crazy again, but I don't think I can." A tear overflowed and dripped on her cheek. "Parker and Mother say I'm too emotional . . . that I get far too upset. It's just that sometimes I get worried and fearful and carried away."

"Oh, darlin' . . ." He hugged her to him, feeling a fierce love in his chest. "Don't you change. Don't you dare change. Of course you're emotional, and that's what I love. I love you just the way you are. I love you crazy, I love you sane. I can't promise you I'll always under-stand or agree, but I can promise to always do my best to love you."

He got so choked up that his voice got hoarse. He wanted to hold her forever and protect her forever, and she clung to him and told him in a ragged whisper, "I won't let a day go by that I don't tell you I love you, Tate Holloway."

It was, he thought, the angel of death who had taught them how to live.

Just then the door of the cabin opened, and Willie Lee stepped out, with Munro right beside him. "There is no schoo-ool, Mo-ther."

"There isn't?" Marilee would have pulled self-consciously from Tate's arms, but he held her. She blinked and did her best to appear her normal self for her son.

Willie Lee shook his head. "It was on the tel-evis-ion. Cor-rine said. There is no 'lect-tric-ity." He struggled with the word as he re-garded her closely. "Are you cry-ing, Ma-ma?"

"Just a bit. It's from happiness, though." She smiled at Tate, and he smiled at her.

He was the most handsome and wonderful man in the world. And he loved her.

"Oh. Look." Willie Lee pointed to the motel office.

It was Mr. Goode coming out with the Valentine City flag to put in the holder on the side of the building.

He hollered over to them, "Y'all want doughnuts, we got 'em. Complemen'ry."

"I am hun-gry," Willie Lee said and started away toward the office.

"Willie Lee, you come get some shoes on," Marilee ordered, imme-diately thinking of a sharp rock possibly cutting his foot, or him catch-ing cold.

But Tate jumped to his feet, grabbed up Willie Lee and hoisted him to his shoulders, saying, "I'll carry him! We'll get chocolate, if we can," he called back to her.

"You don't have any shoes on, either," Marilee hollered, just be-cause it seemed required on her part.

As she stood there, gazing at them and pressing the precious sight of the man and boy she loved into memory, Corrine stepped out beside her. Marilee put her arm around the child, who watched the man and boy, too. Marilee knew suddenly and deeply that whatever came their way in the days and weeks and years ahead, they would face it together and do the best they could. And it was enough.

Marilee and Corrine sat cross-legged on the bed, and Tate and Willie Lee took the two chairs at the rickety table, while Munro lay down between the table and the bed, twisting his head hopefully back and forth, anticipating chunks of doughnut that might come his way.

Eating doughnuts and milk seemed a perfect time for the discussion of an important matter. Marilee asked, "Willie Lee, what did you do to the horse to stop her bleeding?"

Willie Lee, studying the candy sprinkles on his doughnut, said, "I do not know. I just did it, and then she was bet-ter."

"You laid your head on the horse," Tate said, pouring more milk into Willie Lee's glass.

"Yes, I did," Willie Lee said in his helpful manner, then used both hands to drink from his glass.

Marilee looked at his hands, small, with dimpled fingers and not quite the cleanest fingernails.

"Have you done this before, with any other animals?" she asked, when he finished drinking his milk.

Willie Lee looked at her. "It is a se-cret." His gaze slid to Corrine.

Marilee and Tate looked at Corrine.

"Do you suppose you two could tell us this secret?" Tate said. "We won't tell anyone."

Corrine's expression said she did not appreciate being placated like a child. She said, "Beau. Ricky Dale's black dog," she added, when Marilee looked puzzled. "That day, when the mare kicked Beau. Willie Lee told you. Beau looked dead. Willie Lee hugged on him, and Beau got back up."

Marilee remembered the day they had come home from Winston's house, and how Willie Lee had said something about a dog getting kicked.

Corrine went on to tell about Miss Minnie's cat—"It was ver-y old," Willie Lee said—and the titmouse, which Ricky Dale had brought down as an experiment, and Corrine reminded them about the kitten.

"My kit-ten," Willie Lee put in. "He got deaded, but then he got bet-ter. And so did my frog."

"Frog?" Marilee, Tate and Corrine said in unison.

"Yes. But he went away. I have not seen him in a long time."

Marilee, feeling a little dizzy, ran her gaze from Willie Lee to Tate.

Tate asked, "How do you do this, Willie Lee? How do you make the animals better?"

Willie Lee looked thoughtful as he licked chocolate icing from his fingers with the tip of his pink tongue. "I hold them, and I . . . I think a-bout good stuff. Some-times I see the sky, or maybe sunshine." He swung his legs back and forth, and lowered his voice, looking shy. "I think it may be an an-gel. Sometimes she sings to me." He looked downward, then peeked back up. "Can I have one more, Mo-ther—the cher-ry one?"

Just like a normal boy, she thought, leaning over to kiss his head. "You can have one more, my sweet son."

Tate handed him a cherry-filled doughnut, asking gently, "Do the animals always get better?"

Willie Lee looked closely at the jelly hole. "No. Only if I see the light big. Miss Min-nie's cat did not get bet-ter. He was old. He said he was tir-ed. And I do not think the rab-bit did, either."

Corrine said, "You mean Mrs. Yoder's rabbit at school? She's the fourth-grade teacher and has animals," she explained to Tate and Marilee. "The rabbit was losing his hair." She made a face.

"He was old, he told-ed me and Mun-ro," said Willie Lee, and then he bit deeply into the jelly doughnut, sending cherry filling onto his chin. "But the horse got bet-ter, and I am glad," he said, with his cheeks full.

"We're all glad, sugar." Marilee took a napkin and wiped jelly off the healer's chin.

"Does anyone else, other than Ricky Dale, know about Willie Lee's . . . way with animals?" Marilee asked Corrine.

Corrine shook her head. "Ricky Dale won't tell."

Marilee reflected on her niece's answer and attitude. Corrine had already been protecting Willie Lee, whom she loved. Already it was in Corrine to watch the ways of the world, and this was sad, and yet a blessing, too.

It was a sticky wicket to encourage a child to hide the truth. The best Marilee could offer was to say that while in normal circumstances honesty was the best policy, sometimes discretion was kinder and more prudent.

"That's one of those things I'll understand when I'm older, right?" Corrine said.

"Oh, I think you understand it full well right now." Marilee looked into the heart-shaped face of her niece and smiled.

Corrine smiled back.

She was going to be too beautiful by far, Marilee thought, experiencing a pang of worry. *Thank you, God, that you gave her uncommon common sense.*

When they passed Tate's house on the way to Marilee's bungalow, they saw a gathering of people and a van from a television station up in Lawton.

"Don't stop, Tate."

"Have to."

This was because Everett Northrupt flagged them down by running into their path.

"News folks are coverin' the tornado damage, Editor. This is him," Everett called over his shoulder.

A man with a ball cap bearing Channel 2 News and a microphone came hurrying up. "Could we get a comment from you, sir? Just take a couple minutes. Folks say you were in your house, havin' a bachelor party. That's great stuff." He grinned.

Tate gave the steering wheel over to Marilee and told her he would join her later. She hit the accelerator with more pressure than she had intended and headed on to her bungalow, wondering what else folks might say to the newspeople.

It was a little difficult, getting out of the car and going into the bungalow, where she would see Stuart. She told herself her trepidation was silly. There was nothing special for her to do or say; she must simply let this all play out.

The children raced ahead, happy to be home. Marilee saw a rare broad grin on Corrine's face as she took the stairs to the porch two at a time. Even without her things here any longer, this was still home to Corrine, the only real stable home she had ever known.

Franny greeted them just inside the door with hugs, saying, "Come in, come in! No school? Aren't you the lucky ones?"

Stuart, wearing lounging pants and a sweatshirt, came ambling out from the kitchen, a cup in hand. Never a man for mornings, he obviously had not been up long. He needed a shave. She thought he looked thinner, if that was possible.

Willie Lee greeted him, gave him a hug, then wanted to know where his kitten was. The kitten was found, and the children took it out to the tree house, where they went to locate Willie Lee's bird. "I hope Bird-y did not get blown away."

Franny disappeared to take a long bath, she said, and Marilee and Stuart were left alone.

"I can offer you a cup of this tea Franny makes me drink," Stuart said, lifting the cup in his hand. "It's growing on me. There's some left in the pot."

"That's her own brew to stimulate the blood, isn't it? I need some this morning."

When she would have gotten it, he told her, rather sharply, "I'll get it for you." With a self-deprecating grin, he added, "I'm usin' your house. The least I can do is get you a cup of tea."

She followed him into the kitchen. "You don't owe me for the use of the house, Stuart. You aren't taking anything away from us. It is the best thing, you being here. The house isn't big enough for Tate and me and the children, but it is just right for you and Franny right now. I don't want to get rid of it. I love this house," she said rather wistfully.

"Where are you going to live, since your roof was lifted?" he asked her, passing her the cup.

"We're going to find somewhere to rent until details can be worked out." She saw no need to tell him about Tate's house not being insured. "We don't know if the big house can be repaired or will have to be torn down and a new one started from scratch. And we rather like it out at the Goodnight," she added with a grin. "It's quiet, and we get free doughnuts."

He smiled softly, not looking at her, but at the floor. Childish laughter floated in through the open window, and he turned his gaze outside. He *was* thinner. His skin was getting paper-thin.

"Stuart, about what happened with the filly and Willie Lee . . ." She had begun, the words tumbling out, but she didn't know how to continue.

His head jerked around, and his eyebrows furrowed. "What about it?"

"What did you think of it?"

He thought several seconds before he answered. "I think it was quite remarkable to see, the boy holding the dying horse, and I got some great shots. And I think the boy kept her from dying."

Marilee nodded. "Only he isn't *the boy*. He's your son. He's our Willie Lee, who wants more than anything in the world to be considered a normal boy. He won't get that if you do a story about it and spread his name and picture in a magazine and paint a picture of a boy with healing powers."

They gazed at each other. She saw the questioning and considering in his eyes before he looked away out the window.

Seeing he didn't intend to comment, she said, "Willie Lee has a way with animals. He always has had. I've known for a long time that he talks to them, and they talk to him. He said they did, and after a while we all just accepted it. Certainly he can do things with animals that we can't. It seems that he can, on some occasions, have a healing effect on them.

"But I don't want you doing a story on him, Stuart. I don't want his name ending up splashed across magazines and tabloids because a really good story can be made out of it. People don't take kindly to others who are a little different. They poke fun, ridicule, take advantage. He'll face enough of that as it is. Do you remember that girl you did the story on in Tennessee? Do you remember how her family was thrown out of the church, and then another church took hold of them, exploiting that child all over the place?"

He looked at her, his expression carefully guarded.

She considered asking him to promise her that he wouldn't do a story. Would he tell her the truth? Could she believe him?

Then she said what she needed to say. "Stuart, he might be able to help you. I don't know. But I don't want him hurt in the process."

Stuart's eyes narrowed.

Just then the telephone near her shoulder rang. For long seconds she gazed at Stuart and debated about answering, irritated at the interruption. Yet she thought of Tate and finally picked up on the third ring.

"Marilee?"

"Anita?" She was surprised to hear her sister's voice come across the line.

"Oh, Marilee, I'm so glad I got you. I heard the report just this mornin'. Just a blurb on the news. They said a tornado touched down in Valentine. I've been tryin' to get you, but I couldn't get through. . . . I don't know, maybe I got the numbers mixed up. I've been dialing from memory, without my address book. I called Mama, but no one answered there. Is everyone all right?"

At this point she finally had to pause to get a breath, and Marilee took the opportunity to tell her sister to calm down. "We are all fine, Anita. . . . Corrine is fine. The tornado did some damage, but no one was hurt in Valentine."

Seeing Stuart heading for the back door, Marilee had a bit of alarm. "I'll have to call you back, Anita."

"No! You can't! Marilee!"

She heard her sister's voice and caught the tears, and reluctantly put the receiver back to her ear. "I'm here. What is it?" Damn Anita, anyway.

"You can't call me back." Her sister was trying to control her soft sobs. "I'm . . . I'm in the hospital."

"What? What's happened?"

Her sister drew a trembling breath. "I'm in the hospital. In alcoholic rehab," she added in a faint tone.

"Oh, Anita." Marilee leaned back against the wall for support. She pictured her sister, whose ragged chuckles came over the line. Anita always tried to laugh things off. She used to say she would rather laugh than cry. Marilee had seen her after she had been beaten by a boyfriend, and she had quirked that bruised mouth into a grin. Marilee clutched the phone to her ear and listened as Anita told her that she had been given special permission to call Marilee, due to the circumstances, but she was not allowed phone calls for another month.

She had been committed, she said. An order signed by a judge, and Louis had seen to it.

"He must love you very much," Marilee said, surprised at the man, who had admitted to already being married. She wondered how that was working out.

"Yes," Anita said. "Maybe he does." Her tone was filled with ripe doubt. Anita could not believe any man loved her; Marilee understood.

She was to stay in the hospital for at least eight weeks, and she could stay longer, if she chose. "I want to do this, Marilee. I want to give it a try."

"You can do it, sister. You can." Tears streamed down Marilee's face.

"I'll miss your wedding."

Marilee decided not to mention that Anita had said she wasn't coming anyway. "That's okay. There'll be other times." Sober ones, she thought.

"I want to go ahead and give you and Tate temporary custody of Corrine. I'm having Louis draw up the papers. He knows some attorneys up in Oklahoma City, so it will all be handled. All you will have to do is sign the papers."

Marilee was stunned. "Okay." Then she thought to say, "Do you want to talk to her, Anita? I'll call her. . . ."

"No! Oh, no, Marilee, I can't."

"It's okay, honey."

Anita was crying softly again. "Will you tell her—about me being in rehab?"

"Yes, honey, I'll tell her. I'll tell her that her mother is very brave and wants to get well so that she can be with her and be a mother to her."

"Oh, I do, Marilee. . . . I really do."

* * *

When she hung up, Marilee continued leaning against the wall. *Well, God, I don't expect a miracle, but this is going in the right direction.*

She wiped her eyes, and then, remembering about Stuart going out with the children, she raced across the kitchen, through the laundry room to the back door, where she stopped, her hand up to push open the screen door, which she didn't push because of a loud whisper in her heart that said, *Stop!*

There, through the screen, she saw Willie Lee and Stuart sitting on the steps. Willie Lee hugged his father around the neck, his angel face in thick glasses pressed up against Stuart's head, his eyes closed. The sun shone down through the budding tree limbs upon them. Was it healing? Or was it the miracle of love?

She watched for a long second, hardly daring to breathe.

Willie Lee opened his eyes and saw her through the screen. "Hello, Mo-ther."

"Hello, sweetheart. Would you and Corrine like to come in for a proper breakfast, and bring your father?"

It was all she could think of to say.

The children, Franny and Stuart had just sat down at the kitchen table, and Marilee was serving up fried ham and eggs and biscuits and gravy, when Tate arrived through the back door, with a slight, blond-haired young man in tow, whom he introduced as Mike Owen, "From the paper up there in Lawton."

"Mike heard some tales this mornin' about our Willie Lee havin' special powers and healing Leanne's filly."

She stared at Tate and the young man.

"I told him I didn't know about special powers, but to come along and meet Willie Lee, and that Willie Lee would tell how he did it."

She wanted to wring Tate's neck. She only smiled.

Franny said, "Perhaps Mr. Owen would like to breakfast with us, and you could have a chance to speak not only with Willie Lee, but visit with our Stuart James, Willie Lee's father. He's a famous photojournalist. All you journalists can talk shop."

More or less trapped, the young man sat and ate ham and eggs with gusto, and the three journalists talked about the tornado and things that had happened.

Finally Mike Owen asked Willie Lee, "What did you do to save that horse?"

Willie Lee blinked behind his thick glasses. "I hug-ged her," he said, quite seriously.

Mike Owen regarded Willie Lee, then cut his gaze to the others at the table, as if judging that his leg was being pulled.

Tate said, "That filly knew Willie Lee and all the people standing around were pullin' for it. It was just a lot of friendship and love that got that critter back up, right, Willie Lee?"

"Yes," he answered; then he looked at Marilee, "I am go-ing to find my ant farm now, o-kay, Mama? They have mis-sed me."

He was already down from his chair, and Corrine was following him. Marilee called after the two, "Corrine, you get his hands washed so there aren't sticky prints everywhere."

Tate patted the young man on the back. "This is small-town America, where neighbors still care about each other. You can quote me," he added.

Thirty-One

From this day forward . . .

Days of early-evening sunlight shone golden on the church, and Marilee's tears caused her to see glimmering halos on everything—the concrete walk, the heads of all the people, the long, white limousine that everyone at the *Voice* had chipped in to rent to take them all the way to DFW airport.

"Good luck!"

"God Bless!"

"Have a great time!"

"Hallelujah!"

The good wishes of friends and loved ones, as well as bird seed, rained down upon Marilee and Tate as they ran hand in hand down the church steps and along the walk to the waiting limousine. Uncle Perry was just then getting in. It had been decided that Aunt Vella and Uncle Perry would serve in place of a hired nanny. Uncle Perry was being assisted by Sandy Conroy. Sandy had seemed to take on an unusual commanding air with his formal attire. Throughout the wedding and festivities, he had been on the sidelines directing traffic, caterers and band members.

Along the sidewalk, hands applauded and reached out for handshakes and hugs. Her cousin Belinda astonished Marilee by grabbing her in an enthusiastic and teary embrace. Marilee, thoroughly caught up with emotion, hugged her back.

Sheriff Oakes took hold of Tate's hand, pumping it like a pump handle, and then Tate hauled off and wrapped his arms around the big man.

"By golly, you got it done, Editor. You're a brave man."

Marilee wondered about that, and then there was Charlene MacCoy hugging her, followed by Reggie Pahdocony stepping in front of her, with a camera to her face, "Let me get a second shot here! Y'all get out of the way of the bride and groom."

Then Charlotte was taking her hand. "Come on, honey. You and Tate have to get going if you're goin' to make your flight."

"Oh, Charlotte. I love you, friend. Next time it will be your turn."

"Yes, now you all get on. They won't wait the plane," Charlotte said briskly through her tears, tugging Marilee toward the car, where Sandy stood ready with his hand extended, intending to hand her through the wide door.

"Wait! Y'all wait!" It was Franny, hurrying forward with an immense bouquet of forsythia branches. "I promised your mother to get these fixed up so you could take them with you. Here, Tate, hold on to them for her. They'll last till you get to the hotel. Oh, my, you two look beautiful!"

Franny hugged her, and then hugged Tate. Marilee watched them, watched how tenderly Tate held his mother against him, how his tanned face looked against Franny's pale one.

"Miss Marilee?" Sandy beckoned to her.

She started to put her hand in his, to enter the limousine, but someone pulled her around. It was Parker, who said, "I'm not missin' out on my kiss for the bride," and in a grand, sweeping motion, he bent her over backward and planted one on her lips, while the crowd roared and applauded.

When straight up again, she said, "Oh, Parker," and hugged him tight. *Goodbye, into your wife's hands I commit you.*

And then her gaze fell on Stuart, who was standing behind Sandy, leaning a little on the car and taking a picture of her. She paused. He took the shot.

Dropping the camera, he smiled a small smile.

She went to him, going up on tiptoe and putting her arms around his neck. He bent awkwardly, wrapping one arm around her. He felt all bones, so slight, fading away. She pressed her cheek to his for a long moment in which she whispered, "Thank you for Willie Lee. . . . Thank you for coming, so that we got straight with you and me." *All is forgiven, we are free for the journey.*

Pulling back, she looked long into his eyes. He looked back, as straight at her as he was capable of.

Then someone hollered, "Don't forget to throw the bouquet!"

Taking Sandy's hand, she stepped up on the running board of the limousine, braced herself on Tate's shoulder, drew back and gave a great thrust of her arm, sending the bouquet of yellow roses and forsythia and blue cornflowers far up into the bright blue sky, where it seemed to hang in the air and then to float gracefully downward, into thc hands of Bclinda, who ycllcd, "Oh, not mc!" and tosscd it upward like a hot potato to the small cluster of stretching hands.

But Belinda had thrown it harder than anticipated, and it went over the stretching hands to come down right at Zona Porter, who had been standing behind the pack and a little to the side, in order to see. Instinctively Zona caught it, and then she stood there, blinking behind her Coke-bottle lenses.

"Goodbye! Thank you, all!" Marilee blew kisses. She felt, suddenly, like the image of Marilyn Monroe above Tate's desk.

Then she was grabbed by the hips. It was Tate, who pulled her inside and down into his lap, as the doors were closed and the limousine began to roll out of the parking lot.

They were out in the street when Willie Lee and Corrine cried out, "Stop!"

Ricky Dale was in the car, and Munro was not, because he had gotten out to do his business before the long drive.

The limousine stopped. Tate opened the doors for Ricky Dale to hop out, reluctantly, and for Munro to hop inside, eagerly.

Once more the doors closed and the limousine began to roll. Marilee and Tate turned to look out the rear window at their loved ones and friends, who flowed out into the middle of the street, an army of well-wishers sending them off, with Winston Valentine, in his capacity of town patriarch, leading the way.

Marilee's gaze lingered on Winston. In his pale summer suit and with his shock of hair that had finally gone all white, he could be seen from several blocks up the street, until the limousine turned west on Main Street and headed out of town.

Good-night kisses and hugs were exchanged, and hand in hand, Marilee and Tate retired to their bedroom. As Tate was closing the door, there came the sound of the television coming on.

"Perry, you turn that television off and come on over with the children and me to our bedroom."

"But John Wayne is fixin' . . ."

Tate paused, and he and Marilee cocked their ears.

"I don't care what world John Wayne is fixin' to save, shut it off. We are here to watch our great niece and nephew, and to have a wonderful time together. You just keep your eyes on me for a week. I'm sure, if you practice, you can make headway."

"Well, I guess you are entertainment," was Uncle Perry's surprising comeback.

"You bet I am . . . and I'm going to prove it to you," Aunt Vella said in a saucy voice.

If Uncle Perry had anything further to say to this, Tate did not hear it. The door to the bedroom on the other side of the suite closed. Tate closed the door to their own room, and he and Marilee regarded each other in what was for them a moment of surprise.

"Alone at last," Marilee said, and a soft smile bloomed on her lips.

"By golly, we are," said Tate, who had wondered if this night would ever come about. "Feels strange."

Then he saw that the woman who had become his wife was removing her robe in a most seductive manner. She tossed it carelessly to a nearby chair, in a move that sent Tate's adrenaline flowing with such strength as to compel him into the reckless act of sweeping her up into his arms and carrying her to the widest expanse of bed he had ever encountered, where they both practically tore off their clothes and made love in an incredible, mindless fashion, all hot and hard, and fast and furious.

It was a manner Tate had not known himself capable of, and it was so furious for him that Tate thought he should apologize afterward.

He did so, in a whisper, while he held Marilee close against him.

Her response was to rise up and look at him with sex-filled eyes and say, "Oh, Tate . . . do it again."

Tate, who at first wondered if it would be possible for him to do it again, found to his joy that it was. And he thanked God for the miracle of a man and a woman, together.

Two months later:

The Valentine Voice
View from the Editor's Desk
by Tate Holloway

The City Council has designated the coming week Valentine Days, with the theme of *Small Town on the Move.* The question always becomes on the move to where, and after receiving a lot of suggestions in this matter, some not printable, it seems to me that just where this town and each one of us is going is a matter of personal opinion and is not relevant, anyway. Just come on and celebrate our fair town.

Beginning Monday, special prizes will be awarded to customers from various merchants, so shop at home and support your town.

Also beginning Monday, on special display at City Hall will be original photographs by the late eminent photographer Stuart James, as well as historical ones on loan from our files and from a number of our longtime residents. Mr. Winston Valentine and Mrs. Minnie Oakes and some others of our senior citizens will be on hand at certain hours to provide commentary on the historical photographs. Call City Hall for the hours that you can enjoy this rare treat. Then on Saturday will be the great picnic, chili cook-off, dance and fireworks display from the high school grounds, so everyone come on out.

In what is perfect timing, we here at the *Voice* are also celebrating one full year of a new era. It hardly seems possible, but an entire year has passed since I became publisher of the *Voice* and took up residence here in Valentine. In celebration of this milestone, and in conjunction with Valentine Days, we will once again be presenting a series of special inserts each Sunday for the month, in which we give focus on life in our wonderful small town. Don't miss a one! Now revised and updated with comments and memories from our citizenry and pictures by Mr. James, these special features are sure to be collectors' items.

My wife and I would like to say thank you to all who have expressed condolences at our recent and substantial losses. I know the demolition of the great Porter-Holloway house meant the ending of an era for many of you. But I hope the new library to be built in its place will be a fitting substitute, and I'm appreciative to the people of this town for filling a longstanding need of a library for our residents. I am honored to accept the position as chairman of the library committee and promise my utmost effort in getting a facility that suits the tone of the neighborhood and the need.

We are also grateful for the condolences we have received at the passing of our son's father and our friend, Stuart James. We can feel blessed that in the brief time he was among us, Mr. James showed us ourselves and revealed our wonderful gifts of neighborliness.

It seems to me that during our journey through life, it is inevitable that we each have to come often by the corner of love and heartache. I think that corner is a little easier to stand on, here in Valentine.

Tate dropped his pen on his desk and ripped the yellow pages from the legal tablet in order to take them up to Marilee. He preferred her to read his editorials now, instead of Charlotte. Marilee was kinder in her criticism, and she seemed to appreciate his wit so much more than Charlotte.

Charlotte had pointed out that Tate did not want a critic. He wanted agreement. He conceded that this was probably true.

He shut out the light in his office, made sure the ones in the big city room were on that should be on, then stepped out the front door, locking it securely, before heading the couple of yards to the door at the edge of the building—their private entrance to the second floor of the *Voice,* where they were fashioning a temporary apartment.

Just reaching the door was Ricky Dale, lugging a small plastic animal crate, and beside him was a rather tiny girl.

"Well, good evenin', Ricky Dale."

"Good evenin', Editor." The boy set the crate down. "This here's Melody. We come to see Willie Lee. Melody's puppy is deaf. Her daddy won't let her keep him if he's deaf."

"Ah . . . well, come on up." He reached to take the crate, but Ricky Dale said he could carry it. Tate noticed the puppy wasn't all that big.

"It's an Australian shepherd. Sometimes if they're bred too close, they can turn out deaf," Ricky Dale said in a manner indicating he knew about such things. "Dr. Parker told me, when I was over there. I got a part-time job with him now."

"That's good. You're gonna go places."

"Yep."

When they entered the upstairs apartment, Ricky Dale went directly off to Willie Lee's room, already knowing the way.

Tate went into the partitioned kitchen, where Marilee was preparing supper.

"We got another one . . . a deaf puppy."

"Oh, well, maybe Willie Lee can help it."

"Hmm. I wrote my editorial."

He laid it on the table, then took Marilee into his arms and kissed her.

"Do it again," she said, when he lifted his lips. He kissed her again, and kept kissing her even when a puppy raced into the room and around them barking, with children chasing after it. He'd learned not to let children interrupt his kissing his wife.